A Murder Hatched

Murder with Peacocks and *Murder with Puffins*,
the first two books
in the Meg Langslow series

Donna Andrews

THOMAS DUNNE BOOKS

ST. MARTIN'S MINOTAUR 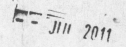 NEW YORK

THOMAS DUNNE BOOKS.
An imprint of St. Martin's Press.

www.thomasdunnebooks.com
www.minotaurbooks.com

Library of Congress Cataloging-in-Publication Data

Andrews, Donna.
    A murder hatched : Murder with peacocks and Murder with puffins, the first two books in the Meg Langslow series / Donna Andrews.—1st St. Martin's Minotaur pbk. ed.
        p. cm.
    ISBN-13: 978-0-312-54190-3
    ISBN-10: 0-312-54190-2
    1. Langslow, Meg (Fictitious character)—Fiction. 2. Women detectives—Fiction. I. Andrews, Donna. Murder with peacocks. II. Andrews, Donna. Murder with puffins. III. Title.

PS3551.N4165 M86 2008
813'.54—dc22

                                      2008028816

First St. Martin's Minotaur Paperback Edition: September 2008

10 9 8 7 6 5 4 3 2 1

Murder with Peacocks

Tuesday, May 24

I HAD BECOME SO USED TO HYSTERICAL DAWN PHONE CALLS THAT I only muttered one half hearted oath before answering.

"Peacocks," a voice said.

"I beg your pardon, you must have the wrong number," I mumbled. I opened one eye to peer at the clock: it was 6:00 A.M.

"Oh, don't be silly, Meg," the voice continued. Ah, I recognized it now. Samantha, my brother, Rob's, fiancée. "I just called to tell you that we need some peacocks."

"What for?"

"For the wedding, of course." Of course. As far as Samantha was concerned, the entire universe revolved around her upcoming wedding, and as maid of honor, I was expected to share her obsession.

"I see," I said, although actually I didn't. I suppressed a shudder at the thought of peacocks, roasted with the feathers still on, gracing the buffet table. Surely that wasn't what she had in mind, was it? "What are we going to do with them at the wedding?"

"We're not going to do anything with them" Samantha said, impatiently. "They'll just be there, adding grace and elegance to the occasion. Don't you remember the weekend before last when we all had dinner with your father? And he was saying what a pity it was that nothing much would be blooming in the yard in August, so there wouldn't be much color? Well, I just saw a photo in a magazine that had peacocks in it, and they were just about the most darling things you ever saw . . ."

I let her rattle on while I fumbled over the contents of my bedside table, found my notebook-that-tells-me-when-to-breathe, flipped to the appropriate page, and wrote "Peacocks" in the clear, firm printing I use when I am *not* in a very good mood.

1

"Were you thinking of buying or renting them?" I asked, interrupting Samantha's oration on the charms of peacocks.

"Well—rent if we can. I'm sure Father would be perfectly happy to buy them if necessary, but I'm not sure what we would do with them in the long run." I noted "Rent/buy if necessary" after "Peacocks."

"Right. Peacocks. I'll see what I can turn up."

"Wonderful. Oh, Meg, you're just so wonderful at all this!"

I let her gush for a few more minutes. I wondered, not for the first time, if I should feel sorry for Rob or if he was actually looking forward to listening to her for the rest of his life. And did Rob, who shared my penchant for late hours, realize how much of a morning person Samantha was? Eventually, I managed to cut short her monologue and sign off. I was awake; I might as well get to work.

Muttering "Peacocks!" under my breath, I stumbled through a quick shower, grabbed some coffee, and went into my studio. I flung open all the windows and gazed fondly at my unlit forge and my ironworking tools. My spirits rose.

For about ten seconds. Then the phone rang again.

"What do you think of blue, dear?" my mother asked.

"Good morning, Mother. What do you mean, blue?"

"The *color* blue, dear."

"The color blue," I repeated, unenlightened. I am not at my best before noon.

"Yes, dear," Mother said, with a touch of impatience.

"What do I think of it?" I asked, baffled. "I think it's a lovely color. The majority of Americans name blue when asked their favorite color. In Asian cultures—"

"For the living room, dear."

"Oh. You're getting something blue for the living room?"

"I'm redoing it, dear. For the wedding, remember? In blue. Or green. But I was really leaning to blue. I was wondering what you thought."

What I thought? Truthfully? I thought my mother's idea of re-doing the living room for the wedding had been a temporary aberration arising from too much sherry after dinner at an uncle's house. And incidentally, the wedding in question was not Rob's and Samantha's but her own. After the world's most amiable divorce and five years of so-called single life during which my father happily continued to do all her yard work and run errands for her, my mother had decided to marry a recently widowed neighbor. And I had also agreed to be Mother's maid of honor. Which, knowing my mother, meant I had more or less agreed to do every lick of work associated with the occasion. Under her exacting supervision, of course.

"What sort of blue?" I asked, buying time. The living room was done entirely in earth tones. Redoing it in blue would involve new drapes, new upholstery, new carpet, new everything. Oh, well, Dad could afford it, I suppose. Only Dad wouldn't be paying, I reminded myself. What's-his-name would. Mother's fiancé. Jake. I had no idea how well or badly off Jake was. Well, presumably Mother did.

"I hadn't decided, dear. I thought you might have some ideas."

"Oh. I tell you what," I said, improvising. "I'll ask Eileen. She's the one with the real eye for color. I'll ask her, and we'll get some color swatches and we'll talk about it when I come down."

"That will be splendid, Meg dear. Well, I'll let you get back to your work now. See you in a few days."

I added "Blue" to my list of things to do. I actually managed to put down my coffee and pick up my hammer before the phone rang a third time.

"Oh, Meg, he's impossible. This is just *not* going to work."

The voice belonged to my best friend and business partner, Eileen. She with the eye for colors. The he in question was Steven, since New Year's Eve her fiancé, at least during the intervals between premarital spats. At the risk of repeating myself, I should add that I was, of course, also Eileen's maid of honor.

"What's wrong?" I asked.

"He doesn't want to include the Native American herbal purification ceremony in the wedding."

"Well," I said, after a pause, "perhaps he feels a little self-conscious about it. Since neither of you is actually Native American."

"That's silly. It's a lovely tradition and makes such an important statement about our commitment to the environment."

I sighed.

"I'll talk to him," I said. "Just one thing . . . Eileen, what kind of herbs are we talking about here? I mean, we're not talking anything illegal, are we?"

"Oh, Meg." Eileen laughed. "Really! I have to go, my clay's ready." She hung up, still laughing merrily. I added "Call Steven re herbs" to my list.

I looked around the studio. My tools were there, ready and waiting for me to dive into the ironwork that is both my passion and my livelihood. I knew I really ought to get some work done today. In a few days, I would be back in my hometown for what I was sure would be a summer from hell. But I was already having a hard time concentrating on work. Maybe it was time to throw in the towel and head down to Yorktown.

The phone rang again. I glared at it, willing it to shut up. It ignored me and kept on ringing. I sighed, and picked it up.

Eileen again.

"Oh, Meg, before you go down to Yorktown, could you—"

"I won't have time to do anything else before I go down to Yorktown; I'm going down there tomorrow."

"Wonderful! Why don't you stop by on your way? We have some things to tell you."

On my way. Yorktown, where my parents and Eileen's father lived and where all the weddings were taking place, was three hours south of Washington, on the coast. Steven's farm, where

Eileen was now living, was three hours west, in the mountains. I was opening my mouth to ask if she had any idea how inconvenient stopping by was when I suddenly realized: if I went to Steven and Eileen's, I could force them to make decisions, extract lists and signatures. I would have them in my clutches. This could be useful.

"I'll be there for supper tomorrow."

I spent the day putting my life on hold and turning over my studio to the struggling sculptor who'd sublet it for the summer. I went to bed feeling virtuous. I intended to spend the next several days really getting things done for the weddings.

Wednesday, May 25

I WAS HOPING TO GET OUT OF TOWN BY NOON, BUT BY THE TIME I packed everything, fielded another half-dozen phone calls from each of the brides, and ran all the resulting last-minute errands, it was well into the evening rush hour. Needless to say I was late arriving at Steven and Eileen's. Eileen, bless her heart, didn't seem to mind. In fact she didn't even seem to notice.

"Guess who's here," Eileen said as she met me at the door wearing a dress of purple tie-dyed velvet, splattered here and there with flour. "Barry!"

"Really," I said, with considerably less enthusiasm. Ever since December, when I'd broken up with my boyfriend, Jeffrey, various friends and relatives had been trying to set me up with their idea of eligible men. Steven and Eileen's candidate was Steven's younger brother, Barry. Barry had taken to the idea immediately. I had not.

"The minute we told him you were coming, he came right up," Eileen burbled. "Isn't that sweet?"

"I really wish you hadn't done that."

"Why, Meg?" Eileen said, wide-eyed.

"Eileen, we've been over this half a dozen times already. You and Steven may think Barry and I are made for each other. I don't."

"He's crazy about you."

"So what? I don't happen to like him."

"I don't see why not," Eileen said. "He's so sensitive. And such a deep thinker, too."

"I'll have to take your word for it. I've never heard him put two consecutive sentences together."

"And so attractive," Eileen went on, while attempting, in vain, to tidy her flyaway mane and succeeding only in covering it with flour marks.

"Attractive? He's an overgrown ox," I said. I could see Eileen bristle. Oops. Not surprisingly, Barry bore a strong fraternal re-semblance to Steven. "All right, he's not as attractive as Steven, but he's okay if you like his type." The hulking Neanderthal type. "But he just doesn't appeal to me."

"But he's so sensitive . . . and such a wonderful craftsman," Eileen protested. "Why, whenever he and Steven have any really delicate carving work to do on a piece of furniture, Barry's always the one who does it. Steven says he has such wonderfully clever hands."

"I don't care how clever those oversized paws are with wood," I said. "I don't want them anywhere near me."

"Oh, Meg, you'll change your mind when you get to know him better."

"What gives you the right to assume I want to get to know him better?" I said, hotly. To empty air. Eileen was skipping down the hall to the kitchen.

"Meg's here!" she trilled. I followed her, fuming inwardly. Calm down, I told myself. She means well, she's your best friend, you love her dearly, and as soon as this damned wedding is over you'll probably even like her again.

Steven and Barry were sitting around the kitchen table talking. At least Steven was. Barry was sitting with his chin in his hand, nodding at whatever Steven was saying. Situation normal. Steven came over and hugged me. Barry, fortunately, didn't try, but his face lit up in a way that made me feel both guilty and depressed.

"Sit down, dinner's almost ready," Steven said. "Meg's come to stay for a few days," he added, as if Barry didn't already know.

"Only tonight, I'm afraid," I said. "Mother's having some sort of party this weekend and I promised I'd come down in time to help her get ready."

A chorus of protests from Steven and Eileen met this announcement, and Barry looked heartbroken.

"Oh, you can't possibly!" Eileen said.

"But we have such a wonderful time planned for you," Steven protested. "You've got to stay."

Even Barry nodded with what in him passed for enthusiasm.

I drained my glass and took another close look at him. No, not even Eileen and Steven's foul-tasting and incredibly potent cider could begin to make Barry look appealing. I didn't share Eileen's besotted view of Steven's charms. Steven was tall, handsome in a rather beefy way, and had a mellow, laid-back personality that perfectly complemented Eileen's ditzy one. But while Steven was definitely not my type, I had to admit that in making him, his parents had done the best they could with the material at hand. And then, flushed with overconfidence, they'd gone and produced Barry. Why couldn't they have left poor Steven an only child? Barry came close to having the same rough-hewn features that made Steven ruggedly handsome (according to Eileen), but everything was just a little coarser and rather haphazardly assembled. And besides, the human head is supposed to be connected to the human body with at least a rudimentary neck.

The rest of the evening, like every other stage of Eileen and Steven's campaign to set me up with Barry, resembled a French farce. I was outnumbered, since the three of them conspired to find ways of throwing me and Barry alone together. But I'd learned that I could neutralize Barry as long as I kept talking. By nine-thirty, I was more than a little hoarse, and found myself explaining to an unnaturally appreciative Barry the reason for the price difference between real engraved invitations and invitations with thermal raised printing.

So much for my quiet interlude in the country.

I did find a few minutes alone with Steven to talk about Eileen's latest addition to the wedding agenda.

"About this Native American herbal purification ceremony," I began.

"I hate to say this, because normally Eileen has such wonderfully creative ideas," Steven said, "but I just think it's a little too much."

"So do I," I said. "Completely ridiculous. You'd be laughing stocks. Guests would be rolling in the aisles. You'd probably make 'News of the Weird'."

"Exactly. So you'll talk her out of it?"

"No, I think you should tell her you agree."

"Agree?"

"Just tell her it's cool with you. I'll tell her I'm researching it. She'll change her mind long before the wedding."

"Do you really think so?"

"Trust me," I said. "I've known Eileen all her life. I guarantee you, by mid-June the Native American herbal purification ceremony will be history." At least I had every intention of ensuring it was.

Steven seemed satisfied. Eileen was overjoyed to hear he'd come around. And I would keep my fingers crossed that whatever new idea she came up with by mid-June was a little less off the wall. Please, I thought, let her become militantly traditional, just for a few months.

To everyone's disappointment, I went to bed at ten o'clock so I could get an early start on the next day's drive. No, I couldn't stay longer; I didn't want Mother to make herself ill getting ready for Sunday's family picnic. No, Mother's health was fine, but she wasn't getting any younger, and she had a lot on her hands this summer. I overdid it a bit; Barry was so touched by my daughterly devotion that he tried to volunteer to come down and help us with the party preparations and was only discouraged with the greatest of difficulty.

It could have been my imagination—or the influence of one too many glasses of cider—but as I was wishing everyone goodnight, I thought I saw something like a snarl cross Barry's usually placid face. Perhaps he was beginning to realize that pursuing me was futile, I thought. And resenting it. Ah, well; even a surly, resentful Barry would be more interesting than his customary bovine self.

Thursday, May 26

WHAT A RELIEF IT WAS THE NEXT MORNING TO GET UP WITH THE chickens (the few who had survived Steven and Eileen's care) and hit the road at 7:00 a.m. By the time I was actually wide awake, I'd put a good hundred miles of winding mountain roads between me and Barry.

Well before noon I found myself driving down the long, tree-shaded driveway to my parents' house. Well, Mother's house, anyway; Dad had moved out. Although I could see him up in a ladder pruning an ornamental cherry tree. I made a mental note to compliment him on the gardens, which were looking superb, and to hint that the house needed painting before all the relatives came for the weddings. On second thought, maybe I should just arrange to hire someone; painting three stories of rambling Victorian house with gingerbread trim was not something a sixty-six-year-old should be doing, though Dad would try if I mentioned it.

Mother was on the porch, her slender frame draped elegantly over the chaise lounge. She was dressed, as usual, as if expecting distinguished visitors, with not a single expensively natural-looking blond hair out of place. I suppressed the usual envious sigh. I'm the same height, and not at all bad-looking in my own fashion, but I'm not slender, I'm not a blonde, and nobody's ever mistaken me for elegant.

Mother wasn't even surprised to see me arrive several days early.

"Hello, dear," she said, giving me a quick peck on the cheek. "There's lemonade in the refrigerator. Why don't you help your sister with lunch? We'll all be able to eat that much sooner."

From the relief on Pam's face when I showed up in the kitchen to help, I suspected she was regretting her decision to pack off her husband Mal and the four oldest kids for a summer with Mal's parents in Australia. I could have warned her that the two youngest, Eric and Natalie, weren't much defense against Mother's tendency to enlist anyone within range as unpaid labor. But she'd known Mother eight years longer than I had; if she hadn't learned by now, there wasn't much I could do.

Dad was the only one who seemed surprised by my early arrival. He came in just as we were sitting down to lunch and took his usual place. Jake, the fiancé, was not here. No one else seemed to find this odd, so I said nothing.

"Meg!" he cried, jumping up to give me a bear hug as soon as he noticed it was me taking the chair beside him. "I thought you weren't coming down till Saturday! You're supposed to be resting at Steven and Eileen's farm! What happened?"

"It wasn't restful. Barry was there."

"Barry who?" my sister, Pam, asked.

"Steven's brother. The one they keep pushing at me."

"The dim one?" Dad asked.

"Precisely."

"Is he nice?" Mother asked.

"Not particularly." I'd explained to her several times before, in excruciating detail, exactly how much I disliked Barry, but since she obviously paid no attention I'd given up trying.

"I can't see how any brother of Steven's wouldn't be nice," Mother said.

"Well, he'll be down for the wedding, so you can see for yourself. For that matter, he'll probably be down for Eileen's family's barbecue on Memorial Day."

"You could call and tell him to come down for our picnic," Mother suggested.

"Mother, I don't want him here for our picnic. I don't like him."

"I suppose it would be awkward, with Jeffrey here," Mother said.

"Jeffrey's not—oh, I give up," I muttered. I'd also failed to convince Mother, who liked my ex-boyfriend for his vapid good looks, that Jeffrey was out of the picture. Dad patted my shoulder.

"I know your mother really appreciates your coming down," he said. "There's such a lot to do."

"Yes, Meg," Mother said, her face lighting with the sudden realization that at least for the moment she had me solely in her clutches, free from the competing influences of Samantha and Eileen.

We spent the rest of lunch discussing wedding details, followed by an afternoon of debating redecorating plans and a supper split between these two equally fascinating topics. I ate both meals with my left hand while scribbling several pages of notes in the notebook-that-tells-me-when-to-breathe. Dad made intermittent attempts to talk them into giving me tomorrow off, and was ignored. After lengthy discussion, Mother, Pam, and I all agreed that a visit to the local dressmaker was the first order of business. I was about halfway through the job of nagging three brides, three flower girls, and fourteen bridesmaids into visiting the dressmaker and had even talked to her on the phone several times, but hadn't actually made it to the shop myself.

"Well, that's settled," Mother said, as Pam and I began clearing the dishes. "Tomorrow morning you'll go down to Mrs. Waterston's shop and make sure everything is going well."

"Yes, that sounds like a wonderful idea!" Dad said, with great enthusiasm. "You'll like that!"

I stared at him, amazed at this sudden about-face. Such enthusiasm from Dad meant that he was up to something, but I couldn't imagine what. He was wearing what he probably thought of as a Machiavellian expression, but since Dad is short, bald, and pudgy, he looked more like a mischievous elf. Ah, well. Perhaps he had decided getting me a day off was a lost cause and was putting a cheerful face on the inevitable. Or perhaps Dad approved of Mrs. Waterston. Perhaps she shared one of his obsessions— bird-watching, or gardening, or reading too many mysteries. Since she'd only come to town the previous September, Mrs. Waterston was one of the few people in the county I hadn't known all my life. That alone made me look forward to meeting her. Yes, a visit to the dress shop was definitely in order.

Friday, May 27

SO, BRIGHT AND EARLY THE NEXT MORNING, I DROVE INTO YORK-town proper to visit the dressmaker.

Mother told me the dress shop was two doors down from the house where her uncle Stanley Hollingworth lived. I've never yet known her to give anyone a set of directions without at least one reference to a landmark that hasn't existed for years. It wasn't until the third time I'd examined every building in the block that I realized she must have meant not the house where he currently lived but the one he'd grown up in, three quarters of a century ago.

Sure enough, two doors down from the old Hollingworth house was a small cottage painted in Easter egg pastels, including a tasteful pink and baby blue colonial-style sign in front reading Be-Stitched—Dressmakers. I walked down a cobblestone path between a low border of immaculately pruned shrubs, opened a glossy sky blue door, and walked in to the tinkling of a small, old-fashioned bell. The whole thing was almost too cute for words. And since I positively loathe cute, I walked in prepared to dislike the proprietor intensely.

And found myself face-to-face with one of the most gorgeous men I'd ever seen in my life. He looked up from the book he was reading, brushed an unruly lock of dark hair out of his deep blue eyes, and smiled.

"Yes?" he said. I stood there looking at him for a couple of embarrassing seconds before pulling myself together. More or less.

"I'm here about a wedding. Where's Mrs. Waterston?" I asked, and then realized how rude that sounded.

"In traction," he said. "Down in Florida. I'm her son, Michael; I'm filling in while her broken bones mend."

"Oh, I'm sorry. I hope she's better soon."

"Not nearly as much as I hope it," he said gloomily. He had a wonderful, resonant voice. Perhaps he was a musician. I'm a sucker for musicians.

"How can I help you?" he asked.

"I'm Meg Langslow. I'm supposed to come here to be measured for a bridesmaid's dress."

"A bridesmaid's dress," he said, suddenly looking very cheerful. "Wonderful! For whose wedding?" He stood up and turned round to pull out the top drawer of a file cabinet on the back wall, giving me a chance to discreetly eye his wonderfully long, lean form. I decided I was looking forward to bringing Eileen in here so I could point out to her that this, not the beefy Barry, was *my* idea of what a hunk should look like. And I peeked at the book he was reading—Shakespeare. Not only gorgeous, but literate, too.

"Samantha Brewster, Eileen Donleavy, or Margaret Hollingworth Langslow. Take your pick."

His hand froze over the files and he looked up warily.

"You're not sure which? Are you, perhaps, comparison shopping to see who has the least objectionable gowns before committing yourself?"

"No, I'm stuck with all three of them. Langslow is my mother, Brewster is marrying my brother, and Donleavy is my best friend. I know it sounds odd, but this is a very small town."

"Actually, after two weeks here, very little strikes me as odd," he said. "And you're right; this is a very small town. I'm surprised I haven't run into you before."

"I don't live here anymore. I've come home for the summer, though, to help with all the weddings. I assume one set of measurements will do for all three; the first and last ones are only two weeks apart."

"Should do," he said. "What a summer you're in for. Here we are. Brewster . . . Langslow . . . and I'll start a file for Donleavy."

"*Start* a file? She's the first one up; you mean she hasn't even *been* here yet?"

"Not since I took over, and if your friend had been in before Mom left for Florida I'm sure she would have started a file."

I closed my eyes, took a deep breath, and began counting silently. I had gotten to three when he asked, "Are you all right?"

"I'm fine," I said. "Eileen always advises me to count to ten when I lose my temper. I generally still feel like throttling her when I'm finished, though."

I opened my eyes.

"She was *supposed* to have come in with one of her other bridesmaids months ago to pick out dresses so your mother could order them in our sizes. I mean, that's what she *told* me she'd done. The measurements were just supposed to be for the fine-tuning, or whatever you call it. Which I thought would be happening this week. She *lied* to me!"

Calm down, Meg, I told myself. Do not lose your temper at Eileen, especially in front of this very nice and extremely gorgeous man. Who was not, I had already noticed, wearing a wedding ring. I made a mental note to interrogate Mother about him; no doubt she and the aunts on the Hollingworth side of the family already knew not only his entire life history but also several generations of his family tree.

"I'm sorry," I said. "It's just that I'm the one who's trying to pull this all together, and she's the one who's unintentionally sabotaging everything."

"We'll manage something," he said, with a smile. "I don't recognize the name—what does she look like?"

"She's about five–ten, frizzy blondish hair down to her waist, a little on the plump side. Kind of looks like she just got in from California, or maybe Woodstock. The original."

He chuckled and walked over to a curtained doorway in the back of the shop and called out something in a rapid, musical tongue. A little wizened Asian grandmother, well under five feet tall, popped out and they chattered at each other for a few moments.

"She was in and looked at all the books several months ago, but didn't decide on anything," he reported finally. "Took down several stock numbers but hasn't called back."

"I'll have her in here Monday. Oh—Monday's Memorial Day. Tuesday, then. She'll be in town by then. You are open Tuesday?"

He nodded. "That would be great. Why don't we have Mrs. Tranh measure you now for the other weddings."

"Fine," I said, my mind still focused on Eileen's iniquities.

"And just what did Mother and Samantha decide on? At least I hope they've both decided on something. They told me they had, but perhaps I shouldn't have trusted them, either."

"Oh, yes, they did. Several months ago. Your mother said she wanted to surprise you and your sister, and we weren't on any account to show you what it was until she had the chance," he said, a little nervously.

"That's Mother for you. I won't ask you to betray a confidence; I won't even ask you if she picked something ghastly. As long as it's underway."

"Oh, definitely," he said. "And it's not ghastly at all, if you ask me."

"And Samantha?" I asked. "She's underway, too?"

"Yes. She hasn't told you anything about what she picked?"

"No, she and the blond bim—the other bridesmaids all got together and decided two months ago. I knew I should have come down for it. How bad is it? Should I be sitting down?"

He pulled a picture out of the file and held it up.

"You've got to be kidding," I said. He shook his head.

"No, and neither is she, apparently."

"Oh . . . my . . . God!"

The pictures looked like publicity stills from *Gone with the Wind*. Enormous hooped skirts. Plunging, off-the-shoulder necklines. Multiple layers of petticoats. Elaborate hairstyles involving many fussy-looking ringlets. And tiny, tiny waists.

"I'll let Mrs. Tranh take you back to the dressing room for measuring," he said. Damn him, he was fighting back a grin. "The corsets, particularly, require a lot of rather intimate details."

"Corsets? In July? Eileen's off the hook. I'm killing Samantha first," I said. Much to his amusement.

Mrs. Tranh, it turned out, was the tiny, gray-haired Asian woman. Vietnamese, I think. Neither she nor any of the other seamstresses would admit to speaking any English. However, she had no difficulty communicating with sign language and firm taps and tugs exactly how I should stand or turn so she and the flock could measure me. There were only five of them, I think, but the dressing room—formerly the kitchen of the tiny cottage—was so small, and they darted so rapidly about the room and up and down the stairs—to the sewing rooms, I supposed—that they seemed like dozens. They were all so short that I felt like a great, clumsy giantess. And knowing that they had previously measured Samantha and my sylphlike fellow bridesmaids, I had to sternly suppress my paranoia. I was sure their soft chattering conversation consisted mainly of unfavorable comments about my more normally female form.

I amused myself by letting my imagination run rampant about their boss, who was hovering attentively outside the curtain, occasionally exchanging rapid and unintelligible remarks with them. I would definitely have to interrogate Mother about him. But discreetly. If she and the rest of the family deduced that I was interested in him, half of them would probably disapprove and make clumsy and embarrassing attempts to interfere. The other half would rejoice and indulge in even clumsier and more embarrassing attempts to throw us together. Matchmaking was a competitive sport in Yorktown, and my family's enthusiasm for it was one of the reasons I had chosen to relocate several hours away.

I would have been tempted to hang about and talk to Michael the Gorgeous, but I knew I should be getting back to keep up with my schedule for addressing the envelopes for Eileen's invitations. Besides, another neighbor had arrived with the twin six-year-old nieces who were going to be flowergirls in her daughter's wedding, and she obviously expected Michael's full attention. I consoled myself with the thought that I would have plenty of future opportunities to see him. As maid of honor, my presence at all future fittings of any member of the three wedding parties could be taken for granted. It would be very considerate to find out when their least busy times were, so I could schedule fittings that wouldn't be interrupted by other customers. Why, choosing Eileen's gown alone would probably occupy several mornings or afternoons next week. I magnanimously forgave Eileen for having lied to me.

I was in very good spirits when I arrived back at the house. I found Mother lounging elegantly on the living room sofa with a box of chocolates and the latest issue of *Bride* magazine.

I hate it when they read the bridal magazines. Every issue is good for at least a dozen new items on my to-do list.

"Well, I went down to the dress shop today, had my measurements taken, and found out that Eileen has *not* decided on her dresses yet," I announced, throwing myself into a nearby armchair.

"You really ought not to have let her wait this long, dear," Mother said. "She could have a very hard time getting anything on such short notice."

"I didn't *let* her wait this long, Mother. I nagged her to go in and order something; I sent her down here to do it under the threat that I'd pick something myself if she didn't, and two days later she came back and told me she'd ordered something. She *lied* to me!"

"She's under a great deal of strain, dear. Be tactful with her. Mrs. Waterston will manage somehow." Bingo! My opening to pry without seeming to.

"By the way, Mother, you told me to ask for Mrs. Waterston, but apparently she's in Florida, recuperating from a broken leg."

"Oh, yes, dear, didn't I mention that?" Mother said. "Her son has come down to run the shop while she's gone."

"Yes, I met him."

"Such a nice boy. I understand he teaches theater at a college somewhere up your way," Mother said, as she poked through the chocolates to see if perhaps there were any left that she liked. "Such a pity, really."

"What's a pity?"

"That he's . . . well, you know. Like that."

"Like what, Mother?" I asked, but had a sinking feeling I already knew the answer. Mother, mistress of pregnant pauses and vague euphemisms, had come just about as close as she ever would to telling me that drop-dead-gorgeous Michael was gay.

"I feel so sorry for his mother sometimes," Mother went on, inspecting a chocolate critically. "She's told several people that she's in no hurry for Michael to settle down because she was a child bride and doesn't want to be a young grandmother. She puts on a brave front. But of course since he came down everyone knows exactly how unlikely it is that she'll *ever* be a grandmother, especially since he's an only child." She nibbled a corner of the chocolate and made a delicate face. "Here, darling, you finish this one; I don't like coconut."

"Neither do I, Mother."

"Oh? Then we'll save it for Eric," she said, putting the candy carefully back in one corner of the box.

"Feed the grandkids the spitbacks?" I snapped. "That's efficient, Mother."

She looked at me in surprise.

"Are you all right, dear? Perhaps you should go upstairs and lie down for a bit; you've been so busy and perhaps the heat is making you just a little out of sorts. So hard to believe it's still May."

Feeling guilty for taking my disappointment out on her, I pleaded a small headache and fled up to my room. Actually I was depressed and wanted to mope by myself. Like Cinderella's golden carriage turning back into a pumpkin, all those impending trips to Be-Stitched to be fitted now turned from golden opportunities back into drab chores. I was already on the verge of tears when the sight of the huge stack of Eileen's envelopes on my dresser sent me over the edge. How symbolic of my summer. Me doing an endless series of chores while other people found happiness.

Obviously I was overreacting to the situation, but damn! My antennae were usually better than this. How could I be so mistaken? Perhaps it was wishful thinking. In the five months since breaking up with Jeffrey, I hadn't really met anyone else interesting. Not that I had much time for meeting people, between wedding arrangements and the extra time I'd been spending at the forge to build up enough inventory so I could take the summer off. The few dates I'd had were with men pushed at me by matchmaking friends, and most of them had been awful. I had pretty much resigned myself to putting my own social life on hold until this summer's weddings were out of the way. Obviously my hormones were objecting to this idea by reacting violently to the first attractive male in sight, without stopping to consider whether he was a suitable target. Or was it possible that Mother could, for once, be wrong?

That hope was dashed rather thoroughly when the Brewsters joined our family for a welcome-home-Meg dinner.

"Imagine," I heard Mother say to Mrs. Brewster, "when Meg went in today to be measured, she found Eileen had *not* ordered her dresses after all. And she told Meg she had done it *months* ago."

"I should have demanded an affidavit." I shrugged. "Well, we're behind the eight ball, but I'm going to drag her down to Be-Stitched the minute she gets here and force her to make a decision."

"So, you've been down to Be-Stitched already," Samantha said. "What did you think of Michael What-a-Waste?"

"Samantha, really," her mother said, but by her tone I could tell she was rather proud of her daughter's wit.

"What-a-Waste?" Mr. Brewster said, as if he had no idea what she was implying.

"Or the last of the Waterstons, if you like," Samantha said. "I mean, you did notice that he's not exactly much of an addition to the town's list of eligible bachelors."

"He seems very nice," I said, noncommittally. I didn't want to get into an argument with Samantha, but didn't see how I could avoid it if she kept on this way. I glanced at Mother. Surely this violated her ironclad rule against discussing sex, politics, or religion at the table? Surely these days one should add genteel bigotry to the list of forbidden topics?

"I do so like what you've done with your hair," Mother remarked to Mrs. Brewster.

"Oh, he's positively charming," Samantha said, relentlessly, "at least if you happen to be a fag hag."

"That's a perfectly hateful thing to say," I began, and then jumped as Mother kicked me under the table.

"Now, Meg," Mother said. As if I were the one at fault.

"He's a very charming conversationalist," Mrs. Brewster said. "Very chivalrous."

"Well, that's a dead giveaway, isn't it," Samantha said. "I mean, how many straight men do you know who have decent manners and can talk about anything other than football and beer?"

Your fiancé and your future father-in-law, for starters, I felt like saying, but Mother was glaring daggers at me, so I counted to three and then said, as calmly as I could, "You all seem to know rather a lot about the private life of someone who's only been here, what, a couple of weeks?"

"Well, it's a proven fact. I mean, several of the bridesmaids who were in being measured have tried to get him interested. I mean, *honestly,* if they're running around half-naked and practically flinging themselves in his lap and the guy doesn't show a spark of interest, what do you think *that* means?"

"He has excessively good taste?" I suggested. "Or——" Mother tapped me again with her foot. Samantha gave me a withering look.

"Oh, sure," she said. "He flat-out told them not to bother 'cause he wasn't interested. Besides, he hangs out with those two old aunties who run the antique store and the decorating shop."

"Now, now, Samantha. That's enough. Little pitchers have big ears," Mother chided, indicating eight-year-old Eric. Eric was too busy stuffing his pockets with tidbits to feed his pet duck to pay any attention to our boring grown-up conversation. "I think it's very sweet of them to make Michael feel more at home."

"And so convenient that they've convinced Michael and his mother to do curtains and slipcovers and such," Mrs. Brewster said. "They've had an awful time finding local help who meet their standards."

"Yes," Mother said. "I'm not sure I'd have dared to go ahead with redecorating the living room without Michael's help. Not the deviled eggs, Eric."

"But Duck likes deviled eggs!" Eric protested.

"You may take a deviled egg to Duck, then," Mother conceded. "But don't put it in your pocket."

Eric took this as permission to leave the table and trotted out to the backyard with the deviled egg.

"Then you're going ahead with redecorating, too?" Mrs. Brewster said.

"Yes, the living room, and possibly the dining room," Mother said. "Michael will be out tomorrow to take measurements."

"The dining room, too?" Jake said, plaintively. No one seemed to hear him.

"We're having the living room and the library done," Mrs. Brewster said. Mr. Brewster sighed gently. "I haven't decided about the dining room yet, although I suppose I should very soon. Perhaps I should have Michael take measurements tomorrow, too."

"If he has time," Mother said. "He will be doing quite a lot of measuring here."

"I'll call to make sure he has time," Mrs. Brewster said. "And no snide remarks when he comes young lady," she said, turning to Samantha.

"Of course; not a word," Samantha said. "What kind of an idiot do you think I am? I mean, you know how vindictive and temperamental they can be; I'm not about to do anything to make him mess up my gown."

Mother kicked me before I could open my mouth. My shins would be black and blue by morning.

What a narrow-minded, prejudiced—no, don't say the word, I told myself. The whole conversation left a bad taste in my mouth. I felt guilty about not having stepped in to defend Michael. On the other hand, if Mother hadn't shushed me, I'd probably have lost my temper and said something that I'd need to apologize for. I had a bad feeling that Samantha and I would end up having a knock-down-drag-out argument about narrow-mindedness before the end of the summer; I'd just try to avoid doing it in front of Mother. Or Rob. I had no idea what he saw in Samantha, but he was madly in love with her, so I'd have to learn to live with her.

In the meantime I vowed to be extremely friendly and hospitable to Michael. To make up for the various indignities and embarrassments he had probably already suffered at the hands of my small-minded relatives and neighbors.

Saturday, May 28

OF COURSE, BEING FRIENDLY AND HOSPITABLE TO MICHAEL WAS going to get a lot easier once I mastered the tendency to drool every time I saw him. I stumbled downstairs at ten Saturday morning to find him sitting in our kitchen. Mother was serving him coffee and pastries and explaining her redecorating plans.

I found myself wishing I'd combed my hair better before shoving it back into a clip. Or put on something other than my oldest jeans. Don't be silly, I told myself crossly, and responded to Michael's heart-stopping smile with as friendly a nod as I could manage before noon. I joined them and listened to Mother chatter about chintz for a while as I sipped my coffee and waited for it to take effect.

"Meg!" Mother said sharply. I started, spilling some of my coffee. Apparently I'd nodded off while sitting upright.

"Sorry, not quite awake yet," I mumbled, mopping at myself with a napkin. Good thing I wasn't trying to impress anyone.

"I know how you feel," Michael said. "During the year I won't let them schedule any of my classes before eleven. I'm still not used to the way people down here get up at the crack of dawn."

"Ten o'clock is hardly the crack of dawn," Mother said, favoring me with a stern look. "Wait till you've been down here for a few weeks, with all the fresh air and proper food, young lady. You'll be getting up with the larks."

"Don't try to reform me, Mother," I warned.

"Of course not, dear," Mother lied, and led Michael into the living room to measure things. He looked as if he would rather stay in the kitchen to ingest more coffee. I could sympathize.

I had another cup of coffee and contemplated the mess Mother had made in the kitchen while serving Michael, the mess she always made in any kitchen. I had learned to cook and clean early, in self-defense. I finished my coffee and swabbed down the kitchen before taking up the phone and my list of things to do. Fourteen phone calls later I had lost my temper twice and succeeded in crossing exactly one thing off my list. I could hear Mother gently but firmly ordering Michael around in the living room. Well, better him than me. My turn would come. I went outdoors for some fresh air and found Dad busily trimming the hedge.

He looked relaxed and happy. Of course he nearly always did. After the divorce, Dad had moved in with my sister, Pam, and her husband, Mal. Or more accurately, into the apartment over their garage. It was all of a mile from the family house, and apart from going home to sleep in a different bed, he made remarkably few changes to his life after the divorce. He still divided his time between gardening at Pam's and at Mother's; doing things with the grandchildren; reading great stacks of books; making anachronistic house calls on the friends, neighbors, and relatives who hadn't yet been persuaded that he'd retired from his medical practice; and, most important, pursuing with wild enthusiasm and single-minded devotion whatever odd hobbies happened to seize his attention.

As soon as Mother decided on a garden wedding, Dad started grooming our yard for the festivities. Once Samantha decided to have an outdoor reception, he began relandscaping the Brewster's grounds. The Brewsters seemed thrilled to have him doing it, though that could change very quickly if all the extra work made their gardener carry out his threat to resign. And Dad was even pitching in occasionally to help Eileen's father prepare for her event.

All of which seemed very odd. Dad was working overtime to make the weddings a success, and yet, he had never liked Samantha. He was constantly complaining that Eileen took advantage of me. And as for Mother's remarriage to Jake—was he really that cheerful about it?

Speak of the devil, I thought, there goes Jake. Predictably, creeping along at five miles below the posted speed limit in his non-descript blue sedan. I waved at him. He screeched to a halt, rolled down the window, and stuck his head out, looking very distraught.

"Yes, what is it?" he asked, his voice trembling.

"Nothing, Mr. Wendell. I was just waving. Sorry if I startled you."

"Off to fetch your sister-in-law?" Dad asked. "She has a fine morning for flying, doesn't she? From Fort Lauderdale, right?"

"Y-yes," Jake said. "How did you know?"

"Mother mentioned it," I said.

"Besides, it's hard to keep secrets in a small town like this," Dad boomed jovially. Mr. Wendell looked alarmed, and more like a startled gray-brown mouse than usual. He rolled his window up, tried to drive away with the emergency brake still on, stopped to release it, and finally rolled slowly off.

Well, that was not a success, I thought. In fact, it was about as much of a bust as most of my attempts to get to know Jake better. Ah, well; I'd have all summer to get acquainted with my future stepfather.

"So, what are you up to this morning?" Dad said, rubbing his back while surveying the parts of the hedge he'd finished clipping.

"Phone calls and errands. Want me to help with that?"

"No, I have a good idea how I want it done."

"Just as well; I have a feeling any minute now I'll get called into a conference about redecorating the living room. Mother has Michael from the dress shop measuring the house."

"Now there's an intelligent young man."

"Yes, he seems nice," I said, wincing. That was all I needed, for Dad to turn his boundless energy and determination to setting me up with the least eligible man in town. It was going to be the longest summer in recorded history.

"He's a professor of drama, you know," Dad went on.

"Yes, well, duty calls," I said, and fled back to the kitchen before he could continue.

I decided that chocolate chip cookies would cheer me up and placate Mother as well, so I took the time off from my list to whip up a batch. Lured by the smell, Rob ambled in, followed eventually by Michael and Mother, who graciously issued an invitation for us to make some lemonade and join her on the porch.

"We always like to have lemonade and cookies on the porch on summer afternoons," Mother said, when Rob and I brought out the glasses.

"Very civilized," Michael said, wolfing down his sixth cookie.

Just then we heard the kitchen screen door slam, followed by frantic quacking.

"Here comes Eric," I said.

My eight-year-old nephew ran in and launched himself at Mother, wailing and holding up a bleeding finger. By the time Mother had calmed him down enough to look at it, the bleeding had mostly stopped, and he had subsided into muted sniffles. Echoed by muted quacking from his pet duck at the back door.

"Would you like Grandma to kiss it and make it better?" Mother asked, smiling down at Eric.

"Grandpa says that the human mouth has more bacteria than even dogs' mouths," Eric said, snatching away his hand and backing off in terror.

"I'm sure your grandpa knows best then, dear," Mother said, with a touch of asperity. "Why don't you go ask Grandpa to suture it?"

"Okay," Eric said, charmed by the idea. Suture, indeed; the child obviously needed more of Dad's vocabulary lessons. Mother sipped her lemonade as Eric ran happily out, armed with a fistful of cookies. Michael was looking oddly at us.

"Dad's very good with childhood scrapes and sniffles," Rob said. "That was always one of his major charms as a parent. How seriously he treated even the most minor ailments."

"It's a wonder you didn't all become raging hypochondriacs," Mother said, shaking her head.

"Other children might run to Mommy and get a Band-Aid," I added. "We'd go to Dad to have sterile dressings for our lacerations and abrasions—after proper irrigation to prevent sepsis, of course. At least Pam and I did."

"I never could stand the sight of blood," Rob said with a shudder.

"Won't that be rather a handicap in your profession?" Michael asked.

"Oh, very funny," Rob said, and buried his face in his bar exam review book.

"Rob's a little sensitive about lawyer jokes," I explained, patting my brother's arm.

"Lawyer jokes?" Michael said. "I'm very sorry; I wasn't trying to make a joke. I could have sworn your father told me Rob was going to go on to medical school. To become a forensic pathologist."

"Oh, God! Dad's at it again!" Rob groaned.

"Dad *wishes* Rob would go to med school and become a forensic pathologist," I said. "He came up with the idea about a week after Rob broke the news that he was going to law school."

"I didn't realize he was going around telling people *that* again!" Rob said, shaking his head.

"*Still,* dear, not *again,*" Mother said. "He never really stopped, you know."

"God, think of all the people he's probably told," Rob moaned.

"I think most of the family understand the situation, dear," Mother reassured him.

"Our family might, but what about Samantha's family?" Rob wailed.

"They'll learn," I said. "The important thing to keep in mind when dealing with any of our extended family," I said to Michael, "is never, ever to believe anything any of us says without corroboration."

"Preferably from an outsider," Rob added.

"Preferably from your own two eyes," I said.

"Are you telling me your entire family are liars?" Michael asked.

"I have no idea what you're talking about, Meg." Mother sniffed.

"Not liars," I said. "Well, maybe a few, and mostly they can't help it. It's just that most of our family are prone to . . . exaggeration."

"Tall-tale-telling," Rob added.

"Creative interpretation of reality resulting from wishful thinking," I suggested. "Like Dad's notion about Rob having a career in forensic pathology. All Rob's life Dad has been dreaming about Rob following in his footsteps. He was depressed about Rob not going to med school until he came up with the forensic pathology idea one day, and after that it took on a life of its own."

"That's the other thing you have to watch out for," Rob said. "With most of the family, once they get an idea into their heads, it's very hard to get them to change their minds."

"We hate letting silly things like reality interfere with our pet notions," I said.

"I think I know exactly what you mean," Michael said. "I've already experienced something of the sort myself."

"Good," I said. "So you'll know to take everything anyone here says with a grain of salt."

"A pound of salt," Rob corrected.

"Honestly, I have no idea why you children insist on filling this poor boy's head with such stories about your own family," Mother said. "You'd think we were a family of lunatics and pathological liars." When the three of us burst out laughing, she shook her head, gathered up her embroidery and her lemonade, and went inside.

"Oh, dear," Rob said. "You don't suppose Mother is upset, do you?"

"I doubt it, Rob."

"I'd better go and see." He sighed, heading for the door.

"Mother is imperturbable, Rob, you should know that by now," I called to his retreating back. Michael chuckled.

"Oh, it's very funny if you don't have to live with her," I said. "Which, thank God, I don't most of the time."

"I wasn't laughing at your mother," he said, hastily. "I was laughing from sheer delight; how often does one meet someone who can use words like 'imperturbable' in casual conversation like that?"

"Yes, I know we can be rather pretentious sometimes. Expanding one's vocabulary is one of Dad's pet projects. He used to pay us by the syllable for new words. He does it with the grand-kids now. That sort of thing has a permanent effect."

"A very charming one, if you ask me," Michael said. I sipped my lemonade and looked at him over the rim of my glass. The more I saw of him, the more I realized why instead of treating him as a pariah when they discovered his sexual orientation the local ladies seemed to have adopted him as a sort of pet. He was not only drop-dead gorgeous, he was absolutely charming. Except for the rather generic Middle Atlantic accent, he could easily have been custom-made to fit their notions of a Southern gentlemen. He was immaculately groomed and casually but elegantly dressed, with impeccable manners. Even Samantha and her mother admitted he was a charming conversationalist—although around here, that could simply mean that he had the ability to listen to others rattle on for hours without any overt sign of boredom. And he had a knack for the formal gallantry and witty flirtatiousness that so many aging Southern belles consider their due. More to my taste, he seemed to have a brain, and a slightly sardonic sense of humor. If only . . . but no. He wasn't very obvious about it, but if both Mother's branch of the grapevine and Samantha's said he was gay, I could see no use wasting time on might-have-beens.

"I'm not sure you should be quite so hard on your family, though," he said. "It seems to me that most of the town shares your tendency to see things the way they want to see them."

"Most of the town are related to us, one way or another. At least the ones who have been here a generation or two. And the rest have just been around us too long."

"That must be it," he said. "You see, shortly after I got here, something happened that seemed to give everyone the bizarre idea that I—" He froze, looking over my shoulder, and I turned around to see Samantha and one of the bridesmaids.

"Hello, Meg," Samantha said. "You look comfortable." I felt as guilty as a night watchman caught sleeping on the job.

"No reason not to be comfortable while I work," I said. "We've been discussing the gowns. Michael has some ideas for making the hoops more manageable."

I felt guilty picking on Michael that way, but he rose to the occasion. After enduring a seemingly endless conversation on how the hoops could be better constructed to allow us to fit through normal doorways, sit in the limos, and go to the bathroom without too much outside assistance, I excused myself and fled outside on the pretext of seeing if Dad needed help. Michael jumped up and followed me out.

"Nice of you to come all the way out here from town," I said.

"It's just down the street, really," Michael said. "I'm staying at Mom's house."

"Which one is that?"

"Your mother calls it the Kaplan bungalow."

"Oh, yes," I said. "Not that any Kaplans have lived there for fifteen years."

As we went out the back door, we ran into Eric, sporting an extremely large and already dirty bandage and followed, naturally, by Duck.

"Hi, Aunt Meg," Eric said. "Who's he?" I suppose he had been too concerned with his finger earlier to notice Michael on the porch.

"This is Michael Waterston," I said, in my best formal manner. "His mother runs the dress shop. Michael, this is Eric McReady, my nephew." Michael leaned down to shake the rather sticky hand Eric was offering. "And this is Duck." Michael won Eric's heart instantly by solemnly turning to Duck and offering his hand, which Duck pecked.

"I've seen you two around," Michael said.

"Yes," I said, "Duck follows Eric around just like a dog."

"Duck's better than any old dog," Eric said, loyally. "Come see what he did."

Eric led us to a spot in the bushes where a single duck egg was resting.

"Duck laid an egg," Eric said.

"That's very smart of her," I said.

"Him," Eric corrected. I decided it wasn't my job to explain that one to him.

"What should we do with it?" Eric asked. I looked at Duck, who showed no apparent interest in sitting on the damned thing.

"Well," Michael said, "I suppose you could always eat it."

"No!" Eric wailed. "I'm not going to let you eat Duck's babies! No, NO, *NO!*" He flung himself down to protect the egg with such violence that I was sure he would crack it. Duck began quacking hysterically.

"Hush, Eric," I said, glaring at Michael. "Nobody's going to eat Duck's babies."

"I didn't mean eat it," Michael said, desperately, "I meant *heat* it! Heat it! So it will hatch."

Eric looked around, still suspicious, but with noticeably less distress.

"That's what you have to do to hatch eggs," Michael went on. "You heat them. Most ducks sit on the eggs to heat them, but Duck seems to prefer following you around, so we have to figure out some other way to keep her . . . his egg warm."

"Like what?" Eric asked, sitting up and cradling the egg in his hand.

"Well, when I was a kid I had a little machine that you plugged in and it kept the eggs the right temperature for them to hatch. An incubator, it's called. I hatched some chicks from hen's eggs that way."

"Where do you get a ink-ink-"

"In-cu-ba-tor," Michael said. Eric mouthed it after him. I could see the dollar signs in his little eyes; he was going to dash right off and collect twenty cents from his grandfather for learning a new, four-syllable word. "Where do you get one?" he asked. Michael and I looked at each other.

"I suppose a pet store would have one," Michael suggested.

"Aunt Meg, *you* could find a pet store with an incubator," Eric said, in the sort of tone that implied that only his incomparable Aunt Meg *could* perform such a miracle.

"I suppose I could try," I said.

"Try real hard!" Eric pleaded.

"I will, I promise."

"And soon!" he wailed. "What if Duck's egg gets cold while you're looking?"

"I'll try real soon. Meanwhile, why don't you keep Duck's egg in your shirt pocket? Of course you'll have to be really careful not to shake it, but that should keep it warm enough."

"Okay," Eric said. He carefully placed the egg in his pocket, and he and Duck trotted off—slowly—to find Dad.

"And what happens if he falls and breaks it?" Michael asked, shaking his head.

"Well, at least he can't blame either of us," I said. "And since there isn't any Mr. Duck around to fertilize the egg, it's not going to hatch no matter how long we incubate it. Eric accidentally breaking it might be the best solution; the kids could have a funeral. Pet funerals are very popular around here, especially since Dad came back from a trip to Scotland with a set of bagpipes for each of the grandkids."

"They really play the bagpipes?" Michael asked.

"No, but they can march around making such an ungodly amount of noise that they completely forget to be upset about the dear departed."

"Let's hope the egg survives. You've got quite enough to do as it is; I'll see if I can find an incubator. Since it was all my fault in the first place."

"You're on."

"By the way, Meg, I was wondering if you would like to go—" Michael began, only to be interrupted by Mother calling and beckoning to us from the porch.

"Michael, you will come to dinner tomorrow, won't you?" Mother asked as we arrived at the porch. "Jake's sister-in-law arrived this morning to spend the summer and help with the wedding, and we want to have a few people over to welcome her. Nothing formal," she insisted, "just a little light refreshment by the pool. Meg, dear, I have something to show you," she said, taking Michael's acceptance for granted and moving to the next item on her agenda. "It's about the dining room . . ."

I waved at Michael and went off with Mother to spend the rest of the afternoon fruitlessly trying to talk her out of totally redecorating the dining room in addition to the living room. I hoped Mrs. Brewster wouldn't up the ante in the decorating competition by decorating three rooms so that Mother would feel obliged to do the family room as well. I hoped Jake was more than reasonably well heeled. I hoped Michael would have the sense to realize that Mother's idea of "nothing formal" meant that guests weren't actually required to wear black tie and tails. I hoped the summer would be over soon.

Sunday, May 29

I'D GONE TO BED SATURDAY NIGHT EXPECTING A RESTFUL SUNDAY. At least the morning, when Mother and all her cronies would gather at Grace Episcopal, dressed to kill and waiting with decorative impatience for the service to be over so they could get down to the serious business of catching up with the week's gossip. I planned to sleep late, read the paper, and rest. But I woke early and got up when I couldn't stop worrying about my to-do list.

I padded downstairs, fixed coffee, and sat at the kitchen table waiting for it to take effect. I was enjoying the peace and quiet of the empty house. I suppose I was halfway asleep again when a noise at the kitchen door startled me. I jumped and whirled, only to see Jake, halfway through the door. He started and looked as surprised to see me as I was to see him. He was clutching a brown paper bag in both hands with a convulsive grip.

"I thought everybody was in church," we said, almost in unison. I laughed when I realized we'd both said the same thing. Jake didn't. No sense of humor, either, I thought. What on earth does Mother see in him?

"I just came by to drop off some things for the party," he said, opening the kitchen door a fraction more and then slipping in sideways and over to the refrigerator. He opened the refrigerator door and surveyed the inside, already crowded with containers of food.

"I suppose I should bring this back later," he said, shifting from foot to foot and rolling the top of the bag a little tighter.

"Oh, no; I'm sure we can find a space," I said. I opened the refrigerator door wider and began shifting around Tupperware containers and foil-covered casseroles. "What is it you've brought? Can we slip it here on top of the ham or——" I heard a slight noise and turned to find the kitchen empty. "Mr. Wendell?" I peered out the back door. I could see Jake scuttling around the corner.

Irritating little man. I seemed to make him nervous. Probably senses that you don't like him, I told myself. Perhaps trying to get to know him was a lost cause. Perhaps I should just ignore him.

On the other hand, if Mother had asked him to bring over something for the party, she would expect to see it. I gulped the rest of my coffee and went after him.

Jake was making better time than I was. By the time I arrived at his house, a block and a half away, he was nowhere in sight. I trudged up the porch steps and was lifting my hand to knock on the screen door when I heard a female voice say, "So there you are!"

I whirled, and saw no one.

"I just went down the street to Margaret's," came Jake's voice from inside the house. I realized the woman was inside, too, and not talking to me.

"To hide something, I suppose?" the voice continued. "Something of Emma's? The missing jewelry, maybe?"

"Just some food for the party," Jake said, meekly. "I told you, Jane; all of Emma's jewelry is in the safety deposit box. Emma was very careful about that. I'm sure the key will turn up."

Ah, I thought. This must be the sister-in-law. Emma, presumably, was Jake's late wife. And here I'd arrived in the midst of a family quarrel. Over missing jewelry, no less. I was tempted to stay and eavesdrop, but my conscience won out. I turned and began sneaking quietly off the porch.

"I'll bet you've given it all to that blond hussy you're marrying," Jane went on. I paused. I'd heard Mother called many interesting things—had called her a few myself—but 'blond hussy' was a new one, even for Mother.

"No, no, no! Margaret doesn't know they're here—or in the safety deposit box, rather. I told her all Emma's good things had gone to pay the medical bills that the insurance didn't cover."

"Well, they've gone somewhere, haven't they? The Sheridan console that used to be here, and the Wyeth——"

"I told you, Jane; it's all in storage."

"We'll see about that. We'll see if your fiancée happens to have a Sheridan console like Emma's."

"Please don't do that. You'll upset her."

"I've a mind to go over there right now," Jane said. Hearing her footsteps coming my way, I whirled and ran pell-mell for home.

I need to exercise more, I told myself, as I sprawled, panting, on my chair in the kitchen, awaiting the onslaught of Jake and his sister-in-law. I'll just have to tell them I was doing my exercises, I thought. Oh, sure; Jake will certainly believe that, having seen me semicomatose in the kitchen a few minutes before. I stood up and did a few jumping jacks to add a note of realism for their arrival. After a few minutes I switched to sit-ups. When five or ten minutes passed with no sign of irate sisters-in-law, I abandoned my charade and went back to the kitchen for more coffee.

Damn Jake, anyway. At least he'd talked his sister-in-law out of storming over here immediately, but I had a premonition that trouble was still coming. Did Jake really think he had to put his late wife's possessions in storage to keep them out of Mother's clutches? And why didn't he just show them to his sister-in-law? Probably no time; she'd only just arrived a few hours ago. I hoped he did it soon. The way she sounded, I suspected that when she didn't find her sister's jewelry and furniture here, she'd accuse Mother of selling them. Which was nonsense. I could see Mother appropriating a piece of jewelry or furniture she thought was about to become hers anyway, and having to be gently but firmly told to give it back. I couldn't possibly see her selling them.

Mother arrived back from church just before noon, followed almost immediately by about fifteen or twenty relatives and neighbors, bearing flowers, extra plates and glasses, and more food in amazing quantities. The expected chaos reigned right up until the party began. I was a nervous wreck, expecting Jake's sister-in-law to arrive any moment shrieking accusations. The fact that she hadn't shown up yet was no relief; I was sure she was postponing the confrontation till the party, where she'd have a bigger audience. At least that's what Mother or any of my aunts would have done.

In retrospect, it seems appropriate that the summer's first known threats of homicide were uttered during the party preparations—although unlike at least one other local resident, I wasn't serious. My nerves were shot, and I was only trying to keep Dad and several of the uncles from decimating the buffet before the other guests arrived.

Mother is fond of remarking that she looks forward to the hour when a party begins because then she can stop working and start having fun. That may be true for her—although Pam and I have noticed that any work she does is purely supervisory. For me, the start of a party only means a change from the tangible, boring, but satisfactory work of cooking, cleaning, and decorating to the unpredictable and far more difficult task of keeping several hundred neighbors and family members from injuring each other or driving me crazy before the end of the evening.

I almost jumped out of my skin when Mother glided over to me with another woman in tow and said, "Meg, this is our guest of honor—Jane Grover, Jake's sister-in-law."

At first glance, Mrs. Grover seemed harmless. She was a short woman with badly hennaed hair and a loud print dress. She and Mother didn't look as if they'd had a quarrel. But after a second I realized that her smile looked artificial and her eyes cold.

"How nice to finally meet you, my dear," Mrs. Grover said, with a look that somehow seemed to insinuate that she had witnessed my shameless eavesdropping on the porch. "We must talk later."

I stammered a greeting and escaped as soon as possible. In the direction of the bar. I watched her and Mother making the rounds of the party. Well, at least they were both on their best behavior.

The party was in full swing, and I'd already confiscated firecrackers from two small cousins and a golf club from an inebriated uncle when Michael arrived.

"Didn't your mother say she was just having a few people over?" he said, incredulously, as he stood at the edge of the sea of guests in our backyard.

"For Mother, this is a few people," I said.

"She doesn't count family," Pam said. "At least half of the horde's family."

"The weirder half," I added.

"Oh, by the way," Michael said, holding out a bunch of flowers.

"Mother will be charmed," I said. "I'll lead you to her so you can present them in person. Don't get in the way of the croquet players," I warned, giving the flying mallets a wide berth. Michael paused to watch the game.

"Croquet!" he exclaimed, taking in the spectacle of a dozen middle-aged and elderly aunts in flowery summer dresses and sun hats posing among the wickets. "It's wonderful! Like something out of a Merchant Ivory film."

"Yes, the croquet clique do tend to dress the part, I'll give them that," I said. "But if you're under the impression that croquet is a genteel, civilized, Waspy way to spend a summer afternoon, don't look too close—they'll spoil all your illusions. It's a blood sport for them."

"Really?" Michael said, incredulously. Just then, one aunt hit another's ball out with a swing that would have been more at home on a golf course than the croquet grounds.

"Ball!" shrieked all the croquet players, and most of the assembled guests—family, anyway—either dropped to the ground or flung their arms over their heads. The ball landed harmlessly in the swimming pool. Its owner, after a few minutes of waving her mallet around and verbally abusing her rival, stormed over to cajole Eric into diving for her ball.

Yes, the party was definitely hitting its stride. One of the uncles had taken his favorite perch on the diving board and was enthusiastically conducting a program of chamber music. My niece was lurking near the CD player in the hopes of slipping the *1812 Overture* into the program and seeing him fall off the board again. About the usual number of relatives had pretended to think the pic-

nic was a masquerade and had come in costume, including Cousin
Horace in his well-used gorilla suit. Eric and Duck were paddling
around in the pool, quacking at each other and bobbing for bits of
food that the guests threw at them. Mother sat fanning herself with
an antique Victorian fan and beaming goodwill near and far.

"Oh, thank you, Michael!" she said, as he handed her the bouquet. "Isn't it nice to have everyone together like this? Though I do
wish Jeffrey could have come down for the holiday weekend," she
added, turning to me. "You should have tried harder to convince
him, Meg."

"Mother, pay attention," I said. "Jeffrey is history."

"Now, Meg."

"Jeffrey has been history for months, and I wouldn't get back
together with him if he were the last human male on earth—which
would be impossible anyway, because Jeffrey is not human, he is
a vaguely humanoid reptile. Please delete Jeffrey from your memory banks. This is a recording."

"I still think Jeffrey is a very nice boy," Mother said.

"Good riddance to bad rubbish I say," Dad put in.

Dad has remarkably sound ideas on what my personal Mr.
Right should be like. I should have known something was wrong
with Jeffrey when Dad didn't take to him.

"Ball!" came the cry again, and we all hit the deck except for
Mother, who watched with mild interest as the croquet ball missed
her ear by two inches and landed in a bowl of potato salad on the
buffet table. This ball apparently belonged to Mother's best friend,
Mrs. Fenniman, who firmly believed that you weren't allowed to
touch the ball with anything other than the mallet. Pam and several
of the saner cousins hurried to move the rest of the dishes off the
table so Mrs. Fenniman could climb up, dig the ball out with the
mallet, and thwack it over the heads of the crowd to the croquet
field.

"It's almost as good as the croquet game with flamingos and

hedgehogs in *Alice in Wonderland,*" Michael said, watching Mrs. Fenniman with morbid fascination.

"Don't give them ideas," I said, noticing absently that since Mrs. Fenniman was dressed in her usual somber colors with a black straw hat precariously attached to the side of her head, her perch made her look even more like a raven than usual. Ravens, flamingos . . . something tugged at my memory. "Oh, Dad, do you know of anyone who sells or rents peacocks?"

"Peacocks? Why peacocks?"

"Samantha wants to have some for her wedding."

"Whatever for?" Michael asked.

"I don't know; loitering about decoratively, I suppose," I said, shrugging. "I mean, that's what peacocks do, isn't it?"

"That sounds very nice," Mother said, thoughtfully. "Very nice indeed."

"Well, if you want them, you can have them after Samantha's finished with them," I said. "Provided I find some to begin with."

"Let's go ask your mother's cousin, the one with the farm," Dad suggested. "He used to have some guinea fowl. Maybe he has an idea where to find peacocks."

"Yes, I think that sounds like a lovely idea," Mother said. "Which reminds me, Michael, about the dining room . . ."

"You're having to spend an awful lot of time on silly details like those peacocks," Dad said, as we left Michael in Mother's clutches and strolled through the crowd looking for Mother's agricultural cousin.

"Well, if I didn't, who knows. Maybe Samantha would get ticked off and cancel the wedding," I said.

"Would that be such a tragedy?" Dad said, vehemently. "If you ask me, it'll be a sad day for Rob when he ties the knot with that one. I know you're working awfully hard to bring this wedding off, Meg, but I hope you won't be too upset if I succeed in talking him out of it, because I certainly intend to keep trying."

I was speechless. I don't know what startled me more, hearing Dad's outburst or realizing that Samantha had come up behind him in time to catch every word of it. If looks really could kill, Dad would be in serious trouble.

"Whatever you think best," I said, steering him gently out of Samantha's range.

We found the cousin, and, after extracting a promise that he would canvass the neighboring farms for peacocks, I left him and Dad deep in a conversation on the relative merits of various kinds of manure. I went to help Pam with her repairs to the buffet table.

"Well, at least they're having a good time," Pam sniffed, watching the winning team perform a decorous victory dance on the croquet field.

"I think everyone is," said Michael. "Anything I can do to help, Meg?"

"Hold these," Pam ordered, shoving several platters into his hands. "Mrs. Fenniman has left muddy footprints all over the tablecloth."

"Having a wonderful time in their own inimitable fashions," I said, watching another aunt who was standing at the very end of the backyard on the bluff overlooking the river, flinging the biodegradable garbage to a flock of seagulls while conversing with them in their native tongue. "With the possible exception of Jake," I added. Jake was standing by himself, a drink clutched in his hand and a nervous expression on his face as he watched the bird-loving aunt.

"I do feel rather sorry for Jake," Pam remarked.

"Jake? Why?" Michael asked.

"Well," Pam said, "about a year and a half ago he has to retire from his job up north somewhere and move down here because his wife is sick and needs a quiet place with a better climate. No sooner do they get here than his wife up and dies. And being pretty much at loose ends, before he's a widower for a year, he falls for Mother."

"Who is apt to be every bit as much trouble for the poor man as an invalid," I said.

"I don't see that there's any reason to feel sorry for him," Michael protested. Pam and I laughed. "I mean, your mother seems to be a very charming woman, and it's not as if she's forcing him to marry her."

"Oh, Mother would never think of such a thing," I said.

"Well, of course she would if she wanted to," Pam said. "But God knows, what reason would she have?"

"But look at him," I said. "I mean, does he *look* happy?" We all three turned to look at Jake.

"No," Michael said, after a moment. "He looks like a nervous wreck. But prenuptial jitters hit some men that way. I was best man for an old college friend a couple of years ago, and I had to stay up all night with him after the rehearsal dinner to keep him from getting into his van and driving to Montana."

"Why Montana?" Pam asked. "Was he from there?"

"No, he'd never been there or ever wanted to that I could remember. But that night, every time I would think I'd talked some sense into him, he'd jump up and say, 'Break the news to her, Michael; tell her I've gone to Montana to herd sheep.'"

"But he didn't go?" Pam asked.

"No, I got him to the church, and the wedding went off as planned. He's never mentioned Montana again. Or sheep. Just a monumental case of prenuptial jitters."

We contemplated Jake a while longer. When one of the neighbors came up and tapped him on the shoulder, he started so violently I was afraid he'd fall into the pool. Pam shook her head.

"If he's got prenuptial jitters already, think how bad he'll be by August," she said. "The man could have a coronary."

"Good point," Michael said.

"Perhaps he's more nervous than usual with his sister-in-law here," I remarked. She certainly made me nervous.

"Does she still count as sister-in-law now that her sister is dead, or is she his ex-sister-in-law?" Pam asked.

"Late sister-in-law, perhaps?" Michael offered.

"No," I said. "She's not dead, her sister is. Maybe he's worried about how she will take it."

"Afraid she won't like your mother?" Michael asked.

"Yes, or won't approve of their marrying so soon after her sister's death."

"Hmph," Pam said. "I'm not sure *I* approve of their marrying so soon." She tossed off the rest of her drink, gave our repair work an approving nod, and stalked toward the bar.

"Do I sense that you and your siblings are not entirely happy about your mother's remarriage?" Michael asked.

"You could say that," I said. "I mean, we could never understand why Mother and Dad divorced. They never argued or anything."

"Then what happened?"

"Who knows?" I said. "All of a sudden one day it was Sorry, children, your father and I are getting a divorce. All very amiable; we all joked that Mother got the house and Dad got the garden, except for joint custody of the tomato patch."

"And you still have no idea why?"

"Pam and I have always felt that it was all Mother's idea, and that she was doing it because of something he did, or didn't do. Or that she thought he'd done or not done. We thought eventually either he'd figure out what it was and set it straight, or she'd forgive him, or both of them would just get tired of the divorce and get back together. But now . . . it's all looking rather permanent."

"And you're not happy about it."

"Well, Jake isn't anyone I would ever have thought of as a possible addition to the family."

"No, I can see that," Michael said. "Compared to your family he seems a little . . . well, bland." He cast an involuntary glance at Uncle Horace.

"He certainly does," I agreed. "Of course, I can't say I've had much time to get to know him. Maybe he has hidden qualities I haven't seen yet." I glanced again at Jake's rather mousy figure. "Then again, maybe bland is what Mother's looking for. I mean he's not likely to startle the guests at a dinner party with graphic descriptions of the symptoms of ptomaine poisoning. Or put a whole truckload of fresh manure on the flower beds just before a garden party for one of her ladies' clubs. Or drag dead and possibly rabid animals into the house to show to the kids. All of which Dad has done, and more."

"Quite a character, your dad." Michael remarked.

"Sometimes a little too much so."

"He does seem to be rather obsessed with poison, doesn't he?" Michael said.

"Ah, I see he's taken you on the garden tour."

"Not exactly, but I overheard enough of what he was telling another guest earlier to get the idea," Michael said. "Pointing out every toxic item in the landscaping, which seemed to be just about every other plant."

"You can never be too careful," I said. "If the buffet had been disappointing you might have been tempted to nibble on the shrubbery."

"But now I know better. I see. Is it a hobby of his, trying to grow every poisonous plant known to man?"

"Well, when my brother Rob was little, he almost died from eating most of a poinsettia, and Dad got interested in the fact that so many common house and yard plants were poisonous. He's made a special study of it. After all, it combines two of his major obsessions: medicine and gardening. Three obsessions if you include mystery books; he's a rabid mystery reader. See, there he is at it again."

"Enlightening one of the neighbors, I see."

"Actually, that's Mrs. Grover, the sister-in-law," I said. Dad was pointing at one of the shrubs and gesticulating enthusiastically. "Hydrangea." I said absentmindedly. "Contains cyanide, mostly in the leaves and branches, although I wouldn't advise sampling the flowers, either."

"Charming," Michael said.

"That's mountain laurel next to it. I forget what it has in it, but if Socrates had been a Native American, that's what they would have fed him instead of hemlock. And then the oleander, which contains a drug similar to digitalis."

"Is this a family obsession as well?" he asked.

"Not at all," I said. "But it's hard not to pick up a few tidbits over the years."

"I won't need your dad's tour, then. You can do the honors."

"Ah, but Dad would tell you the scientific names of each poison and describe the effects in vivid, clinical detail."

"Sounds as if it takes a strong stomach," Michael said, with one eyebrow raised.

"Yes. Mrs. Grover seems to be enjoying it more than most people do," I said. She was asking rather a lot of questions and peering with those cold eyes at each plant as if committing it to memory. Perhaps some of her sister's shrubbery was missing as well.

"Could it be her way of flirting with your dad?" Michael asked.

"More likely she's planning on poisoning someone herself," I replied. "Seems in character."

"Poisoning someone? Who?" Michael and I both turned in surprise to see a startled Jake behind us.

"No one's poisoning anyone, Mr. Wendell," I said, gently. "It was only a joke; we were both commenting on how patient your sister-in-law is being about listening to Dad's lecture on poisonous plants."

"Ghastly," Jake said, and edged away.

"Do I sense that he didn't enjoy his tour?" Michael said, chuckling. I frowned slightly at him; Dad was coming over with Mrs. Grover in tow. I braced myself.

"And this is my daughter Meg, who's down for the summer to help her mother with the wedding, and Michael Waterston, who's filling in this summer for his mother, who runs our local dress shop. How's your mother's leg?" he asked.

"Fine," Michael said. "Making good progress the doctor says. I'm hoping it won't quite be all summer before she comes back."

"Well, tell her not to rush it," Dad said. "You'd be amazed how many people do themselves a permanent injury trying to do too much too soon."

"Her sister is looking after her," Michael said. "Aunt Marigold won't let her get away with anything she shouldn't."

"Marigold? Tell me, is your mother Dahlia Waterston?" Mrs. Grover asked.

"Yes," Michael said, startled. "Do you know her?"

"Yes," Mrs. Grover said. "I come from Fort Lauderdale, you know. I know your aunt Marigold, and as it happens, I saw your mother not very long ago."

"Really," Michael said, oddly nervous.

"It must have been just before her accident," Mrs. Grover said. "Her leg, was it?"

"Yes," Michael said. "Quite a bad fracture."

"Really," Mrs. Grover said. "We must talk about her sometime."

I found myself rather disliking her sly, insinuating manner. She seemed to say one thing and mean another, and I wondered what there could be in that short conversation to make Michael so uneasy. Perhaps he was afraid that Mrs. Grover had found out he was gay and would reveal it to his mother when she went home. Perhaps she'd found it out from his mother and he was afraid she would reveal it here, not knowing that it was already common knowledge. Or perhaps . . . oh, but don't be silly, I told myself. She's just a woman with a rather unpleasant manner. Stop letting your imagination run wild.

"Speaking of Florida, we have some very interesting tropical plants over here," Dad said, hauling the conversation by brute force back to his pet topic. He trotted over to another section of the yard with Mrs. Grover in tow. Michael and I both breathed sighs of relief.

"What an irritating woman," Pam said, appearing at my elbow. "If her sister was anything like her, perhaps even Mother would be an improvement."

"Why, what's she done?" I asked.

"What hasn't she done?" Pam countered. "One of the aunts leaves in tears after Mrs. Grover tells her how natural her wig looked——which it does, but you know how sensitive people are when they've lost their own hair, and Mrs. Grover goes and announces it in front of at least a dozen people who probably didn't realize it was a wig. She suggests that perhaps Mrs. Fenniman has had enough wine, which she has, but you know how contrary she is; she's off swilling it down now and will probably have to be carried home. And then——well, she said something very unkind about Natalie's looks, so I suppose you have to call me a biased witness. Oh, no, she's talking to Eric," Pam said, cutting short her tirade. "Excuse me while I rescue him; I don't fancy seeing her torture both kids on the same evening."

But before Pam had gone two steps, Mother swept over and led Mrs. Grover off. For the rest of the party, whenever I saw Mrs. Grover, she had Mother at her elbow and a vexed look on her face. Bravo, Mother.

That evening, as I was preparing for bed, I found myself getting depressed. I wasn't quite sure why. The anticipated explosion from Mrs. Grover hadn't happened. I'd actually enjoyed myself far more than I usually did at a family party. I'd spent much of the time with Michael. We had a great many interests in common, not to mention similar senses of humor. He seemed to enjoy the company of my eccentric relatives without actually appearing to be laughing at them. Unlike most of the theater people I'd ever met he didn't seem to have an overdeveloped ego and an underused brain— although maybe that was because he was a theater professor, not a working actor. And he was certainly easy on the eyes. Just my luck that I was the wrong gender to suit the only genuinely attractive, intelligent, witty, and interesting male to come along in years. I told myself that it was definitely destructive to my peace of mind to spend too much time with Michael What-a-Waste. I vowed that tomorrow, at Eileen's party, I would mingle. After all, while her father's guest list was unlikely to include anyone as gorgeous as Michael, it might offer someone who was not only unmarried but actually eligible.

Monday, May 30

HOWEVER, I RECKONED WITHOUT MICHAEL'S APPARENT ENTHUSI-asm for my company. Obviously he'd decided I was a kindred spirit here in the wilderness. Or perhaps only the least unpalatable female camouflage available. Whatever. In the light of day, surrounded by dotty relatives, my resolution not to waste time on ineligible bachelors evaporated rapidly. And so from the start, the second party seemed almost as a continuation of Mother's.

"I have a sense of deja vu," Michael said, shortly after arriving. "Didn't I picnic with these same people yesterday?"

"Yes, and ate much the same menu you'll get today," I said. "Welcome to small town life."

"Speaking of food," Rob said, and he and Michael headed for the buffet table.

"Michael's right," I told Pam. "This picnic has almost the same cast of characters as Mother's."

"It's a pity the return performances include Mrs. Grover," Pam said. "After all the stories I've heard about her antics yesterday, I'd have thought she'd be persona non grata everywhere in town."

"She does have a gift for offending people, doesn't she," I replied. "I suppose we're underestimating the local dedication to Southern hospitality."

"Or Mother's ability to twist arms."

"Also a pity Barry had to come," I said, glancing around to see if he was nearby.

"Oh, which one is he?" Pam asked.

"The one following Dad around like a puppy," I said, pointing. "He's been doing it all afternoon."

"Is Dad that entertaining today?" Pam asked.

"I don't know," I said. "I've been avoiding them. Actually, I think Barry's doing it to make a good impression on me. Steven and Eileen probably put him up to it."

"Hmph," Pam said. "I don't see them."

"They stopped over on Cape May on the way back from a fair."

"So we're partying without the guests of honor."

"Yes. Theoretically, they're supposed to be down here tomorrow so we can go pick her dress."

"I'm not holding my breath," Pam said.

"Neither am I." .

I felt it was very shortsighted of Eileen not to come. Both other brides were using the occasion to assign me new projects and extract progress reports on the old ones. Although if I reciprocated by trying to get either of then to make a decision or cough up information, they would gently rebuke me for being a workaholic and ruining such a nice social occasion. I hadn't expected to need the notebook-that-tells-me-when-to-breathe at a party, dammit, so

I was taking notes on napkins. With two out of three brides present at the picnic, my pockets were getting rather full of napkins.

I joined the mob at the buffet table and discovered, to my irritation, that there was only a small bowl of Pam's famous homemade salsa, and that was nearly gone. Rob and Michael were
industriously shoveling down what little remained.

"Is that all the salsa left?" I demanded. Michael and Rob froze,
then edged away guiltily.

"Dad got into it," Pam explained.

"He always does," I said, scraping a few remnants off the side
of the bowl. "You should have made two bowls and hidden one."

"I always do," she retorted. "It's not my fault he found them
both this time. He's getting better at it."

"You mean your dad ate two whole bowls of salsa?" Samantha
asked incredulously.

"Dad's very fond of my salsa," Pam said.

"It's very good," Barry pronounced.

"Wonderful digestion for someone in his sixties," Jake remarked. "I can't even look at the stuff without having heartburn for
days."

"Dad can eat everything," Pam remarked.

"And frequently does," I said. "How well did you hide the
desserts?"

"Here, Meg," Mother said, handing me a plate. "Have some
potato salad."

"I don't like potato salad, Mother," I said.

"Nonsense, it's very good," Mother said. "Mrs. Grover made
it." Not, to my mind, a recommendation. I examined it for telltale
signs of ground glass or eye of newt.

"Oh, Meg, there's your friend Scotty!" Mother said, pointing
out a new arrival. "Scotty and Meg grew up together," she explained to Michael, who was looking dubiously at Scotty's disheveled, potbellied form.

"I've been a little more successful at it," I said. "Scotty's in training to become the town drunk."

"Meg!" Mother said. "Is that necessary?"

"Well, somebody has to do it. Scotty's certainly the best qualified."

"He's had a little trouble finding himself," Mother said. "I'm sure he'll do just fine as soon as he finds something that suits his abilities."

"Mother," I said. "Scotty is thirty-five years old. If he hasn't figured out what he wants to do when he grows up by now, I would say the chances of his ever doing so are slim and getting slimmer by the minute."

"I'm sure he'll turn out all right," Mother said. "He just needs encouragement." She floated over to talk to some newly arriving cousins, graciously bestowing an encouraging word on Scotty in passing. He jumped guiltily away from the beer cooler at the sound of her voice and began combing his unwashed hair with his fingers. Then, when he realized she was gone, he furtively fished out another can.

"Actually, he doesn't usually need much encouragement at all," I said as Scotty had caught sight of me and hurried over. Scotty cherished the fond delusion that we were childhood buddies.

"Meg," he said, approaching with open arms.

"Hello, Scotty, have some potato salad," I said, shoving my plate into his hand to ward him off. He didn't seem to mind. Scotty was used to rejection.

"Isn't it great?" Scotty said. "We're going to be in a wedding together."

"Scotty's an usher in Samantha and Rob's wedding," I explained.

"His father is a partner in the firm," Samantha added, giving Scotty a withering look. He sidled off. I wondered, not for the first time, why Samantha had ever included Scotty as an usher. Granted he was rumored to be reasonably presentable when sober and washed, but other than that . . . well, his father must be a great deal more important to Mr. Brewster's law firm than I'd previously thought. Samantha marched off haughtily in the opposite direction. Scotty looked as if he might return, but noticed that Dad was organizing an impromptu work detail to weed Professor Donleavy's flowerbeds. Scotty vanished around the side of the house. He was all too familiar with Dad's tendency to find work for idle hands. Barry, Eric, and one of Eric's classmates had already begun weeding.

"I see Dad's putting Barry to some good use," I said.

"They seem to be getting along pretty well," Michael remarked with a frown.

"Stuff and nonsense. I suspect Eileen has told Barry to get in good with Dad if he hopes to make a favorable impression on me, which is why he's been hovering over Dad even more than me since he got here."

"And getting in good with your Dad isn't important to making a favorable impression on you?" Michael asked. Dad saw us, waved, and began walking our way.

"It is, but I doubt if Barry has any chance of doing it," I replied.

"What a remarkably obtuse young man," Dad said, shaking his head as he joined us. Michael chuckled.

"I quite agree," I said. "Mother thinks he's very sweet."

"Really," Dad said.

"Of course, she has incredibly bad taste in men—present company excepted, of course."

"Of course," Dad said.

"She always liked Jeffrey, she's very taken with Barry, and she's even rather fond of Scotty the Sot," I said.

"Your mother strikes me as the sort of person who would be a sucker for stray animals, too," Michael remarked.

"Oh, she is." Dad beamed.

"But since we kids started going off to college and weren't around full time to feed them for her, she's gotten very good at getting other people to adopt them," I added.

I left Dad and Michael to entertain each other and strolled through the lawn, greeting friends and neighbors and adding to my napkin collection. One of Eileen's aunts gave me the new address for sending her invitation. A neighbor knew a calligrapher. Mrs. Fenniman knew a cheaper one. An aunt's new (third) husband was starting a catering business. By midafternoon I had to make a trip into the house to empty out my napkin collection.

When I came back out, I paused and looked over the lawn, bracing myself to dive back into the crowd. I noticed Samantha and Mrs. Grover standing a little apart at one end of the pool. From the looks of it, they weren't exchanging pleasantries.

I admit it, I'm nosy. I went over to join them.

"I'm sure you wouldn't want that to get out," Mrs. Grover was saying as I strolled into earshot.

"I have no idea what you could possibly be referring to," Samantha said in an icy tone.

"Well, we'll talk about it some other time, dear," Mrs. Grover said, so softly I could barely hear her. For a few seconds, she and Samantha appeared to be having a staring contest, and although neither appeared to take any notice of me, I knew perfectly well that both were acutely conscious of me and that my arrival had interrupted—what? As far as I knew, Samantha and Mrs. Grover had only just met. What could possibly be causing this undeniable antagonism between Samantha and her fiancé's future stepfather's first wife's sister? What did Mrs. Grover know that Samantha wouldn't want to get out?

"Aunt Meg!" My melodramatic speculations were interrupted by Eric, who had appeared at my side and was tugging at my arm. "Come see what Duck did!"

"I can't imagine," I muttered, following him to a spot in the shrubbery. Mrs. Grover tagged along.

"What is it?" she asked.

"Duck laid another egg," Eric said. "Aunt Meg, what am I going to do with it? I don't have another shirt pocket, and I could put it in my pants pocket, but——"

"In warm weather like this, I think it will be fine until we get the incubator," I said. "Don't worry about it."

"Okay," Eric said. Spotting some newly arrived cousins, he ran off to play, presumably entrusting the care of Duck's egg to me.

"He's remarkably dependent on that bird," Mrs. Grover said, in a disparaging tone.

"Children are devoted to their pets," I said.

"Not exactly a normal sort of pet, though, is it?" she said, in a slimy, insinuating tone that seemed to imply that most arsonists and ax murderers started on the road to ruin through unnatural attachments to waterfowl.

"They have a number of dogs, too," I said, defensively. "But only one Duck."

"Yes, and I rather think we can keep it that way, don't you?" Mrs. Grover said, and before I realized what she was doing, deliberately squashed Duck's egg with the heel of her shoe.

"Don't! Eric's pet laid that!"

"Ugh," she said, as the contents of the egg splattered her foot. "The nasty thing is all over me."

"Well, what did you expect? Did you think ducks laid hardboiled eggs? Don't touch that!" I said, swatting her hand away as she reached to strip a clump of leaves off one of Professor Donleavy's more fragile tropical bushes. "Don't touch any of the bushes; hasn't Dad warned you about all the galloping skin rashes you can get from the foliage around here?"

"Then get me some napkins," she ordered, shaking her foot and spattering me with droplets of egg, while scrubbing her hand on her dress.

"Get your own napkins," I snapped. "And don't let Eric see you. We're going to have a hard enough time explaining why the egg's gone; you have no idea how upset he'll be if he sees you with egg all over your foot."

I snagged a few napkins from the buffet table, cleaned the splatters of egg off my dress as best I could, and retreated to the opposite side of the yard to fume.

"What's wrong, Meg?" Michael asked, appearing at my elbow. I jumped.

"Don't sneak up on me like that!" I said. "Especially when I'm already feeling guilty about contemplating homicide."

"Really," he said, handing me a fresh glass of wine. "Who's the intended victim?"

"Mrs. Grover."

"You may have to stand in line," he replied. "What's she done to you?"

"She deliberately smashed Duck's latest egg. I know it's trivial, but she very nearly did it in front of Eric, and you saw how upset he was at the very idea of something happening to the first egg. It was just so . . ."

"Cold," Michael said. "Very cold. I know exactly how you feel. She sets my teeth on edge."

"Who's that?" asked Dad appearing so suddenly that I jumped again. "Goodness, you're nervous today, Meg."

"That's understandable," Michael said. "She's contemplating homicide."

"Mrs. Grover, of course," Dad said, nodding. "I do hope she won't come to visit often when they're married. I hate to think of Margaret having to put up with her all the time."

"Mother's probably the only one of us who's a match for her," I said.

"Meg!" Dad exclaimed. "Your mother is nothing like Mrs. Grover!"

"I didn't say she was *like* her," I protested. "I said she was a match for her. As in, I defy Mrs. Grover to get Mother's goat the way she's getting to everyone else around here."

"Your mother feels things more than she shows sometimes," Dad said, reprovingly. "I plan to do whatever I can to see that she doesn't have Mrs. Grover on her hands any more than necessary this summer. She doesn't need that with everything else she has to do to get ready for the wedding."

"All the things *she's* doing!" I began, but before I could get much further, Dad had trotted off.

"He looks like a man with a purpose," Michael remarked.

"Yes, but what purpose, I have no idea," I said. "Not to rescue Mother, certainly. Mrs. Grover seems to have latched on to Barry at the moment, and I'm all for letting him go unrescued for as long as possible."

"Amen," said Michael.

In fact, I was definitely hoping no one would interrupt Mrs. Grover's tête-à-tête with Barry, since she seemed to be accomplishing the hitherto unknown feat of getting him hot under the collar. He was frowning and getting very red in the face; you could almost see the steam pouring out of his ears. He seemed to be looking for rescue. He kept glancing in my direction and then frowning all the harder. He would have to wait a long time before I rescued him. Unless—a sudden thought hit me. He wasn't just glowering at me, he was glowering at us. Michael and me. I would be willing to bet almost anything that Mrs. Grover was trying to make him jealous of Michael. Only Barry would be dim enough to fall for that one, I supposed. But the ridiculousness of it wouldn't necessarily prevent Barry from taking some violent action if he got much madder. He should avoid getting angry, I thought. It didn't suit him at all. His eyes got small and piggy and he reminded me more with each passing moment of the bull in a cartoon bullfight, snorting and pawing the earth and preparing to charge. Michael, who would be playing the part of matador if Barry did charge, didn't seem the least bit alarmed.

I finally decided that it would be better to rescue Barry, for Michael's sake if nothing else, and had actually gotten within earshot when Dad bustled up.

"I have a wonderful idea!" he said. "You don't mind, do you, Barry?" he said, taking Mrs. Grover by the elbow and leading her off. No, Barry didn't mind a bit, though Mrs. Grover looked rather like a cat when you take away a wounded bird that the cat's not quite finished playing with.

"Fetch some punch, Barry," I said, rather brusquely, thrusting my cup into his hand and giving him a shove in the direction of the food and drink. I watched to make sure he was really leaving, then dashed off after Dad and Mrs. Grover, partly to avoid being around when Barry returned with the punch and partly to hear what Dad's wonderful idea was. I was appalled to see that he appeared to be making a date with her. To go bird-watching.

Since Dad's bird-watching trips start an hour before dawn and include trekking through some of the local streams and marshes to view the waterfowl, Mrs. Grover was proving less than enthusiastic, even after Dad offered to lend her his spare pair of hip boots. But from the way Dad persisted, I realized he must have some ulterior motive. Very few people can hold out when Dad persists. Mrs. Grover finally agreed, with a visible reluctance that seemed to escape Dad, to meet him in Mother's backyard an hour before dawn for a few hours of nature appreciation.

"Now, tell me why you're so eager to go hiking through the woods with Mrs. Grover," I said, when she finally escaped Dad's clutches.

"I think a little taste of healthy, outdoor exercise would be beneficial," Dad said. "Perhaps a fishing trip in the rowboat would be a good idea, too."

"You could borrow an outboard motor from someone."

"No, that wouldn't do at all," Dad said. "The rowboat's the thing. I could teach her how to row."

"Dad, I doubt if Mrs. Grover has any interest in learning how to row. If you're trying to chase her out of town, why don't you take her over to Mother's cousin's farm and show her the hogs."

"That's a splendid idea," Dad said. "Perhaps he could arrange to slaughter a few while we're there. Any other little ideas you have to keep her out of your mother's hair and make her homesick for Fort Lauderdale, you just speak up anytime." And he trotted off happily in search of the hog-owning cousin. I sighed.

"What now?" Michael asked, once more appearing at my elbow. He was getting very good at that.

"Dad has found a new purpose in life," I said, pointing to where Dad was enthusiastically talking to Mrs. Grover.

"Mrs. Grover?" he said, incredulously.

"In a way. He's decided Mother needs protecting from Mrs. Grover."

"*Your* mother?" he said, even more incredulously.

"Precisely. He's planning to kill her with kindness. Strenuous dawn nature hikes, visits to cousins who live under rigorously rustic conditions—all sorts of supposedly fun things that aren't. Keeping her out of Mother's hair and if possible, encouraging her to flee."

"She could always refuse to go along."

"You don't know him yet," I said, shaking my head. "Dad's the only human being on the face of the earth who can talk Mother into doing something she doesn't want to do. Mrs. Grover's a pushover compared to Mother."

"Well, I must say, I won't be sorry if he succeeds in running her out of town," Michael said. "She keeps coming up to me and insisting she knows me from somewhere. I'm sure if she does she remembers me from my acting days. Before I went back to school for my doctorate, I was one of those rare actors who actually earned a living at it. Mostly in soap operas. I assume that's how Mrs. Grover knows me."

"Have you told her that?"

"Yes, but she keeps saying 'No, that's not it. But it will come to me sooner or later.' As if she expects me to break down and confess, 'Yes, yes, you've seen through me! It was I on the grassy knoll, and what's more, I can tell you where Jimmy Hoffa is buried!' "

"Really? I always heard it was somewhere on the New Jersey Turnpike," said a cousin who was the family's leading conspiracy enthusiast. His uncanny ability to turn up at moments when his pet subjects are mentioned is one of the most persuasive arguments for mental telepathy I've ever known. I confess, I abandoned Michael to him and hunted down Dad.

"Dad, about your trip to the farm with Mrs. Grover," I said. "Do they still have that old outhouse around for local color?"

"Yes," Dad said, a blissful smile spreading over his face as he dashed off to talk to the cousin.

Maybe it wasn't going to be such a bad summer after all.

I kept one eye on Mrs. Grover's progress through the crowd—it was easy to track her by the comparatively bare spot in the crowd that tended to form around her whenever she paused anywhere for more than a minute. I was surprised she hadn't yet burst forth to accuse Mother of robbing her dead sister, but perhaps she was saving that for the grand finale. I wandered over to where Mother and Samantha were talking to the current and former rectors of Grace Episcopal Church. The retired rector, the aptly named Reverend Pugh, was an old family friend. Mother had recently granted tentative approval to his successor after a mere eighteen-year probationary period. She now referred to him as "that nice young man" rather than simply "that young man." At this rate, he had a very real chance of achieving "dear rector" status by the time he retired.

"And here's Meg," the rector said, as I strolled up. "Your mother and Samantha have been telling me about all the things you're doing to get ready for their weddings." Telling him in mind-numbing detail, I suspected, from the desperate note in his voice. I'd long ago stopped wondering why all three brides showed such a distressing inability to understand how anyone they came in contact with could fail to be fascinated with the minutiae of their weddings.

"I'm sorry I'll have to miss them all," he continued, somewhat disingenuously, I suspect. "The day after tomorrow I'm taking the wife and kids on that trip to the Holy Land. Finally going after all these years!"

"Do you mean you're not going to *be* here in July?" Samantha demanded. "Then who's going to do my wedding? I've booked the church." The rector and I exchanged worried glances.

"Yes, well, if you'd talked to me I'd have told you I was going to be gone this summer," he stammered. "When you didn't, I assumed you were making your own arrangements with my substitute."

"And who is that?" Samantha asked.

"Why, me, of course," Reverend Pugh answered, beaming. Fortunately his eyesight was very bad—not unusual at ninety-seven—and he failed to notice the expression of outrage that crossed Samantha's face. I could see she was horrified at the mere thought of his decrepit and highly unaesthetic self officiating at her wedding.

"Don't worry, Samantha dear," he said, reaching to pat her hand and getting Jake's by mistake. "I've got it down in my calendar already. I wouldn't miss it for the world!"

I'd often heard of people having conniption fits, but I'd never actually seen a genuine, unmistakable example before. I was briefly tempted simply to let things run their course, but reason prevailed, and I knew I had to defuse the situation. Nothing brilliant came to mind, so in desperation I made a conspiratorial gesture to Samantha and whispered the first thing that came to mind: "Just humor him! I'll fill you in later."

And spent most of the rest of the party avoiding Samantha while racking my brain for some explanation that would satisfy her. By the time she finally cornered me, much later in the evening, we'd both had rather a lot of champagne, and I managed to spin a convincing yarn about Reverend Pugh's mysterious illness, and how Dad had said a positive mental attitude was important and of course it would keep his spirits up to look forward to the wedding, but that we'd round up a substitute and have Dad order bed rest at the last minute. It sounded highly convincing to me, though it could have been the champagne. Either she bought it or she allowed me to believe she had, after issuing the stern warning that I had better find the substitute ASAP.

I had changed my mind; it was going to be an interminable summer.

Tuesday, May 31

ALTHOUGH I HADN'T EXACTLY MADE A WILD NIGHT OF IT, I HAD stayed up rather late at the picnic, plotting pranks against Mrs. Grover, averting disasters, and drinking a few glasses of wine and champagne. All right, more than a few. I was not at all happy when one of the bridesmaids showed up at the house shortly after dawn. The caterer was acting up and Samantha wanted my help.

"I'm sure Meg will be able to take care of it," Mother said soothingly as she adjusted her hat in the hall mirror. "Jake and I are following your orders today, dear. We're going down to get him a new suit for the wedding, and then we're going to run a whole lot of little errands."

"What sort of little errands?" I asked. Perhaps it was paranoid of me, but I couldn't help suspecting that, as usual, some of Mother's errands would later turn out to involve major amounts of work on my part.

"Oh, this and that," Mother said, vaguely. "Some things for the house. I don't have a list yet. We're going to make a list over a nice breakfast, and then see how much we can get done by lunch."

"Wonderful," I said, insincerely. Mother turned loose on the unsuspecting county. I much preferred her indolent.

"There's Jake now, dear," she said, and floated out toward the front door just as Dad came in the back.

"Meg," he said. "Have you seen Mrs. Grover this morning? She was supposed to meet me here at six A.M. to go bird-watching. She's half an hour late."

"She probably decided to be sensible and sleep in. That certainly was what *I* had in mind this morning," I said, looking pointedly at the bridesmaid.

"Probably so. Well, if she shows up, or if anyone needs me, I'll be in the side yard." I nodded; my mouth was filled with one of Pam's blueberry muffins.

"Okay," I told the bridesmaid, as I finished filling my traveling coffee mug. "Let's go get Samantha and bring the caterer to heel."

The neighbors two houses down had recently put up an eight-foot fence to keep in their Labradors. When we started down the street, I saw Michael trying to pull a small furry dog away from that very fence. The little dog was barking almost hysterically and leaping repeatedly at the fence. We heard an occasional bored bark from one of the Labs. Michael finally succeeded in dragging his dog away, and they headed in our direction. When the dog caught sight of us he quickened his pace.

"Oh, what a cute little dog," the bridesmaid cooed as we came near them.

"If you say so," Michael said. "I consider him—*don't!*" he shouted, as she bent down to pet the dog. "He'll take your nose off," he explained, as the dog went into a frenzy of snarling and snapping. "Bad dog, Spike," he said rather mechanically, as if he had to say it rather often.

"Oh, his name's Spike," she said inanely.

"No, actually Mother calls him Sweetie-cakes, or Cutesy-poo, or something like that," Michael said, with disgust. "I don't think even a nasty little dog like him deserves that, so I've decided to call him Spike. After a bully I knew in grade school." As if he understood what Michael was saying, Spike glanced up at him balefully and curled his lip.

"Charming," I said. Spike was a small dustmop of black and white fur with a petulant, pushed-in face. I prefer cats and collies, myself.

"Mom rescued him from an animal shelter where she was doing some volunteer work."

"Oh, that's so nice," the bridesmaid said.

"She is fond of remarking that he must have been mistreated," Michael said, "and will mellow when he learns to expect food and kindness instead of ill treatment."

"Oh, then she hasn't had him long," I said.

"Only seven years. At this rate, I think he'll go senile before he mellows."

Spike trotted over to the neighbors' mailbox and lifted his leg. However, he lifted the wrong leg, and instead of watering the post came perilously close to spraying the bridesmaid and me.

"We'd better go," she said, wrinkling her nose. "Samantha will be getting impatient."

"The caterer is showing signs of rebellion," I said. "We're gathering a posse to deal with him."

"Good luck. Are you bringing your friend Eileen in later today?"

"If she shows up," I said. "Mother took a garbled message from her yesterday. Something about her and Steven running away to the beach."

"Perhaps they're eloping."

"Don't get my hopes up."

We dealt with the caterer by phone, and then spent what seemed like hours in earnest discussion over whether or not there should be finger bowls, and if so, whether they should have flowers or paper-thin lemon slices floating in them. Left to my own devices, I could have settled this in thirty seconds.

When this weighty issue had been decided and I had my marching orders, Samantha and her bridesmaid went off to meet yet another bridesmaid for lunch. Probably going to split a lettuce leaf between the three of them, I thought, guiltily remembering the muffin with which I'd already undermined my day's calorie count.

I went home, fixed myself an early and depressingly meager lunch, and spent the next few hours on the back porch swing with the phone, racking up long distance charges. One of Eileen's bridesmaids, from Tennessee, had provided two completely contradictory shoe sizes, and I had to elicit the truth. One of Mother's more elusive cousins had to be tracked down—as it turned out, to a commune in California. After failing miserably to find out through any other means the phone number of the Cape May bed and breakfast where Eileen and Steven were reputed to be hiding, I called Barry at Professor Donleavy's and managed to extract the information without actually promising to go out with him. And finally, I reached Eileen and Steven and made Eileen promise to come home within a day or two to decide on her dress and ours.

Having reached the end of my patience, I retired to the hammock and addressed envelopes for a few hours. When Mother hadn't shown up by six o'clock, I began fixing some dinner. When she hadn't shown up by seven-thirty, I ate it. Jake finally dropped her off after nine, tired but happy and laden with parcels.

Not a wildly exciting or productive afternoon, but trivial as my activities were to the progress of the weddings, they loomed large in the light of subsequent events.

Wednesday, June 1

SUBSEQUENT EVENTS BEGAN HAPPENING THE NEXT MORNING AT breakfast.

"Meg, have you seen Mrs. Grover?" Mother asked while waiting for me to finish fixing her a fresh fruit salad.

"Yes," I said. "I met her at the party, remember? At both parties."

"Yes, but have you seen her since? Jake called a little while ago to say she didn't come home last night. He wanted to report her missing to the sheriff, but for some silly reason you can't do much until she's been gone for twenty-four hours."

"Does he think something could have happened to her?" I asked. Trying hard not to sound too hopeful.

"Goodness, I hope not," Mother said. "I think perhaps he's worried that she may have gotten a little vexed at his leaving her alone all day yesterday. While he and I did all our little errands."

"Maybe he's right. She is supposed to be his houseguest."

"Yes, but good heavens, half the neighbors had invited her to visit them or offered to take her places. Your father even came out early to take her bird-watching and she never showed up."

"Well, let's call some of the neighbors and see if anyone has seen her."

We called all the neighbors. No one had seen Mrs. Grover. I went over and searched Jake's yard and the small woods in back of it, in case she'd fallen, broken her hip, and been unable to move, as had happened to an elderly neighbor the previous year. No Mrs. Grover. We braved the dust of the attic and the damp of the cellar to see if she might have been overcome by illness while indulging in a bit of household snooping. Still no Mrs. Grover. There were dishes in the sink and half a cup of cold coffee on the bedside table in her room that Jake didn't think had been there when he left yesterday morning, but he couldn't be sure. She had left three suitcases and quite a lot of clothes, but there was no way we could tell if anything was missing. I was quietly amused by the number of small but valuable household items that seemed to have found their way into her suitcases. Things she considered part of her rightful inheritance from the late Emma Wendell, I supposed. Having met the woman, I could easily believe that she would storm off and leave Jake to have fits worrying about her. But that didn't mean she couldn't have gotten ill or had an accident. And I privately doubted that she would have gone off, even temporarily, and left all her loot behind where Jake could reclaim it.

While we were searching, the sheriff turned up at Jake's house. It was rather unsettling; the sheriff was a cousin, and dropped by quite a lot, but usually his conversations with Mother revolved around family gossip, not police procedures.

"We're going to list her as officially missing first thing in the morning," he announced.

"Anything could happen between now and then," Jake said.

"Frankly, I decided not to wait to start checking around," the sheriff assured him. "She's not in any of the local hospitals or morgues, and there are no Jane Does remotely fitting her description. She can't have taken a plane or train or bus; none of them have a credit card transaction in her name and these days the ticket agents tend to remember anyone who pays in cash. I got in touch with the police department down in Fort Lauderdale, and they'll let me know if she shows up at home. We could try to get some dogs in here to try to track her in case she's . . . wandered off and lying ill someplace."

"I'd appreciate that," Jake said. "I only hope I'm not putting you to all this trouble for nothing. I mean, I'd feel terrible if she just showed up tomorrow and we find out that she forgot to tell me she was going to visit some friend who lives down here. It just has to be some kind of silly mix-up like that, doesn't it?"

He looked hopefully up at the sheriff.

"That's very probable, Mr. Wendell, but I'd feel terrible if we didn't do everything we could to make sure she's all right," the sheriff replied in the earnest tones he usually reserves for the election season. "If you hear from her, you let us know straight away, you hear? And we'll call you the minute we find out something."

I spent most of the rest of the day trying to do a few wedding-related chores in between fielding phone calls about Mrs. Grover, helping coordinate the search for Mrs. Grover, and reassuring an increasingly anxious Jake that I was sure nothing serious had happened to Mrs. Grover.

"I certainly hope she really is all right," I told Dad as we sat on the porch after dinner. "She's totally wrecked my week's schedule and probably taken ten years off Jake's life, the way he's worrying, but I will feel guilty about resenting it all until I know she's all right."

"Yes," he said. "I feel mildly guilty for all the little pranks I was planning to play on her."

"Let's resolve to be especially nice to her when she shows up again," I said.

"Agreed," said Dad. "No more little pranks."

Thursday, June 2

I WOKE UP EARLY, COULDN'T GET BACK TO SLEEP FOR WONDERING if anyone had heard from Mrs. Grover, and finally gave up and came down for breakfast.

"Any news of Mrs. Grover?" I asked.

"No, but Eileen called," Mother said.

"Make my day; tell me she's coming home to pick out a dress."

"No, she and Steven are staying over at Cape May," Mother said. "Such a nice place for a honeymoon."

"Yes, but they're not honeymooning yet. Or ever will be, if she doesn't get down here to pick out a dress."

"There's still time, dear. Why don't you fix us a nice omelet?"

We heard a knock and saw Michael's face at the back door.

"Have you seen Spike?" he asked, slightly breathless. "You know, Mom's dog?"

"No," I said. "Damn, we don't need any more disappearances."

"If you see him running around loose, just give him a wide berth and call me," Michael said. "He's not really vicious, just terminally irritable."

"You might try going down to the beach," I said, following him out. "Dogs always seem to like that. Lots of smelly seaweed and dead fish to wallow in."

"Your nephew and your father suggested that," he said. "Searching the beach for Spike, that is, not wallowing there. They went down to look."

"Or wallow, knowing Dad and Eric."

Just then we saw Eric running toward us.

"Maybe you're in luck," I said.

"Meg!" Eric called, running up to us. "We found something down on the beach! I think it's a dead animal. Grandpa's down looking at it!" He ran over to the edge of the bluff and teetered there, pointing down.

"Stay away from the edge!" I shouted, grabbing for him. "You know it's not safe. It could cave in."

"Come see, Meg!" Eric pleaded.

"We'd better go," I told Michael. "We may have to carry Dad up the ladder."

"Ladder?" Michael said.

"It's a shortcut down to the beach," I explained over my shoulder as Eric tugged me along by the hand to the next-door neighbors' yard. "Most people go down to the Donleavys' house. They have an easy path down to the beach. But Dad likes to go down this rather precarious series of ladders our neighbor built straight down the side of the bluff to his dock.

"Dad!" I called as we reached the top of the ladder. "Do you need us for anything?"

"You keep the kids back, Meg," Dad called up.

"There's only Eric."

"Just keep him back, you hear?" Dad repeated, sounding anxious.

"Go on back to the house and see if your grandmother has the cookies ready," I told Eric, who trotted off eagerly.

"Is she baking cookies?" Michael asked, with interest.

"Mother? It's extremely unlikely. But by the time she convinces Eric of that, he'll have forgotten all about whatever it is Dad doesn't want him to see. It's very odd; I wonder why he's so worried about keeping the grandkids away."

"Surely he wouldn't want them to see a dead animal."

"I don't see why not. He was always dragging Pam and Rob and me to see dead animals and using them for little impromptu biology lessons. He does it all the time with the grandkids. Unless it's one of their animals, of course; even Dad has more sense than to do that. Oh, I hope it's not Duck; he wasn't following Eric."

"Or Spike," Michael said. "Mom would have a fit."

"Meg," Dad shouted up. "Who else is that with you?"

"Michael," I shouted back. "We sent Eric back to the house."

"Good!" said Dad. "Michael, would you mind climbing down here for a minute?" Michael shrugged and started down the ladder. A little too quickly.

"Take it slow!" I said. "That's an old ladder; there are a few rungs missing, and a few more will be very soon if you aren't careful."

"Right," he said, and continued at an excessively cautious pace. I stood at the top of the ladder peering down, rather idiotically, since the bushes were too thick for me to see anything. I could hear Dad and Michael talking in hushed tones.

"Meg," Dad called up. "We've found Mrs. Grover. Go call the sheriff."

"The sheriff," I repeated. "Right. And an ambulance?"

"Yes, not that they need to rush or anything," Michael said.

"And tell him to come prepared," Dad added. "There are some rather suspicious circumstances."

"Oh, dear," Mother said, after eavesdropping shamelessly on my conversation with the sheriff. "Poor Mrs. Grover. And here we all were so irritated because we thought she'd disappeared on purpose to annoy us. I suppose it should be a lesson to us."

I felt rather guilty about the uncharitable thoughts I'd had about Mrs. Grover—now, presumably, the late Mrs. Grover. But while I felt very sorry indeed for her, I couldn't help thinking that if she was going to die under suspicious circumstances, she couldn't have picked a better place to do it.

Of course, having met her, I felt sure that she'd have made every effort to die elsewhere if she'd had any idea of the deep personal and professional satisfaction a mystery buff like Dad would feel at the prospect of helping investigate her death.

Dad examined the body, both on the scene and again at the

morgue, once the coroner had arrived from the county seat. He kept trying to discuss the findings at the dinner table and was sternly and repeatedly repressed. I could understand it in Jake's case; he wasn't used to Dad, and it was, after all, his sister-in-law. But I found it hard to see how Mother and Rob could still be so squeamish after years of living with Dad.

Rob and Jake fled after dinner, and Pam and Eric joined us for dessert, and Dad was at last able to discuss what Mother was already referring to as "your father's case."

"And just what is that in English?" Pam queried, after Dad had given a detailed, polysyllabic description of Mrs. Grover's injuries.

"There was no water in her lungs, so she didn't drown," I translated. "She had a fracture on the left rear side of the top of her skull, apparently from a rounded object; she died within minutes of the fracture; and the way the blood settled in her limbs indicated she may have been moved after death. Right?" I asked.

"Very good, Meg," Dad said. "Of course, the moving may have been due to being washed about in the water; hard to tell yet whether it's significant. And they'll have to do more tests to determine the precise interval between the fracture and her death; that's just my estimate. Incidentally, I estimate the time of death as sometime during the day on Tuesday, but, again, the medical examiner's office will be able to tell more accurately. An examination of the contents of the stomach and the digestive tract as well as—"

"James," Mother warned.

"Well, anyway, they'll be able to tell," Dad went on, unabashed. "But there's one more important thing about the fracture."

"What's that?" I said.

"Consider the location and angle," Dad said. Pam and Mother frowned in puzzlement. I fingered my own skull with one hand, recalling Dad's description.

"You think it's homicide," I said.

Dad nodded with approval.

"Homicide? Why?" Pam demanded.

Dad looked expectantly at me.

"Try to visualize it," I said. "The fracture was on the top of her skull. It's a little hard to figure out how she could do that falling. Unless she fell while trying to stand on her head. Sounds more like what would result if someone hit her on the head with a golf club or something."

"She fell off the cliff," Pam said. "If she was falling head over heels, couldn't she have landed smack on her head?"

"From forty feet up? It would have been like dropping a melon on—"

"James!" Mother exclaimed.

"Well, it would have," Dad protested. "Consider the velocity of a straight fall. She would have sustained far more extensive injuries, particularly to the cranium if that's where she landed. And if her fall was broken one or more times by the underbrush or by intermediate landings, why were there no significant abrasions or contusions elsewhere on the body? No torn clothing, no leaves or twigs caught in her hair or clothes? I don't believe she fell from that cliff, before or after her death," he stated firmly. "I believe she was murdered and then left on the beach. The sheriff may not realize it yet, but I do. And I'm going to do my damnedest to prove it."

Well, at least someone was happy. I went to bed trying to fight off the uncharitable thought that thanks to Mrs. Grover's inconveniently turning up dead almost in our backyard, I was now yet another day behind in my schedule. And I had no doubt further interruptions would be coming thick and fast.

Friday, June 3

EITHER THE SHERIFF HAD COME AROUND TO DAD'S WAY OF THINK-
ing or he was taking no chances that Dad might be right. When I
woke up the next day, the bluffs were swarming with deputies.
Well, six of them, anyway, which was a swarm by local standards,
being exactly half of the law enforcement officers available in the
county. They were searching the beach and the top of the bluff, and
had even gotten the cherry picker from the county department of
public works, which they drove down to the beach and used to
search the side of the bluff. About the only thing of interest they'd
found was the missing Spike.

One of the deputies spent several hours and a whole truckload of Police Line — Do Not Cross tape cordoning off the bluff
and the beach for half a mile on either side of where Mrs. Grover's
body was found. Which seemed idiotic until the crowds began
showing up.

Everyone in the neighborhood turned out to watch the excitement, and not a few people from the rest of the county. Mother
organized about a dozen neighboring ladies to provide tea, lemonade, and cookies, and the whole thing turned into a combination
wake, block party, and family reunion, with Mother holding court
on the back porch.

The only good thing about the gathering was that I met Mrs.
Thornhill, the inexpensive calligrapher Mrs. Fenniman had rec-
ommended, and turned over Samantha's invitations and guest list
to her. What a nice, motherly woman I thought, as I watched her
drive off, her backseat piled high with stationery boxes. Of course
Samantha was paying her, but it still felt as if she were doing me a
favor by lifting that enormous weight off my shoulders.

The forces of law and order knocked off at sunset, leaving a lone deputy standing guard. The festivities went on long after dark. About ten o'clock I snuck off to my sister, Pam's, to sleep.

Saturday, June 4

THE SHOW RESUMED AT DAWN, AND SINCE IT WASN'T A WORK DAY, the crowds were even larger. I pointed out to the sheriff that anyone he might possibly need to interrogate about Mrs. Grover's death was probably milling about in our yard or the neighbors', rapidly replacing whatever genuine information they might have with the grapevine's current theory—which seemed to be that Mrs. Grover, arriving early for her appointment with Dad, either fell over the bluff or was coshed on the head and heaved over the edge by a prowling tramp.

So the sheriff was using our dining room as an interrogation chamber and enthusiastically grilling a random assortment of witnesses, suspects, and fellow travelers. He was concentrating on our whereabouts on May 31, and what we had seen then. Mother and Jake were of no use, of course, since they'd spent the entire day together running errands. I thought it was a very lucky break for Jake that they had. Dad is fond of remarking that in small towns, people tend to kill people they know. The sheriff had heard this often enough to have absorbed it, and Jake was the only one who really knew Mrs. Grover. And might have had reason to do her in, considering the quarrel I'd overhead. But if her death did turn out to be a homicide, not only Mother but half a dozen sales clerks and waitresses would be able to prove that he hadn't been within fifteen miles of our neighborhood between 7:00 A.M. and 9:00 P.M.

The sheriff was particularly interested in the fact that between ten and two-thirty or so I'd been sitting on our back porch making phone calls. Evidently that was a critical time period, and the stretch of the bluff I could see from the porch was the most likely spot for Mrs. Grover to have gone over the cliff, if that was indeed what happened to her.

"And at no time did you see Mrs. Grover or anyone else enter the backyard," he said.

"No," I replied. "I didn't see anyone except for the birthday party going on in the yard next door and Dad on the riding lawn mower."

He didn't look as if he believed me. Dad, on the other hand, believed me implicitly, but that was because my evidence supported his theory that Mrs. Grover had not fallen or been pushed but had been deposited on the beach.

With the exception of Mother and Jake, nobody else in the neighborhood had anything that even vaguely resembled an airtight alibi for the time of the murder. Of course, the sheriff had yet to uncover anything vaguely resembling a motive, either, so the dearth of alibis was not yet a problem for anyone in particular. I began to wonder if there was a homicidal maniac hidden among the horde of locals, who, from their sworn statements, appeared to have spent the day after Memorial Day wandering aimlessly through the neighborhood, borrowing and lending cups of sugar and garden tools and feeding each other light summer refreshments.

Before Mother could organize another neighborhood soiree, I hid in our old treehouse with a stack of envelopes and a couple of good books. I couldn't concentrate on either, though, and found myself gazing down on the crowd, wondering if Dad was right and one of them was a murderer.

I didn't buy the idea of a wandering tramp. I doubted any stranger could pass through our neighborhood without getting noticed by at least half a dozen nosy neighbors and being reported to the sheriff long before he'd had the chance to knock anyone off.

Even residents would cause talk if they did anything out of the ordinary. Long before we noticed Mrs. Grover's disappearance and had reason to be suspicious, someone like Mrs. Fenniman would be sure to ask, "What on earth were you doing standing around in the Langslows' backyard waving that blunt instrument?"

But a neighbor doing something perfectly normal would be ignored. People wouldn't be suspicious—in fact, they wouldn't even remember seeing an everyday sight like—what? I pondered, wondering if I'd done the same thing myself: omitted mentioning a possible suspect.

A bird-watcher. No one would notice a habitual bird-watcher like Dad strolling along the bluffs with binoculars, I thought. Or a gardener. Gardeners also tended to wander rather casually from yard to yard, borrowing tools and admiring each other's vegetation. A dog owner could pretty much wander at will, I realized, seeing Michael stroll into our yard leading Spike. At least as long as he or she had a pooper scooper of some sort. Or a neighbor carrying something that looked like prepared food and heading for Mother's kitchen, I thought, seeing three more neighbors arrive with covered dishes.

This is not getting anywhere, I told myself. Ninety percent of the neighborhood falls into one or another of those categories.

Besides, even if I'd forgotten to mention a passing bird-watcher or food-bearing neighbor, I'd have noticed someone getting close to the bluff. The edge is fragile and crumbling; I grew up having it drummed into me to stay away from the edge of the bluffs. And I admit, I've been a little hyper about it myself ever since the Fourth of July when Rob was seven and got carried away while watching the fireworks over the river. Watching your kid brother suddenly disappear, along with a large chunk of ground on which he had been standing, and then seeing him excavated, undamaged except for a broken arm, from a mound of rubble—that sort of thing tends to stay with you. I'd have noticed anyone even approaching the edge of the bluffs, much less someone getting close enough to shove a person, live or dead, over the edge.

So perhaps I should start from the other end. Who had reason to kill Mrs. Grover?

I didn't like the answers. Aside from Jake, secure behind his alibi, most of the other possible suspects were people I knew and liked. Hell, half of them were family. Although Mother was graciousness itself, I could tell she had taken an intense dislike to Mrs. Grover. I didn't suspect my own mother, of course, but someone else might. And while she had been gallivanting about the county with Jake at the time of the crime, I could think of several friends and relatives who would throw themselves over a cliff—to say nothing of an unpleasant stranger—if they thought it would please Mother.

The sheriff would be high on that list, which could account for his being so slow off the mark investigating. But if he was a cold-blooded killer he was certainly a much better actor than I'd imagined. He'd established what he called an observation post on our diving board, and was standing with a glass of iced tea in his hand, watching his deputies' frenzied activity with a mixture of pride and bewilderment. Then again, it could simply be that he was a little out of his depth dealing with a murder other than the occasional domestic dispute down in the more rural end of the county.

I suspect Dad might have brought himself to dispose of Mrs. Grover if he thought it was absolutely necessary to protect Mother's life, but his idea of how to deal with Mrs. Grover as an annoyance was the mild-mannered, rather entertaining plan of harassment we'd developed during the party. He was rational enough to realize that he would be overreacting if he killed Mrs. Grover merely to spare Mother embarrassment and irritation. At least I thought he was. And no matter how much Dad had always longed to have a homicide to investigate, I knew he wouldn't go overboard and actually commit one. That would be crazy, even for Dad.

Pam. Ordinarily, my sister would be the last person I'd expect to do anything as outlandish as murdering somebody. She could shrug off nearly anything; if someone really did cross her, Pam's natural reaction would be to toss off a few witty remarks and then make sure the culprit's name was mud throughout the county. But if she thought Mrs. Grover was harming one of her kids? She'd be capable. Where they were concerned, she could exterminate a hundred Mrs. Grovers as matter-of-factly as she would an equal number of cockroaches. Pam was not crazy, but she was very, very focused.

Mrs. Fenniman, now. She was a little crazy. Fond as Mother was of her, Mrs. Fenniman was indisputably crazy enough to fit right into my family. In fact, she was a relative, more or less. After twenty-five years of intense genealogical discussion, she and Mother had finally found that the sister of one of our ancestors had apparently been married to the nephew of one of Mrs. Fenniman's forebears, so they'd declared each other relatives. I could see Mrs. Fenniman taking matters into her own hands. During a visit to Richmond, she had once discouraged an armed mugger by stabbing him with her hatpin. And she was convinced that she had never been burgled because everyone in the county knew she slept with her great-grandfather's Civil War saber at her bedside, ready to deal with any intruders. The fact that at least 99 percent of the townspeople had never been burgled either was, of course, irrelevant.

Mrs. Fenniman was wandering about in the yard below, wearing—good heavens, no!—a deerstalker hat. That was all we needed, another would-be amateur detective. I was relieved when she spotted Dad and hurried over to deposit the deerstalker on his shining crown. Dad beamed gratefully. He and Michael were talking, somewhat apart from the crowd—though it was hard to tell whether this was because they were sharing inside information on the crime or simply because people tended to steer clear of Spike, who lunged, snarling and snapping, at any human who came within a few feet.

Michael. He wasn't a relative or an old friend, but I found myself strangely reluctant to consider Michael in the role of suspect. But what, after all, did I really know about him? He seemed like a nice person. But who knew what secrets he might be concealing? Secrets worth killing for? As I watched, he offered Spike a sliver of cheese. Kind-hearted of him, considering how nasty the little beast was. Spike gobbled the cheese, and then, when he'd barely swallowed it, lunged at the hand that had just, literally, fed him. What a pity there was no possibility of Mrs. Grover being killed by a wild animal. We could make Spike the fall guy; he certainly qualified.

Then again, Spike had his uses. He whirled and nearly took a chunk out of Barry, who was still dogging Dad's footsteps.

Barry. One of the few people who might possibly be large enough to have heaved Mrs. Grover into the river. Or over it, if he wanted. Or tucked her under his arm and hauled her down to the beach as easily as I could carry a loaf of bread. He was staying at Eileen's father's house, with the path to the beach not ten feet away. He'd had a run-in with Mrs. Grover at one of the parties. He and Dad alibied each other, but incompletely. Barry claimed to have been with Dad all day, helping in the garden, but I overheard Dad explaining to the sheriff that he'd done his best to "park" Barry whenever possible — to find a chore Barry could do unsupervised and then leave him there where he was out of Dad's hair. It didn't work all that well, I gather — Barry seemed to need to hunt Dad down at regular intervals to ask rather idiotic questions. But still, there were vast stretches of time during which Dad was reveling in Barry's absence and Barry could have been doing away with Mrs. Grover. I would be crushed to find out that any of my family or friends was a murderer. But I thought I could bear up under the loss if it turned out to be Barry. I briefly contemplated life without Barry, or rather with Barry behind bars. I liked the prospect. No more having Barry hang around my booth at craft fairs, scaring away any other, more attractive men who might want to talk to me. No more showing up at Steven and Eileen's to find out they'd arranged to have Barry over at the same time.

Whoa. Steven and Eileen. They would be crushed if it turned out to be Barry. Ah, well, I suppose I would have to hope it wasn't him either, for their sakes.

"Hi, Aunt Meg!" I started; I hadn't even noticed my nephew Eric climbing the tree with Duck under his arm.

"Hi."

"Samantha was looking for you." Drat.

"Don't tell her where I am," I said. I tried to think of a reason to give him, but Eric didn't seem to find my request at all strange.

"Okay," he said. Sensible child. He and Duck settled down beside me.

I scanned the crowd until I found Samantha. She was striding purposefully around, stopping from time to time and questioning people. Still looking for me. I drew back a little from the edge of the platform and made sure I was well hidden behind some leaves. Samantha had also argued with Mrs. Grover during the party. Perhaps she was the murderer, I thought, and then was appalled to realize how much savage, triumphant joy that thought gave me.

I really don't like her, I told myself. I could take her or leave her when she and Rob were dating, but after five months of helping her organize the wedding, I truly didn't like her. By the end of the summer, I would probably loathe her. Of course my relationship with Eileen was a little strained at the moment——or as strained as a relationship could be between two people when one of them was so charmingly oblivious. But that was different. After the wedding was over, Eileen and I would still be good friends. But Samantha. I realized I'd somehow been looking forward to her wedding day as if it were the end of my relationship with her instead of only the beginning. I felt sick to my stomach at the thought of having to see her year in, year out. And felt guilty about feeling that way. I was beginning to suspect Samantha's friendliness toward me when she first got engaged was all a fake. A deliberate ploy to sucker me into doing for her the million and one things I was doing for my own mother and for Eileen, who was not only motherless but perpetually disorganized. Samantha's mother was about on a par with Eileen when it came to practical matters, but I was beginning to think Samantha could have organized her own wedding singlehanded if she had to. But she didn't. She'd trapped me into doing it all instead. I sighed.

"What's wrong, Aunt Meg?" Eric said. "Are you worried about the bad man?"

"What bad man?"

"The one who hurt Mrs. Grover."

"No, I'm just tired. I think I'll take a nap."

"Okay," Eric said. He closed his eyes and curled up to take a nap, too. I was glad. I wasn't sure what I could tell him if he kept asking questions. That there wasn't a bad man? That there was nothing to worry about? I'm not big on lying, even to protect kids. There could be a bad man out there. Or a bad woman.

Please, let it have been an accident. Maybe she was walking on the beach and a stone tumbled down the cliff and hit her on the head. I made a mental note to discuss this idea with Dad, just before I dropped off to sleep.

Sunday, June 5

ATTENDANCE AT GRACE EPISCOPAL WAS UNUSUALLY HIGH THE NEXT morning, almost rivaling Christmas and Easter. I went with Mother largely to keep her in line. She was trying to plan an elaborate funeral for Mrs. Grover; I wanted to get Reverend Pugh to contact

Mrs. Grover's clergyman or friends back home to make arrangements. I wondered if, knowing Mother, he could be persuaded to utter a small white lie and tell Mother that Mrs. Grover wanted to be cremated quietly, with no service or other fuss. Preferably back in Fort Lauderdale.

Reverend Pugh correctly deduced that Mrs. Grover's death was the reason for the high attendance and preached a very moving sermon on the general theme "Even in the midst of life we are in death." At least I suppose it was moving for those who were able to hear it. I was sitting in the back, where Mrs. Fenniman and the other professional town gossips were busily updating each other on new developments in "the case."

I fled home immediately after the service, but my hopes of getting anything done were dashed by an unusually large infestation of visiting relatives.

Monday, June 6

EVEN ON MONDAY, ACCOMPLISHING ANYTHING WAS AN UPHILL battle. No one wanted to talk about weddings; everyone wanted to hear about Mrs. Grover. I stopped by the Brewsters' house after lunchtime to give Samantha some photographers' samples.

Of course, since my arms were completely full, no one answered when I knocked. I juggled the books with one arm and let myself into the kitchen.

"Anyone home?" I called, poking my head into the family room. I interrupted Samantha in the midst of a phone call.

"I'll have to call you back later," she said, and hung up in a distinctly furtive manner. How odd; furtive wasn't usually Samantha's style at all.

"Coordinating your alibi with your co-conspirators?" I teased. To my surprise, she jumped.

"Alibi! What do you mean alibi?" she snapped.

"Where were you on the afternoon of May 31 when the late Mrs. Grover disappeared?" I said, melodramatically.

"I don't think that's the least bit funny. The poor woman is dead."

"I'm sorry. I don't think it's particularly funny either; I've just had it up to here with people putting on their lugubrious faces and wanting to hear all about it."

"Who wants to hear all about it?" Samantha asked. "Hasn't everyone around here heard enough already?"

"Yes, but all day, everyone with whom I've tried to discuss menus, flowers, photo packages, and tuxedo sizes has wanted to hear all about Mrs. Grover before doing any business."

"That's so tacky," she sniffed.

"Yes, but in a small town, one can't afford to offend the limited number of vendors available," I pointed out. "So I give them a thrill by telling them the inside scoop, and with any luck I can turn it to our advantage."

"Well, that's sensible, I suppose," Samantha said, absently. I gave her the photographers' books and beat a retreat. She seemed to want to be left alone, which was highly unusual. Normally she'd have wanted to interrogate me on my progress and natter on for hours about her latest inspirations. Perhaps I had been too hard on her, I thought, as I strolled home. Perhaps she had really been affected by Mrs. Grover's death. I doubted she could have gotten to know Mrs. Grover well enough to be mourning her personally, but perhaps the death had momentarily jarred her out of her monumental self-absorption. A sobering reminder of mortality in the midst of celebration and plans for the future and all that. Maybe that was why she had seemed so furtive; perhaps she was embarrassed to have her frivolous preoccupation with finger bowls and flower arrangements compared with the grief suffered by Mrs. Grover's loved ones. Whoever they might be.

Then again, perhaps Samantha's touchiness on the subject of the murder was due to irritation about the attention it was drawing away from her wedding. And as for behaving furtively, she was probably up to something. Coming up with some new complication—another one of those "small details that really make the occasion"—as well as making mountains of work for me. Doubtless she'd unveil her new plan, whatever it was, as soon as she was sure she'd figured out how it could cause the maximum amount of trouble for me.

I spent the afternoon fretting alternately about what Samantha was up to and what the sheriff was up to, becoming so preoccupied that I actually misspelled several relatives' names on their invitations and had to rewrite them.

"Meg," Dad said that evening, "I'm having a hard time convincing the sheriff how extremely unlikely it was for Mrs. Grover to have fallen from the bluff without sustaining a more serious injury. Could you help me for a while tomorrow?"

"Why not?" I said, rashly. If I couldn't forget about the murder long enough to address a few envelopes properly, I might as well help Dad out and perhaps get it out of my system. And of course my brother, Rob, who was supposed to be studying for the bar exam, was up for anything that didn't involve sitting indoors with his law books, so Dad succeeded in recruiting him as well.

Tuesday, June 7

I WAS GETTING READY TO THROW AN IMPOSSIBLY HEAVY SANDBAG off the bluff the next morning when Michael came along walking Spike.

"What are you doing?" Michael said.

"Helping Dad help the sheriff with his investigation."

"Ready!" Dad called up from the beach.

I took a deep breath and then grappled with the sandbag.

"Here, let me help you with that," Michael said, looking for somewhere to tie Spike's leash.

"No, no!" I said. "That would spoil the test."

"Test? What test? That thing must weigh a ton."

"A hundred and five pounds, actually," I puffed. "Stand clear." I wrestled the bag as close to the edge of the bluff as I dared, gave it a desperate heave over the side, and fell back panting. I heard the bag crashing through the brush on the way down. "One more to go," I said, as I collapsed onto the ground by the last sandbag.

"I assume this has something to do with the murder?" Michael said, sitting down on the grass beside me. "Was that all she weighed, a hundred and five pounds?"

"Was that all? You try lugging one of these," I said. "Actually, a hundred and two, according to the medical examiner, but Dad decided to add three pounds for clothes. We're doing some testing for the sheriff."

"Ready!" Dad called again.

"Testing what?" Michael asked. "And why do you have to throw them?"

"If you want to throw some next, that would be fine with Dad. And great with me, I'm done in, and Rob's beat, too, and we both want to keep Dad from doing too much of the throwing. He's very fit but he's not invulnerable. But seeing how much strength it would have taken to have thrown her over is one of the things we're testing. I'm pretty damned strong for a woman, and it's about as much as I can do to drag them to the edge and shove them over. Here goes."

I slung the bag over the side, but this bag didn't go as far and stuck in the bushes. "Damn," I said, and grabbed up the garden rake. I shoved at the bag until it finally toppled over and went crashing down the side.

"All gone!" I shouted over the side.

"You said how much strength it would take was one of the things you were finding out," Michael said. "What else is this intended to discover?"

"All sorts of grisly things. Could the underbrush or the water break Mrs. Grover's fall enough to result in the relatively minimal injuries she sustained?"

"And could it?"

"Not bloody likely. And how much noise a hundred-and-five-pound object makes when landing, on sand and in the water, and how far away you can hear the noise, and the answers are less than you think, and not with the riding lawn mower running."

"Was it running?"

"Much of the time, yes. And whether there's any possibility she could merely have tripped and fallen over."

"Somehow I doubt that."

"Yes, it's so unlikely that we can pretty much discard it, no matter where you try it. Similarly, it's highly unlikely that anyone could have shoved her over. It very much looks as if the only way she could have gone over under her own steam would be if she took a running broad jump at the edge. And even then she'd have to be pretty athletic for a fifty-five-year-old."

"Aren't you afraid of destroying evidence?" Michael asked.

"They've been all over this stretch of the cliff, and found nothing," I replied. "No sign of one-hundred-five-pound weights having crashed through the brush, no scraps of clothing, no stray objects. At least none that could reasonably be assumed to have fallen off Mrs. Grover. That's another thing Dad wants to prove, how unlikely it would be for Mrs. Grover to have fallen over the cliff without leaving any traces on her or the cliff."

"How do you know this is where she went over?" Michael asked. "I thought she was found a little further downstream than this."

"We're trying it at all the likely places along the bluff. All upstream from where she was found, of course. Next he's planning to do some tide and current tests to see if it would be plausible for a dead body dumped in the river to wash up where hers was found."

"Using what?" Michael asked, dubiously. "I mean, sandbags obviously won't cut it."

"Rob and I are trying to convince him just to use a whole bunch of floats instead of actual dead bodies. Of animals, of course," I added, hastily, seeing the look on Michael's face. "He's been talking to meatpacking houses."

"Lovely," Michael said, just as Dad and Rob came puffing up the ladder. I hoped Michael wouldn't laugh when he saw that Rob was carrying a camcorder.

"Michael!" Dad said, enthusiastically, as he flung himself down by us, mopping his face with his handkerchief. "Glad to see you; we could certainly use your help!"

"So Meg was telling me."

"Oh, Meg, how about some lemonade or iced tea?" Dad said. "Or a beer. Anything cold."

"Meg's been playing stevedore," Michael said. "How about if I fetch the refreshments?"

"Good idea." Dad approved. "And when you get back I'll tell you what you can do."

I don't know whether Rob's videotapes and the meticulous notes Dad had been taking impressed Michael with the value of our efforts or whether he allowed himself to be recruited for the entertainment value. There are people in town who gladly help Dad out with his most hare-brained projects and then dine out on the stories for months afterwards. Or maybe it was the camcorder. Michael was an actor; perhaps the ham in him couldn't resist the chance to be in front of a camera. Whatever the reason, for the next couple of hours Michael joined in energetically as we shoveled sand into the bags, dragged them up from the beach with a winch the next-door neighbors had installed to haul their boat up to their driveway, weighed them, and then heaved them down again while Dad scribbled more pages of notes. Jake came over to watch briefly at one point, and Dad tried to enlist his help, but as I pointed out, it was his sister-in-law's demise we were trying to reenact, so he could hardly be blamed for feeling a little squeamish about the prospect.

It's always entertaining to watch a couple of men who've been bit by the macho competitive bug and are earnestly trying to outdo each other at something relatively pointless, like heaving giant sandbags over cliffs. Once he got the hang of it, Michael proved to be slightly better at sandbag-heaving than Rob, and so it was Michael who got to demonstrate for the sheriff when he came out that evening.

The sheriff couldn't help smiling at Dad's enthusiasm, but I could tell Dad was beginning to convince him.

"So you see, I think we've pretty clearly established that Mrs. Grover did not fall from the cliff accidentally," Dad pontificated over lemonade on the porch after our demonstration. "There was nothing on the cliffside to indicate the passage of a falling object the size of a body."

"There is now," Michael said.

"Don't worry, young man," the sheriff said. "We searched it pretty thoroughly for a couple days. Nothing to be found."

"No traces of leaves or dirt on her body," Dad went on, relentlessly. "And, as you can see from the effect on the sandbags, it is highly unlikely that she could have fallen, either postmortem or antemortem, without significantly greater injury. I postulate that she was taken to the beach, probably by the Donleavys' path, possibly by the neighbors' backyard staircase."

"Or by boat," Rob suggested.

"Yes, it's possible," Dad conceded, frowning. "Of course it's unlikely. Unless someone risked discovery by bringing her by boat from quite a distance. They'd have been just as noticeable carrying her down to a boat anywhere near here as they would simply carrying her down to the beach to dump her body. But you're right; we can't overlook the possibility of a boat."

He looked very depressed. Doubtless the possibility of a boat either contradicted his pet theory or, more likely, emphasized how difficult it would be to catch the culprit. I felt sorry for him.

"Call the Coast Guard," I said. "Maybe they're still staking out suspicious inlets for potential drug runners."

The commandant of the local Coast Guard station was convinced that his colleagues had made landing in Florida too risky for the Colombian cocaine merchants. He thought a small, unassuming town like Yorktown would be the perfect base for a major drug smuggling ring. So far his intense surveillance of the local waterways had not produced any stray smugglers. However, fishing out of season and poaching from other people's crab pots had fallen to an all-time low.

"Yes, it was the Coast Guard who arrested young Scotty Ballister and your cousin," Dad said, happily. In addition to being caught crab poaching, which wasn't actually illegal but hadn't won them any friends, the two of them had been arrested for possession of marijuana——the closest the commandant had actually come to a drug raid. But although the baggie of grass had inconveniently floated long enough for the Coast Guard to fish it out, the prosecutor's office couldn't prove that Scotty or the cousin had tossed it overboard——at least, not after Scotty's father the attorney had finished with them. Rumor had it the Coast Guard were patrolling the beaches of our neighborhood intensively, in the hope of catching Scotty and the cousin redhanded.

Dad trotted off to call the commandant.

"Excellent thinking, Meg!" he reported a few minutes later. "There were no craft other than the Coast Guard cutters anywhere near the beach any night this week. They'd had an alert, and have been putting on extra patrols." Translation: they were, indeed, still lurking off the shores of our neighborhood, hoping to catch Scotty and my cousin. "It looks as if our criminal must have delivered the body by land after all."

"Unless she got there on her own," the sheriff added, shaking his head.

"I'm just glad I didn't somehow overlook seeing someone shove her over," I said. "That idea really bothered me."

"Of course there's the question of whether she was killed there, or moved there after her death," Dad continued. "And if she wasn't killed there, whether she was put there for a reason, such as to cast suspicion on someone, or merely because it was the most convenient place in the neighborhood to dispose of a corpse."

"And regardless of where she was killed, where was she all morning?" I put in.

"Good point," Dad replied. "How come no one saw her either walking or being carried down to the beach?"

"And for that matter, has anyone remembered searching the beach that day we were all looking for her?" I asked. No one, alas, had; so the question of whether she was on the beach on June 1 or put there sometime later remained unanswered.

"We're going to start the current tests tomorrow, to see how far it's feasible for her to have drifted before she was found," Dad said, turning back to the sheriff. "Did you bring the tide tables?"

Wednesday, June 8

DAD SPENT MOST OF WEDNESDAY PREPARING HIS TIDE AND CURrent tests. In the morning, he cruised upriver for several miles, noting every place where someone could have dropped a body into the river. Rob weaseled out, pretending to study. So since Dad's mechanical ineptness is particularly pronounced with outboard motors, I ended up as pilot, with Eric as crew. Eric could have run the boat himself, but it took both of us to fish Dad out whenever he got carried away and fell in.

Thursday, June 9

"EILEEN STILL HASN'T SHOWN UP," I REPORTED BY PHONE TO Michael Thursday afternoon. "I've begun to wonder if she and Steven might have eloped after all."

"Well, just bring her in as soon as you can."

"Roger."

"Or maybe you'd like to come in and do some preselecting for her, eliminating things that you know wouldn't work for her body type and so forth."

"Sounds like a good idea. I'm rather stuck out here today, but maybe I should do that as soon as I'm free."

"I could bring some of the books out to the house for you now," he offered, eagerly. Evidently he was more anxious about the deadline than he was letting on.

"Thanks, but I'm not at the house right now."

"Where are you, then?" he asked. "They need to get their phone checked, wherever you are; this is a lousy connection."

"I'm in a rowboat in the middle of the river. I'm using Samantha's cell phone." There was a pause so long I thought we'd been disconnected.

"I know I'm going to regret asking, but why are you in a rowboat in the middle of the river?"

"Dad's driving up and down the bank, releasing flocks of numbered milk jugs at intervals. To test the speed and direction of the current and narrow down the sites where Mrs. Grover's body could have been dumped into the water."

"That'll take forever, won't it?" he asked. "After all, she was missing for several days before we found her."

"Yes, but she couldn't have been in the water for more than a few hours. Trust me on that. If you want to know why, ask Dad, although I advise not doing it just before dinner."

"I'll take your word for it. So you're out helping your Dad release bottles?"

"No, he and Rob are doing that, and keeping a log of exactly where each one was released. I'm out here to record my observations. Scientifically."

"And what have you observed, so far? Scientifically speaking."

"That there are getting to be a truly remarkable number of milk jugs bobbing around out here, but unless they start showing a great deal more enthusiasm, none of them are going to make it to the beach anytime this century. Most of them don't seem to be going anywhere at all. Except for the ones the sheriff is dropping into the current in the middle of the river. They're travelling rather briskly, but they're not coming anywhere near the beach."

"Oh, the sheriff's involved, too?"

"I don't know whether Dad's convincing him or he's humoring Dad, but yes, he's out in the powerboat releasing jugs. That's why I'm in the rowboat."

"Rather tedious for you," Michael sympathized.

"Oh, it's all right. It's peaceful out here, and it's also amazing how much you can get done even in the middle of the river with a cellular phone. And I brought the stationery so I can keep on with the addressing for Mother."

"Well, come in when you can. With or without Eileen."

"Roger."

I had a quiet day, but on the bright side, Barry took off to meet Steven and Eileen for a craft fair in Manassas. Good riddance.

Friday, June 10

I SPENT FRIDAY IN MUCH THE SAME WAY——BOBBING ABOUT ON THE water watching Dad's latest crop of milk jugs. I found I couldn't write invitations after all; the sunscreen smeared them. I'd made all the phone calls possible. All I could do was fret about the identity of the murderer, if there was a murderer. I resolved that once I was released from my observation post, I was going to go around to question some of my friends and family. With subtlety. The sheriff was about as subtle as a plowhorse.

Saturday, June 11

AFTER TWO DAYS OF BOBBING ABOUT ON THE RIVER HERDING milk jugs, I devoted Saturday to helping Dad with the roundup—tracking down as many of the milk jugs as possible and recording where we'd found them. We even started getting calls from people down river, claiming the small reward we had offered for turning in the jugs that got past us. Most of these, as expected, were the ones the sheriff had dumped into the current. None of the jugs washed up anywhere near the beach where Mrs. Grover was found, which Dad and the sheriff concluded was convincing enough proof that her body had been dumped there rather than washing up there. I had to admit, I was convinced. Thanks to the vigilance of the Coast Guard and the contrariness of the currents, we now knew that Mrs. Grover must have arrived on the beach by land, not by sea.

But for the moment I'd decided to let Dad investigate alone. Wonder of wonders, Eileen had showed up Saturday afternoon, even more sunburnt that I was, but in one piece, and presumably available for measuring and gown selecting. If she didn't take off before Monday morning.

"Having trouble with your car?" Michael asked. He came across me peering under the hood of my car, owner's manual in hand, so I suppose that was the logical assumption.

"I'm trying to figure out where the distributor cap is, and how one removes it."

"You're having trouble with your distributor cap?" he asked.

"No, but I want Eileen to have car trouble if she tries to leave before I get her in to pick out her gown. In the movies, they're always removing the distributor cap to keep people from leaving the premises, but I can't even figure out where the darned thing is."

After much effort, we succeeded in locating something that we thought was the distributor cap; more important, we confirmed that, whatever it was, once it was removed the car wouldn't start. After considerably greater effort, not to mention some help from Samantha, who happened to be passing by, we managed to get it reinstalled and start my car again.

We then staged a daring midnight raid on Eileen's car.

Sunday, June 12

I SLEPT IN SUNDAY MORNING AND THEN FLED BEFORE MOTHER AND her court arrived for the midday dinner. I didn't want to face what the assembled multitudes had to say about either the murder or the Langslow family's latest eccentricities. Instead, I went over to Eileen's house to read her the riot act about staying in town until the gown business was finished. We arranged to go down to Be-Stitched bright and early Monday morning. She promised repeatedly that of course she wouldn't think of leaving town before the gown was settled. Cynic that I am, I took more comfort in the thought of her distributor cap safely stowed in a shoebox at the very back of my closet.

As I was walking down her driveway, Eileen came back out and called to me.

"Oh, by the way, Meg," she called, "Barry's coming in tonight. He called to say he's dropping by on his way home from the show and can stay around for a few days."

"How nice for him. I'll pick you up at five of nine tomorrow."

I rejoined Mother, Dad, and Pam on the porch of our house. Dad had several dozen medical texts scattered about. He kept reading bits in one, then switching to another, all the while nodding and muttering multisyllabic words to himself. I hated to interrupt him, but—

"Dad," I asked. "Do you have any heavy yard work that needs doing?"

"I need to saw up that fallen tree, but I don't think you'd want to do it."

"Besides, dear, don't you have enough to do with the invitations?" Mother hinted. "All this excitement over Mrs. Grover seems to have taken such a lot of your time."

"I wasn't volunteering for yard work," I said. "But Eileen says Barry is dropping by on his way back from the craft fair to spend a few days."

"How nice of him," Mother purred.

"Good grief," Pam said.

Dad snorted.

"And I see no reason why he should be loitering around underfoot, getting in everyone's way," I continued. "He could make himself useful. He's a cabinetmaker; he should feel right at home with a saw. Have him cut up the tree."

"He could come with me up to the farm," Dad said. "They've promised me a load of manure if I help haul off a few more truckloads of rocks. Barry's a big lad; he should be able to handle the rocks."

"What a good idea," I said. "Barry spends a lot of time at the

farm with Steven and Eileen. I'm sure he'd love one of your manure trips." Perhaps we could also take Barry on all the little ex-
peditions we'd dreamed up to help run poor Mrs. Grover out of
town. Waste not, want not.

"By the way, Dad," I added, "remind them about the peacocks."

Monday, June 13

"EILEEN WILL BE CHOOSING A GOWN THIS WEEK," I ANNOUNCED
over breakfast to Mother and Mrs. Fenniman—who had dropped
by shortly after dawn to borrow some sugar and had now been discussing redecorating schemes with Mother for several hours.

"That's nice, dear," Mother said. "Does she know that?"

"She will soon," I replied. "I am picking her up at five minutes
to nine. We will drive in to Be-Stitched and stay there until she se-
lects something. If she hasn't decided by lunchtime, I will go out
for pizza. If she hasn't decided by closing time, we will do the
same thing Tuesday if necessary, and Wednesday, and Thursday.
If by noon Friday she hasn't picked anything, I will select whatever
Michael tells me can be most easily completed between now and
mid-July, and she will have to live with it."

"This I gotta see!" chortled Mrs. Fenniman.

"Eileen is so fortunate to have you taking care of things,"
Mother remarked. "Perhaps Mrs. Fenniman and I could help. We
could try to gently influence her toward some gowns that would
be appropriate and flattering."

"With no hoops!" Mrs. Fenniman snorted.

I considered the offer. Logically speaking, one would assume
that having more people involved would prolong rather than stream-
line things. But Mother could not only talk anyone into anything, she
could probably make Eileen think it was her own idea. The trick was

to get Mother properly motivated. I needed a mother determined to help Eileen reach a quick decision, not a bored mother finding entertainment by helping Eileen dither for the rest of the week.

"If you wouldn't mind, that would be a help. Perhaps the problem is that Eileen doesn't quite trust my advice on clothing, but of course with you two there that wouldn't be a problem. And it would save time in the long run. As soon as I've gotten a decision from Eileen, I can really concentrate on getting the rest of your invitations out and running all those errands you need for the redecorating."

I was afraid I'd been a little too obvious, but they fell for it. It only took me ten minutes to put on my shoes and find my car keys, but when I went outside they were standing impatiently by the car in their full summer shopping regalia (including hats), and had begun jotting down a list of criteria for Eileen's dress. I felt encouraged that the first item was "No hoops!"

"We've all come to help Eileen decide on her dress," I announced to Michael as the parade filed into the shop. Mother and Mrs. Fenniman settled on either side of Eileen on the sofa in the front window and dived efficiently into their task.

"I'm not holding my breath," Michael said, too quietly for the others to hear.

"Have faith," I muttered back. "The end is in sight. I've pretended to Mother that I'll have absolutely no time to work on her wedding till Eileen's gown is chosen. Five bucks says she has a decision by lunchtime."

"No bet," Michael said, laughing.

By eleven-thirty, I was beginning to be glad we hadn't wagered. I wouldn't exactly say Mother and Mrs. Fenniman had been unhelpful. They'd talked Eileen out of a number of truly horrible dresses, usually with graphic descriptions of how awful Eileen would look in them. But we didn't really seem any closer to a decision.

"Perhaps it's time to order in lunch," I said.

"Good idea," Michael said, and strolled over to the counter to pick up the phone book.

"They have lovely salads and pastries at the River Cafe," Mother said brightly. "It's just two blocks down."

"Do they do carryout?" I asked. "We're not leaving till Eileen makes a decision."

"I suppose they might, but you can't carry out a nice pot of tea. Why don't we just——"

"Tea?" Michael said. "I'll be happy to make some tea. Mom and the ladies have quite a selection. Earl Grey, jasmine, Lapsang souchong, gunpowder, chamomile, Constant Comment, plain old Lipton tea bags . . ."

Deprived of the prospect of an elegant luncheon, Mother lapsed into decorative melancholy after I placed our sandwich order with the cafe. Even Mrs. Waterston's best jasmine tea in a delicate china cup produced little improvement.

"I can see why Eileen is having so much trouble." She sighed to Mrs. Fenniman. "They simply don't make gowns like they used to. I mean the styles, of course," she said quickly to Michael.

"I like to split a gut laughing the first time I saw a bride in a miniskirt," Mrs. Fenniman cackled. "And that Demerest girl last year—out to here!" she exclaimed, holding her hand an improbably three feet from her stomach. "It's a wonder she didn't go into labor right there in the church, and her in a white gown with a ten-foot train."

"I always thought the gowns Samantha had made for her other wedding were really sweet," Mother mused.

"Her *other* wedding?" Michael and I said in unison.

"Oh, dear," Mother said. "That's terribly bad luck, two people saying the same thing like that. You must link your little fingers together, and one of you has to say, 'What goes up a chimney' and then the other has to say, 'Smoke.' " Michael was wearing the you've-got-to-be-kidding look that was becoming habitual these days. At least when my family was around.

"Just do it," I said, extending my little finger. "For the sake of all our sanity. What goes up a chimney?"

"Smoke."

"I hope that was in time," Mother said. "Well, you'll know next time; at least you will, Michael. Meg is *so* stubborn."

"I'll work on it," he said. "Tell us about Samantha's other wedding."

"You remember, Meg, it was supposed to be at Christmas, a year and a half ago. She was engaged to that nice young boy from Miami."

"Oh, yes, the stockbroker," I said. "I remember now. And how many millions of dollars was it he embezzled? Or perhaps I should say cruzeiros; he skipped to Brazil if I remember correctly."

"No, dear, that was his partner. They arrested Samantha's young man in Miami before he got on the plane. And he said his partner got away with all of the money. The partner claimed otherwise, of course, but they never found a penny of it."

"Poor thing! So Samantha dumped him and went after Rob," I said.

"That's so cynical, Meg," Eileen said, looking up from her catalog.

"That's me, town cynic," I said.

"Anyway, I do think her first gowns were lovely," Mother continued. "Not that the new ones aren't lovely too. But these were rather unusual, too, and your mother's ladies did such lovely work on them."

"Mom made them?" Michael asked, surprised.

"Why, yes," Mother said. "They might still be here; I remember when we told her about Samantha and Rob's engagement she said something about hoping Samantha would finally take them off her hands, but of course Samantha didn't want anything to remind her of that ill-fated first engagement."

"I'm beginning to wonder if your mother breaking her leg just now was entirely an accident," I said to Michael.

"What do you mean?" he asked, with a start.

"Perhaps subconsciously she *preferred* to break it rather than stick around for Samantha's second wedding." He laughed.

"Why blame her subconscious? Seems like a rational decision to me."

"I thought it was her arm she broke," Mother said.

"No, I'm sure Michael said it was her leg," Mrs. Fenniman said. They both looked at Michael.

"Both, actually," he said, nervously. "They knew the leg was broken right away, and at first they only thought the arm was sprained, but then when they x-rayed they found the leg was a simple fracture and the arm was some sort of more serious kind of break so we were more worried about the arm and I might have forgotten to mention the leg at that point, but now we know they're both broken, but mending nicely." Only a trained actor could have gotten that out in one breath, I thought.

"Poor thing," Mother said. "How did she do it, anyway?" Michael looked nervous again and hesitated.

"To tell you the truth, I don't really know," he said finally. "She's told me several completely different stories, and I've decided she probably did it while doing something she thinks I would disapprove of or worry about. We may never know the whole truth." He walked over to the curtained doorway and called out something in——Vietnamese? Whatever. Mrs. Tranh appeared and they talked rapidly for a few moments, then Mrs. Tranh disappeared behind the curtain.

"Mrs. Tranh says the gowns Samantha originally ordered are, indeed, here, and she's going to bring some of them down."

"Oh, how interesting," Mother said.

"If by some miracle they appeal to you, Eileen, we can probably give you a really good deal. At cost, even; they've been hanging around taking up space for nearly eighteen months now."

And tying up cash, no doubt; I felt sure that if Samantha's family had paid for them, they'd have the gowns in their possession. I wondered how they managed to weasel out of paying. I would have to consult the grapevine on that one. If it were my wedding I would never stoop to taking Samantha's castoffs, but I suppressed the thought. At this point, I'd like *anything* Eileen could be persuaded to choose. Mrs. Tranh and one of the other ladies appeared lugging garment bags taller than they were, and Samantha's rejects were pulled out and lovingly displayed.

"Oooohhhh," Eileen said as the bridal gown emerged from the bag. I hurried over to see what we were in for.

Maybe it was seeing the actual garments instead of a lot of pictures. Maybe she'd had a brief attack of frugality and focused on the words "at cost." Probably it was because Eileen has always longed to live in another century—any other century—and these gowns were in a rather ethereal pseudomedieval style. The more Eileen looked at the bride's dress, the more infatuated with it she became, and she was just as enchanted with the bridesmaids' dresses. Mother and Mrs. Fenniman were also oohing and ahhing. The owner of the River Cafe, arriving with our lunch, was equally enthusiastic. Mrs. Tranh and the other lady were beaming and pointing out wonderful little details of the construction and decoration and I was the only one paying any attention to the practical side of things.

"Eileen," I said. "They're made of *velvet*. Your wedding is in *July. Outside!*" I was ignored.

"I'm so sorry," Michael said.

"Correct me if I'm wrong," I said, "but even at cost, those things aren't going to be cheap. All that velvet and lace, and the pearls and beads stitched on by hand." He winced and shook his head. "And they look as if they were made either for Samantha's current flock of bridesmaids or one similarly sized. I don't suppose you've noticed this, but Samantha's friends are all borderline anorexics and Eileen's friends tend more to be earth mother types, so they'll need alterations. *Major* alterations. You may even have to make some of them from scratch." He nodded.

"If I'd had any idea——" he began.

"Skip it," I said. "It's done."

"Look on the bright side. She's made a decision."

"In front of plenty of witnesses," I added.

"And Mrs. Tranh and the other ladies will be so happy."

"True."

"And Mom won't have to take the Brewsters to small claims court as she's been threatening."

"Or hold Samantha's new gowns for ransom a couple of days before her wedding, which I hate to admit is what I'd be tempted to do if the Brewsters still owed me for the last set."

"See? Everybody's happy," Michael said.

"Ah, well," I said, softening. "They are beautiful." Michael went over to the happy crew and extracted a dress. The bride's gown was white velvet trimmed with white and gold brocade and ribbon, the bridesmaids' gowns dark blue velvet with blue and yellow, and this one, the maid of honor's dress, in deep burgundy and rose. He spun me around to face one of the mirrors and held it in front of me.

"Look how good that is with your coloring," he said, coaxing. "You're going to look smashing!"

"Assuming I can ever get into it."

"Oh, I've seen Mrs. Tranh and the ladies pull off bigger miracles. It's not that far off, really. Take a look." He slipped the dress off the hanger and had me hold it at the neckline while he fitted it snugly to my waist with his hands. "Not bad at all," he murmured, looking over my shoulder at my reflection in the mirror, and then down at me for my reaction. I found myself slightly breathless, even though I knew that the flirtatiousness in his voice was meaningless and that the warmth in those incredible blue eyes was probably due to his relief at getting a decision out of Eileen *and* unloading the unsold dresses.

"Yeah," I said, reluctantly pulling away and handing him back the dress. "We'll all die of heatstroke, but we'll make beautiful corpses. Why don't we leave them alone to coo while we discuss our no doubt very different definitions of the phrase 'really good deal'?"

It wasn't such a bad deal after all. Either Michael was a lousy bargainer, or he was very eager to unload the unsold dresses. Or eager not to have Eileen underfoot dithering for another whole day. Although the total was going to be significantly more than we'd originally planned, Eileen was so deliriously happy that I didn't worry about it. I'd figure out somewhere else to skimp. We'd gotten her to choose a dress, the last major outstanding decision. I figured the worst was over.

I figured wrong.

We dropped her off at her dad's house to call Steven. Several hours later she showed up with Barry in tow, just in time to join Mother, Pam, Mrs. Fenniman, and me for a light supper.

"Steven loves the dresses," she announced happily.

"Steven hasn't even seen them yet," I said.

"Yes, but I've told him about them and he loves the idea. Meg, we've decided—that's going to be our theme!"

"What, letting Steven make decisions sight unseen? Sounds efficient."

"No! The Renaissance! Isn't it wonderful!" Eileen said, clasping her hands together. "We'll have an authentic period wedding!"

"It's a complete change of plans," I protested. In vain. During the rest of the meal, I watched, helpless, as the four of them made plans that rendered every bit of work I'd done over the last five months totally useless.

After dinner I fled to my room and began major revisions to my list of things to do. Okay. Renaissance music wouldn't be too bad. I knew some craftspeople who worked the Renaissance Fair circuit; I could probably find some musicians through them. Or the college music department. The florist wouldn't be a problem. Flowers are flowers. Decorating the yard wouldn't have to change much. Floral garlands and perhaps a few vaguely heraldic banners. I was sure I could work something out with the caterer. Perhaps a suckling pig with an apple in its mouth would lend a proper note of Renaissance splendor to the festivities. Later on I could probably talk Eileen into using plastic goblets; if not, her grand scheme of making several hundred souvenir ceramic goblets and inscribing them with the date and their initials would keep her harmlessly occupied and out of my hair for the next few weeks. I was reasonably sure that in the light of day the notion of hiring horse-drawn carriages for the arrival and departure of the bridal party would seem excessive. They'd been rewriting the language of their vows for months now, and I shuddered at the thought of their very politically correct script rewritten in pseudo-Shakespearean language. But, then, it wouldn't make any work for me, so the hell with it. And, on the bright side, it would probably kill the Native American herbal purification ceremony, and perhaps Dad would obsess about the Renaissance instead of true crime.

I'd gotten into the habit of looking at my list each evening and rating the days as well or badly done, depending on how much further ahead or behind I'd gotten. As I looked at the three-and-a-half pages of new items that Eileen had just added to the list, I felt seriously depressed.

Tuesday, June 14

I CALLED MICHAEL FIRST THING IN THE MORNING TO KICK OFF THE costuming side of things.

"Michael," I said. "Are you sitting down?"

"I can be. What's wrong?"

"We've created a monster. Eileen has decided to redo the entire wedding in a Renaissance theme."

"Oh," he said, after a pause. "That's going to take some doing, isn't it?"

"Do you think there is any possibility that your seamstresses can cut down one of the extra dresses to make a flowergirl's dress and make seven doublets or whatever you call them—six adult and one child—to coordinate with the dresses? By July Thirtieth?"

"Let me check with Mrs. Tranh."

"Great. I'll see what I can do about getting the ushers in for measuring as soon as possible."

"Good idea."

"If Barry's still loitering with intent, I'll send him in tomorrow. If it should happen to take an unconscionably long time to measure him, no one around here will mind."

"If it'll make you happy, I'll keep him around the shop long enough to pick up conversational Vietnamese," Michael offered. "As for the rest, I assume you had them measured somewhere for tuxedos or whatever else they were originally going to be wearing."

"Ages ago."

"Maybe those measurements would be enough for us to get started. Normally I stay clear of Mrs. Tranh's area of expertise, but as an old theater hand I can testify that they never have as much trouble making the costume fit the understudy in a Shakespearean production, what with all the gathers and lacings."

106

"I'll try," I said. "But we haven't yet finished notifying them all of the change of plans yet. There isn't really any point in sending you measurements for an usher who categorically refuses to prance around in tights and a codpiece."

"Good point. We'll stand by. I hate to add a note of gloom, but what if you can't find enough ushers willing to prance around in tights?"

"Steven knows a lot of history buffs who like to dress up in chain mail on weekends and thwack each other with swords. He's sure he can find enough volunteers."

"Oh, well, if there's going to be swordplay involved, you can count me in if all else fails," Michael said with a chuckle.

I spent most of the rest of the day in futile attempts to track down Steven's footloose ushers. And the priest, Eileen's cousin, who reacted to the news that Eileen wanted him in costume with suspicious enthusiasm. He offered to mail me a book with pictures of period clerical garb. Another would-be thespian. But he was the one bright spot in an otherwise ghastly afternoon. By dinnertime I was in an utterly rotten mood, incapable of uttering a civil word. Fortunately I wasn't required to; Dad had come to dinner and monopolized the conversation with a complete rundown of his theories on Mrs. Grover's death. As long as I kept an eye on him so I could dodge flying food whenever he gesticulated too energetically with his fork, I could wallow in my lugubrious mood to my heart's content. I wallowed.

"Anyway, I'm going up to Richmond next week to see the chief medical examiner," Dad said finally, as he picked up his coffee and headed out to the porch. Sighs of relief from those family and friends present whose appetites were depressed even by euphemistic discussions of forensic evidence. "I'll see that we get some straight answers or I'll raise a ruckus they'll never forget."

"Oh, dear," Mother murmured.

Dad's voice floated back from the porch.

"Yes, sirree, I'm going to go over the evidence and insist that they come right out and declare this a probable homicide, so the sheriff will take the investigation seriously."

"I hope your father won't really cause a scene," Mother said. "That would be so mortifying."

"Don't be silly," I said. "You know perfectly well that half an hour after Dad storms in there, he and the ME will be down at the nearest bar having a few too many beers and repeating all their old med school stories."

"They went to med school together?" Jake asked in surprise.

"No," I said. "Same med school, several decades apart."

"But med school stories don't change much," Pam added. "Especially the pranks. Like singing ninety-nine bottles of formaldehyde on a wall, ninety-nine——"

"Pam," Mother chided.

"Or putting a stray cadaver in——"

"Meg!" Mother and Rob said together. Pam and I collapsed in giggles. Jake shuddered and looked, not for the first time, as if he were having serious second thoughts about the upcoming wedding. At least I hoped so.

Out on the porch, I could hear Dad expounding his plans for a trip to the medical examiner to someone. I peeked through the curtains, saw that Dad's audience was a rather weary-looking Barry, and decided that I would go to bed early with a mystery book.

Wednesday, June 15

I SPENT MOST OF WEDNESDAY VISITING THE VARIOUS HIRED GUNS involved in Eileen's wedding to tell them about the Renaissance theme. Like Eileen's cousin, the caterer was suspiciously enthusiastic. He was losing sight of the practical, financial side of things.

I laid down the law and made a mental note to keep an eye on him. The florist was quite rational, so I suppose he shared my notion that flowers were flowers. The newly booked photographer seemed to find it all hilarious, until I broached the idea of putting him in costume, which he seemed to find unreasonable and insulting. I decided to give him twenty-four hours to come around before starting to look for another photographer. Eileen was paying him for this, after all. Eileen was inexplicably adamant on having the photographer in costume. It seemed idiotic to me: he would be taking pictures, not appearing in them, and even the most spectacular costume couldn't hide the camera, film, lights, and other glaring anachronisms. Ah, well; mine not to reason why. I headed for the peace and quiet of home.

Michael was walking Spike past our yard as I drove up, and came over to say hello.

"I hate to bring up business," I said, "but have you and the ladies figured how you're going to manage Eileen's gowns and the doublets? Without throwing your entire summer's schedule off?"

"It kept them pretty busy yesterday, but they gave me the list of materials they needed this morning, and I've already called in the order. They'll be starting tomorrow. We'll manage."

"That's a relief."

"And the beastly Barry's measurements have been duly entered into the files," Michael said. "It took us rather a while, as expected."

"His absence was duly noted and much appreciated."

"How was your day?" he asked, shifting Spike's leash to the hand farther from me.

"I only managed to tick off three items from my list. But that's life."

"I'll come with you, if you don't mind," Michael said. "I had something I wanted to ask you."

"If you're willing to risk being shanghaied by Mother to talk about upholstery, be my guest."

"Doesn't look as if there's anyone home at your house," Michael said, falling into step beside me. "Only the porch light is on."

"That's odd. Mrs. Fenniman was supposed to come over for dinner."

When we got closer to the house, I could see that it was completely dark, except for the front porch, where Mother and Mrs. Fenniman were rocking by candlelight.

"Hello, Michael," Mother said. "How nice of you to drop by. Meg, why don't you get us some lemonade. Take one of the candles from the front hall." I began carefully making my way across the cluttered porch toward the front door. "The power's out," Mother said brightly, if unnecessarily, to Michael.

"Out like a light," Mrs. Fenniman said, a little too brightly.

"When did it go out?" Michael asked. "I had power when I left the house to walk Spike."

"Damn!" I said, as I barked my shins on an unseen object while climbing the front steps. "And yuck!" In grabbing the nearest step to keep from falling, I'd put my hand into something lukewarm and squishy. What on earth?

"I only left the house about twenty minutes ago," Michael continued.

"Watch out for the Jell-O, Meg," Mother said belatedly. "It's just our house, apparently. I've called the electrician."

"What seems to be the problem?" Michael asked. He tied Spike to a post and perched on the porch railing.

"The houshe is haunted," Mrs. Fenniman said, spilling a little of her wine.

"Probably the fusebox," Mother said. "I'm afraid we'll have to hold dinner until the power is back on." Considering how infrequently Mother actually cooked anything, especially in the summer, I saw no reason why we couldn't have had our usual cold supper from the deli by candlelight, but I knew better than to argue with Mother.

"Maybe we should all have another glash of wine while we're waiting," Mrs. Fenniman hinted.

"I'd be happy to see if I can do anything about the fuse box," Michael offered. "Let me have one of the candles, Meg."

"Woooo-ooooohhhh," Mrs. Fenniman intoned, spookily, then spoiled the effect by giggling.

"That's all right, dear," Mother said. "Meg's father is the only one who ever seems to be able to figure it out. I have no idea where he is; I looked around for several hours and then gave up and called Mr. Price, the electrician. Meg, have you seen your father?"

"Really, it's no trouble," Michael said. "I'm not exactly a wizard with mechanical things, but fuse boxes I can handle."

"We could tell ghosh stories," Mrs. Fenniman suggested. "I know plenty."

"Dad said something about getting some more fertilizer," I said.

"Oh, dear." Mother sighed. "Not another trip to the farm?"

"It's really no trouble," Michael insisted. "I'd be happy to go look."

"That won't be necessary, dear," Mother said. "There's Mr. Price now. Meg, have you got the candles? You can light the way for him."

"I expect he has a working flashlight," I suggested.

"Don't let him break his neck," Mrs. Fenniman warned. "Only dam' man in the county knows how to fix air conditioners. Year he had his gall bladder out the whole damn county like to fried."

"You're right, he probably does," Mother said. "And he brought his boy to help him. Meg, see if you can get some coffee from next door or perhaps you could go up to the Brewsters. We're going to need some caffeine to stay awake till dinner time."

"I'll go along with you and help," Michael offered.

"I'll get a thermos," I said, and shuffled off behind Mr. Price back to the kitchen.

"Whole place could use new wiring, like most of these old houses," I heard the electrician remark from the utility room, where the fuse box was. "Shine that flashlight here."

Michael followed me into the pantry and held the candle while I rummaged for a thermos.

"As if it isn't enough the power is out," I grumbled, "we have to have Mrs. Fenniman getting soused. Mother should know better than to serve her wine. Last time she ended up in Eric's tree-house singing arias from *Carmen*. Dad and I had to lower her down with a sling made out of a blanket and carry her home."

"Sounds like fun," Michael said. "If you'll feed me, I'd be happy to stick around and help, in case your father doesn't show up in time."

"A little to the right," came Mr. Price's voice from the utility room.

"You don't have to, you know," I remarked. "I mean, you're welcome to stay for dinner. But I think your mother's business will still survive if you occasionally take a night off from being the neighborhood jack-of-all-trades and guardian angel."

"That's not why I offered," Michael said.

"Well, I'll be damned," said the unseen voice. "What the dickens . . ."

"Meg, I realize this is going to come as a surprise to you," Michael continued. "But——"

He was interrupted by a loud explosion from outside the pantry door. It was followed almost immediately by a sharp thud, a second explosion from somewhere outside the house, and the sound of the assistant shrieking, "Oh my God! Oh no! Oh my God! Oh no!" over and over.

Michael and I ran out to find Mr. Price slumped against the

wall opposite the fuse box while the assistant tried to put out the flames that were dancing over his boss's clothing. Michael grabbed the doormat and began beating out the flames, while I ran to the stove to grab the fire extinguisher. Dad picked that moment to reappear.

"Meg, were you fooling with the fuse box?" he asked.

"No, Mr. Price was," I said. "See if he's all right."

Michael and I extinguished the flames. Dad found that far from being all right, Mr. Price had stopped breathing. I called 911 and yelled for someone to bring Dad's medical bag while Michael took the increasingly hysterical assistant outside to calm him down and Dad administered CPR. Dad managed to get Mr. Price breathing again, and then the ambulance drove up. Dad took Michael aside for a few quiet words before jumping into the ambulance and riding off to the hospital with Mr. Price. I found myself wondering why in a crisis Dad always turned not to me but to the nearest male, even if it happened to be Michael, who was, after all, practically a stranger.

"I don't see why your father had to go to the hospital with him," Mother complained, as we watched the ambulance driving off. Apparently I wasn't the only one in a cranky mood. "Perhaps we should go over to Pam's for dinner."

"Might as well; you're not going to get any hot dinner around here tonight," chimed in Mrs. Fenniman cheerfully. "When your fuse box fried Price, it knocked out the whole neighborhood!"

Just then Eric came running up.

"Grandma! Grandma!" he cried. "The doggie bit me."

"You mustn't tease the doggie, dear," Mother said. "Let's go see if your mommy can fix us some dinner."

"I'm so sorry," Michael began.

"Spike's fault, not yours," I said.

"But I'd still better take him home," Michael said. "Meg, I need to ask you something."

I strolled back to the house with him.

"Your dad wanted one of us to keep everyone away from the fuse box," Michael said. "He wants to get someone in to make sure it wasn't . . . tampered with. He's going to call the sheriff from the hospital. Could you keep your eye on it while I take Spike home? Then I'll come back and spell you."

I stood on the front porch for a few minutes, watching Michael and Spike disappear in one direction and Eric and Mother and Mrs. Fenniman in the other. Then I walked down to the edge of the bluff where I could enjoy the breeze from the river while keeping my eye on the fuse box through the open back door. It was a beautiful night, and with the power out there were no radios, TVs, or air conditioners to drown out the slapping of waves against the beach, the songs of the cicadas, and the first warbling notes of Mrs. Fenniman's rendition of the "Ride of the Valkyries."

Thursday, June 16

WE DISCOVERED THE FOLLOWING MORNING THAT THE POWER WAS out not only on our street but throughout the neighborhood. It wasn't until midafternoon that they finished repairing the relay station or whatever it was that short-circuited. Mr. Price survived, thanks to Dad's quick intervention, but his recovery was expected to be slow. When the temperature had reached ninety degrees well before noon, ill-feeling began to spread through a neighborhood contemplating a summer without a capable air-conditioning repairman at hand. I was sure the local weatherman was gloating when he reported the National Weather Service's prediction that temperatures for the coming month would be above average. If anyone blamed us, they could take consolation in the fact that we were suffering more than most. Dad and the sheriff insisted on taking the fuse box away to be examined by an expert to see if it had been tampered with. It was going to be a few days before we could have another fuse box installed and get our power back. Mother went to stay with Pam, who had plenty of room with Mal and most of the kids away. I stayed on at the house. With the answering machine out of commission, I didn't feel I could leave the phone for too long. I might miss a vital call from a caterer, a florist, or someone who had peacocks.

Friday, June 17

"IT'S AMAZING HOW INTERESTED EVERYONE IN TOWN IS IN THE FUSE box incident," Michael said, as we ate Chinese carryout on the porch Friday evening. When he found out I was holding down the fort at the house, he'd gotten into the thoughtful habit of showing up several times a day with care packages of food, cold beverages, and ice.

"Nearly everyone who comes into the shop wants to hear all about it," he went on. "And a lot of people are coming in on remarkably flimsy pretexts."

"That's small-town life for you."

"Seems to have driven Mrs. Grover's death quite out of everyone's head. I haven't mentioned your dad's suspicion that the fuse box might have been tampered with, of course."

"Of course," I said. "Too bad the distraction is likely to be temporary. People were starting to get hysterical about the idea that a murderer could be running around loose, so if it weren't for Mr. Price's close call, I'd have called the fuse box incident a lucky thing."

"It was certainly a lucky thing for Mr. Price your dad showed up when he did."

"And lucky for Dad that he didn't show up earlier," I added. "If he had, he'd have been the one who was electrocuted, and there wouldn't have been a doctor around to revive him."

"Where was he all day, anyway?"

"In Richmond, at the medical examiner's office. He announced at dinner the night before that he was going next week to try to get some more definite action on Mrs. Grover's case. And then, as usual, he changed his mind on impulse and decided to take off the next morning."

"Had he talked to the medical examiner's office before?"

"On the phone. But he seemed to think he wasn't going to get anywhere unless he went down and kicked up a fuss in person. He also seems to think he has some evidence the ME hasn't really seen."

"The sandbag graphs, perhaps," Michael said. "And the results of the milk jug flotilla. I can't wait to see if the fuse box really was sabotaged."

"Perhaps it's my overactive imagination. But it has occurred to me to wonder if it's really an accident that this happened the day after he went around announcing to the immediate world that he was going to see the ME about Mrs. Grover's death."

"If I were your dad, I'd watch my back," Michael said. "As a matter of fact, I intend to watch my own back. I tried to talk your mother into letting me mess with the fuse box, remember?"

Saturday, June 18

THINGS WERE QUIET. TOO QUIET, AS THEY SAY IN THE MOVIES. THE local grapevine still didn't see the connection between Mrs. Grover's death and the fuse box incident, and none of us who did felt like setting off panic by mentioning the possibility. I wished I didn't see a connection. I felt as if I were waiting for the other shoe to drop, but had no idea whether the shoe would be another murder or another explosion or merely another catastrophic change in one of the brides' plans. I tried to avoid looking over my shoulder every thirty seconds as I sat in the quiet, airless house all day, writing notes and calling caterers and florists and the calligrapher who had had Samantha's invitations for quite some time now. Of course, everybody in town and in both families already knew who was invited; the invitations were just a formality. But a necessary one, in Samantha's eyes.

"What on earth do you think could have happened to Mrs. Thornhill," I fumed to Dad when he dropped by in the evening to tell me the good news that he had finally located a substitute electrician to replace the fuse box. The bad news, of course, was that the electrician wasn't coming by until sometime Monday. I didn't plan on holding my breath.

"Why, who's Mrs. Thornhill?" Dad asked, looking startled. "And why do you think something may have happened to her?"

"The calligrapher who's holding Samantha's invitations hostage, remember? I can only guess that something must have happened to her. She hasn't answered any of my calls, and believe me, I've had plenty of time to call. We are now seriously overdue mailing out those damned invitations."

"But you don't know that anything's happened?"

"No. Good grief, I'm not suggesting she's another murder victim. Although wasn't there a story in the *Arabian Nights* where the wicked king was killed because someone knew he licked his finger to turn the pages when he read and gave him a book with poison on all the pages? Maybe we should interrogate the printers; maybe they were intending to poison Samantha and accidentally bumped off Mrs. Thornhill."

"I know you think this is ridiculous, Meg," Dad said, with a sigh. He took off his glasses to rub his eyes, and then began cleaning them with the tail of his shirt. Since this was the shirt he'd been gardening in all day, he wasn't producing much of an improvement. He looked tired and depressed and much older than usual.

"Here, drink your tea and let me do that," I said, grabbing a tissue and holding out my hand for the glasses. With uncharacteristic meekness, Dad handed over the glasses and leaned back to sip his tea.

"I don't think it's ridiculous," I went on, as I polished the glasses and wondered where he could possibly have gotten purple glitter paint on the lenses. "I'm just trying to keep my sense of humor in a trying situation."

"Yes, I know it's been difficult for you, trying to get these weddings organized and having to help me with the investigation."

"Not to worry; it's probably kept me from killing any of the brides."

"It's just that it's so maddening that despite all the forensic evidence, the sheriff still believes I'm imagining things."

"Well, consider the source. I'm sure if I were planning a murder, I wouldn't worry much about him catching me," I said, finally deciding that the remaining spots on Dad's glasses were actually scratches, and giving the lenses a final polish.

"No," Dad said, glumly.

"But I would certainly try to schedule my dastardly deeds when you were out of town," I said, handing him back his glasses with a flourish. Dad reached for them and then froze, staring at them fixedly.

"Dad," I said. "Are you all right? Is something wrong?"

"Of course," he muttered.

"Of course what?"

"You're absolutely right, Meg; and you've made an important point. I don't know why I didn't think of that."

"Think of what?"

"This completely changes things, you know." He gulped the

rest of his tea and trotted out, still muttering to himself. With anyone else I would have wondered if they were losing their marbles. With Dad, it simply meant he was hot on the trail of a new obsession.

It was getting dark, so I lit some candles and spent a couple of peaceful hours addressing invitations by candlelight.

Sunday, June 19

.DAD DROPPED BY THE NEXT MORNING WITH FRESH FRUIT. HE WAS looking much better, smiling and humming to himself. Obsession obviously suited him.

"Oh, by the way, I'm going to borrow Great-Aunt Sophy," he said, trotting into the living room.

"You're going to what?" I said, following him.

"Borrow Great-Aunt Sophy."

"I wouldn't if I were you; Mother is very fond of that vase," I said, watching nervously as Dad lifted down the very fragile antique Chinese urn that held Great-Aunt Sophy's ashes.

"Oh, not the vase, just her. I'm sure she wouldn't mind."

"What makes you think Mother won't mind?"

"I meant Sophy," Dad said, carrying the vase out into the kitchen. "We won't tell your mother."

"I know I won't," I muttered. "Here, let me take that." Dad had tucked the vase carelessly under his arm and was rummaging through the kitchen cabinets. "What are you looking for?"

"Something to put her in."

I found him an extra-large empty plastic butter tub, and he transferred Great-Aunt Sophy's ashes to it. Although ashes seemed rather a misnomer. I'd never seen anyone's ashes before and wondered if Great-Aunt Sophy's were typical; there seemed to be quite a lot of large chunks of what I presumed were bone. After Dad finished the transfer, I cleaned his fingerprints off the vase and put it back, being careful to position it precisely in the little dust-free ring it had come from. I still didn't know what he was going to do with Great-Aunt Sophy. I assumed he'd tell me when he couldn't hold it in any longer. He trotted off with the butter tub in one hand, whistling "Loch Lomond."

I decided that vendors and peacock farmers were not apt to call on a Sunday and went over to Pam's at noon for dinner. Pam had air-conditioning.

"What on earth is your father up to?" Mother asked as we were sitting down.

"What do you mean, up to?" I asked, startled. Had some neighbor told her about Dad's visit earlier that morning? Could Dad have revealed to someone what he was carrying around in the plastic butter tub?

"He went down to the *Town Crier* office yesterday, and even though it was almost closing time, he insisted they drag out a whole lot of back issues."

"Back issues from the summer before last? While he was in Scotland?"

"Why, yes. How ever did you know that?"

"Just a wild guess," I said, feeling rather pleased with myself for putting together the clues. Dad was obviously pursuing the theory that Mrs. Grover's murder had something to do with something that had happened while he was away. Though what Great-Aunt Sophy, who had been quietly reposing in Mother's living room for three or four years, could possibly have to do with current events was beyond me. I couldn't think of anything odd that had happened that summer. No deaths other than people who were definitely sick or definitely old.

Or definitely both, like Jake's late wife.

How very odd.

Could Dad possibly suspect Jake of killing his wife? And if so, what could it possibly have to do with Mrs. Grover's death, for which Jake, at least, had a complete alibi?

Perhaps he suspected someone else of killing the late Mrs. Wendell. Someone who also had a motive for killing Mrs. Grover? And of course, if someone was knocking off the women in Jake's life, Dad would certainly want to do something about it, in case Mother were at risk.

At least I assumed he did. I toyed briefly with the notion of Dad going off the deep end and trying to frame Jake for his late wife's murder so he could get Mother back. And then disposing of Mrs. Grover when she found out his plot.

Or Mother, knocking off Mrs. Wendell in order to get her hands on Jake, and then doing away with the suspicious Mrs. Grover who called her a blond hussy and tried to stop the marriage.

I sighed. Dad couldn't possibly carry off such a scheme; he'd have been visibly bursting with enthusiasm and would have dropped what he thought were indecipherable hints to all and sundry. Mother would never have done anything that required that much effort; she'd have tried to enlist someone else to do it for her.

No, I couldn't see either parent as a murderer. But then, I was a biased witness. For that matter, like most children, I had a hard time seeing my parents as sexual beings, despite the evidence of Pam, Rob, and myself. Perhaps I was missing all the telltale signs of a passionate geriatric love triangle being played out in front of my nose.

I glanced over at suspect number one. She was looking at me with a faint frown of genuine concern on her face.

"Are you all right, Meg?" she asked.

"A little tired," I lied. "The weather, I'm sure."

"Perhaps you should stay here this afternoon, where it's cooler. Jake and I are going over to have tea with Mrs. Fenniman, so you'll have some quiet. Or you could come with us; Mrs. Fenniman's air-conditioning is working."

I was touched by her concern, but realized in that instant that I had other plans for the afternoon.

"No, I have a few things to do." With Jake and Mother safely out of the way, I was going to play detective. After all, if Dad could do it, why not me?

I waited until Mother and Jake took off. Then I grabbed an unfamiliar-looking dish—one that I could plausibly claim I had mistaken for something of Jake's—and trotted over to his house. Quite openly; just one neighbor returning another's pie plate.

I knocked, in case someone was there. Then I reached out, heart pounding, to open the door.

Which was locked. Unheard of. People in Yorktown don't lock their doors.

Searching Jake's house was going to be a little harder than I thought. I wandered around to the back door, calling "yoo-hoo" very quietly. The back door was locked, too.

But he'd left the window by the back door open.

I had pried open the screen and was halfway in the window when I heard a voice behind me.

"Lost your key?"

I started, hitting my head on the window frame, and turned to find Michael behind me. Holding Spike's leash.

"I know what this looks like," I began, turning to look over my shoulder and lifting the tips of my sneakers out of Spike's reach.

"To me, it looks very much as if you've been reading too many of the same books your dad has. And why Jake? Isn't he the one local who's not a suspect? Or is this only one in a series of clandestine searches?"

"He's not a suspect, but he has a whole roomful of the victim's stuff. I want to see Mrs. Grover's stuff."

"Surely the sheriff took any important evidence?"

"The sheriff wouldn't know important evidence if it walked into his office and introduced itself. Look, either call the cops or go away; I'm getting very uncomfortable hanging half-in and half-out of this window."

"I have a better idea," Michael said. "I'll give you a cover story. Here." He picked up Spike and, before the little beast could react, tossed him over my leg into the house. Spike shook himself, looked around, and then ran out of sight, growling all the way.

"You were helping me retrieve Spike," Michael said, offering me a leg up and then jumping nimbly in after me. "Don't ask how he got into Mr. Wendell's house. The place obviously needs to be vermin-proofed."

Now that I'd succeeded in getting in, I felt temporarily disoriented. I had a whole house to search, and I had no idea what I was looking for.

Of course there wasn't that much to search. It was a rather bare house. There seemed to be even less furniture and fewer decorations than the last time I'd seen it, just after Mrs. Grover disappeared. I reached under the sink and fortunately found a pair of kitchen gloves.

"Here," I said, handing them to Michael. "You wear these. I brought my own."

"So where do we start?" he asked, following me from the kitchen into the living room.

"I'll look in the guest room," I said, more decisively than I felt. "You search his desk."

"What am I looking for?"

"How should I know? Discrepancies. Anomalies. The missing will. Blunt objects still bearing telltale traces of hair and blood. We're working blind here."

Michael chuckled and sat down at Jake's desk. He began deftly rummaging through the desk, whistling "Secret Agent Man" almost inaudibly.

"Smart aleck," I said, and went into the guest room.

It wasn't a complete loss. I continued to be amazed at the

number of small, portable valuables Mrs. Grover had appropriated while at Jake's. I did find an envelope containing two thousand dollars in cash, mostly in hundreds. Perhaps evidence of a blackmail scheme, although it must have been a penny-ante one if this was all she had collected. Still, perhaps she had been stopped before she'd hit her stride. Then again, perhaps she just didn't believe in traveler's checks. And I found nothing else of interest. No diary with a last entry announcing her intent to meet X on the bluff before dawn. No list of suspects' names with payoff amounts jotted beside them. No incriminating letters or photos. Nothing out of the ordinary.

Well, one thing out of the ordinary. I found the late Emma Wendell. What remained of her, anyway. I opened a rather non-descript box marked Emma, expecting to find another piece of silver or china bric-a-brac and found something greatly resembling Great-Aunt Sophy, only slightly less lumpy.

"Yuck!" I said, rather loudly. Michael was at my side in an instant.

"What is it?" he asked eagerly.

"The first Mrs. Wendell."

"I see," he said, showing no inclination to do so. "Is this significant?"

"Not that I know of." Although it began to give me ideas about why Dad had borrowed Great-Aunt Sophy.

"Let's leave her in peace, then. What else have you found?"

I showed him the cash, which he agreed was poor pickings for a blackmailer. He showed me his findings. Sales receipts, complete with the date and time, that tended to confirm Jake's alibi rather thoroughly. A bank book and other papers showing that Jake was in no danger of starving no matter how many valuable little knickknacks the late Jane Grover had purloined. An envelope marked Jane containing a key to a self-storage unit and a neatly itemized list of oriental rugs, antique furniture, and other objects that were certainly more than knickknacks. Another envelope marked Safety Deposit containing a key and an impressive itemized list of jewelry. I made a mental note to suggest that the sheriff see who inherited Mrs. Grover's estate. A framed certificate of appreciation on the occasion of Jake's retirement from Waltham Consultants, Inc., whatever that was. Neat stacks of promptly paid bills and perfectly balanced bank books.

"Commendably businesslike," Michael said.

"But not very illuminating," I said. I stood up and looked around. "Something's missing here."

"Like any sign that the man has a personality." Michael had wandered over to the shelves on either side of the fireplace. They were largely empty, except for a few pieces of bric-a-brac that were presumably either too large for Mrs. Grover to hide or too cheap for her to bother with. There were maybe two dozen books, all paperback copies of recent best-sellers.

"Doesn't he have any more books?" Michael asked.

"Good question."

We looked. Not in the guest room. Not in the bedroom, which looked more lived in than the rest of the house but still depressingly tidy. Not in the dining room or the upstairs bath or the kitchen. Not in the basement, where Spike lay in wait for us under the water heater, growling. Not in the attic.

"Depressing," I said. "Irrelevant, but depressing."

Just then we heard a car go by, and peering out, I saw it was Jake's.

"We'd better leave; Jake may drop Mother off and come back soon," I said.

We lured Spike out from under the furnace and left the way we came.

"That was a bust," Michael said.

"Well, we do have corroboration for his alibi."

"I thought we had that already."

"The sheriff had it," I said. "Now that I've seen it myself, I believe it."

And, as I admitted to myself before falling asleep that night, I was more than a little hoping to find some evidence against Jake because deep down I just didn't like him. How much of that was justifiable and how much due to my resentment that he was taking Dad's place, I didn't know. But I had to admit, I'd found nothing against him, other than further confirmation that he was a bland, boring cipher.

I pondered the other, more viable suspects. I could certainly find the opportunity to sneak into Samantha's room . . . Barry's van . . . even Michael's mother's house, although if I were seriously considering him a suspect, I had already made a big mistake by letting him find out I was snooping. Two big mistakes if you counted letting him paw through Jake's things. It all seemed rather pointless.

"I give up," I told myself. "Let Dad do the detecting. I have three weddings to organize."

Monday, June 20

ON MONDAY MORNING, I COERCED PAM INTO WAITING FOR THE electrician while I traipsed down to Be-Stitched for some fittings— along with Samantha and Mother and half a dozen hangers-on. I wondered for the umpteenth time if my presence was really necessary at every one of Samantha's fittings. Having to stand perfectly still while Mrs. Tranh and the ladies did things with pins and tape measures seemed to throw Samantha's brain even further into overdrive, and she used the energy to cross-examine me on my progress (or lack thereof).

"How is the calligrapher doing?" she asked, as Mrs. Tranh

frowned over some detail of the sleeves. "Are the invitations back yet?"

"She wanted a full week," I said, glossing over the fact that the week had been up the previous Friday and I'd had no luck getting in touch with Mrs. Thornhill, the calligrapher, over the weekend. Best not to upset Samantha until absolutely necessary.

"What about the peacocks?" she asked.

"I've got some leads."

"It's nearly the end of June," she complained.

"Yes, have you been to see Reverend Pugh for the premarital counseling yet?" I asked, partly to change the subject, partly to see her squirm, and partly because it was another item I'd like to get checked off my list.

"Yes, you really must get that out of the way," Mother chimed in. Samantha looked uncomfortable.

"Well, not yet," she admitted. "We have been wondering if he is quite the right minister," she added, glaring at me because she didn't dare ask aloud how the search for a substitute was going.

"Fat chance finding another this late," Mrs. Fenniman remarked.

"Why shouldn't he be?" Mother asked.

"Well, isn't he rather . . . elderly?" Samantha said. "Are you sure he's up to the strain?" What a very tactful way of saying that he was older than the hills, looked and acted peculiar even by local standards, and she didn't want him within five miles of her elegant wedding.

"Oh, he'd be so hurt if we didn't let him," Mother said. "And he still does a lovely ceremony."

"He's had so much practice," I said, trying to imply that even the eccentric Reverend Pugh could probably manage to get through something as well known as the standard Book of Common Prayer wedding service without difficulty. "Besides, the Pughs have been marrying, burying, and baptizing Hollingworths for generations."

"Though not in that order, I hope," Michael said under his breath.

"Generations," Samantha repeated, looking very thoughtful. "Well, if it's a family tradition." I'd hoped she would fall for that one. She disappeared into the dressing room, still pondering, followed by the mothers and Mrs. Fenniman.

"Reverend Pugh, eh?" Michael said. "Should be a hoot."

"You've met him?"

"No, only heard stories. So has Samantha, apparently; clever the way you brought her round."

"I've found that with Samantha nothing works like snob appeal. Bet you five bucks that before the week is out, Samantha will find at least half a dozen occasions to remark, 'But of course, the Pughs have performed all the Hollingworth family weddings for generations.' Hooey."

"You mean it's not true?"

"Oh, it's true. For about two generations; before that the Hollingworths were Methodists and considered the Pughs carpetbaggers. But no need for her to know that."

"My lips are sealed," Michael said, raising an eyebrow at me.

"They'd better be. Anyway, I'm getting nowhere trying to find a substitute, and I've got to find some way to convince her to put up with Reverend Pugh. There seems to be a puzzling shortage of clergy in this part of the country at the moment; or perhaps not so puzzling if word has leaked out about what Yorktown is like in the summer."

"Or word about what Samantha is like all year round," Michael muttered through a fixed smile as the bride in question sailed out of the dressing room.

Thanks to my rapidly improving talents for prevaricating and changing the subject, I managed to get through the rest of the day without taking on more than two small new jobs and without admitting to Samantha exactly how slowly I was progressing on some of her odder requests. When I arrived home and found that Barry had shown up and invited himself for dinner and I'd missed a call from the calligrapher, I decided that I was feeling poorly and retired to my room with a cold plate and a hot new mystery. I fell asleep over chapter two.

Tuesday, June 21

THANKS TO ALL THE TIME I'D HAD TO WASTE OOHING AND AHHING over Samantha's and the bridesmaid's gowns, I'd managed to spend the better part of Monday in Be-Stitched without getting anywhere near the inside of a dressing room myself. After making a quick return call to the calligrapher—who wasn't home again; I was going to have to find the time to drop by her house in person—I headed down Tuesday morning to see if I could squeeze in a fitting before a series of appointments with assorted caterers and florists. Unfortunately, I let Eileen tag along.

"How are the rest of my costumes going?" she asked, before I could get a word out. I thought her choice of words accurate; they were very beautiful, but much more like costumes than normal wedding garb.

"Splendidly!" Michael said. "They've already done most of the priest's outfit. Would you like to see it? I can try it on for you; your cousin and I seem to be much the same size."

Of course she wanted to see it. It was for her wedding. Like Mother and Samantha, she would happily spend hours contemplating a placecard holder for her own wedding, while begrudging every second I spent on anyone else's wedding, even something as critical as finding out if I would fit into my dress. But I had to admit I was curious about the priest's outfit, especially if Michael was proposing to model it. Michael disappeared into the dressing room. We heard a few words in Vietnamese, muffled giggles, and the jangle of a dropped hanger. Eileen browsed in a few of the magazines— which made me nervous; one of them had a rather spectacular article on a wedding with a Roaring Twenties theme that I was hoping would not catch her eye until after her wedding. If ever.

Suddenly, the curtain was thrown violently aside, and out stepped Michael, in costume and very much in character. The long, flowing vestments were all black velvet, white linen, and gold lace, and made him look even taller and leaner than usual. He'd obviously decided to adopt the persona of a powerful, sinister prelate—perhaps one of the Borgias, or a grand inquisitor of some sort. He stalked slowly across the floor toward us, catlike, Machiavellian, almost Mephistophelean, and I found myself imagining him in a dark, paneled corridor in a Renaissance palazzo, lit by candles and flaring torches—a secret passage, perhaps—and he was striding purposefully along to . . . to do what? To foil a devious plot, or arrange one? Counsel the king, or betray him? Rescue a fair maiden, or seduce one? And as he turned and looked imperiously at us—

"Oh, it's absolutely fabulous!" Eileen gushed, jarring me from my reverie. Suddenly I became aware once more of the mundane real world around me, the steady mechanical humming of a sewing machine, a scrap of incomprehensible conversation from behind the curtain, and the heavy, oppressive heat of a Virginia summer. Or perhaps it wasn't the heat I felt so much as a blush, when I realized how ridiculous I must look, staring at Michael with my mouth hanging open. I really would have to see him act sometime, I decided.

"Think your cousin will like it?" he asked, reaching to answer the phone. "Be-Stitched. Yes, Mrs. Langslow, she's right here." He handed the phone to me. "Your mother. Something about peacocks?"

"Meg, dear," Mother trilled. "I have splendid news! Your cousin has found us some peacocks, but you'll have to go over there today to make the arrangements."

"Over where?" I said. "And why can't we just call?"

"He doesn't have a phone, apparently, or it's not working. I'm not sure which. And he won't take a reservation unless he has a cash deposit, so you'll have to go there immediately to make sure they're available. Think how terrible it would be if after all this we finally found the peacocks and someone else snapped them up just before you got there, which I'm sure could happen if anyone else finds out about them. There are two other weddings in town the same weekend mine is, and—"

"All right, Mother. I'll go and put a down payment on the peacocks."

I couldn't prevent Mother from giving me directions, which I ignored because she was sure to have gotten them mixed up. I called my cousin to get real directions, rescheduled all the other appointments on my list, and dashed off into the wilds of the county. Even with directions, I got lost half a dozen times. How can you turn right at a millet field if you have no idea what millet looks like? But I found the farm and only stepped in one pile of manure while I was there. The peacocks' owner agreed to bring them over a week or so before Samantha's wedding, so they'd have time to settle down, and leave them till a few days after Mother's wedding. I managed not to yawn during his lengthy stories about how he came to have a flock of peacocks and the difficulties of breeding them and how they were better than dogs for warning him whenever strangers came to the farm. And I left a deposit that would still have seemed excessive if the damned peacocks were gold-plated. Considering the cost involved, his lack of a telephone must have been sheer cussedness rather than a sign of economic hardship.

I was feeling very pleased with myself until bedtime, when I realized I'd spent the entire day running around in order to cross off just one item. I tried to reach Mrs. Thornhill, the calligrapher, so I could cross that off, but there was no answer. Again. Ah, well. Tomorrow was another day. I wondered, briefly, where Dad had been for the past several days, and what he had done or was doing with Great-Aunt Sophy. Cool it, I told myself. Let Dad play detective. You have enough to do.

Wednesday, June 22

I GOT AN EARLY START AND HAD CRAMMED A TRULY AWESOME number of caterer and florist inspections into the morning. Not to mention half a dozen unsuccessful attempts to reach Mrs. Thornhill, the feckless calligrapher. Although still suspicious of what Dad was up to, I was just as happy to have heard nothing about homicide for several days. I was feeling optimistic about the possibility of getting back on schedule when Eileen showed up unexpectedly to have lunch with us. I immediately wondered what she was up to.

"Are you doing anything this afternoon?" Eileen said, finally. Here comes the bombshell, I told myself.

"I'm going in to Be-Stitched for a fitting. My dress for Samantha's wedding."

"I'll go in with you," Eileen said. "I have something I want to ask Michael about."

Doubtless another sign of rampant paranoia on my part, but on the way, as Eileen chattered happily about Renaissance music, I worried about what she wanted to ask Michael. Doubtless some new scheme that would make more work for me. I would have interrogated her then and there, but thought it might be more tactful to wait and see. Besides, I felt sure Michael would help me out if she pulled anything really outrageous.

"Michael," she said, as we came in, "I've had the most wonderful idea, and I wanted to see if it was okay with you first."

"What is it?" he asked, surprised and a little wary. Not actually suspicious, but then he didn't know Eileen as well as I did.

"I'm going to have *everyone* in costume," she announced happily. "I want to see if you can make the costumes if necessary."

"I thought we already were having everyone in costume," Michael said. "Bride, groom, maid of honor, best man, father of the bride, ring bearer, flower girl, four ushers, and four bridesmaids. And your cousin the priest. The musicians, you said, would be providing their own costumes. Who else is there?"

"Eileen, not the guests," I said.

"Yes!" She beamed. "Won't it be splendid?"

"Oh, God, no," I moaned.

"How many people have you invited?" Michael asked.

"Six hundred and seven," I said. "At last count."

"Of course they won't all come," she said, looking a little hurt and puzzled at our obvious lack of enthusiasm. "And some of them already have Renaissance costumes."

"How many?" I asked. "A dozen or two? That still leaves several hundred costumes, even if half the guest list doesn't show up."

"Well, yes," Eileen admitted.

"Have you considered how much it would cost for guests to buy, rent, or make their costumes? It could be several hundred dollars apiece. I don't think you can ask people to spend that much just to come to your wedding. On top of what they'll already have to spend in airfare and hotels. A lot of people would stay away and feel hurt. Unless you're thinking of sticking your father with the bill. I'm sure he'd like that; feeding *and* clothing the multitudes."

"Maybe we could rent a bunch of costumes from a theater," Eileen said, looking hopefully at Michael.

"I suppose you might be able to," Michael said, "But you certainly wouldn't want to."

"Why not?"

"Most theatrical costumes are designed to look good from a

distance," he said. "Up close, the way guests would see each other, they don't look so hot, even if they're brand new, and if they've been used they could be more than a little ragged around the edges. Also, up close, no matter how well cleaned they were, you'd probably be able to tell that people had been wearing them and sweating under hot lights for hours on end. You'd smell more than just the greasepaint." Bravo, Michael, I thought.

"Perhaps we could send them all patterns," she suggested. "So they could make their own costumes."

"I'm sure the few who know how and have the time have other things they'd like to be sewing," I said.

"I'm sure there must be some way we can manage it," Eileen said, turning stubborn.

"Tell you what: let's ask Mother," I said. "She's the best one I know to tell us whether it's suitable and if so, how to get it done. Michael, why don't you let Eileen take a look at how her dress is coming while I call to see if Mother's home or at Mrs. Fenniman's."

Eileen cheered up again at this, and obediently followed Michael back to the sewing room while I phoned home to enlist Mother.

"She's going to try the dress on while she's here," Michael said, reappearing a few minutes later.

"Good," I said. "That will give Mother time to round up Mrs. Fenniman and Pam and meet us back at the house to talk Eileen out of it."

"Are you sure they'll talk her out of it?" Michael asked. "No offense, but it seems to be just the sort of . . . charmingly eccentric idea your mother would encourage."

"Charmingly eccentric," I said. "That's tactful. Totally loony, you mean. Yes, it's just the sort of circus Mother normally likes to encourage, and normally she'd be the first one down here trying to make sure her costume outshines all the rest. But I have carefully explained to her how much time this would take to coordinate. How much of *my* time, which Mother would rather have me spending on *her* wedding. She'll talk Eileen out of it, never fear."

"I see why you wanted to get your mother involved," Michael said. "Brilliantly Machiavellian."

"If all else fails, I'll try to convince Eileen that costumes would be more fun for one of the prewedding parties. Last I heard she was still planning several of those."

"You know, some people pay other people good money for what you're doing for these three weddings," Michael remarked.

"Not enough," I said, fervently. "They can't possibly pay them enough."

"I don't mean to be nosy," Michael said, "but your mother does seem to have a lot of very definite ideas about what she wants done, and you always seem to be the one who ends up doing everything. I was wondering . . . uh . . ."

"Is she always like that, and why do I put up with it?"

"Well, yes, more or less."

"She's not usually this bad," I said, with a sigh. "I think it's sort of a loyalty test."

"Loyalty test?"

"She's making me pay for having taken Dad's side in the divorce."

"Did you really?" Michael asked. "Take his side, I mean."

"All three of us did," I said. "At least, Mother wanted a divorce and Dad didn't, and neither did Pam or Rob or I. If that counts as taking Dad's side, then yeah, I took his side. Still do. So it's my theory that Mother's making us all jump through hoops to pay for it."

"If the question ever comes up, I am firmly on her side in any and all disputes, no matter how ridiculous," Michael said.

"Good plan," I replied.

"Unless, of course, you're on the other side."

"Foolhardy, but I appreciate the thought."

It did take most of the afternoon to squelch the costume idea, even with Mother, Mrs. Fenniman, and Pam helping out. Somewhere along the way, Mother promised Eileen that we would hold a costume party sometime between now and her wedding. I left them trying to settle on a date and retired to the hammock to fall asleep over chapter three of my mystery.

Thursday, June 23

AND SO FOR THE FOURTH STRAIGHT DAY IN A ROW I DROVE IN TO Be-Stitched. Alone. Without telling anyone where I was going. Maybe that way I could finally sneak in my own fitting.

Michael looked up at the sound of the bell and I could see him suddenly grow tense. Or tenser; he hadn't really looked relaxed when I came in. Great, I thought, we're driving *him* crazy too.

"Yes?" he said, and glanced behind me at the door. I turned and looked, too. No one was there. Odd.

"Which one is it now?" he asked.

"Which one what?"

"Which one of them? Your mother, or Eileen, or Scarlet O'Hara—I mean, Samantha—"

"Just me. I was supposed to come by for a fitting, remember?"

"And no one else found any reason to come along? Like the last three days? No last-minute inspirations? No urge to ask how the latest alterations are coming? No kibitzing?"

"Just me."

"Amazing," he muttered. "An absolute bloody miracle."

"You're in a good mood."

"Sorry. We just had an absolutely horrible fitting with another bride. I had to stand there and be polite while her mother accused me of everything from incompetence to lunacy, and then when she started on Mrs. Tranh and the ladies, I lost my temper. I don't care if the whole town thinks *I'm* an idiot on top of everything else, but I won't have the ladies blamed for something that's not their fault."

"I saw them on my way in; let me guess: the dress was much too small, particularly in the waist, and according to the mother you must have messed up the measurements."

"Are you psychic?" he asked in surprise.

"No, but I have Mother and the Hollingworth grapevine."

"They just left ten minutes ago; don't tell me the old . . . lady was on the phone already telling everyone about it."

"No, although I'm sure that's on her afternoon agenda. But it's been all over the grapevine for two weeks that her daughter is pregnant, which could certainly tend to make the measurements you took a month or two ago obsolete."

"Wish I was on the grapevine," he complained. "I had no idea why she was so touchy about my suggestion that the kid had gained a few pounds until Mrs. Tranh explained it to me."

"I just found out this morning myself. You have to be able to translate. No one comes right out and says 'So-and-so is getting married because she's pregnant.' They talk about a 'sudden' marriage, with a little pause before the word *sudden.*"

"So they got married suddenly merely means that it surprised the hell out of everyone, where as they got married . . . suddenly means at the point of Daddy's shotgun."

"Precisely. He died suddenly meant nobody expected it; he died . . . suddenly means call the medical examiner; it could be homicide."

"Do you have a lot of homicide around here?" he asked.

"This summer is practically a first. That was just a hypothetical example."

"I see."

"If you listen closely for that little beat, you can start picking up all sorts of useless information. Being down here for the summer, I seem to be regaining all my lost small-town survival skills."

"Any advice for dealing with the irate mother?" he asked.

"Let Mrs. Tranh and the ladies handle it. Now that they know, I'm sure they can guesstimate what size she'll be in two weeks."

"I'm sure they can, but what if her mother starts bad-mouthing the shop all over town?"

"Don't worry about it; everyone knows being abused by that particular grand dame is a normal rite of passage for the local merchants. Besides, she and Mother loathe each other, so I'll tell Mother about it at lunch. By dinner, your side of the story will be all over town.

"I'd appreciate that. I'd hate to be responsible for running Mom's business into the ground while she's laid up. And speaking of business," he said, briskly changing tone, "let's have Mrs. Tranh get your dress."

Having seen the pictures, I thought I would be prepared for Samantha's hooped monstrosity. But I'm sure Michael and Mrs. Tranh were disappointed at the look on my face when she came trotting out with the dress and held it up.

"Oh, dear," I said.

"I'm crushed." He chuckled. "You'll break the ladies' hearts."

"Don't get me wrong. It's lovely. Lovely fabric. Wonderful workmanship."

"But not the sort of thing you'd ever think of wearing."

"Or inflicting upon an unsuspecting friend." I walked around and looked at it from another angle. "Somehow I wasn't expecting the hoops to be quite so . . . enormous."

"Although my experience is limited to this summer," Michael said, "I've evolved a theory that bridesmaids' gowns are generally chosen either to make the bride look good at her friends' expense, or to force the friends to prove their devotion by having their pictures taken in a garment they are mortally embarrassed to be seen wearing in public."

"You've left out inflicting acute physical torment," I added. "Think of Eileen and her velvet and these damned corsets."

"True. When I publish the theory, I'll put you down as co-author."

"Well, let's get this over with," I said, following Mrs. Tranh behind the dressing-room curtain.

Several of the ladies had to help me get into the dress. I made a mental note to ask Michael if we could hire some of them to help out on the wedding day. And when we finally got me into the thing, I realized that in my dismay over the enormous size of the skirts, I had failed to notice the correspondingly tiny size of the bodice.

"I feel as if I'm falling out of this," I said, more to myself than anyone else, since obviously Mrs. Tranh and the other ladies could not understand me. I twitched the neckline slightly, and Mrs. Tranh slapped my hand.

"I don't see why you don't have mirrors back here," I called out.

"So you won't be tempted to look until the ladies are satisfied it's ready," Michael called back.

So we won't run away screaming, I added, silently. The ladies finished their manipulations, and I was surrounded by their smiling, bobbing faces. Mrs. Tranh began shooing me toward the doorway.

"Well, here goes," I muttered. I swept aside the curtains, awkwardly maneuvered my hoops through the doorway, and planted myself in front of the mirror.

"Oh, my God," I gasped, and gave the neckline of the dress a few sharp upward tugs. "I really *am* falling out of this." Surprisingly, the dress wouldn't budge, although the neckline looked even lower and more precariously balanced in the mirror than it felt.

"The effect is historically accurate, I believe," Michael drawled. He was grinning hugely, enjoying my embarrassment.

"Sadist! I don't care if it's required by law, it's just not gonna work. I can't possibly walk around like this. Especially in church. And around drunken relatives."

"On Samantha and the others, this style gives to meager endowments a deceptive appearance of amplitude," Michael said, pedantically. "However, we may have miscalculated the effects of this amplification on your . . . radically different physique. Let me talk to the ladies," he added quickly, and backed away as if he suspected how close I was to swatting at him.

He exchanged several rapid sentences with Mrs. Tranh, punctuated by gales of giggles from the ladies. Mrs. Tranh and two of the other seamstresses surrounded me and began pulling and tweaking at the bodice of the dress, applying measuring tapes to one or another angle of me or it and pointing to or even poking my troublesome endowments. The fact that the tallest of them still fell short of my shoulder only compounded my feeling of being huge, awkward, and ungainly. Michael was carrying on a running dialogue with the seamstresses. I assumed he must be a very witty conversationalist in Vietnamese as well as english; every other sentence of his provoked a fresh crop of giggles. Or maybe they were just all enjoying themselves at my expense. Michael wasn't giggling with the rest, but he couldn't suppress a huge grin.

"They think they've got it figured out," he said at last.

"Good; does that mean I can take it off? I feel like Gulliver among the Lilliputians."

"Sorry," he said, choking back laughter. "I had a hard time convincing them that anything needed fixing, and once I did, they kept trying to talk me into letting them not change it until Samantha had seen it. They don't like her very much, and they kept insisting they wanted to see her face when she saw it."

"You're right; she'd have a cow. And then she'd probably put the evil eye on me or something."

"That's more or less what I told the ladies," Michael said. "And they agreed that it would be a shame, since they like you at least as much as they dislike Samantha. They're going to fix the dress so you look beautiful, but in a somewhat less spectacular manner, and Samantha will have nothing to complain about. Don't worry," he added, momentarily serious, "Mrs. Tranh will manage; she's really very good."

"Thanks," I said, feeling a little bit better as I ducked back into the dressing room to take off the dress. The giggles of the seamstresses seemed somehow friendlier, as if they were laughing with me at the ridiculousness of the dress rather than at how I looked at it. Of course he might have been lying outrageously, but since I would never know, I decided to think positively. Well, I told myself, at least Michael is in a better mood than when I walked in. For that matter, so was I—at least until I got home and tried, for what seemed like the millionth time, to reach the calligrapher. Surely, by now, she had found the time to finish addressing Samantha's wretched invitations.

Dad was also incommunicado. Like the parents of a small and mischievous child, I had learned to be most suspicious when Dad was seemingly quiet and on his best behavior. I was beginning to regret having let him abscond with Great-Aunt Sophy.

After my search of Jake's house, I deduced that either Dad was planning to steal Emma Wendell's ashes and leave Great-Aunt Sophy behind in her place, or he wanted to run some kind of test on Emma Wendell and was using Great-Aunt Sophy to rehearse. Neither one of which seemed like a particularly pleasant thing to be doing. And considering there wasn't much left of either lady but ashes and a few bits of bone, I wasn't sure what on earth he thought he was going to test for, anyway. I decided to drop by and see him tomorrow.

I would have tried to call him, but I had to fight Mother for the phone to call the calligrapher. She was busy putting the word out about the costume party. Apparently she and Eileen had decided to hold it in ten days' time.

"Before any of us gets too busy," Mother remarked. Apparently it had escaped her notice that some of us were already rather busy.

Friday, June 24

I SPENT THE MORNING PHONING TENT RENTAL COMPANIES AND THE afternoon tracking down a supplier for the mead that Steven and Eileen had decided was the only appropriate drink to serve at a Renaissance banquet.

I was tired by the end of the day, but the fact that Steven and Eileen had taken Barry with them to a craft fair in Richmond raised my spirits considerably. I decided to take the weekend off, doing only the most necessary tasks—like continuing to hunt for the errant calligrapher. And keeping an eye on Dad.

Which was harder that I thought. I tried to hunt him down after dinner, and he was definitely nowhere to be found. Not in our garden, not in his apartment over Pam's garage, not in her garden. So I dropped in on Pam.

"Pam," I said. "What's Dad been up to recently?"

"Up to? Why, what should he be up to?"

"Has he been doing much gardening?"

"No, come to think of it, he hasn't," she said, looking out at the rather shaggy grass in the backyard. "That's odd."

"Has he been performing experiments?"

"What kind of experiments?"

"You know, chemical ones."

"How would I know?"

"Noticed any funny smells? Heard any explosions?"

"No," Pam said. "And he hasn't been dragging home stray body parts, or putting out a giant lightning rod on the roof, or drinking strange potions and turning bad-tempered and hairy. What do you mean, experiments?"

"Never mind," I said. "Can I borrow your key to the garage apartment?"

I wanted to check out Dad's lair. I could always pretend that Pam had asked me to help her clean up.

There were several hundred books lying about, apparently in active use. Medical books. Criminology texts. Electricians' manuals. Heaps of mysteries. Bound back issues of the *Town Crier,* the weekly local newspaper, for the past five years. All of them fairly stuffed with multicolored bookmarks. Dad's messy little laboratory looked recently used. His bed didn't. I saw no signs of Great-Aunt Sophy.

I sat down on the cleanest chair I could find with the old *Town Criers* and began checking out Dad's bookmarks.

I found Emma Wendell's obituary, two years ago this month. She'd died in her sleep of heart failure, following a long illness. She'd been quietly cremated and memorialized in a service at the nearby Methodist church. Jake and sister Jane were the only survivors.

I also reread the articles about what the *Town Crier* had called the "Ivy League Swindlers"—Samantha's ex-fiancé and his friend. It had a list of local residents who had been bilked out of large sums. Including, I was surprised to note, Mrs. Fenniman, who was quoted as saying she'd lost a few hundred thousand and was glad they'd been exposed before she'd invested any real money with them. Interesting. I knew Mrs. Fenniman must be well off if she lived in our neighborhood; I'd had no idea she was that well off. And apparently Samantha's father's law firm had been involved as local legal counsel for the Miami-based swindlers—although the articles made it clear they had been duped just as the investors had—in fact, had lost some of their own funds. I noticed only one very distant relative among the list of fleeced locals. Apparently Hollingworth solidarity had kept most of Mother's family using one of the half-dozen relatives who were brokers or investment advisors. Lucky for us.

Dad had bookmarked all of these articles. He'd also bookmarked Mrs. Fenniman's "Around Town" columns for the summer. I read them, too, but did not find any enlightenment in Mrs. Fenniman's meticulous recountings of who entertained whom, who was engaged to whom, and who had returned from vacationing where.

I saw an interview with Michael's mother on the opening of Be-Stitched. No picture, alas, and not much personal information. Widow of an army officer. She'd moved to Yorktown from Fort Lauderdale to be nearer her only child, Michael, who was an Associate Professor in the Theater Arts Department of Caerphilly College.

I was impressed. Caerphilly was a small college with a big reputation located about an hour's drive north. Michael was doing all right.

As I moved back in time, I saw the occasional reference to people visiting Mrs. Wendell in the hospital or Mr. and Mrs. Jacob Wendell being honored for their generous donation to various local charities. Quite the philanthropist, Jake—or was it Emma? I checked the columns since her death. If Jake was still supporting the local charities he was doing it more quietly.

Moving still further back, I found a short article welcoming the Wendells to town. Emma Wendell was the daughter of a wealthy Connecticut state supreme court justice. Jake had just retired from Waltham Consultants, a Hartford-based engineering consulting firm where he'd held the post of senior executive administrative partner in the special projects training division. Whatever that might be. A desk jockeying bureaucrat, no doubt; it was hard to picture Jake as an executive. They were overjoyed to be in York-town, and hoped that the milder winters would be good for Mrs. Wendell's delicate health.

Beyond that, Dad had only marked the occasional article. One or two mentioning Mr. Brewster's law firm. One or two about various neighbors and relatives. One about the use of natural plant dyes in colonial times that I presumed he'd marked because he'd found it interesting, not because it had anything to do with the case.

I didn't feel I'd learned anything in particular. Dad's investigation seemed to have been following the same frustrating dead-end paths as mine.

I thought of tidying up a bit, then thought better of it and returned the key to Pam.

On my way home, I ran into Eileen's dad.

"Meg! Thank goodness!" he said. "I was looking for you."

"Why, what's wrong?"

"We've got to do something about these wedding presents!"

"What about them?"

"They're all over the house, and people are starting to call to ask if we've gotten them. We need to do something."

"Why doesn't Eileen do something?"

A stricken look crossed Professor Donleavy's face.

"She says she won't have time, and asked me to take care of it. And I have no idea what to do."

I thought he was overreacting, but I let him drag me back to the house and he was right: the presents were taking over the house. The professor had started piling them in the dining room, and had run out of room. The living room was filling up fast, and some of the larger things were overflowing into the den.

"I wish Eileen had mentioned this," I said. "This would have been a lot easier to deal with gradually."

I promised him that I'd come around tomorrow to unpack and inventory the presents. So much for taking the weekend off.

Saturday, June 25

I WAS ALREADY IN A BAD MOOD WHEN I SHOWED UP AT THE DON-leavys' to unpack and inventory the presents. Imagine my dismay when the front door was opened, not by Eileen's father but by Barry.

"What are you doing here? I thought you were in Richmond with Steven and Eileen."

"Helped set up," he said, with shrug. "Don't need me till tomorrow afternoon. It's only two hours."

Wonderful. Well, if Barry was going to be underfoot, I was going to do my damnedest to see he didn't enjoy it. First I had him move all the presents from the dining room into the living room. Then I had him bring in a few at a time. I unwrapped them—what was wrong with Eileen, anyway? Present opening wasn't work un-less they were someone else's presents—and made up an index card with a description of each present and the name and address of each giver. It took hours. Even Barry began showing signs of restlessness toward the end.

"That's it," I said finally. "I guess I should take the index cards with me; they'll only get lost around here."

I turned to leave the dining room only to encounter an obsta-cle. A very large obstacle. Barry's arm.

"Don't go yet," he said.

"I have things to do, Barry," I said, backing slightly away from the arm. "Let me go."

"Stay here," he said. I backed up a little further, against the din-ing room wall, which was stupid, because it gave him the chance to put an arm on either side of me. I looked up and saw on his face the unmistakeable, slightly glassy-eyed look of a man who has made up his mind to make his move. The sort of look that sends pleasant shivers down your spine when you see it on the face of the right man. And on the wrong man, makes you mentally kick yourself and wonder why the hell you didn't see this coming and head it off.

"Don't even think of it," I said.

He reached up to take my chin in one hand. I put my hand against his chest and shoved slightly.

"Go away," I said.

He didn't budge. I felt suddenly a little afraid. Barry was so much larger than me, and stronger, and so aggressively determined, and Steven and Eileen were not around to provide a calming influence . . . and then a wave of temper replaced the fear.

"I mean it, Barry. Move it or lose it."

He leaned a little closer.

I mentally shrugged, grabbed his arm with both hands, and twisted. Hard.

"Owwwwwwwwww!" he yelled, and jumped back, nursing his arm. Thanks to self-defense courses, I knew exactly how to do it. Thanks to my iron-working, I'm strong for my size. And I'm not small. Barry glared at me, resentfully.

"You didn't have to do that," he said, taking a small step closer. "What's wrong?"

I lost it.

"What's wrong!" I yelled. "What's wrong! I told you to let me go, and I meant it. Did you think I was kidding? Flirting with you, maybe?"

"Don't be like that, Meg," he said, taking another step closer.

I grabbed a candlestick off the buffet. A nice, heavy iron candlestick that wouldn't fall apart if you banged it around a little. I should know; I made it. I got a good two-handed grip on it and waved it at Barry.

"Come one step closer and I'll use this," I said.

Barry paused, not sure what to do.

"Am I interrupting anything?"

I glanced at the doorway to see Michael. He hadn't adopted his usual pose of leaning elegantly against the frame with one hand in his pocket. He was standing on the balls of his feet, looking wary, alert, a little like a cat about to pounce. More than a little dangerous.

"Barry was just leaving," I said. Barry looked back and forth between Michael and me. I gestured to the door with the candlestick. Barry finally slouched out.

I put the candlestick down and sank into a chair.

"That was stupid," I said.

"I thought it was rather impressive. Remind me not to bet against you in an arm-wrestling contest."

"Yeah, I'm stronger than I look," I said. "Fringe benefit of my career."

"I didn't realize pottery was quite so strenuous."

"I'm not a potter; I'm a blacksmith."

"You're what?"

"A blacksmith," I said. "I work with wrought iron. That's my work," I said, pointing at the candlestick.

"I'm impressed. But obviously confused; I thought your mother said you and Eileen were partners."

"We share a booth and sometimes collaborate," I said. "Mother hates to tell people what I really do; she thinks it's unladylike."

"Ladylike or not, it's useful. I was on the porch and heard you telling him to let you go, so I rushed in to rescue you. Only to find you didn't need rescuing at all."

"I don't think he'd have gone as easily if you hadn't come along. Thanks."

We strolled out. Barry, fortunately, was nowhere to be seen. I'd be just as happy if I never saw Barry again.

Michael walked home with me and stayed for several hours, amusing Mother and me with his banter. I had the feeling, though, that he was keeping a lookout in case Barry showed up to pick up where he'd left off.

Which was silly. Barry was obtuse but not dangerous or violent.

Or was I being obtuse?

I pondered briefly how satisfying it would be to catch Barry red-handed with a blunt instrument in one fist and a tampered fuse in the other.

I suppressed that train of thought and tried to call Mrs. Thornhill, the calligrapher, a few more times before going to bed. I tossed and turned for a while, remembering the sullen anger on Barry's face when he left the dining room. I knew I'd handled the situation badly, but I wasn't sure what I could have done that would have turned out better.

Sunday, June 26

SAMANTHA AND MOTHER, HAVING HEARD WHAT I'D DONE FOR Eileen, insisted on the same service. Since their weddings were one and two weeks behind hers, respectively, they didn't have quite as many presents. Yet.

Pam had only seen Dad in passing, and Mrs. Thornhill was nowhere to be found. On the positive side, Barry made himself scarce.

Monday, June 27

BY MONDAY, I WAS BEGINNING TO THINK THAT MRS. THORNHILL, THE calligrapher, had skipped the country, taking Samantha's envelopes with her. At her rates, the 50-percent down payment Samantha had made would certainly cover plane fare to Buenos Aires, and probably a few nights at a moderately priced hotel. I decided to go over and confront her in person. If she wasn't there, I would wait for her. I could make use of the time; I took my clipboard and my notes for another batch of the thoughtful, warm, personal invitations Mother wanted me to ghostwrite for her. I wasn't sure how early to go—I wanted to catch Mrs. Thornhill before she could disappear for the day, but not wake her up. I finally decided on eight. If she hadn't already missed her deadline I might have given her till nine. If I had to go a second time, I'd go at seven. Maybe six.

When I got there, I saw Mrs. Thornhill's car parked in the driveway—somewhat carelessly—and heard a television blaring away. I'm in luck, I thought. She's home. But as I walked to the front door, I noticed half a dozen copies of the *Daily Press* scattered on the lawn and a Jehovah's Witness flyer stuck behind the screen door. Perhaps she wasn't home after all. Perhaps she left the TV on at top volume to discourage burglars. If so, her neighbors would be ready to strangle her when she got back.

I rang the bell several times, and since the television kept me from hearing whether it worked, knocked a few times for good measure. At last some impulse inspired me to turn the knob. The door was unlocked.

Had something happened to Mrs. Thornhill? I had laughed at Dad's melodramatic suggestion when he made it, but what if he was right? Could that be why she hadn't answered any of my calls this week? Was I about to walk in and discover a horrible, bloody corpse?

Nonsense, I thought. But still, I braced myself before carefully reaching to push the door open—

And hurriedly jumped aside to avoid a tidal wave of cats. They swarmed out of the door and scattered to the four winds. About a dozen of them, I thought, although it seemed like more. I waited until they were out of sight . . . waited a little longer while one extremely fat cat waddled slowly out, hissed at me, and disappeared into the bushes. Then, very cautiously, I entered the front hall.

There were still cats left indoors, and the place reeked of cat urine and fish. Two or three cats wound themselves sinuously around my ankles, and several others scattered from my advance. There were sedate cats sitting at the top of the stairs, and half a dozen playful kittens scampering up and down.

I peered to the right into a dining room that was more or less empty of cats, but filled with debris. Empty catfood cans strewed both the floor and the mahogany dining room table, which they shared with a number of Royal Doulton plates holding crumbs of catfood. I went back though the hall into the living room and found Mrs. Thornhill. She was on the couch, unconscious, with a gin bottle in her hand, and half a dozen cats draped companionably over various portions of her body, some sleeping and others washing whichever parts of her or themselves were handy.

Oh, please, let her have finished the envelopes *before* she started drinking. Or at least let her have left them in a safe place. Somewhere the cats couldn't get to them.

A prayer destined to remain unfulfilled. Scattered among the cats, cans, bottles, and plates in the living room were a number of cream-colored envelopes. I began gathering them up.

Most of them were in the living room, though a few had migrated into the kitchen, or upstairs into the bedroom. She had gotten as far as the S's, unfortunately. The lettering on the A's was absolutely gorgeous. B through D were a little less precise, but still had a kind of aristocratic dash about them. By E she was definitely going downhill, and I could only guess what names some of her late scribbles were intended to represent. Unfortunately, the envelopes that had been completed first had also been lying around longer at the mercy of the cats. I couldn't find a one that hadn't been chewed on, slept on, peed on or blotched with fishy-smelling grease stains. The blank envelopes were a dead loss; several of the cats had used the carton as a litterbox. I made sure I collected all forty-seven pages of Samantha's guest list. Thank goodness I had numbered the pages. I thought I still had a copy somewhere, but with my luck Natalie and Eric would have used it as kindling.

Having gathered up all the envelopes and list pages and deposited them, as appropriate, either in my car or in the overflowing trash can, I turned to consider Mrs. Thornhill. However exasperated I was with her, I couldn't leave her here unconscious. What should I do?

I called Mother.

"Mother, I'm over here at Mrs. Thornhill's."

"That's nice, dear. How is she?"

"She's passed out on the sofa, dead drunk and covered with cats."

After a short pause, I heard Mother's patient sigh.

"Oh, dear. Not again. We were all so hoping she was doing better this time," Mother said, infinitely sorrowful. Great. Why hadn't someone bothered to mention that our calligrapher was a dipsomaniac cat freak? I should have known better than to hire one of Mrs. Fenniman's cronies.

"Do you have any idea who I should call?" I asked. "I can't just leave her there. Does she have family, or should I find one of the neighbors?"

"Oh, dear, I don't think the neighbors. Such intolerant people." I felt a sudden surge of solidarity with Mrs. Thornhill's long-suffering neighbors. "I'll call her son and his wife. You look after her till they get there."

And so I spent the rest of the day baby-sitting Mrs. Thornhill. I realized I hadn't asked Mother where the son lived—in-state, I hoped—but when I tried to call her back the line was busy. For several hours. Presumably the grapevine was disseminating and analyzing Mrs. Thornhill's fall from grace. I checked periodically to make sure she was all right, but the last thing I wanted to do was wake her.

I called Be-Stitched to let Michael know I would miss the afternoon's fittings. I browbeat the printer into promising that he'd find some new envelopes for me in twenty-four hours. I tuned into the Weather Channel, saw a long-range forecast for July and began calling caterers to discuss making menus mayonnaise-free and otherwise heat-proof. I made every other call on my to-do list. I opened a can of cat food for any cat who wandered in and meowed at me. I finally got fed up with the mess and spent the last few hours cleaning. I hauled out a dozen trash bags full of cat food cans, bottles, newspapers, and other debris, changed ten litter boxes, and vacuumed—it didn't seem to bother Mrs. Thornhill. Halfway through the dusting, a car screeched up outside and a frantic couple rushed in. I met them at the door, dustrag in hand.

"Mr. and Mrs. Thornhill?"

"Oh," said the woman, "I thought you came on Tuesdays."

"No," I said, puzzled, "I've never been here before."

"Aren't you the new cleaning lady?"

I explained who I was and why I was there. They overwhelmed me with apologies and thanks. I went home and took a shower, followed by a long hot bath.

"Meg," Mother said over dinner that evening, "you haven't touched your salmon."

I didn't even try to explain.

Tuesday, June 28

MOTHER TAGGED ALONG THE NEXT MORNING WHEN I FETCHED THE new envelopes, and then shanghaied me to help her pick out some upholstery fabric. Unfortunately, by the time I staggered home carrying five giant bolts of blue fabric, Samantha had already heard about Mrs. Thornhill from parties other than me, parties who had no interest in breaking the news to her gently and putting the best face on it. The ensuing tantrum was not pretty. I had to promise that the invitations would be out by Friday to calm her down. My mood was not improved when Mrs. Thornhill the younger called me up and tried to hire me to "do" once a week for her mother-in-law. And to top it all off, Mother decided the blue in Great-Aunt Sophy's vase was the exact shade she wanted for the living room. She spent several hours dragging it and the bolts of fabric around, looking at them together and separately in daylight and lamplight. I was a nervous wreck, waiting for her to detect Sophy's absence. Once she actually tipped the vase and dropped the top on the top on the sofa. I replaced it quietly and she never seemed to notice that nothing had spilled. After Mother finally lost steam and went to bed, I stayed up until two addressing envelopes, fretting all the while because I hadn't seen Dad in several days.

Wednesday, June 29

THE NEXT DAY, MOTHER DECIDED SHE HAD CHOSEN THE WRONG upholstery fabric. I had to lug the bolts back down to the store and exchange them. Not, of course, without endless time-consuming consultation with Mrs. Fenniman. I caught a glimpse of Dad as Mother and I drove to the fabric store, so at least I knew nothing had happened to him. I discovered, to my vast irritation, that Barry had brought down all his tools and set up a shop in Professor Donleavy's garage, thus giving him less reason than ever to leave town. Professor Donleavy was about as thrilled as I was, but several relatives and neighbors had already given Barry commissions. I tried calling Dad when I got home, with no luck, and was up until two-thirty addressing invitations.

Thursday, June 30

MOTHER THEN DECIDED THE FIRST FABRIC HAD BEEN RIGHT, AFTER all. At least she thought it was. I had to chauffeur her and half a dozen friends to half a dozen fabric stores before we were sure, though. Back home with the original five bolts of fabric. Mrs. Thornhill the younger called to up the ante on her offer. I refrained, with difficulty, from resorting to unladylike language. No word from Dad. After Mother went to bed, I snuck down to Pam's house with the five bolts of blue fabric and asked her to hide them. While I was there, I asked her if she'd seen Dad.

"Only in passing," she said. "He's behaving very oddly."

"What do you mean oddly?"

Pam thought for a moment.

"Furtively," she said at last.

Great.

I only managed to stay up till midnight before falling asleep over Samantha's beastly new envelopes.

Friday, July 1

BY THE TIME I WOKE UP FRIDAY MORNING, MOTHER AND THE AD-visory board had decided they needed to exchange the upholstery fabric again. However, my foresight in hiding the fabric at Pam's thwarted them. I told them I'd be glad to ferry them back to the fabric store when they found the bolts, and retired to the hammock with the remaining invitations, leaving them twittering over the sample swatches. I was able to finish all the invitations and drop them off at the post office before noon. On my way back, an inspiration struck me, and I stopped at Be-Stitched just as Michael was taking off for lunch.

"Meg!" he cried. "I've hardly seen you all week."

"Is that why you've given up shaving?"

"I'm getting ready for the costume party tomorrow," he said, with enthusiasm. Drat; I'd completely forgotten the party.

"I'm going as a pirate," Michael said. "What about you?"

"I haven't decided yet."

"But it's tomorrow!"

"Now that I've finally finished Samantha's invitations, I'll think about it."

"Have you been doing those bloody envelopes all this week?"

"That, and running a fabric delivery service," I said. I explained about the blue fabric I'd been shuffling back and forth. "Any chance you could drop by this weekend, look at the swatch I left lying around, and convince Mother she's made the right decision?"

"Your wish is my command. Tell you what: I'll drop by tomorrow and do it, and bring you a costume to boot. I'll have the ladies throw something together; they've got your measurements."

"You're on. As long as it's not made of velvet and doesn't have hoops."

I was relieved when Dad dropped by for dinner that night, proving he hadn't yet fallen victim to the local homicidal maniac. Jake and Mrs. Fenniman also showed up, as did Reverend Pugh, making it yet another of those dinners that should have been more awkward than it was.

Although Dad did his best to make it awkward. His obsession with homicide seemed to have mutated into a fixation on death and funerals. He spent the entire meal talking about them. Once Mother realized there was no stopping him, she gave in gracefully—nay, aided and abetted him—and we were treated to lengthy discussion of the final illnesses, deaths, and burials of both her parents, together with amusing anecdotes about the departures of a dozen or so collateral relatives.

Mrs. Fenniman told several improbable but entertaining anecdotes about the last words or deeds of several of her cronies. Reverend Pugh related poignant or amusing stories about the deaths of past parishioners. Dad discoursed eloquently on funeral customs in a variety of cultures. Whenever the conversation threatened to veer off on a nonmorbid tangent—for example, the amusing incidents that occurred at the wedding of a relative whose death we'd just discussed—Dad would drag it back on course. Everyone got into the act, except Jake. He looked distinctly uncomfortable and resisted all temptation to join the conversation. And just as Mother was dishing out peaches and ice cream for dessert, it suddenly dawned on me. Dad was trying to find out what Jake had done with his wife's ashes.

I burst out laughing, right in the middle of one of Reverend Pugh's more touching anecdotes. Everyone looked at me disapprovingly. Including Dad, damn it.

"Sorry," I said. "I don't know what came over me." And I fled to the kitchen to get the giggles out of my system, smothering my mouth with a dish towel so I wouldn't further embarrass the family.

And as I expected, very shortly Dad found his way to the kitchen.

"Of course, wakes today aren't the same thing at all," he said over his shoulder as he walked in. I could almost hear the sighs of relief in the dining room when the swinging door swung closed.

"Any more peaches?" he asked.

"In the fridge." And while he was poking about in the refrigerator, I slipped up behind him and snagged a large brown paper bag that was hanging out of his jacket pocket.

"I don't see any peaches," he said, turning.

"You were about to lose this," I said, while squeezing the bag slightly to verify its contents.

"Oh, good job, Meg! I wouldn't want to misplace that," Dad said, snatching at the bag. I whisked it away.

"First tell me why you're carrying Great-Aunt Sophy around in a paper bag."

"It's a long story."

"I have time," I said, wiggling the bag just beyond his grasp. "Give me one good reason not to put her back where she came from. No, on second thought, you'd just steal her again. Give me one good reason not to hide her where you'll never find her."

"I need her."

"So I gathered; what are you going to do with her?"

"I'm going to switch her with someone else . . . in a similar condition."

"Going to? You've had her for nearly two weeks; what are you waiting for?"

"To tell you the truth, I haven't located the other party," Dad said, looking discouraged. "I've looked everywhere I could."

"If you mean the late Emma Wendell, she's in a cardboard box in Mrs. Grover's suitcase. In Jake's guest room. Unless Jake has moved her for some reason. That is what this ridiculous charade has been all about, isn't it?"

Dad's face lit up. "Meg, that's wonderful! But how do you know?"

"Michael and I burgled his house. We didn't find anything incriminating, I should point out."

"No, of course not. But are you sure it was Emma Wendell?"

"Can you think of anyone else whose remains Mrs. Grover would be lugging around in a box marked Emma? I think the odds are good."

"Yes," he said. "And Michael helped you."

"In a manner of speaking."

"Good man, Michael," Dad said, warmly. "That was very enterprising of both of you, not to mention brave and very thoughtful."

"Foolhardy and futile were the words I would have used," I said. "But thanks anyway. Now that you know where to find her, what are you going to do with her?"

"Run some tests."

"Is that what you've been doing all this time with Great-Aunt Sophy?"

"Well, no. Actually, I've been on a stakeout."

"A stakeout?" I echoed.

"Yes," he said. "You see, I realize that Jake couldn't possibly have killed Jane Grover, but I still think he was mixed up in it somehow. Maybe he hired someone to do it. Or maybe he knows something he's afraid to tell. Something that might mean that your mother's in danger. So I've been staking his house out for the last ten days."

"Staking it out from where?"

"The big dogwood tree in his yard. His phone's just inside the window on that side of the house, and I can hear every conversation he has and see anyone who comes to the front door. And I've rigged a mirror so I can keep an eye on his back door. Jake can't move a muscle without my finding out about it. At least while I'm there."

I closed my eyes and sighed. I wondered if Jake had really failed to notice Dad perching in his dogwood tree for the past ten days. None of the neighbors had mentioned it. That was a good sign, wasn't it? I made a mental note to cruise by Jake's house later to see how well camouflaged Dad was. Perhaps I should start building a cover story in case someone noticed him. Babble about some rare species of bird Dad suspected of nesting in the neighborhood. Yes, the sheriff would probably buy that.

"Sooner or later, he'll leave the house unlocked and I can pull the switch, now that I know where his late wife is," Dad continued. "I didn't have that much time to search the one time I could get in. But now——"

"Let me do it, Dad," I said. He looked doubtful.

"I'm not sure I should let you. If he finds out we're on to him——"

"I'll get Michael to help me," I said. As I suspected, that did the trick.

"Oh, well, that's all right, then," Dad said. "Just let me know when you've pulled it off."

And he trotted off. Presumably to continue his vigil.

Saturday, July 2

MICHAEL DROPPED BY AS PROMISED THE NEXT MORNING AND TALKED Mother into keeping the blue fabric. In fact, he convinced her that she had picked out the one fabric in the world that would do her living room justice.

"I'm in your debt for life," I said, as we left Mother and Mrs. Fenniman to contemplate the future glories of the living room.

"Good," he said. "Hold that thought. But I have something to show you. Follow me."

I followed him down the driveway. I began to suspect where he was taking me.

"Jake's house, right?" I asked.

"Right. You already knew about this?"

"I only found out last night. How bad is it?"

He rolled his eyes. I winced inwardly.

When we got to Jake's house, Michael stopped, and bent down as if to tie his shoe.

"Up there in the dogwood."

I pretended that I was idly looking around the neighborhood

while waiting for Michael. Dad wasn't quite as obvious as I'd feared. If you knew what to look for, you could rather quickly spot the lump of slightly wilted dogwood leaves and wisteria vines that was Dad. But it actually wasn't all that noticeable. I thought.

"He's been there all morning," Michael said, standing up and pretending to inspect the other shoe to see if it needed tying. Both of us were carefully avoiding looking at Dad.

"As a matter of fact, he's been there on and off for ten days," I said.

"Really!" Michael said, barely stopping himself from turning around to stare at Dad in surprise. "I had no idea. I only noticed this morning. Spike thought he'd treed him."

"In case anyone does see him and mentions it, mutter something about a rare migratory bird that he wants to scoop Aunt Phoebe with."

"Rare migratory bird," Michael repeated. "Aunt Phoebe. Right. Just for curiosity, is he investigating Jake or guarding him?"

"He's not sure himself."

"I see," Michael said, as we began walking on past Jake's house. "Tell him to let me know if he needs any help. Not necessarily with the actual stakeout," he said, quickly, noticing the sharp look I gave him. Right. I could see it now: two suspicious lumps in the dogwood tree, one short and round, the other long and lean. And Michael and Dad getting so caught up in conversation that they forgot to keep their voices down. Just what we needed.

"By the way, I have a costume for you," Michael said. "The ladies helped me pull it together. Do you want to go in and try it on now, or shall I just come by a little early for the party and bring it?"

"Just bring it. Right now, I want to get the yard ready for the party while Dad's out of the way."

"I thought the yard was your Dad's territory. I offered to help him out by mowing the lawn, and he wouldn't hear of it."

"Dad adores riding the lawn mower," I said. "Usually the yard's all his, but if I get out this afternoon and festoon all the trees with little twinkly electric lights, it might keep Dad from trying to fill the yard with torches and candles. He nearly burns the house down every time we let him decorate for a party."

"I can come over and help if you like," Michael offered.

"It'll be hard work," I warned.

"Yes, but in such delightful company," he said.

No accounting for taste, I suppose. By now, I was actively looking to avoid spending too much time in my family's company. Although as it turned out, Pam and Eric were the only other family members I succeeded in recruiting. The four of us spent the whole afternoon climbing trees and perching on ladders.

"Once we've got these up, I think we should just leave them up till Mother's wedding," I said, as we surveyed our handiwork. "One less thing to do that week."

Of course Dad insisted on putting out a few dozen candles, but not nearly the number he would have otherwise.

And Michael brought over my costume. He called it a lady pirate costume.

"You can be either Anne Bonney or Mary Read. Both famous lady pirates. Piracy was an equal opportunity career."

I examined it. A tight corset, topped by a skimpy bodice and finished off (barely) with a short skirt. All ragged, with picturesque fake bloodstains and strategic tears. I'd have turned it down, except that his concept of a lady pirate included a cutlass and a dozen daggers of assorted sizes.

"I don't think much of the dress," I said. "But I like the cutlery. If things keep going as they have been, you may not get the weapons back till I leave town. And I want your eyepatch."

Even after I divested him of his eyepatch, Michael made a very picturesque pirate. With the three or four days' growth of beard he'd cultivated, he ought to have looked scruffy, but he only looked more gorgeous than usual. Rather like the cover of a romance book. It wasn't fair.

Dad came dressed as Sherlock Holmes. Fortunately he felt inspired to act the part as well. Since Mrs. Grover's murder and the other unfortunate events of the summer were a century out of his period, he feigned complete ignorance of them.

Mother outshone everyone. She came as Cleopatra, with Barry and one of her burlier nephews to carry her litter. I suspected that Barry had built the litter as well. Perhaps that was the excuse he'd used to con Professor Donleavy into letting him set up the carpentry shop. I sighed. I hadn't realized he'd started buttering up Mother as well as Dad. Barry and the cousin were standing around in their skimpy Egyptian slave costumes, flexing their muscles, looking as if they, too, were posing for the cover of a romance. To me, they looked more like low-rent professional wrestlers. Or extras from a Conan flick.

About the only person with a mediocre costume was Jake, who wore a tuxedo and carried a cane and periodically performed a few clumsy dance steps to show that he was Fred Astaire.

Even Cousin Horace, though predictably attired in the usual gorilla suit, had apparently gotten himself a brand new gorilla suit. I approved. The old one had become loathsome, its fur frayed and matted and covered with wine and salsa stains. Perhaps he was feeling self-conscious about the new suit, though; I noticed him slipping around the corner of the house in a manner that was remarkably furtive, even for Horace.

Being armed to the teeth was an excellent idea for future neighborhood parties. The cutlass wasn't sharp, but waving it at anyone who misbehaved tended to get my point across. Some of the daggers actually were sharp, which I used to advantage when Barry, having too much to drink, foolishly grabbed me by the waist. And the weaponry made me feel irrationally safer whenever I remembered the fact that one of the cheerful party guests gamboling on the lawn might well be a killer.

Everyone was having a good time. Well, Barry was off somewhere sulking and nursing his cut. It wasn't much of a cut, and I was sure he didn't really need the elastic bandage on his wrist, either. I hadn't twisted his arm that badly the other day; he was blowing these things out of proportion. Jake was off somewhere sulking, too; someone had mistaken his Fred Astaire impersonation for a penguin. And Samantha had proclaimed herself mortally embarrassed and gone home in a huff after seeing Rob dressed in what he called his legal briefs—a pair of swim trunks with pages from a law dictionary stapled all over them. But everybody else was having a great time.

"Hello, Meg," came a muffled voice. I turned to see Cousin Horace. Who appeared to have changed back into his old gorilla suit. He was waving a paw at me. I could see a familiar set of blueberry stains on his left palm. How tiresome; if he had to wear the suit, why couldn't he have stayed with the new, improved model?

"What happened to your new suit?" I asked.

"New suit?" he asked, puzzled. He was eating watermelon through the gorilla mask; an amazing feat, but one I would really rather not have watched.

"Didn't I see you earlier in a new gorilla suit?" I asked, irritably. Well, perhaps to give him credit he preferred not to stain his new suit. Perhaps we could get him to change back when he'd finished eating.

"I don't have a new suit."

"Are you sure?" Dumb question; of course he'd know if he had a new gorilla suit. But if it wasn't him . . .

"Who was it?" Cousin Horace asked, suspiciously. I gave him an exasperated look.

"How should I know? I thought it was you."

Who, indeed. I left Cousin Horace muttering threats against the imposter and moved through the party, scanning the crowd for another squat, furry figure.

"Looking for someone?" Michael asked, coming up beside me.

"Yes; someone in a gorilla suit," I said, standing on tiptoes to look over the crowd.

"Your cousin Horace is back there, by the buffet."

"Not him," I said, shortly.

"You mean there's someone else wearing a gorilla suit? Is it contagious?"

"I have a bad feeling about this," I said.

"About what?" asked Dad, who had just appeared on my other side.

"Someone is sneaking around in a gorilla suit," I said. "Someone other than Horace."

"Well, it's not as though he has exclusive rights to it," Dad said. "Although I'm sure Horace finds it upsetting."

"You don't understand," I said. "I saw whoever it was sneaking around the corner of the house. With everything that's going on, I don't like the idea of someone sneaking around."

"Someone dressed in a costume that hides its wearer's identity," Michael added.

"Sneaking in or out?" Dad asked.

"Out, I think. Unless I scared him away."

"Let's check the house," Michael suggested.

We did, though it didn't seem too useful to me, since we had no idea what we were looking for. We didn't even know if we were looking for something missing or something added. Nothing seemed amiss downstairs, other than the normal chaos that comes from preparing for a large party and then having several hundred people tramping in and out to use the bathroom. I sighed at the thought of the cleanup we'd be doing tomorrow. The few people currently in the house remembered seeing the gorilla suit, but thought it was Horace. Was I the only one who noticed the new suit? Then again, presumably Horace could have gone inside to use the bathroom. We scrutinized the fuse box, but none of us knew what a booby-trapped one looked like, and anyway the lights were working.

It was upstairs that we found it. In my room.

"Dad! Michael!" I hissed. They came running, and I pointed to the object lying on my bed.

A small wooden box, like a shoebox propped up on one end. Made of some highly polished wood, with delicate asymmetric carving on two sides. Leaning against one side was a card that said, in large, bold letters: For Meg.

"Looks like Steven's and Barry's work," I said.

"Really?" Michael said. "It's quite impressive."

"Could you have mistaken Barry for Horace?" Dad asked.

"Doesn't seem likely," I said. "It was a new gorilla suit, but it still didn't seem that large a gorilla. Then again, I didn't get a really good look, and I assumed it was Horace."

We were circling the bed, peering at the box from all sides. I finally reached out to take the card—

Lifting the card triggered some hidden mechanism. The lid flew open, and something leaped out like a jack-in-the-box. I didn't see what, at first; we all hit the floor. After a few seconds, when nothing happened, we peeked over the side of the bed. A large bouquet of silk flowers had popped out of the box and was still swaying slightly. A card that said Love, Barry was twined in the foliage.

"That's certainly very ingenious," Dad said, peering at the box with interest.

"And rather romantic in a way, I suppose," Michael remarked, frowning.

"Of all the idiotic things," I began. My heart was still pounding at twice the usual rate. And then I noticed something about the box.

"Gangway," I yelled, grabbing it and running. I scrambled through my window onto the flat porch roof outside, and hurled the box as far as I could toward the river. I have a good, strong throwing arm; it actually ended up in the bushes at the edge of the bluff.

"Meg, that was uncalled for," Dad said, following me out onto the roof. "I don't like Barry any more than you do, but——"

Whatever else he was saying was drowned out by the loud explosion at the edge of the bluff. Part of the bluff flew up into the air, disintegrating as it went, and began raining down in small chunks on the guests in the backyard. A small tree wobbled and disappeared over the edge.

"It was ticking," I said. "I see no reason for jack-in-the-boxes to tick. And someone had ripped open the lining and put something under it and sewed it back up, clumsily. Of course he could have decided at the last minute to put in a music box, and done it in a hurry, but I didn't think that was too likely, and I'm glad I didn't stop to find out. What kind of an idiot would leave something like that where anyone could find it, Mother or Eric or——"

"Sit down, Meg, you're babbling," Dad said. I sat. "Michael, fetch her a glass of water. And then——"

"Yes, I know," Michael said. "Find the sheriff."

"And Barry," Dad said. "I think I see them there in the crowd."

I looked up. People were swarming near the edge of the bluff. Much too near the edge. I leaped up.

"Get away from the bluff!" I shrieked. "Everybody away from the bluff! Now!"

They paid attention. Clowns, hoboes, gypsies, and furry animals of all kinds scattered madly and dived for cover. No doubt they thought I'd finally lost it and was planning to lob more grenades.

"Good," Dad said approvingly. "We need to preserve these crime scenes better."

"I'll fetch the sheriff now," Michael said.

He brought them right out onto the roof. The sheriff didn't mind; he could keep an eye on his deputies—several of whom, conveniently, were also relatives and thus already here to begin the investigation.

"What is going on here?" the sheriff began.

"Barry," I said. "Did you leave me a present? Carved wooden box with a pop-up bouquet?"

"Yes," Barry said, his face brightening. "Did you like it? When you didn't say anything before I thought you didn't like it."

"Before? I only just found it a few minutes ago."

"But I left it on your porch last night."

"And I only found it a few minutes ago, here on my bed."

"But I left it on the porch," Barry insisted. "Last night."

"I think it's obvious what happened," Dad said. "Someone found the box Barry left, took it away, and added their own little surprise."

"Surprise?" Barry said.

"The explosion. Someone put a bomb in your box."

Barry turned pale and gulped. He looked at me, opened his mouth, then closed it and sat down on the roof, his head in his hands.

"I'm sorry," he moaned. "It's all my fault."

"Don't," I said, patting his shoulder. "It was a very beautiful box. It's not your fault." Unless, of course, he *had* put the bomb in it.

"I'm so sorry," he repeated. "If I'd had any idea . . ."

The party disintegrated, although many of the guests hung around watching long after the sheriff's merry men finished interrogating them. The sheriff decorated the house with a lot of cheerful yellow crime scene tape and kept us out until he could arrange for a special bomb detection squad to come down from Richmond to search the premises. The team turned out to be a laid-back state trooper with a hyperactive Doberman.

"Shutting the barn door after the whole herd of horses have been stolen," I muttered.

"You'd feel differently if they'd found a second bomb," Michael pointed out.

"I'm so sorry," Barry said. Again.

Clearly it would be hours before the police and firefighters left and we could get some peace and quiet. Or what passed for peace and quiet these days. Mother and Rob went off to Pam's. I thought someone from the family ought to be around, so I collapsed in the backyard hammock, out of the way but within call. I was too tired to keep my eyes open but too hyper to sleep. How had I managed to attract the attention of the killer? Had my sporadic attempts to help Dad with his detective work made the killer nervous? Or were Mrs. Grover's murder, the booby-trapped fuse box, and now the bomb the work of a lunatic who didn't care who he killed?

I was not in the mood for company. Well, I didn't mind having Michael around; he was making entertaining conversation on a variety of subjects that had nothing to do with homicide and he didn't mind if I just listened in silence. Barry, on the other hand . . .

"It's all my fault," he said—not for the first time—during a lull in the conversation.

"It's alright, Barry," I said, mechanically.

"If only I had just given you the box."

"You had no way of knowing," I said, through gritted teeth.

"You could have been killed, and it would have been all my fault. Well, partly my fault."

"Barry," I said, "if you put the bomb in the box, tell the sheriff. If you didn't, stop apologizing and go away."

He opened his mouth and stared at me for a few moments, his

mental gears almost audibly turning. Then he closed his mouth and went away rather quickly.

I settled back in my hammock. After a few minutes, I opened one eye. Michael was sitting, watching me with a worried look on his face.

"So?" I asked. "You were telling me how you dealt with the soap opera queen who tried to upstage you."

He grinned, and went on with his story. I closed my eyes. It was a funny story. I could feel myself relaxing. And if I managed to drift off before he got to the punchline, I could ask him to tell it again tomorrow. Michael was certainly good company; I was going to miss him when the summer was over.

Sunday, July 3

IT WAS NEARLY THREE WHEN I TOTTERED UP TO BED, SO I WAS HOP-ing to sleep in the next morning. But the thought of all the mess left over from the party and the bomb wouldn't let me. About nine, I got up and went down to survey the cleanup ahead of us. Was hunting down a cleaning service that would work on Sunday less trouble than doing it ourselves? Perhaps we should relocate this afternoon's tea for the bridesmaids to Pam's house. Fortunately tomorrow's shower was at the Brewsters'.

First, coffee and the Sunday paper. I padded out to the front door and looked out to see if by chance the paperboy had hit our porch for a change, instead of the goldfish pond.

And saw a small box sitting on the porch with a tag on the top that said For Meg.

I ran back to the kitchen and called the sheriff. Then Dad. Luckily, the trooper and his bomb-sniffing Doberman had stayed over. The sheriff was able to catch them before they took off for Richmond and drag them back out to our neighborhood. Also luckily, most of the neighborhood were still either asleep or in church, so we didn't have to contend with a large crowd. Just Dad, Michael, Rob, me, and nine assorted law enforcement officials. Ten if you counted the Doberman.

"Does this look like the other bomb?" the sheriff asked.

"No, the other was a wooden box about the size of a shoebox," I explained. "And it seems like a different handwriting. But the other one also had a tag that said For Meg.

The Doberman was going wild, barking madly at the box. This seemed to alarm his handler and the deputies. Did that mean it was a particularly large and powerful bomb? For that matter, Spike was going wild, too, but probably all that meant was that he wanted to attack the Doberman.

"We're going to put the box in a special container and then take it out where we've got room to detonate it without hurting anybody," the sheriff said. "We're just waiting for the special equipment."

Waiting for the special equipment was getting on my nerves. I found myself staring obsessively at the box, as if I could figure out by looking at it who had planted it there. I began to realize that there was something familiar about the box. It was a stationery box. A battered, grease-stained box that had once held envelopes. And there were holes punched in the side. And where had I seen that neat, elegant handwriting before? I suddenly realized what it was.

"Oh, for goodness' sakes," I said. I strode over to the steps—the deputies were too startled to stop me—and picked up the box.

"No—don't—put it down—look out!" came shouts from Dad, Michael, and the assembled lawmen. I opened the box.

"Mrrow?" A small white kitten was staring back at me with wide green eyes.

"Call off your dogs," I said.

"Mrrow!" said the kitten, and extended a head to be scratched.

"I knew I'd never seen him act like that before," said the Doberman's handler, with disgust.

"It's from Mrs. Thornhill," I told Dad and Michael, who still looked shaken as they approached.

"Mrs. Thornhill?"

"The tipsy calligrapher. I suddenly recognized the handwriting."

I explained about Mrs. Thornhill and the invitations, to the great amusement of the deputies and firefighters. We were all bursting with the nervous laughter of people who have been badly scared. Some of the deputies began suggesting names like Boomer and Dynamite for the kitten. I refrained from telling them that the kitten would be going home to Mrs. Thornhill as soon as possible.

We did, however, decide that from now on we wouldn't open any wedding presents until we'd had them tested. Except for Eileen's, of course; no one would have any reason to harm her. The sheriff went off to discuss the arrangements with the Doberman's handler.

"So who are these people, anyway?" I overheard the trooper ask. "The local mob or something?"

I let the sheriff defend the family honor. I went off to intercept Mother and warn her that her yard was once more filled with police and firefighters. Warning her didn't seem to help much; she was still decoratively distraught and her recovery seemed to require that Jake take her and several of the aunts out to an expensive restaurant for Sunday dinner. On the bright side, while the chaos was at its height, I did manage to convince her to postpone her tea for the bridesmaids until the following weekend. And before I called all the bridesmaids to cancel, while I was sure she and Jake were still out of the way, I went down to Jake's house for another spot of burglary.

"Here," I said, sotto voce to Dad that evening. "I've got the goods."

"Great-Aunt Sophy?" he asked, looking into the bag.

"No, Emma Wendell. I pulled the switch this afternoon."

"That's splendid," he said, peering more intently into the bag. "This will be a great help."

"If it makes you happy," I said, as Dad trotted off, bag in hand.

We had a violent thunderstorm that night. The power went out just as we were about to fix dinner. The kitten, whom I hadn't gotten around to returning, turned out to be terrified by lightning. It was not a restful night.

Monday, July 4

UNFORTUNATELY, THE THUNDERSTORM THAT TOOK OUT THE power Sunday night failed to cool down the air. By nine o'clock Monday morning, the day of Samantha's bridal shower, the power was still out. The temperature was pushing ninety and still rising. Tempers were wearing thin all over the neighborhood, but particularly at the Brewster house. Those of us trying to help out in the kitchen spent most of the afternoon bickering over which foods were going to be safe to eat by the time the guests arrived and which contained ingredients like mayonnaise and were not to be trusted. As time passed and the mercury soared, the list got shorter, the trash cans got fuller, and we began to wonder if canceling would be a good idea.

Then, by a stroke of luck—possibly a bad stroke, although we didn't realize it at the time—the power came back on at five in the afternoon and we didn't have to cancel after all. In the hour before the first guests arrived, we ran the air conditioners full blast and changed the atmosphere from an oven to a mere steambath by the time things got underway. Mother sent Rob and Jake to the store to bring back an assortment of cheese, chips, crackers, and luncheon meats to replace the foods lost to the heatwave, and Pam, whose end of the neighborhood got back power a little sooner than ours, endeared herself to everybody by showing up with several huge bowls of fresh onion dip and salsa. I suspected that Dad must still be crouched in Jake's dogwood tree; for it was nearly the first time all summer we actually served party food that Dad hadn't picked over in advance. Which meant, of course, that there was so much food we'd probably end up calling him in to help get rid of it afterwards.

Once the shower got underway, I suppressed my mutinous wish that we'd cancelled after all. Watching Samantha unwrap and wave about frothy bits of lingerie ranked very low on my list of ways I'd like to spend one of the hottest days of the summer. I envied Mother, who had pleaded a headache and gone home already. Looking at Samantha's carefully matched set of bridesmaids depressed me. They were all there: Jennifer, Jennifer, Jennifer, Kimberly, Tiffany, Heather, Melissa, and Blair. I'd made a little rhyme of it to help me remember all the names, and was working on matching them to faces.

I was in a lousy mood, but I was the only one, and as far as I could see, the shower was going fine until Samantha vomited into the onion dip.

One minute she was chatting and laughing with Kimberly and Jennifer II, and then, suddenly, she bent over and puked right onto the dip platter. Conversation, naturally, screeched to a halt.

"Oh, dear," she said, faintly, putting her hand to her mouth. And then she turned and fled upstairs. I was still staring after her, wondering if I should go and see if she was all right, when suddenly I heard more retching. In stereo. Kimberly on my right, and one of Samantha's college friends on my left, were also throwing up.

It was the beginning of a mass exodus as, one after another, the guests either threw up and ran out or turned pale and walked unsteadily to the door. I considered going after them and rejected the idea. I'm not much of a nurse. And my stomach was beginning to feel a bit queasy. I hoped it was my imagination. I went out to the kitchen, told the housekeeper and Mrs. Brewster what was going on. The housekeeper fainted. Mrs. Brewster dialed 911. Good move. I began gathering paper towels and spray cleaner to mop up the living room as my penance for not going to the aid of the patients.

Just as I was beginning to think that perhaps luck—or my finicky eating habits—had been on my side and that I wasn't going to be sick, I felt the first faint tremors.

You'd think that in a house with seven bathrooms you could find a toilet to puke in when you wanted one, but after trying the hall powder room door—locked, with audible retching sounds emerging—I passed by the kitchen and saw three guests fighting for room at the sink while another was lying on the floor with her head propped over the dog's waterbowl. That's it, I told myself. I'm going home while I still can.

It wasn't easy. My head was beginning to ache badly, and even though it was twilight, the light hurt my eyes. I made it up the Brewsters' driveway and almost to the end of the next yard when the dizziness got so bad I had to stop and clutch the fence to stay upright. A horrible cramp went through my stomach, and I felt a sudden, uncharacteristic urge to strangle whichever of the Labs was barking just inside the fence.

"Meg?" I opened one eye to see Michael, with Spike in tow. Spike was trying to claw his way through the fence to get at the Labs. Serve him right if he succeeded, I thought.

"Meg, are you all right?" I shook my head, then wished I hadn't.

"Samantha's poisoned us all," I gasped. "At the shower. Food poisoning."

"For God's sake, why didn't you stay there if you're sick."

"No place to be sick," I muttered. "Can't even squeeze into a john. Everyone's having hysterics. Going home to be sick in peace." I began to lever myself off the fence and toward home.

"Hang on a minute, damn it! Let me set Spike loose and I'll help you. He can find his own way home." He caught up with me before I'd gone two steps, and picked me up remarkably easily, considering that I'm neither short nor skinny.

"What if I throw up on you?" I protested feebly.

"It'll wash out."

I shut up so he could save his breath for carrying me. Mother, Dad, Jake, and Mrs. Fenniman were sitting on the porch chatting when he staggered up with me.

"Someone should get over to the Brewsters' house right away," Michael ordered. "Apparently all the guests are dropping like flies from food poisoning. Don't worry, I'll take care of Meg."

All four of them took off immediately. Even, wonder of wonders, Mother. Dad had his ever-ready black bag, so I figured I could stop worrying about the others. Michael carried me upstairs, correctly figured out from my feeble gestures which bathroom I wanted and deposited me there just in time.

It was a long night. About the time I thought I had finished throwing up, some of the neighbors began setting off their fireworks, and for some reason that set me off again. Maybe it wasn't the neighbors' fault; maybe I was destined to get the dry heaves at about that point anyway, but the light hurt my eyes, the noise made my headache worse, and I wasn't in the mood for celebrating anything.

I think Dad came by once or twice to check on me. Michael stuck it out to the end, holding my head when I threw up, and then always ready with a glass of water, a clean washcloth, or a cold compress. It's a good thing it's Michael seeing you puking, I told myself, and not Mr. Right. I couldn't bear to think of Mr. Right, whoever he might turn out to be, seeing me heave my guts up seventeen times in succession. It was embarrassing enough having Michael see it.

Tuesday, July 5

I SPENT THE NEXT DAY IN BED, AS DID MOST OF THE REST OF THE guests at the shower. I was one of the lucky ones; some of the other guests had also had diarrhea and convulsions. Dad had to send some of the worst cases off to the hospital. To Mrs. Brewster's complete mortification, the local paper ran a story about the incident, making it sound a great deal more hilarious than any of us in attendance thought it had been. I slept a lot. Mother and Eileen were too worried about me to mention any of the thousand tasks that weren't getting done, and Samantha was in the hospital. What a pity I spent most of this unexpected respite sleeping. And playing with the kitten, since no one had found the time to take him back to Mrs. Thornhill.

Wednesday, July 6

PERHAPS THE WORST THING ABOUT BEING SICK IN BED IS THAT everyone knows exactly where to find you. Barry attempted to smother me with attention. Dad shooed him out as often as possible, along with various neighborhood ladies who dropped by to report how bravely poor Samantha was holding up and how she was still doing everything she could to keep the wedding plans moving. Since the only thing I could discover she'd done was call me up three or four times to issue new orders and complain about the things I hadn't felt well enough to get done, a certain lack of cordiality tended to creep into these conversations.

But Dad liked Michael, or at least found him entertaining, and so didn't shoo him away as he did with most of the people who came to visit. In fact, Michael made me feel much better by reporting that he had convinced Mother that the blue fabric still in hiding at Pam's was the perfect thing for the living room, if only it could be found. He brushed away my repeated grateful thanks—about the fabric and his nursing services—and regaled me with the outrageous antics of the various bridal parties who'd been in and out of the shop all week. I was actually in a reasonably good mood when Dad dropped by with news that only he would have considered cheering for a recovering invalid.

"It wasn't food poisoning, you know," he said, with enthusiasm.

"Then what was it?" I asked. "Surely we weren't all simultaneously overcome with the force of Samantha's personality? After all, she was a victim, too."

Michael sniggered, but Dad, full of his news, ignored my sarcasm.

"Some sort of vegetable alkaloid in the salsa," he said.

"How does that differ from food poisoning?" I asked.

"It wasn't something that ought to have been in the salsa to begin with," Dad explained. "Probably something in the amaryllis family. I've had the residue sent to the ME in Richmond, but we may not be able to tell much more. It was out in the heat rather a long time before anyone thought to preserve it."

"How remiss of me," I said. "Poor Pam! She must be frantic; it was her secret recipe for the salsa, after all."

"The sheriff and I have both questioned Pam about the salsa, and it's hard to see how she could have done it by accident," Dad said. "The dishes she used to prepare it were still in her kitchen and showed no traces of poison, so it must have been added after she put it in the two serving bowls. And none of the kids admit to having played any tricks with it, and I believe them. There's just one thing that bothers me."

"Just one?" Michael muttered.

"The rigged fuse box was probably directed at me," Dad said. "But these last two incidents—the bomb and the poisoned salsa— they were directed at you, Meg."

"Not necessarily," I said. "The bomb, yes; but the salsa was probably aimed at you."

"I wasn't even invited to the shower," Dad protested.

"Yes, but the killer could have guessed you'd show up to nibble on the food before the party started," I said. "Everyone in town knows to fix more food than they need for a party, to feed the nibblers. And you're king of the nibblers."

"That's ridiculous," Dad said, but his face had turned a bright red that suggested he saw the truth, even if he wouldn't admit it.

"It's a good thing you were busy elsewhere all day," I went on. "If two bowls of salsa split among twenty people did all that damage, imagine what it would have done to you if you'd scarfed down a whole bowl the way you usually do with salsa. The only reason we had two bowls of the stuff is that you usually finish off one before the guests get to it, so Pam always makes one for you and one that she hopes you won't find."

"Oh, well," Dad said, looking shaken and not bothering to protest. "Good point, I suppose. Anyway, there's no way Pam could have accidentally introduced a potentially fatal dosage of a highly toxic vegetable alkaloid into the salsa."

"That's a relief."

"The question is, who tampered with the salsa after Pam finished with it?"

"And why? Was it aimed at you, or Meg, or just at causing maximum death and injury?" Michael put in.

"Dad, you've got to be careful," I said. "We all do."

"Right. No nibbling." Michael said.

"Yes, we should all be very careful indeed," Dad said. And with that, he patted my hand and trotted away, no doubt to confer with the sheriff and the ME.

"Why the hell hasn't your sheriff done something?" Michael asked, with irritation. "Called in the FBI or something."

"Well, up until the bomb, I don't think anyone was that worried," I said. "The sheriff still seemed to think the fuse box incident and Mrs. Grover's death could have been accidents. And after all, when it comes to homicides, Dad has rather a history of crying wolf."

"I wasn't sure I believed him myself, before," Michael said. "But after this weekend, I'm sold. Whatever you and your dad have been doing with your detecting, you've definitely scared somebody. And that somebody's after you."

I closed my eyes briefly and shuddered at the idea of a cold-blooded killer stalking my occasionally demented but thoroughly lovable Dad. I didn't want to believe it. And I hadn't even begun to sort out how I felt about joining Dad on the killer's most wanted list. Why me? Had I found out something vital? If I had, it was news to me.

"I really don't need this," I said. "I have enough on my mind without this. These damned weddings are enough to worry about, without having a homicidal maniac on the loose."

"Yes, life in Yorktown is getting very complicated," Michael said. "Don't walk on the bluffs, don't play with fuse boxes, don't open any packages, and don't eat the salsa. Anyway, you look tired; I'll let you sleep. I think I'll go home and start harassing some law enforcement agencies to take action."

"Good idea."

"Anything I can do for you on my way out?"

"Yes," I said, handing him a bag. "Take this herb tea and ask Dad to take a look at it to see if it's safe to drink."

"You think someone is trying to poison you again?" he asked, holding the bag as if it contained another ticking bomb.

"Not deliberately, but I've learned to distrust Eileen's home remedies. And take these damned lilies of the valley away, too. Give them to Mrs. Tranh and the ladies if you like."

"Are they poisonous too?" he joked.

"Actually, yes. Highly toxic. Warn them not to eat them. Even the water they've been soaking in could kill you."

"I can see why you don't want them around."

"I don't want them around because they're from Barry," I said, rather peevishly. "I thought he was safely off at a craft fair with Steven and Eileen for the weekend, but he showed up here instead. I'd be tempted to feed him the damn flowers and be done with him if I thought there was any chance they could decide on a new best man in time. But come July Sixteenth, Barry had better watch out."

"Until they catch whoever spiked the salsa, all of us better watch out," Michael said gravely. "Be careful."

Thursday, July 7

FORTUNATELY FOR MY PEACE OF MIND, IT WASN'T UNTIL THURSDAY afternoon that I was reminded of what was in store for me over the weekend. Undeterred by the dramatic events at the shower, the Brewsters were going full steam ahead with plans for a weekend house party for a number of Samantha's and Rob's friends. Actually, mostly Samantha's friends. Rob was being firmly but gently detached from any of his circle of friends of whom Samantha did not approve. Which generally meant the interesting ones, as far as I could see.

The house party had seemed like such a good idea when Mrs. Brewster first suggested it. I'm not, as a rule, a keen party goer, and spending the evening in a roomful of Samantha's friends was on a par with visiting one of the lower circles of hell. But I had been having difficulty getting some members of the wedding party to come in for final fittings. It occurred to me as soon as the party was suggested that it would be just the thing to lure any holdouts into town where they could be fitted and, if necessary, read the riot act while I had them in my clutches. So Samantha and her mother had planned a fun-filled weekend of parties and picnics, and I had suggested that they pay overtime to have Michael's ladies on standby all weekend.

But I'd completely forgotten about the whole wretched thing until Mother glided into my room early Thursday morning. Considerably earlier than I had been intending to wake up.

"I think you should plan on getting up today," she said. "You need to start getting your strength back." She was probably right. I sighed.

"Pammy is fixing us a nice breakfast," she continued. I was touched.

"And after breakfast you can both help me plan a new menu for the tea party I'm giving for Samantha and her little friends on Sunday."

I pulled the covers back over my head and refused to budge until noon. Which only meant that we did the menu-planning after lunch.

"Meg, I'm beginning to think that blue fabric has been stolen," Mother said that evening. "We should go down tomorrow and see if they can order some more."

"Why don't you let me look for it first," I said. Great; now I had to find a way to lure Mother out of the house, sneak down to Pam's, lug the fabric back, and hide it someplace where Mother could be convinced she hadn't already looked. I didn't feel up to it. I collared Dad and Michael after dinner and asked them if they would take care of it.

"Of course," Dad said, patting my hand.

"Provided you'll vouch for us if we're caught," Michael added.

"I'll keep Mother well out of the way," I said.

"I wasn't thinking of your mother," Michael said. "I was thinking of how the neighbors will react when they see the two of us sneaking about with wrapped parcels about the size and shape of human bodies."

"We won't sneak," Dad said. "You can get away with almost anything as long as you act as if you have a perfect right to be doing whatever you're doing."

"Perhaps that's how our murderer got away with it," I said.

"I should think that even around here it would be a little hard to shove someone over the bluffs without exciting comment from the neighbors," Michael objected.

"Not if they thought shoving that particular someone was the reasonable thing to do," I said, testily, spotting Samantha heading down the driveway.

"And besides," Dad protested, "I thought I'd made that clear: she couldn't possibly have been shoved over the cliff."

"True, but what about Meg's theory that she was walking on the beach when a stone hit her on the head?" Michael replied.

They ambled off to Pam's house, cheerfully debating their various theories about Mrs. Grover's death. I eluded Samantha and went to help Mother prepare for her Sunday afternoon tea. By dint of looking wan and pale—I'd had a lot of practice over the past several days—I managed to talk her out of having me cook all kinds of complicated goodies. We drove down to three of the local bakeries and placed orders with each for a supply of their specialties.

Driving home, I wondered if placing the order several days ahead of time was such a good idea. Plenty of time for anyone to find out, duplicate one of the pastries we were serving, and prepare a doctored batch. I'd have to pick them up myself. And then hide them until the party. Perhaps there was some way I could mark them so I'd know they were the ones I'd picked up. And then if I saw someone lifting a pastry without the telltale mark, I could dash it from her hands . . .

You're just being silly, I told myself. At least I hoped I was. Then again, if I were one of the out-of-town bridesmaids who'd lived through last weekend, I wouldn't be that quick to eat the local cuisine. Or open any packages. Or come to Yorktown at all, for that matter.

Friday, July 8

I SPENT MOST OF THE DAY SUPERVISING THE CLEANING CREW MOTHER hired to get ready for Sunday's tea. And then trying to keep Dad from tracking in garden debris. And cleaning up after the kitten, whom I really would have to return before everyone got too attached to him. And sorting out wedding presents. The sheriff's office had been very cooperative about testing all the packages before we opened them, but they had failed to grasp the importance of keeping the cards with the presents. In some cases I had to figure out not only who sent the present but also whether it was for Mother or Samantha. I made a note to stay and supervise their inspection of the next batch.

Despite all this, I was ready early for the Brewsters' party, largely because Mother was out for the evening and I could dress without any nuptial or decorating interruptions. I went over to see if the Brewsters needed any help. When I walked in, I wasn't surprised to find Dad and Reverend Pugh parked by the buffet, discussing orchids. They had finished off a huge bowl of shrimp cocktail and were starting in on the bean dip.

"I thought we'd all agreed to avoid nibbling," I said with some irritation. Dad froze, holding a stick of celery loaded with bean dip. The reverend shoveled in another mouthful. Well, if it hadn't already killed him, one more bite wouldn't hurt.

"After last weekend's poisoning, you know," Dad said, putting down the celery—which had already lost its load of bean dip to his lapel.

"Oh," Reverend Pugh said, reluctantly moving away from the bean dip.

"You promised," I said, fixing Dad with a stern glare.

"I suppose it's all right for someone else to be poisoned instead of me," Dad said, indignantly. "I suppose I should have let Pugh eat some of it and waited to see if he keeled over."

From the way the rector was eyeing the ham croquettes, I expected he was about to volunteer to put his life on the line again for the good of the party.

"I suppose that's why Mrs. Brewster asked us to guard the food," he said, brightly.

"Guard, not devour," I said. The two nibblers made a quick retreat. I concentrated on figuring out which neighbor would either have some shrimp around or be able to get some in time to replace what they'd eaten before Mrs. Brewster noticed.

I shouldn't have bothered. With the exception of a few dozen oldsters like Dad and the Pughs, who left early, most of the crowd wasn't seriously interested in food. In fact, most of Samantha's friends focused on getting drunk as rapidly as possible and crawling off somewhere private with the most presentable person of the opposite sex they could get their hands on. Not only did I have to dodge the ever-present Scotty, but apparently not all of Samantha's male friends went for the bleached blond anorexic type. By the time the third keg was being opened, I dodged a particularly persistent (and intoxicated) suitor by literally crawling out a bathroom window.

As I turned up the driveway toward home, I heard a shout.

"Meg! Wait up!" It was Michael. I waited for him to catch up with me.

"I'm surprised," he said. "Not even midnight and you're home from the party. I thought you were supposed to be a night owl."

"Oh, not you, too. Officially I'm still a little under the weather from the poisoning. Unofficially, Samantha's friends can be a real drag. Where's Spike? Lost again?"

"At home, as far as I know. I dropped by on the chance either you or your mother would be here. She said you had found the jacquard and I should come by to pick it up. What is jacquard, and what am I supposed to do with it when I've got it? I presume it's something to do with the shop?"

"Jacquard? Oh, I suppose she means those five bolts of blue fabric you and Dad retrieved from Pam's. I think I shoved them in my closet; hang on and I'll haul them down. Mother must still be out at her cousins'," I added, seeing that the house was dark.

"I can do the hauling if you show me where they are," Michael offered.

"Ordinarily, my stubborn independent nature would compel me to insist on doing it myself. But after a week like this one, I'll even let people open doors for me."

"I gather the other bridesmaids are fully recovered from the shower, then?" Michael asked, as we climbed the stairs.

"Mostly recovered," I said. "Of course, most of them aren't worrying about saving any energy for the second party tomorrow night, Mother's tea on Sunday, and whatever nonsense we're going to have to go through with the fittings tomorrow," I added.

As we walked into my room, Michael and I were both startled to see the closet door fly open. Scotty jumped out, holding half a dozen bedraggled roses and wearing nothing but a tipsy grin.

"Meg, baby," he cried, opening his arms wide. Then he saw Michael. The smile faded slowly, and after a few moments, it occurred to him to use the roses in place of a fig leaf.

"I could leave if you like," Michael said, with one eyebrow raised.

"If you do, I'll kill you," I told him. "Scotty, what on earth are you—never mind, stupid question. Those are from Mother's rose bushes, aren't they?"

"Yes," he said, the smile returning.

"She'll be very upset when she finds out they've been cut," I said. "She was saving them for her wedding."

"Oh." His face fell again, and he clutched the roses nervously, as if he expected me to demand that he hand them over.

"You'd better apologize to her."

"Okay."

"Tomorrow," Michael put in.

"Right," Scotty said.

"I think you should leave now," I said. Scotty slouched out. Michael watched carefully until the screen door slammed downstairs, then shook his head. "Hope those roses don't have thorns," he remarked. I giggled at that.

"It would serve him right if they do. That's the material, those bolts he was standing on. I hope the mud washes out." Michael hoisted the bolts and turned to leave. "Hang on a second and I'll get the doors for you," I told him. "I want to have a vase full of water handy just in case."

"In case he brings back the roses?"

"God, no! I'd throw them back in his . . . face. In case he starts singing under my window."

"Does he do that often?" Michael asked, peering over the bolts at me.

"He's never done it to me before. But it's what he usually does when someone he's interested in tells him to get lost. He fixated on Eileen when we were in high school, and it became a regular nightly routine for a while. Her father tried to set the dogs on him, but all dogs like Scotty."

"No doubt he makes them feel superior."

"There, you see?" From down in the backyard, we could hear Scotty launching into an off-key version of "Hey, Baby."

"Scotty!" I yelled out the window, waving the vase. "If you don't shut up this minute I'll throw this!"

"Is he dressed?" Michael asked, peering over my shoulder.

"Unfortunately not. Scotty! I mean it!"

Scotty continued to bray, so I threw the contents of the vase at him.

"Good shot," Michael observed. "But it doesn't seem to be working. Try this," he said, fishing a small plastic squeeze bottle out of his shirt pocket and handing it to me. I aimed it at Scotty and was pleased to see that when the contents of the bottle hit him, he stopped in midverse, looked up at me reproachfully for a few moments, then sighed and stumbled off.

"Ick, what was that?" I asked, wrinkling my nose at the rank smell rising from the bottle.

"I have no idea," Michael said. "Some esoteric brew Mrs. Tranh concocts for Mom. It's supposed to repel dogs. The idea is to squirt it at any larger dogs who fight back when Spike picks on them."

"Well, it did the trick," I said, handing back the bottle. "At least for now. Oh, please let this be a temporary aberration! First Steven's Neanderthal brother and now this. I just can't deal with Scotty on top of everything else. If one more oaf comes near me . . ." I said, shaking my head and leading the way to the stairs.

"Define oaf," Michael said, moving away slightly.

"The way I feel at the moment . . . any member of the male sex."

"No exceptions?" he asked, plaintively.

"Dad. He's totally bonkers, but he's not an oaf."

"Agreed," Michael said.

"Rob . . . I think."

"You think? Your own brother and you're not sure?"

"His taste in women is highly questionable," I said.

"No argument there. Anyone else?"

"Michael, if you're fishing for compliments, I'll grant you pro-visional exemption from oafhood on the grounds that you helped rescue me from Scotty, and have refrained from asking what I could possibly have done to encourage him to leap out of the closet at me like that."

"Like you said before, somehow I don't think Scotty needs much encouragement."

"The wrong men never do."

"What about the right ones?"

"I'll let you know if I ever meet one," I said.

"Speaking of which, have you ever considered—" Michael began, and then was drowned out by a frightful commotion in the yard. Scotty, still unclad, suddenly burst through the azalea patch and streaked across our yard, closely pursued by all three of the Labradors from next door.

"That's odd," I said, "the Labs usually like Scotty." Spike popped out of the azalea patch, barking fiercely, and disappeared in the direction Scotty and the Labs had taken.

"Oh, God," Michael said. "It must be Mom's dog repellent. Though why a dog repellent should make dogs chase him I have no idea. I suppose I should go see if he needs help." I wasn't sure whether he meant Scotty or Spike, but I didn't feel much like help-ing either of them, so after watching Michael lope off in the gen-eral direction of the furor, I went to bed. After making a note in my indispensable notebook to borrow the so-called dog repellent from Michael before the next time Barry showed up.

Tired as I was, I had a hard time tuning out the barking noises, steadily increasing in volume and variety, that seemed to come first from one end of the neighborhood and then the other.

HAVING GONE TO BED BEFORE MIDNIGHT, I WAS UP BY EIGHT AND feeling virtuous about it. I joined Mother for breakfast on the porch, and felt suitably rewarded when Dad dropped by with fresh blueberries and Michael with fresh bagels.

"We certainly had a lively time around here last night," Mother remarked over her second cup of tea. Michael and I both started. I had thought Mother safely out of the way during Scotty's unconventional visit, the ensuing mad dash around the neighborhood, and the countywide canine convocation that had reportedly dragged the sheriff and the normally underworked dogcatcher out of their beds at 3:00 A.M. Michael had a suspiciously innocent look on his face.

"Could you hear the party all the way down at Pam's?" I asked.

"Oh, no, dear," Mother said. "But I think some of Samantha's friends must have gotten just a little too exuberant."

"Most of them were totally sloshed, if that's what you mean," I said. "But that's nothing new."

"Yes, but it really is too bad about the side yard," Mother said.

"What about the side yard?" I said. Had Scotty and the pack returned to our yard after I dropped off?

"So very thoughtless," she continued. "And not at all what one would expect from well-brought-up young people."

"What, Mother?" I asked, beginning to suspect it would be easier to get an answer from the side yard.

"Someone has torn up some of your father's nice flowers. You know, dear," she said, turning to Dad, "those nice purple spiky ones."

"Purple spiky flowers?" Dad and I said in unison, looking at each other with dawning horror.

"Oh, no!" I gasped, and Dad exclaimed "Oh, my God!" as we simultaneously jumped up and ran out to the side yard. Mother and Michael followed, more slowly.

"I'm sorry, dear," Mother said, looking puzzled. "I had no idea you'd be *that* upset about it."

"They were fine when I watered them yesterday afternoon," Dad said.

"A lot of the damage is trampling," I said, as Dad and I crouched over the flower bed.

"Yes, but I don't think all the plants are here," Dad said. "I think some of them are missing. What do you think?"

"I think a lot of them are missing," I said. "Whoever did this did a lot of trampling to cover it up—or maybe someone else came along and trampled it afterwards—but there are definitely a lot of plants missing, too."

"Does it really make that much of a difference whether the vandals dragged them off or not?" Michael asked. "They look pretty well ruined to me; you couldn't replant them or anything in that condition, could you? And are they really that valuable?"

"It's not that they're valuable," Dad said. "They're poisonous."

"Why does that not surprise me, in your garden?" Michael said, with a sigh. "What are they, anyway?"

"Foxglove," I said. "Which means that if it wasn't just vandalism—"

"Which I don't believe for a minute," Dad fumed, shaking a fist full of limp foxglove stalks.

"Then someone—"

"Someone who's up to no good—" Dad put in.

"Has just laid in a large enough supply of digitalis to knock off an elephant."

"Several elephants," Dad added. "This is very serious."

"Digitalis!" Michael exclaimed.

"Is it dangerous, dear?" Mother asked.

"Meg and her friends might very well have died if that salsa had contained digitalis," Dad said.

"It felt as if we were going to anyway," I said.

"I do hate to criticize, dear," Mother began. "But we wouldn't have this little problem if you wouldn't insist on growing all these dangerous plants." She looked over her shoulder with a faint shudder, as if half expecting to find a giant Venus flytrap sneaking up on her.

"I'd better call the sheriff," Dad said, trotting off with Mother trailing behind him, gracefully wringing her hands.

"You know," Michael said, as we watched them leave, "your mother's right. Your dad's garden is rather a dangerous thing to have around."

"Nonsense," I said, automatically parroting the Langslow party line. "I'm sure more people die in car accidents every year than from eating poisonous plants." But I must admit that I said it with less conviction than usual. Somewhere, probably very nearby, someone could be concocting a deadly potion out of Dad's plants. I had no idea how one would actually do this, but that didn't ward off the vivid visions of a determined poisoner bent over a black kettle on his—or her—stove, distilling digitalis from Dad's beautiful little purple flowers. Probably highly inaccurate, but I couldn't shake the picture.

"Let's go and find out what you would do with foxglove to make it into a poison," I said, starting for the door.

"You're not serious."

"Deadly serious. The more we know about how the poison is made, the better we can watch for signs that anyone we know is up to no good."

Dad gave us a highly technical lesson on the chemistry of digitalis. He was partial to the idea of our plant thief distilling the foxglove leaves to extract the poison, but it sounded to me as if almost any way you could get the plant into someone's system would be highly effective. Michael and I were both in a depressed state when we headed off to the day's tasks—the shop for him, and for me, frog-marching wedding participants into the shop to be fitted. Samantha and her friends spent their day racketing up and down the river on speedboats, so I spent most of mine dashing up and down the river in Dad's not very speedy boat, capturing recalcitrant ushers and bridesmaids and ferrying them back to shore and hauling their wet, bedraggled, beer-bloated carcasses into Be-Stitched.

"No offense," Michael said, toward the end of the day, "But your brother has highly questionable taste in friends."

"On the contrary. Rob has excellent taste in friends. These are Samantha's friends."

"That would account for it," Michael said.

"I have to keep telling myself that it would do no good to throttle them; we'd only have to detain and outfit a new set."

"Let's hope our foxglove bandit isn't targeting them too. I'm not sure I could take another day like this."

Samantha was having another party that night. I passed. I stayed home. I did my laundry, balanced my checkbook, and cleaned the bathrooms. I had a lot more fun than I'd had Friday night.

Sunday, July 10

BY THE NEXT DAY, EVERYONE IN THE NEIGHBORHOOD—PROBABLY everyone in the county—knew about the theft of Dad's foxglove plants. Dozens of people called up wanting to know what foxglove looked like. Five of the more notable local hypochondriacs dropped by to be examined for symptoms of digitalis poisoning. The leading local miser, an elderly uncle of Mother's who had a heart problem, dropped by to insist that Dad give him instructions for making his own digitalis, so he could "cut out the middleman and stop lining the pockets of the big drug companies." He went off mad because Dad tried to talk him out of it, and it was weeks before we were really convinced he wasn't going to experiment on himself. I don't know if our family was typical—I suspect that for once it was—but we spent the greater portion of an otherwise lovely Sunday dinner discussing digitalis. The more squeamish souls, like Rob and Jake, ate sparingly.

The whole neighborhood also knew the details of Scotty's misadventure. Apparently the next-door neighbors had seen his unclad form leaving our yard. I had been forced, in self-defense, to reveal the whole story, calling Michael as a witness.

"Sorry to drag you into this," I said, after the seventeenth time he'd been forced to produce the little squeeze bottle for inspection and say that no, he had no idea what was in it, but he'd be sure to ask his mother the next time he called her.

"It gives me great pleasure to defend your honor against this rank calumny," he said, with a sweeping bow.

"Hang my honor. It's my taste and my sanity you're defending. And possibly Scotty's life; if I see him around here anytime soon, I'll probably rip up the remaining foxgloves and shove them down his throat."

"Don't exaggerate, Meg," Mother said.

"I'm sure you wouldn't do that," Barry chirped up.

I looked around the porch at the assembled family and friends. They were all smiling and nodding as if they thought Scotty's behavior were the most amusing thing in the world. Except for Michael, who looked as exasperated as I felt. And Jake, who was cringing back in the shadows at the edge of the porch as if he were afraid I would confuse him with Scotty.

Just then—speak of the devil—Scotty appeared around the corner of the porch.

"Hi," he said cheerfully, waving at me. I could hear muffled titters from several places on the porch. Scotty had the good grace to look embarrassed.

"I came to apologize," he said, still looking at me. I crossed my arms and glowered at him.

"That's all right, Scotty," Mother said, graciously. "Just be more careful in future."

Careful? I gave her an exasperated look. So, I noticed, did Samantha. Obviously Scotty's fitness for usherhood was seriously in question.

"I saw the oddest thing last night," Scotty went on. He glanced at Dad, who had his nose buried in the Merck manual, and then back at me.

"Really? You too?" I said, coldly. More titters from somewhere on the porch.

"Saw? Or hallucinated?" Samantha said, even more coldly. Scotty looked startled.

"No, saw," he said. "I wanted to tell you, Meg."

"Some other time," I said, losing patience. I went back to the kitchen and took my irritation out on some greasy pots and pans. Michael followed shortly afterward.

"Need some help?" he asked. I handed him a soap pad and a particularly awful pot. He tackled it energetically.

"Aren't you curious what the odd thing was?" Michael asked.

"Not particularly, but tell me anyway."

"He didn't say," Michael replied. "He left after you did."

"Probably nothing important."

"And you're not the least bit curious?"

I sighed.

"I suppose I ought to go find out what it is," I said. "After all, I suppose it is possible that he saw the foxglove bandit and wasn't too drunk to remember who it was."

But by the time I got back outside, Scotty was long gone. I'd tackle him later.

Eileen and Steven arrived late that night from their last craft fair before the wedding. They called up to invite me to go to dinner with them the next day. I agreed to meet them at Eileen's house at five o'clock the next evening. I had plans for them.

Monday, July 11

MOTHER, PAM, AND I SPENT THE MORNING HELPING DAD PICK OUT a new gray suit for Rob's wedding. He'd ruined his last gray suit a few weeks ago, shinnying up a pine tree to look at a buzzard's nest. We planned to hide this one until the day of the wedding. Then I spent the afternoon ferrying back another enormous pile of inspected wedding presents from the sheriff's office and inventorying them.

Steven and Eileen were a little surprised when I showed up at Professor Donleavy's house at five sharp, bearing a bag of sandwiches and a large stack of their notecards.

"I thought we were going to take you out to dinner," Steven said.

"Our treat," Eileen added.

"I thought of something that will be an even bigger treat for me," I said. "You're going to write thank-you notes for your presents."

They turned a little pale, but once they realized I had already gotten a list of donors and gifts all organized for them—or perhaps once they realized there was no escaping—they gave in and cheerfully sat around writing notes.

I stood over them, doling out the index cards on which I'd written the name and address of each donor and what they'd given, then taking back the finished notes, proofing them, addressing them, and sealing them.

It was slow work, much like forcing restless children to do homework.

"What's an ee-perg-nay?" Steven would ask.

"A what?"

"E-p-e-r-g-n-e," Steven said.

"Oh, epergne," I said, correcting his pronunciation. "Eileen's aunt Louise sent it."

"Yes, I see, but what is it?"

"What do you care?" I said. "Just thank her for it."

"How can I thank her if I don't know what it is?"

"It's that giant silver compartmented bowl on a pedestal."

"Oh, that thing," he said, frowning. "What on earth will we ever do with it?"

"You serve fruit or desserts in it."

"You've got to be kidding," he said.

"Then stuff it in the attic, unless you want to trip over it the rest of your lives," I said. "Just tell her you'll think of her whenever you use it."

"Well, that's honest," he said.

"Do you think there's a market for these if I did them in clay?" Eileen said, holding up a set of silver placecard holders."

"An exceedingly small one," I said. "Who cares? Just write."

"Another silver tray?" Steven said. "How many does this make."

"You have twelve in all," I said. "Don't worry, you can return them."

We finished up around midnight, and I turned down their offer to see me home. They looked as if they'd rather be alone, anyway. I was cutting through their yard to the street when I saw a familiar figure.

Jake. Carrying a box that looked suspiciously like the one I'd found in Mrs. Grover's room. The box that he probably did not suspect now contained Mother's great-aunt Sophy rather than his late wife.

How odd. Jake was taking the path to the beach.

I lurked in the bushes until he'd passed. Then I put down the box of thank-you notes and quietly followed him. It wasn't hard; I had been using that path since I was a small child and knew every stone. I could follow it very silently. Jake was trying to sneak, but having a hard time. Every few steps he'd trip over a root or stone and swear quietly.

He finally made his way down to the beach, although I could tell he was going to have some bruises in the morning. I did some more lurking in the shrubbery a little way up the path. He went out to the end of the Donleavys' dock. He peered up and down the shore. Then, evidently thinking no one was watching, he opened the box and flung the ashes out. Without any particular ceremony, as far as I could see. I felt a pang of guilt. Great-Aunt Sophy deserved better.

Jake then ripped the cardboard box into a dozen or so pieces and flung those into the river. He watched for a few minutes— waiting for the pieces to sink, no doubt—then turned and headed back for shore.

I scampered back up the path. By the time Jake arrived at the street, I was back to skulking in the roadside bushes. I watched as he nonchalantly strolled down the street that led to his house.

I couldn't wait to tell Dad about this, although I knew it would have to wait till morning. Dad went to bed early, and it was already twelve-thirty. Closer to one by the time I found where I'd left the thank-you notes.

As I was approaching Samantha's house, I noticed a car waiting at the end of their driveway. Skulking was getting to be habit-forming; I slipped into the bushes and watched. After a few minutes, I saw a figure slipping out of the car. Samantha. She shut the door, being careful not to slam it, and tiptoed down the driveway. The car started up and drove off. Perhaps the driver simply forgot, but I noticed that the headlights stayed off until it was well out of sight.

Curiouser and curiouser, as Lewis Carroll would say. I could sympathize if Rob and Samantha had decided to sneak away from the neighborhood to get some privacy. The cloak-and-dagger antics were a bit over the top, but perhaps Rob was growing into the family penchant for theatrics. But I really didn't think that had been Rob's car. It was smaller than Rob's battered gray Honda, and ran a lot more quietly. It wasn't Samantha's red MG either, that much I could tell. And it had headed away from our house, not toward it. Anyway, Rob was supposed to have gone with a friend to the bar exam review course.

I extracted myself with difficulty from the Brewsters' holly bushes and continued on home, very thoughtful. When I reached our driveway, I confirmed that Rob's car was still there. Odd. What was Samantha up to?

Just as I was entering the front door, I heard a car again. Another car, older and noisier than the one that had dropped Samantha off. It paused at the end of our driveway, a door slammed, and then it drove off.

I heard careful footsteps coming up the driveway. I waited inside the front door until I heard the footsteps just outside, then I turned on the porch light and flung open the door. There was Rob, blinking against the sudden glare, with a pile of books and papers under his arm. Law books. How odd; why would he feel the need to sneak in after a bar exam review session?

"Hi, Meg," he said, with studied casualness. And then he jumped as the kitten climbed his trouser leg. The pile slipped, papers flew everywhere, and a small box fell to the floor, where it popped open, spilling out a clutter of lead figures and brightly colored four-, six-, ten-, and twenty-sided dice.

"Role-playing games?" I asked. He winced. "I thought you were studying for the bar exam. What are you doing playing games?"

"But I'm not playing," he protested. "A classmate and I have invented a game. We're calling it Kill All the Lawyers. Or possibly Lawyers from Hell. I thought of it during finals, and we've been working on it all summer. We're running a test session now. Everyone loves it, and we think we can market it to one of the big game companies."

"Rob," I began. And then gave up. If he wasn't worried about what Samantha would do if she caught him inventing games instead of studying for the bar, I certainly wasn't worried. Maybe it would be the best thing.

But if Rob was sneaking out to play Lawyers from Hell, where had Samantha been? And with whom? And why had Jake suddenly decided to scatter his wife's ashes?

I would have to have a talk with Dad tomorrow.

Tuesday, July 12

"HAVE YOU DECIDED WHAT YOU'RE GOING TO WEAR FOR ROB AND Samantha's wedding?" I asked Mother over breakfast. Besides getting out another large batch of Mother's last-minute additional invitations, my day's to-do list included taking her in to Be-Stitched to let Michael and Mrs. Tranh talk her into something if she hadn't yet made a decision. Otherwise Michael's ladies would still be sewing when Rob and Samantha's grandchildren got married.

"Not exactly, dear," Mother said. "I was thinking of that suit with the lace-trimmed jacket."

"Mother. It's white. You can't wear white to a wedding unless you're the bride."

"Yes, dear, I know. I wasn't thinking of doing that." The hell she wasn't. "But I was thinking I could dye it a nice pastel. Or perhaps Michael's ladies could make something just like it in a pastel."

"Excellent idea. You've always looked great in that suit, and it's so unusual that there's no way Mrs. Brewster will have anything even similar. Pink would look great."

"Ye-es. In a nice raw silk, I think."

"Let's go down to Be-Stitched and talk to them this morning."

"After lunch, dear. Mrs. Fenniman and I are going to visit your aunt Phoebe this morning. Would you like to come?"

"Love to, but I still have some invitations to do," I lied. The last time we'd visited Aunt Phoebe, I'd gotten ill listening to her descriptions of operations—hers and other people's. Or possibly from drinking her truly vile homemade dandelion wine.

After seeing Mother and Mrs. Fenniman off I took my stack of notepaper and Mother's instructions and settled down under my favorite shade tree on the lawn. When I heard the riding lawn mower start up, I ran over to talk to Dad, but for once he'd let someone else use his favorite toy. Scotty Ballister was merrily cruising up and down the front lawn on the mower. I returned to my lawn chair, keeping a weather eye open for Dad so I could tell him about all the night's adventures.

I had paused over a note to a cousin who lived in Santa Monica. I was lost in a reverie of a trip to California several years ago, when I'd spent hours on the beach watching the surf with no responsibilities hanging over my head. I was relaxed, at peace—all right, I was nearly asleep—when Michael's voice jolted me awake.

"I'll join you if I may," he said, setting up a lawn chair next to mine. "I came to drop off some fabric samples for your mother, but she's not here."

"She'll be back for lunch," I said, jerking upright. "I don't suppose you'd be interested in addressing a few envelopes while you're here?"

"Sure," he said, obligingly taking a stack and a pen. "I thought the invitations were all out by now."

"Mother thought of a few more intimate friends and immediate family members."

"The more the merrier."

"That's easy for you to say," I shouted over the lawn mower as Scotty came round the corner on the lawn mower. "They're not your family."

Michael said something in reply, but I couldn't hear him for the lawn mower.

"Sorry, I missed that," I said, when Scotty was far enough off. "It figures."

"What figures?" I asked. Scotty cruised by, slightly closer.

"I thought your dad never let anyone else ride the mower," Michael shouted.

"He usually doesn't," I shouted back. "Especially not Scotty."

We gave up on conversation and worked away quietly—except for the buzz of the lawn mower, but by this time I had gotten so used to it that it seemed just another pleasant part of a sunny summer afternoon. Scotty was working his way steadily toward us, driving a more or less straight line back and forth, rattling quickly down the slope to the bushes at the edge of the bluff and then grinding slowly uphill again to the pine trees at the other side of the yard. As he got closer, he would slow down each time he drove past us to wave or wink.

"At least he's dressed today," Michael remarked. "I only hope he's reasonably sober."

"Dad wouldn't have let him on the mower if he weren't. I'm more worried about whether he'll be sober for the wedding. Or so hung over from the party the night before that he can't walk down the aisle straight."

"That's right; he's in one of the weddings, isn't he?" Michael asked.

"Samantha's. Usher," I said. "His father's a partner in Mr. Brewster's firm."

"Must be an important partner," Michael remarked. "I can't imagine why else Samantha would put up with him."

"He's rumored to be reasonably presentable when properly clothed," I said. Michael chuckled.

"I suppose we should move and let him get this part of the lawn," I said finally, beginning to gather up my envelopes and lists, while keeping an eye on Scotty, who had once more narrowly avoided hitting the trees when he turned at the top of the yard and was heading downhill toward us again.

"Give it one more pass," Michael said, putting down his stack and stretching luxuriously. I did the same.

"I have an idea," Michael said. "Let's go—"

But just then he saw my look of surprise and turned to see Scotty careen past us at full speed, waving his arms and legs wildly, and then crash through the bushes to drive straight off the bluff.

"What the hell—" Michael began. We heard the lawn mower, still running, ripping through the underbrush on the way down, and then a wet, gurgling noise as the motor choked and died.

"I'll go down and see if he's all right," Michael said, running in the direction of the ladder in the neighbors' yard. "You go dial 911."

"Dialing 911 is getting to be a habit around here," I muttered as I raced to the house.

Scotty was not all right at all. I could tell that much from the top of the bluff. His unwilling dive had ended on a large rock at the foot of the bluff.

"You don't want to go down there," Michael said, appearing at the top of the ladder looking very shaken. "You don't want anyone going down there. I think we should post a guard at each end of the beach to keep people away. And for what it's worth, I'm sorry I ever doubted your dad; he's right, there's no way Mrs. Grover fell over that cliff."

I called some neighbors to arrange guard details, and then we waited. The rescue squad showed up too late to help poor Scotty. They were followed shortly by the sheriff and Dad. The sheriff and Dad seemed to find our description of Scotty's last wild ride highly interesting.

"Waving both arms and both legs, you say?" the sheriff asked. For about the thirteenth time.

"That's right," I said. Michael nodded.

"You're sure," the sheriff persisted.

"Absolutely," I said.

"That's certainly what it looked like," Michael said.

"Then I think we'd better have a look at that lawn mower when they fish it up," The sheriff said. "Those things have a dead-man switch on 'em. No way it could just keep going without his foot on the pedal . . ."

"Unless it was tampered with," Dad finished. They both looked grim and headed off in the direction of the bluff.

Needless to say, we did not make it in to Be-Stitched that afternoon. The lawn mower was examined, and the sheriff hauled it away to be examined some more.

"And just think, we still have the foxglove to look forward to," Michael said that evening.

Wednesday, July 13

NOTHING IMPROVES SOMEONE'S CHARACTER IN THE PUBLIC MIND like dying suddenly and young. The same people who last week criticized Scotty's family for not kicking him out to earn his own living were now remarking what a waste it was and what potential Scotty had. Potential for what they didn't say.

We were treated to another up-close-and-personal look at our local law enforcement officials in action. I was not impressed. If I were still a registered voter in York County, I'd be looking for a new candidate for sheriff come the next election. I'd even vote for

Mrs. Fenniman, the only opposition candidate who'd come forward so far.

The state police were a lot more impressive, but either the law or the unwritten code of the old boys network seemed to keep them from getting too involved without the sheriff's consent. And the sheriff definitely wanted to squelch any talk of murder.

"First Mrs. Grover and now Scotty," Mother said, "and that nice Mr. Price, too."

"Mr. Price wasn't killed, Mother," I said.

"It was a near thing. What if there's a murderer among us?"

"I grant you, we've had a run of unfortunate accidents this summer," the sheriff said, cautiously. "But it's a long stretch from there to murder."

"You know, I really do think it most odd of Mrs. Waterston to just go off like that. So suddenly, and right at the beginning of the wedding season," Mother said.

"Mother! She didn't just go off, she broke her leg while visiting her sister and she's staying there till she recuperates," I explained to the sheriff.

"But it was very odd of her to just go off to visit her sister at the last minute and abandon her clients."

"She didn't go off at the last minute; she went off in May."

"Well, that was the last minute for all the June weddings, dear."

"Yes, but anyone with any sense picked out her dress months ago. And she didn't just abandon you. She left Michael to take care of things."

"Yes, he does seem to have taken hold and settled right in."

For a paranoid moment I wondered if Mother was evolving a theory that Michael was the murderer. Perhaps she was about to suggest that Michael's mother was not down in Florida with a broken leg, but dead somewhere. That he planned to worm his way into our confidence, then announce that his dear mother had died of complications, and take over her business. Perhaps he wasn't even her son. And Mrs. Grover and Scotty had been killed and Mr. Price nearly killed because they somehow discovered his secret. For a few moments, I found myself seriously considering Michael as a cold-blooded killer. And rejecting the idea outright.

"Mother," I said, "what on earth are you suggesting?"

"I think," she said, leaning closer to the sheriff and me, "that Mrs. Waterston may have had a Premonition."

"A premonition," the sheriff repeated.

"A Premonition of Danger," Mother elaborated.

"Ah," the sheriff said, nodding sagely. I have often wondered if he ever realizes how much being Mother's cousin has contributed to his success as an elected official. After five decades of dealing with Mother, he can listen with a perfectly straight face to almost any inanity uttered by a constituent.

"I don't want to worry your mother," he said to me as I showed him out. "We can't be one hundred percent sure, but there is something real strange about Scotty's death. You keep an eye on your folks, you hear?"

Did the man think I was an idiot? I intended to keep a very close eye on my parents, particularly Dad. Scotty had been killed riding a lawn mower that everyone in the neighborhood knew Dad almost never let anyone else use. Scotty had died, but I would bet anything Dad was the intended victim.

And I remembered the night Scotty had dropped by to apologize to me. He'd said something about seeing something odd. And I'd cut him off. I mentally kicked myself. Scotty had probably seen something that would have solved Mrs. Grover's murder and the other strange incidents. And had been mistakenly killed instead of Dad before he could reveal it.

Then again, what if the murderer had heard Scotty say that and deliberately killed him? Even if the odd thing Scotty saw had noth-

ing to do with the murder, what if the killer's guilty mind jumped
to that conclusion? In which case the killer might have been aiming at Scotty after all, and not Dad.

I thought of mentioning it to Dad, but decided not to. Whatever Scotty had seen, it was gone for good now. Reminding Dad
that we'd had a chance to hear it and failed would only frustrate
him further.

And of course, there was the depressing task of recruiting a
suitable usher to replace Scotty. After much discussion of the can-
didates, Samantha dragged in Rob to rubberstamp her choice:
someone named Ian who, although apparently not a close personal
friend of either of the principals, was tall, dark, and handsome
enough to please the bridesmaids and well connected enough to
suit Samantha and her mother.

Thursday, July 14

THE NEXT CASUALTY——NOT, FORTUNATELY, A FATALITY——WAS
from Eileen's wedding party.

"Oh, Meg, my nephew Brian has the measles!" she wailed.

"Well, so much for a ring bearer," I said.

"Oh, Meg, we have to have a ring bearer," Eileen said. "The
costume is so darling, and I don't want poor Caitlin to have to
walk down the aisle alone." Caitlin, I suspected, would rather prefer to have the limelight all to herself, but I doubted Eileen would
see this.

"Don't you have any other little boy cousins?" I asked.

"There's little Petey, but he's only two."

"No way. What about Eric? I think he'll fit the costume."

"Oh, that would be perfect, Meg!" Eileen enthused, and hung
up reassured.

Now all I had to do was talk Eric into it. I ended up having to promise to take him and several of his friends to ride the roller coasters at the nearest amusement park as a bribe. Dad was so touched by this show of auntly devotion that he offered to foot the bill. No one else volunteered a damned thing.

"By the way, Dad," I said, "one more thing."

"I have to run, Meg," he said. "I have to talk to the medical examiner."

"Fine. I'll tell you later about Jake scattering Great-Aunt Sophy in the river, and Samantha sneaking out of her house late at night with someone other than Rob, and what Rob's been doing instead of studying for the bar exam."

That got his attention. His listened intently as I gave him a dramatic account of everything I'd witnessed while skulking about the neighborhood.

"How odd," he muttered, when I was finished.

"My words exactly."

"This doesn't add up at all," he said. He wandered off, looking very puzzled.

"Well, don't bother telling me anything," I said to his departing back. "It's not as if I've contributed anything to this investigation."

He didn't seem to hear me. The hell with it. Let Dad detect; I had to go over to the Donleavys' to keep Steven and Eileen from getting up to anything. Like changing the theme of the wedding at the last minute.

Like everyone else in town, I kept looking over my shoulder, watching for sinister figures lurking in the shadows. And seeing them; although so far all the reports of prowlers had turned out to be plainclothes state police scouting the neighborhood.

Friday, July 15

MICHAEL AND THE LADIES MANAGED TO GET ERIC'S OUTFIT READY for Friday evening's wedding rehearsal. We'd decided to hold it in partial costume, so everyone could get used to some of the unusual gear they'd be wearing. The bridesmaids adapted easily to the trains, but it took a while for the men to learn to walk without tripping over the swords.

"What do you think?" Michael asked, as we surveyed the bridal party.

"I think most of these men ought to have known better than to agree to wear tights. And arming them was another mistake," I added watching two of the ushers draw their supposedly ornamental swords and strike what I'm sure they thought were dashing fencing poses.

"Let's go and straighten them out," Michael said. "The same thing happens whenever we do a period play with weapons. Everyone starts thinking he's Zorro."

"Oh, give it a few minutes," I said, as one overzealous usher narrowly missed skewering the beastly Barry in a particularly painful place. "Maybe his aim will improve."

I glanced at Michael, who was leaning elegantly against a tree trunk and watching the ushers' antics with lofty amusement. I sternly suppressed the distracting mental picture of how much better he would look in tights than any of the ushers.

Or, for that matter, in the elaborate Renaissance priest's costume he'd modeled for us in the shop. Like Michael, Father Pete was inspired by the costume to do a little swashing and buckling. Unfortunately, aside from his height, he bore no resemblance at all to Michael. He was only a little on the pudgy side, but his round, fair, freckled face, and thinning sandy hair looking distinctly incongruous atop the elegant sophistication of his costume. Ah, well.

The rehearsal went about as well as could be expected, which meant it fell slightly short of being an unmitigated disaster.

"A bad dress rehearsal makes a good performance," Michael remarked to anyone who fretted.

"It damn well better," I muttered through gritted teeth. Having Barry hovering over me was not helping my mood. Or having to listen to Eric gloating over the payment he was getting for his bit part as ring bearer.

"Aunt Meg is taking me and all my friends to ride the roller coaster!" Eric informed Barry. Not for the first time.

"Not all of your friends," I said. "One. And only if you behave yourself during the wedding and the reception."

"Right!" Eric said, and trotted off, no doubt to be sure I couldn't actually catch him doing anything that constituted not behaving.

"I think that's great," Barry said, and then in an apparent non sequitur, added, "I want a large family myself."

"How nice for you," I said. "Personally, I prefer being an aunt. You can take your nieces and nephews out and have fun with them and then dump them back on their parents when they're tired and hungry and cranky."

Barry blinked a couple of times and then wandered off.

"You don't really feel that way about kids," Michael said, over my shoulder.

"No, as a general rule, I like children," I said. "But I'm sure I could make an exception for any offspring of Barry's."

We ran through the proceedings a second time with slightly better results. I decided to leave well enough alone.

"Okay, everyone, you can leave now," I said. "But be back here at eleven tomorrow. No exceptions."

"You'd make a great stage manager," Michael remarked.

"Or a drill sergeant," I replied. "I think everything we can control is under control."

"As long as we don't have a thunderstorm we'll be okay," Eileen's father said, frowning at the sky.

As if in answer, the sky rumbled.

"Uh-oh," Michael said.

"Red sky at morning, sailors take warning," Mrs. Fenniman chanted. "Red sky at night, sailor's delight."

"Was there a red sky tonight?" Michael asked.

"Who had time to look?" I said.

"Meg, we're not going to have a thunderstorm, are we?" Eileen asked. As if there were something I could do about it if we were.

"Not according to the weatherman," I said. "Not according to all three of the local weathermen."

"Weatherpeople, Meg," Mother corrected. "Channel Thirteen has a weather lady."

"Whatever," I said. "All the weatherpeople say sunny skies tomorrow, thank goodness."

"But what if they're wrong this time?" Eileen wailed. "It would absolutely spoil *everything* if we had a thunderstorm!" Then why did you dimwits shoot down every backup plan I suggested, I said to myself, and then immediately felt guilty.

"Don't worry," I said. "They'd be able to tell us if it were going to rain cats and dogs all day. If it's only scattered thundershowers, all it can do is delay us slightly. And that's no problem. I mean, nobody's going to kick us out of your yard if we run late. Your cousin the priest isn't going anywhere. The guests are there for the duration. It'll be fine."

"Oh, I just know it's going to rain," she moaned. And repeated, several times, while the rest of us were exchanging farewells. In fact, as I walked down the driveway with Dad and Michael, the last thing I heard was Eileen, plaintively wailing, "Oh, I just know the rain's going to spoil everything." Followed by my mother, in her most encouraging maternal tones, saying, "Don't worry, dear; if it does, Meg will think of something."

"Please, let it be nice and sunny tomorrow," I muttered.

Saturday, July 16. Eileen's wedding day.

ONE SHOULD BE CAREFUL WHAT ONE WISHES FOR, AS MOTHER AL-ways says. Eileen's wedding day did, indeed, dawn nice and sunny. Nice was over by nine o'clock, when the temperature hit 90 degrees and continued climbing. But it certainly was still sunny. By two o'clock, when the ceremony was supposed to begin, it would be absolutely hellish.

"Oh, for a thunderstorm." I sighed, fighting the temptation to look at the thermometer again. What difference did it make if the temperature had broken into triple digits or was still hovering at 99? It's not the heat, it's the humidity, and we had more than enough of that.

"I'm afraid the air-conditioning's busted," Mr. Donleavy apologized. For about the fifty-seventh time. As if I thought his air conditioner normally shrieked like a banshee while emitting a tiny thread of air not appreciably cooler than the air outside. "And with Price still in the hospital . . ."

"It's okay," I said, as graciously as I could manage. "Not your fault."

One good thing about the heat, it tended to keep the members of the wedding party under control. Virtually comatose, in fact. No clowning about with the swords today. The men lounged around in the kitchen with their doublets off, or at least unbuttoned, waiting for the first guests to show. And resentfully swilling quarts of iced tea. Eileen's elderly aunt had caught two of them with beer cans earlier and was now sitting in a corner, sternly enforcing sobriety. I wondered if so much iced tea was a good idea. If all these tights-clad men waited to hit the bathroom at the last possible moment before the wedding started, they'd find out why women's trips to the john take so much longer. I thought of warning them, but it was too hot to bother. Let them learn the hard way.

Two of Be-Stitched's seamstresses were perched in another corner, waiting to make repairs or adjustments as needed. Michael had another two stationed upstairs to help stuff the women into our velvet when the time came. All four beamed and nodded whenever they caught sight of me. Nice to know I was such a hit with Michael's ladies.

Inside the house, the cloying smell of the patchouli incense Eileen was burning for luck warred for dominance with the smell of damp, sweaty humans. If you walked outside, the reek of citronella smoke hit you like a wall, from the dozens of mosquito repellent candles Dad was lighting throughout the yard.

"Everything under control?" Michael asked when I ran into him at the iced tea pitcher.

"So far," I said. "Just so I can say I told you so to someone, I hereby predict Eileen's last attack of prenuptial jitters will occur between one-forty and one-forty-five."

"How can you be sure it will be the last attack?" Michael asked.

"After about two-thirty, they'll be postnuptial jitters, which makes them Steven's problem, not mine."

"Good point," he replied. "Any predictions on how many heatstroke cases we'll have?"

"I'm trying not to think about it. I'm worried about Professor Donleavy in that velvet tent."

To spare Eileen's father the indignity of tights, we had clad him in a long, voluminous royal blue velvet robe that would have been suitable wear for a wealthy, middle-aged Renaissance man. He took it surprisingly well. He was a professor, after all. Perhaps having to march in academic robes in the graduation ceremonies every year made the costume seem less ridiculous to him than it might to most men. Or perhaps after thirty-four years, he'd given up arguing with Eileen. At any rate, he was pacing up and down in the front hall, his elaborate Renaissance footgear looking very odd with the Bermuda shorts and William and Mary T-shirt he was wearing. He didn't argue for a second when we decided to wait till the last possible minute to put the velvet gown on him.

Father Pete was the only person already in full costume. If vanity was still a deadly sin, he'd have a busy time in his next confession. We'd had trouble prying him out of costume the night before, and today, long before anyone else could even look at their gear, he was completely togged out in the black velvet gown with gold and lace trimming that had looked so spectacular on Michael. He'd spent the last two hours strolling around the house striking poses and checking his appearance surreptitiously in any handy reflective surface. His only concession to the heat was to mop his forehead occasionally with a lace-trimmed handkerchief that he'd probably filched from a bridesmaid.

"Am I doing all right?" he asked me, in passing. "Looking authentic and all?"

"You look fabulous," I lied. Actually, he looked rather like Elmer Fudd in drag, but he was entering into the spirit of the thing so enthusiastically that I didn't have the heart to say anything else.

At one-twenty-five, Eric ran in, with Duck in his wake, to report that the first car was approaching. I sent him out to put Duck in her pen for the afternoon. I shooed the ushers out to earn their keep. There was the anticipated logjam in the bathroom. I waved a signal to the musicians. Gentle harmonies began wafting up from the garden, the sound of the lutes and recorders drowned out occasionally by faint rolls of thunder. I peered out at the first guests in amazement. What on earth had possessed them to show up here thirty-five minutes before the ceremony when they could be riding around with their air-conditioning on, or at least their windows open? Ah, well, it was their funeral. Though not, I hoped, literally.

Inside, the tension level ratcheted up significantly. Although giving Eileen away only required one line, Professor Donleavy was obviously getting stagefright. I could hear him muttering, "I do. I do," with every possible variation in tone and inflection. Father Pete was humming along with the music and improvising a stately dance. I trudged upstairs to check events in the women's dressing rooms.

The bridesmaids donned their gowns and then sat around with their skirts up over their knees, fanning themselves or rubbing ice cubes wrapped in dish towels over any accessible skin. Good thing this crew was heavily into the natural look; makeup would have been running down our faces in sweaty streaks in five minutes.

Mrs. Tranh and the ladies were coaxing us all into the remaining bits of our outfits. Michael, looking annoyingly cool and comfortable in a loose-fitting white shirt and off-white pants, supervised and translated.

"Oh, God, I'm not sure I want to do this," Eileen said, ripping her velvet headpiece off.

"Well, let's not spoil the show," I said, rescuing the headpiece before she could ruin it and catching her hands to keep her from removing her gown. I glanced at a bedside alarm clock: one-forty-five on the dot. "After it's all over, if you decide it's been a mistake, we can get it annulled and send back the presents. Right now we need to get downstairs and into position."

"How can you be so calm about this when I may be making the biggest mistake of my life!"

I wanted to say, "Because it's your life, not mine," but I didn't think it would go over that well. Eileen went on in much the same vein for the rest of the time it took to replace her headpiece and put the finishing touches to her outfit. Mrs. Tranh and the ladies seemed to grasp what was going on, despite the language barrier, and made sympathetic noises while ruthlessly forcing her into the remaining bits of clothing. Always nice to see real professionals in action.

Ten minutes to go. We dragged Eileen, still babbling, downstairs and out the side door to where we had curtained off a makeshift foyer with a moss-green velvet curtain. I peeped out through a small tear in the fabric and saw that the only empty spots on the lawn appeared to be the places where the guests had rearranged the folding chairs to avoid unusually large mud puddles. I tried to tune out the chaos around me, including the seamstress trying to make my damp puffed sleeves look a little less limp. I concentrated on keeping Eileen calm and recognizing our cue. Which wasn't as easy as it usually was in weddings. Nothing ordinary like "Here Comes the Bride" would do for Eileen, of course. She'd chosen a stately pavane to accompany our muddy procession down the makeshift aisle. Unfortunately, she was the only one who knew it well enough to tell when the musicians began playing it. Every time they started a new piece of music, at least one bridesmaid would look panicked and hiss, "Isn't that it?" It all sounded twittery and slightly flat to me, and I was as clueless as the rest of them, but I began calmly asking Eileen the name of each tune. Having to search her memory and come up with a name seemed to bring her temporarily back to sanity. We had been through "Pastime with Good Company," "La Mourisque," "Jouyssance Vous Donneray," and a lute solo of "My Lady Carey's Dompe" when finally she replied.

"Oh, that's Le Bon Vouloir!" She looked panic-stricken. Must be our cue.

"I'll get Eric and Caitlin going." I grabbed Eric with my left hand and Caitlin with my right.

"Slow and steady," I stage-whispered, "just like we rehearsed it."

Caitlin looked excited but not nervous. Good. Eric looked bored and only marginally cooperative.

"Roller coasters," I hissed at him. He assumed a look of pained innocence and exaggerated cooperativeness. I mentally crossed my fingers and gave both kids a gentle shove.

I peeked as they slipped through the curtains and set out down the makeshift aisle. They were more or less in time with the music, and I could hear oohs and aahs and exclamations of "Oh, aren't they precious?" Father Pete appeared behind the altar, beaming with enthusiasm. I turned to check that the first pair of bridesmaids were ready. I was beginning to relax when I heard the first titters. I whirled back to my peephole. At first I couldn't see anything wrong. Eric and Caitlin were doing splendidly. Then I realized that Duck had escaped from her cage somehow, and was waddling sedately down the aisle behind Eric.

"Oh, God," I moaned, turning away from my peephole. Michael took my place.

"At least she's in step with the music," he remarked. I reclaimed my peephole and saw that Eric and Caitlin had reached the altar.

"First pair, on three," I hissed. "One, two, *three.*"

I marshaled the other two bridesmaids out and took my bouquet. Mr. Donleavy was being buttoned into his robe. Eileen looked shell-shocked.

"Send her out in another——" I began.

"I know, I know," Michael said. "I'm a showbiz veteran, remember? Go!"

I stepped out on cue and marched down the aisle, head high, shoulders squared, trying hard to ignore the little trickles of sweat running down my neck, back, and legs.

Eileen looked radiant as she walked down the aisle. At least I hoped it was radiant. It could very easily have been early warning signs of heat stroke. But when I saw the looks on her face and Steven's as she reached the altar, I suddenly felt, at least for the moment, that all was right with the world and everything I'd gone through all summer was infinitely worthwhile. I stood there for a few minutes, beaming sappily as they began taking their vows, until I caught a glimpse of Barry, beaming just as sappily at me. I came down to earth with a thud.

Fortunately, just then something happened to distract me from my sudden, almost irresistible urge to throw something at Barry. Duck, who had been sitting sedately at Eric's feet, suddenly rose and began walking toward the center of the aisle, quacking loudly. When she reached the absolute center of Eileen's train, she sat down and continued to look around and emit an occasional quack. I debated whether to leave her alone or not, and decided I'd better get her off the train before she laid an egg or answered any other calls of nature. In as dignified manner as possible, I tucked my flowers under one arm, walked out, picked Duck up, and returned to my place. There were titters from the audience, and Father Pete was overcome with a fit of coughing. Duck seemed to calm down after that, but I held her bill closed for the rest of the ceremony, just in case.

The minister pronounced Steven and Eileen husband and wife, and we began exiting to the triumphant strains of a royal fanfare. When Barry tried to take my arm, I handed him Duck instead. Duck didn't appear to like it any more than he did.

We marched into the side yard and formed a receiving line. Although they could just as easily have circumnavigated the house, most of the guests played by the rules and ran the gauntlet before going to the backyard for champagne and hors d'oeuvres. Unfortunately, this kept us standing around for rather a long time under the inadequate shade of a flower-trimmed bower. I found myself silently cheering whenever someone sneaked out of the line.

The Renaissance banquet, once we finally got to sit down for it, was much admired, especially the spit-roasted pigs. Eileen did manage to set her veil on fire with one of the votive candles decorating the head table, but Steven put it out immediately with a tankard of mead. Only a few of the die-hards joined in the period dancing, but the tumblers, jugglers, and acrobats were a great hit.

I was increasingly glad that I had talked Eileen and Steven out of some of their more bizarre ideas of Renaissance authenticity. The dancing bear, for instance, would have been a bit too much. Although I wasn't entirely sure that the substitute was much of an improvement—Cousin Horace, risking heat stroke in his moth-eaten gorilla suit, which he'd ineptly altered in the vague hope of making it look bearlike. Ah, well. Horace had fun, anyway. After dinner, the rest of the program was largely the usual agenda, in costume. There was much to be said for the usual agenda. The guests knew it, and could carry on without a lot of instructions. Already guests were beginning to coagulate for the bouquet and garter throwing. Then we would have changing into going away clothes and pelting the departing van with organic birdseed. Followed by the utter collapse of the maid of honor. My responsibilities for the day would be over and I could swill down a couple more glasses of champagne. Maybe a couple of bottles.

Eileen had chosen to throw her bouquet from the Donleavys' front stoop, which was gussied up to look like yet another bower. All the unmarried women were being chivvied into a semicircle at the base of the stoop. I took a safe place at the outskirts, hoping the lucky recipient of the bouquet would be a perfect stranger with no reason even to invite me to her wedding, much less recruit me as a participant.

Eileen teased the crowd with a few fake throws.

"Come on, Meg," someone behind me said, "you'll never catch it like that."

I was turning to explain that catching it was the last thing on my mind, when something struck me violently on the side of the head. I was actually somewhat stunned for a few seconds, and then people began hugging me and clapping me on the back, and I realized that without even trying I had caught the bouquet. In my hair.

In fact, the thing had become inextricably tangled with my hair and the intricate floral headpiece that Mrs. Tranh and the ladies had anchored in place with about a million hairpins. Everyone seemed to find this hilarious except me; I had to hold onto the damned thing tightly to keep my hair from being torn out by the roots. Steven headed up to the stoop to remove the garter from Eileen's leg and fling it to the crowd. I was not about to sit still for having the garter put on my leg with a basketball-sized shrub stuck to my head. I fled inside to untangle myself. They would just have to wait till I was finished; if they got impatient, someone could come and help me, dammit. I found a hand mirror in the hall powder room and went out to the kitchen, where by resting my head on the kitchen table and propping the hand mirror against a vinegar cruet I could free up both hands and still see what I was doing.

What I was doing was going nowhere fast. In fact, I was making it worse, and the last few shreds of my patience evaporated. I heard gales of laughter outside. Steven must be really hamming up the garter bit. I rummaged through the kitchen cabinet drawers—one-handed—until I found a pair of scissors, and was reaching up to hack off the bouquet, hair and all, when I felt someone grab my wrist. I shrieked.

"Now, now," Michael said. "Let's not be hasty. You have two more weddings coming up; you'd regret doing that in the morning."

"Right now I just want to get the damned thing out of my hair," I said, close to tears.

"Sit down and I'll do it," he said, pulling up a chair and easing me into it with one deft motion as he began the tedious business of untangling the bouquet. "However did you manage this?"

"I didn't, Eileen did. I always thought you were supposed to give the bouquet a gentle toss and let fate decide who caught it. Eileen must have hurled the thing at my head with the speed and accuracy of a Cy Young award winner." Just then I saw Eileen and a couple of the bridesmaids flit by on their way upstairs. "Damn, I'm supposed to be helping her change!"

"I'm not sure that's either possible or necessary," Michael said. "Like all the local inhabitants, Eileen is an original; you don't want to tamper with that."

"Very funny," I said—all right, snapped. "Change her clothes, I mean, of course. God only knows what she'll do in the state she's in."

"Don't worry, Mrs. Tranh will take care of it. Though that does mean you're stuck with me to untangle this thing. Are you sure you wouldn't rather just wear this as a trophy till it grows out?"

"Just hack a chunk out," I said, reaching again for the scissors. "I can wear a flower or a bow over the spot in the other two weddings."

"Leave those alone," Michael ordered, slapping my hand away from the scissors. "I was only joking; I've almost got it." Sure enough, in another few minutes my hair and the bouquet parted company.

"I'm sorry," Michael said, as he saw me rubbing the spot. "I was trying not to yank out quite so much hair by the roots."

"Don't feel bad; I think most of the yanking happened when the thing landed. Besides, it's not the hair, it's the thorns on the roses that really hurt. Well, at least there's one consolation."

"What's that?" Michael asked, while rummaging through the debris on the kitchen counters.

"I seem to have missed the damned garter throwing ceremony."

"If it's any consolation, there wasn't one."

"What do you mean, there wasn't one? We have a garter; I know because I had to exchange the red one Steven bought for the pink one Eileen wanted."

"When Steven went to take the garter off Eileen's leg, they realized they'd never put it on her leg. The beastly Barry left it in his trunk, and can't find his car keys. Ah! Champagne?" he said, unearthing a full bottle that had somehow been left in the kitchen and brandishing it triumphantly.

"I give up," I said, holding out my hand for the glass. "After all the trouble we went through picking out the perfect garter, and they give it to that Neanderthal Barry for safekeeping."

I stretched out with my feet up on a second kitchen chair and sipped. However inadequate the air-conditioning was, it was better than outdoors. I was just beginning to feel relaxed when, speaking of the devil, Barry bounded in with all the grace of a half-grown Saint Bernard.

"Look what I've got!" He dangled the garter from his finger and leered in what I suppose he thought was a charming manner.

"It's you, Barry," I said. "Wear it in good health."

"You know what I get to do with it!"

"Get lost, Barry," I said, holding out my glass for more champagne.

"Ah, come on," he said, reaching for my leg. I grabbed the scissors and feinted at his hand with the point. He froze.

"Barry, if you lay one hand on my leg, I will stuff that garter down your throat and then cut it into shreds. I am not in a good mood, and besides, I know damn well that you didn't catch that thing, you just finally found your car keys. Now run along."

Barry did, though not without looking back reproachfully at me a few times. When the screen door slammed behind him, I sighed.

"I'm so glad he's gone, but now I feel as guilty as if I kicked a puppy."

"He'll live," Michael said. "I think."

"Why do I always end up using weapons on Barry?" I wondered.

"Seems perfectly sensible to me."

"Oh, God, I am so tired of Eileen and Steven throwing Barry at me. Why don't they see that he's just not my type."

"What is?" Michael said.

"What is what?"

"What is your type?"

"I don't know. Probably nonexistent; it's too depressing to think about."

"Come on," he said, "I'll make it easy. Tell me some of the ways in which Barry falls short of the mark. What would you have to do to Barry to make him even remotely resemble your type?" Bizarre, I thought; was Michael catching the local mania for matchmaking? I certainly hoped not.

"He'd have to be smarter," I said. "More articulate. Dare I say intellectual? With a better sense of humor. Not always so politically correct. And physically . . . I don't know; I prefer lean, muscular men to that beefy jock type. It's weird, whenever I try to tell Eileen why Barry doesn't appeal to me, she thinks I'm trying to knock Steven. I'm not; I think Steven's very nice, and they're a great couple. But Steven isn't my type, and the beastly Barry even less so."

"I can see that. Although he's not actually an ogre, he certainly doesn't strike me as your type. On the other hand—"

"Only this commendation I can afford him," I said, paraphrasing some lines from *Much Ado About Nothing,* "that were he other than he is, he were unhandsome; and being no other but as he is, I do not like him."

Michael laughed and struck a pose.

" 'Rich she shall be, that's certain,' " he quoted back. " 'Wise, or I'll none; virtuous, or I'll never cheapen her; fair, or I'll never look on her; mild, or come not near me; noble, or not I for an angel; of good discourse, an excellent musician, and her hair shall be of what color it please God,' " he finished with a flourish, using some strands of my hair he'd removed from the bouquet as a prop.

"Who's that?" said Jake, who had come in while Michael was speaking and was looking confused. Which was more or less his usual state as far as I could see.

" 'You are a villain!' " Michael declaimed in yet another speech from *Much Ado*. He grabbed the scissors and struck up a fencing position. " 'I jest not: I will make it good how you dare, and when you dare. Do me right, or I will protest your cowardice. You have killed a sweet lady, and her death shall fall heavy on you. Let me hear from you!' "

Jake turned pale and began backing out of the room. "Is everyone here completely crazy?" he asked.

"He's just quoting me some lines from a Shakespeare play he appeared in, Mr. Wendell," I said, soothingly. To no avail. Jake reached the door and fled.

"That man's damned lucky to have an ironclad alibi," Michael remarked. "Have you ever seen anyone so hysterical?"

"For two cents I'd frame him for either murder, just to have him out from underfoot," I said. "And what's more, he's too big."

"Too big! He's shorter than you are, and I doubt if he weighs more than one hundred fifty pounds. Too big for what?"

"Too big for me to toss over the bluff," I grumbled. "We've already proven I can barely handle one hundred five pounds."

Michael gave me an odd look, but Eric's arrival cut off whatever answer he might have made.

"I did good, Aunt Meg, huh?" Eric said, grabbing my arm and swinging on it.

"You were a marvel."

"So we're going, right?" he demanded.

"You've got it."

"When?"

"We can't do it tomorrow; there's Samantha's party. And I may not feel like getting up early Monday. I thought Tuesday."

"Great! I'll go call Timmy and A.J. and Berke!"

"Timmy and A.J. and Berke? I thought—never mind," I said, closing my eyes and holding out my champagne glass. "How much worse can four of them be?"

"Four of what?" Michael asked, filling my glass.

"I had to bribe Eric to get him to take Brian's place. I'm taking him and, apparently, three other eight-year-old boys to ride the roller coasters."

"Roller coasters?"

"Yes, at whatever's the nearest huge amusement park," I said, with a shudder. "I hate riding roller coasters."

"Can't somebody else actually ride with them?"

"Strangely enough everyone else in the family is completely tied up all next week," I said. "Rob's taking the bar exam, but most of them seem to be going to the dentist. Isn't that odd? You'd think toothaches were contagious. Dad has offered to pay for the trip, though. I suppose that's something."

"Not enough. Did you say Tuesday?"

"Yes. Why? Do I have a fitting or something?"

"No," he said. "There's nothing important going on at the shop Tuesday. I'll go with you."

I opened my eyes and stared at him. "You must be mad. Or you've had too much of that," I said, pointing to the champagne. "We're talking about four eight-year-olds, here."

"Yes, and if you take them all by yourself, you'll be outnumbered four to one. If I go, we'll only be outnumbered two to one. Better odds."

"You're mad," I repeated. "Stark, raving mad."

"Oh, come on, it'll be fun," he said.

"You have a very warped idea of fun, then."

"Consider it part of Be-Stitched's superior customer service," he said. "We not only make your gown, we make sure you stay alive and sane enough to wear it."

I SLEPT LATE. THE ONLY THING I ACTUALLY HAD TO DO WAS HELP Professor Donleavy cope with the cleanup crew he'd hired. And pack a few things to return to rental places. And log in a few more gifts. And field all the phone calls from people who'd lost things at the party. And find a box that would hold all the things Eileen had forgotten and called home already to ask that we ship to her. Well, maybe it wasn't going to be such a quiet day after all. Thank goodness Michael had arranged for the ladies to capture all the costumes at the end of the party and was having them cleaned and returned to their owners. I spent most of the day over at the Donleavys'. Professor Donleavy was pathetically grateful for everything I was doing.

Nice to see that somebody was.

"Meg, where have you been?" Dad said, when I strolled up the driveway. "I needed you to help out with the investigation."

"What do you want me to do?" I said, trying to feign an interest in his detective work that I was too tired to feel at the moment.

"It's too late now. But——"

"Besides, I need you to help me," Mother said. "I was looking for you hours ago. Michael brought the new drapes and the recovered furniture. We're rearranging the living room."

Michael and Rob were in the living room, leaning wearily against the couch, looking very sweaty and disheveled. They'd obviously been shoving around the newly upholstered furniture for quite a while. It's not fair, I thought, as Michael flashed me a tired smile. No one that sweaty and disheveled should be allowed to look that gorgeous.

"Now, I want Meg to take a look at the different arrangements we've tried," Mother said.

Rob and Michael both became a little wild-eyed. They looked at me, obviously hoping for rescue.

"What's wrong with this arrangement?" I said. "It's fine."

"Yes, but . . ."

Mother described her alternate arrangements. I improvised compelling reasons why none of them would work. Rob and Michael watched us, heads moving back and forth with the fanatic intensity of spectators at Wimbledon. I finally convinced Mother to leave the living room alone. Michael and Rob began to look a little cheerful.

"Now about the dining room," she said. Rob and Michael slumped back into despondency.

"We can't possibly do the dining room at night," I said. "It's no good even trying until we see what it looks like in daylight."

"Can't we just—"

"Tomorrow, Mother," I said, firmly.

"I suppose," she said, with a disappointed look. Rob fled. Michael looked as if he were thinking of it. Mother wandered around the dining room twitching the new curtains and flicking invisible dust off the furniture. Dad dashed in.

"Meg, can you—" Dad began.

"Tomorrow."

He looked disappointed, but left. Not without a few reproachful backward glances. I slumped back on the couch, closed my eyes, and sighed.

"Having a bad day?" Michael asked. I felt the couch shift slightly as he sat down beside me.

"It wasn't particularly bad until I got home. I'm sorry; I can't help them tonight. I'm beat."

"Not your fault," he said.

"Of course it is. I'm supposed to be Wonder Woman. I'm supposed to be able to leap tall buildings with a single bound." I paused. "Actually, I think the real problem is that I'm supposed to be here. Back in the hometown. Like Pam. Available when they need me. And I can't do that."

"Yes, we never are quite what our parents want us to be, are we?" Michael said. With perhaps a little bitterness? I had a sudden sharp mental image of a frail little gray-haired lady, peering over her bifocals at Michael with a look of mild reproach in cornflower blue eyes whose beauty was only slightly dimmed by age. Like Barry Fitzgerald's tiny Irish mother tottering down the aisle in *Going My Way.*

"How is your mother?" I asked, to change the subject. He sighed. I frowned in dismay. Perhaps this was a tactless subject. Perhaps his mother was not doing well.

"Fine, just . . . fine. The bandages are off, and she's actually showing her face in the dining room already."

"Bandages? Don't you mean cast?"

"No." He paused for a few moments. "Don't you dare repeat this."

"Cross my heart."

"She didn't break her leg. Or her arm."

"No?"

"She had . . . a face-lift. That's why she couldn't come back here to recuperate. She's checked into a hotel in Atlanta and she's not going to come back until all the bandages and stitches and swelling are gone, and if anyone says anything about her looking different, she'll claim she went on a diet while she was convalescing. Not that she ever needs a diet, thanks to all the aerobics and iron-pumping. Next to Mom, Jane Fonda is a couch potato."

"Oh." A face-lift. My mental picture of sweet, kindly, gray-haired little Mrs. Waterston was undergoing radical revision.

"Don't tell anyone," he warned. "She'd kill me if she knew I'd told anyone."

"Don't worry; I'm not into gossip." Mother and Mrs. Fenniman, on the other hand, would have it all over the county within twenty-four hours of her return. Nothing I could do about that. "I'm the oddball around here; I like secrets as much as anyone, but prefer keeping them to myself and snickering at people who aren't in the know."

"I can certainly relate to that," he said. "But sometimes . . . well, there's a big difference between simply not telling a secret and having to run around lying and pretending to cover it up. This summer I've gotten very tired of *pretending*. In fact——"

Just then we heard a blood-curdling shriek. We both jumped up and ran out of the study and toward the front door, the direction from which the shriek seemed to have come. Other family and friends were peering over the upstairs banister and popping out of doorways all up and down the hall, although I didn't see any of them venturing down to help us. Michael grabbed my grandfather's knobby old walking stick from the umbrella stand in the front hall. I flung open the front door and peered out to see——

A small, nondescript man in overalls and a John Deere cap standing on the front steps holding a much-creased piece of paper and frowning at us.

"Is this the Langslow house?" he asked.

"Yes," I said, rather tentatively. He looked vaguely familiar, but I couldn't quite place him.

"About time," he growled, turning on his heel and walking down the steps to the driveway, where a large, battered truck, like a small moving van, was parked. "I'd like to have a word or two with whoever drew up this map," he said over his shoulder, shaking the piece of paper vaguely in our direction. "Been driving around the county with these damn things for hours now."

"What damn things?" Michael asked, still keeping the walking stick handy.

Instead of answering, the man flung open the back door of the truck and banged the side a couple of times with his fist. A chorus of unearthly shrieks rang out and then half a dozen shapes exploded from the back of the truck and scattered across the lawn, still shrieking.

"Ah," I said. "I see the peacocks have arrived."

Mr. Dibbit, the owner of the peacocks, gave Dad, Michael, and me a brief rundown on peacock care while the rest of the family ran off into the night to hunt them down. Mr. Dibbit assured us this was unnecessary; they'd find someplace to roost tonight and would show up for breakfast when they got hungry enough. Or if they didn't, we wouldn't have any problem finding them; you could hear them for miles. Or follow the droppings. I sensed that Mr. Dibbit was not a peacock owner by choice, or at least was no longer a proud and happy one. I began to suspect he was secretly hoping we would manage to lose or do in his peacock flock so he could be rid of it. He unloaded a couple of sacks of what he called peacock feed—actually Purina Turkey Chow, I noticed. He told us just to treat them like any other big bird. And then he drove off into the night—rather hurriedly. Or perhaps he was still miffed about the map. Mother had drawn a beautiful map, elegantly lettered, with many little sketches of the houses and gardens in the area. But since she'd left out or misnamed most of the critical streets and drawn most of the rest out of scale or perpendicular to the way they really ran, I could well understand Mr. Dibbit's frustration.

Dad and Michael began lugging the peacock chow into the garage. I was not a bit surprised to see Dad sampling it, but I hadn't realized how much he was influencing Michael. Men. At least Michael had the grace to look sheepish when I caught him nibbling. I went upstairs to change. The rest of the family could amuse themselves chivvying the peacocks through the neighborhood or devouring the poor birds' breakfast. The peacocks had arrived, taking care of one more of what Samantha called "those little details that really make an occasion." I was filled with a sense of accomplishment, and I planned to get all dressed up and go to Samantha's party.

Why I bothered I have no idea. Within half an hour of my arrival I was wondering how soon I could sneak out. As usual, most of the people at the party were Samantha's friends, not Rob's. I wondered if Rob realized how much his life was going to change after the wedding. And not for the better if it meant hanging out with this crowd.

By one in the morning, I was through. I was running out of ways to dodge Dougie, the particularly persistent unwanted suitor I'd ditched at Samantha's last party. I decided to leave. But I didn't want to have him follow me home, so I decided to hide out upstairs for a little while, in the hope that he'd think I was gone. Then I would go back down and sneak out.

I didn't want to stumble into a bedroom that might be occupied, so I headed for Mr. Brewster's library at the end of the hall. Luck was with me; the door was open, and I was able to duck inside before anyone else appeared in the hall.

Just as I was breathing a sigh of relief, I heard a noise behind me. I whirled about and saw a couple half reclining on the library sofa. Rob, and one of the bridesmaids. She was wearing a tight, red strapless dress, although there was a great deal more of her out of the dress than in it at the moment. I tried to remember her name, but after several glasses of wine it was impossible. Not one of the Jennifers, anyway. Rob looked somewhat disheveled as well, but instead of the angry stare the woman in red was giving me, Rob's flushed face showed mostly embarrassment with, I was pleased to note, perhaps a hint of relief. I decided that he needed rescuing, and that the best way to do it was to ignore whatever they had been up to.

"Oh, good, there you are, Rob," I said, walking over to the sofa. "Samantha was looking for you for something." Rob jumped to his feet and began putting his clothes to rights. I helped him by retying his tie as I continued. "I think they want to take some pictures. With the peacocks, if they're still awake." What a stupid thing to say, I told myself, but it was the first thing that came to mind. Actually I hoped they didn't want Rob for anything else tonight; as I drew his arm through mine and began leading him to the door, I realized that he was stumbling and lurching badly. Rob never did have much of a head for drink. I was babbling something inane about peacocks and wondering how on earth I was going to get him downstairs, when I ran into Michael at the landing.

"Help me with Rob," I hissed, glancing back at the door of the study. Sure enough, the vamp was standing in the door, looking daggers at me and trying to stuff herself back into the bodice of the dress. Michael took in the situation and immediately propped up Rob from the other side.

"We need to get him downstairs and back home," I said.

"Maybe you'd better zip his fly up before we take him back out in public. I'll hold him steady while you do." I did, made a few more futile efforts to make him look presentable, and then we more or less carried him down the stairs. Fortunately there were only a few people to stare as we lugged him out the front door.

Our luck held at first; the fresh air seemed to revive Rob a little, so he wasn't a dead weight on the walk home. But getting up the porch steps took a lot out of him, and he passed out in the front hall.

"Allow me," Michael said, and he heaved Rob up in a fireman's carry and hauled him up to his room, with me running ahead to show the way. Michael deposited his burden on the bed. After I pulled off Rob's shoes and loosened his tie, I decided to call it quits.

"Thanks," I told Michael. "Once again, I don't know what we'd have done without you. You seem to be making a career out of hauling incapacitated Langslows home."

"You're welcome. I only wish we could get some aspirin in

him. I learned in my misspent youth that a couple of aspirin the night before does more than a dozen the morning after. But I don't think he'd thank us for waking him up to feed them to him."

"He should thank us for getting him out of there. I don't know what I would have done if you hadn't happened to come along."

"I didn't just happen to come along. I saw you go upstairs, and I remembered that you'd seemed to be trying to lose that Doug character, and I thought I'd tag along in case he followed you."

"And what if I'd been heading for a rendezvous with him?" I teased.

"I would have been frightfully embarrassed. But somehow I can't see you slipping upstairs for a rendezvous with Dougie."

"No, actually he was waiting for me in the gazebo."

I'd never actually seen anyone do a double take in real life.

"He was what?"

"Waiting for me in the gazebo."

"You agreed to meet him in the gazebo?"

"No, but about the seventeenth time he asked me if we could go somewhere more private, I told him to be in the gazebo in fifteen minutes. If he chose to believe I was planning on showing up there, that's his problem."

"Why not just tell him to get lost?" Michael asked.

"I did. Several dozen times. The man just won't take drop dead for an answer."

"I'm relieved," Michael said. "I didn't think he was your type. In fact, I was wondering—"

Just then Rob stirred, rolled over on his back, smiled seraphically, and spoke.

"Kill the lawyers," he said. "Kill *all* the lawyers." Then he began snoring loudly. Michael and I tiptoed out of the room.

"Did he say what I thought he said?" Michael asked.

"Yes. Kill All the Lawyers," I said. "It's a role-playing game. Also known as Lawyers from Hell."

"I've never heard of it."

"That's because Rob and a friend have been inventing it this summer."

"That's great!"

"While they should have been studying for the bar exam."

"Oh," Michael said. "How do you think Samantha will like that?"

"Not at all, but then after tonight, it may be irrelevant. If anyone tells her what Rob's been up to."

"True. Let me know as soon as you know what happens. Not that I'm trying to be nosy—"

"But if Samantha cancels another wedding you'd like to know immediately. Before the Brewsters stick your mom with another set of unused dresses. I understand."

He chuckled and went off. I went to bed wondering how Samantha would react if she found out about Rob. And how he would feel about it. If she threw his behavior in his face, should I bring up her clandestine expedition of the other night?

No. Stay out of it. It's his life; let him ruin it himself. Then again, he'd been awfully subdued recently. Maybe this was more than just prenuptial jitters. I'd never been able to figure out what he saw in Samantha. And they weren't billing and cooing much anymore. Maybe, subconsciously, he wanted out.

Monday, July 18

AMONG HER MANY FAILINGS, SAMANTHA WAS NOT ONLY A MORNING person but an intolerant and inconsiderate one. At least Eileen saved most of her crises for the afternoon. And she would never have awakened me at dawn the morning after a party. All right, it was eight o'clock, but I'd been up until well past one, looking after Rob. And Mother—the traitor—let her in and insisted I get up and talk to her: I found the two brides calmly sipping tea when I stumbled downstairs to the kitchen.

"Meg," Samantha said. "See if you can locate Michael Waterston. We need to schedule a fitting for Ashley. Today if possible, and if not, first thing tomorrow."

"Ashley?" I said groggily. "I didn't know we had an Ashley." Samantha looked at me as if I were feebleminded. I counted them off on my fingers: "Jennifer, Jennifer, Jennifer, Kimberly, Tiffany, Heather, Melissa, and Blair. I'm right; we don't have an Ashley." I nodded triumphantly, turned to the refrigerator, and began rooting around for a diet soda to wash down my aspirin. It was already too hot for coffee.

"Heather will be unable to participate," Samantha said, in a brittle tone. "Ashley has very graciously agreed to take her place."

"That's rather inconsiderate of her," I grumbled. "Heather, I mean, not Ashley. Dropping out at the last minute like this. What happened? She was at the party last night, wasn't she?"

"Yes, I think so," Samantha said, tight-lipped. Suddenly, memory returned. Heather. Of course. The she-beast in the red dress.

"I'm sure she was," I said. "Wearing that rather tacky strapless red dress."

"Yes," Samantha said, with a thin, satisfied smile. "It was rather tacky, wasn't it?" And I very much doubt if she meant the dress. Ah, well; I hadn't really expected Rob's little encounter with the Lady in Red to go unnoticed.

"Do you think Ashley's approximately the same size as Heather?"

"Oh, yes," Samantha said, very businesslike. "Heather and Tiffany are exactly the same size, and Ashley was Tiffany's roommate in school and they always used to share all their clothes. So the dress should only need minor alterations."

I was impressed. Not eight hours after the event and Samantha had already rounded up not only a replacement bridesmaid but
one in a convenient size. And I bet Ashley was a blonde, too.

"Leave it to me," I said.

Samantha gave me Ashley's number and promised me that
Ashley could be down at Be-Stitched on half an hour's notice. I
strode out of the kitchen, leaving the two of them chatting away.
When I was out of sight, I grabbed a lawn chair and Dad's wide-
brimmed gardening hat and went down to the end of the driveway,
where I plunked myself down in the lawn chair with the hat over
my face and fell asleep.

Actually, I only intended to sit and think until Michael and
Spike came along on their usual morning walk, but the next thing
I knew my shoulder was being shaken and I heard Michael's voice.

"Meg! Are you all right?"

"Morning," I said, "I thought you'd be coming along soon."

"And you were lying in wait for me. I am immensely flattered.
And if you'll only tell me it has absolutely nothing to do with nuptial attire, my happiness will be complete."

"Sink back into the depths of despair, then," I said, getting up
and falling into step beside them. "We need to schedule a fitting for
a new bridesmaid. Samantha has decided to dispose of her prede-
cessor."

"Not another suspicious death," he said, only half joking.

"No, just a summary dismissal. I suppose it was too much to
hope for that Samantha wouldn't hear about last night's escapade."

"At least it's the bridesmaid who's dismissed, not Rob. She
wouldn't be casting another bridesmaid if she intended calling off
the wedding."

"I'm not sure that would be a tragedy," I muttered. "And anyway, I hope he's not too hungover to do some heavy groveling
today."

"Wonder what she said to Heather?"

"I'm impressed; you actually remembered her name. I have a hard time telling them all apart sober, and last night after a couple of drinks I'll be damned if I could remember which one she was."

"I have reason to," Michael said, "I had a run-in with her myself. She's as subtle as a pit bull, and about as appealing. As a matter of fact, it was because of Heather that—oh, damn!"

Spike had slipped his leash again and was running merrily toward the peacock flock in the side yard. We chased him for a while, but it was too hot.

"I give up," Michael said, as we collapsed, panting, on the lawn. "He's too small to do them any real damage; he'll come home when he's tired of chasing them."

It was a long day, and I was dead tired when I got home. Replacing one indistinguishable blond bimbo with another shouldn't be this difficult, should it? Of course, I'd also had to play wise older sister to a depressed, guilt-ridden and very hungover Rob. And deal with Samantha, who was treating me with a watered-down version of the same icy, condescending calm she was using with Rob. Had everyone forgotten, by the way, that Rob was going to be taking his first day of bar exams tomorrow? It would be a miracle if he passed after all this.

A thoroughly rotten day. I stopped to rest for a moment on the porch steps.

The peacocks were crossing the lawn. Actually, I suppose I should say the peafowl, since we had three peacocks and six peahens. I watched with satisfaction. Many things had gone wrong this summer, and many more probably would. I was sure to be blamed for most of them, and some of them would actually be my fault. But the peafowl situation was shaping up nicely. They had settled in. We had found that we could lead them from one yard to another with a small trail of food and more or less keep them in place by putting a supply out. Establishing them in the Brewsters' yard for Samantha's wedding and then reestablishing them in our yard for Mother's would not be a problem. I leaned against the railing and smiled contentedly. Then my contentment was shattered by a voice from the porch.

"I don't suppose you could find some different peacocks," Mother said.

"Different peacocks? I had a hard enough time finding these. What's wrong with them?"

"Only three of them have tails," Mother pointed out.

"That's because only three of them are peacocks, Mother. The rest are peahens."

"Well what do we need *them* for?" Mother asked. "They don't add anything to the impression. They're not very attractive."

"Maybe not to you, but apparently they are to the peacocks. If we didn't have them around, the peacocks would sulk and wouldn't spread their tails. You know how men are."

Mother digested that in silence.

"Besides, one of them's shedding," she said.

"Shedding?"

She pointed. One of the peacocks—the smallest—was beginning to look a little bedraggled.

"I think it's called molting. Either that or he lost a fight with one of the bigger peacocks." Or perhaps Spike had been chewing on him.

"It's not very attractive," Mother said. "What if they all do that?"

"Then we call Mr. Dibbit and get our money back. If you don't like them, we can take them back after Samantha's wedding."

Mother pondered.

"We'll see how they look by then," she said finally, and swept off.

I looked at the peafowl again. Were the other two peacocks showing signs of molting? Would they start shrieking during the ceremony? It would probably be a good idea to keep them out of the Brewsters' yard until the day before the ceremony. To minimize the number of droppings on the lawn. That way the guests would only be stepping in fresh peacock droppings. I saw a slight movement in the shrubbery. A small, furry white face peeked out. The kitten was stalking the peafowl. Should I go out and rescue him? Or was it the peafowl who needed rescuing?

The kitten attacked. The peafowl scattered in all directions, shrieking. Mother slammed the front door closed. I sighed. So much for things going right.

Tuesday, July 19

ERIC WOKE ME UP SHORTLY AFTER DAWN TO REMIND ME THAT WE were going to the amusement park and ask me if I thought it would rain. I restrained the impulse to throttle him and sent him down to watch the Weather Channel. The weather, alas, was clear, and the other small boys would arrive at seven. So much for sleeping late.

By the time Michael strolled up, looking disgustingly alert for a professed night person, I was inventorying the stuff I'd packed— snacks and games to keep the small monsters happy while getting there, sunblock, dry clothes for everyone in case we went on any water rides too close to closing time, the inhaler A.J.'s mother had provided in case his asthma acted up, a large assortment of Band-Aids, aspirin for the headache I suspected I'd have by the end of the day, and several dozen other critical items.

Hannibal crossed the Alps with less baggage.

"Dad should be by any minute with his car," I said.

"How big is his car?" Michael asked, eyeing our charges.

"It's a great big Buick battleship; we can stuff them all in the backseat."

Eric and his friends were running about shooting each other with imaginary guns and competing to see who could achieve the noisiest and most prolonged demise, and I was watching them with satisfaction.

"Rather a lively bunch, aren't they," Michael said, continuing to watch them.

Aha, I thought. Second thoughts already. Well, he wasn't drafted.

"I egged them on. The more energy we bleed off now, the less hellish the drive will be."

"Good plan. You did bring the stun gun, I hope?"

"It's all packed."

"By the way," he said, "have you seen Spike? He never came home yesterday."

"No, not since we lost him chasing the peacocks."

"Maybe I should ask someone to keep an eye out for him," Michael said. "Feed him when he shows up."

"I'm sure Dad would do it; we'll ask him." Just then I saw Dad's car turn into the driveway.

To my surprise, instead of slowing down as he approached the house, Dad began blowing his horn at us. We jumped aside as he whizzed by at nearly forty miles per hour and, instead of following the curve of the driveway back out to the street, plunged full steam ahead across the yard, sending the peacocks running for their lives in all directions. He lost some speed going through the grape arbor, then plowed through the hedge that separated our yard from the one next door and came to a halt when he ran into a stack of half-rotten hay bales left over from when the neighbors used to have a pony.

"Something must have happened to him," I said, dropping my carryall to run to the scene.

"Grandpa!" Eric shouted. "You wrecked your car!"

The car was, indeed, something of a mess, but once we'd gotten him out from under the hay, Dad was unharmed. In fact, he was positively beaming with exhilaration.

"Grandpa, why did you wreck your car?" Eric asked as we hauled Dad out. Good question. The approaching next-door neighbors would soon be asking similar questions about their hedge and haystack. The peacocks had disappeared but were shrieking with such gusto that I was sure the entire neighborhood would be showing up soon to complain.

"Call the sheriff," were Dad's first words. "I think someone's tampered with my brakes."

Pam, who had come running out when she heard the commotion, ran back in to call. Eric and his friends looked solemn.

"Grandpa, what's tampered?" Eric asked. His grandpa, however, was crawling under the car. As was Michael. I didn't know about Michael, but I knew perfectly well Dad was incapable of doing anything underneath a car but cover himself with grease. Fascinating the way even the most mechanically inept males feel obliged to involve themselves with any malfunctioning machine in their immediate vicinity. And usually, at least in Dad's case, making things worse. The small boys were crouching down and preparing to join their elders.

"Tampered means Grandpa thinks somebody messed around with the car to make it crash," I said. "So all of you stay away from that car until Grandpa and Michael are sure it's safe." They were ignoring me. The lure of male bonding beneath an automobile was too strong. Then Michael's voice emerged sepulchrally from beneath the car.

"Anyone who does come under here will be *left behind!*"

The herd backed up to a respectful distance. About then the sheriff turned up. Dad and Michael emerged from beneath the car for a conference with him. The sheriff crawled under the car, popped out long enough to ask Pam to call a tow truck, and then disappeared again, followed by Dad. And then one or two deputies.

"You seem very calm about this," Michael remarked, as we watched the growing number of feet sticking out from under various parts of the car.

"I'll postpone my hysterics until later," I said, feeling a little shakier than I'd like to admit. "I think it's important that we stay calm and avoid traumatizing the children."

"Are we going soon, Aunt Meg?" Eric asked. The children didn't seem particularly traumatized. The excitement of the car wreck was evidently fading. There was a growing herd of small boys swarming over the haybales and getting in the deputies' way. I made a mental note to make sure only four of them came with us to the amusement park.

"Yes, let's maintain a façade of normality," Michael said. "I'll get Mom's station wagon. They'd kill each other stuffed in the back of your Toyota, and my car's a two-seater."

By the time we got the boys loaded into the station wagon and drove off, Dad was recounting his wild ride through the yard for the third time, to a spellbound audience of deputies. The sheriff was down at my sister Pam's house, interviewing any neighbors who might have seen someone tampering with the car. The cousin who ran the local plant nursery and gardening service was working up an estimate for replacing the damaged portions of the hedge for the neighbors' insurance agent, who happened to be another cousin. A wonderful day in the neighborhood.

Although I'm sure Eric and his little friends would disagree, I found our trip to ride the roller coasters blissfully uneventful—at least compared to how the day began. Oh, I was exhausted by the end of it, of course, and was trying hard to hide a tendency to jump at loud noises. But no new bodies were discovered. Apart from the sort of mayhem that small boys routinely inflict on each other, no one tried to murder anyone. Only one of the kids threw up. And the only new item added to my list of things to do was "Hit Dad up for reimbursement."

"Where do they get the energy?" I asked, as we watched them careening around in the bumper cars for the fifth or sixth time. "I don't want to sound like a stick in the mud, but I just can't keep up with them."

"Oh, don't worry," Michael said. "They don't think of you as a stick in the mud. I overheard A.J. telling Eric how great it was that his aunt Meg wasn't scared to go on the big rides like most girls."

"I'm flattered. Even if A.J. is a little male chauvinist pig."

"And Eric told A.J. that his aunt Meg wasn't scared of anything."

"I wish that was true." I sighed.

"You're worrying about your Dad," Michael observed.

Eric and the horde bounded up demanding food just then, cutting off my answer. Which would have been that I was worried about all of us. If someone was trying to kill my Dad, he—or she—might already have killed at least one innocent bystander in the process by tampering with Dad's lawn mower. Michael and the four little boys and I might have just missed becoming victims ourselves.

Michael brought up the subject again on the way home, after a glance to make sure that Eric and his friends were curled up asleep in the back of the station wagon.

"Wonder if they've had time to found out anything about your dad's car?" he said quietly. "Brake line cut, or brake fluid drained, or whatever."

"Did it look suspicious to you?" I asked.

"I'm not exactly a master mechanic," he admitted. "Your dad seemed to find something of interest."

"Dad's no master mechanic either. In fact, anything he might possibly know about how car brakes work would pretty much have to have come from a detective story. But I'd be willing to bet that either they find the brakes had been tampered with or at least that they can't rule out sabotage."

Michael nodded.

"I'm going to have to give Mom a hard time when this summer is all over," he said. "I distinctly remember her telling me this was a quiet, peaceful little town where nothing ever happened."

"Until we got our own serial killer."

"If that's the right name for it."

"True. Serial killer does seem to imply some sort of random, sick, purposelessness, and I get the feeling there is a very rational purpose to everything that's gone on this summer, if only we knew what it was."

"So what *do* we know?" Michael asked. "I mean *really* know—"

"As opposed to Dad's highly imaginative speculations?" I asked.

"Right."

"Not much," I admitted. "On the day after Memorial Day, a visitor from out of town either was killed or died in a freak accident. And while she managed to alienate a significant portion of the county before her death, the only person who would seem to have known her well enough to want to do her in has a cast-iron alibi."

"Is it so cast-iron?" Michael asked. "I mean, apart from the alibi, Jake's so perfect for it."

"If it were just Mother giving him his alibi, I'd say no. Not because I think she'd lie, but because she's too spacey."

"What a thing to say about your own mother," Michael said.

"Do you disagree?"

He shrugged.

"But anyway," I continued, "Since they spent the entire day billing and cooing in front of half a dozen waiters and salesclerks, the sheriff can say with complete confidence that Jake couldn't have been within twenty miles of the neighborhood for hours before or after the time Mrs. Grover died."

"Hard to argue with that." Michael sighed. "Pity. There's something about Jake that gets on my nerves. He's so aggressively banal. I'd love to see it turn out to be him."

"You and me both."

"Not to mention your dad."

"Right. Though for different reasons."

"Like disqualifying Jake as a suitor for your mother."

"Exactly. But unless he's sitting on some really dynamite evidence, I think he'll have to find some other way of breaking up the match. As a murderer, I'm afraid Jake's a nonstarter."

"Sad but true."

"Getting back to what we know: two weeks after Mrs. Grover's suspicious death, an electrician is nearly killed in a freak electrical accident that *may* have been a booby trap. And if it was a booby trap, the most logical person for it to be aimed at was Dad, who would have fixed the fuse box if he hadn't been AWOL."

"And a little more than two weeks after that, we're all nearly blown up by a bomb, just before you and a dozen other women are made severely ill by what appears to have been poison that may have been deliberately placed in a bowl of one of your dad's favorite foods."

"Thank God for the bomb. All the rest could possibly be accidents, although the number of accidents is beginning to make even the sheriff suspicious. But there's no way to argue with that bomb."

"True; I think about it whenever I'm tempted to doubt your dad."

"And shortly afterward, a harmless neighborhood layabout is killed in what again may have been sabotage, and again the more logical target would have been Dad."

"And now today your father has a car wreck that he thinks may have been due to sabotage. So maybe the big question is, who is trying to kill your father, and why?"

"Either he knows something or the killer is afraid he'll find something out," I said. "Dad's the one who kept the sheriff and the coroner from declaring Mrs. Grover's death an accident. Dad's the one who points out the suspicious side of all these so-called accidents. Dad keeps turning over stones, and maybe the killer is afraid he'll eventually find something."

"If that's the case, it all goes back to Mrs. Grover. If we figure out who killed her, we know who's trying to kill your dad."

"Or, conversely, if we figure out who's trying to kill Dad, we'll know who did in Mrs. Grover." We rode a while in silence, no doubt both trying to come up with a plausible suspect.

"Maybe I'm too close to this," I said with a sigh. "I can think of dozens of people who would have been capable of doing all this, but I can't for the life of me see why any of them would want to kill Mrs. Grover. And I have a hard time seeing most of them as cold-blooded murderers."

"Is there anyone you *can* see as a murderer?" Michael asked.

"Samantha," I said, only half joking. "I can see her killing anyone who seriously inconvenienced her. I certainly go out of my way to avoid crossing her."

"I can see that. But what could Samantha have against Mrs. Grover? Granted, Mrs. Grover was a supremely irritating person, but that's hardly grounds for murder."

"They had some kind of small run-in at the Donleavys' picnic. But then who didn't? I know I did."

"So did I," Michael said.

"Maybe she knew something damaging about Samantha. Although I can't imagine what. She was here less than a week before she died. Even Mother would have difficulty unearthing any juicy skeletons after only five days in a strange city."

"Maybe it was something she knew about Samantha before she came here," Michael said. "I seem to recall being an object of mild suspicion myself because she knew my mother from Fort Lauderdale. Was Samantha originally from Florida?"

"No, but her fiancé was. The one before Rob."

"The bank robber?"

"Embezzler. But that was Miami, not Fort Lauderdale."

"It's the same thing," Michael said. "All part of the same metropolitan area. Like Manhattan and Brooklyn."

"Is it?" I said. "Geography was never my strong point. So they both had ties to the Miami/Fort Lauderdale area."

"Samantha through her shady former fiancé," Michael expanded. "This is much more promising."

"If I remember correctly, the fiancé claimed his partner had gotten all the money, and the partner claimed that the fiancé had gotten the lion's share."

"Wouldn't it be funny if Samantha'd somehow gotten her claws into most of the loot? Played both of them against each other and made off with the loot under their greedy noses?"

"It's probably beastly of me, but I can definitely imagine Samantha doing it. Or killing, for enough money," I said. "And the estimates of how much they milked out of their clients range between ten and fifteen million dollars."

Michael whistled.

"There's a motive to be reckoned with. But do you really think she'd try to kill her future father-in-law to keep it quiet?"

"She's never much liked Dad," I said. "And besides, I can also see her disposing of anyone who tried to get in her way about the wedding."

"What, has your dad tried to butt in on the wedding? Insisted on a nonpoisonous wedding bouquet, perhaps?"

"She's probably overheard him trying to talk Rob out of marrying her. I know I have. And come to think of it, even if she didn't hear him talking to Rob, I know for a fact that at the picnic she overhead him tell me he thought the marriage was a bad idea and he was going to keep trying to talk Rob out of it."

"Oh," Michael said.

"You can see how she might resent that."

"Definitely. Samantha goes at the top of the list of people on whom I will not willingly turn my back. And on whom I will keep an eye when your father's in the neighborhood. Any other suspects?"

"It's a pity we can't frame the Beastly Barry for it," I said. "I thought we'd be rid of him, at least for a little while, after Eileen's wedding, but it begins to look as if he'll never leave. At least that's the way it looks to poor Mr. Donleavy. I'm surprised he didn't try to join us today."

"I doubt if his enthusiasm for small children extends to doing anything with or for them that involves actual work," Michael said, glancing at the backseat where the small boys appeared still asleep. "Is he frameable, do you suppose?" he added, with seemingly genuine interest. Civil of him to adopt my dislike of the Beastly so enthusiastically.

"Well, he was here for the Donleavys' Memorial Day picnic when Mrs. Grover was killed. I remember she did something or other that ticked him off pretty seriously, and he's normally about as excitable as a house plant."

"Maybe he's one of those people who's slow to anger but even slower to get over it, and he's been plotting revenge," Michael suggested.

"And he was here shortly before the fuse box incident. It was just after Eileen went on the Renaissance kick, and I remember you had him measured for his doublet that day."

"He could have put the bomb in the jack-in-the-box and lied about it," Michael said.

"And he could have poisoned the salsa; he was hanging around here for the whole Fourth of July weekend, and some days after-ward—I remember he kept trying to come up and read to me while I was recovering. He's had plenty of time to have rigged the lawn mower or the car since he practically moved into the Don-leavys'."

"The hell with framing him," Michael said. "If he has even a shadow of a motive, he's worth suspecting for real."

"I'm afraid I have a hard time believing that he's capable of ra-tional thought, much less planning two murders and several at-tempted murders."

"Well, they weren't very *well* planned," Michael said. "The killer seems to have missed his intended victim at least three out of four times, and missed altogether all but two attempts. Hell, maybe Mrs. Grover wasn't the intended victim. Maybe he missed that time, too."

"That would explain why we're having such a hard time figur-ing out why she was killed."

"Maybe it would help if we eliminated some more suspects. We've more or less eliminated Jake and your mother for lack of opportunity. And as the intended victim, your father's pretty much out of the running."

"Unless you like the theory that Mother and Jake are in ca-hoots, or alternatively, that Dad is the murderer and is trying to di-vert suspicion by staging a series of crimes that appear to be aimed at him. I mean, it has been remarkable how he's escaped every time."

"Do you really see either of your parents as a multiple mur-derer?" Michael asked.

"No. But I can't expect the rest of the world to take my word for it."

"We'll classify them as highly improbable."

"I would have called Pam a likely suspect at one point," I said. "Mrs. Grover was horrible to Natalie and Eric."

"That's no reason to kill someone," Michael said.

"Not in and of itself, no," I said. "But if she caught Mrs. Grover doing something she felt was seriously damaging to her kids—mentally or physically damaging—then yes. Pam thinks child molesters should be executed. Preferably at the hands of their victims' parents."

"That's a little extreme, but I see her point," Michael said.

"But there's no way Pam would sabotage a car the kids ride in all the time, or poison salsa they might find as soon as Dad."

"True. You know, come to think of it, the way the murderer has kept missing your Dad does suggest one interesting thing about his or her personality."

"I'm all ears."

"The murderer has come up with a number of rather clever ways to bump off your Dad in the course of his usual activities. So we know the murderer has a relatively good idea of your Dad's tastes and habits. But each of the attempts failed—or succeeded with the wrong person—because your father didn't happen to be doing what the murderer expected him to be doing at any given time."

"Always a serious mistake, expecting Dad to be where he's supposed to be."

"Exactly. I've only known him since the beginning of the summer, but I've picked up that much. The murderer, however, despite knowing rather a lot of useful details about your Dad, has apparently not grasped this critical aspect of his character. I suspect the murderer is a person of limited imagination and very regular habits. Enough imagination to come up with a series of ideas, but not enough to think them through and make them foolproof. Not enough to recognize that there were going to be an awful lot of external events around this summer to interrupt everyone's usual habits. And that your dad doesn't have very many usual habits anyway."

"So the murderer, who has a highly organized but pedestrian

mind, knows Dad reasonably well but doesn't really understand him."

"Precisely," Michael said.

"Unfortunately, it seems to me that the people who best fit that description are the very suspects we've already been looking at."

"True," Michael said. "We need more."

"He or she has some basic knowledge of poisons."

"Thanks to your dad, that doesn't eliminate anyone in the county." We both thought in silence for several miles.

"Mechanical ability," Michael said at last. "Whoever did it knew how to tamper with cars and lawn mowers and fuse boxes. That should eliminate a few people."

"Mother, certainly, if we hadn't already counted her out. And Dad, for that matter."

"Samantha, too, I should think," Michael said.

"Now, don't you be a chauvinist like A.J. I know she gives the impression that she'd die before she'd lift a finger to do anything mechanical, but that only applies when there's someone else around who'll do it for her if she bats her eyes. Remember how she bailed us out when we were trying to reinstall my distributor cap?"

"I stand rebuked. Return her to the top of the suspect list. What about the bomb? Surely most of our suspects have little or no experience with bombs."

"No, but I hear you can build one with fertilizer, which everyone in town has by the ton, and these days I'm sure any eight-year-old could find step-by-step instructions on the Internet."

We both glanced at the back of the car, where the troop of eight-year-olds appeared to be sound asleep, oblivious to the new level of destructiveness they could be achieving with a little initiative.

We continued to dissect the case all the way home, without coming up with anything else useful. Was the murderer really that brilliant, or were we all being particularly dense?

Wednesday, July 20

I WAS HELPING DAD WITH SOME GOPHER STOMPING THE NEXT MORN-
ing when Aunt Phoebe showed up to introduce a visiting cousin.

"Cousin Walter?" Dad said. "I don't remember a Cousin Walter."

"I'll explain the genealogy to you later, Dad," I said, poking
him with my elbow.

Cousin Walter was about six two, very physically fit, with a
crew cut and a bulge under one arm of his bulky, unseasonably
heavy navy sports coat. I'd never heard of Cousin Walter either,
but if the FBI or the SBI or the DEA or whatever law enforcement
agency sent him wanted us to pretend he was a cousin, that was fine
with me.

No one in town would be fooled—we were all chuckling already about the half-dozen locals who'd introduced relatives nobody had ever met before or even heard of. Everybody was going
along with the joke—we were glad to have them. I apologized for
not inviting our newfound cousin to the wedding, he graciously accepted an oral invitation, and Dad and I returned to our gopher
stomping. We were still at it when Michael showed up.

In my book, gopher stomping is useless but fun. Dad is convinced that if you systematically destroy a gopher's tunnels by
treading on them to cave them in and then stomping to pack the
dirt, the gopher will eventually get discouraged and go elsewhere.
I think that far from discouraging them it probably pleases them immensely; they get to have the fun of digging all over again. But Dad
likes to do it, and I help him out. Besides, with an outdoor wedding coming up, to which at least half a dozen middle-aged or elderly relatives would insist on wearing spike heels, reducing the
pitfalls in the yard seemed like a good idea.

"I've come to a fork," Dad announced. "Are you at a dead end, Meg?"

"No, I'm still going strong," I replied.

"Michael, would you like to take one?"

"One what?" Michael asked.

"One fork of the gopher trail," Dad explained, stopping for a moment and mopping his face with a bandanna. "Come over here and I'll show you." After Dad demonstrated the basics of gopher stomping, we all three stomped a while in silence. Michael looked as if he wasn't sure whether or not we were putting him on.

"By the way," Michael said, pausing to stretch, "I was actually looking for Spike. Have you seen him?"

"No, not for several days," Dad said. "How did he get loose?"

"Took off after the peacocks and hasn't been seen since."

"Do I detect a note of concern?" I asked. "Don't tell me you're actually getting fond of the beast."

"I wouldn't say fond," Michael replied. "But after two months of feeding him and walking him and giving him so many doggie treats Mom will probably have to put him on a diet when she gets back, we've reached a sort of truce."

"That's great," I said.

"Yeah," Michael said. "He hardly ever bites me anymore. Unless I try to take away something he ought not to be chewing. Or give him a flea bath. Or wake him suddenly. Or sometimes when he gets too frustrated at not being able to kill the postman."

"Next thing you know he'll be fetching your pipe and slippers," Dad remarked.

"Hardly." Michael snorted. "But just when I was beginning to think we could get through the summer without one of us killing the other, he disappears like this. What am I going to tell Mom?"

"We'll put the word out on the neighborhood grapevine," I said.

"And we'll add that you've offered a small monetary reward for information leading to his capture," Dad added.

"Every kid in the neighborhood will be scouring the bushes for him," I said.

"Remember to warn them he bites," Michael said.

"I think the entire county has figured that out by now," Dad remarked. "Well, I think that will discourage the little critters for a while," he added, finishing off his trail with a crescendo of stomping around an exit hole. "Let's go find the local urchins."

The local urchins had a lively afternoon looking for Spike, but things quieted down by late afternoon. The storm we'd been expecting all day broke about five o'clock. The power went out almost immediately, of course. It always did when we had a thunderstorm. Mother had had the foresight to be visiting a cousin in Williamsburg, and called to say she'd be staying the night.

Rob went out with his bar exam review group to celebrate getting through the bar exams. Celebrating was a little premature if you asked me; he wouldn't know for months if he'd passed. But even if he hadn't, at least he wouldn't have to study night and day for a while, which I suppose was worth celebrating. I didn't expect him home till the wee hours, if at all.

Usually I like a good thunderstorm, especially since there was hope that it would break the latest heat wave. But tonight the candles I'd lit made the house look unfamiliar and creepy, and I was abnormally conscious of being by myself. The kitten was under the bed, spitting and wailing occasionally. The peacocks, who by rights should have been roosting somewhere, were awake and shrieking. I found myself starting at shadows, jumping at every clap of thunder, and straining to hear the suspicious noises that I was sure were being muffled by the steady drumming of the rain. Or drowned out by the menagerie.

When the rain let up at about nine-thirty, I decided to go out for some air. The ground was soaked, and it looked as if it would start raining again any time, but I couldn't stand being cooped up in the house any more. I put on my denim jacket and fled to the backyard. I found myself staring down at the river from the edge of the bluff, wondering if we'd ever find out the truth about Mrs. Grover's death. Morbid thoughts. Here I was in the backyard of the house I'd grown up in, and yet I found myself looking over my shoulder for shadowy figures. But it was only because I was so on edge, and straining to hear the slightest noise, that I heard the faint whining coming from somewhere down the bluff.

I peered down. I caught a faint glimpse of movement, a flash of something white.

"Hello," I called. I heard a feeble little bark.

Spike.

I suppose I should have waited until I could find someone else to help me, but Michael had been looking for Spike for several days. The poor animal could be starving, injured—I couldn't wait. I rummaged in Dad's shed until I found a rope that seemed sound, tied one end to a tree and let myself down, half rappelling and half climbing hand over hand down the rope, toward the whining sounds. It was starting to rain again, of course. About twenty feet down, I found a vine-tangled ledge that I could stand on, and there at one end of the ledge, was Spike.

He cringed away from me, whining softly. His collar was caught on a branch, and I could see that he'd rubbed his neck raw trying to get out of it. Upon closer examination, I began to doubt that Spike had gotten into this mess by accident. It almost looked as if someone had deliberately buckled his collar around the branch. I felt a surge of anger. How could anyone treat a helpless animal that way! The poor thing was sopping wet, trembling like a leaf—

And still as nasty-tempered as ever. When I reached toward him, he lunged at me, teeth bared, and I jerked back. As I did, a long, horribly sharp blade about two feet long snapped out of the pine-needle-covered floor of the ledge between me and Spike and buried itself in the side of the bluff. It passed through the place where my throat would have been if I hadn't suddenly leaped back to avoid Spike's teeth.

Spike and I sat there for a while in silence. He looked as stunned as I felt. When my pulse had slowed down to a mere twice its normal rate, I leaned over and examined every square inch of the ground around me as carefully as I could without touching anything. The machete was attached to one side of a set of steel jaws that must have come from an animal trap. The other side was anchored in place, so when you tripped the spring the blade sprang up from the ground, sliced through the air in a lethal semicircle and buried itself in the side of the bluff. The whole contraption was invisible, hidden under leaves and pine needles on the floor of the ledge. The spring that made it snap shut like a mousetrap had been placed just where I'd have put my hand if Spike hadn't lunged at me. In an unprecedented display of common sense, Spike waited patiently while I searched. The rain and darkness didn't make the job any easier, and I was still more than a little nervous when I finally gave up the examination, prodded the machete—or whatever it was—with a stick to make sure it wasn't going to move anymore, and turned back to Spike.

"Seeing as how you saved my life, I might forgive you one or two little nibbles," I told him. "On the other hand, I wouldn't object to a little gratitude."

He only snapped a few times, not even really trying, while I untangled his collar. As soon as I freed him, he kicked dirt in my eyes trying to scramble up the bank before falling back onto the ledge, panting with exhaustion. He made several more feeble attempts to climb up, then subsided, and looked at me, shivering piteously, with a peevish, expectant look on his face.

"I suppose now you expect me to haul you up the bank," I said. He growled, then whined and cringed at a particularly violent clap of thunder. It was raining steadily now, and dozens of little waterfalls and rivulets were making the side of the bluff even more slippery than ever.

"Oh, all right." I took off my jacket and managed to wrap him up in it—without getting bitten—so that only his head stuck out. I buttoned it up, tied the arms together, slung it over my shoulder, and began the precarious climb up to the top of the hill. Hoping that whoever put that blade there considered one booby trap enough.

I slipped and nearly fell half a dozen times, skinned my hands badly on some rocks, and was covered with mud to the teeth. At least Spike was too exhausted to cause trouble. I could feel him shivering against me. I was just pulling myself over the edge of the bank when suddenly a figure loomed up above me. I almost lost hold of the rope and gave a small, startled shriek, and then a flash of lightning showed that it was Michael.

"My God, what happened?" he said, hauling me up the last few feet.

"Found Spike," I panted. "Oops!" I was so tired from all my climbing that my knees gave out when I tried to stand. I had to grab onto Michael to keep from falling.

"I can't believe you'd risk your life to save that damned little monster," Michael said, wrapping an arm around me to keep me upright. "You're incredible. Are you all right?"

To tell the truth, I was light-headed, partly from exhaustion and partly because I was rather irrationally enjoying the feeling of having Michael's arm around me. Don't be an idiot, I told myself, and I could tell that Michael felt uncomfortable as well, because his smile was suddenly replaced with a very serious look. But before I could pull back to a more suitable distance—

"Damn!" I yelped, as Spike suddenly became impatient and bit me on the arm. Snarling and growling, he wriggled out of the sling I'd carried him in and ran barking off into the night. Of course when he bit me, I'd jumped, and that caused the bank to start crumbling under my feet, and I would have fallen over the bluff if Michael had not pulled me after him to safety.

"Thank you," I said, as I examined my latest wound. "Unlike Spike, I appreciate having my life saved."

"He's had his shots," Michael said. "I'd better come and help you clean it, though."

"Don't be silly, Michael," I said, pulling away. "I crawled fifteen feet up the damned bluff; I can crawl a few more feet to my own back door."

"Sorry," he said.

"No, I'm sorry," I said. "That was uncalled for. It's just that— is your phone working?"

"No, it went out hours ago," he said. "Why?"

"Never mind, I'll tell you in the morning."

And calling the sheriff would have to wait until the morning, too. I decided that any clues not already washed away would still be there in the morning. I was so exhausted that I barely managed to pull my clothes off and make it to the bed before I fell asleep.

Thursday, July 21

THE NEXT MORNING I CALLED MICHAEL AND DAD AND ASKED THEM to meet me at the bluff, and then called the sheriff. I had to leave a message; the dispatcher had no idea where he was or when he'd be back. By the time I'd convinced one of the deputies to hunt the sheriff down, Michael was already waiting by the bluff.

"The suspense is killing me," he said. "What is the life-or-death matter you mentioned over the phone?"

"Wait a minute," I said. "Here comes Dad; I wanted him to see this, too."

"Is this important, Meg?" Dad said. "I really ought to be over at the Brewsters. Their gardener has no idea how to get the lawn ready for an outdoor event. And I want to finish before everyone gets here tomorrow afternoon."

"I'll help you stomp gophers later, Dad," I said. "This is very important."

My rope was still tied to the tree, but I didn't think I wanted to climb down it again, and I didn't think Dad should. Under my direction, the two of them maneuvered Dad's longest ladder into place against the bluff and we climbed down that way.

They were both appalled at the sight of the booby trap.

"You're lucky to be alive," Michael said, looking pale.

"And I hope you took a shower last night before you went to bed," Dad said, in what seemed, even for him, a monumental non sequitur.

"Dad, I was bone tired and already soaking wet," I said. "What does it matter if I took a shower or not?"

"Meg, these are poison ivy vines!" Dad exclaimed.

"Oh, no," Michael and I said in unison.

"Don't worry, Michael," Dad said, shooing us back up the ladder, "If you take a long, hot shower with plenty of soap, you should have no trouble. Washes off the sap that causes the irritation."

"I can't possibly have poison ivy," I wailed. "I have to be in a wedding in two days."

"Just as soon as the sheriff has finished looking at this, I'm going to hack down all of the poison ivy," Dad announced. "Of course the children shouldn't be down here, but you can't always keep them from wandering. And Michael, you'd better wash that dog of yours. He could be carrying the sap on his fur." With that, he trotted off to shower.

"Oh, great," Michael said. "Do you have any idea how thrilled Spike is going to be when I try to wash him?"

"Probably about as thrilled as he was to be tied up on that ledge. If we want to find out who set that trap, I think we should keep our eyes open for anyone with fresh Spike bites."

"I guess that makes me a suspect," Michael said. "I'm always covered with fresh Spike bites."

"And poison ivy," I said. "Don't forget the poison ivy."

With these comforting thoughts, we both headed off for the showers. To no avail, at least in my case. By evening, I was starting to break out in blisters all over my arms and shins. The sheriff, wisely, inspected the booby trap from afar. When Dad showed up around dinnertime, I asked him to prescribe something for the itching.

"I have some interesting new ideas for treating poison ivy with natural herbs," he announced with great satisfaction. "Don't put anything on the left arm; we'll use that as a control and divide the right one up into patches so we can see which course of treatment works best."

"Nothing doing," I said. "I want heavy-duty chemicals, and I want them now. Give me a shot of whatever it was you gave Rob when he had hives."

"Benadryl," he said. "But really, Meg, that isn't necessary."

"If you won't give me something I'll find someone who will."

"Now, Meg," Dad began.

"Mother, explain it to him," I said. "If I don't have something to stop this itching, not only will I be too nasty and evil-tempered to live with but I will probably become very distracted and screw up some of the last-minute arrangements for one of the weddings."

"She does have a lot on her hands," Mother said.

"Several hundred blisters," Mrs. Fenniman said, giggling.

I shot her an evil look.

"I'm sure someone else will come down with a case soon," Mother said, soothingly. "There will be so many extra people around for the weddings, and so many of them will be from the city and will have no idea what poison ivy looks like."

Dad brightened visibly, and reluctantly agreed to prescribe some conventional medicine for me.

"Is it likely to spread?" Samantha asked, being careful to stay at least ten feet away from me, and upwind. Just my luck to have her drop by tonight; now I was sure she was calculating whether I was going to be presentable enough for her wedding.

"It will probably be all over my entire body by tomorrow," I said. "I'll look like a leper."

"Don't be silly," Mother said. "It can't possibly spread much more by tomorrow. Luckily it's a long dress," she said, glancing at my lotion-smeared legs.

"And no one will be able to see all the blisters on your arms once you have those elbow-length gloves on," added Michael, who had stopped by on his way back from Spike's walk and was show-ing, in my opinion, just barely enough sympathy, considering how narrowly he had escaped sharing my affliction. He was lounging against the porch rail, cool and blister free, while Spike sniffed around the flower beds.

"Oh, that's a great comfort," I said, "And I suppose—ahhhh!" I jumped back as Spike suddenly lunged toward me. To my sur-prise, however, instead of taking a bite out of me, Spike began licking my shins, tail wagging in delight.

"Isn't he cute?" Mother said. "He wants his aunt Meg to know how much he appreciates her saving him, doesn't he?"

"He probably just likes the smell of the ointment," I said, try-ing to push Spike away. "Maybe it's got bacon grease in it or some-thing."

"I've never, ever seen him do that before," Michael said, as he tried to restrain the now-affectionate Spike.

"I must be going," Samantha said, stepping around me on her way down the steps. When she got close to him, Spike suddenly put his tail between his legs and began whining and trying to hide behind me.

"Nasty little beast," Samantha hissed, glowering at the cring-ing Spike.

"Spike's suddenly showing incredibly good taste," Michael murmured to me as he gave the dog an encouraging pat.

Good taste or good sense, I thought. The only other time I'd ever seen Spike act scared was the previous night, when he was trapped on the ledge. What if Spike was acting the same way because he'd suddenly caught sight of the very person who'd tethered him by the booby trap? There wasn't a whole lot of time to worry about it.

The house was beginning to fill up with elderly relatives from out of town and Pam's husband and kids had arrived back from their trip to Australia. One of the few benefits of my poison ivy was that no one was particularly eager to bunk with me, so Mother sent the elderly aunt who had been destined to share my room off to sleep at Mrs. Fenniman's. Definitely a good thing; I was going to need peace and quiet and privacy to keep from losing my mind. And while the extra guests created a lot more work, that had the advantage of distracting me from my itching for whole minutes at a time.

But at the end of the day, despite a cool baking soda bath, the itching kept me awake for quite a while. I was finally drifting off to sleep when I heard an unearthly shriek.

I started upright in panic before realizing that it was the same damned unearthly shriek we'd been hearing repeatedly for the past several days.

"Damn those peacocks," I muttered.

Several more of the birds joined in. I hoped the visiting relatives were all either too deaf to hear them or too tired from traveling to wake. The peacock chorus was definitely building to a crescendo.

"I thought they weren't supposed to be nocturnal," I said to the kitten, who was standing with her back arched, spitting.

And then I suddenly remembered something Mr. Dibbit the peacock farmer had said. About not worrying about trespassers with the peacocks around.

I jumped out of bed, pulled on my clothes, and crept downstairs without turning on any lights. The peacock shrieks were coming from the back door. I would creep to the back door and turn on all the floodlights in the yard and then——

"Yrroowrrr!" I tripped over the kitten, who leaped out of the way with a surprisingly loud screech. I fell flat on my face on the kitchen floor, knocking the glass recycling bin into the aluminum can recycling bin.

I think I heard footsteps. Soft, quick footsteps disappearing down the driveway, and maybe an occasional crunch of gravel. But perhaps it was my imagination. It would have been hard to hear, anyway, over the clinking glass, clattering cans, and howling livestock. By the time I got the floodlights on, the yard was empty. I turned them out again so the peacocks would settle down.

"What on earth is going on?"

Mother had appeared in the kitchen doorway.

"Something scared the peacocks," I replied, as I began to gather up the spilled cans and bottles. "I came to see what."

"I really think we should send those creatures over to the Brewsters'," Mother said.

"I'd rather keep them here. I think what scared them was a prowler."

Mother closed her eyes, and leaned against the doorway. She looked very unlike herself——almost haggard. And scared.

"What is going on here?" she asked, faintly. "What on earth is going on here?"

"I wish I knew. I'm going to have some tea to calm down. Want some?"

"The caffeine will only keep us up," she said, sitting down at the table.

"You can have Eileen's herbal muck if you prefer."

"I'll have Earl Grey, thank you," she said, more like her usual self.

We sat together, quietly sipping our tea. I was kicking myself for not having caught the prowler, desperately curious to find out what the prowler wanted, and generally distracted. I noticed that Mother, too, seemed preoccupied. I wondered what was bothering her——the possibility of a prowler, or something else?

You'll probably never know, I told myself. I could sometimes predict what Mother would do, but I'd given up trying to figure out what she was thinking. Unless, of course . . .

"Mother," I began, "Can I ask you something?"

"Of course, dear? What did you want to know?"

What did I want to know? The answer to about a million questions. What do you think's happening around here? With all your sources of gossip and information, do you know anything that might help solve the murders? And why did you divorce Dad, anyway, and why are you marrying Jake? What do you see in him? What do you know about him? Do you really approve of Rob marrying Samantha? Do you trust her?

But she suddenly looked so vulnerable that I realized there was no way I could ask her any probing questions. Or any questions that would upset her.

"When are you going to let me see the dress I'm wearing in your wedding?"

She smiled.

"Not till the wedding day," she said. "I want it to be a lovely surprise."

We squabbled amiably about this for a little while, which seemed to put her in a much more normal, cheerful mood. We went to bed well past midnight. I locked all the doors and windows. I felt almost guilty doing it. Here in Yorktown, it just wasn't done.

But then, here in Yorktown it had never been open season on my family before.

Friday, July 22

NONE OF THE AUNTS, UNCLES, AND COUSINS SAID ANYTHING ABOUT the noises in the night. Did they all sleep through it, or did they all assume this was just a normal occurrence around the Langslow house?

Michael dropped by after breakfast, leading a creature that looked, at first glance, like a small pink-and-white spotted rat.

"What on earth is that?" I asked, looking at it with alarm.

"Spike. Clipped and daubed with lotion for his poison ivy. The vet says he must be unusually sensitive; dogs aren't normally affected."

He was certainly unusually subdued. His tail was between his legs, and his head hanging down near the floor. I knelt down beside him.

"I know just how you feel, Spike," I said, tentatively patting him. He whined and wagged his tail feebly.

"So, are you looking forward to the rehearsal and the dinner?" Michael asked.

"I'd rather have a root canal. Something is sure to go horribly wrong."

Famous last words.

The rehearsal went well enough, considering. It was a good thing I'd insisted on trying out our costumes, because we only discovered at the church that the hoops were too wide to allow the bridesmaids to march in side by side. The organist would just have to play another half-dozen verses of "Here Comes the Bride." We had to do some ingenious arranging to find enough space for us all to stand around the altar. It was hot, the church was stuffy, and Samantha was in a touchy mood.

"If we can't do this properly, we might as well not do it at all," she said, not once but several dozen times during the rehearsal, whenever anything went wrong. If I hadn't known better, I'd have thought she was looking for an excuse to cancel.

It was a relief when we turned over our costumes to the waiting hands of Michael's ladies and piled into our cars to go to the hotel for the rehearsal dinner.

The festivities started with what was supposed to be a cocktail hour—actually hour and a half—and seemed more like a wake. Samantha's ill temper had poisoned the atmosphere, and despite the presence of air-conditioning and alcohol and the promise of food, no one seemed particularly jolly. Though some of us were trying. Mother glided about the room, telling everyone how beautiful they looked, how well they had done, and how nice tomorrow's ceremony would be. Dad bounced from person to person, cheerfully predicting that it wouldn't be quite as hot tomorrow and reciting the wonders of the coming dinner.

"There's going to be caviar on the buffet, and cold lobster, and a Smithfield ham," I heard him tell several people near me. I grabbed his arm and dragged him to one side.

"What was that you were saying about the buffet?"

"They've got caviar and lobster and—"

"Any escargot? Mango chutney?"

"I don't know; I'll go and check."

"No, you won't," I said. "You're not going anywhere near the buffet until everyone else does."

"That's silly. The sheriff and his men are keeping an eye out—"

"If you eat one bite of it before the dinner begins, you'll be sorry," I said.

"Now, Meg—"

"I mean it, Dad," I warned. "One bite, and I tell Mother what you did with her great-aunt Sophy."

He turned pale and disappeared—not, I noticed, in the direction of the supper room. One small victory. Of course, he was right; the sheriff and his deputies and all the clean-cut pseudo-cousins were swarming about keeping an eye on things, but still, no harm in making sure Dad behaved himself.

I checked my watch. Still half an hour to go. Perhaps the hotel manager could start the dinner earlier than planned. At least when everyone started eating, their disinclination to talk would be less obvious. Assuming anyone was still vertical after another half an hour.

"Meg?" I looked up to see Michael at my shoulder. Mr. Brewster suddenly appeared before us.

"We still have time before dinner," Mr. Brewster said with false heartiness, handing us each another glass of champagne. "Drink up!"

"Cheers," Michael said, taking a healthy swig from the glass. "Meg, can I talk to you about something?"

"Sure; why not?"

"Not here," he said, taking my arm and tugging me toward the hall door.

"Careful of my poison ivy."

What the hell, I wondered, as I followed Michael down the hall. The party's a bust, anyway. He pulled me into the Magnolia Room, where we would be dining shortly. A deputy lurking in the hall gave us a sharp glance and then relaxed when he recognized us.

The outsized chandeliers were not turned on yet, and no waiters were scurrying about, but the table was already set. The silver and crystal of the place settings gleamed even in the dim emergency light, and steam was rising from a couple of covered dishes whose lids were ajar.

"Good," he said, glancing quickly around. "The coast is clear. Lock that door behind you."

"Good grief, Michael," I said. "You're acting very strangely. How much of the champagne have you had?"

"Enough, I hope," he muttered. "Enough to make me decide to—Meg, are you listening to me?"

I confess; I wasn't, really. I was looking over his shoulder. I lifted my finger and pointed at an ominously still figure slumped at the head table.

"Michael, look," I said in a quavery voice. "I think it's the Reverend Pugh."

Michael whirled, swore grimly, and leaped over one of the tables to reach the minister. I followed more slowly. Reverend Pugh, seated in a chair near the center of the table, was face down in a bowl of caviar. His left hand was clutching his chest, and his right hand dangled down beside him, still holding a small piece of Melba toast.

"Call 911," Michael said. "There's a phone on the wall."

I ran to the phone, but I had a feeling it was useless. Michael lifted the minister's head out of the bowl, and I could see that the old man's eyes were wide and staring and there was an expression of great surprise fixed on his face—or as much of it as I could see under the coating of caviar. The phone only connected with the front desk, but I figured that would do just as well. The Reverend Pugh had gotten the jump on his fellow diners for the last time.

"Call 911," I said, slowly and clearly. "One of your guests seems to be in cardiac arrest in the Magnolia Room." I was surprised at how calm I sounded.

"I'll see if Dad is here," I said. Michael nodded; when I left the room he was still staring at the reverend and absently wiping caviar from his hands with one of the napkins.

By the time I returned with Dad, trailed by the many of the wedding party, the hotel manager was already on the scene, obviously torn between his desire to express sympathy and his panic at the thought of the litigation and negative publicity that the hotel could suffer. Dad pronounced the reverend dead, and shook his head grimly at Mother's suggestion that he try to resuscitate the patient.

"Too late for that," he said. "But I think we'll need to call the sheriff in on this."

"Oh, dear," Mother said. "Not again." Dad scanned the crowd and then turned to the hotel manager.

"Please page the sheriff," Dad said. "He's probably in the bar. Tell him what has happened, and tell him Dr. Langslow believes that due to medical evidence found on the scene this death should be treated as a potential homicide."

The hotel manager amazed us by proving it was possible for him to turn even paler than he had already, and vanished without a word.

"Got homicide on the brain if you ask me," someone at the back of the crowd muttered.

"Let's all clear out of here," Dad said. "The sooner we get things organized, the less chance we'll all end up staying here all night." I failed to see what we were going to organize or how clearing the room would get us all home any earlier. Obviously Dad just wanted to get us all out from underfoot.

"We will all wait in the lounge while Mrs. Brewster and I see the manager immediately to arrange a change of rooms," Mother announced firmly, taking Mrs. Brewster by the arm and guiding her out. The rest followed, sheeplike. Dad stopped me as I started out.

"The sheriff will want to talk to you and Michael about finding the body," he said apologetically.

I found a window seat just outside the Magnolia Room and watched the comings and goings of the sheriff and his deputies for what seemed the millionth time. The various clean-cut pseudo-relatives were blowing their cover to join the investigation, and looking chagrined that another murder might have happened right under their noses.

Mother came back to tell me that they had decided to cancel the dinner after all, and the guests were going home. Michael went and fetched us both sandwiches. From outside the hotel.

"Thanks," I said, through a full mouth. "I didn't realize how hungry I was."

"I think we're all a little in shock."

"And I feel so guilty."

Michael started.

"Guilty? Why?" he asked. "You didn't have anything to do with his death."

"No. But I keep thinking I ought to be feeling grief. Or empathizing with his family. Or concentrating on what the sheriff might need to know. And instead, all I can think about is getting this over with so we can start getting the wedding back on track. Do you have any idea how hard it is going to be to find a minister less than twenty-four hours before the ceremony?"

"Don't scratch your arms," Michael advised. "You'll only make your blisters worse."

It was clear that by the time the sheriff was finished with all of us and we could go home, it would be late. In fact, it was already too late to call anyone. So I collared Mother, Mrs. Brewster, and Mrs. Fenniman. We compiled a list of possible substitute ministers. Mother and Mrs. Fenniman thought of most of the names, of course. I coaxed Michael into helping me look up their addresses and numbers in the phone book. Mother and Mrs. Fenniman even had very definite—and I hoped accurate—ideas of how early we dared call each minister without offending. Since Mother and Mrs. Fenniman knew most of them, they ranked the names, divided up the calling list according to who was best acquainted with each potential victim, and agreed to meet at our house at 6:00 A.M.

Saturday, July 23. Samantha's wedding day.

I DRAGGED MYSELF UP AT FIVE-THIRTY TO HELP WITH THE MINISTER search. We got Mother installed in her study and Mrs. Fenniman in the living room with the Brewsters' cellular phone. I transcribed their notes on to our master list, kept strong coffee flowing, and started cooking breakfast to keep from biting my nails.

Samantha and Mrs. Brewster came over about eight.

"The bad news is that they're nearly through the original list and haven't found anyone yet," I reported, pouring coffee for them, although I wondered if I shouldn't have made it decaf, given the obvious state of their nerves. Or iced tea; apparently the weather gremlins wanted Samantha's wedding day to be at least as hot as Eileen's and were getting an early start. "The good news is that the few ministers we've been able to reach have suggested another couple of dozen, and there are a few more in the phone book that we could just call blind."

"We'll have to cancel the wedding," Samantha said, tight-lipped. It was only about the hundredth time she'd said that since we found Reverend Pugh. If I hadn't known better, I'd have thought she *wanted* to cancel the wedding.

"Oh, no, dear," Mother said, coming in to refill her coffee cup and nibble on the fruit I had laid out. "You could always have the wedding at home. If we run out of ministers, there's always Cousin Kate. She's a justice of the peace; she could perform the ceremony. And it would be no trouble, since she's coming to the wedding anyway." I could see a look of panic cross Samantha's face. Cousin Kate is five feet tall and twice my weight. She has a hog-caller's voice, and what my mother tactfully refers to as an earthy sense of humor. She'd been known to boom out no-nonsense advice about the procreative side of matrimony in the middle of the ceremony. I could just see her officiating at Rob and Samantha's wedding, but I suppressed the grin that the thought provoked. Apparently Samantha had met Cousin Kate as well.

"Oh, I couldn't ask that. Not when she's been invited as a guest. It would be an imposition. Besides," she said, warming to the topic, "I'm sure she would perform a lovely ceremony, but it just wouldn't really feel like a wedding to me if it wasn't in church."

"I understand, dear," Mother said. "I'm sure we'll find someone. I just wanted you to know that there's really no reason to worry. You'd better run along home before Rob comes down and sees you. I know you young folks think that's a silly superstition, but it never hurts to be careful." She finished filling a plate with fruit—including all of the strawberries I'd set out—and drifted back to her study. Samantha, gauging more accurately than Mother the likelihood of Rob rising before ten, stayed around to eat a hearty breakfast—including the rest of the strawberries we had in the house.

Michael arrived about nine o'clock, walking Spike.

"I was just going to take off to pick up Mrs. Tranh and the ladies," he said, peering through the screen door. "I thought I should come by to make sure there hadn't been any changes in plan."

"We don't have a minister yet if that's what you mean," I said. "But we have a justice of the peace on call, and if we reach the drop-dead point and have to relocate the ceremony to the Brewsters' lawn, we'll track you down either at the shop or at the parish hall as soon as we know."

"Oh, my," Mrs. Brewster muttered. "I hope we don't have to do that. The place will be swarming with caterers from ten o'clock on." She and Samantha were just getting up to leave when Mother and Mrs. Fenniman came in to share what they blithely assumed was good news.

"I've found a minister," Mother announced. "Cousin Frank

Hollingworth. I don't know why I didn't think of him before. And I've gotten the vestry's permission for him to perform the ceremony at the church, just as a formality. Given the circumstances they were all perfectly understanding. Now if someone can just go and pick him up, we'll be fine."

"Where is he?" I asked, warily, as I mentally traced family trees, trying to place the Rev. Frank Hollingworth. Samantha and her mother were breathing sighs of relief. Prematurely, in my opinion. The Reverend Frank, whoever he might be, was not in our clutches yet.

"In Richmond," Mother said. "It's an hour's drive, so we'd better get someone started immediately."

"Do we have to send someone for him?" Samantha said, peevishly. "I mean, Dad would be happy to reimburse him for the mileage."

"He doesn't have a car, dear," Mother said.

"He could rent one," Samantha countered.

"I'm not sure he has a license anymore," Mother said. "And anyway, I had to promise the director of the home that someone from the family would pick him up at the door and then deliver him back tomorrow."

"Someone from the home," I said. "What home is that? A nursing home?" Samantha and her mother looked taken aback.

"Don't worry, dear. They're sending someone to look after him. To see he that takes his medication and all that."

"Mother," I said, as the light dawned, "You aren't talking about *crazy* Frank, are you?"

"That's no way to refer to your cousin," Mother chided. "Besides, Sarah says that he's been coming home for the occasional weekend for several months now, and he's been a perfect lamb. All the visits have been absolutely uneventful." I wondered, fleetingly, how badly three decades of being a Hollingworth by marriage had warped Cousin Sarah's definition of uneventful.

"Who is this Uncle Frank?" Mrs. Brewster asked, dubiously. "I mean, is he a duly ordained, practicing minister?" I wondered if she thought we were kidding about the crazy part. She'd learn.

"Oh, yes," Mother said, brightly. "Ordained, at any rate, twenty-five or thirty years ago."

"Is he Episcopalian?" Mrs. Brewster asked.

"Well, no," Mother said. "I can't remember the name, but it's a small, progressive-thinking denomination. Such a spiritual man. But he had to retire early and come home. He always had rather delicate nerves, and the stress of parish life was simply too much for him. He was pastor of a very large church in San Francisco then."

"Haight-Ashbury, actually," I said to Michael, in an undertone. Michael was suddenly overcome with coughing.

"He'll do wonderfully for the wedding," Mother said, handing Michael a glass of water.

"As long as he's given up his theory that wearing clothing is a sinful attempt to hide oneself from the stern but just eye of the Lord," I said. Now that I remembered who Cousin Frank was, I thought Cousin Kate would definitely be a safer bet.

"I'm sure everything will be fine," Mother said, shaking her head as if to imply that I was teasing. "He's looking forward to his release so eagerly that I'm sure he won't do anything that might delay it. Of course," she went on thoughtfully, "It might be just as well to dispense with the sermon. No sense tempting fate."

"What a pity," I remarked. "I was looking forward to hearing the latest on the theological implications of UFOs and other extraterrestrial manifestations." Michael appeared to be choking in earnest; I had to pound him on the back several times before he could speak.

"If you're really stuck for a volunteer, I could go after I deliver Mrs. Tranh and the ladies to the parish hall," he offered, when he'd recovered.

"No, that's very sweet of you, Michael, but we don't want to send anyone who already has something useful to do," Mother said. "I'll have Jake do it," she decided, and trotted out to issue Jake his orders.

I think it said a great deal for their sense of desperation that Samantha and Mrs. Brewster threw themselves into the arrangements for transporting Cousin Frank without saying a word about his suitability for the role into which we'd just drafted him.

With the problem of the minister taken care of, we raced to get everything else done on schedule. We ferried everyone over to the parish hall, leaving Mrs. Fenniman at the Brewsters' to harry the caterers, decorators, and musicians until shortly before the ceremony.

Samantha kept sending me back and forth to check on details. "It's the little details that really make the occasion," she said primly.

The press arrived, in the form of Mother's cousin Matilda who wrote the society column for the *Town Crier*. She kept trying to interview various members of the wedding party about the Reverend Pugh's death. She and I had some harsh words on the subject of the First Amendment when I finally kicked her out of the parish hall.

"Meg?" Pam asked, sticking her head in the door. "Are you busy?"

"Of course not," I snapped. "What is it now?"

"Jake's back with Cousin Frank and his . . ." Pam gestured vaguely as she looked for a suitably diplomatic word. "Keeper" would have been my choice. "Attendant" would have been reasonably polite. Before she could make up her mind on a word, the gentleman in question popped into the room.

"Meg," Mother said sternly. "We simply can't have Cousin Frank and his assistant wearing the clothes they've traveled in." As if it were my fault that Cousin Frank arrived in jeans and a sports coat, accompanied by a burly uniformed orderly.

"Of course not. I called Richmond while Jake was on his way and found out their sizes. We have one of Rob's suits for Cousin Frank, and we've borrowed one from Mr. Brewster for the assistant. They're not quite the right size, but two of Michael's seamstresses are ready to do any minor alterations. They'll be fine."

"Well, that's all right, then," Mother said.

"Gentlemen, if you'll follow me," I said. Cousin Frank and the . . . assistant obediently followed me down to the basement of the parish hall where the men were dressing.

They cleaned up well, I had to admit. Once we had them in the suits, it almost looked as if we'd brought in a pair of distinguished clerics for the occasion, one white and one black. Cousin Frank was behaving impeccably, and Mr. Ronson, the attendant, was either a very good-natured man or found us all highly amusing. Possibly both. He followed Cousin Frank around unobtrusively and cheerfully, creating a small and unfortunately temporary trail of calm in his wake.

I went upstairs to report to Samantha that the minister was present and accounted for. When I stuck my head into the room she was, surprisingly, alone. Perhaps all the bridesmaids had gone off to gawk at Cousin Frank. Samantha had her back to the door and was talking on the phone.

"After the ceremony," I heard her say into the mouthpiece. "Yes. Yes, it's all arranged."

I ducked back into the hall, prepared to eavesdrop a little more, and then heard footsteps coming up the stairs. Drat. I bustled into the room as if I had just arrived.

"Oh, sorry," I said. "Just wanted to tell you the minister has arrived."

"Thank you, we'll talk later," she said into the phone. In a very different tone of voice than the one I'd overheard.

What could she be up to? Arranging some sort of surprise?

Well, luckily it wasn't likely to be for me. I wasn't in the mood for surprises.

We struggled into our dresses with the help of two of Michael's ladies. At least Samantha didn't need to be jollied out of last-minute jitters. She was icily calm, and no detail escaped her eye. Nothing shook her. At the last minute, we discovered a run in her pantyhose. No one could possibly have seen it, unless she was planning on dancing the cancan at the reception, which I doubted, but she insisted she couldn't go out with a run. Fortunately, I'd brought over an extra pair.

"Thank you," she said. "That was very organized of you."

High praise from Samantha, and probably the only thanks I'd get for the past six months of effort. I found myself wincing as she slit open the plastic on the pantyhose package with one swift, graceful slice of her nail file.

It took a while for all the bridesmaids to totter down the stairs. And a while for us all to negotiate the rather damp walk to the door of the church. The atmosphere was humid as a jungle, and we heard occasional ominous rumbles of thunder in the distance. The impending storm, together with stage fright, seemed to set everyone on edge. There was much whining about ruined shoes and frizzing hair. Perhaps it would be better after the storm broke, although I dearly hoped that wouldn't happen until after the reception.

We marched in one by one, an interminable procession of pink ruffled dolls. I found myself slightly teary-eyed when we walked into the church, thinking of all the times I'd seen Reverend Pugh in the pulpit. I wondered if I was the only one thinking of him. There was a lot of sniffling in the congregation, but then there usually is at a wedding. I was momentarily startled when I thought I saw tears running down several people's faces. Then I realized it was probably only sweat; the church was an oven. I'll think about Reverend Pugh later, I told myself. The ceremony was beginning, and I had to concentrate on not fainting.

"If anyone here can show just cause why this man and woman should not be joined in holy matrimony," intoned Cousin Frank, "Let him speak now or forever hold his peace." He paused and looked around pugnaciously, as if daring anyone to speak out. Mr. Ronson, at his side, beamed at the congregation as if he were rather hoping someone would.

One of the ushers on my side of the circle picked that moment to faint. He fell over backwards, striking a large flower-twined candelabrum on his way down. The candelabrum fell, taking down two others with it in a chain reaction, and in leaping away from the falling candelabra, some of the wedding party set still more candelabra in motion. For a few moments, burning candles were flying through the air in every direction. Bridesmaids shrieked, ushers grabbed vases and doused small flames with the water they contained, without bothering to remove the flowers first. After a minute or so, when all the fires had been put out and stray candles and vegetation kicked aside, we noticed that the offending usher was not only still unconscious, but had managed to gash his head rather badly on the altar step. I stage-whispered orders to the remaining ushers to carry him out. Four of them got the idea immediately: they lifted him on their shoulders and marched decorously out. Perhaps a little too decorously; they rather resembled absentminded pallbearers who had mislaid the coffin. Fortunately the sight of Dad, trotting briskly and cheerfully down the aisle after them, diluted the funereal effect. After leaving the victim in the vestibule with Dad, they marched back in again quite beautifully and closed ranks with the rest of the bridal party as if the whole maneuver had been rehearsed in advance. I was proud of them.

For the rest of the ceremony, it was obvious from the cold precision of Samantha's voice during her responses that she was furious with the world in general and looking to take it out on someone at the first opportunity. It was equally obvious from the shakiness of Rob's tone that he fully expected to be the someone. The occasional sounds from the vestibule of Dad matter-of-factly ministering to the fallen usher didn't help. But Cousin Frank carried on splendidly in his wonderfully sonorous voice, and had almost succeeded in restoring some shreds of dignity to the proceedings when, just as he was about to pronounce them husband and wife, the ambulance pulled up, siren screeching, to take the felled usher away.

Samantha looked truly grim as she and Rob walked down the aisle, and I decided it was a lucky thing we were having all the photos taken after the actual event. She would have time to calm down and an incentive to remove the Lizzie Borden look from her face.

It began to pour just as we got out of the church, so we all milled back in again, causing total gridlock as guests trying to head for the reception tried to squeeze through the squadron of hoop skirts. After the guests finally cleared out, the photographer put us through our paces for about an hour. Of course, on the bright side, it had stopped raining by the time we took off for the reception, and when we arrived the guests were just beginning to venture out from under the tent and most of the food hadn't been set out.

I was mildly depressed when we arrived at the Brewsters' house. Even with the interruptions, it had been a gorgeous ceremony. The dresses were ridiculous, but in a bizarre sort of way the overall effect was beautiful. Once he'd gotten over his disappointment at not being allowed to give a sermon, Cousin Frank had really thrown himself into the occasion and performed a beautiful ceremony. After the charming eccentricity of Eileen's Renaissance music on virginals and lutes, I'd actually enjoyed hearing a really big church organ boom out "Here Comes the Bride" and other old standards.

But I kept remembering Eileen's and Steven's faces during their ceremony. Samantha's face didn't light up when she saw Rob standing at the altar. I got the distinct impression she was checking him out to see if he was properly combed and dressed. And Rob didn't look transfigured. Just nervous.

I tried to enjoy the reception, or at least look as if I were enjoying it. But I had the nagging feeling there was something I ought to have done that would blow up in my face any minute. Perhaps it was a side effect of the poison ivy.

Barry was hovering, as usual. For once, he was proving useful.

"I'm not sure this is real Beluga," I said to Barry, handing him a cracker heaped with caviar. "Does it taste right to you?"

Barry downed the cracker.

"Tastes fine to me," he said.

"No, you ate it too fast. Here, try another one. Roll it around in your mouth for a while. Get the full flavor."

Barry obligingly did so.

"Still tastes fine," he said, when he'd finished.

"Maybe it's the crackers. They have a strong flavor. Just try some by itself." I handed him a heaping spoonful.

"It's fine," he said, again.

"Here, clear your palate with this water," I said, handing him a glass. "Now try again. Are you sure it tastes like real Beluga?"

"I'm not sure I know what real Beluga tastes like," he said finally. "But this stuff tastes great."

"Go take some to Mrs. Fenniman, will you? See what she thinks."

Barry lumbered off with a plate of caviar and crackers for Mrs. Fenniman.

"Well, the ceremony went off," Michael said, arriving at my side.

"I notice you didn't say anything about how it went off," I said, craning over his shoulder. "The less said about that the better."

"What are you looking for?"

"Barry. Does he look healthy to you?"

"As a Clydesdale," Michael said, frowning. "Why?"

"I've just fed him a vast quantity of caviar. If he doesn't keel over in the next ten minutes or so, I'm going to have some myself."

"Bloodthirsty wench," was his comment.

"Has he tried the shrimp yet?" Dad asked, plaintively. "And the salsa?"

"I'm sure he'll wander back in a minute," I said, reassuringly. "We'll have him graze his way through the whole buffet if you like."

"Not a bad idea, at that," Michael said. "The guests seem curiously reluctant to eat today."

He was right. Usually by this time the buffet would have been decimated. Now, most of the crowd sat around sipping drinks and surreptitiously watching Barry, Cousin Horace, and the few other hardy souls who'd already braved the buffet. I decided to load up my plate while the coast was clear. I could always stand around and hold it until enough people had dined that I felt safe.

"Damn, I'll be glad to get out of this dress," I said. I tried to scratch my blisters unobtrusively and then realized that I shouldn't have. Scratching set everything revealed by my décolletage into jiggling motion.

"You look very nice," Dad said approvingly. "Michael, you'll have to tell your ladies what a fine job they've done."

"Thanks; I will," he said.

"It may look nice, but if I ever wear a dress this low cut again, I'm going to put a sign at the bottom of my cleavage," I said. "I've seen a bumper sticker with the wording I want: If you can read this, you're too damn close."

"It's not really that bad," Dad said, as Michael spluttered on his champagne.

"Oh no?" I said. "Watch what happens when he comes over,"

I said, pointing to Doug, my nemesis from parties past, who seemed to be looking in our direction. Michael and Dad looked at him, and he seemed to change his mind.

"Did one of you glare at him?" I asked. "If so, you have my eternal thanks."

"I think we both did," Michael said, as he and Dad burst out laughing.

"Well, at least for the moment all I have to worry about is stray bits of food," I said, as I caught a bit of caviar before it disappeared into the bodice. I noticed that more people were eating, and Barry was showing no signs of distress, so I'd begun nibbling from my plate.

It took a while for the guests to find their way to the buffet, but after a few centuries the party began to show signs of life. Especially after word spread through the crowd that the county DA's date was an FBI agent she'd met during the bureau's local investigation on Samantha's former fiancé. I had to give Samantha credit: she hadn't turned a hair when he came through the reception line. Maybe she didn't remember him. I could spot half a dozen of the preternaturally clean-cut new "cousins" cruising the crowd like eager human sharks, waiting to pounce. I was torn between hoping they'd find someone to pounce on and hoping everything went off quietly.

Dad was installed by the punch bowl, and from his gestures I suspected he was relating the graphic details of the usher's injury to anyone who would listen. I was trapped by a long-winded aunt who was telling me every moment of the weddings of each of her four daughters. I was smiling and making polite noises while daydreaming of pulling off my dress, scratching my poison ivy, and then flinging myself naked into the pool. I almost jumped out of my skin when Mrs. Brewster suddenly appeared behind me.

"Where's Samantha?" she asked. "Shouldn't she be getting ready to throw her bouquet?"

"She's——she was right over there," I stammered. Mrs. Brewster frowned. Losing the bride was not acceptable behavior for a maid of honor. "I'll just go and find her and hurry her up," I babbled.

I cruised through the crowd. Samantha was nowhere to be found. Everyone had just seen her a few minutes ago and expected she'd be right back. I could see Mrs. Brewster fuming by the punch bowl. Evidently Dad's adventures in the emergency room were failing to charm her. I decided to check the house. Perhaps she'd gone in to use the bathroom. Or to cool off.

I grabbed a few hors d'oeuvres on my way past the buffet and trudged upstairs to Samantha's room. She wasn't there. I saw only Michael and the two little seamstresses staring out the window.

"Where's Samantha?" I asked. Michael pointed out the window. I managed to find enough space to peer out over the seamstresses' heads.

"Dashed out without even changing," he muttered.

Mother and Mrs. Brewster came in.

"So where is she?" Mother gushed. "I can't wait to see her in that lovely suit!"

It was a long driveway, but down at the other end we could see that Rob, still faintly elegant in his damp, limp gray morning suit was helping Samantha into the passenger's seat of her red MG. Stuffing her in, actually; she was still in her bridal gown, hoops and all, and he was bashing armfuls of expensive fabric down around her. God knows how he was going to find the gearshift under all that froth. He didn't even try to deal with the veil, just took it off, crumpled it into a ball, and shoved it down in the space behind the seats.

It was a lucky thing their backs were to us; they couldn't see the venomous looks they were getting from the two seamstresses. Or hear Michael sighing, "Oh, shit." I echoed his sentiments: what, pray tell, had happened to the bouquet throwing? We'd had a special throwing bouquet made, a slightly more compact version of

the one Samantha had carried down the aisle, thereby nearly dou-
bling the bouquet budget. Perhaps she'd held an impromptu
throwing while I'd been looking for her. I peered down the driveway. No signs of a bouquet. But I did see Mrs. Fenniman pop up,
apparently from the azalea bed, and begin throwing birdseed at
them from one of the little lace-trimmed bags, and Rob was just
getting into the car when——

"Where's Samantha?" Rob said, sticking his head in the door.
Wearing his traveling clothes.

"Rob?" I said.

"If Rob's here——" Mrs. Brewster said.

"Who the hell is that?" I asked.

"Such language!" said Mother.

"Who the hell is who?" asked Rob.

"Who the hell is that driving off with Samantha?" Mrs. Brewster and I said, in unison.

"Oh, dear." Mother sighed. "That's very bad luck when two
people say the same thing. You must both link your little fingers together and say——"

"Not now, Mother," I said, on my way to the door.

Despite the handicap of my hoop skirts, I won the race to the
end of driveway, finishing a hair before Mrs. Brewster. Michael
came loping along close behind us, while Mother and Rob, not
being quite sure what the fuss was all about, finished in a dead heat
for last. Mrs. Fenniman, who had obviously gotten rather heavily
into the Episcopalian punch, still had a great deal of birdseed left,
so she chucked some at us as we pulled up. But, of course, we were
all too late. As Mrs. Brewster and I reached the end of the driveway, we could just see the MG disappearing around the corner.
And catch a few bars of a Beach Boys song blaring from the radio.
"I Get Around."

That's Samantha for you. Always a stickler for those appropriate little details that really make an occasion.

As we stood, dumbfounded, something fell out of the dogwood trees above us and bounced off my head onto the gravel. Samantha's wedding bouquet. I heard a burst of high musical laughter from the upstairs window and looked up to see the seamstresses bobbing back out of sight.

"So that's what she did with it," Mrs. Brewster said triumphantly, as if the discovery of the bouquet more than made up for Samantha's absence.

"You seem to have an affinity for these things," Michael remarked, as he picked up the now-battered bouquet and handed it to me.

As soon as Rob understood what was going on, he insisted on dashing after them in the first car available. Mine. Several other birdseed-bearing guests had arrived at the end of the driveway, and they and Mrs. Fenniman cheered and pelted him as he pulled out. As word of the——was elopement the appropriate word? Flight, I suppose, was more accurate. As word of the flight spread, most of the male guests felt compelled for some reason to drive off in pursuit. No one was too clear on who they were pursuing, Rob, or Samantha and her fellow traveler, who turned out to be Ian, the last-minute substitute usher. There was a great deal of coming and going as cars drove up to report on where they'd been and what they'd seen, or hadn't seen and then set out again fortified with food and drink from the buffet. Mrs. Fenniman and her fellow harpies stood around by the driveway, swilling punch and sniping at the passing cars with handfuls of birdseed, giggling uproariously all the while, until at last they reached the point where they couldn't open the little bags and began throwing them whole, at which point somebody had the good sense to confiscate the remaining birdseed. They tried to keep up the barrage with acorns and pine cones, but that took most of the fun out of it and they lost interest fairly quickly.

Except for a couple of bridesmaids who considered themselves entitled to have hysterics and the mothers or friends who evidently felt compelled to cater to them, most of the women gathered around the food tables like a twittering Greek chorus. The peacocks, unsettled by all the chaos, adjourned to the roof for a filibuster. Mrs. Brewster retired to her bedroom with a migraine. Jake undertook the job of running around fetching her cold compresses, relaying her messages to Mr. Brewster (who had locked himself in his study with a bottle of Scotch), hunting down and locking up valuable items Mrs. Brewster feared might disappear in the confusion, and generally serving as chief toady and errand boy. I had no idea why—maybe it was a role he was used to playing with Mother—but he certainly made points with me for taking it off my hands. Personally, I had my doubts at first whether Mrs. Brewster's headache was real or merely convenient. I decided it was probably real—she did, after all, have reason—when she emerged looking absolutely ghastly and demanded, imperiously, that someone Do Something About Those Peacocks. Which was how I found myself at about seven o'clock, sitting on the roof of the Brewsters' house with Michael.

He was the only male who was neither half-drunk nor off in pursuit of the elusive trio. Instead, he had been lounging elegantly around the house, sipping punch, supervising the seamstresses' packing, flirting with me, eavesdropping shamelessly on every conversation within earshot, and obviously enjoying the hell out of the whole situation. But with a straight face, I had to give him that. When Mrs. Brewster issued her ultimatum, he volunteered to help me with the peacock roundup. We changed into jeans, unearthed Dad's ladder, and together managed to chase the birds back down into the yard. Some of the men who were tipsy enough that their wives had restrained them from driving off in search of Rob, Ian, and Samantha took over the roundup.

"I vote we let them handle it from now on," I said. "After all, someone's got to stay here, to repel the peacocks if they attempt another boarding."

"Fine by me," Michael said. "I think there's actually a breeze up here."

He stretched out luxuriously on a flat part of the roof with his head propped up against a second story dormer. He was right about the breeze. It was ruffling the lock of hair that had fallen over his forehead. I decided at that moment that I'd had enough punch.

"Everyone seems to be getting on rather well in spite of everything," he remarked, startling me out of my reverie.

"Why shouldn't they?" I asked. "I mean, what did you expect?"

"I don't know. His friends at one end of the yard reviling her, her friends at the other darkly hinting that he drove her to it, the minister darting back and forth striving in vain to prevent bloodshed, people storming off in outrage. Everyone seems rather . . . I don't know. Cheerful?"

"I expect they are, really. I mean, for one thing, half the people here have known both of them all their lives, so the friends of the brides versus friends of the groom thing is out. The main debate is between the people who are saying 'I told you so' and the ones saying 'Well, I never!' And no one's going to leave now; they might miss the next disaster. Samantha surprised us all, she really did throw the event of the season, although not quite in the sense we expected. Cheerful is an understatement; they're having the time of their lives."

A cheer went up from the side yard. Somebody had dragged the nets off Dad's strawberry beds and trapped one of the peacocks. Unfortunately, two guests had gotten entangled as well, and the peacock, somewhat the worse for wear, escaped before the guests did.

"If they deduct for damages, you're going to lose your deposit on those peacocks," he remarked.

"Not *my* deposit," I replied. "The Brewsters are footing the bill for the livestock."

"Aha! The first crack in the facade of interfamily solidarity. But somehow I expect you'll still be the one who has to cope with their owner."

"Probably," I replied. Perhaps I hadn't had enough punch after all. Then again, maybe my suspicions were right and Mr. Dibbet didn't really want them back.

Just then Rob burst back into the yard. He was disheveled and slightly bloody, attempting to shake Uncle Lou and Cousin Mark from the death grip they seemed to have on his arms. And trailed by several deputies.

"Now what?" I moaned.

Just then one of the peacocks gave a particularly ghastly shriek. Both deputies drew their weapons and swung into a defensive formation in an impressively calm and efficient manner. Michael and I crouched behind a dormer until that misunderstanding had been settled and then climbed back down the ladder to catch the next act.

Samantha and Ian had apparently gone to the airport and taken a commuter flight to Miami. Uncle Lou and Cousin Mark had restrained Rob from taking the next flight and had escorted him back home. They were still standing guard over him. Presumably, so were the deputies. Silly, if you asked me. Did they think he would rush out onto the runway at Miami International to challenge Ian to armed combat, with Samantha going to the victor? An aunt who owned the local travel agency was on the phone using her connections to find out if they'd booked a continuing flight.

"They don't need to book one," I pointed out. "They've got the honeymoon tickets."

"Surely she didn't give Ian Rob's ticket," Mother said incredulously.

"She ran away with him," I countered. "Why shouldn't she give him Rob's ticket?"

"She didn't even wait to see if I passed the bar exam," Rob kept saying, in an indignant tone.

"Rob," I said, when I could get his attention, "where's my car?"

"Car?"

"You were driving my car," I said. "Where is it?"

"Oh, God, I left it at the airport."

"At the airport? You drove away and left my car parked in the airport parking lot?"

He winced.

"Well, in the loading zone, actually."

"Good heavens, Rob," Uncle Lou said. "Why didn't you tell us that? They'll have towed it by now."

"Was that Meg's car?" Cousin Mark asked. "I saw them towing away a little blue car when we drove off."

"You left my car to be towed?" I said. Rob hung his head.

"Don't scold your brother, dear," Mother said. "Think what a trying day he's had."

"What do you mean a trying day?" I said. "Trying day? He's just had one of the luckiest escapes in history. What the hell is trying about—"

"Meg," Michael said, grabbing my arm with one hand and steering me toward the house, "let's go call the airport."

"Trying!" I shrieked back over my shoulder as Michael dragged me away.

"We can find out where they've towed your car—"

"Talk about trying! How about someone trying to find out if Samantha and Ian happen to be carrying a suitcase full of embezzled cash!"

"I'll give you a ride," Michael went on relentlessly.

"How about trying to find out if she knows anything about digitalis—"

Michael managed to drag me away from the reception, though not before I'd made a fool of myself shrieking several more wild accusations about Samantha. We collected his convertible and sped out to the airport to find where they'd towed my car. And then across the county to the towing company's lot. Which was run by one of Mother's more feckless cousins. And was closed tight when we arrived, with a sign on the gate: Back Soon.

"I wonder how soon is soon," Michael said.

"Great," I said. "He hauls my car out here in the middle of nowhere and then dashes off looking for another victim."

"Well, relax. Look at the bright side: it's probably a great time not to be around your neighborhood."

"I'm sorry to drag you out like this."

"The fun was just about over at the house," he said. "And I wanted the chance to talk to you."

"I'm not very good company right now."

"Understandable," he replied.

"Do you think she did it?" I demanded.

"Who?"

"Samantha."

"Run away? I'm sure she did it."

"I didn't mean that; I meant the murders."

Michael shrugged again.

"You've got me. Forget about the murders for now. And Samantha."

"Easier said than done," I muttered. I was getting sleepy—I had gotten up at five-thirty, after all. I leaned back in my very comfortable seat. I closed my eyes.

"Meg," Michael said, in a firm tone.

"Mmm?" There was a pause. Whatever Michael wanted to talk to me about, he was in no hurry. Neither was I. It was very peaceful out here in the middle of nowhere, with just the frogs and crickets. Much more peaceful than it would be back home. The tow truck driver could take his time.

Suddenly I felt my shoulder being shaken.

"All right," I growled. "I'm not going to sleep."

"You did already," Michael said. "You've been asleep for hours. The tow truck driver is finally here. Are you awake enough to drive home?"

I was. And fortunately, by the time I got home, things were fairly quiet around the neighborhood.

Sunday, July 24

SUNDAY WAS A BUSY DAY. ALSO AN AWKWARD ONE.

"Should we go over to help the Brewsters with the cleanup?" Pam wondered.

"They've already got a cleaning service coming" I said. "They can afford to pay for it and still bail out Samantha, I'm sure."

"We don't want to look as if we're avoiding them," Pam countered.

"Why? Aren't we?"

"You can't exactly blame them for what Samantha did," she protested.

"Why not? They raised her. Besides, if you were the Brewsters, wouldn't we be the last people you wanted to see right now?"

"Hmm," she said.

"Don't you think you should go over to start sending back the presents?" Mother asked.

"Surely the Brewsters can do that."

"One does want to make sure it's done right," Mother said. Translation: make sure all the family members who sent valuable or antique gifts got their stuff back safely.

"I think we should wait a day or so, Mother," I said. "I can get a head start making up some labels; I've got the index cards with the record of who sent what." Translation: the Brewsters won't be able to put anything over on us and abscond with any valuable presents.

"I imagine they've got a lot of food that they don't feel like eating just going to waste," Dad said. "Do you suppose I should go over and offer to help them with it?"

"No, Dad."

The Brewsters weren't picking up the phone or answering the door, anyway; I'd tried the one and Mrs. Fenniman the other. I left a polite message on their machine apologizing for intruding when they had so much on their minds and asking them to let me know if there was anything that needed to be done.

"I think they're packing," Mrs. Fenniman reported with glee.

The only person in the house behaving normally was Rob. Which was a little abnormal, considering that he'd more or less just been deserted at the altar. Granted, he couldn't officially start the annulment process until Monday morning, but still, you'd think he'd be spending a little time reflecting on the whole disaster. But he came down at ten, ate a hearty breakfast, and spent the day curled up in his hammock with his books and papers. Working on Lawyers from Hell, I realized.

"I thought he'd already taken the bar exam," Mrs. Fenniman commented.

"He's working on a . . . related project," I said.

"He's taking this so bravely," Mother said. Dad and I looked at each other.

"You could say that," Dad said.

"If you ask me, he's relieved," I muttered to Dad.

"I agree," Dad said. "But don't upset your Mother. She likes fussing over him."

The sheriff dropped by to tell us that there had, indeed, been digitalis in the caviar at the rehearsal dinner. And that it would probably be ten to fourteen days before they released the reverend's body, which was a relief. Callous as it may sound, we had enough on our hands with the cleanup from Rob and Samantha's ill-fated wedding and preparations for Mother's event; we didn't need a funeral on top of everything else.

Monday, July 25

MONDAY MORNING, WHILE THE FAMILY LEGAL MINDS DRAGGED ROB off to begin the annulment proceedings, Mother hauled me into Be-Stitched and insisted that I be blindfolded while I tried on my bridesmaid's dress for her wedding.

"This is totally ridiculous," I said.

"Humor me, Meg dear," she said.

"Don't I always?"

All I could tell about the dress was that the material was some kind of butter-soft silk that made you want to stroke it, and that it didn't have either hoops or an excessively low-cut front. Mother was ecstatic with its appearance, which didn't reassure me in the slightest, and Mrs. Tranh and the ladies seemed pleased, which did reassure me, but only a little.

"How does it look, really?" I asked Michael, who came back to the house to have lunch with us.

"Fantastic," he said. "Really, you're going to like it."

"I damn well better."

"You really don't like giving up control of things, do you?" Michael asked.

"No, I don't," I said. "That sounds like Dad's capsule analysis of my character flaws. What else has he been telling you?"

"He thinks you intimidate most men—he's not sure whether it's deliberate or not—and on those rare occasions when you meet someone who's not intimidated by you, you run for cover."

"Really."

"He's decided that the best thing for you would be to meet

the right guy under circumstances that would allow you to get to know each other as friends before the possibility of anything else comes up."

"Please tell me he's not about to start playing matchmaker," I said, wincing.

"I . . . think he's perfectly happy to leave things alone for the moment. Until all the weddings are all over."

"That's fine; after the weddings are all over, I can escape."

"We'll see," Michael said.

I wondered if he was planning on helping Dad. Just great. Dad and Michael, sitting around discussing the sorry state of my love life and trying to do something about it. The idea depressed me. And seeing Jake at one end of the family dinner table—timid, bland, ferret-faced Jake—was enough to complete the depression. Mother may have good taste in bridesmaid's dresses—the jury was still out on that—but her taste in bridegrooms had certainly gone downhill.

"I'm going to sit outside and be idle," I announced as lunch ended. "I'm going to lounge in one of the folding lawn chairs, sip lemonade, and leaf through whatever magazines I can find that I can feel reasonably sure have no pictures of brides in them."

"I'll join you, if you don't mind," Michael said, following me out the door.

"They won't miss you at the shop?" I asked.

"They're at a point on this set of dresses where they can manage without me right now. As a matter of fact, they're at a point where I would be very much underfoot."

"Then you can amuse me with witty conversation," I said.

"I don't know how witty it will be. But I have been meaning to talk to you about something. Now that things are settling down a little."

We gathered up the lemonade and lawn chairs and found a

nice shady spot under the largest oak tree on the lawn. But just as
we were setting up our chairs, a peacock leaped out of the tree and
began strutting up and down the lawn with his tail spread. We
looked around and saw a peahen behind us.

"I think we're in his way," I remarked.

"He has my heartfelt sympathy," Michael said. "Let's give them
a little privacy. God knows that can be hard enough to find around
here."

We picked up our lawn chairs and moved down the lawn to an
almost-as-shady spot. The peacock followed and resumed his mating display in front of us.

"He seems to be a little confused," Michael observed.

"We could split up and see which one of us he's really interested in," I suggested.

"I'm not sure I want to know," Michael said. "I thought they
were just rented for Samantha's wedding. Did you decide to keep
them around for your mother's after all?"

"We decided to keep them around permanently." I sighed.
"The grandchildren put up such a fuss this morning when Mr. Dibbit came to pick them up that Dad talked him into selling them. I
think Eric has them confused with turkeys. He's walking around
bragging about having rescued them from somebody's dinner
table."

"Every home should have a few peacocks."

"If you really feel that way, I could write your name on a couple of the eggs."

"Eggs?"

"Of course, I've only seen one so far, and I have no idea how
many they hatch at one time. But if you keep your eyes open,
you'll notice you don't see most of the hens. They're off . . . somewhere. Incubating, we think. Dad and Eric have put in a special
order at the bookstore for books on peafowl and general poultry

care, so within a week or two the entire family will be walking experts on peacock husbandry."

"I can hardly wait," Michael said.

"I can."

"I think you need to get away from your family for a little while."

"That's what I'm doing right now," I explained.

"Out here in full view, where anyone who wants to find you can just walk right up and find you?"

"Well, what do you suggest?"

"Let's go to dinner someplace," he said. "Someplace that is not run by any of your mother's family or anyone who even knows you and will come up and start babbling about the weddings."

"I wish I could," I said. "But I shouldn't. Not until after the wedding. Things are too crazy. I shouldn't be sitting here doing nothing now."

Still, I was considering changing my mind and taking him up on it when Dad and Pam came running out of the house.

"Meg! Michael! You'll never guess what's happened?" Pam called.

"They've tracked Samantha down in Rio de Janeiro and are trying to get her extradited for Mrs. Grover's murder," I said.

"Rats! Who told you?" Pam said crossly. "But you're wrong about Rio; it was the Caymans."

"Are you serious?" Michael asked.

"Yes! I suppose the sheriff told you," Pam said.

"I actually thought I was kidding," I said.

"Perhaps you knew it, subconsciously," she said. "After all, the sheriff said it was your idea."

"It was?"

"Yes. After she and Ian ran off. Don't you remember? You said to search her room for evidence," Pam said. "The sheriff took you seriously and went to Uncle Stanley to get a search warrant. And do you know what they found?"

"Two years' worth of back issues of *Bride's* magazine?"

"Evidence!" Pam chortled. "Books about poisons! Samples of some of the poisons she's used this summer! Books about car maintenance and electrical wiring. And stuff that she probably used to rig the fuse box and the lawn mower and Dad's car!"

"Books? Doesn't sound like Samantha's style," I mused.

"And some papers that the sheriff thinks may prove that she and Ian really did steal the money her first fiancé was supposed to have embezzled. Ian was an old college friend of his, you know."

"You were right all along," Michael said.

So why didn't I feel happier about the outcome?

Tuesday, July 26

I WAS PLANNING TO SLEEP LATE. I'D DECIDED THAT EVERYTHING really essential that needed to be done for Mother's wedding had been done, and the more I worked, the more things she would think of for me to do. I managed to sleep though her departure for a facial and was planning to drag myself out of bed just in time to greet the relatives she'd invited over for lunch.

But around nine o'clock, when I turned over, stretched, and prepared to go back to sleep for the second time, I heard Spike barking outside my window.

Damn. Couldn't Michael keep the little monster quiet?

Apparently not. The barking continued. I rolled out of bed, stumbled over to the side window, and peered down at the yard. Spike was dancing around the foot of a large dogwood tree, barking frantically.

Damn. I heard no outraged peacock shrieks, so I assumed Spike had finally intimidated and treed the kitten. I turned to put on some clothes so I could go downstairs to rescue the kitten. I'd have to name the kitten sooner or later, I reminded myself.

But the kitten was inside. When I turned around, I saw him. Peeing on a silk blouse I'd neglected to hang up.

Perhaps I wouldn't be naming the kitten after all, I thought, as he stepped delicately off the blouse, shaking his paws. Perhaps Pam's household could absorb another animal. Perhaps the animal shelter was open today.

But wait. If the kitten was inside, what had Spike treed?

I peered out at the dogwood again. There was a lump swaying in its upper branches, directly opposite my window. Not a small, round, Dad-shaped lump, festooned with vines. Not a long, thin, Michael-shaped lump either. An enormous, ungainly, disgustingly bovine lump. It could only be—

"Barry!" I shrieked. "You pervert!"

He had the grace to look embarrassed.

I grabbed some clothes, quickly dressed—in the bathroom— and ran downstairs, stopping on my way through the kitchen to pick up a piece of cheese for Spike.

"Good dog, Spike," I said, flicking the cheese at him. He gobbled it and resumed barking.

"Take him away, can't you?" Barry whined.

"Me? Are you crazy? Michael's the only one who can do anything with him. You'll have to wait till Michael shows up."

And wait we did. I fetched the mystery I'd been trying to read all summer and settled in a lawn chair. Spike got tired of barking after a while and curled up under the tree where he could keep an eye on things and resume barking whenever Barry moved a muscle. I tossed Spike a bit of cheese from time to time, to keep his energy up, and devoted myself to my book. Barry, showing greater sense than I'd previously given him credit for, remained very, very quiet.

Michael showed up around noon.

"So there he is," Michael said, in exasperated tones. "What's going on anyway?"

"Spike has treed a desperate criminal," I said, tossing the dog another bit of cheese. Spike took this as a signal for renewed vigilance and began barking energetically.

"A desperate criminal?" Michael said, peering upward. "Isn't that Barry?"

"Yes."

"What's he done?"

"He's a peeping Tom," I said. "A low-down, sneaking, miserable, perverted peeping Tom," I added, loudly, shaking my fist at the tree.

"Meg, I'm so sorry," Barry began.

"Save it for the sheriff," I said.

"The sheriff?" Michael said. "You're going to call the sheriff? Good!"

I heard a whimper from the dogwood.

"No need to call him," I said. "He's coming over for lunch, I believe."

Sure enough, the sheriff showed up a few minutes later, along with fifteen or twenty other ravenous relatives—some, fortunately, bearing covered dishes. I related Barry's misdeeds as dramatically as possible—somewhat exaggerating the state of undress I'd been in when he'd spied on me. Considering my family's tendency to barge into rooms, day or night, with minimal warning, I'd learned better than to sleep in anything see-through or skimpy.

The sheriff took me aside.

"Are you planning to press charges, Meg?"

I sighed.

"I'd say hell, yes . . . but he is Steven's brother. Can you just take him down to the station and scare the hell out of him? Don't let anyone hurt him or anything, but make him think twice before he does something like this again?"

The sheriff pondered.

"I'll do that, but while I'm scaring him, I'm going to check for priors. And where does he live?"

"Goochland County."

"Great; the sheriff there's an old hunting buddy of mine. I'll just have a word with him, see what he thinks. If I hear anything that gives me second thoughts about letting him off so easy, I'll get back to you this afternoon."

The sheriff might be weak in the area of homicide investigations, but he had few equals when it came to inducing guilt and putting the fear of God into wayward fifteen-year-olds. Which as far as I could see was about Barry's emotional age. I had a feeling the sheriff was about to solve my long-standing Barry problem.

The family dissected Barry's sins and shortcomings over lunch. Apparently everyone had had their doubts about him all along, but had politely refrained from voicing them. He was *too* nice. He had shifty eyes. Lucky for Barry that they'd unmasked Samantha, or they'd be stringing him up for the murders as well. Needless to say, lunch was a resounding success.

Everyone in the neighborhood was in a wonderful mood except for me. Well, and possibly the Brewsters, who after a talk with the sheriff had remained in residence, but in hiding. No one was sure whether to commiserate with them for the way their daughter had treated them or consider them her accomplices.

Everyone assumed that seeing the FBI agent at the reception triggered Samantha's flight. I wasn't so sure. I didn't think she'd reacted at all when she saw the agent. I thought she'd planned to run away all along. Well, for some days anyway.

"That's silly," Pam said. "If she planned to run away, why did she go through with the wedding?"

"She spent months arranging it; I can't see her letting a little thing like having chosen the wrong groom spoil it."

Everyone seemed to think I was joking.

I couldn't account for the bad mood I was in. The local serial killer was out of business. Rob had been saved from a truly disastrous marriage. Barry was probably out of my hair for good. In less than a week, all my wedding chores would be over. Well, okay, maybe two or three weeks if you count all the cleanup. So why was I alone in such a lousy mood?

Well, maybe not quite alone. Dad was moping.

"What's eating you, anyway?" I asked him.

"It's Emma Wendell," Dad said. "They've run any number of tests, but they haven't found anything."

"Maybe that's because there isn't anything to be found."

"I suppose," Dad said. He sighed. "It all seemed to fit together so nicely. This really has messed up all my theories."

"I don't think you're going to be able to prove that Jake's a cold-blooded murderer," I told him. "You might have to find some other way of changing Mother's mind. If that's what you want."

He wandered off, giving no sign of having heard me.

I went off to run last-minute errands and perform last-minute tasks. Everywhere I went, people congratulated me. They seemed to think that it was my suggestion that made the sheriff search Samantha's room. And that I was solely responsible for catching her.

"And how clever of you not to let on to anyone until you had the goods on her," one aunt enthused.

I protested that if I'd known she was a murderer, I'd have told the sheriff about her before Saturday, and spared us all the trouble of the ceremony. And poor Rob all the bother of getting an annulment. No one listened. Everybody thought I was just being modest. I gave up trying.

But I couldn't help wondering if it wasn't all a little too convenient. Samantha disappears, and suddenly we discover that she's responsible for Yorktown's homemade crime wave. Somehow it didn't quite add up.

Something suddenly struck me: what if Mrs. Grover showed up early that morning to meet Dad for a bird-watching trip and saw a furtive figure lurking in the trees outside my room? What if she was the first to unmask Barry as a peeping Tom, and threatened to call the police or tried to blackmail him? What if Barry had taken drastic measures to avoid exposure?

What if we had the wrong murderer?

I began to wonder if letting Barry off with a warning was a good idea after all. I called and left a message on the sheriff's answering machine: "call me—I'm having second thoughts about letting Barry go."

Wednesday, July 27

BUT I DIDN'T HEAR FROM THE SHERIFF THE NEXT DAY, AND HE WAS nowhere to be found. Only more hordes of relatives bent on congratulating me. Rumor had it that the missing millions had been found with Samantha, and everyone who'd lost money was going to get it back. My popularity was reaching new heights.

"I'm really tired of being hailed as Yorktown's answer to Nancy Drew," I told Michael when he dropped by during his morning walk with Spike.

"Well, you did have her pegged as one of the prime suspects," he said.

"Yes, but I didn't find any evidence of anything. I was just mouthing off when I suggested searching her room. And I'm beginning to have serious doubts about whether—"

"Michael!" Dad exclaimed, popping round the corner of the house. "Just the man I was looking for! My wedding present for Margaret should arrive tonight, and I was wondering if you could help me with it?"

"Sure," Michael said. "How?"

"Well, could we park the truck behind your house so she won't see it?"

"I don't see why not," Michael said, shrugging.

"What kind of truck?" I asked, suspiciously.

"One of your cousin Leon's trucks," Dad said.

"We're talking an eighteen wheeler, then," I said, looking at Michael.

"As long as it doesn't block the driveway, I guess it's fine."

"And if you'd like to help us put it up tomorrow, you're welcome," Dad said. "Mrs. Fenniman is going to go with Margaret to the beauty parlor and then take her to lunch, so as soon as they leave, everyone we can find will be coming over to put it up so it will be there when she comes back."

"Sure," Michael said. "Just what will we be putting up?"

"You know how I've been trying to get the yard in shape so it will look really nice for the wedding?" Dad said. "Well, I thought of one thing Margaret likes that would make it just perfect, so I called some cousins in South Carolina—"

"Oh, no," I said.

"And they agreed to help, so I sent our cousin Leon down there with the truck—"

"Dad, do you have any idea how much you can fit into one of those trucks?"

"That's why I'm getting as many people as possible to put it up, Meg," Dad said.

"Put *what* up?" Michael asked.

"Spanish moss." Dad beamed.

"Spanish moss?" Michael said, incredulous.

"It's that gray, trailing stuff you see hanging from all the trees in the Deep South," Dad explained.

"Yes, I know what it is," Michael said. "You're having a truckload of Spanish moss brought in as a wedding present?"

"Yes," Dad said. "Margaret loves it; she says it always makes her feel she's living at Tara. Whenever anyone in the family comes up here from further south, or if anyone goes down there to visit, they bring back a little of it."

"I don't recall seeing any," Michael said.

"It doesn't survive," I said. "What the cold doesn't kill in the winter the birds drag away in the spring to make nests."

"But she thinks it's so pretty while it lasts," Dad said. "So I decided just once to drape every tree in the whole yard with the stuff. She'll love it. I'll give you a call when the coast is clear. Refreshments for everyone who helps out of course, and you're already coming to the party Friday, I assume? Oh, and if you have a ladder we could use, that would be splendid. We need all the ladders we can get."

Dad trotted off happily.

"Unusual sort of wedding present," Michael remarked.

"It's damned peculiar to be giving your ex-wife a wedding present to begin with," I said.

"Do you think she'll like it?"

"Oh, she'll adore it. I hope it doesn't cause trouble with Jake. That *is* who she's supposed to be marrying, last time I heard."

"Just one question," Michael said. "Why the hell *is* she marrying Jake?"

When Cousin Leon and the truck finally arrived, Dad came by and dragged me down to Michael's to inspect the Spanish moss.

"Isn't it wonderful!" he said. "Now tomorrow, as soon as your mother takes off, we'll drive the truck over—"

"Er, I can't stay that long," Cousin Leon said. "I have to start back tonight. Can't we just go over and unload it now?"

"No, that would spoil the whole surprise," Dad protested.

"No way round it," Leon said, shrugging. "You want us to put it somewhere else?"

Dad thought for a minute.

"Michael," he began.

"Dad," I warned.

"It's no problem," Michael said. "What can it hurt to have a few piles of Spanish moss in the yard for a few days?"

We all got pitchforks and began unloading the truck. It took three hours, working at top speed. Michael's mother's house was painted a cheerful pink and blue—perhaps with leftover paint from the shop? Anyway, by the time we'd finished, Michael's mother's house looked like an Easter egg in a bed of excelsior.

"That truck holds a lot more than you'd think," Dad said, as we waved good-bye to Cousin Leon and stood surveying Mrs. Waterston's backyard.

"I'll say," Michael replied, no doubt wondering whether we'd ever succeed in hauling all of it down to our house and getting it hung up.

"I'll go call the volunteers," Dad said. "We'll all meet at Pam's house and come down here as soon as Meg calls us to let us know that her mother has gone to the beauty parlor."

"It's going to take quite a while," I said. "Maybe I should arrange with Jake to keep her out all afternoon, too."

I waited until Mother had settled in for a nice long after-dinner gossip with Mrs. Fenniman and several of the visiting aunts and then snuck down to Jake's.

I knocked on his door. He opened the door a crack and peered out.

"Yes?"

"It's Meg."

"Yes, I see." He didn't open the door any wider. I could have told him that he didn't have to worry, I'd already seen his depleted possessions and his shoddy bachelor housekeeping.

"I was wondering if you could keep Mother away from the house tomorrow afternoon while we hang some Spanish moss in the backyard."

It took quite a while to explain it to him, and at the end, I still wasn't sure he believed me. What if Dad's idea of a wedding present made him think we were too crazy to cope with? What if he called off the wedding?

Well, I could always hope.

Thursday, July 28

I GOT UP IN TIME TO SEE MOTHER AND MRS. FENNIMAN GETTING ready to leave. Mother seemed a little depressed. Or was she perhaps not feeling well? She seemed preoccupied, anyway, which was a good thing. Dad kept popping into the kitchen every five minutes with an air of badly suppressed excitement. He looked at his watch; he made highly visible (though incomprehensible) hand signals to me; he all but shouted, "Is she gone yet?"

"Go back to Pam's and wait," I hissed at him. "I'll call you."

That kept him out of our hair. For about ten minutes.

Finally, Mother and Mrs. Fenniman drove off. I was lifting the phone to call Pam when I saw four wheelbarrows dash into the yard, propelled by four of Pam's kids. Three ladders followed, carried by Dad, Michael, Rob, and Pam's husband and sons. Neighbors and relatives began arriving. More ladders appeared. The wheelbarrows disgorged their loads and were trundled off for a refill. Cousin Horace's pickup pulled into the driveway, laden with Spanish moss. I sighed, and went out to grab a pitchfork and help them unload.

Everyone had a lot of fun for the first hour or two, chattering happily as they hauled or hung moss. Things got a little quieter as it began to dawn on everyone how very much moss these was to be hung and how determined Dad was to get it all hung. By noon, the less hardy souls were beginning to sneak away. Not a disaster; the lower, easily reachable limbs were almost too thoroughly covered, and we were down to a dozen diehards on ladders, trimming the middle and upper branches. And of course the kids, who trundled doggedly back and forth from the moss pile to the ladders, keeping the hangers supplied. Mrs. Fenniman arrived back, having turned over to Jake the duty of keeping Mother away. In the middle of the afternoon, I drove the pickup back for another load and realized that there was a highly visible trail of moss leading from Michael's mother's house to ours. One glance at that and Mother would know something was up. I grabbed a few of the slackers who'd snuck away and set them to work sweeping the street and policing the neighborhood.

Late in the day, Jake called to say they were on the way home. We hadn't even finished the backyard, so we decided to try to keep Mother from looking out and drag her away from the house tomorrow as well, so we could finish the rest of the yard Friday. I did another spot inspection for stray bits of moss and sent everyone off to shower and change.

I then corralled my nephews and got Mother interested in rearranging the furniture again, which kept all of them out of trouble till bedtime.

Friday, July 29

JAKE CLAIMED TO HAVE IMPORTANT ERRANDS FRIDAY MORNING. HE positively put his foot down and insisted that he couldn't haul Mother around for another day. I was so pleased to detect some sign that he had a backbone I almost didn't resent inheriting the task of keeping her distracted. As luck would have it, she made my job easier by coming up with eight or ten absolutely urgent errands that had to be done before the wedding. Pam managed to keep her from wandering out into the backyard until I was awake enough for us to get on our way. I took the cellular phone along so I could call home from time to time during the day to check on the progress of the moss-hanging effort.

"Don't worry, we're getting along just fine without you," Pam would say every time I called. Translation: for heaven's sake, don't come home yet; we're nowhere near finished.

I saw Jake once, in passing, coming out of the local branch bank and heading into the travel agency. Well, at least he was presumably doing something useful about the honeymoon. I had no idea where they were going; Mother had assigned him the job of arranging the honeymoon and surprising her. Presumably she had dropped enough not-so-subtle hints that it would be a welcome surprise.

At about seven in the evening, I called from the candy store and hinted that they'd better wrap things up.

"We're going to be finished soon," I said.

"For heaven's sake, we still have a lot of moss left; can't you stall her some more?"

"No, we're not going to be much longer, don't worry," I said.

"Drat. Well, don't forget to pick up the cake."

"The what?"

"The cake," Pam repeated.

I glanced at Mother. She was absorbed in selecting boxes of chocolates to send to various relatives too ill or too far away to come to the wedding; I put as much space between us as possible.

"What do you mean, the cake?" I hissed into the phone. "We don't want the wedding cake till tomorrow."

"No, no; this is cake for the rehearsal party. Didn't I tell you the last time you called? Cousin Millie was going to deliver it, but her van broke down."

"Well how am I supposed to get it home? I'm keeping Mother out of the way, remember? Whither I goeth, she goeth, and she's not blind."

"Well you've got to think of something! I can't find anyone else who can get down there."

I thought of something.

"Have Cousin Millie take it to the garden store. It's just two doors down from her shop. I'll pick it up there. I'll tell Mother that Dad wants me to pick something up. Some manure; she won't want to come inside and help with that."

"Okay. Can you sneak it into the house when you get home?"

Can't anybody but me do anything?

As I expected, Mother was irritated at having to stop at the garden store.

"Why can't your father run his own errands?" she complained. "Whatever does he want now?"

"Some manure," I said. "You know how he is when he gets his heart set on putting down some manure. And he can't pick it up because he's mowing the lawn for your party tonight."

"He's not going to put manure on the yard today!" she gasped in horror.

"No, it's for Pam's vegetable garden, next week. But the sale ends today. I don't suppose you want to help me carry it out?"

I supposed right. Mother waited patiently in the car, leafing through the latest issue of *Modern Bride*. She never saw me lugging two sacks of manure and a remarkably large sheet cake out to the trunk. I hoped the cake's wrapping was air tight.

Eventually both of us ran out of errands, and I called home on the cellular phone. Pam answered.

"Hi," I told her. "I just thought I'd let you know that we're finished and heading home. Maybe you could have some tea and sandwiches ready?"

"They're coming! They're coming," she bellowed. Audibly, even to Mother. I cut the connection. Mother seemed absorbed in playing with her purchases. Perhaps she hadn't noticed.

When we arrived back at our neighborhood, I was astonished

to find a large fallen tree blocking the direct route home. It was getting dark; I was lucky not to run into it.

"Wherever do you suppose that came from?" Mother asked.

"Maybe they had a local thundershower here," I said. "We'll have to go the long way round." I dialed home on the cell phone.

"Pam, hi, there's a tree down blocking our way," I said.

"Oh, really?" she said. "Imagine that!" I glanced back at the street behind the log. Despite the fading light, I could see a few telltale shreds of pale Spanish moss littering the pavement. A head popped out from behind the Donleavys' fence and then back in again.

"I'll have to go the long way, by your house, so I'll stop by and put the manure in the shed. Have you got that? I'm putting the *manure* in the *shed.*"

"Oh, what a great idea! Dad can come there and get it!"

"Yes, that's the idea."

I turned around and took the long way home. I glanced in the rearview mirror and saw the fallen tree crawling swiftly off the road into the Donleavys' yard, on eight or ten mismatched legs.

When we got to Pam's yard, I backed up to the garden shed.

"I'll just be a minute," I said. I blocked Mother's view by opening the trunk, threw open the garden shed door—

"Aaaaaaah!" I was so startled to find Dad crouching in the corner of the tiny shed that I uttered a small shriek.

"Meg, dear? Is anything wrong?" Mother called.

Dad put his finger to his lips and shook his head.

"No, why?" I called back.

"I heard a scream."

"Must have been the peacocks," I called, shoving the cake into Dad's hands. "I hardly notice them anymore." Dad, attempting to help with the deception, began giving remarkably authentic peacock shrieks. I frowned him into silence.

I unloaded the two manure sacks, closed the shed door—resisting the temptation to lock Dad in and keep him out of mischief—slammed the trunk down, and drove off.

This time, when I glanced in the rearview mirror, I saw Dad galloping across the backyard toward our house with the cake in his arms. I sighed.

"Is anything wrong, dear?"

"It's been a long day," I said, truthfully. Mother patted my arm.

"Well, you'll be able to rest this evening," she said. "The rehearsal won't take long at all."

Sure.

When I got to the end of the driveway, I was startled. There were two very large iron lanterns with burning candles in them posted on either side of the entrance. I turned into a lane literally dripping with Spanish moss and lit by dozens of strings of twinkly lights.

"Oh, my goodness!" Mother said. "It's wonderful!"

Even as tired as I was, I had to admit it was impressive. We drove up to the house, which was lit with candles on the inside and more strings of lights on the outside. Several more lanterns outlined a path to the backyard.

Everyone yelled "Surprise!" when we got there. Only about two hundred of our nearest and dearest, which made it positively cozy compared with what tomorrow would be like. Everyone was complimenting Dad on his brilliant idea and each other on how well it had turned out. Everyone had brought food and drink, and they were all behaving themselves beautifully. Even Cousin Horace had showed up in coat and tie.

I dragged a lawn chair and a Diet Coke to a quiet corner of the yard, put my feet up on an empty beer keg, and collapsed.

"Why so glum?" Michael asked, appearing at my side, as usual.

"Do you know how many miles I've walked today?" I asked.

"Do you know how many wheelbarrow loads of Spanish moss I've hung?" he countered.

"You didn't have Mother cracking the whip over you."

"I had your Dad and Pam."

"I almost ran into that fallen tree."

"I fell off the ladder twice."

I couldn't help giggling. "All right, you win," I said.

"Beautiful, isn't it?" he said, waving his arm at the yard.

"Yes," I said. "Absolutely, positively, ridiculously beautiful."

We sat in silence, watching the guests drift across the yard in the flickering candlelight, hearing the murmur of conversation and the occasional ripple of laughter. Mother and Dad were standing near each other at the center of the party. Dad was explaining something to several cousins, gesturing enthusiastically. Mother was watching him with approval. Everyone was relaxed and happy. At the time like this, it became really obvious how much of a pall the unsolved murders had cast over everyone's mood this summer, I thought. And looked around once more for the sheriff. Where on earth was he? I still had nagging doubts about Samantha's guilt, and I wanted to make sure that the sheriff, in his zeal to convict Samantha, didn't overlook any evidence that pointed to Barry as the culprit.

A figure stepped between us and the rest of the party. Jake. He was strolling along, looking up at the trailing fronds of moss with bewilderment.

"What do you think of the moss?" Michael asked him.

Jake started.

"The moss? Oh, it's all right if you like the stuff. I suppose it's pretty enough." He picked up the end of a frond, looked at it critically, and then dropped it again, as if dismissing it. "Very odd," he said, as if to himself, and wandered off.

I forced myself to mingle for a while, then retreated back to brood in peace in my observation post at the edge of the yard.

"You're worried about something," Michael said. He was definitely turning into a mind reader, as well as my faithful shadow.

"I keep having this nagging feeling I've forgotten something. Or overlooked something. Something important."

"Something for your mother's wedding?"

"I suppose it must be. I mean, the murders are solved, the other two weddings are over, one way or another. It must be something about Mother's wedding, right?"

"What did you do today? Maybe we can figure what you've forgotten by process of elimination."

I related all the errands we'd done, made Michael chuckle at the clever way I'd gotten the cake into the car under Mother's very nose, made him laugh outright at my description of Dad lurking in the tool shed and shrieking like a peacock.

"I can't see Jake doing anything ridiculous like that," I said with a sigh.

"Ridiculous!" Michael said. "I like that; if you ask me your dad's the ultimate romantic."

"I agree," I said, looking around at all the moss, candles, and Christmas lights. "In a bizarre way, it's very romantic how he'll happily do the most ridiculous things to please Mother."

But I still felt a nagging unease. Perhaps it was the assembled relatives. They were all too well behaved. Surely someone was contemplating something really stupid that we wouldn't find out about until the worst possible moment tomorrow. Like the night before Pam's wedding, when some of the cousins had gotten Mal, the groom, completely plastered and put him on a plane to Los Angeles with a one-way ticket and no wallet. I was keeping a close eye on the cousins in question tonight, despite my sneaking feeling that it wouldn't really be a bad thing if something delayed this

wedding. Or called it off entirely. If I saw the practical jokers leading Jake off toward the airport, would I really want to interfere?

But no one was doing anything suspicious. Everyone seemed
to be having a wonderful time.

Except, possibly, Jake. I saw him, a little later, hovering near
the edge of the group around Mother, looking rather forlorn.

"I could almost feel sorry for Jake," I said. "It is supposed to be
his wedding, too."

"Yes," Michael said. "Which reminds me: wasn't the party actually supposed to follow the rehearsal?"

"Oh, damn! I can't believe we forgot the rehearsal!"

"We could go and remind them."

"No," I said, shaking my head. "It's nearly ten already. Everyone needs their rest. Mother, especially. And I can't go to bed
until we chase everyone out and put out all the candles and Christmas tree lights. Mother and Jake have both done this before; they'll
manage."

"Famous last words," Michael said.

"Oh, don't be silly. After all, it's supposed to be a short, simple ceremony. What could possibly go wrong?"

"Well, now we know what you've forgotten."

"I hope so," I said. "I really hope so."

Saturday, July 30. Mother's wedding day.

I WOKE EARLY, AND CROSSED THE LAST BLOCK OFF MY CALENDAR.
All I had to do was get through today and I was home free.

I fixed Mother some breakfast. She picked at her food. She
seemed anxious. She didn't want to talk. We carried out last-
minute tasks in an awkward silence.

Caterers arrived. Why we'd bothered, I don't know; every
neighbor and relative invited had insisted on bringing his or her

specialty. The men came to set up the tents in case of rain. The cousins who would be playing their musical instruments arrived early and began a much-needed rehearsal. The florist fussed about the effect the heat was having on the flowers, which was silly; it was no hotter than either of our previous weddings. By now we'd all forgotten what unwilted flowers looked like. The peacocks were now definitely molting and looked thoroughly disgusting, so we lured them down to Michael's mother's yard for the day. Cousin Frank, who had behaved impeccably throughout the chaos of Samantha's wedding, was hauled back from Richmond for a return engagement.

Through all this, Mother remained preoccupied. She failed to respond to any of my conversational gambits. If she was having second thoughts, she was keeping them to herself and not letting them slow the momentum of the day.

"What's wrong?" Michael asked when he arrived in the early afternoon.

"I have this strange feeling Mother's having second thoughts."

"Is that so bad?"

"No, except that it's a little inconveniently late. I mean, I really wish people would think things like weddings through before they go and ask their friends and relations to spend literally months of their lives working like dogs to arrange ceremonies they have no intention of going through with."

"Or following through with, in Samantha's case," Michael said.

"Precisely," I said, testily. "If you're not entirely sure you want to spend the rest of your life with someone, it seems to me that the last thing you'd want to do is to set in motion a very lengthy, time-consuming, expensive, and highly public process designed to lead inexorably to just that."

Michael nodded sympathetically and went to supervise the arrival of the Be-Stitched ladies, along with (in addition to our dresses) their husbands, children, and extended families. At the last

minute, Mother had invited them en masse. Why not? It wasn't as
if we'd really notice a hundred or so extra people.

Mother finally allowed me to see my dress, although she did
make me put a paper bag over my head until the ladies put it on
me. I held my breath as she reached to whisk off the bag. I stared
into the mirror, astonished.

"Do you like it, dear?" Mother asked, a little nervously.

"It's beautiful," I said. And, for a wonder, it really was. The
rose color went perfectly with my complexion and the cut made
the best of my figure. Mother looked more cheerful as she went off
to put on her own dress.

"I told you so," Michael said. "You look really great; I knew
you would."

"This almost makes up for the velvet and the hoops," I said.

Relatives began arriving in the middle of the afternoon, well
aware that the parking would run out long before five. I'd arranged
to have two vans available so Rob and Mal could run a shuttle service for guests who'd had to park half a mile away. The sheriff had
borrowed some deputies from two neighboring counties to carry
out the regular patrol work for the day so his entire staff could direct traffic and then attend the wedding.

Jake looked positively cheerful. I almost didn't recognize him.
Perhaps he really was deeply in love with Mother and finally felt
confident that the wedding was really going to happen. Or perhaps
he was merely looking forward to getting the ceremony over with
and leaving town. He kept looking in his inside jacket pocket and
patting an airline ticket folder with obvious satisfaction.

Dad, on the other hand, was wandering about looking forlorn, with periodic intervals during which he had obviously told
himself to keep his chin up. I found myself siding with Dad. If one
of the weddings had to misfire, couldn't it have been this one? I really didn't want this one to come off.

And so, of course, before you knew it we were marching

down the aisle——Pam and I, followed by Mother on Rob's arm. At the last minute, Mother had decided to have Rob give her away.

"To take his mind off everything, poor dear," she said.

I'd have thought that the best thing to take his mind off the everything in question was to have nothing whatsoever to do with weddings. I hoped he was really as cheerful as he seemed. I hoped Dad wouldn't be too depressed. I hoped Mother really knew what she was doing. If she didn't, it was a little late to do anything; the wedding was underway.

"If anyone here can show just cause why this man and woman should not be joined in holy matrimony," Cousin Frank intoned, "Let him speak now or forever hold his peace."

Seemingly expecting no reply, he was drawing breath to continue when Dad spoke up.

"Actually, I have one small objection," he said. The wedding party turned around to look at him, and in the back of the crowd you could see people craning for a better view and shushing each other. After a suitably suspenseful pause, Dad continued.

"You see, I have a pretty good idea that old Jake here bumped off his first wife, and I really don't want to see him do the same to my Margaret."

A hush fell over the entire crowd. I looked at Dad, who was beaming seraphically at us. At Mother, who was gazing from him to Jake with rapt attention. At Jake, who had turned deathly pale. At the miles of Spanish moss festooning every tree in the yard. At the masses of out-of-season flowers, the regiment of caterers gamboling over the lawn, at the bloody $1200 circus tent on top of which, despite all our diversionary tactics, the least decorative of the newly acquired Langslow family peacock flock was now roosting.

"Honestly, Dad," I said, "couldn't you have brought this up a *bit* sooner?"

Smothered titters began spreading through the audience, and

Dad brought down the house by replying, "But Meg, I've *always* wanted to see someone do that in real life."

"I have no idea what he's talking about," Jake said. "The man must be crazy."

"I think an analysis of your late wife's ashes might prove very interesting, don't you?" Dad said. Had the chemists finally found something, I wondered.

"*If* you could analyze them," Jake countered. "You'd have a hard time doing it; I scattered them, just as she wanted."

"No," I said. "You scattered Mother's great-aunt Sophy. Dad has your wife."

Jake looked a little shaken.

"Well, if someone did poison Emma, I'd like to know about it. But it wasn't me."

"You can prove he did it, can't you?" the sheriff said to Dad.

"Moreover, I believe you're really responsible for Mrs. Grover's death," Dad went on. More oohs and ahhs from the crowd. Jake looked pale. I cringed inwardly. If Dad had proof that Jake had murdered his first wife, he'd have produced it. He was changing the subject. He was bluffing.

"That's impossible," Jake said. "You know very well I was nowhere near here when she was killed."

"Yes, but I suspect an analysis of your financial records will show you hired someone to do it."

"Nonsense," Jake said, much more confidently. Bad guess, Dad. "Look all you want."

Dad looked crestfallen. No doubt he was expecting Jake to jump up and confess when accused, the way people do in the movies. People don't do that, Dad, I wanted to say. The crowd was shuffling around, looking embarrassed, and I imagined that any minute now, Cousin Frank would call things to order and suggest they get on with the ceremony. Do something, Dad! But he was simply staring at Jake, obviously waiting for something. Jake stared back, unruffled. He wasn't going to make a slip.

Or had he already? Something that had been tugging at the back of mind suddenly clicked into place. Don't worry, Dad, I think we've got him.

"That was an interesting slip of the tongue, Mr. Wendell," I said. Jake whirled to face me. Dad's face brightened.

"You said that you'd like to know if anyone poisoned your wife," I continued. "Dad didn't say anything about poisoning. He just said he thought you killed her. I think 'bumped off' was the exact phrase he used."

"Well . . . I assumed . . . from the ashes . . ." Jake spluttered. The sheriff looked interested, but unconvinced.

"But you're right, it's a long time ago," I went on. "It would be very hard to prove he did it anyway. So, Sheriff, why not just arrest him for murdering Mrs. Grover?"

"If you have any idea who he hired, I'd be happy to look into it," the sheriff replied.

"He didn't have to hire anyone," I said. "He did it himself."

"But how?" Dad said, eagerly. I could hear the words "cast-iron alibi" muttered from several directions in the crowd, and the sheriff was shaking his head regretfully.

"I wasn't anywhere near here when Jane was murdered," Jake said, smugly. "So how could I possibly have done it?"

"The storage bin," I said. "That's how you did it. And where you did it."

Jake froze.

"She was accusing you of selling her sister's possessions or giving them to Mother," I went on. "I overheard you telling her that the jewelry was in the safety deposit box and the furniture and paintings were safe in your storage bin. She didn't want to wait, did she? The bank wasn't open on the weekend, but you promised her that you'd take her to the storage bin as soon as the party was over. And you did. But she never came back. Not alive, anyway."

"This is ridiculous," Jake said. But his voice was shaky.

"Did you drug her coffee with her sleeping medication? Or did you hold a gun on her and force her to take it? Either way, you knocked her out, drove her out to your storage bin, tied her up, and left her there. Then the next day, in between a couple of errands, you asked Mother if she'd mind if you dropped by your storage bin for a minute. What was it you said you wanted?"

"His golf clubs," Mother said, frowning slightly. "He wanted to take them with us on the honeymoon."

"And of course Mother didn't want to go inside your stuffy old storage bin. Right? I bet she stayed in the car reading a bridal magazine while you bashed Mrs. Grover's head in with a blunt object— I'm guessing one of the golf clubs—and stowed her in the trunk of Mother's car."

"In my car?" Mother said, faintly. "We were riding around with a dead body in my car?" I saw gleams in the eyes of the two cousins who sold cars.

"He couldn't use his, Mother," I said. "It's a hatchback. And then that night, after we all went to bed, you snuck back and put her on the beach. You figured it didn't matter that the autopsy would show she'd been moved from wherever she'd been killed, because everyone would know you weren't anywhere nearby to have killed her. The fact that the body wasn't found for another whole day made it even harder to prove anything."

"That's all very interesting, Meg," the sheriff began. "But I think you're letting your imagination run away with you."

"Check his storage bin," I said, turning to the sheriff. "The U-Stor-It on Route Seventeen, bin number forty-three. Check his golf clubs for traces of blood. I bet you'll also find a lot of other interesting things in his bin, things he didn't plant in Samantha's room, like traces of foxglove plants and leftover stuff from that bomb he planted in Barry's jack-in-the box and a brand-new gorilla suit and—"

Suddenly I felt an arm grab me around the neck and a cold, metal circle pressed against the middle of my back.

"Everyone stay away! I have a gun!" Jake shouted, dragging me with him as he backed slowly away from the sheriff.

"Now, Mr. Wendell," the sheriff said, in his most soothing tone. "You don't want to make things any worse for yourself."

"Any worse! I like that! You're going to put me away for murder, and it's all his fault," Jake shrieked, pointing at Dad with the gun for a moment before sticking it in my back again. Everyone looked at Dad in bewilderment. "When we got home from the damned party, Jane told me that she knew how I'd done it," Jake said. "It was Langslow and his damned garden that tipped her off. He was going on about common household poisonings. She recognized Emma's symptoms."

"And she threatened to turn you in?" the sheriff asked. Good. Get him interested in talking and maybe he'll wave the gun again. I was too surprised to make a break the first time, but if it happened again. I'd be ready.

"She said she'd tell if I didn't pay her off," Jake said.

"She tried to blackmail you?"

"She said if I didn't pay her five-hundred-thousand dollars, she'd give Emma's ashes to the sheriff. She seemed to think you'd still be able to tell she'd been poisoned."

"So Dr. Langslow inadvertently enlightened Mrs. Grover on how you killed her sister, your late wife, and you killed Mrs. Grover to prevent her from blackmailing you?"

"You can't give in to blackmailers," Jake said, very earnestly. "They're like crabgrass; you never get rid of them. And I already had one on my back. It was going to be hard enough to get rid of her."

"Someone else was blackmailing you?" Dad asked.

"Of course," Jake shouted, jerking his head in Mother's direction. "She was!" There were murmurs of astonishment from the crowd. Jake seemed to be enjoying himself now. It was nice that someone was. The crowd was hanging on his every word, and in case they missed anything the first time around, Aunt Esme was repeating everything he said at the top of her voice into Great-Aunt Matilda's good ear. I hoped the sheriff and his deputies weren't getting so interested that they'd forget to rescue me if the opportunity came up.

"Well, I never!" Mother said, in her chilliest manner. "I can't imagine what would ever have given you *that* idea."

"She kept at me," Jake continued. "She kept telling me that she knew exactly what I had done, and it was all for the best. She even told me she knew all about the rice pudding." Everyone looked at Mother.

"Well, I did," Mother said, perplexed. "I knew how much Emma liked it, and you were so good to learn how to make it for her. So few men would go to that much bother. I don't see what rice pudding has to do with it, anyway."

"That was what I fed her the poison in," Jake shouted. Please, Mother, I thought; don't get him any more excited. "I thought you *knew* that! And I almost had a heart attack when I found out you expected me to marry you to keep you quiet!"

"I can't imagine what could possibly have given you that idea," Mother said stiffly.

"You kept going on about married couples keeping each other's little secrets."

"I'm sure you were asking something highly personal about Dr. Langslow."

"I was asking if he knew what you knew."

"Knew what?" Mother asked.

"About Emma!" Jake shouted.

"You needn't shout, Jake," Mother reproved. "If he did, he

certainly didn't tell me, or I would never have accepted your proposal."

"Are you suggesting," Pam asked, "that although Mother knew you had killed your first wife, she was so eager to marry you that she was willing to blackmail you into doing it?" Put like that, it seemed so implausible that even Jake was taken aback.

"Well," he waffled, "it seemed so at the time."

"And then Mrs. Grover tried to blackmail you, and you killed her," Dad picked up the tale. "But you realized that you'd never feel safe as long as I was around asking difficult questions about Mrs. Grover's death. So you decided to shut me up by getting rid of me. And Meg, once you decided she was a threat."

"No you don't," Jake said, suddenly, dragging me with him as he whirled about to look behind him. Some of the deputies had edged their way around there. I assume they were trying to surprise him.

"Get out of my way," Jake snarled, and dragged me with him until he had his back to the garage. "Someone bring my car around. We're leaving."

Great. From maid of honor to hostage. I suddenly realized that I was still holding my bouquet in the hand that wasn't clutching at the arm that was choking me.

"Jake, you don't have to do this," Mother said in her most soothing tones, and started to walk toward us as she talked. "I'm sure Dr. Langslow knows a psychiatrist who could help get you off. Why don't you just turn Meg loose and we'll sit down and talk to him—"

"You stay away from me," Jake wailed. "Stand back or I'll shoot her! I swear I will!"

Everybody stood back. Stalemate. What did Jake have in mind—fleeing the country with me as his hostage?

Suddenly we heard the usual unearthly peacock shrieks coming from directly overhead. Two peacocks were fluttering down from the roof toward us. Jake dodged to one side to avoid them, dragging me with him, and I could feel that the barrel of the gun was no longer pointed at my back. The peacocks were followed almost immediately by Michael, who landed with a thud where Jake would have been if he hadn't dodged. But the diversionary tactic worked—Jake loosened his grip on me and started to point the gun at Michael.

Here was my chance! I jerked Jake's arm skyward, the gun started firing, guests began screaming and dropping to the ground.

Luckily my ironwork had given me a great deal more upper body strength than most women have. A lot more than Jake, too. I could keep the gun pointed harmlessly in the air until it was empty. Then I shoved Jake away from me and watched as he was tackled, first by Mother, then by Michael, and then, belatedly, by the sheriff and most of the deputies and ersatz cousins. The lawmen began fighting over who got to handcuff him, their efforts hampered by Mother, who had one knee on Jake's neck and was beating him over the head with her wedding bouquet.

"Of *all* the *nasty, mean* things!" Mother said, punctuating her remarks with blows. "I hope they put you *under* the jail!"

"Now, Margaret," Dad said. "I think the sheriff can take care of him. Come and have some champagne."

Mother allowed Dad to help her up and, after they were sure I was unharmed, they waltzed off toward the refreshment tent. A few guests stayed to gawk as Jake was led away to the car by six of the deputies, or to shake my hand or pat me on the shoulder soothingly. Most of the herd wandered off behind Mother and Dad and started in on the champagne and the buffet. I shooed away the well-wishers, sat down in one of the folding chairs, and put my head in my hands.

"Here, have some champagne," Michael said, waving a glass of it under my nose. "Or I could get some water if you're feeling faint."

"I'm not feeling faint," I said, glancing up. He looked worried.

"Sorry I ran away with your rescue attempt," I said.

"Once again, you didn't need much rescuing," he said, with a grin. "I don't know why I bother with these useless acts of chivalry."

"It gave me the chance I was looking for," I said. "And now I know what was bothering me last night. Leaving Mother in the car while I went in to fetch the cake, and then seeing Dad hiding in the tool shed. It was staring us all in the face. I should have realized then how Jake got away with it. He was miles away from here when Mrs. Grover was killed—but so was she. He knew exactly how to manipulate Mother to give himself that cast-iron alibi."

"Well, he didn't get away with it, thanks to you. If you hadn't figured it out, the rest of us would still be wondering. Cheer up!"

"Yes; after all, no one will ever ask me to be their maid of honor again. After Samantha's wedding and now this, I will be considered a complete and total jinx. People will pay me to stay out of town for their weddings." I took the glass of champagne and drained it.

"Oh, it's not that bad," Michael said soothingly. "I'm sure it will all blow over."

"I don't want it to blow over. I never, ever want to be involved in a wedding again."

"At least not as a maid of honor."

"Not in any capacity. Ever."

"What about your own?" he asked. "Assuming, of course, you're interested in having one?"

"I'm not. If I ever get married, I shall elope. That has now become my prime requirement in a husband. Willingness to elope."

"Sounds perfectly sensible to me," he said, surveying the chaos around us. "Which reminds me, for some strange reason, and apropos of nothing in particular except that I've been trying to drag the conversation around to the subject for what seems like half the summer, do you think there's any possibility that you might—"

"What on earth is Dad doing?" I interrupted.

"What an odd coincidence," Michael remarked. "He seems to be proposing to your mother." Dad was down on one knee at Mother's feet, and as we watched, she said something to him that provoked applause and raised glasses from the surrounding relatives.

"Hardly coincidental at all. I'm sure he's been planning this for days."

"Weeks," Michael replied. "Possibly months. I always found it slightly odd that he was going to so much trouble to make your mother's remarriage a success. Of course, you realize this probably means another wedding."

"No, I think not," I said. "All they have to do is drag the guests back in and take it from the top."

"Without a marriage license?"

"I imagine they'll manage. The man shaking Dad's hand right now is Judge Hollingworth—Mother's cousin Stanley. Dad is probably arranging some sort of special license."

"I do like your family's style," Michael remarked.

"That's because you're not related to them. You'd feel different if they were your crazy relatives."

"We'll see," he said, cryptically.

The sheriff and his remaining deputies used their bullhorns to reassemble the guests. After a pause while Dad gathered an impressive new bouquet to replace the one Mother had destroyed on Jake's head, the revised wedding went forward. I made my absolutely, positively final appearance as a maid of honor.

After the ceremony, the sheriff and the deputies drove off with their prisoner, and the rest of the friends and family settled down to celebrate in earnest.

Rob, I was glad to see, had already found someone to console him for the loss of Samantha. A tall, slightly gawky young woman with bright orange hair.

"Meg, this is Red," he said, in a tone that would have been quite appropriate for presenting the Queen of England.

"How do you do," Red said, pushing her spectacles up off the end of her nose. "Nice bit of deduction, that."

"Too bad I didn't deduce it till the last minute," I said.

"Better late than never," she said, shrugging. "Are you really a blacksmith?"

"More or less."

"Cool!" Red looked impressed. I decided I could get to like her.

"Red's going to help me turn Lawyers from Hell into a computer game," Rob said. They went off discussing RAM and mice and object-oriented programming and other things that I had no idea Rob knew anything about. Well, he was happy, anyway.

The party was definitely hitting its stride. Aunt Catriona tried to convince Natalie to play her bagpipes, but reason——or stage fright——prevailed. Undeterred, Aunt Catriona performed her justly notorious highland fling unaccompanied. With her final kick, she lost one of her spike heels, which arched across the dance floor to lodge in Great-Aunt Betty's bouffant hairdo.

Despite the fact that their usual grounds were occupied by at least four hundred people, the croquet crowd were wandering about with their mallets in hand, trying to set up wickets.

I sat on the edge of the patio wall and gazed over the lawn. These were my family. My kin. My blood. I felt a strong, deeply rooted desire to get the hell out of town before they drove me completely over the edge.

And I could now. The sculptor still had my house till Labor Day, but there was no earthly reason for me to stay here. I could go . . . anywhere! I began to feel more cheerful.

Out of the corner of my eye, I saw Mother standing at the edge of the rock garden, preparing to launch her bouquet. I gauged the distance, satisfied myself that there was no way Mother's delicate arm could possibly throw the bouquet anywhere near me, and snagged a glass of champagne with a strawberry in it from a passing waiter.

"Aren't you going to try for it?" Michael said, startling me by appearing at my elbow.

"No. I've sworn them off. I've sworn off everything connected with weddings; I told you that already." I deliberately turned my back on the charming tableau of Mother gracefully waving her bouquet over the heads of a sea of laughing, chattering women.

"I don't care if she's had the damn thing gold-plated," I said. I daintily raised my champagne flute to take a sip—when Mother's well-aimed bouquet bounced off my head and landed in the hands of a startled Michael.

"You touched it first," he said, quickly stuffing the bouquet into my hand.

Hordes of relatives swarmed over to congratulate me on my detecting ability, my wedding organizing ability, my bouquet-catching ability. I smiled and murmured thanks and sipped my champagne.

"You're in a very good mood," Michael said.

"The damned weddings are over. I can finally think about something else for a change."

"I'll drink to that," Michael said. "Speaking of which—"

"I can't drink to it, I'm out of champagne."

"Your wish is my command," he said. "Back in a jiffy."

I glanced up at the sky. It was clouding over. Maybe a short, sudden shower would slow down the coming riot. I looked back over the sea of relatives. Then again, maybe it would take a deluge.

The band was playing an Irish jig, and many of the crowd were dancing, although most of them obviously had no earthly idea what a jig was like. I particularly liked Mrs. Tranh's interpretation, though.

"Charming," Michael said, coming up behind me so suddenly that I nearly fell off the wall.

"My God, you startled me," I said.

"Sorry," he said. "I need to talk to you."

"So talk," I said, watching two of my great-uncles, who were perched on the diving board beginning some sort of arm-wrestling contest.

"Not here. Come with me," Michael said, taking me gently but firmly by the arm.

"Where?" I asked.

"This way," he said, dragging me around the other side of the house to a point out of sight of the wedding festivities.

"Michael, I adore masterful men," I said sarcastically, "but what on earth is this about?"

"Sit here," he said, pointing to a picnic bench that had some-how not been requisitioned for the reception.

"I can't see what's going on from here," I protested.

"We know what's going on," he said. "Your family are eating and drinking and doing bizarre things. This is important."

"What if someone needs me?"

"They can do without you for a few minutes. This is important. I want to explain something to you."

"So explain."

"No, first you have to promise me something. Promise me you'll hear me out."

"Okay."

"I mean it," he insisted. "No interruptions. If one of the kids comes running up with a broken arm you'll send him off to your father. If your mother needs something, you'll let your sister take care of it. If a dead body falls out of the trees you'll ignore it until I finish."

"Michael, whatever it is, you could probably have explained it by now. I promise you, I'll ignore an earthquake; get on with it."

"Okay," he said. And sat there looking at me.

"Well?" I said, impatiently.

"I'm suddenly speechless."

"That must be a first," I said, starting to rise. "Look, while you're collecting your thoughts——"

"No, dammit, hold on a minute, let me explain," he said, pulling me back down to the picnic bench. And as I turned to protest, he grabbed me by both shoulders, pulled me close . . .

And kissed me.

It was a thorough, expert, and fairly lengthy kiss, and by the end of it I would have fallen off the picnic bench if Michael hadn't put an arm around me.

"I've been trying to explain to you all summer," he began.

"Yes, I think I'm getting the picture. Explain it to me some more," I said, pulling his head back down to mine.

It was during the second kiss that the first of the fireworks hit us. Quite literally; the grandchildren had begun setting off an impressive array of fireworks, and one badly aimed skyrocket went whizzing by and sideswiped Michael's ear.

"They're doing it again," he exclaimed, jumping up.

"Have the kids been shooting fireworks at you? You should have told someone; that's strictly against the rules."

"No, I mean they're interrupting us," he said. "They've been doing it all summer. The whole town has, for that matter."

"You can't really accuse everyone of interrupting us," I said. "I don't suppose it ever dawned on anyone there was an us to interrupt. It certainly never dawned on me. Was there a particular reason you decided to pretend to be gay all summer? Research for a part or something?"

"I didn't decide; it just happened," he said. "I turned down some pretty disgustingly blunt propositions from a couple of

Samantha's bridesmaids and then I found they'd spread it all over town that I was gay."

"You could have said something."

"I didn't really give a damn at first. I figured, who cares, and it would keep the matchmaking aunts and predatory bridesmaids at bay. But then you came along, and they convinced you, and every time I tried to explain to you, someone would come along and drag you away to do something for one of the weddings, or something would explode, or a dead body would turn up. It's been driving me crazy."

"That's my family for you," I said, nodding.

"Let's go someplace," he begged, pulling me up from the bench. "Someplace where we can be alone. Come on. There's no one at my mother's house. Let's go there. We need to talk."

Actually, I thought we'd done enough talking for the moment, but I figured we'd work that out when we'd ditched the rest of the wedding guests.

As we rounded the corner of the house, watching warily for anyone who might waylay us, a spectacular flash of lightning and an almost simultaneous burst of thunder dwarfed the fireworks, and the heavens opened.

We were ignored as everyone began running for shelter, either in the tent or the house. But then, one end of the tent sagged dramatically as part of the bluff collapsed beneath it, sending buffet tables ricocheting down the cliff. Guests and caterers nearly trampled each other evacuating the tent as larger and larger portions of the bank dropped off. A sudden gust of wind caught the out-of-balance tent and sent it flying out onto the water, while with a final rumbling, one last, enormous chunk of bluff subsided into the river, taking the shallow end of the swimming pool with it. Several mad souls cheered as the contents of the pool spilled over the side of the bluff in a short-lived but dramatic waterfall.

As we watched, the tent drifted gently down the river, with

one lone, wet, bedraggled peahen perched atop it, shrieking irritably until the tent finally disappeared below the waves and she flapped to the shore.

"Oh, my God," I said.

"Pay no attention," Michael said.

"We've got to do something."

"No one's hurt, and there's a thousand other people here to do something. Come on!"

We dashed through the downpour down to Michael's mother's house. Which now looked like an Easter egg in a bed of very wet excelsior. With several damp, irritable peacocks sitting on the peak of the roof. We ignored their plaintive shrieks.

"Alone at last!" Michael exclaimed, slamming the door shut. We stood there, looking at each other for a moment.

Looking into Michael's eyes, I wondered how I could ever have been so blind all summer, how I could ever have been so mistaken about him, and whether he'd ever let me hear the last of it.

Time enough to worry about that later. He reached out to pull me close and—

"Michael? Is that you?" came a voice from deeper within the house.

Michael dropped his arms, leaned back against the door, and closed his eyes.

"Not now," he muttered. "Please, not now."

"Michael! What on earth have you done to the dog? And why is there Spanish moss all over the backyard? And where did all these peacocks come from? What is going on around here?"

Michael sighed.

"Your turn," he said. "Come and meet *my* mother."

Murder with Puffins

Acknowledgments

♡

With thanks:

• To Dad, for inspiring Meg's dad.

• To Mom, for being nothing whatsoever like Meg's mother. (Well, except for the bit about the coconut.)

• To Stuart and Elke, for holding your wedding on Monhegan.

• To Monhegan and its residents—although a hurricane and a homicide must seem poor thanks for your hospitality.

• To Ruth Cavin and the crew at St. Martin's, and to Ellen Geiger of Curtis Brown, for helping steer me through the perils of publishing.

• To my friends and family everywhere, including the Misfits, Queen Bees, Teafolk, Wombats, fellow writers, and fellow readers.

Chapter 1

My Puffin Lies over the Ocean

"I see land ahead," Michael said.

"I'm sure they said that often aboard the original *Flying Dutchman*," I replied, my eyes tightly shut.

"No, really; I'm sure of it this time," he insisted.

I kept my eyes closed and didn't relax my death grip on the rail while the ferry's deck bucked and heaved beneath my feet. The rain and spray had soaked me to the bone, but I wasn't going into the cabin unless the swells grew dangerous. Way too many seasick people inside. Of course, those of us on deck were seasick, too, but at least out here the wind kept the air fresh, if a little damp.

"The next time I have an idea like this," I mumbled, "just shoot me and get it over with."

"What was that?" Michael shouted over a gust of wind.

"Never mind," I shouted back.

"I really do think that's land ahead," Michael repeated. "Honestly. I don't think it's another patch of fog."

I debated, briefly, whether to look. My seasickness seemed a little less intense if I kept my eyes closed. But if an end to our ordeal was in sight, I wanted to know about it. I opened one eye a crack and peered in the direction Michael pointed. To me, the vague shape ahead looked like the same ominous cloud bank we'd been staring at for hours. Maybe it made him feel better to think he saw land. Maybe he was trying to make me feel better.

"That's nice," I croaked, and closed my eyes again, blotting out the gray sky, the gray sea, and the disturbing lack of any clear line of demarcation between the two. Not to mention the gray faces of the other passengers clinging to the rail.

"We must be getting close," Michael said, sounding less confident. "Monhegan's only an hour off the coast in good weather, right?"

I didn't answer. Yes, normally it took only an hour by ferry to reach Monhegan, where we planned to stay in my aunt Phoebe's summer cottage. But there was nothing normal about this trip. If Michael still believed we'd reach dry land soon, I wasn't going to discourage him. Even though deep down I knew that we really *had* boarded the *Flying Dutchman* and were doomed to sail up and down the coast for all eternity, or at least until we ran out of fuel and had to be rescued by the Coast Guard.

"Well, maybe not," I heard Michael murmur.

I pried my eyes open to check on him. He stared out over the water with a faint frown. I felt a twinge of jealousy. I probably looked as ghastly as I felt, but even in the throes of seasickness, Michael was gorgeous. A little paler than usual, and the hypnotically blue eyes were a bit bloodshot. But still, were I an artist, looking for just the right tall, dark, handsome cover model for a nautically themed romance, I'd look at Michael and shout, "Eureka!"

"I'm sorry," I said instead. "This was a bad idea."

"It'll turn out all right," he said with a smile. Only a faint ghost of his usual dazzling smile, but it made me feel better. "But next time we set out on an adventure, let's remember to check the weather first, okay?"

Well, that was encouraging. At least he was still talking about "next time." And next time I took off on a trip with Michael, I promised myself, we'd go someplace warm and tropical, where the nearest large body of water was the hotel swimming pool. Not on a boat in the middle of the Atlantic—well, several miles off the coast of Maine anyway. Hurricane Gladys had now headed out to sea and now subsided to a mere tropical storm, but if I'd bothered to check the Weather Channel before Michael and I set out for our weekend getaway, I could have picked a more promising spot. In fact, I could probably have done better just by sticking a pin in a map.

"It's a deal," I said, smiling back as well as I could. He put his hand on mine for a few seconds, until another wave hit the boat and he had to grab the rail again. But I felt better. Mentally anyway. Physically . . . well, I was trying to ignore another set of warning signals from my stomach.

"Meg Langslow? Is that you?"

I opened my eyes and turned, to see two figures standing to my left, both wrapped from head to toe in state-of-the-art rain gear. They looked like walking L. L. Bean catalogs and were probably toasty warm and reasonably dry underneath. I tried not to resent this.

"Yes?" I said, peering through sheets of rain at the small portion of their faces visible under their hoods.

"Meg, dear, don't you remember us? It's Winnie and Binkie!"

"Winnie and Binkie?" Michael repeated.

I finally placed the names. Mr. and Mrs. Winthrop Saltonstall Burnham, aka Winnie and Binkie, owned a cottage on Monhegan Island and were old family friends. Childhood friends of my grandparents, if memory served, which made them fairly ancient by now. And yet there they stood, two sturdy round figures in yellow slickers, seemingly undisturbed by the driving rain, the frantic rocking of the boat, and the near–gale force winds.

"Bracing, isn't it?" Winnie said, throwing out his chest and taking a deep breath, which was at least one-quarter rain.

"Don't mind him, dear," Binkie whispered, noticing my reaction. "Rough weather always makes him a little queasy, and he likes to put a brave front on it."

"Oh, I don't mind the crossing," Winnie said. "I'm just hoping the weather doesn't spoil the bird-watching."

"Bird-watching?" Michael said. "You're going out to Monhegan in the middle of a hurricane for bird-watching?"

"Yes, aren't you?" Winnie asked.

"It's been downgraded to a tropical storm," Binkie said. "And this is the fall flyover season."

"Oh, of course," I said.

"The what?" Michael asked.

"The fall flyover season," Binkie explained. "Monhegan lies right in the path the birds take when they migrate north and south. There's a short time every spring and fall when the bird-watching reaches its peak, and birders come here from all up and down the Eastern Seaboard."

"We have a cottage on the island," Winnie said. "We've been bird-watching here for fifty-three years." He and Binkie exchanged fond smiles.

"But if you're not here for the bird-watching, why are you going out to Monhegan?" Binkie asked.

"We wanted to get away from things," Michael put in. "Get some peace and quiet."

"Some what?" Winnie shouted over a gust of wind that had evidently carried away Michael's words.

"Peace and quiet!" Michael shouted back.

"Oh."

They still looked at us with puzzled expressions. I sighed. I wasn't sure I even wanted to try explaining.

The trip had seemed so logical a few days ago. My romance with Michael had reached the point where we wanted to spend a little time alone together—okay, a lot of time—just at the point when neither of us had a place to call our own.

As a bachelor professor of theater in a college town with a chronic housing shortage, Michael had lived in relative luxury for the last several years by renting houses from faculty members on sabbatical. This year, alas, his landlords had suddenly realized they couldn't afford to spend a year in London—not with their seventh child on the way. They'd been very nice about letting Michael sleep on their sofa until something else turned up, but it was no place for the logical conclusion to a romantic candlelight dinner. We'd already ended enough dates watching Disney videos and dodging blobs of peanut butter.

And I was temporarily homeless, as well. Subletting my cottage and ironworking studio for several months to a struggling sculptor had seemed like a good idea at the start of the summer. I'd known I would be down in my hometown of Yorktown, organizing three family weddings; and with my career as an ornamental blacksmith on hold, I could use the rent money.

But when I tried to move back in, I couldn't get rid of my tenant. He was in the middle of an important commission; he would ruin the whole piece if he had to move it; he needed just one more week to finish it. He'd been needing just one more week for the past six weeks.

So I was still staying at my parents' house. Mother and Dad weren't there, of course; they were off in Europe on an extended second honeymoon. But the house was filled with elderly relatives. They'd come for the weddings and stayed on to watch the legal circus unfold as the county built its case against the murderer whose identity I'd managed (more or less accidentally) to uncover.

That was another problem. I'd become notorious. I couldn't go anywhere in Yorktown without people coming up to congratulate me for my brilliant detective work. More than one romantic candlelight dinner with Michael had been interrupted by people who insisted on shaking my hand, having their picture taken with me, buying us drinks, treating us to dinner—it was impossible.

"Too bad we can't just run away together to a desert island," Michael said after one such interruption.

Inspiration struck.

"Actually, we can," I said. "What are you doing next weekend?"

"Running away to a desert island with you, evidently," Michael said. "Did you have a particular island in mind?"

"Monhegan!" I said.

"Never heard of it. Where is it?"

"Off the coast of Maine."

"Won't that be cold this time of year?"

"The cottage has a fireplace. And a gas heater."

"Cottage?"

"Aunt Phoebe's summer cottage. Actually, it's an old house. And hardly anyone stays on the island after August; it's too rugged." Which meant we wouldn't have half a hundred neighbors and relatives looking over our shoulders and reporting who said what to whom and how many bedrooms were occupied.

"What about Aunt Phoebe?"

"It's a summer cottage, remember? Which she isn't using, partly because summer's over and partly because she's having much more fun down here, waiting for the trial and keeping me awake with her snoring."

"And she won't mind if you use her cottage?"

"She wouldn't mind if she knew, and she won't have to know. Dad has a spare key. She's always inviting us to go up anytime. We haven't for years, but the whole family knows they have an open invitation."

"And how can we be sure the whole family won't be there?"

"In September? Like you said, it's cold this time of year. Besides, most of the family finds it a little too Spartan for their tastes. Mother won't go at all; she refuses to go anywhere that doesn't even have electricity, much less ready access to a deli and a good hairdresser. Michael, this is not a tropical paradise. But it's empty, it's free, and there's nobody else around for miles except for a few dozen locals who winter there."

"I'm sold," he said. "I can't skip Wednesday night's faculty meeting, but I'll get someone to cover my classes for the rest of the week, come by for you early Thursday morning, and we'll drive up."

As I said, it seemed like a good idea at the time. Even the two flat tires that stranded us in a Motel Six near the New Jersey Turnpike for the first night of our getaway hadn't dimmed our enthusiasm. But standing there on the deck of the ferry, I wasn't sure any of that would make sense. I focused back on the present, where Winnie and Binkie were still patiently waiting for an answer. From the way they looked at us, they probably thought we were on the run from something.

"Well, things were so hectic down in Yorktown, and I told Michael about what a great place Monhegan was for getting away from it all," I said finally. "I didn't really stop to think how far past the season it is."

"Yes, you've had quite a time," Winnie said. "We had a note from your father when they were in Rome, and he mentioned your detective adventures. You'll have to come over for dinner and tell us all about it."

Michael winced. I could almost hear his thoughts: So much for anonymity and privacy.

"Yes, that's a wonderful idea," Binkie said. Then her smile suddenly vanished, and she flung her hand out to point over her husband's shoulder.

"Bird!" she cried.

Winnie whirled, and they both produced gleaming high-tech waterproof binoculars from beneath their rain gear. They plastered themselves against the boat rail and locked their lenses on their distant prey. I couldn't see a thing. I glanced at Michael. He shrugged.

I had assumed that the other passengers clinging to the rail were seasick, like us, and either optimistically hoping the fresh air would make them feel better or pessimistically placing themselves where the weather could take care of the inevitable cleanup. But up and down the rail, a forest of binoculars appeared, all trained on the distant speck.

"Only a common tern, I'm afraid," Binkie said. "Still, would you like to see?"

Under Binkie's guidance, I managed to focus on a small black dot atop a distant buoy. Even with the binoculars, you could recognize the dot as a bird only if you already knew what it was.

"Poor thing!" Binkie said "Imagine being out in weather like this!"

I didn't need to imagine; we *were* out in it.

"Oh, there's another tern at three o'clock!"

Dozens of binoculars swerved with the uncanny accuracy of a precision drill team. Binkie redirected my binoculars to another, closer buoy. This one definitely had a morose bird perched on top. I deduced that terns must be closely related to seagulls; this looked like just another seagull to me. The buoy gave a lurch, and the tern had to flap its wings and scramble to keep its footing before hunching down again. It cocked its head and looked at the boat. In the binoculars, it seemed to stare directly at me. It shook its head, pulled it farther back between its shoulders, and looked so miserable and grumpy that I identified with it immediately.

"Poor thing," I said.

"Oh, they're fine," Winnie said. "Coming back very well."

"Coming back from where?"

"Extinction, dear," Binkie said. "Things looked very bad for them at the beginning of the century, poor things, but we've managed to turn that around."

"We have several hundred nests on Egg Island, and, of course, nearly a dozen pair of puffins," Winnie said. "If you get a chance, you should take the tour. The boat leaves from Monhegan and anchors off the island for several hours."

"In the spring, love," Binkie said. "I imagine they stop running after Labor Day. The puffins would be mostly gone by now."

"True," Winnie said. "But if there are still a few puffins there, perhaps we could arrange a special tour for Meg. If the weather lets up a bit," he added, glancing up.

I forced a smile and handed Binkie her binoculars. The weather would have to let up more than a bit before I'd set out from Monhegan again in a boat. But if by some misfortune Winnie and

Binkie succeeded in convincing a suicidal boat captain to take them out puffin-watching, I'd find some excuse.

"Just what is a puffin anyway?" Michael asked.

I winced. Dangerous question. The Burnhams and several nearby birders pulled out their field guides and began imparting puffin lore.

If I'd been explaining, I'd have said to keep his eye out for a black-and-white bird about a foot high that looked like a small penguin wearing an enormous clown nose over his beak and bright orange stockings on his feet. The birders did a good job of describing the beak——a gray-and-yellow triangle with a wide red tip——but they went into too much detail on the chunky body, the stubby wings, the distinctive, clumsy flight, and the precise patterning of the black-and-white feathers. I doubt if Michael needed to know quite so much detail on how to tell immature puffins from other birds he'd never heard of, or if he cared in the slightest about puffins' breeding and nesting habits. When Winnie and another birder began competing to see who could more accurately imitate the low, growling *arr!* that the usually silent puffins make when their nests are disturbed, I groaned in exasperation.

"Don't worry, dear," Binkie said, patting me on the shoulder. "It always gets a little rough when we're this close to the harbor."

"Close to the harbor?" I said. "You mean we'll be landing soon?"

"Thank God," Michael muttered. I wasn't sure whether the ocean or the bird lore made his exclamation so fervent.

And sure enough, within minutes we saw the ferry dock. Quite a crowd of people stood on it with great mounds of luggage. More birders, I supposed, since at least half of them peered through the rain with binoculars. Like the birders on the boat, they scrutinized the gulls that wheeled overhead——hoping, I suppose, to spot a rare species of seagull. The two sets of birders also scanned one another. As we approached the dock, they began pointing, waving, and calling greetings.

"Good Lord, Binkie, look who's on the dock," Winnie said. "Just beside the gift shop."

"Oh no not Victor!" Binkie exclaimed. "How awful! I did so hope we'd seen the last of him."

"No such luck," Winnie growled. "Turns up like a bad penny every few years. Wonder what the old ba—scoundrel's up to this time."

"Never borrow trouble," Binkie said. "We don't know for sure that he's up to anything."

"Like hell we don't."

I peered at the dock, wondering who Victor was and how he could possibly have aroused this much animosity in the normally mild-mannered Burnhams. But without binoculars, I couldn't see many details; if the docks held a sinister villain twirling his mustache or sporting cloven hooves, I couldn't spot him.

"Oh, look, Dr. and Mrs. Peabody," Binkie said—no doubt to distract Winnie from his irritation with the nefarious Victor. "What rotten luck; they're leaving just when we're getting here."

"I wouldn't count on it," Winnie replied, inspecting the Peabodys through his binoculars. "I overheard the captain speaking rather sharply to someone over the radio. Said he'd never have set out if they'd accurately predicted the size of the swells."

I was glad Winnie hadn't mentioned this until after we could see the dock.

"You think he'll ride out the storm here, then?" Binkie asked.

"If he has any sense," Winnie replied.

"Luck was certainly with you two," Binkie said, turning to Michael and me. "You very nearly missed the boat!"

The boat picked that moment to make a sudden free-fall drop into the trough of a wave.

"Lucky us," Michael muttered.

Chapter 2

The Puffin Has Landed

"So this is Monhegan," Michael said as he stood in the middle of the dock, inspecting the landscape.

I was relieved to see that he looked better already. Entirely due to being back on dry land, I was sure. Certainly nothing about our surroundings would cheer anyone up. Did the Monhegan dock always look this seedy and run-down, I wondered? Or were the weather and my queasy stomach still coloring my view of things?

After the boat docked, we had the usual mad scramble to sort out the enormous piles of luggage. Michael and I were luckier than most; the birders tended to favor battered rucksacks and ancient suitcases covered with peeling travel stickers from unpronounceable foreign birding meccas. Our more sedate urban luggage was comparatively easy to spot.

"What next?" Michael asked when we had all our gear.

"Next, we negotiate for someone to take our luggage to the cottage."

I pointed to the island's half a dozen pickup trucks lined up, fender-to-fender, on the dock, with their tailgates open toward the arriving crowds. Beyond the trucks, a steep gravel road, already swarming with birders, led up toward the village proper.

"The two hotels each have a pickup truck to take their guests' baggage," I said. "If you're staying at a bed-and-breakfast or a cottage, you hire one of the freelance pickups to haul your stuff."

"Just our stuff?" Michael said. "What about us?"

"We walk," I said. "Unless you want us to get a reputation as lazy city folks."

Michael and I stood back, though, until the logjam of birders cleared. Which didn't take long: As soon as the birders realized the ferry wasn't going anywhere, they all panicked and scurried up the hill. Birders who had planned to leave set out to reclaim the rooms they had recently vacated before the newly arrived birders checked in. The new arrivals hurried after them to wave their confirmation letters and credit cards before their stranded colleagues established squatters' rights.

Within minutes, the dock lay deserted. The few travelers, like Winnie and Binkie, who owned cottages and didn't have to worry about someone else displacing them had gone into the small shop at the foot of the hill to drink hot tea and catch up on the local gossip. Lucky that Michael and I weren't staying in a hotel; I didn't think I could have beaten even the oldest and most arthritic birder up the hill. But we declined an invitation to join the Burnhams and found ourselves alone on the dock, surrounded by mountains of luggage higher than our heads.

"Are they all just going to leave their luggage here?" Michael asked.

"Why not?" I said. "Who would steal it, and where could they possibly hide it if they did? There's no getting off the island until the ferry starts running again."

We found a truck with room for our larger bags, and paid the exorbitant hauling fee. Despite my warnings, Michael tried to talk the driver into giving us a ride.

"No room," said the driver. His broad face looked vaguely familiar. He was about my age, which meant if he was a local, I'd probably played with him as a child. Or, more likely, beaten the tar out of him for picking on my much younger brother, Rob, if my memories of some of the other children we'd played with on the island were accurate. His clothes smelled of cigarette smoke and beer, and he had a seedy, furtive air that made me wonder, just for a moment, if letting him have our baggage was really a good idea.

"We could wait till you come back," Michael said.

"Not coming back," the driver replied. "Not for a while anyway. You could walk there sooner."

"I'm not sure my friend is up to the walk," Michael said, putting a protective arm around me.

I did my best to look frail and in need of protection as the driver peered at me. I could tell I wasn't succeeding. Which didn't surprise me; when you're nearly five foot nine, people tend to look at you and think, Sturdy. Unless you're model-thin, which I'm not. Even with Michael looming half a foot taller beside me, I obviously didn't look like the driver's idea of a damsel in distress.

"She's getting over a broken ankle," Michael said. "She's not supposed to overdo it."

I switched from frail to suffering stoically. The driver still wasn't fooled.

"Only a quarter of a mile," he said. "Ain't even uphill most of the way."

With that, he jumped into the cab of the truck and gunned the engine.

The truck took off, spinning its wheels a little before the tires got enough traction to climb the steep slope up from the docks. Little blobs of mud spattered us.

"Bloody little weasel," I snapped. "Bad enough he wouldn't give us a ride—"

"Don't worry," Michael said, wiping a bit of mud out of his left eye. "It'll wash off by the time we get to the cottage."

"Yes, it is beginning to drizzle a bit more heavily, isn't it?"

"We follow him?"

I glanced over. Michael was staring up the hill.

"Strange," I said. "The hill didn't seem as steep when I was a kid."

Michael chuckled.

"I remember it always used to drive me crazy how long it took for us to get to the cottage from the docks."

"Oh great."

"But that was mostly because Dad insisted on stopping to talk to everyone along the way. We'd take two or three hours, sometimes. But really it's only a fifteen-minute walk."

"The sooner we begin, the sooner we'll get warm and dry," Michael said, hoisting his carry-on bag to his shoulder. "Lead on, Macduff."

We trudged up the hill. Ahead of us, we could see the last two birders hiking stoutly toward the crest. The rest had no doubt reached their hotels or bed-and-breakfast lodgings long ago and were now watching whatever birders watch when the weather deprives them of their natural prey.

At the crest of the hill, we turned right on the island's main thoroughfare—another dirt and gravel road, but this one slightly better maintained. It wound through a seemingly haphazard scattering of buildings, most made of weather-beaten gray boards. I tried to see the place through a stranger's eyes, and cringed. You forget little details over time, like how many yards contained untidy stacks of lobster traps in need of mending. Or how the utilitarian PVC pipes that brought water down from the central reservoir lined every road. I could see Michael darting glances around, and I suspected he was wondering why the devil we'd come all this way to such an unprepossessing place. The picturesque charm of the island definitely came across better on a sunny summer day than in the wake of a fall hurricane.

The drizzle had escalated to a light shower by the time we turned down the lane to Aunt Phoebe's cottage. About time; a little later and we'd have had to stumble along in the dark. Monhegan has no streetlights. And Aunt Phoebe thought repairing the ruts in her lane a citified affectation, which made finding your way in the dark a nightmare.

Only it wasn't dark. I could see light ahead of us——coming from the house. And was that music playing? I felt a twinge of panic. Surely Aunt Phoebe hadn't rented it, had she? She was always so adamant about having it ready at any time the family wanted to use it.

"Someone's already here," Michael said.

"No one's supposed to be," I said. "Maybe it's just the cleaners. I know Aunt Phoebe has someone local come in every two weeks or so to keep the place from getting too dirty."

A burst of laughter rang out from inside the cottage.

"Wish I enjoyed cleaning that much," Michael said. He shifted his carry-on bag from one shoulder to the other.

I noticed that the rest of our luggage hadn't arrived yet. Michael's attempts to bribe the driver into giving us a ride had probably irritated him to the point that he'd make sure ours was the last off the truck. He might even pretend to forget about it until the morning, with our luck. I sighed.

"Well, there's no sense standing out here wondering," I said. I marched up the steps, ready to deal with whatever the cottage contained——burglars? Squatters? Cleaners who had gotten into the bar and decided to hold an impromptu hurricane party?

I squared my shoulders and knocked firmly on the door.

Chapter 3

All My Puffins

No one answered. I waited briefly, then knocked again.

Another burst of laughter greeted my knock.

"What's going on in there?" I called.

Still no answer.

"Well, here goes," I said.

I flung open the door.

The cottage was empty. But someone, obviously, had been there, and not very long ago.

"I guess someone was expecting us," Michael said.

Evidently—but who?

We looked around. A fire crackled briskly in the fireplace. Enough candles burned in various parts of the room to cast a warm, romantic glow. Both sofas were piled high with down pillows and fuzzy afghans. Two teacups stood on the coffee table, and a hint of steam and a faint odor of jasmine indicated that the quilted cozy concealed a fresh pot of tea. A battery radio sat on the mantel; as we stood there gaping, a final burst of laughter signaled the end of a commercial and an announcer with a beautiful spun-silk baritone voice assured us that W something or other would now continue with its Friday-night light classical program. The strains of "The Blue Danube Waltz" filled the room.

"Hello?" I called.

I stepped inside. I could smell something cooking. Right now, my stomach objected strenuously to this, but, even so, I could tell that when I'd fully recovered from the ferry ride, whatever was going on in the kitchen would turn out to be intensely interesting. A bottle of champagne stood on the table, beads of sweat running down its sides, with a corkscrew and two glass flutes nearby.

"You know, this is a lot less primitive than you described it," Michael said, dropping his bags by the door. "In fact, now that we're off the boat, I think I'm starting to like this place."

He looked around appreciatively. The place did look its best by candlelight. The living room was two stories high, with stairs curling around one wall, leading to a balconylike upper hall, off which the three bedrooms opened. Downstairs, under the bedrooms, were a large bathroom and a larger kitchen. I remembered the place as tiny and cramped—which it usually was in the summer, with every bedroom filled, a carpet of sleeping bags in the living room, and a typical hour-long wait to use the bathroom. But for two people looking for peace and quiet and a place to get away from it all, the cottage suddenly looked like a palace.

"Let's worry about the luggage later," Michael said, sitting down on one of the sofas and patting the cushion beside him. I joined him, and for a few minutes we sat there in silence, enjoying the warmth, the music, the whole ambiance.

Although I did wonder who had opened up the cottage and set everything up for us. Had Winnie and Binkie made a quick call from the gift shop and sent some helpful neighbor over? Or had Aunt Phoebe noticed the missing key, done a head count, and decided to arrange a lovely surprise? Whoever it was, they had my thanks. In my exhausted state, I kept remembering the version of "Beauty and the Beast" in which the disembodied hands set the table and served dinner, and I wondered if something similar had happened here.

No matter, I thought, sinking back against Michael's arm. This is heavenly.

The door suddenly opened with a bang.

"I'm back!" caroled a voice.

Michael and I whirled about in astonishment.

"Dad?" I said.

My father stood in the doorway with a load of wood in his arms. Water flew everywhere as he shook himself like a dog.

"Meg!" he cried. He dumped the wood on the hearth with a thump, then enfolded me in a soggy bear hug. "What a wonderful surprise!"

"You think you're surprised," I muttered. "You have no idea."

"And Michael," Dad added. "How grand! Margaret, come look; it's Meg and Michael here to join us."

Mother appeared at the top of the stairway, delicately suppressing a yawn, carrying her embroidery and a European fashion magazine.

"Meg, dear," she cried. She floated gracefully down the stairs and bent over to kiss my cheek. "This is so nice! And how lovely to see you, Michael."

Not a single improbably blond hair had strayed out of place, and she looked, as usual, as if she could replace any of the models in the magazine on a moment's notice.

Just then, I heard a loud pop, and something whizzed past my nose and bounced off Michael's chin.

"Sorry about that, Michael," Dad said, waggling the champagne bottle. "Nothing broken, I hope?"

"No, I'm fine," Michael said, rubbing his chin.

"Here we go," Dad said, handing Mother a glass of the champagne and taking a sip from his own glass. "Would you two like any?"

"No thanks," Michael and I chorused. I closed my eyes. I wasn't quite ready to watch people eating and drinking.

The door slammed open again.

"Well, I see the ferry's in," said Aunt Phoebe, appearing in the doorway with a dripping canvas tote in each hand. "You've missed dinner, but there's plenty of leftovers. Smithfield ham, potato salad——"

"No thanks," I said.

"Maybe later," Michael added.

"Hell, they just got off the ferry; they're probably sick as dogs," cackled Mother's best friend, Mrs. Fenniman, appearing behind Aunt Phoebe with her own pair of tote bags. "Leave them in peace till their guts stop heaving."

Although Mrs. Fenniman was absolutely right, I wished she hadn't emphasized the word *heaving* quite so forcefully. My stomach gave a queasy lurch, as if to say, Okay, time to pay attention to me.

"Is the ferry going back tonight?" came a voice from above our heads. I looked up, to see my brother, Rob, standing on the upstairs landing, rubbing his eyes as if he'd just awakened.

"My God," I said. "Is everyone in Yorktown up here? Yikes!"

I jumped as something cold and wet touched my ankle.

"What the devil is Spike doing here?" Michael asked, looking down at the small black-and-white fur ball at my feet. Although Spike was Michael's mother's dog, he had never liked Michael. He looked up for a moment, curled his lip at Michael, and returned to his favorite pastime of licking me obsessively. He didn't seem to mind the mud.

"Your mother asked me to baby-sit him for the weekend," Rob said. "And when I had to drive up here, there wasn't anything I could do but bring him along. You want to take charge of him?"

"Thanks, but you'll probably get back to Yorktown before I do," Michael said. He didn't like Spike any more than Spike liked him. Of course, Spike didn't really like anyone but Michael's mother and me. And I'd never figured out why he liked me. The feeling certainly wasn't mutual.

"True, I'm heading home as soon as possible," Rob said.

"Speaking of which, I'd probably better get my bag and head down to the ferry."

"I doubt the ferry's going anywhere tonight," I said. "And trust me, if it was, you wouldn't want to be on it. For a tropical storm that's heading out to sea to die, this one still has a lot of life left in it."

"That's because it isn't heading out to sea to die," Mrs. Fenniman said, pouring herself some tea. "It just went out to sea long enough to pick up steam. It's back up to a hurricane again and has turned around to take another run at the coast."

"What?"

"It's true; I just heard it on the radio," Mrs. Fenniman said with the good cheer she usually displayed when she had managed to scoop everyone else with news of a scandal or disaster.

"Oh great," Rob said. "I guess that means I'm stuck here for the duration."

He threw himself down on one of the couches and assumed a martyred air. Along with Mother's slender height and aristocratic blond looks, he'd inherited her talent for self-dramatization.

"Don't be gloomy," Dad said. He stood before the hearth, apparently trying to set the back of his pants on fire. His short, round form and the way the firelight played on his bald head made him look like a mischievous gnome. "Look on the bright side," he added. "After all these years, we'll finally get to see what really happens here during a hurricane!"

"Yippee," Rob mumbled without enthusiasm.

"Oh dear," Mother murmured.

"Don't worry, Margaret," Aunt Phoebe said. She had shed her dripping rain gear and was tying a green-and-orange-flowered apron over her stout khaki-clad form. "We've got plenty of food and fuel. We may have to rough it for a bit, but we'll come through just fine."

Mother looked relieved. After all, she knew better than anyone that Aunt Phoebe's idea of roughing it meant using the checked gingham napkins instead of the starched linen, and that the caviar might be tinned instead of fresh.

"Time we got busy," Mrs. Fenniman said. She had donned a flowered apron identical to Aunt Phoebe's, though it looked odd over her usual black clothes and scrawny frame. The two of them hefted their tote bags and disappeared into the kitchen.

"We can go out on the cliffs at Green Point and actually see the storm hit!" Dad went on. "Won't that be fantastic!"

"Oh, James, you mustn't!" Mother protested.

"Won't that be dangerous?" Michael asked. I looked at him with astonishment and more than a little dismay. He sounded as if he might actually be considering Dad's suggestion. Much as I adored my father, I'd always sworn never to get involved with someone who did the kind of crazy things Dad did. And yet, there it was again: I could see on Michael's face that same look of lovable but daft enthusiasm. Oh dear, I thought. Dad had spread a small map of Monhegan over the coffee table and was scribbling madly on it—apparently trying to calculate the best spot to await the hurricane's arrival. Michael leaned over to watch.

"Count me out," Rob said. "I have to work on Lawyers from Hell."

Mother sighed. The whole family was still anxiously waiting to see if Rob had, by chance, passed the bar exam in July. Since he and his bar exam review group had whiled away the summer inventing a role-playing game called Lawyers from Hell instead of doing anything that even vaguely resembled studying, the odds were slim.

"I really ought to be back in Yorktown working on it," Rob said. What he meant was that he wanted to be back in Yorktown talking about bits and bytes with Red, his new girlfriend, who was helping him turn Lawyers from Hell into a computer game.

"How on earth did you get here anyway?" I asked, taking Rob aside.

"We came over on the ferry yesterday," he said.

"Well, I figured out that much," I said. "I meant, what are all of you doing up here in the first place?"

"Dad called to say they were flying home from Paris and could I meet them at Dulles Airport," Rob said. "Their plane got in very early yesterday morning. And Aunt Phoebe and Mrs. Fenniman hitched a ride up to Washington with me so they could catch a flight to Maine to go birding. But the flight got canceled because of the hurricane, and instead of going back to Yorktown, Aunt Phoebe convinced Mother and Dad to come up here with her. What are you doing here?"

"Looking for a little privacy," Michael put in.

"Good luck," Rob said with a snicker, and slipped out of the room—probably to call Red and indulge in a little long-distance whining. Or heavy breathing.

Well, Rob isn't the only one doomed to disappointment in his love life for the immediate future, I thought, glancing at Michael as I sat back down beside him. Here I was, sitting with the man of my dreams on an overstuffed sofa by a roaring fire, just as I'd imagined in my fantasies about this weekend. But having to share the experience with my entire family took a lot of the fun out of it.

I felt guilty about resenting their presence. They were all trying so hard to make us feel better. Of course, this meant that every five minutes one of them would pop up with either a new remedy for seasickness or a new tactic for preventing pneumonia. And I'd taken a head count and compared it to the number of bedrooms and figured out that I'd probably be sleeping on one of the sofas.

"Now the phone's out," Rob announced, shuffling back into the room and throwing himself on the other sofa.

"Usually happens in a storm," Aunt Phoebe said, shoving a cup of herbal tea into my hands.

"I wouldn't mind so much if I could just use my laptop," Rob said.

"Can't you just run it on battery?" Michael asked.

"I could, except the battery's old; it only holds about a fifteen-minute charge," Rob said. "And it takes me ten minutes to boot up and figure out how to open my word processor."

"I tell you what," Dad said. "Let's run an extension cord up to the Dickermans' house. I'm sure they wouldn't mind."

Whether the Dickermans would mind or not was irrelevant; I doubted they could resist Dad when he got his mind set on doing something.

"Ugh," Rob said, and sneezed. A patently phony sneeze, I thought; obviously designed to serve as an excuse for not sloshing out in the rain with Dad. But it served its purpose. Mother, Aunt Phoebe, and Mrs. Fenniman immediately turned their full attention to medicating Rob. I took advantage of the distraction to pour my herbal tea into an already-moribund potted plant.

"Come on, Meg; you can help me run the extension cord," Dad said, picking up a flashlight. "You, too, Michael. Fresh air will do you a world of good."

I didn't really want to go back out into the rain. I wanted to curl up someplace quiet and sleep for a few years. But it didn't look as if I'd get any peace and quiet in the cottage for a while, with Aunt Phoebe and Mrs. Fenniman arguing about the weather and trying to pour their potions and philters into me. Not to mention the way my stomach reacted to the smell of all the food. Maybe fresh air was a good idea. I sighed, then got up and followed Dad and Michael to the coatrack beside the kitchen door, where we rummaged through a rather random collection of rain gear. We finally found slickers for all three of us, though Michael's was too short, mine nearly dragged the ground, and Dad's was glow-in-the-dark pink with lime green and yellow spots.

Then we repeated the rummaging, this time in the garden

shed. Underneath a hand-cranked ice-cream freezer, a collection of antique life jackets, a gas grill, odd parts of three unmatched croquet sets, and several dozen mildewing stacks of *Life* magazines from the forties and fifties, we finally unearthed three bright orange industrial-weight extension cords.

"That should do the trick," Dad said, and we set off for the Dickermans' house.

I'd forgotten how dark Monhegan nights could be. In clear weather, you could see three times as many stars as in the city, and the sight of the moon rising over the ocean could inspire even me to poetry. But when clouds obscured the moon and stars, as they did tonight, you could really understand the deep-seated human tendency to fear the dark.

The darkness relented only slightly when we passed by our nearest neighbors, with whom Aunt Phoebe shared her treacherous, muddy little lane. Like Aunt Phoebe, they had only oil lamps and gas appliances. Some residents ran their own small electrical generators—including, apparently, the Dickermans—but these contraptions were noisy and generally less reliable than the old-fashioned alternatives—not to mention so expensive that their owners tended to keep their wattage low to avoid bankruptcy.

The flashlight wasn't much help, and I felt strangely comforted by the luminous glow of Dad's raincoat as he bobbed along ahead of us.

Suddenly, just as we reached the head of the lane, the glow disappeared.

"Dad?" I called, and hurried to reach the point where I'd last seen the glow-in-the-dark raincoat. I tripped over something large and hard and fell flat on my face in the gravel road.

"Your luggage is here," Dad said. The glow hadn't disappeared entirely, I realized; it was now—like me—horizontal.

"Are you two all right?" Michael said, coming up beside us.

"I will be if you take your foot off my hand," I said, trying not to make it sound like an accusation.

"Sorry," he said. "I can't see a thing."

"Damn that little weasel," I said. "He might at least have run the luggage up to the house."

"Maybe he was scared of getting stuck in the mud," Michael suggested.

"Well, we can take it up on the way back," Dad said. "Let's get up to the Dickermans' house before they go to bed."

The Dickermans, to my surprise, were thrilled to have Dad run a power cord down to our house. Of course, Dad had forgotten to mention that this was a commercial arrangement, the Dickermans being the founders and owners of the Central Monhegan Power Company.

"I didn't know Monhegan even had a central power company," I said. "Of course, it's been several years since I've spent much time on the island," I added hastily, seeing the hurt look on Mr. Dickerman's broad, friendly face.

"Well, really it's only one generator," Mr. Dickerman said. "Quite a bit larger than the ones individual households and businesses use, of course."

"And a bit quieter, obviously, if you've got it anywhere around here."

"Oh, it's noisy enough, but we've put it up on Knob Hill," Mr. Dickerman said. "It's pretty much out of the way up there, and the noise doesn't bother folks as much. Jim does most of the work on it; he's always been handy that way, Jim has."

"And so nice that he's found something to do without leaving the island," Mrs. Dickerman put in. She was a sweet, motherly person; I never could figure out how she and her mild-mannered husband had managed to produce so many rowdy and unpleasant sons, at least half a dozen of them. "All my other birds have flown the coop, but Jimmy's happy as a clam, staying here with us, where he can tinker with the generator. Does you good to see how happy he is, up at the electric plant, when he's working on those machines of his."

"Don't forget Fred," Mr. Dickerman put in.

"Fred's only here between jobs," Mrs. Dickerman said. "You remember Jimmy, don't you, Meg?"

I did, actually, with something that approached fondness—he was the one Dickerman of my generation who wasn't loud, extroverted, and an inveterate bully. The worst had been Fred, whom I now recognized as the driver of the truck and kidnapper of our luggage. But Jimmy had been a small, intense, bespectacled little boy, whose main interest in life was taking things apart. He and Dad got along well that way, although, unlike Dad, Jimmy could also put the things back together again. When he felt like it, which was seldom. I wondered how much time the Central Monhegan Power Company's generator ran and how much time it spent disassembled for maintenance, enhancements, and general tinkering.

"Maybe if she sees how useful the electricity can be, Phoebe might see her way clear to hooking on," Mr. Dickerman suggested.

"Maybe," Dad said. "But then again, you know what a traditionalist Phoebe is."

"She is that," Mr. Dickerman agreed. "We could have used her here this spring, when the town council was squabbling over what to do about Victor Resnick's new house."

"Victor Resnick? The landscape artist?" Michael asked.

"That's the one," Mr. Dickerman said. He didn't sound all that fond of the local celebrity, and I suspected Resnick was the Victor Winnie and Binkie Burnham had been so dismayed to see on the docks.

"Monhegan has quite a lot of famous artists," I said aloud. "One of the Wyeths lives here, too; or at least he used to. I forget which one."

"I thought Resnick had moved to Europe," Dad said, frowning.

"Came back last fall and built himself a new house," Mr. Dick-erman said. "A real eyesore. Ought to run the bastard off the island."

"Frank!" Mrs. Dickerman scolded.

"Well, they ought to," Mr. Dickerman said.

Dad seemed unusually subdued as he and Mr. Dickerman fin-ished hooking up the extension cord and making the arrange-ments for payment. He was deep in thought during the whole return trip to the cottage—which wasn't exactly a bad thing. Instead of returning by the road, we had to run the extension cord as directly as possible to Aunt Phoebe's—which meant slog-ging through the Dickermans' overgrown backyard, followed by a brier-filled gully, and then the cord barely reached the living room. Even in our debilitated state, Michael and I probably man-aged it much better by ourselves than we would have if Dad had insisted on taking an active hand.

Rob pounced on the cord with glee, hooked up his computer, and began tapping away on the keyboard—though whether he was doing useful work or merely composing an e-mail he could send to Red when the phone lines returned, I had no idea. Dad took advantage of the power supply to hook up his portable CD player and put on his beloved Wagner. And then he scurried out of the room again, after turning up the volume enough that he could hear it from anyplace in the cottage. From anyplace on the island, probably; lucky for us the phones were down, or ours would have rung off the hook with noise complaints.

I glanced at Michael to see how he was taking all this. At least so far, he seemed more amused than annoyed. That was one of Michael's charms: his tolerance for my father's eccentricities seemed as great as mine.

Possibly greater, I thought as the orchestra sank its teeth into a loud, rousing passage of the overture.

The opera was just hitting its stride when the music stopped in the middle of one of Brünnhilde more appalling shrieks.

Chapter 4

A Portrait of the Puffin as a Young Man

In the sudden absence of Wagner, we heard Aunt Phoebe's voice bellowing in the kitchen.

"Never would have come out here in the first place if we'd had any idea we'd run into that son of a——"

"Sshh!" Mrs. Fenniman hissed, and then, a little louder, she called out, "What happened to the power?"

"Oh dear," Mother said, looking up from her magazine. "Not the generator already?"

"I hope I can save in time," Rob said, fingers flying over the keyboard.

"Maybe someone tripped over the cord," I said. "We should go see if——"

"Damnation!" came a voice just outside the windows.

"I don't think you'll have to go far," Michael remarked.

The music came back on, almost drowning out the loud footsteps stomping up the porch steps. Carrying Michael's and my suitcases, Dad appeared in the doorway with blood running down his face from a cut on the top of his head.

"James! What happened?" Mother cried, leaping up.

"Tripped over the extension cord," Dad said. "Don't fuss; it's not serious. Scalp wounds do bleed a lot."

"The suitcases," Michael said, rushing over to take our luggage from Dad. "I'm so sorry; I forgot they were there. I should have gone back for them."

"Not to worry," Dad said. He picked up his black doctor's bag and scurried off to clean up his cut, with Mother trailing in his wake.

Dad brushed off all our attempts at sympathy.

"I'll be fine," he said when he returned, sporting a picturesque dressing on his head. "I'll just sit here and listen to my Wagner and I'll feel better in no time."

After that, of course, guilt prevented us from even asking him to turn it down a little.

Dad hummed and conducted with his fork quite happily for what seemed like an eternity but must have been only an hour or two. Fortunately, before the neighbors showed up at our door bearing torches, like the villagers in a bad horror movie, the power went out again.

"Probably just someone else tripping over the extension cords," Dad said.

We waited for a few minutes, but no sounds of cursing came from the yard.

"I suppose I'll have to follow the line up to the Dickermans," Dad said with a sigh.

"I don't think so," I said, peering out a window. "The Dickermans' house is dark. And listen."

Everyone cocked their heads and listened intently for a few seconds.

"I don't hear anything," Mother said finally. "Just the wind."

"That's just it," I said. "I've heard this persistent rhythmic humming noise ever since we got to the island. I thought the hurricane was doing it. But now I realize it's the generator."

"She's right," Aunt Phoebe said. "I've complained to the town council about that noise. You don't notice it as much when a hurricane's approaching, but in normal weather, it's a menace. Much more peaceful like this, when the generator stops."

Deprived of his Wagner, Dad decided he was tired, and Mother agreed that perhaps an early night would be a good idea. Since by my calculations they'd covered more than three thousand miles by plane, boat, and automobile over the last forty-eight hours, I wasn't surprised. And the thought occurred to me that if the rest of the family got tired and went to bed, Michael and I might still rescue some shreds of our romantic evening by the fire.

Unfortunately, no one else seemed the slightest bit fatigued. Aunt Phoebe and Mrs. Fenniman were still out in the kitchen, cooking under the soft glow of the oil lamps. Rob wandered about restlessly for a while. Eventually, I could hear him opening the trapdoor and letting down the ladder to the attic. He scuffled around up there for a while, then reappeared with an armload of old volumes.

"What are those?" Michael asked.

"Photo albums that Aunt Phoebe likes to keep around at the cottage," Rob said. "She says when people have electricity, they're too busy with TV and computers and stuff to look at old photos."

"Well, she's right, isn't she?" Michael said. "What were you doing before the power went out?"

Rob shrugged sheepishly and picked up an album.

"Actually, Rob usually does spend time with the photo albums," I said. "It must be the charm of seeing variations on your own face, wearing so many old-fashioned hairdos and clothes, Rob."

"You could be right," Rob said. "Look at this. Great-Uncle Christopher."

He held up a picture. But for the handlebar mustache and dandified Edwardian clothes, you could easily have mistaken it for a picture of Rob.

"He looks rather dashing in the uniform on the next page, too," Michael said. "World War One?"

"Yes," Rob said, assuming a solemn air. "Poor Uncle Christopher!"

"He never came back?" Michael said. Rob shook his head and

sighed, as if the whole thing were a tragedy from which the family had never recovered.

"Yes," I said. "Killed in a brawl in a French bordello, apparently; though they made up something else to tell his mother."

Michael laughed, and Rob looked as insulted as if I'd impugned his character, instead of that of our late and little-lamented greatuncle. He pointedly buried his face in the album. Michael picked up another volume and began to flip through it.

"Don't you enjoy the albums, too?" he asked. "Seeing your face through history and all that?"

"I suppose I would, but apparently I look like Dad's side of the family," I said. "None of the pictures look much like me."

I didn't mention the other reason: that looking in the albums usually triggered a temporary but acute resurgence of the inferiority complex I'd fought all my life. Far too many of my female ancestors had been tall, thin, aristocratic blondes, like Mother; and the albums contained far too many pictures of them surrounded by the swarms of beautiful, wealthy, and sometimes famous men who'd courted them.

The album Michael had picked up, for instance. Looking over his shoulder, I could see that it held hundreds of photos from the late forties and early fifties, all neatly arranged and held in place with old-fashioned black paper photo corners. The early pictures, featuring the angelic preadolescent Mother, were bad enough. But looking at her at thirteen, when she'd already acquired a figure and a flock of admirers, I could feel myself fighting off those old feelings of inadequacy.

It helps a little that none of the men were as gorgeous as Michael is, I thought, looking fondly at him and curling a little closer. And that many of them ought not to have allowed themselves to be photographed in swimsuits, although I suppose I was applying today's fitness standards to bodies not considered unattractive fifty years ago. Perhaps the kind of lean, tanned, muscular body modern women consider attractive in a man would have been a dead giveaway, back in those more class-conscious times, that its owner earned his living from some kind of badly paid manual labor.

But still; seeing picture after picture of Mother surrounded by half a dozen obviously smitten men—well, it got depressing. And the occasional suitor whose face appeared a little too often, who always wangled a place right beside Mother in the group shots, who occasionally managed to ditch the crowd and have his picture taken with Mother, as a couple—for some reason, they made me anxious. I couldn't help wondering if but for some strange accident or other she might have married one of them. And where would I be then?

"I think some of them have fallen out," Michael said, coming to a page with several empty sets of corners.

"More likely, they're pictures Mother considered unflattering," I said. The other nearby pictures were all of Mother posing in a two-piece bathing suit. While the suit looked demure enough by today's standards, I suspected that forty-odd years ago, it had been daring enough to give my grandfather conniption fits.

We stayed up for a while, looking at the albums—at least Rob and Michael were looking, and I was half-dozing against Michael's shoulder. Even after Rob yawned his way upstairs with an album under his arm, Mrs. Fenniman and Aunt Phoebe kept bustling in and out of the living room at frequent intervals to make sure Michael and I weren't getting ill. Michael finally said good night. He found about a dozen excuses to pop back downstairs when everything seemed quiet, but we finally gave up trying to find a few moments alone together and said an awkward good night, with Mrs. Fenniman at our elbows, pressing cough lozenges into our hands.

If I hadn't been doomed to spend the night on the sofa, I'd have felt very sorry for Michael. He was sharing with Rob what we referred to as "the children's room"—a former walk-in closet fitted with a set of rickety bunk beds half a foot too short for either of them. Far from ideal, but since no one could reasonably expect Aunt Phoebe or Mrs. Fenniman to scramble into an upper bunk, they were stuck with it.

I made a bed for myself on the less lumpy of the two living room sofas. But I didn't get to sleep right away. Mrs. Fenniman and Aunt Phoebe continued their culinary efforts until well past midnight. Either they planned to invite the whole island over very soon or they expected to be stranded for a very long time. Both prospects appalled me.

They kept trying to talk me into sleeping on a floor pallet in their room. Since Aunt Phoebe's snoring had helped inspire my flight from Yorktown, and Mrs. Fenniman was just as bad, I resisted their suggestions with every argument I could muster, including the pretense that I still felt dizzy from the ferry and didn't want to risk the stairs, which let me in for another round of foul-tasting herbal remedies.

They finally tramped up to bed, still arguing about whether Hurricane Maude or Hurricane Ethel had been the most devastating storm to hit the island in previous years. After another hour or so of people stumbling in and out of the bathroom, dropping their flashlights, barking their shins on things, and swearing with varying degrees of verbal ingenuity, the house finally settled down and I dropped off to sleep.

I'd probably gotten a whole hour's sleep by the time the Central Monhegan Power Company's generator started up again. And I'd have slept through that easily if Dad, while trying to turn his Wagner off, hadn't turned the CD player's volume dial the wrong way and cranked it up to the maximum.

My second awakening of the morning was quieter, although no less nerve-racking. I woke up realizing that I needed to go to the bathroom. Luckily, before I leapt off the sofa, I noticed a small, warm weight lying on top of me. Spike.

Because I'd once rescued him from dire peril, Spike had decided I was the one person in the world he liked, other than Mrs.

Waterston. Unfortunately, since his memory was as bad as his temper, Spike periodically forgot who Mrs. Waterston and I were. Which made him more dangerous to us than to the people he didn't like. At least they could keep their distance. He was always trying to climb into our laps to be petted, which brought us within easy chewing distance when he suddenly decided to mistake us for the dreaded mail carrier.

Mrs. Waterston took this a lot more philosophically than I did. Why couldn't Michael's mother have adopted a cat, for heaven's sake, instead of an overbred nine-pound dust mop?

I knew from experience that Spike was a lot more likely to bite you if you woke him up suddenly than if you let him wake up at his own pace. And you learned to give him a wide berth for the first hour or two, until he'd had his walk and his breakfast.

I lay there, growing increasingly uncomfortable as Spike slumbered, unbelievably loud snores issuing from his tiny pushed-in nose. Finally, around dawn, he heard Aunt Phoebe rattling pans in the kitchen and ran off to see if it was raining food in there.

"You look tired," Michael said over breakfast.

" 'The Ride of the Valkyries' is not my idea of a lullaby," I said, frowning at Dad. "It's a wonder I have any hearing left, as loud as that damned thing was."

"Remarkable speakers, aren't they?" Dad said.

"Hurry up with breakfast," I whispered to Michael. "We need to talk."

"Okay," Michael said—a little too loudly, for he found he'd agreed to a second helping of Mrs. Fenniman's undercooked grits.

"Well, the damned storm's stalled again," Mrs. Fenniman announced.

"Is the ferry running?" Rob asked.

"I said stalled, not gone away," Mrs. Fenniman replied. "Just close enough to keep the ferry from running, but not close enough to bother us much. Not yet anyway. Looks like we'll have good weather for another day."

I glanced out at the gray sky and the faint but steady drizzle. Yes, this would be Mrs. Fenniman's idea of good weather.

Michael and I managed to escape the house without anyone else tagging along, although Dad insisted that we each shoulder a backpack filled with several pounds of survival gear that we might need if we got lost for a few weeks. And Aunt Phoebe gave us a long list of errands she wanted us to run down in the village.

"You'd think the village was in Siberia," I complained as we finally escaped down the lane. "It's not as if it would take them ten minutes to walk down here themselves."

"If it keeps them happy," Michael said. He looked a lot more rested than I felt, and when he shook the water out of his hair, he resembled a hunk from a commercial for deodorant soap. I could feel my hair, initially frizzy from the damp, being matted down by the rain; no doubt I'd soon resemble a drowned rat.

"How did you sleep?" I asked.

"Your brother snores," he said.

"So does Spike."

"Spike doesn't talk in his sleep."

"Did Rob say anything interesting?"

"No, and if I hear another word about Lawyers from Hell . . ."

"I'm really sorry," I said. "It's all my fault; I should never have suggested coming here."

"Let's make a deal," Michael said. "I won't blame you for anything that goes wrong if you promise to stop apologizing for bringing me here. After all, if my damned car hadn't had those two flats, we might have spotted them before boarding the ferry the day before yesterday, and we could have changed our plans and found a bed-and-breakfast on the mainland."

"It's a deal," I said.

"So let's go down to the grocery store and see if they still have any of the things your aunt wants."

"We should probably hit both grocery stores," I said as we squelched down the road.

"Both grocery stores? How can an island this small possibly support two grocery stores?"

"The two of them together are smaller than a Seven-Eleven back home. And they serve slightly different clientele. There's the upscale grocery store—in that salmon pink building with the turquoise trim," I said, pointing down the road. "Caters more to the artists and the summer people; probably does a lot less business this time of year. Sells Brie and whole-grain bread from an organic bakery on the mainland. Nice selection of wines. The place that looks like a bait shop is the other grocery. More like a general store, really. Bologna and Wonder Bread, and a good variety of beers. They do a lot more steady year-round business, I should think."

"Let's start with the down-to-earth place," Michael said. "There's something obscenely decadent about eating Brie in the eye of a hurricane."

Decadent or not, it sounded perfectly lovely to me, but Michael was obviously getting into the spirit of things, roughing it here on the island, so I didn't argue.

"Actually, since we already have more food than we'll ever eat, I thought we could leave the grocery store till later." I said. "Maybe we should start with our other mission."

"Other mission?"

"Finding you a room of your own. One without a roommate."

"One where I might possibly entertain a friend without being interrupted every five minutes to drink another cup of herbal tea?" he said, raising one eyebrow.

"You've got the idea."

"I like the way you think," he said.

Chapter 5

These Puffins Were Made for Walkin'

We tried. We really did. The Monhegan House's three dozen rooms were filled with birders. The Island Inn was full, as well. Overflowing, in fact. I'd forgotten about the oversupply of birders.

"We've called up everyone on the island, trying to find rooms for them all," the owner of the Island Inn explained. "We even have a bunch of birders camping out down in the church."

"Well, so much for peace and quiet and privacy," Michael said. "I assume on an island this size, everyone has a pretty good idea who has a vacancy and who doesn't?"

"On an island this size, everyone has a pretty good idea who's running low on corn flakes and toilet paper," I said. "I think we can take it as a given that there's no room at the inn. Any inn."

So by 9:00 A.M.—an hour when I normally prefer to be fast asleep—we had already given up on our search. We sat for a few minutes on a soggy wooden swing on the front porch of the Island Inn and watched the pedestrians hiking up and down the streets. The rain had temporarily slacked off to a mere icy mist, and both birds and birders made the most of it. I only caught fleeting glimpses of the birds, but I was getting to know the plumage and feeding habits of the common New England bird-watcher pretty well.

Actually, at first glance, it was hard to tell the locals from the bird-watchers. Everyone had some kind of waterproof footgear, with the unfortunate exception of Michael and me. Rain ponchos

and down vests were commonplace. I wondered if it had occurred to any of them how many birds had given their all to fill
those vests.

But while most of the locals scurried about with canvas tote
bags full of supplies and bits of lumber for boarding things up,
the birders carried enough waterproof surveillance hardware to
equip a squad of Navy SEALS. Binoculars, telescopes, cameras,
tape recorders, video cameras—you name it, they had it.

Every couple of minutes, a troop of birders would swarm up
the steps of the inn and ask us where we'd been and what we'd
seen and whether we'd spotted the kestrels up on Black Head
yet. When we explained that we hadn't been anywhere or seen
any birds and thought the kestrels up on Black Head had enough
company already, they would look at us oddly and slip inside to
refill their thermoses with hot coffee.

"Apart from going back to the cottage and listening to more
Wagner, what else is there to do on the island?" Michael asked.

"We could stroll through the village and see the sights," I said.

Just then, Fred Dickerman rattled by in his pickup truck, leaning on the horn, while a quartet of birders sprinted just ahead of his
bumper. Monhegan has no sidewalks; any pedestrian walking in the
road when a truck approached was expected to step aside to let the
vehicle pass. Or jump aside, if the driver was Fred. Most truck
drivers took it slowly when they went through the village, but Fred
evidently enjoyed chivvying tourists into puddles and brier patches.

"Reminds me of running before the bulls at Pamplona," Michael remarked as the birders finally reached a wide spot in the
road and hurled themselves to safety.

"Oh, have you actually done that?"

"No, and I'm not about to start now," he said. "Doesn't look
too restful, strolling through the village. Anything else?"

"Mostly healthy, outdoorsy things like hiking around the cir-
cumference of the island."

"All right, let's hike," Michael said, standing up and holding out his hand.

"You've got to be kidding. In this weather?"

"It's not actually raining now, and the weather's going to be a lot worse in a few hours," he said. "Let's go and see the sights before it gets bad."

"You're serious, aren't you?"

"Why not? At least once we've done it, when the birders ask us if we want to go to the South Pole with them to see the penguins, we can say, 'No thanks, we've already circumnavigated the island.' "

"Okay," I said. "You're on."

I could tell after the first fifteen minutes that circumnavigating the island was a lot less fun to do than to brag about afterward. But I wasn't about to confess that I couldn't handle it, so for the next hour or two, we squelched and slopped up and down the muddy parts of the trail and inched our way gingerly over the rain-slick rocky parts.

And invariably, every time we paused, panting, to catch our breath, a covey of middle-aged or elderly birders would breeze past us.

"I always thought bird-watching was a sedate pastime," Michael said as we took temporary refuge beneath a rocky outcropping that sheltered us from the worst of the drizzle. "These people could probably ace an Iron Man competition."

"Yes. Stirs up all my deep-seated feelings of inadequacy," I said, panting slightly.

"Oh, I don't know," Michael said, putting an arm around my waist. "You look pretty adequate to me."

It wasn't exactly the tropical beach of my dreams, but this was the closest I'd gotten to being alone with Michael since we'd arrived on the island. I snuggled closer, and he bent his head down toward mine. Then he froze.

"Why are those people watching us through their binoculars?" he muttered.

I followed the direction of his eye.

"I think they're looking at that bird at our feet," I whispered back.

"Why? Is that some kind of rare and exotic bird?"

I glanced down. The bird was moderately large, light brown, with a black-and-white mask over its face. It had bits of red and yellow on its wings, and the end of its tail had been dipped in yellow.

"How the devil should I know?" I said. "It looks like a paint-spattered female cardinal; cardinals certainly aren't rare."

"Damn," Michael said, a little more loudly this time.

The bird, whatever it was, took flight.

The three birders removed the binoculars from their eyes and stared at us accusingly.

"That was a Bohemian waxwing," one of them said.

"Did you get any photos?" the second asked.

"No," said the third. "They frightened it off before I got the chance."

"Oh, you mean that bird with the yellow-tipped tail?" I asked.

The birders nodded and frowned at us. Madame Defarge looked more kindly on her victims.

"We've seen them around here a lot," I said.

"They're quite rare in this part of the continent," one of the birders replied.

"Yes, that's what I was telling Michael," I said. "How rare to see so many Bohemian waxwings here. If you just stay quietly where you are, you'll probably see dozens."

With that, Michael and I fled down the path, until we had rounded a corner and could collapse in gales of laughter.

"Bohemian waxwings?" Michael spluttered. "That can't possibly be a real bird."

"I'm sure it is," I said, peeping around the corner. The three birders had hunched down by the path and were on the alert, scanning the landscape through their binoculars, one looking left, one right, and the third straight out toward the ocean.

"Come on," I said. "Let's get out of here, in case the Bohemian waxwing has flown the coop completely."

We giggled intermittently over the antics of the birders for the next hour or so. But the day got colder and damper, and every time we rounded a headland that I thought would bring us to the end of our journey, we'd encounter another stretch of path. And another flock of birders.

In one place, I spotted the remains of a campsite back in the trees, some distance from the trail.

"How odd," I said. "Let's go take a look at this."

"What's so odd?" Michael asked. "Looks like someone camped here."

"Definitely," I said, using my foot to rake leaves away from a charred spot. "You can see where they had a fire, right here, and they buried something over there. Garbage, I guess"

"Beer cans, mostly," Michael said, looking down at the trash-disposal area. "Someone had quite a party."

The unknown campers had buried their empties on the side of a hill, and the heavy rain had washed away a good deal of the covering dirt, exposing a vein of silver-and-blue aluminum cans.

"Definitely odd," I murmured.

"Yes, I should think conditions back in the village are primitive enough to satisfy even the most discriminating masochist. What kind of nut would come all the way over to this side of the island for even more Spartan conditions?"

"Well, I'm sure some people want to," I said. "But it's illegal. No camping permitted. To protect the fragile ecosystem on the undeveloped side of the island. And definitely no open fires. Normally, they're very quick to chase off anyone who tries."

"Maybe they did," Michael said. "Whoever did it is long gone."

Still, I couldn't help fretting as we hiked, and looking for further signs of neglect or environmental damage. I thought of summers past when Dad, Aunt Phoebe, and the rest of their generation would denounce some new change to the island. I'd thought them tiresome, a little cracked on the subject of keeping Monhegan unspoiled. And yet, here I was, fretting about the same thing.

At least until my energy began to flag again.

"Maybe it's my imagination," I said, stopping to pant. "But the path around the island seems longer than it did when I was a little kid."

"Your father used to let you walk around this path?" Michael said, peering over the edge of a precipice to the surf crashing twenty feet below.

"Let us? He'd insist on it. He thought it was good exercise. If we didn't voluntarily hike around the island every few days, he'd drag us along on a nature walk."

"And he was never prosecuted for child abuse? Amazing. I hope he at least insisted that you learn to swim before turning you loose on these cliffs."

"Technically, yes; though I don't see what good swimming would do anyone who fell off the cliffs. The undertow could drag away a small submarine, and if the undertow didn't get you, the waves would pound you to death against the rocks."

"What a vacation paradise," Michael said, chuckling as we resumed our hike. "I see why he brought you here; the place is as escapeproof as Alcatraz. He wouldn't have to worry about you sneaking over to the mainland and getting into any trouble."

"We managed anyway," I said. "The sneaking over to the mainland part anyway; we never could find much trouble when we got there. But you can reach the mainland quite easily if you know someone with a small boat. Not in weather like this, of course."

"Oh, the weather's not that bad," Michael said. "Great weather for sitting around by the fire."

"Sorry. Hiking wasn't that good an idea, was it?"

"Nonsense. It was a great idea," Michael said, smiling over his shoulder at me before turning and beginning to climb the next hill. "The scenery's fantastic, and when we get back to the cottage, I'll appreciate the fire all the more."

If only we could appreciate it by ourselves, I thought, pausing for a moment to enjoy the view of Michael's long legs as he jumped over a small gully that interrupted the path. Perhaps if all the rest of the family went hiking. But no, the weather would soon be too foul for hiking. And anyway, Mother never hiked. Turn her loose in a mall, or, better yet, on a street lined with quaint boutiques and expensive shops, and she could walk combat-trained marines into the ground, but here on Monhegan, there wasn't much shopping, even in the summer. How could we possibly get Mother out of the house? I sighed.

"Tired?" Michael asked, looking down at me. I shook my head.

"Just figuring where we are," I said. "It can't be too much farther. I'm sure we're getting close to the village."

"You said that an hour ago," he said, chuckling.

"That was wishful thinking," I said. "Now that I've gotten my bearings back, not to mention my second wind, I know exactly where we are. Just over the next hill we're going to see a quaint little shack that's been converted to an artist's studio. It's on a headland with one of the most spectacular views of the island."

"Over this hill?" Michael said. He had reached the top and paused to catch his breath.

"Yes. Look a little to your right. You should be able to see it peeping through the trees."

"Yes, that's quite a quaint little shack."

I reached his side and looked down, expecting to see one of my favorite rustic Monhegan landscapes. Instead, I saw a glittering, spiky forest of steel beams and glass plates.

"Wrong hill again?" Michael said.

"No, it's the right hill. I recognize the view, at least what little we can see of it behind that monstrosity. What the hell is it anyway? Some horrible new piece of weather equipment from the Coast Guard?"

"A rather large and very modern house," Michael said.

He was right, of course; when I'd stared at it a few minutes, the jumble resolved itself into something resembling doors, walls, and windows.

"I wonder how in the world they got permission to build it," I said. "The town council is very conservative about new development. It took Aunt Phoebe two years to get permission to expand her deck."

"We did hear the Dickermans saying that someone's new house was an eyesore."

"Yes, but around here, that just means someone painted the house the wrong shade of blue," I said. "Or painted it at all, instead of just allowing it to fade to the usual, tasteful weather-beaten gray. This is more than an eyesore; it's an abomination."

"I don't think the house itself is all that bad," Michael said, squinting at it. "Not my cup of tea, but you have to admit it's striking."

"True," I said, sighing. "Anywhere else I might actually find it interesting, although I can't imagine living in something that that bare and modern. But here on Monhegan, it's completely out of place."

"No argument from me," Michael said.

"I was going to suggest stopping to enjoy the view, but I've changed my mind," I said. "Let's hurry up and get past that eyesore."

"Fine by me," Michael said.

We started down the hill, Michael again in the lead. I was craning my neck, trying to see something of sea and sky beyond the abomination, and mentally composing scathing letters to the town council, when—

"Look out!" Michael yelled. He ran back up the path a few

feet, knocked me to the ground, and threw himself on top of me. I heard a sharp noise somewhere, and then a lot of sand and pebbles sifted down on us from higher up the hill.

"What's going on?"

"Some lunatic is shooting at us!" Michael said.

Chapter 6

They Shoot Puffins, Don't They?

Another shot rang out. Wonderful, I thought; now I know what getting shot at sounds like. Michael flinched, and I thought for an awful moment he'd been hit.

"Are you all right?" I asked.

"I'll be fine as soon as I know we're out of gunshot range."

"Excellent idea," I said. "Let me up; I can't get out of gunshot range with you on top of me."

"Right," he said. He jumped up, pulled me to my feet, and began dragging me up the path.

"Hang on a minute," I said, looking back over my shoulder when we got to the top of the hill. "He's not shooting now. Let's see what's going on."

"Keep your head down, then."

We both crouched on the path, peeking over the top of the rise at the lunatic below: a tall, gaunt man, all angles and elbows, with a bushy beard and long gray-streaked hair that looked as if he'd attempted, with limited success, to cultivate dreadlocks. He wore a baggy, shapeless, partially unraveled fisherman's sweater over paint-splattered olive corduroys. He stood with his left hand on his hip while his right held a long gun—a rifle or a shotgun, I supposed. He wasn't aiming it at anything, but he looked ready to. He stared up the path as if waiting for us to emerge again. If he planned on standing there with the gun, he'd have a long wait.

"He looks familiar," I said.

"Don't tell me he's one of your relatives?"

"Good heavens, no!" I said. "Do you really think my relatives would do something like that?"

Michael didn't answer.

"Okay, some of them *might* be crazy enough to shoot at the tourists, but none of them would have the bad taste to build that house."

"You have a point there," Michael said, chuckling. "So what do we do now?"

"Good question," I said. "We could turn around and go back the way we came."

"God no," Michael muttered. Perversely, it made me feel a little better that he hadn't enjoyed the last few rain-soaked, mud-infested hours of hiking quite as much as he'd pretended to.

"Let's try to talk to him, then."

"Talk to him?"

Just then, the man started up the path toward us.

"Damn," Michael said, "We'd better turn back after all."

"Don't come any closer!" I shouted.

The man with the gun ignored me.

"Stay where you are! I mean it!" I shouted, and lobbed a baseball-sized rock down at him. Well, not directly at him—I could have hit him if I'd wanted to—but in his general direction. Close enough to get his attention.

The rock bounced and tumbled down, taking quite a collection of pebbles and sticks with it. The man stopped and then backed up a few paces. I grabbed another rock and held it at the ready.

"Why the hell are you shooting at us?" I yelled.

"This is private property," he yelled back. "You're trespassing!"

"Trespassing?" I shouted. I stood up, ignoring Michael's frantic gestures. Foolish, perhaps, but somehow I didn't think that the man was going to shoot us. Not in front of witnesses. I could see a flock of birders peeking out of the woods at the other edge of his property, snapping away with their cameras.

"Trespassing?" I repeated. "Excuse me, quite apart from the fact that this trail has been a public right-of-way for generations, and assuming you do have some legal claim to keep people out, which I very much doubt——and I assure you that I intend to investigate very thoroughly——quite apart from that, were you planning to post any signs, or were you just going to kill off anyone not psychic enough to guess that you don't want them hiking here?"

"Meg," Michael said. He tugged on the leg of my jeans. I shook him off.

"There's a sign right there——" the man began, raising his hand to point and then stopping when he saw there wasn't a sign after all. "What the hell have you done with my sign?"

"Don't look at us," I said. "We just got here."

The man snorted in exasperation. He walked forward a few paces, then leaned his gun against a tree and reached down. He pried a battered sign out of the mud beside the path, picked up a large rock——possibly the one I'd thrown at him——and began hammering the sign back into the ground.

"I'm not kidding," he said, looking up from his work. "I'm fed up with people trespassing. And people knocking down my signs. I've served notice that this is private property, and I intend to enforce it."

"Well, serve notice a little more visibly from now on," I said, dodging Michael, who had despaired of making me crouch down again and was trying to put himself between me and the lunatic. "And speaking of serving notice, exactly who are you anyway? I'd like to know whom I'm going to ask the police to charge with attempted murder."

"You know perfectly well who I am!" the man shouted. He threw the rock in my direction, then reached for his gun. I quickly followed Michael's advice and we ducked behind the crest of the path, but instead of firing, the man stormed back toward the house. I suppressed a giggle; he was getting himself even grimier than before, stomping through the mud like that. And when he slammed the door, I burst out laughing: the huge, pretentious——and, no doubt, expensive——front door didn't fit quite right. Perhaps all the dampness had warped it. He had to spend several minutes wrestling it closed, his struggles clearly visible through the sweeping glass wall and slanted glass roof of the entrance hall.

"I'll refrain from saying anything about people who live in glass houses," Michael said. "But they shouldn't shoot rifles at people, either."

"And they definitely shouldn't live this close to the ocean," I said, giggling. A seagull had just flown in from the ocean, banked gracefully over the house, and landed, with a clumsy thud, on the glass roof of the entranceway, which was somewhat sheltered by the rest of the house from the full brunt of the wind. Several other gulls followed, and enough bird droppings coated the glass to show that this wasn't the first time the birds had discovered this refuge. The lunatic suddenly appeared behind the glass of the entranceway, causing both Michael and me to jump. The gulls, however, stared down unmoved as he thumped with a broom handle on the heavy plate glass beneath their feet.

"Serves him right," I said. "I hope that creep has to wash all those windows every day."

And he certainly had a lot of windows. In addition to the main house, we saw a smaller glass building nearby. A studio, apparently; while off-white curtains screened the lower six feet or so of its glass walls, from our place on the hill we could see the tips of several easels peeking over the top of the fabric. Even the nearby woodshed, while not made of glass, looked considerably newer, not to mention more expensive and stylish, than most of the actual houses on the island.

"Who on earth could possibly afford to build a place like this on Monhegan?" I wondered aloud. "Do you have any idea how much it costs to bring supplies and workmen over here?"

"Well, whoever he is, I'm sure he can afford to pay for a lawyer," Michael said. "Let's go back to the village and file charges against him."

"No sense tempting fate, though," I said. "Let's retrace our steps a bit; I think I can find a shortcut through the interior of the island."

As we retreated along the trail, I saw a flash of lavender disappear around a rock ahead of us. Somebody else watching our encounter with the mad hermit, no doubt. I nodded with satisfaction; it looked as if we'd have plenty of witnesses.

My shortcut didn't seem much shorter than going all the way back around the island, but at last we arrived at the village.

"I don't recall seeing a police station," Michael said. "Where are we going to report that lunatic?"

"There isn't a police station," I said. "They call the police over from the mainland when they need them. But a local resident acts as constable until the police arrive. Let's go into the general store and ask who it is."

We squished down the main drag until we reached the general store, then squelched up the front steps.

"I remember him," I said, pointing to a sign in the window that said JEBEDIAH BARNES, PROPRIETOR. "His family's run this place for two or three generations now."

"That's good," Michael said. "Maybe he'll remember you; otherwise, we may have a hard time making him believe what just happened."

The store was blissfully warm inside; an old-fashioned potbellied stove burned full blast, and a small crowd of local residents sat or stood around the stove, drinking coffee and listening to what sounded like an all-weather radio station. Hurricane Gladys still hovered offshore, according to the announcer.

Michael headed for the coffeepot while I strode over to the counter where the storekeeper stood.

"Where do I find the constable?" I asked him.

"You're looking at him," he said. "Jeb Barnes. What can I do for you?"

"I'd like to report an assault," I said.

Chapter 7

I Fought the Puffin and the Puffin Won

At the word *assault,* Jeb Barnes's jaw dropped, and the desultory conversation around the stove stopped cold. I could almost hear their ears turning in our direction. Jeb glanced nervously at Michael. He'd jumped to a very wrong conclusion, obviously; but at least I'd gotten his attention.

"Some lunatic fired a gun at us," I went on. "I realize you probably can't do anything until the storm passes and the ferry's running, but I'd like to make a report now so you can contact the mainland police as soon as possible."

"Fired a gun at you?" Jeb repeated. "Where?"

"We were trying to follow the public path around Puffin Point," I said.

The constable closed his eyes and sighed. Michael handed me a steaming cup of coffee and put some money down on the counter.

"Resnick again," said one of the locals by the stove.

"Crazy bastard," said another.

"Going to kill someone one of these days," said a third.

"He's done this before?" I asked. "And you haven't done anything?"

"We've formally warned him he has no right to block the path," Jeb Barnes said defensively. "And we're looking into the possibility of a lawsuit about that pile of junk he calls a house. We can't do anything about the alleged shooting incidents. No one who lives here wants to tick him off any more, and none of the damn fool tourists want to stay around to testify, so we haven't found anyone willing to press charges."

"Well, I will," I said. "I'm self-employed, so I can arrange my schedule to be here for the trial. And I'm sure Aunt Phoebe will let me use the cottage when I come back."

The constable sighed again. Here I was, offering to press charges against his biggest local scofflaw, and he wasn't acting the least bit grateful.

"You're Phoebe Hollingworth's niece?" he asked finally.

"Meg Langslow," I said, holding out my hand. Jeb Barnes shook it with obvious reluctance.

"One of them Hollingworths," I heard one of the locals mutter. "They'll take him on."

I was glad to see Mother's family name was still a force to be reckoned with here on Monhegan.

"Yeah, they're all crazy enough," agreed another local.

Well, I couldn't exactly argue with him. I heard Michael make a noise that sounded like a cough but had no doubt started out life as a chuckle. I decided to bring him onstage. Why should I have all the fun?

"And this is Michael Waterston, a family friend. I'm sure Professor Waterston will also want to press charges."

"Naturally," Michael said. "What a pity I haven't been admitted to the bar in Maine."

I had to hand it to Michael: he carried that off beautifully. Jeb Barnes turned pale.

"What about that cousin of yours in Bangor?" I said, picking up on the improvisation.

"He doesn't practice anymore," Michael said.

"Oh, I like that," I said. "Elect the guy to the legislature and suddenly he's too good to represent us common people."

"He has to avoid conflict of interest," Michael said. "But as soon as the phones are working again, I'll give him a call; I'm sure he knows someone who can help."

"You've got a cousin in the legislature?" asked one of the locals.

"A very distant cousin," Michael said.

Our joke had backfired, big-time. We spent the next half hour listening to a point-by-point analysis of a bill pending before the state legislature that Monheganites considered the last hope of preserving their lobster industry. By the end of the discussion, I still didn't understand the issue, but I had grasped that if anyone asked me where I stood on the lobster bill, I should express enthusiastic support for the town proposal and apologize for not being a registered Maine voter. Either that or turn tail and run the minute they brought up the subject.

We finally escaped, after Michael had promised to fill his cousin in on the details of the Monhegan bill. I had to admire the way he'd changed the conversation every time anyone tried to ask which legislator his cousin was. It wasn't as if we could make a name up; Maine had fewer than two hundred legislators, and the townspeople knew exactly how every one of them felt about their bill.

"And another thing," Jeb Barnes called out, following us out onto the front porch of the store. "Don't you listen to that Resnick fellow. He's got investments in foreign lobstering interests. Been spending a lot of money trying to kill our bill."

"Considering that he takes potshots at us whenever we get near him, it's not very likely we'll discuss it, now is it?" I said. "Don't forget to file my complaint with the mainland police if the phones come back up."

As I suspected, this sent Jeb scurrying back into the store.

"Everyone's quite impassioned about this lobster thing," Michael remarked.

"Well, it is the main local industry," I said.

"I thought that was tourism."

"Okay, the other main local industry. And no one's going to get all worked up about anyone preying on the tourists; they're not in short supply."

"But what am I supposed to do if someone corners me and asks about my cousin?"

"We'll ask Aunt Phoebe; she's sure to know a legislator on the right side of the issue, and she'll persuade him to adopt you."

"Speaking of your aunt Phoebe, shouldn't we get back to the house?"

"You want to go back to the house?" I said. "We'll be cooped up with my family soon enough when the hurricane actually hits. Do you really want to get a head start?"

"Well, it is warm and dry there," Michael said, pulling up the hood of his parka.

"It's warm and dry in the house," I said. "But right now I doubt if they'd let us stay inside."

"Why on earth not?"

"Look around you," I said. "What do you see?"

"Birders," he said automatically.

"Aside from the birders."

Just then, Fred Dickerman drove by at his usual breakneck speed. We leapt into some bushes by the side of the road while a flock of lady birders squawked and scattered like geese before his honking horn.

"The natives are getting hostile?" he asked.

"The natives are busy." I pointed out the half a dozen locals boarding or taping their windows, trudging back from the grocery stores with bags and boxes of supplies, and frantically trying to tie down or carry indoors every object smaller than a Volkswagen.

"With the exception of that crowd of old-timers killing time in the general store, you're right."

"If we go home now, Aunt Phoebe will find half a hundred chores for us to do, most of them outdoors," I said.

"And those same chores won't be waiting for us when we get back?"

"With any luck,, she'll manage to get Dad and Rob to do quite a few of them while we're gone."

"So what should we do?" Michael asked. "I'll tell you straight out—I'm not up for another hike around the island, even if it wasn't infested with armed lunatics."

"We're going shopping," I said. "Monhegan has a few artists' studios and craft shops. You're not going to go back to Yorktown without a present for your mom, are you?"

"Now that's a good idea," Michael said.

We spent the next hour inspecting the remarkable number and variety of CLOSED FOR THE SEASON signs in the windows of the island shops and studios. Some of them were genuine works of art in their own right, but I wasn't having a lot of fun viewing them on water-soaked, locked doors or through rain-splattered windowpanes while my feet remained firmly planted in the mud.

At one point, we actually saw Victor Resnick stalking down the street in a disreputable mackinaw that made him look more like a scarecrow than ever. We ducked behind a building until he'd passed.

"He doesn't have his gun," Michael reported, peering around the corner. "If I were the constable, I'd tackle him now."

"I wouldn't count on it, though," I said, getting up the nerve to poke my head out.

Resnick stood in front of the general store, talking to someone—a young Asian man.

"Who do you suppose that is?" Michael said. "Doesn't have binoculars, so I doubt he's a birder."

"Definitely not a birder," I said. "He's wearing a necktie underneath his raincoat."

"The men at the general store did say something about Resnick having ties with foreign lobstering interests," Michael said. "Maybe he's from some Japanese seafood conglomerate."

"That's possible," I said. "Although around here, the word

foreign just means 'not from Monhegan.' But he definitely looks corporate."

Resnick's discussion with the corporate man had grown heated. They stood nose-to-nose, both talking and gesturing furiously. Resnick's complexion grew redder and redder, and he shook his finger in the Asian man's face. Obviously, our visitor from the East hadn't heard about Resnick's readiness with firearms; he gave back as good as he got. A pity the wind, rain, and surf kept us from hearing what they said. Well, if the argument turned violent, we'd have plenty of witnesses, I realized. I could see at least three other people hiding behind nearby buildings, although I had no idea whether they wanted to avoid Resnick or eavesdrop on his conversation.

Suddenly, Resnick whirled and began striding down the street the way he'd come—toward us.

Chapter 8

The Little Puffin Around the Corner

"Oh my God, he's coming this way," I whispered. We both jerked back, but not so far that we couldn't see what went on.

"You can go to hell for all I care!" Resnick shouted over his shoulder.

The Asian man opened his mouth as if to reply, then stopped, took a deep breath, and shoved his hands in the pockets of his raincoat. He stood there for a few moments, staring after Resnick, then turned on his heels and began walking in the other direction.

About then, Michael and I scurried around the corner of the building to avoid Resnick. When we peeked out a minute or two later, both he and the Asian man with the necktie had disappeared.

After that brief flurry of excitement, we resumed our shopping quest and finally ended up down by the ferry dock in the only gift shop still open—probably because it doubled as the island-side office for the ferries.

We flung open the shop door, shook ourselves like large dogs, and said good morning to the shopkeeper and her one other customer. The shopkeeper was a stout sixtyish woman, sensibly dressed in boots, jeans, and several layers of sweaters. I couldn't remember her name—probably a subconscious form of revenge, since during my last visit to Monhegan I'd tried, without success, to get her to sell my ironwork in her shop.

The other occupant was a rather odd-looking woman in her

forties, dressed in a peculiar multilayered medley of black, purple, and violet, topped with a limp lavender-trimmed straw hat. Not one of the birders, obviously; probably an artist or craftswoman.

"My God," Michael said, looking round. "Is the puffin the state bird here or something?"

He had a point; the shop was a puffin lover's paradise. Puffin posters, puffin T-shirts, puffin sweatshirts, puffin key chains, and so many stuffed toy puffins of all sizes that the place looked like Santa's workshop on December 23.

"We're very proud of our puffins," said the shopkeeper. "Maine is the only state in the union that actually has nesting puffins."

"Yes, so Meg's aunt Phoebe has told us," Michael said, breaking in to stem the tide of puffin lore.

"Oh, you're Meg?" the shopkeeper said. "I didn't recognize you; it's such a long time since you've been here. Your father's told us about all your detective adventures this summer."

I winced. I should have known that my mystery-buff dad couldn't spend five minutes anywhere without bragging about his daughter, who had actually solved a real live murder. Listening to Dad, you'd think any minute I'd quit my career as a smith and open up a detective agency.

"You know, we never did finish those arrangements for selling some of your ironwork here in the shop," the woman went on.

I snapped to attention. A more accurate statement would be that I'd never convinced her my occasional summers on the island constituted enough of a local tie to warrant my inclusion in the "Crafts of Monhegan" section of the shop. But if my past summer's adventures had made me notorious enough to interest her, thus opening up a profitable new market—well, I wasn't about to let the opportunity go to waste.

In minutes, the shopkeeper and I were deep in discussions of the quantity and type of merchandise she thought she could use and whether she would buy them outright or take them on consignment. Michael wandered off to inspect the puffin paraphernalia, and after a few minutes, the woman in lavender picked up her purse.

"Bye, Mamie," she whispered, and slipped out of the store.

"Oh, I'm sorry," I said. "I didn't mean to drive a customer away."

"Oh, she's not a customer," Mamie said. "That's one of our other island celebrities. That's Rhapsody." From the tone of voice, I suspected Rhapsody was one of those people who strenuously resisted admitting that they owned a last name. And that she was somebody I ought to have heard of.

"Rhapsody?" I said.

"You know, she does the children's books. They call her the 'Puffin Lady of Monhegan.' "

"Oh, the Happy Puffin Family," I said.

"That's right," she said, beaming.

I hadn't actually heard of the Happy Puffin Family before, but though my detective skills are overrated, they were sufficient to let me spot the giant display of Happy Puffin Family books right beside the cash register.

"I keep meaning to read one of her books," I said. "I'm sure my sister, Pam, has some around the house for her kids, but I never find the time when I'm home."

"Oh, they're wonderful!" Mamie exclaimed.

While Michael continued to inspect puffin tea towels and puffin ashtrays with a suspiciously serious look on his face, I poked through the display rack. Evidently, the Puffin Lady was reasonably prolific; the shopkeeper had at least a dozen titles displayed.

Even as a child, I had what Dad called a "deplorably literal streak." When presented with a book that was part of a series—*The Borrowers,* for example, or *Little House on the Prairie*—I would insist on beginning with the first in the series and working my way through in order. I therefore examined the copyright dates and passed up *Puffin in the Rye* ("The Happy Puffin Family Visits a Farm!") *The Daring Young Puffin on the Flying Trapeze!* ("The Happy Puffin Family Visits the Circus!"), and *Snow Falling on Puffins* ("The Happy Puffin Family Goes Sledding!") in favor of the original volume, *Hark the Herald Puffins Sing* ("Christmas with the Happy Puffin Family!").

I hoped the Puffin Lady's artistic and literary skills had improved over time. I wasn't much impressed with either in her first opus. The puffins looked vaguely inauthentic—either she didn't draw all that well or perhaps she had taken liberties with their anatomy to make them more anthropomorphic. Or perhaps it was the props and costumes. She liked decking the poor birds out in brightly colored bits of human clothing, or having them carry things like yo-yos and lollipops. They were colorful and eye-catching. But she hadn't succeeded in making them all that appealing, as far as I could see; in fact, they looked faintly reptilian. I saw more charm in one mass-produced plush stuffed puffin from the gift shop than in Rhapsody's whole book.

It was the beaks and the eyes. The puffins' beaks might be picturesque and unusual, but they weren't designed for expressing human emotion. Whatever charm the Puffin Lady had tried to create with cute little props and costumes, she hadn't managed to make those huge cartoonlike beaks look any different. Happy, sad, angry, or surprised, the puffins all had the same lack of expression. And the eyes—maybe it's just me, but I've always found birds' eyes a little cold and alien. You get the feeling they're off thinking strange, fluttery little splinter thoughts; and you hope it's all about seeds and nuts and where to find a birdbath, and not something like acting out in real life their great-great-grandfathers' starring roles in *The Birds*. Maybe I'd done her artistic skills an injustice. Rhapsody had captured everything I disliked about birds' eyes so accurately that a chill went down my spine.

"You're not really thinking of buying that," came a voice, interrupting my thoughts.

I looked up, to see one of the birders, a matronly woman who had both the inevitable binoculars and a pair of reading glasses dangling over her ample bosom, not to mention a camera hanging by a strap from her wrist. I wasn't sure, but I thought she might be one of the birders who'd snapped pictures of the lunatic shooting at us, so I resolved to be as polite as possible.

"Just trying to see what the fuss is all about," I said. "She seems such a local celebrity."

"I can't for the life of me see why," the birder said. "It's not as if she's particularly good at it."

Actually, I agreed, but the birder's bullying manner irritated me, so I said only, "Oh, really? How so?"

"Her stuff's shockingly inaccurate," the birder said with a sniff. "Shoddy research all around. Worse than useless from a scientific point of view."

I looked back at the brightly colored page, where the Happy Puffin Family was sitting down to Christmas dinner. The little Puffins, complete with napkins tied bib-fashion around their necks, looked eagerly toward their mother—you could tell her by the flowered hat. Mama Puffin stood beside the table, holding a giant covered dish with the tips of her wings. I flipped the page. The dish now rested in front of Papa Puffin, who was about to wield a carving knife on its contents—not turkey, thank goodness, but an enormous smiling fish. The small Puffins jumped up and down in their seats, and even the main course looked implausibly cheerful, as if they hadn't quite gotten around to telling him exactly what role he was to play in the upcoming feast.

"I didn't realize she intended to be accurate," I said, flipping the page again and holding up a scene of the Happy Puffin Family sledding. "I mean, I'm sure she realizes that puffins don't actually wear little red mufflers and woolly caps."

"I'm not talking about the anthropomorphizing," the birder said. "That's silly, but not actually harmful, considering the age group. But look at their bills! And their plumage!"

A plump beringed finger, quivering with indignation, planted itself just below the picture of little Petey Puffin. I had to admit, I didn't like the look of him, but I had no idea what she thought was wrong with him. I noticed that, like bird guidebooks, the Puffin Lady never showed her subjects head-on. The Puffin Family invariably stood in profile. She must copy them from bird books, I realized. That would account for the strangely mechanical and puppetlike quality. But no; if she copied them from bird books, then they'd be accurate, wouldn't they? And then the birders wouldn't complain.

"I'm sorry," I said. "I'm not awfully knowledgeable about puffins. What's wrong with it?"

"This is not the picture of an immature puffin," the birder said. "An immature puffin looks like this." She plopped one of the ubiquitous blue bird guides open atop *Hark the Herald Puffins Sing* and pointed out a black-and-white shape. "And he's in breeding plumage. By Christmas, adult puffins have long since shed their colorful bill plates and their faces darken. Like this," she added, indicating yet another black-and-white shape.

I studied the page before me. Yes, the puffin in winter was a drab bird indeed compared to what he would look like in mating season. I'd almost have taken him for a different species. And all the Puffin Family were in breeding plumage, right down to diaper-clad baby Patty.

"I see what you mean," I said. I didn't add that I didn't see what was so important about the distinction. Perhaps they planned to haul Rhapsody before the Audubon Society on morals charges for turning an infant puffin into some kind of avian Lolita.

I was relieved when Michael joined us. Probably not an accident; we'd both become a little wary of the more rabid birders.

"Found something interesting," he said, holding up the back cover of another book. "Look familiar?"

He held out an oversized art book—a collection of Victor Resnick's paintings. On the back of the book was a picture of our gun-toting lunatic. Only in the picture, he wore a clean fisherman's sweater, his hair and beard were combed, and he looked quite distinguished. The picture was in three-quarters profile. Resnick's chin was lifted, and he gazed into the distance with a lofty, otherworldly look. He really appeared every bit the distinguished artist, already planning his next brilliant work.

"Yes, that's the jerk," I said. "Almost wouldn't have recognized him."

I turned the book over and began leafing through it. I sighed. The man might be a jerk, but he was definitely a talented jerk.

"Someone should do something about that horrible man," the birder said.

"Well, Mrs. Peabody, that's very difficult," Mamie said. "He's quite an important person. . . ."

"That's irrelevant," I said, glad to find a conversational topic other than puffins. "I don't care how important they are, people can't run around shooting off rifles or shotguns or whatever he's using."

"My God!" exclaimed Mrs. Peabody. "He's not shooting them, is he? I'd heard about the electric shocks; we've gotten up a petition about it. But this is beyond all belief! Shooting the birds!"

She whirled and ran for the door, knocking down a stack of stuffed puffins on her way.

"We can't let him get away with this," she shouted. "There's not a moment to lose!"

Chapter 9

Twelve Angry Puffins

"Wait," I called, starting after her. "I didn't say he was shooting the birds; I just said he was shooting at us!"

But Mrs. Peabody didn't hear me. And the electric lights chose that moment to flicker and die. In the sudden near darkness, I tripped over the fallen puffins and sent the rack of Rhapsody's books sprawling. Mamie scurried over to pick them up while Michael leapt to my side and spent rather more time than strictly necessary making sure I'd suffered no damage in the fall. By the time he finally relented and helped me to my feet, the birder had vanished.

"Don't worry about it," Michael said as we pitched in to put the book display back together again.

"She'll tell everyone Resnick is shooting birds," I said. "They'll probably all go hiking up to confront him."

"And either they'll lynch him or he'll shoot one of them, and either way, maybe you won't have to file charges against him."

"Are you going to file charges against him?" Mamie asked, wide-eyed.

"Yes, at least if Constable Barnes ever takes me seriously."

"Good," she said, patting my shoulder with approval. "Someone needs to do something about that man. He's absolutely beastly to poor Rhapsody. She had a one-woman show here last summer of some of her paintings from the books. You should have heard some of the things he said to her. Absolutely savage. Someone really ought to do something. Do you have any matches?"

I thought for a moment she was enlisting us to help burn Resnick at the stake, but apparently she'd decided the power wasn't coming back anytime soon. She pottered through her drawers until she found some matches, then began lighting oil lamps.

I glanced back at the book of Resnick's paintings. I'd paused at a painting of the Black Head. He'd precisely captured the way the sky had looked all day; only slightly cloudy, but somehow full of vague future menace. I could imagine what he would have to say about poor Rhapsody's puffins.

"She went into quite a slump and almost missed her deadline for *Puffin in the Rye!*" Mamie said. "I really thought for a while she'd give up painting entirely."

I continued to leaf through the book of Resnick's work while Michael bought a puffin sweatshirt for his mom. I was torn. The more I looked at the paintings, the more I wanted to buy the book; Resnick had really captured the beauty of the island in a way that photographs couldn't quite manage. But I didn't want to risk the shopkeeper's disapproval. And for that matter, I had mixed feelings about giving any support, financial or otherwise, to the wild-eyed lunatic who'd fired a gun at me and built that horrible eyesore on one of my favorite parts of the island. Ironically, the book even included several paintings of the picturesque shack he'd demolished.

"Aha!" I cried, snapping the book shut. "I'll take this, please," I said to Mamie, handing over the book and fishing my Visa card out of my purse.

She looked at me as if I'd just declared myself a vivisectionist.

"Take a look here, on page one hundred and ten," I said. "See the caption—'View of Puffin Point from the Public Path.' That proves it."

"Well, of course," she said. "Everyone knows it's a public path."

"Yes, but this proves that he knows it. He said so in the title of one of his very own pictures. I can use this in the court case; if Jeb Barnes won't take my assault charges, I'll file a civil suit."

"Oh, I see," Mamie said. "Your father was right; you have become quite the detective."

She rang up the book with enthusiasm, then waved cheerfully to Michael and me as we stepped outside again.

"Now where?" Michael asked.

"Back to the cottage, I think," I said. "Aunt Phoebe will try to put us to work, but we can get her to feed us first."

"Sounds like a plan," he said.

But when we neared the top of the hill, we saw Aunt Phoebe in heated conversation with several birders, including Mrs. Peabody.

"Oh damn," I said. "She's probably telling Aunt Phoebe a lot of inaccurate information about Resnick."

"You're probably right," Michael said. "And your aunt doesn't look too happy."

In fact, while we struggled up the last few feet of the hill, Aunt Phoebe broke away from the birders and began storming up the path toward Resnick's cottage.

"The man deserves a good thrashing," she called over her shoulder, brandishing her blackthorn walking stick.

"Aunt Phoebe! Wait!" I wheezed. She probably couldn't hear me.

"I'll show him a thing or two," she shouted as she disappeared around a bend in the road.

"Shouldn't we go after her?" Michael asked, puffing.

"Yes, but I don't think we could possibly catch her." I, too was panting.

"True. She hasn't been hiking around the island all morning."

"Actually, she probably has, but never mind," I said. "Let's go tell the constable. It's downhill from here to the general store."

"And we can get those groceries your aunt wanted," Michael said.

While Michael gathered the items on Aunt Phoebe's list, I tried to convince Jeb Barnes to go after Aunt Phoebe. I wasn't having much luck.

"I'm sure there's no reason to worry," he said.

"Did you hear what I said?" I demanded. "She's going up there to confront Victor Resnick! She thinks he's been shooting birds."

"Probably has," one of the locals commented.

"I'm sure Phoebe can take care of herself," Jeb said.

"She probably can, but what about Resnick?" I said. "What if she carries out her threat to give him a good thrashing?"

"Call up and warn him," someone suggested.

"Phones are out," someone else said.

"Serve him right if she did," commented a third.

The lights flickered on at that moment, and everyone looked up with a hopeful expression. Then the lights winked out again and the locals sighed and huddled a little closer to the stove.

Just then, we heard the sound of a truck engine outside.

"That must be Fred," Jeb Barnes said. "I'll get him to take me up to Resnick's. We'll head her off."

He darted out of the store, flagged down Fred Dickerman, and the two of them roared off up the gravel road.

Michael and I watched as the truck careened off, scattering birders on both sides.

"Should we follow?" Michael asked.

"Let's go back and find Dad," I said. "Maybe he can figure out a way to calm her down."

We made rather slow progress, though. We had our arms full of grocery bags, and we had to push through throngs of birders, all of whom wanted to know if Victor Resnick was really slaughtering birds with his shotgun. At first, they seemed curiously unalarmed by the fact that Resnick had been shooting at Michael and me.

"We didn't actually *see* him shoot any birds," I said finally. "But

he certainly shot at us. Probably thought we were birders trespassing on his land."

This tactic generated a satisfactory level of sympathy and outrage. Especially after one of the birders informed the rest that
Resnick's land was the only place on the island where some rare
bird had been sighted a day or two earlier.

Leaving the assembled birders debating whether the once-in-a-
decade chance to add the bay-breasted warbler to their life lists was
worth the risk that it might become the last bird they ever saw, Michael and I escaped and headed back to Aunt Phoebe's cottage.

We ran into Winnie and Binkie on the way.

"Meg, dear," Binkie called. "How are you enjoying your stay?"

"Well, it's not quite what we expected," I said. "We didn't
expect to run into the whole family here."

"No, and I'm sure your mother and father weren't expecting
that dreadful Resnick person to be here," Binkie said. "Terribly
awkward, under the circumstances."

"Awkward?" I repeated. *Awkward* didn't even begin to describe
the sensation of having a gun fired over one's head.

"Oh, leave it alone, Binkie," Winnie said. "It's all over and
done with."

I felt a little miffed at their quick dismissal of our ordeal.
Unless by "awkward" they meant some past conflict—perhaps
this wasn't the first time Victor Resnick had taken violent measures against trespassers. Perhaps it wasn't the first time Aunt
Phoebe had attempted to thrash him.

"And do be careful," Binkie added. "I've heard reports of an
imposter running around the island."

"An imposter?" I echoed.

"Yes, someone carrying binoculars and a bird book and pretending to be one of us, when he doesn't know a tern from a
seagull," Winnie said, frowning. "Up to no good, whoever he is,
if you ask me."

But before I could ask what possible harm the so-called imposter could do, Winnie and Binkie spotted another party of
birders down the road and tripped off to compare notes.

I shrugged. The fake birder wasn't my problem; my family,
on the other hand . . .

"I wonder if it was wise, letting Aunt Phoebe run off like that,"
I said, fretting.

"She's a grown woman," Michael said as we turned into the
lane to the cottage. "She can take care of herself, and besides,
the constable will referee. Let him take care of her."

"I suppose we'll have to," I said.

"Look, there's Rob," Michael said. "What's he doing there on
the beach?"

"Posing," I said. "He probably saw us coming."

Rob stood on the narrow strip of beach, hunched against the
cold, one hand jammed in his pocket, staring out to sea. Trying,
no doubt, to achieve an air of picturesque, Byronic melancholy.
Someone should break the news to Rob that blondes can't do
Byronic. Michael, on the other hand, managed it without even
trying; I particularly liked the way the breeze ruffled the lock of
hair that had fallen over his eyes.

Then again, Michael wasn't handicapped by Spike. Rob held
one end of a very long leash; on the other end, Spike was chasing
the waves. When a wave fell back toward the ocean, Spike would
pursue it, barking bravely, convinced he had terrified the water
into flight. When the water turned and thundered back toward
the beach, Spike would turn and run away, tail between his legs,
howling in terror. Rob was pretending to be oblivious to the
whole spectacle.

"Well, at least Spike's having fun," I said as I drew up beside
Rob.

"Miserable little mutt," Rob muttered. "Sorry, Michael."

Michael shrugged.

"Don't look at me," he said. "The miserable little mutt belongs to my mom."

"You think he'd get tired of it," Rob said, frowning, as Spike chased the water back and forth again.

"I'm sure he will after a while," I said.

"I've been here two hours," Rob said. "He's not getting tired. Just hoarse."

"Well, hoarse might be an improvement," I said. "Why on earth have you been standing here for two hours? Is something going on?"

"Not much," Rob said. "Everyone's getting hysterical about some guy who's running around shooting the puffins. That's about it."

"He's not shooting the puffins; he's shooting us. At us anyway," I said.

"Us? You mean you and Michael?" Rob asked.

"Yes."

"Wow, are you going to file charges?"

"Yes," Michael said. "And when you've passed the bar, you can handle the civil suit, if you like."

"Cool," Rob said. "So what's going on with the puffins?"

"Nothing. They've left the island," I said.

"Lucky them," Rob muttered. "Here, take him for a while, will you?"

"No thanks," I said, backing away. "We've got our hands full of groceries."

Which was true, but Rob still glowered at me as he strode off down the beach, Spike skittering along at his heels. Michael and I headed back to the cottage.

"I wish Aunt Phoebe would come back," I said, glancing down the lane.

"Don't worry," Michael said. "Everything will be fine."

I always get nervous when people say that.

Chapter 10

The Puffin Before the Storm

"There you are!" Mrs. Fenniman said, pouncing on us the second we entered the cottage. "It's about time someone showed up to do some work around here!"

Before we knew it, Mrs. Fenniman had drafted us into hurricane preparations. Apparently, Dad had vanished shortly after Michael and I left, leaving her with only Rob to order around.

Fortunately, Aunt Phoebe's house was built along sensible lines, with working shutters. All you had to do was close them and make sure the latch was secure, thus sparing us the nightmare of boarding and taping that some residents had to do. Rob and Dad had apparently managed to deal with the shutters before they debunked. Probably took them all of half an hour.

Michael and I weren't so lucky with the lawn and deck furniture. Before dashing off to deal with Victor Resnick, Aunt Phoebe had left orders for us to bring every movable object inside. Mrs. Fenniman took her quite literally. The deck alone housed a dozen plastic chairs, three tables, a gas grill, half a dozen sets of wind chimes, and several dozen wooden planters or clay pots, with or without vegetation. The yard contained two picnic tables, three birdbaths, a rain gauge, a sundial, a second grill, a badminton net, a croquet set, a set of horseshoes, a pair of flag-poles, several dozen more flower boxes, an awesome assortment of lawn ornaments, and a never-ending supply of bird feeders and birdhouses. We finally convinced Mrs. Fenniman that the slate flagstones and the bricks bordering the flower beds could probably cope by themselves. And since the garden shed was already overflowing with junk not actively in use, we had to drag everything into the house and shove the furniture around until we could fit it all in somehow.

We had nearly finished and were looking forward to resting when Mother suddenly appeared on the upstairs landing, her hair falling down her back. She was wringing her hands, looking fit to give a bang-up performance of Ophelia's mad scene.

"Have you seen your father?" she demanded.

"Not since this morning," I said.

"Don't worry, Margaret," Mrs. Fenniman said. "He'll be fine."

"Where's Phoebe?" Mother asked.

"Up at the village," I lied, not wanting Mother to start worrying about Aunt Phoebe, too.

"You go back to your nap," Mrs. Fenniman put in. "She'll be back anytime now, and James, too."

"What if something has happened to him?"

"What could happen to him?" Michael asked.

"He said he was going to go out to Green Point and watch the hurricane hit the island," Mother said. "I told Phoebe not to let him go, and now she's gone, too."

"Oh Lord. I thought he was kidding about that," I said.

"You should know your father by now," Mother said pointedly.

"Well, at least he didn't go off with your aunt Phoebe to tackle Victor Resnick," Michael put in.

So much for not worrying Mother.

"Victor Resnick?" Mother repeated. "Is he on the island?"

"Yes, why wouldn't he be?" I asked. "He owns a house here."

"Oh dear," Mother said. "Your father doesn't know Resnick is here, does he?"

"Of course he knows, Mother," I said. "We all heard it from the Dickermans last night."

"Oh dear me," Mother said. She drifted down the stairs, looking preoccupied.

"Where did you say Phoebe was?" Mrs. Fenniman asked.

"Probably up at Victor Resnick's house, giving him a good thrashing," I said.

"I'm sure your father is doing no such thing," Mother said. "That's absolute nonsense."

She strode out into the kitchen, leaving the swinging door flapping wildly.

"Not Dad—Aunt Phoebe," I called after her. "Why on earth would Dad want to thrash Victor Resnick?"

"Well, he's a birder, too, isn't he?" Michael said. "Probably upset about what everyone thinks Resnick's doing to the birds."

"Birds! Don't be silly," Mrs. Fenniman said with a cackle. "The green-eyed monster, more likely."

"Green-eyed monster?" Michael and I said in unison.

"They were quite an item, your mother and Victor Resnick," Mrs. Fenniman said. "Of course, that was a few years ago, before she met your dad."

"Over forty years ago, if it was before she met Dad," I said. "What makes you think Dad would still be jealous of Victor Resnick after all this time?"

"Quite a famous man, Victor Resnick," Mrs. Fenniman said. "Bound to make a man a little nervous, his wife's old beau showing up like this. And still single."

With that, she disappeared into the kitchen.

"*He* didn't show up; Mother and Dad did," I said as the door swung to again.

I heard a smothered chuckle from Michael, who sat there as calmly as you please, flipping through one of the old family photo album. Men.

"Very funny," I said. "You don't really think Dad is off confronting Victor Resnick, do you?"

As if in answer, Michael held out a photo album, pointing to one of the pictures. I glanced down and saw Mother, posing arm in arm with a tall, gawky young man who looked dreadfully familiar. Something about the hawklike nose and the pugnacious expression. I flipped the page. And the page after that. Picture after picture of Mother with the same young man. In several, they were affectionately entwined in a manner that wasn't particularly shocking today but probably was back then. Particularly since the fashions and the ages of some of the younger cousins showed that Mother wasn't more than fourteen or fifteen. In one photo, he held a sketch pad and Mother had assumed an exaggerated cheesecake pose.

"Resnick." I said. "Damn."

The kitchen door swung open again.

"Meg, go and find your father at once!" Mother said. "Make sure he doesn't do anything foolish."

"Mother, he's probably just gone to Green Point to watch the hurricane hit the island," I said.

Mother looked at me in silence for a moment.

"*Anything* foolish," she repeated, and disappeared into the kitchen.

Mrs. Fenniman stuck her head out a few seconds later.

"Keep your eye out for Phoebe, too," she said. "She ought not to be out in this weather. Hurricane's moving again."

"Is it going to hit the island?" Michael asked.

"No, but it's going to come close enough to make things pretty nasty," Mrs. Fenniman said. "Don't forget your knapsacks; you may need some of that gear out there!"

With that, she popped back into the kitchen.

Michael and I looked at each other. For a moment, I could see a look of utter exhaustion on his face, and I felt a sudden surge of anger. Why on earth couldn't my family behave like sensible human beings for once? Then his face relaxed into a tired smile and he reached down to pick up his knapsack.

"Well, no one ever called life dull with your dad around," he said, turning to open the door. "Once more into the breach, my friends."

I sighed, picked up my own knapsack, and followed him out.

"So where do we go first?" he asked. "Green Point or Resnick's house?"

"It's the same general direction," I said.

We hurried through the village, asking passing birders if they'd seen Dad. No one had. We peered into the dimly lit general store and saw Jeb Barnes had apparently just arrived back. He was shedding his wet wraps by the stove.

"Have you seen my dad?" I asked.

"No, nor your aunt Phoebe, neither," he said. "I thought you said she'd gone up to Resnick's."

"She did."

"Well, she'd left by the time we got there, and he wasn't too happy to see us, either," Jeb said. "Mad as a wet hen about something, so we didn't stay long."

The electric lights flickered on and off again.

"Jim's not having much luck with that thing today, is he?" one of the locals said.

"Too much rain," Jeb said. "He might as well give up till the storm's past. Go ahead and light some more of those oil lamps, will you?"

"Come on," I said to Michael. "I guess we'll have to look for Dad by ourselves. Before he breaks his neck or something."

The men huddled by the stove looked uncomfortable, but none of them volunteered to help. I stomped outside. The rain was growing worse by the minute. The birders had all gone somewhere to roost, and the only local we saw as we passed through town was Fred Dickerman, trying to ease his truck out of a mud hole in the road. We gave him a wide berth and squelched up the road in the same direction we'd last seen Aunt Phoebe hiking.

"We're not really going back to Resnick's, are we?" Michael asked.

"We can claim we've come to rescue him from Aunt Phoebe," I said. "And we'll try to detour around the edge of his property."

Michael still looked dubious. I wasn't sure which prospect worried him more, meeting Resnick again or taking another of my detours.

The closer we got to Victor Resnick's house, the more anxious I felt. Michael reacted the same way, although since he didn't know the local landmarks, this meant he'd been in a constant state of anxiety since about five minutes after we left the village.

"Are we getting close to that lunatic's property line?" he kept asking.

"Yes," I said finally. "We'll start our detour in a few minutes. I just want to go a little farther up this path. There's a lookout point where we can see quite a way down the shore."

"Damn!"

I whirled, to see Michael sprawled facedown in the mud.

"Michael! What's wrong?"

"Tripped over another of these damned water pipes," he said. "Why don't they bury the damned things where they'll be out of the way?"

"Well, for one thing, half the places the pipes run don't have enough topsoil to bury a matchstick, much less one of these pipes," I said, pausing in the path to get my breath. "And for another, they take the pipes up in the fall to prevent them from freezing. They'd have a hard time doing that if they buried them."

"Take them up?" he echoed. "What do they do for water in the winter?"

"Use cisterns," I said. "And practice rigorous water conservation."

"When in the fall?" he asked. "They're not going to take them up while we're here, are they?"

"Not unless there's a freeze predicted," I said. "Make sure you didn't disconnect the pipe you tripped over, by the way."

"Right," he said. "You go on; I'll catch up in a second."

As Michael bent over to examine the pipe, still shaking his head in disbelief, I trudged up the path until I emerged from the trees into the open and could see along the shore to the end of the point of land on which Resnick's house and studio stood. I was hoping to see Dad, alive and well and ready to come back to the house to dry off and warm up.

Instead, I saw a dead body.

Chapter 11

From Puffin to Eternity

The body lay facedown in a shallow, rocky pool, but my money wasn't on drowning as the cause of death.

"Michael," I yelled. "Could you come up here a second?"

I stood looking down the slope at the tidal pool where the body floated. I was shivering, from nerves as much as the cold rain, as Michael scrambled out to the cliff's edge and stood beside me.

"Meg, maybe we should just go back to the house," he said, his voice raised to be heard over the wind and surf. "Your father's probably back there by now; I'm sure he was only kidding about wanting to stand on Green Point and watch the hurricane hit the island."

"I'm sure he wasn't, but never mind that now," I said. "Look down there."

"Oh my God," Michael said. He tried to pull me away so I couldn't see the body. "It's not him, is it?"

"You mean Dad? Heavens no! Look at all that hair."

"You're right," Michael said. "Sorry. I panicked for a second. So who is he?"

"I think it's Resnick."

Michael craned his head to look at the body from another angle.

"I think you're right. Well, that's a relief, for us at least."

"Not much of a relief, considering he was almost certainly murdered."

"Murdered! What makes you think that? I mean, why not drowned?"

"Look at that gash on the back of his head."

Michael peered through the rain.

"Oh," he said. "Not so much of a relief after all, I suppose; and before you say anything, I only meant a relief because it wasn't your dad. I didn't mean I was glad Resnick was dead or anything like that."

"Although I have a feeling a lot of people will be, even if they don't admit it."

We just stood there for a moment, staring at the body.

"We'd better go and tell somebody," Michael said. "The helpful Constable Barnes, I suppose."

"We'd better haul the body up first," I said with a shudder.

"We can't; we'd be disturbing a crime scene," Michael protested.

"I think the storm's going to do more than disturb the crime scene by the time we could get down to the village, much less bring anyone back. If we don't haul him up, he's going to wash out to sea."

As if to emphasize my point, the crest of a particularly big wave washed over the rocks into the tidal pool. The body rocked slightly, and the right arm moved back and forth, as if Resnick were waving to us.

"See, the tide's rising," I said. "We'd better hurry."

"Right," Michael said. He took a deep breath and then began easing himself over the side of the ledge, feeling for a foothold on the rocky slope.

"I'm sorry," I said.

"Not your fault," he replied, looking up with a reassuring smile.

"Yes, it is," I said. "I got us into this. Coming here was my idea. Some romantic getaway."

"Well, you never promised me a tropical paradise."

He gave me a hand over the edge of the cliff, and I began carefully following him down the slope. It wasn't all that steep; if there had been solid ground at the bottom, I'd have just slid and slithered down in a hurry. But considering what waited below—a dead body and a rapidly rising ocean—I very definitely didn't want to lose my footing.

"Getting him up again is going to be a real headache," Michael said, looking around. "I don't suppose there's another way back."

"There's a path that goes back toward Resnick's house," I said. "But I don't think the tide's low enough."

"You're sure?" Michael said. "Where is it? Maybe we can pick a time between waves."

I pointed to the narrow path hugging the side of the cliff. As we studied it, a wave sloshed over the path, stranding a wire-mesh lobster trap. A few seconds later, a larger wave broke over the path, crushing the trap against the side of the cliff and sucking the fragments back as it retreated.

"Okay, I guess the cliff's it," Michael said. He looked up at the cliff, frowning, and then back at the body. Water sloshed over our feet.

"Hang on a second," I said, pulling the knapsack off my shoulders. "I never thought I'd give Dad the satisfaction of hearing this, but for once this damned hiking emergency kit of his will come in handy."

I dug through the contents of the pack, passing up a hefty first-aid kit, a large bottle of SP35 sunscreen, plastic bottles of water and Gatorade, several packages of freeze-dried food, and a flare gun that probably dated from the Korean War. Sure enough, there at the bottom of the pack I found a long length of slender nylon rope.

"We can tie this to him and haul him up," I said. "There should be another rope in your pack, if we need it."

"He'll get a little battered," Michael observed.

"I think he's past caring."

"Yes, but it will complicate the autopsy, won't it?"

"Good point. We can hoist him up over there," I said, pointing a little to the right, where the cliff overhung the beginning of the submerged path. "We can keep him away from the cliff until the very top."

"I'll bundle him up," Michael said, taking off his parka and spreading it out on the rocks. "You find something up there to tie the other end of the rope to."

"Right," I said. But before I started scrambling back up the slope, I paused, took a breath, and tried to look around very methodically and fix the scene in my mind.

In the sunlight, the rocky shoreline would have looked rugged and picturesque, but in the gloomy half-light, I could think only what a bleak and cheerless place it was to die all alone.

Well, not quite all alone. Out of the corner of my eye, I saw the sudden bright flash as a beam of sunlight broke through the clouds and reflected off the lenses of a pair of binoculars. Some-where, farther up the slope, birders were watching. I only hoped they had been watching long enough to see that Resnick had been dead when we found him. Awkward if they'd only seen us mess-ing around with a dead body.

"Meg? Is something wrong?"

"No," I said. "Just looking around to see if there's anything unusual we should report to the police. I mean, you're probably right about this being a crime scene. Want me to help you pull him out?"

"It's okay," Michael said. "I can manage."

He didn't sound too happy about it, but if he wanted to play strong, protective male, I didn't plan to argue. It was one thing to talk about corpses and autopsies around the dinner table when Dad went off on one of his true-crime tangents and quite another to haul a body out of the briny deep.

Michael frowned down at the corpse.

"Michael, I'm—" I stopped myself. He looked up and raised an eyebrow. I couldn't help smiling; I loved the way he did that.

"Having promised that I wouldn't apologize for anything that went wrong," I said, "I'm trying very hard to think of anything else to say right now."

He chuckled.

"I was just thinking what great research material this is for my acting," he said. "I had a part in a TV show once where I had to discover a murder victim. Had a tough time making it authentic, given the fact I'd never even seen a dead body. But since I've met you, I've seen more stiffs than a mafioso in training."

"Is that a good thing?" I asked.

"Well, it's useful."

With that, he bent down and began pulling at Resnick's body. I coiled the rope over my shoulder, replaced the pack on my back, and headed toward the cliff.

As I reached for the first rock in my climb, I saw a piece of paper fluttering on the ground at my feet. I stooped to pick it up. Force of habit—growing up with Dad, you tended to think the eleventh and twelfth commandments were "Thou shalt not litter" and "I don't care if you didn't put it there; pick it up anyway; it won't kill you to bend over."

I found myself staring at a familiar piece of paper; the map on which Dad had scoped out the best place on the island to watch the hurricane. It was soggy and some of the ink had smeared, but I recognized Dad's printing instantly. His handwriting achieved a degree of artistic illegibility that made him the envy of less accomplished physicians, but his printing was precise, elegant, more readable than most typefaces—and absolutely distinctive. I'd figured out the real scoop on Santa Claus one year when I realized that the note thanking me for the milk and cookies was in Dad's inimitable printing.

Oh damn, I thought. If anyone else found this, and figured out it belonged to Dad—and anyone who'd ever seen his printing would figure it out in a heartbeat . . .

"Meg?" Michael called.

"Sorry. I'm going," I said, stuffing the map in my knapsack and reaching again for the cliff.

"Hang on a second. Do you think we should take this, too?"

I glanced back. Michael had laid Resnick's body on a flat rock and was pointing down at something floating in the pool. I scrambled back down to see what it was.

A NO TRESPASSING sign, minus its post, bobbed just below the surface.

"It was under the body," he said.

"We'd better take it, I suppose," I said. "It could be evidence."

I tried a couple of times to snag it, using the rope so as not to touch it and leave fingerprints. But in the end, the only way we could manage to reach it without wading into the icy water was for Michael to hold on to my waist while I reached out and grabbed it, and even then both of us got half-soaked by the waves.

"Definitely time to make tracks," Michael said as I secured the sign to my backpack and he turned back to deal with Resnick.

Hauling the body up the slope took forever, and then we decided to put Resnick someplace out of the rain, since we'd moved him so far already. We picked him up—I took the feet, which seemed less personal somehow—and lugged him down the path to his house.

I didn't like the glass and steel monstrosity, but I couldn't help thinking it looked a little forlorn already. The wind had plastered the glass with wet leaves and mud, and the way the windows rattled made me glad I wouldn't be inside the house when the storm really broke.

We found room in the woodshed, put the body out of the storm, pulled a canvas tarpaulin over it, and stashed the sign in a corner.

Now that we were out of the rain, we paused for a moment.

I took my flashlight out of the knapsack and played it over Resnick's face. In the struggle to get his body up above the tide line and under cover, I hadn't had much chance to inspect him. Now, in the harsh illumination of the flashlight, I had much too good a view. The angry gash on the back of his head didn't show, of course, since he lay faceup, but he had a nasty-looking bruise on his forehead, just at the hairline. And he definitely looked very dead. And very unhappy. Was the look on his face anger? Pain? Fear? Surprise? Probably a combination of all of them.

"Let's get out of here," Michael said, echoing my thought. "I mean, we need to get back to the village and report this."

As we stepped out of the shed, I tripped over something and went sprawling.

"Are you all right?" Michael asked.

"I'm fine," I said. "Just tripped over something Resnick must have left lying around."

"Even dead, that man's dangerous," he said.

Before I got up, I felt around to find whatever had tripped me—I didn't want to repeat the experience again immediately. My hands finally touched something—a thick, slightly damp nine-by-twelve envelope, curled up into a half cylinder. Was that what I'd tripped over? Odd that it was only slightly damp if it had been lying around in the rain for any amount of time. Perhaps the overhanging roof of the shed had sheltered it until I'd tripped over it. Or perhaps Resnick had carried it rolled up and stuffed into one of his pockets and it had fallen out when we moved him.

I stowed it in my knapsack for later examination; then Michael and I hiked back to the village, looking over our shoulders about every third step.

Jeb Barnes wasn't happy to see us again.

Chapter 12

A Puffin Is Announced

"We haven't seen your father," Jeb said, hunching toward the woodstove and holding his coffee closer to his face.

"Neither have we," I said. "That's not why we're here."

"Phoebe's not here, either," one of the locals said.

"We've come to report a murder," Michael said in his most resonant stage voice.

The group around the stove froze, and one dropped a coffee mug, which shattered on the gray wooden floor.

"Who did that crazy fool shoot?" Jeb Barnes asked when he finally found his voice.

"Resnick? He didn't shoot anyone," I said. "Someone smashed his skull in first."

I didn't imagine the faint sighs of relief from several of the locals.

"Who did it?" Jeb demanded.

"How should we know?" Michael said. "We just found him facedown in the water."

"In the water?" Jeb echoed.

"In a tidal pool a little down the shore from his house," I said. "We had to move him; the tide was about to wash him away, so we carried him up and put him out of the rain."

"My God," Jeb said. "What are we supposed to do now?"

Why does everyone look at me when people ask questions like that?

"I suppose you can't call the police over from the mainland until the storm's over?"

"The phones are down," Jeb said. "I could try radioing the Coast Guard, but even if I got through, I doubt they could come till after the storm. It's headed our way now."

"No, it's not; it's going to miss us by at least fifty miles," another local put in.

"Fifty miles is nothing to a hurricane," Jeb said. "Why, in '24—"

"So aren't you going to do something about the body?" I interrupted. "To preserve it until the police get here?"

They all stared at me.

"Is there anyplace on the island with a working generator and a big refrigerator you can empty out?"

They looked horrified.

"One of the restaurants, maybe?" I suggested. "Most of them have closed for the season. And most of them have emergency generators, don't they? Because of the food?"

"Yes, but—" a local began, and then stopped. They looked at one another. I could read their thoughts. Having its refrigerator serve as a temporary morgue wouldn't enhance a restaurant's ambiance if it got out—and it would certainly get out in a community as small as Monhegan.

"I hear the Anchor Inn's probably going out of business unless the Mayfields get an extension on their loan," one said finally.

"Mayfields went back to the mainland, though," another said.

"They're having the Dickermans look after the place," Jeb Barnes said, looking relieved. "Fred, you've got a key, right? You take care of it."

Fred was tucked away behind the stove, nursing a mug with a protective air, which made me suspect it contained more than just coffee. He looked up, nodded, chugged the remaining contents of his mug, and slouched over to the coatrack beside the door.

"And someone official should take charge of the scene," I said, looking at Jeb. "Supervise bringing the body down."

Jeb sighed and began struggling into his raincoat and hat, as well.

"Sam, you see if you can raise the Coast Guard," he said. "I'll fetch the mayor and we'll go up to the crime scene."

"And can you have someone start a search for my dad and Aunt Phoebe?" I asked. "With a killer running loose on the island, I'm getting very worried about them."

"There's no way we can send anybody out right now," Jeb said. "If they have a lick of sense, they'll find someplace and stay put till morning. Can't have search parties risking their necks out on those rocks. Where did you say you left the body?"

"We'll show you," I said. Michael and I climbed in the back of the truck, which rattled over the gravel road and finally pulled up in front of a small gray saltbox house whose windows were tightly boarded against the storm.

"Why are we stopping here?" I asked nervously. "Doesn't the idiot even know where Resnick's house is?"

Jeb Barnes got out and began knocking on the door of the house.

"Mamie!" he yelled. "It's Jeb; we've got a problem."

The door opened, and the owner of the puffin-infested gift shop peered out.

"Problem?" she repeated. "What sort of a problem?"

"That damn fool Resnick's gone and gotten himself killed."

"Murdered, most likely," I called from my place in the truck.

"How awful!" Mamie said, her voice implying she didn't really think it was particularly awful at all.

"Those two found him," Jeb Barnes said, jerking a thumb over his shoulder at Michael and me. "We'd better secure the body until the mainland authorities can get here."

"Right," Mamie said. "Hang on a minute while I put on my rain gear."

Jeb climbed in the back of the truck with Michael and me.

"Why are we bringing Mamie?" I asked.

"Well, like you said, we need the local authorities to take charge of the body. She's the mayor."

Her Honor reappeared, dressed in a battered rain slicker, got into the cab of the truck with Fred, and we clattered off—this time, to my relief, in the direction of Resnick's house.

Jeb didn't say much—not that we'd have heard him, given the rising wind and the rough ground the truck rattled over. I had nothing to distract me from my thoughts, which were pretty grim. If the police didn't quickly figure out who had bashed Victor Resnick's head in, suspicion could start falling on far too many of my nearest and dearest. On Aunt Phoebe, last seen dashing off to Resnick's house, announcing her intention of giving him a good thrashing. On Michael and me, since we'd made no secret of our anger over Resnick taking potshots at us. And since we had no proof yet that we'd only discovered the crime, instead of committing it. And, worst of all, on Dad. Even though I'd pocketed the telltale map, I doubted if Mrs. Fenniman was the only one on the island who knew Resnick was an old beau of Mother's. And now that I thought about it, Dad had seemed in a rather strange, quiet mood after he'd heard that Resnick had returned to the island. What if some detective who didn't really know Dad jumped to the wrong conclusion?

Then again, with both Dad and Aunt Phoebe missing, I also had ample reason for worrying about what might be happening to them. I couldn't help fretting that if Hurricane Gladys didn't get them, the unknown killer would. And occasionally, just by way of a change, I glanced over at Michael and worried a little about what he thought of all this. Bad enough I'd dragged him off for a so-called vacation under cold, wet, primitive conditions that offered even less privacy than we'd had in Yorktown. Now I'd dragged him into the middle of another homicide.

Stop worrying, I told myself, though I might as well have told the wind to stop blowing. I come from a long line of Olympic-caliber worriers.

When we got to the gravel path to Resnick's house, Fred Dickerman stopped his truck and we all climbed out.

"We'll have to send someone up to the power plant to fetch Jim," Mamie boomed at us. "Hate to take him away from his repair work, but the Mayfields have a small backup generator; I think he can get that going to run the cooler."

"Can't Fred do that?" Jeb asked.

Fred shrugged.

"Jim's the one knows generators," he said.

"We'll fetch him," I volunteered. "You'll have no trouble finding the body; it's in his woodshed."

"You have to show us where you found the body," Mamie said.

"We can't," I said. She looked up with a frown. "Not until low tide anyway. We found him facedown in a tidal pool at the foot of the cliffs."

"Good thing you came along when you did, then," she said. "He'd have washed away by now if you hadn't brought him up."

I wondered if she was sincere or if, like me, she'd realized how much less trouble we'd have if Michael and I hadn't found Resnick. If the storm had washed his body away, they might never have found him. Or if they had, they'd probably have assumed the gash on the back of his head happened in the storm. Nonsense, I told myself; you've prevented a murderer from getting away with his crime.

"We'll show you tomorrow," I said. "After it's light. And after we find my dad and Aunt Phoebe."

"Good Lord, don't tell me they're still out there," Mamie said.

"Jeb says we can't send out search parties until the storm blows over," I said.

"No, we can't," Mamie said. "Let's go get the body."

As she headed down the path toward Resnick's house, I could have sworn I heard one of the three mutter, "Damn fool tourists."

Maybe I was imagining things. Maybe not. And they needn't have muttered; I'd have agreed with them.

Michael and I toiled up the road a little farther, heading for the power plant.

"We should come back up here when the storm's over," I said as we rested before the final, nearly vertical stretch of road. "You get a beautiful view of this whole end of the island from up here. The village on this side, and the wild, unspoiled landscape on the other. At least you could the last time I came up here," I added with a frown. "Who knows—maybe between the power plant and Resnick's monstrosity, there isn't much unspoiled view left."

With that cheerful thought, we attacked the last hill. Up this high, we had little shelter from the wind, which blew the raindrops nearly horizontal at times. We could never have found the shed housing the power plant if not for the flickering lantern light in the windows. We felt our way around the side of the building until we came to a door, then began pounding as loudly as we could.

"I don't suppose it would occur to anyone to build a front porch to this thing," Michael shouted as we pounded.

"It's only a shed," I shouted back. Although I did think that even with a shed, any sane builder would have gone to the trouble of putting up gutters—so when it rained, you could get inside without walking through sheets of water running straight off the steeply slanted roof.

The door finally opened and a bearded face peered out from considerably above my eye level. Could this be little Jimmy Dick-erman?

"I'm working on it," he said, and started to shut the door.

"Wait," I said, inserting my foot in the frame. "What do you mean, 'I'm working on it'? You don't even know why we came up here."

He looked at me as if I were crazy.

"Same reason everybody else comes up here when the phones are out," he said. "To ask when the generator's going on-line again. And the answer's the same I'd give anybody: I don't know yet, and I'm working on it."

"Fine," I said. "Except that's not why we're here. Mamie sent us. Can we come in? It's pouring out here."

Jim looked at us for a minute, then nodded and turned to walk back into the shed. Michael and I followed.

"Good Lord!" Michael exclaimed, looking around. The shed contained a jungle of odd-shaped metal tools, parts, and machines. I remembered Jim, as a child, filling the Dickerman house with odd bits of half-assembled machinery that he was tinkering with or saving for some inscrutable purpose. He'd expanded the scope of his operations considerably since then. I once saw a picture of an elephant graveyard, littered with the skeletons and tusks of elephants who'd gone there to die. Jim had created the mechanical equivalent. No wonder Mrs. Dickerman had sounded so happy when she talked about her Jimmy up here tinkering with his machines. At least she had her living room back.

Jim had returned to pottering with one large machine. It looked old, but less abandoned than most of the objects in the room.

"That the generator?" I asked.

He nodded.

"What's wrong with it?"

Jim looked up.

"You really want to know?"

I had a feeling if I said yes, I'd regret it for at least the several hours he'd take to explain.

"Not really," I confessed. "Aunt Phoebe's not even hooked up to your power company yet, so it's academic to me how long it'll take to fix it."

"Good for you, then, 'cause it's going to take awhile," Jim said. "Specially if the mayor keeps sending people up here to pester me. What is it this time?"

His surliness irritated me.

"Murder," I said.

Chapter 13

Zen and the Art of Puffin Maintenance

Okay, it was a cheap trick, but Jim Dickerman got on my nerves. I enjoyed the way his head snapped around when I said that, and how he stared at me, openmouthed.

"Murder," he repeated finally. "Who?"

"Victor Resnick."

"Least it's nobody anyone's going to miss," he said, recovering his poise. "What's that got to do with me anyway?"

"The mayor wants you to go down and get the generator at the Anchor Inn going," I said. "They're storing the body there in the meat locker until the police can get here."

Jim chuckled.

"Mayfields know about this?" he asked.

"The Mayfields aren't here to object," I said. "The mayor's exercising her authority and commandeering it."

"Should have exercised her authority when the old bastard started putting up that eyesore of his," Jim commented. "Well, now he's gone, maybe the town can get it condemned, tear it down."

Not a very eloquent eulogy, but typical, I suspected, of what the townspeople would say when news of Resnick's death got around.

Jim poked around the shed for a while, gathering tools. I didn't mind the delay. I wasn't looking forward to going back out into the storm. And Jim's workroom was rather interesting.

The more I stared around, the more I could identify the bits and pieces. Over in one corner were the parts to an old lawn mower. Did anyone on Monhegan actually mow lawns? Another large pile would probably turn into a golf cart when reassembled. I saw two pair of binoculars, one more or less intact and the other in pieces. Or maybe it was the disassembled pieces of several sets of binoculars; I doubted all the parts would fit into one. The pile of radio parts also contained enough components to assemble two or three objects, as did the piles of fragments from televisions, VCRs, cameras, and outboard motors. He had a few intact things, too: propane tanks, Coleman lanterns, and, in one corner, a large glistening-wet coil of the familiar industrial-weight orange power cords Monheganites used when they wanted to borrow some electricity from a more wired neighbor.

"Your dad would love this place," Michael said.

Yes, he would. I shuddered at the thought of the havoc he could wreak.

"Don't want anyone barging in here right now when I'm work-ing on the generator," Jim said, looking up from his tool bench.

"Don't worry," Michael said. "At the moment, Dr. Langslow's lost somewhere on the island. By the time he's found, you'll probably have the generator running again."

"Dr. Langslow?" Jim repeated, looking at me. "You're Meg, then?"

I nodded. Jim looked at me with a frown. I suppose he was trying to connect my thirty-something self with the teenager I'd been when he'd last seen me. He shrugged as he threw on several layers of wraps and rain gear. Then he picked up a tool box and stepped out into the storm.

Jim set off briskly, head down against the rain, ignoring us trailing behind him. When we got to the edge of the hill, I paused briefly to look around. Apart from my desire not to spend any more time than necessary with the mortal remains of the late Victor Resnick, I'd wanted to come up to the power plant be-cause I knew it had a view of half the island. From this vantage point, I'd hoped I could spot Dad or Aunt Phoebe. But I could see only the occasional flickering lights of candles and oil lamps, and not many of those. I sighed and began scrambling down the slope after Michael and Jim.

When we got to the Anchor Inn, Jim disappeared into the back shed to tinker with the generator while Michael and I stepped into the front room to take a break before the rest of our hike back to the cottage.

A nice place, the Anchor Inn. Of course, the heat and power were off. But it was solidly built, and insulated well enough to keep out not only the wind but also a good deal of its noise. We stumbled past a number of tables with the chairs stacked upside down on their tops and peered into the shadowy kitchen.

Mamie had gone, but Jeb Barnes and Fred Dickerman still stood guard. Jeb stood beside the cooler door, looking around as if he expected body snatchers to leap out from behind the cabinets. Fred sat as far from the cooler as possible, smoking a cigarette. I wouldn't have pegged him for the squeamish or superstitious type, but I noticed that his hand shook a bit.

"You find Jim?" Jeb asked.

"He's out back," Michael said.

"Are the police coming over?" I asked.

Jeb snorted.

"In this weather? Hell no. Maybe tomorrow, but probably not till Monday."

A sudden rumbling noise filled the building. A light over in the far end of the kitchen came on, and the meat locker began humming.

"Well, that's taken care of anyway," Jeb said. He stood up and began donning his rain slicker. "You and Jim keep an eye on the place, make sure the generator's running."

"Right," Fred said. He still had all his rain gear on, and from the haste with which he buttoned his slicker on his way to the door, I had a feeling he'd keep an eye on the place from a distance.

"Shall we go?" Michael asked.

I started. I'd been lost in thought. If the police couldn't come out for a day or so, all the better, as far as I could see. I wanted time to find out some things before the authorities showed up. Like how Dad had managed to drop his map of the island at the murder scene. And where he and Aunt Phoebe were, and what really had happened when she confronted Resnick. After all, we were longtime summer people, but we were only summer people. Which in the local hierarchy put us only one step above day tourists, and considerably below lobsters and puffins. And I had a feeling that even the mainland police would rather have their internationally famous corpse bumped off by tourists or summer people instead of by some good, solid, salt-of-the-earth Monheganite.

The weather outside had gone beyond frightful. The wind drove the rain into our skin like cold needles, and at times we had to clutch fences and buildings to keep from being knocked down.

We seriously contemplated taking refuge for a while in the village church. Candlelight flickered invitingly in the windows, and the birders camping inside were having a splendid time, despite the lack of creature comforts. We could hear a spirited rendition of "Kumbayah" in three-part harmony.

"I'm not looking forward to going back to the cottage without Dad," I shouted over the wind as we struggled down the lane. Is the wind really that much worse, I wondered, or does it just seem that way this close to the water?

"Your mother will be frantic," Michael shouted back as we paused for a moment to steady ourselves.

"I'm already frantic," I bellowed back. "But there's no way we can keep looking when the storm's like this. We'll just have to hope that he's got the sense to—my God, what was that?"

Michael raised his arm instinctively to shield me as a gust of wind slammed a large metal object down in the road a few inches in front of our feet and then swept it over the side of the road and down toward the beach. I could hear a metal clanging noise as it hit the rocks of the breakwater below.

"An aluminum lawn chair, I think," Michael answered, staggering over to the edge of the road. "It almost—oh no!"

I struggled to his side and peered over the edge of the road. I could see someone crouching on the rocks, perilously close to the edge of the water.

Mother.

Chapter 14

A Long Day's Journey into Puffins

"Why on earth is she out in this weather?" I asked. Normally, we could barely coax Mother out on the deck on a perfect summer day, and even then she'd be well nigh invisible beneath the sunblock, the giant sunglasses, the parasol, and the mosquito hat. But for her to go out in the hurricane . . .

"She must be in a panic about your dad," Michael said, echoing my thought. "We'd better go rescue her."

We crawled down the breakwater toward her. She clung to a rock with one hand, but when she saw us coming, she waved at us with—What the devil did she have in her other hand?

An umbrella. Or what remained of one after the wind had turned the frame inside out and ripped away all but a few shreds of fabric.

"Hello, dears," she said when we reached her side. "I'm very glad to see you. I've hurt my ankle and I was beginning to wonder how I'd get home."

"What on earth are you doing out here?" Michael asked.

"Looking for James. Have you found him yet?" she asked. Beneath her usual calm tone was an edge of panic. Or was it pain? Either way, I'd have given anything to have some good news to tell her.

"Not yet, and there's no way we can keep looking at night, not in this weather," I said as calmly as I could manage. "I'm sure he's holed up somewhere and we'll find him in the morning."

She looked at me for a few seconds, and I tried to project

calm, reassurance, and confidence. But after thirty-odd years, I should have known better than to try fooling her. She nodded slightly, and I could see her jaw clench.

"Let's continue this back at the house," Michael said. "Can you walk?"

"No, dear," she said. "I think I must have done something unfortunate to my ankle."

I twitched up the hem of her skirt and took a look. Yes, *unfortunate* was a good word; the ankle had swollen to the size of a grapefruit. I also noticed that she wore the battered remains of a pair of high-heeled leopard-print sandals.

"Good grief," I said. "It's no wonder you hurt yourself, wearing these things. Why didn't you put on a pair of sneakers or something? Something practical you could walk in."

"I walked all over Paris in these," she said. "They're the most practical ones I have with me."

"You should have borrowed a pair of mine."

"At least these fit," she retorted. She had a point; her feet were three sizes smaller than mine. But still . . .

"We'll have to carry her," I said, turning to Michael.

Just then a wave, slightly larger than the rest, lapped over Mother's foot.

"I think I'm ready to leave now," she said, clutching Michael's hand.

I couldn't help thinking, as we half-pulled, half-carried Mother home, how much easier it had been with Resnick—even though he'd been a deadweight and Mother helped as much as she could. But the storm had gotten so much worse in the last couple of hours. And then again, we didn't have to worry about hurting Resnick; Mother was fighting back tears of pain by the time we finally staggered up the front steps of Aunt Phoebe's cottage.

Mrs. Fenniman leapt up from the couch when we sloshed into the living room.

"Good heavens, Margaret," she exclaimed. "I thought you were upstairs napping!"

"Napping?" Mother snapped back. "Napping, with James out there in the storm, and for all we know——" She stopped, and settled for frowning at Mrs. Fenniman.

"Well, what do you two have to say for yourselves?" Mrs. Fenniman said, turning on us. "Have you managed to find anyone?"

"We haven't found Dad, we haven't found Aunt Phoebe, and someone knocked off Victor Resnick," I said.

" 'Knocked off'?" Mrs. Fenniman exclaimed. "As in murdered?"

"Oh my God," Mother murmured. "You should be out looking for your father."

"That's what we've been doing," I said. "But we can't possibly do any good right now; we'll go out again in the morning, assuming the storm has let up and there's a ghost of a chance of finding him without killing ourselves in the process."

"But we can't just leave him out there in the storm!" she protested, blinking back tears.

"Mother, he has his knapsack," I said. "Which means he's got supplies—food, water, Gatorade, flares, a flashlight, a first-aid kit, and even that silver blanket that's supposed to help you retain ninety-five percent of your body heat. He's got everything he needs to survive."

Except, of course, for the common sense that would have kept him from venturing out into the storm in the first place, but I wasn't going to bring that up.

Just then, the front door burst open and Rob stumbled in, bringing a gust of wind and spray with him. He had to struggle to close the door, then leaned against it, panting.

"It's impossible out there," he said finally. I glanced at Mother's face and had to look away.

"Come on, let's get you patched up," Mrs. Fenniman said, helping Mother toward the stairs. Mother stopped at the bottom step and fixed me with her sternest glance. She looked at me for a full minute, as if it were my fault Dad had gone off on another crazy expedition.

"First thing in the morning," she said. And then she shook off Mrs. Fenniman and limped up the stairs by herself, leaning heavily on the banister all the way.

Michael, Rob, and I fetched dry clothes and they chivalrously insisted I take first turn in the shower. I would have loved to stand under the spray for an hour, until I felt really warm again, but I knew the meager hot-water supply would barely let all three of us wash off our coatings of mud.

"I suppose I should fix something for us to eat," I said, slumping on the couch as I dried my hair.

"I'll do it after my shower," Michael said.

"Leave the cooking to me," Mrs. Fenniman said. "You come and tell me about the murder."

"Dinner sounds like a good idea," Rob said, disappearing into the bathroom. "I'll be out in half an hour."

"Don't you dare use all the hot water, Rob," I called. "Leave some for Michael."

"Don't worry about it," Michael said. "I'll manage."

"Rob's like Mother," I said. "You have to be firm with him."

"Like you are with your mother," he said with a smile, and disappeared into the kitchen.

Good point.

I slumped on the sofa and listened to the increasing wind, the rattle of pans, the rise and fall of Michael's voice as he narrated our day's adventures, and the occasional exclamation from Mrs. Fenniman. I couldn't actually make out Michael's words, thanks to the wind, which suited me just fine. I wanted to think about something other than lost relatives and dead bodies for a while. Not that I had the slightest chance of doing so. My brain was

running like a hamster in a wire wheel, wondering where Dad
and Aunt Phoebe were, and what they were doing, and whether
they were all right, and occasionally, just by way of a change,
wondering who had done in Victor Resnick.

Every few minutes, Mrs. Fenniman would pop out of the
kitchen and bring me the next course of what was rapidly turning
into an epicurean feast. I managed to put away a ham and cheese
sandwich, a bowl of chili, a bowl of soup, a plate of mixed fruit,
and a baked potato before I called a halt. Mrs. Fenniman didn't.
She kept bringing out more food and insisting I needed to eat to
keep my strength up. I got tired of arguing with her and started
shoving the new arrivals under the coffee table. Spike was in
ecstasy, alternating between devouring the food and licking my
ankles. After an hour, Rob finally ceded the bathroom to poor
Michael and settled onto the other sofa to be fed.

At one point, Mrs. Fenniman bustled upstairs. I could hear
her and Mother squabbling about something, and then she
stormed down again.

"Finally got her to take one of my Valium," she said. "Calm
her down a little. Only way she's going to make it though tonight
without going crazy."

As the night wore on, I became convinced that whoever had
prescribed Mrs. Fenniman's Valium had actually slipped her a
placebo. Mother didn't calm down in the slightest. Periodically,
she would limp out of her room and lean over the balcony. She
would stand motionless until she had attracted everyone's attention. Then she would look pointedly at the door and even more
pointedly at me.

I should have just ignored her, but every time, I patiently
explained that we had spent several hours searching all over the
island before the storm made it too dangerous. That if Dad had
any sense, he'd found someplace to hole up for the night. That
as soon as it was light enough to see six feet in front of our faces,
we'd go out and start hunting all over again.

She would look reproachfully at me, heave an enormous sigh, mutter something like "Your poor father!" and disappear. For about fifteen minutes. Then we'd go through the whole thing all over again.

Dad always says a person's true character comes through in a crisis. Judged by his own standard, Dad didn't come off too badly. Unless the crisis was a medical one, he was generally of no practical use and had a tendency to run around getting underfoot and making implausible suggestions. But he remained so cheerful and optimistic that no one really minded having him around. In fact, they almost invariably spoke of him afterward as a tower of strength and a real inspiration.

Mother ignored crises as long as possible, on the assumption that of course someone else would take care of them. Usually me. On those rare occasions when Mother felt a situation needed her attention, she would go into what Rob and I called the "off with her head" mode—making decisions and issuing orders with a ruthlessness that made Robespierre look benign. Once Mother took charge, crises tended to work themselves out quite satisfactorily—at least if you agreed with Mother's definition of a satisfactory outcome. That Mother could think of nothing to do except pace the floor and lay a guilt trip on me disturbed me almost as much as Dad's absence.

So far, Michael had shown a great deal of grace under pressure. He'd kept his sense of humor when the trip hadn't turned out to be the private, romantic getaway we'd planned, and if he was grumbling about the primitive conditions here on the island, he'd kept it to himself. Since Dad had gone AWOL, Michael had run himself ragged helping me search, all the while remaining supportive and upbeat, without displaying the sort of mindless, cheerful optimism that would have sent me over the edge. Over the last few weeks, Mrs. Fenniman had decided that Michael was, as she put it, "a keeper." Her habit of telling me this loudly, repeatedly, and in front of Michael had grown irritating, but I couldn't exactly argue with her.

I only hoped he felt the same way about me. I like to think that in a crisis I'm the cool, collected one who really gets things done with calm efficiency. I'm afraid that I'm really a lot more like Dad, with occasional touches of Mother at her worst. Well, I'd worry about that when the crisis was over; all I could do now was wait the storm out. For lack of something better to distract my mind, I picked up one of the bird books that perched on every available horizontal surface and began thumbing through it, trying to concentrate on the contents. Despite my agitated state, I couldn't help marveling at both the incredible variety of birds in the world and the incredible subtlety of some of the variations. I leafed through page after page of birds largely indistinguishable from one another unless you happened to have memorized minute differences in the amount of white on the head or red on the wing. And the way they were arranged—all the birds on the same page in the very same pose, like some avian chorus line—was particularly daunting.

"What's that?" Michael asked, sitting down beside me and handing me a cup of hot tea. He had a towel draped around his neck and smelled faintly of soap. He seemed in fairly good spirits for someone who had probably just taken a cold shower. I held up the bird book so he could see the cover.

"Thinking of taking up bird-watching?" he asked.

"Not on your life," I said. "I'd go crazy. Look at this!"

I pointed to a page entitled "Small Hooded Gulls."

"Seagulls," he said. "Lots of seagulls. So?"

"Yes, but that's only one page of seagulls. There are five or six more, not to mention the terns. And look at these: the laughing gull and the Franklin's gull? Can you tell them apart? What if one of them gets a spot of tar on the red beak? You'd probably think he was a Bonaparte's gull, the one with the all-black beak."

"Does it really matter?" Michael asked, giving me an odd look.

"That's my point," I said. "I just don't get it. They're gulls; they eat garbage and scream at the ferry. Does it really matter that much which particular kind of gull they are? I can't figure out why the birders get so obsessive."

"See, I knew we had a lot in common," Michael said. "I promise I will never take up bird-watching."

"Here, take a look at this," I said, flipping to another page and pointing to a bird. Michael glanced at it.

"That's *not* a seagull," he said.

"No," I said. "It's our friend the Bohemian waxwing. *Bombycilla garrulus.* You know, the one those bird-watchers got so upset at us for scaring away this morning."

"If you say so," Michael said, putting his arm around my shoulder. "It seems like days ago, not this morning, and anyway, my mind wasn't on the damned bird at that point."

"I was just thinking about how fanatical some of those birders are," I said. "Do you think one of them could have lost all sense of proportion and attacked Resnick because of what they all thought he'd done to the birds?"

"It's possible," Michael said. "I think the lobstermen have a more down-to-earth reason."

"Oh, did you understand all that about the bill?" I asked.

"Not one word in ten, but I got the idea that they thought he'd spent a lot of money supporting a cause that would put them all out of business."

"It's a motive all right," I said. "And anyone who cares about preserving the unspoiled charm of the island has a motive every time they look at that horrible house of his. Anyone he's taken potshots at could have a motive. Somehow, I can't see the Puffin Lady of Monhegan bashing anyone's head in, but I wouldn't put it past Mayor Mamie."

"Yes, she's very protective of poor little Rhapsody," Michael said.

"I'm sure she sells a lot of her books."

"Is there anyone on the island who doesn't have it in for the guy?"

"Probably not," I said. "Maybe we're looking at a real-life reenactment of *Murder on the Orient Express*."

"Well, let's forget about it for now," Michael said. He used his bare toe to nudge aside some of the plates on the coffee table and then propped both feet up on it. "We can't do anything now, and we'll have to get up early to search. Let's unwind and get some rest."

It sounded like a good idea to me. I took a sip of my hot tea, leaned back into Michael's arm, and sighed. As long as I kept my eyes closed, I could pretend that everything was just the way I'd imagined it when I planned our getaway. Michael and I sitting warm and cozy on a soft couch in front of the fireplace, listening to the crackling of the fire and the pounding of the surf outside the cottage.

And my brother sneezing, and Mrs. Fenniman rattling plates in the kitchen, and, of course, the wind periodically slamming large objects into the side of the house. So much for cozy.

"You haven't had any coleslaw yet."

I opened one eye and saw a large, virtually untouched bowl of coleslaw floating just under my nose. I had given up telling Mrs. Fenniman that I hated coleslaw.

"No thanks," I said, closing my eye again.

"It was great, really," Michael said. "But I'm stuffed."

Mrs. Fenniman sighed and moved on to thrust the bowl under Rob's nose. I heard a sudden crash.

"What was that?" came a voice from above.

We all looked up to where Mother was standing on the balcony above us.

"I just knocked over another one of Phoebe's damned flowerpots," Mrs. Fenniman grumbled, picking her way through the shards of pottery toward the kitchen.

Mother disappeared back into her room.

I felt something cold and wet on my ankle. Spike, having investigated the remains of the flowerpot and found them inedible, had returned to my feet and now resumed licking me obsessively. I discouraged his attempts to climb into my lap. For one thing, he'd probably bite Michael, and for another, if he'd eaten even half of the food I'd stuck under the coffee table, he'd probably start throwing up later in the evening. Better on my ankle than in my lap.

I looked around. The living room looked more like a consignment shop for used lawn and garden equipment than the cozy retreat of my vision. If I peeked over the forest of flowerpots and garden gnomes infesting the coffee table, I could see Rob reclining on the other sofa, reading a law book and adding to his thick sheaf of notes. Part of me wanted to shriek at him for being so lost in his role-playing game when we had no idea if Dad was even alive—and another part of me envied him.

His side of the coffee table was covered with plates and bowls containing samples of all the various foods Mrs. Fenniman had dished out. Mrs. Fenniman seemed to work on the theory that the hurricane wasn't going away until we'd emptied out the larder, but even Rob was long past the point where he could help her out.

She reappeared with a broom and dustpan and a plastic ice-cream tub. She plopped the orphaned plant and some of its dirt into the tub and began sweeping up the rest of the dirt and the bits of broken pot. I jumped to move a birdbath out of the way before she knocked it over with the broom handle. Mrs. Fenniman continued flailing away with the broom, and I stood by, ready to rescue anything else that got in her way.

But she lost energy; with a final flourish, she swept a few more specks of dirt into the dustpan, then marched off into the kitchen, leaving a trail of potting soil behind her. I sighed and slumped down, shoving my hands into my pockets.

And my fingers encountered a piece of damp paper: the map.

I pulled it out and studied it. Traveling in my pocket had made it even more damp and wrinkled than when I'd found it, but you could still recognize Dad's distinctive printing.

"Meg? Is something wrong?"

Michael looked up at me with an anxious expression on his face.

"I need to talk to you for a moment," I said.

We both glanced upstairs, saw Mother limping dramatically past the railing, looked at each other, and shook our heads in unison. We could hear Mrs. Fenniman singing sea chanties out in the kitchen, so that was out.

"The garden shed?" Michael suggested.

"We're going to check how the shutters are holding up," I told Rob. He barely looked up as Michael and I donned our slickers. On the way out, I grabbed my flashlight and, remembering the envelope I'd picked up outside Resnick's shed, my knapsack. We trooped out the door and over to the garden shed and managed to clear enough space to squeeze inside and close the door.

"Alone at last!" Michael said, putting his arms around me.

Chapter 15

The Agony and the Puffin

Okay, we allowed ourselves a brief distraction from the original purpose of our visit to the garden shed. But—call me unromantic if you like—there are limits to how successfully I can be overcome with passion when I'm sopping wet and shivering in an unheated shed that I'm half-convinced won't survive the next strong wind.

"I hate to spoil the moment," I said, "but could you move a little to the left? There's a croquet mallet digging into my kidney."

"If I move to the left, I'll probably drown; the leaks are much worse over there."

"Sorry," I said.

"So much for my hopes that we'd found a hideaway suitable for romantic trysts," Michael said, shoving aside several life jackets and a lobster pot to clear a space for us to sit on a stack of old magazines in the driest part of the shed. "You wanted to talk about something? Or was that just an excuse to get me alone?"

"No, there was something. Here," I said, handing him the map as I perched beside him. He turned on his flashlight and peered down at the paper.

"Your dad's map of the island," he said. "Does this mean you've got some idea where he is?"

"Unfortunately, no."

"Then what's the big deal?"

I took a deep breath.

"I found it down on the shore. Near where we found Resnick's body."

"Damn," Michael said. He closed his eyes and leaned against the side of the shed. "The police will find this very suspicious."

"The police!" I said, startled. "We can't give this to the police!"

"Meg, we can't not give it to them," Michael said, sitting up again. "That would be concealing evidence."

"Evidence that would make my dad the primary suspect in Resnick's murder. You saw how Jeb and Mamie reacted when they heard Dad had disappeared. For some stupid reason, everyone thinks Dad has some kind of grudge against Resnick because he used to date Mother fifty years ago, before she even met Dad. You heard them. The map will clinch it."

"That doesn't give us the right to conceal evidence. You do realize that, don't you?"

I sat staring at him. I felt betrayed. I'd trusted Michael with something that could hurt Dad, and here he was threatening to squeal to the authorities.

"Meg," Michael said, gently taking my hand. "I don't believe he did it any more than you do. But you have to see that we can't help him by concealing evidence. I mean, for all we know, that map could be what the police need to find and convict the real killer."

I sighed. I didn't like it. I didn't know the local police, wasn't sure I trusted them to find the real killer. But much as I hated the idea, I had to admit he was right.

"Okay," I said. "We'll turn in the map. But to the police, when they get here. Not to Constable Jeb or Mayor Mamie or anyone else on the island when Resnick was killed."

"That's sensible enough," he said.

"Which gives us a day or two to find the real killer," I said.

"You know, you're more like your dad than you want to admit," he said, grinning. "Never pass up a chance to play detective, right?"

"Michael, this is serious," I said. "We've all heard about cases where the police find a likely suspect and don't look any further. We can't let that happen to Dad."

"Of course not," he said. "Though I'm curious how we're going to find the killer in the middle of a hurricane. Not to mention—well, never mind."

I suspected I knew what he hadn't said: that right now, finding Dad—alive—was more important than proving his innocence.

"I'll keep this safe for now," Michael said, folding the map and taking out his wallet.

"Don't trust me not to destroy it?" I said.

"I wasn't thinking that at all," he said. "But you can't keep carrying it around in your pocket; it'll turn to mush. And we can't just leave it lying around where someone could get hold of it prematurely, and, unlike your purse, my wallet almost never leaves my body."

"Well, that makes sense," I said, slightly mollified by his tone.

"Shall we go back in?" Michael asked. "Much as I'd enjoy being alone with you under other circumstances, this shed's getting colder by the minute. And damper," he added as a large drop of water splattered his nose.

"Hang on a second," I said, opening up my knapsack. "As long as I'm confessing to my crimes against humanity, I may as well make a clean breast of it. I found an envelope in Resnick's yard after we put his body in the shed—tripped over it, actually. It didn't seem wet enough to have been there long, and I wondered if it fell out of his jacket while we were moving him."

"Let's have a look at it, then," Michael said.

I pulled out the envelope and we both pointed our flashlights at it. It was an ordinary nine-by-twelve brown clasp envelope, with no markings on the outside. Inside we found an inch-thick sheaf of papers held together with a giant binder clip as well as a smaller Tyvek envelope.

The top sheet of the papers held a title, centered, in all caps:

VICTOR S. RESNICK: UNHERALDED GENIUS OF THE DOWN EAST COAST. A BIOGRAPHY. By James Jackson.

"Wonder who James Jackson is," Michael said, flipping to the next page.

"I don't know, but the Tyvek envelope is addressed to him," I said. "In care of General Delivery at the Rockport Post Office."

"My God, listen to this," Michael said. " 'In this tome will be related the story of a great man whose genius has gone largely unappreciated in our century, a century in which the degradation of artistic taste has led to the exaltation of lesser artistic talents and those whose talents lie less in art than in publicity and the pursuit of notoriety, while alone, at the head of a small contingent of artists who still adhere to the tradition of representational art and the tenets of artistic quality that have prevailed, until now, since the Renaissance, Victor Resnick holds back the bulwark against the barbarians of popular culture and the deliberate obfuscations of an outworn academic community; unsung, unheralded, unappreciated, in recent years largely neglected, Victor Resnick nevertheless—' Arg!"

"Was that really all one sentence?" I asked.

"No, only about a third of one," Michael said. "I'm not sure which is worse, James's writing or his blatant toadying."

"I'll give you odds this is the authorized biography," I said.

"Definitely authorized," Michael said. "Our friend Victor has begun making some rather pungent comments on the first couple of pages. 'Small contingent of artists' used to be 'small contingent of artists, such as Andrew Wyeth and Edward Hopper.' Jamie boy might have crossed out the names himself, but only Resnick would scrawl 'Stupid! Don't mention those clowns!' Speaking of odds, I'll give you odds no one ever publishes it unless Jamie boy does a lot of rewrites."

"Looks like he already has," I said. "We've got draft seven, according to the footer. Oh my God!"

"What's wrong?"

"Jackson's got a time/date stamp in the footer—he printed this yesterday at six P.M. The ferry had stopped running by that time. He's on the island!"

"Lucky him, then; not every biographer gets a ringside seat at his subject's murder."

"We've got to find him."

"Why?" Michael asked. "To give him our editorial comments?"

"He's Resnick's biographer; he must know everything about his life," I said. "He'll know better than anyone who might have it in for Resnick."

"We've already decided that's a long list."

"Well, Jamie boy can tell us who's at the head of it. For that matter, we can probably get some ideas from the biography."

"Of course to do that, we'll have to read it," Michael said.

We both stared down at the manuscript in Michael's lap. I flipped over a page. Someone—Resnick, I suspected—had crossed out a paragraph with such violence that his red pen had torn the paper, and he had scrawled, "No, no, *no*!!!" in the margin.

"My sentiments precisely," Michael said.

"You know, we shouldn't lose sight of the fact that James Jackson is a suspect, too," I said.

"He's lucky he wasn't the victim," Michael grumbled. "Writing this badly ought to be a capital offense."

"Maybe Resnick finally realized that the guy can't write and so decided to fire him, or unauthorize him, or whatever you'd call it when you stop cooperating with a biographer. And Jackson saw his years of hard work go down the drain, and he lashed out and killed Resnick."

"We'll keep it in mind," Michael said. "Meanwhile, I guess we should start reading. I'm sure it's no worse than some of my students' papers."

I read over Michael's shoulder for the first twenty or thirty pages. Okay, I confess, I skimmed a lot. When you chucked out the excess verbiage—was the man paid by the word, or only by the adverb?—and untangled the convoluted sentences, Resnick's story was really pretty simple. He'd grown up in a small midwestern town, a sensitive, misunderstood child, the butt of every bully and jester in town, until the day he first picked up a pencil and began to draw. At which point, to judge from James Jackson's account, the earth trembled, comets were seen in the skies, three-headed calves were born, and wise men came from the east bearing gifts in the form of a scholarship to study art at the Boston Conservatory. By the time we reached the detailed description of the physical ailments that had kept him, despite his intense patriotism, from serving in World War II, my head was spinning.

"I need a break," I said. "I think I'll see what's in Jamie boy's mail."

"It's a federal offense to open mail!" Michael protested.

"Well, I know that," I said, in exasperation. "It's already opened, and I've never heard it was a federal offense to read stuff that people leave lying around in their yards. So there."

"Sorry," he said. "Must be the demoralizing effect of Jamie boy's prose. Carry on."

I opened the envelope, to find another sheaf of papers—slimmer, fortunately, and not written by James Jackson. The first sheet was a cover letter to Jackson from a Boston private investigation firm, dated a few weeks earlier, stating that the information he had requested was enclosed and that if he required any other assistance, he should contact them.

I turned to the next sheet. A list of names, all with birth dates and some with dates of death. Some of them were people I knew—Mary Ann ("Mamie") Dawes (Benton). Elspeth ("Binkie") Grayson (Burnham). Lucinda Hart Dickerman. Others sounded vaguely familiar. Old island names, many of them. All women, born between 1925 and 1940. Some were crossed out in bright red ink. Others had question marks or checks beside their names. No clue what the list was for.

I finished scanning the first page and flipped to the second, shorter page. Along with the crossed-out, checked, and question-marked names, one was circled heavily in bright red pen: Margaret Hollingworth (Langslow).

What the devil was this list, and why was Mother on it, so prominently singled out?

I went on to the rest of the papers. A series of reports from the detective agency on the whereabouts of the women on the list during their teenage years.

How odd.

I scanned the reports, fascinated. Binkie had gone from a posh boarding school to an equally posh women's college, and from there to Harvard Law School. Not what James Jackson wanted, apparently; he'd crossed her name out on the main list. Several other names had similar histories—summer people, I noticed; their lives contrasted starkly with those of the year-round island residents, many of whom were married and had had several children by the time their wealthier counterparts graduated from whichever of the Seven Sisters they'd chosen.

I came across Mother's sheet, finally, and double-checked it. The private investigator had his facts correct, as far as I knew. Right address, and the dates she'd stayed on Monhegan seemed consistent with what Mother always related of her vacations on the island. High school and college data correct. And in the center of the report, the beginning and end dates of the two years she'd spent in Paris, living with Aunt Amelia, attending a French lycée, taking art and music lessons, and achieving a level of poise and sophistication I knew even as a toddler I'd never match.

I had sometimes wondered how different Mother's life (and mine) would be if when she was fifteen Grandfather hadn't finally given in to her pleas to see Paris. If instead he had, for instance, sent her to stay for a few months on Cousin Bathsheba's farm, learning to milk the cows and feed the chickens. That first trip to France was undoubtedly the watershed event in Mother's life.

So why had the private detective circled it in red? And printed five little exclamation points after it?

And why had the biographer clipped a Polaroid of Mother to the back of the page—the present-day Mother, stepping off the Monhegan ferry, wearing a scarf I'd given her three months ago?

I had a bad feeling about this.

"Michael," I said.

"Mmm?" he replied absently. I glanced up. He was lost in the manuscript.

"The biographer's style must be improving," I said.

"What's that?" he said, looking up with obvious reluctance.

"What's so fascinating? I thought it was a lousy book."

"Oh, it is! The writing anyway; but the contents—You've got to hear this. Wait a second; let me get back to the beginning of this chapter."

He flipped back several pages and began reading.

" 'It was at this formative stage of his life that young Victor Resnick underwent an experience, the impact of which would last for the rest of his life, an experience that, while producing no outward change in his demeanor or his countenance, would nevertheless affect the sensitive young artist in the most profound and permanent fashion imaginable. Who could have predicted this event, at once so joyous and so tragic? Who can calculate the import this occurrence would present upon his life and art? Who can possibly discern . . .' Well, you get the idea. It goes on like that for about another page and then Jamie boy finally gets around to dropping a few actual facts. Apparently, young Victor fell in love."

"Don't tell me; I know what's coming. She told him to get lost."

"No, apparently the attraction was mutual."

"That's a little hard to buy."

"According to this, young Victor was quite a hunk and a rising star of the art world to boot."

"According to the biographer, who we already decided was telling Resnick's decidedly one-sided version of events."

"Well, I suppose," Michael said, running his finger down the page. "Here we go: 'She saw beneath his gruff exterior the sensitive artist whose soul had been blighted by calumny and neglect; she alone appreciated not only the force of his artistic genius but also the inner light that he had previously shown only through his brushes, and, bravely scorning the rigid strictures of her upbringing, daringly risking the calumnies and slings and arrows of outraged society that would be flung at her if discovered, she at last surrendered to their mutual passion.' "

"Ick," I said. "So she slept with him. I suppose there's someone for everyone, even Victor Resnick."

"And no matter what the boomers may think, sex wasn't invented with the pill. Anyway, we now have several pages about the progress of the affair, a little light on concrete details, but heavy with descriptions of things heaving and throbbing—the sort of stuff that might be mildly titillating if better written."

"Let me see that," I said, looking over his shoulder.

"Be my guest," Michael said. "And if you should find any of it inspirational . . ."

"You can forget the rerun of the *From Here to Eternity* surf scene," I said as I scanned the text. "It's vastly overrated, even on a tropical beach."

"You know this from experience?"

"I know this from common sense," I said. "And do you have any idea how rocky the Monhegan beach is, not to mention the subarctic temperature of the water?"

"So we won't be doing Burt and Debbie this trip?"

"More to the point, I doubt Victor Resnick and his lady love ever did."

"We take this passage with a grain of salt, then. Want to bet the writer learned his—or, more likely, her—trade writing romances?"

"No—most romances are far better written. And most romance writers have a better grasp of reality; that, for example, is anatomically impossible," I said, pointing to one particularly florid paragraph.

"Are you sure?" Michael said, quirking one eyebrow.

"Positive, as I'll happily demonstrate later. He's obviously unreliable about the details—probably embroidered them over the years. This only tells us that some poor woman had the bad taste to sleep with Resnick, and he remembers her fondly, perhaps because that kind of thing was a rare event in his life. And then she came to her senses and broke his heart, or, more likely, dented his ego."

"It's a bit more than that," Michael said. "According to this, she was underage."

"Well, I'm not surprised," I said, fishing out my Gatorade and opening the bottle. "No woman old enough to have any sense could possibly fall for him. How underage?"

"Fifteen. Just barely."

"He's scum."

"Resnick was twenty-five," Michael added.

"Pond scum."

"And her parents forced them to part, then packed her off to Paris to get over her broken heart. And then—Meg, are you all right?"

"I'm fine; you can stop pounding my back," I said, wheezing, once I'd finally cleared enough Gatorade from my windpipe to speak.

"You're not fine; I can tell," Michael said. "What's wrong?"

I handed him the detective's reports and sat back to cough a little more while he scanned them.

"Oh, damn," he said when he got to Mother's sheaf.

"He thinks Mother was Victor Resnick's secret love."

"Obviously," Michael murmured. He picked up the biography again and flipped over a few pages, frowning.

"It's ridiculous," I fumed.

Michael didn't say anything, and his eyes remained ostentatiously glued to the manuscript.

"Okay, it's not ridiculous; it sounds plausible enough. I certainly don't believe it, but people would if they heard it. And as long as Victor Resnick was alive, or even if he died of natural causes, the odds are no one would ever publish this travesty. But with his murder, they're going to want to drag all the skeletons out of his closet."

"Including a few that just might belong to your family."

We sat there for a few minutes, with me staring at the wall, trying to absorb what I'd read, while Michael continued to read the manuscript.

"Oh, bloody hell," he said suddenly.

"What's wrong?"

"Here," he said, handing me the manuscript and indicating a paragraph with his finger. "Read this."

I tried, but between the biographer's tangled grammar and his overly florid style, I couldn't make heads or tails out of the passage. Something flowery about a token of love, lost many years ago, that Resnick had sought ever since.

"I don't get it," I said. "What's this token thing anyway? Some kind of locket or something?"

"Sorry," Michael said. "It's a little hard to follow out of context. Back up and start reading a couple of pages sooner."

"I'd rather not," I said. "Since you've already suffered through it, why don't you give me the gist?"

"Okay," Michael said. "The biographer thinks Resnick fathered a child with his underage girlfriend. And she went to Paris to conceal her pregnancy."

"Impossible," I said.

"Impossible how?" Michael asked.

I knew what he meant. Impossible for Resnick to have fathered a child with his girlfriend? No. These things happened, even circa 1950. But impossible for the girlfriend to be Mother? Yes, if you asked me. I remembered all the tales Mother told of her years in Paris—the art and music lessons, the exhibitions, the galleries, the fashion shows, the opera, the ballet, the midnight meals in bistros, the flirtations in cafés. How could even Mother talk so blithely of that time if she'd spent the first nine months of it waiting out an unwanted pregnancy?

"I still don't believe it," I said. "But if he publishes that damned book, someone will believe it. Think of the embarrassment."

"Oh, I don't know," Michael said, the corners of his mouth twitching. "I'm not sure your Mother wouldn't like a wild un-substantiated rumor that in her youth she was the mistress of a famous artist."

"She'd eat it up," I agreed. "But Dad would be mortified. And the cops would have yet another reason for suspecting him of Resnick's murder."

"True," Michael said. "Look, it's freezing out here; can't we finish reading this inside?"

"What if someone sees it!" I protested.

"I'll pretend it's a master's thesis from one of my students," Michael said. "I won't let anybody else read it, and I'll hide it in my suitcase, under the dirty socks, where no one would want to touch it even if they found it."

"Oh, all right," I said, smiling in spite of myself. "I have to admit, I'm not sure I can take much more of this cold."

And is Dad out in this cold? I wondered as we walked back to the house. Or has he hung on to his knapsack, with the chem-ical hand warmer and the body heat–conserving blanket? Is he curled up warm and dry somewhere? Is he . . .

No, I'd worry about that tomorrow.

When we arrived back in the living room, Rob had disap-peared. Michael settled down with the manuscript. I picked up the photo albums and leafed through them until I found the pages that showed Mother and the young Victor Resnick, and brooded over the smiling black-and-white images.

Mrs. Fenniman appeared occasionally with plates of food, sighed when she saw our third helpings of everything were untouched, and clomped back out into the kitchen without speaking.

Suddenly, a shower of plaster rained down on our heads. I looked up, to see a large muddy Reebok protruding from the ceiling.

"Oh damn," came Rob's voice from beyond the Reebok.

"Rob? Are you all right?"

The Reebok wiggled slightly, dislodging more plaster. I adjusted my plate to make sure my unwanted coleslaw got its fair share of debris.

"Yeah, I guess so."

"Do you need any help?" Michael called.

"No, I'm fine," Rob answered.

The Reebok gyrated wildly for a few seconds, then dropped down another six inches and was joined by its mate.

"Actually, I guess I could use a little help after all," Rob said.

Michael and I abandoned our plates, grabbed our flashlights, and climbed upstairs, where, at the end of the hallway, the trapdoor in the ceiling gaped open and a small rickety ladder led up into the attic.

The attic didn't have a floor, just a rolling meadow of fluffy pink insulation crisscrossed by the two-by-fours that formed the rafters. Here and there, large flat pieces of plywood placed across the rafters formed storage spaces for boxes and trunks. None of them anywhere near the ladder, unfortunately. Evidently, Rob had stepped on a piece of plywood too light to hold his weight. Both feet disappeared into a rough-edged hole in the plywood, while he lay sprawled backward on the pink insulation.

"I see you found the jigsaw puzzles," I remarked. Several cardboard puzzle boxes lay nearby, and Rob lay half-covered by the brightly colored pieces of several enormous puzzles.

"I was looking for something to do," Rob said. "I saw the puzzles up here when I fetched the photo albums."

"You're lucky you didn't fall through," Michael said. "You're in the part of the attic over the living room. It'd be a long way down."

Rob shuddered.

"What's going on up there?" came Mrs. Fenniman's voice.

We extricated Rob from the plywood, helped him back to the trapdoor and watched as he limped away to be patched up and cosseted by Mrs. Fenniman. Michael was about to follow him, but he turned to see why I wasn't coming.

"I'll be down in a little bit," I said.

"You've found something?" Michael asked eagerly.

"No, but it occurs to me that there's an awful lot of old junk in the attic besides the photo albums," I said. "I'm just going to poke around for a while and see what turns up."

"I'll go down and guard the manuscript," Michael said.

Nothing much turned up in the first dozen boxes I opened. Actually, I'd have found some of the stuff fascinating at another time. Vintage clothes, trinkets, and souvenirs of bygone eras. More photos, this time in boxes. Even letters and diaries. A collection of taxidermy, including a stuffed squirrel wearing a jeweled collar and a wolverine in a Groucho Marx nose and a neon Hawaiian-print shirt. Fascinating stuff, really. But most of it more than fifty years old and none of it relevant.

At the bottom of the last box I found about a dozen faded brown manila file folders, tied in a packet with some string. I was struggling to untie the knot when I suddenly heard a commotion down in the main part of the house.

Now what? I thought, tucking the file folders under my arm and carefully walking along the rafters to the trapdoor. I heard Mother's voice wailing.

"I don't believe you; she's lost, too!"

I stuck my head down out of the trapdoor. Mother stood at

the edge of the upper hallway, one hand clutching the railing, the other pressed to her forehead, and her eyes raised heavenward. Vintage Sarah Bernhardt.

"How could you let her do it, Michael?" she asked mournfully. "How can you sit there when Meg is out there in the storm, frantically searching for her father?"

"Because I'm not out there in the storm, Mother," I said. "I'm up here in the attic."

Mother turned, looked at me, and blinked.

"Well, what are you doing in the attic?" she asked in an aggravated tone. "Why aren't you doing something useful? Looking for your father, for example?"

I could see her working up to another dramatic scene, and I was tired of the game. I'd been calm, patient, and reassuring the last million times she'd popped out of her room. So by way of a change, while she continued to wail about poor Dad out in the storm, I stuck the folders under my arm, climbed down the ladder, and went downstairs, where I stepped over a pile of croquet mallets, dodged around an upended picnic table, and jerked open the front door.

A gust of wind burst in, carrying with it a half-crushed lobster pot, sending Rob's papers flying like giant snowflakes, knocking flowerpots and other breakable objects onto the floor, and spraying showers of rain halfway across the room.

"Damn it, Meg, close that door!" Rob shouted, snatching at his notes. Mrs. Fenniman and Michael tried to grab as many breakable objects as they could and hold them down. Mother simply sighed and limped back into her room.

Having presumably made my point about the impossibility of searching for Dad in the middle of a hurricane, I stuck the folders under the umbrella stand, got a better grip on the door, and began forcing it closed. But suddenly, I suddenly noticed something outside.

There was a body on the porch.

Chapter 16

Travels with My Puffin

I let the door crash open again and staggered outside.

"What the hell are you doing out there?" Rob shouted.

"Michael, Rob, come here and help," I said, crouching over the still form on the porch. "It's Aunt Phoebe."

Aunt Phoebe moaned slightly at the sound of my voice.

"Meg?" she whispered.

"It's all right," I said. "You're home."

Rob, Michael, and I carried her in and laid her on the sofa. She was soaking wet, her clothes were ripped and filthy, and after the first dozen I gave up counting the cuts and bruises on her face and arms.

"I'll get her some clean, dry clothes," Mrs. Fenniman said, knocking over a stack of plastic lawn chairs on her way to the stairs.

"Phoebe!" Mother cried, looking down from the balcony. "What's wrong? Where have you been? Have you seen James?"

"James? Why, isn't he here?"

Mother limped down the stairway and over to the sofa. She sat there patting Aunt Phoebe's hand and giving the rest of us orders to go and do what we'd already started doing—fetching blankets, clothes, hot tea, the first-aid kit.

"You boys come out in the kitchen while she changes," Mrs. Fenniman said.

"A nip of brandy in this wouldn't hurt," Aunt Phoebe said, inhaling the steam from her tea.

"Good idea," Mrs. Fenniman said, crashing her way toward the kitchen.

"And some of that leek and potato soup, while you're there," Aunt Phoebe added.

"And some toast?" Mrs. Fenniman asked.

"Is there jam left?"

I relaxed a little. Aunt Phoebe's injuries couldn't be that bad if she showed such an interest in food. Rob, Michael, and Mrs. Fenniman clattered about in the kitchen and Mother supervised while I helped Aunt Phoebe change, cleaned her wounds, and wrapped an elastic bandage around her hugely swollen knee. I hoped she hadn't dislocated it or done something else serious, since we couldn't possibly get her to the hospital for a day or two.

"So where have you been all this time?" I asked when Michael and Rob had returned and Aunt Phoebe, under Mrs. Fenniman's approving eye, was making serious inroads into a six-course banquet.

"Damn fool thing to have happen," Aunt Phoebe said, plopping a generous dollop of homemade jam on her toast. "Slipped on the path up above the Dickermans' and fell into a gully. Took me forever to crawl out."

"Why didn't you call for help?"

"I did, but who can hear a thing in all this wind? Finally got myself back on the path, then had to half-crawl home. Lost my walking stick."

"Well, why didn't you stop and ask for help at the Dickermans'?" I asked. "Or those people next door, whoever they are?"

"Didn't want to impose on strangers," she said. "My own damn fault, falling in that gully; didn't want to cause them any bother."

"The Dickermans are hardly strangers," I said in exasperation. "You've only known them thirty or forty years."

"Now, Meg," Mother said.

"What were you doing gallivanting up that way anyway?" I

asked. "The last time we saw you, you were running up to Victor Resnick's to give him a piece of your mind."

Everyone else in the room froze and looked anxiously back and forth between me and Aunt Phoebe. She paused in the middle of helping herself to another pint of potato salad and cackled.

"I gave him a bit more than a piece of my mind," she said. "Scoundrel had the nerve to wave that blunderbuss of his in my face. Had to take it away from him."

"You did *what?*" Rob said.

"Oh lord," Michael muttered.

"Took away that fool gun of his," Aunt Phoebe said through a mouthful of potato salad. "Threw it off the cliff."

"I'm not sure she should say any more," Rob said.

"Cool it, Rob," I said. "Now's not the time to play lawyer."

"I'm not playing; she may need a lawyer."

"Why, has that fool complained about me?" Aunt Phoebe said. "That rap on the noggin I gave him when he tried to take the gun back is nothing. Look at this bruise where he grabbed my arm! And this cut here—I got this when he tripped me."

"Self-defense," Rob said. "She has a very good case for self-defense."

"Aunt Phoebe," I said, "exactly what happened when you went up to Resnick's house?"

"Why, what does he say happened?" she asked.

"Just tell us."

Aunt Phoebe thought for a moment.

"All right," she said. "I walked up and knocked on his door a couple of times, and nobody answered. I was about to leave when he came charging around the corner of the house, waving his gun. Wasn't aiming it at me, but the way he was waving it around, who knows what could have happened. So I grabbed it, and we played tug-of-war for a bit, until he lost his grip. He tried to twist my arm to make me give it back, so I whacked him sharply on the noggin, and he let go, and I ejected all the shells and threw the thing off the cliff. After that, he yelled for a while, and I yelled back, and then he stomped back into his house and tried to slam the door."

She shrugged and bit into a large ham and cheese sandwich.

"And that was the last you saw of him?" I asked.

She nodded as she chewed and swallowed, then chuckled.

"Fool hadn't put up a single board or a scrap of tape, as far as I could see when I was up there. Wonder if he's still up there trying to ride the storm out in that fishbowl."

"No," I said. "Actually, he's down in the meat locker of the Anchor Inn."

Aunt Phoebe stopped chewing.

"What's he doing there?" she asked through a mouthful of sandwich.

"Waiting to be autopsied," I said. "Michael and I found him floating facedown in a tidal pool earlier today."

Aunt Phoebe swallowed hard and then coughed a few times.

"Are you saying he's dead?" she asked when she could finally speak.

"That's generally a prerequisite for autopsying someone."

"Good Lord! You think that rap on the head killed him?"

"We won't know what killed him until the autopsy," I said.

"He was fine when I left him," Aunt Phoebe said. "Just as loud and obnoxious as ever."

"Maybe he had a delayed reaction," I said. "Or maybe you had nothing to do with it. Was he bleeding very badly when you left him?"

"Didn't see that he was bleeding at all," she said. "I didn't smash his skull in, just rapped him sharplike to let him know I wasn't going to stand for him trying to lay hands on me."

"Rapped him with what?" Michael said.

"My walking stick, of course."

"Well, they can examine the walking stick and compare that

to the wound," Michael said. "Maybe someone else hit him later. It's not as if the guy didn't have other enemies."

"If I still had the stick," Aunt Phoebe said. "I told you—I lost it."

"In the gully?" I asked. "We could go look for it in the gully."

"No, somewhere between Resnick's house and the gully," she said.

"That only covers half the island," I said. "I don't suppose you could widen the search area a little?"

"I wasn't thinking about my stick," she said. "I was hopping mad, and I took the long way around to blow off steam. I know I'd lost my stick by the time I got to the gully, because I remember thinking I wouldn't have fallen in if I'd had it. Careless damn fool thing to do."

Or incredibly clever, if the walking stick was the murder weapon. She had only to toss it off the cliff and no one would ever see it again. Except that I couldn't quite picture Aunt Phoebe as a murderer.

We were all silent for a few minutes.

"There's no way they could prove first-degree murder," Rob said, finally.

"Not now, Rob," I said.

"I mean, manslaughter's probably the most they could even hope to—"

"Shut up, Rob!"

"You didn't see James on your way home, did you?" Mother asked.

"Haven't seen him since he took off for Green Point to watch the hurricane hit the island," Aunt Phoebe said. "Have you looked there?"

"Yes, that's how we came to find Resnick's body," I said.

"I'm sure something has happened to him," Mother said.

"He'll be fine, Mother," I said. "He'll turn up in the morning, full of enthusiasm about what an exciting adventure he's had."

I tried to sound as if I really believed it. I wasn't sure I'd fooled anyone. Probably not, since Michael chose that moment to take my hand and give it a reassuring squeeze. Aunt Phoebe had fallen very silent, and, worse yet, she'd stopped eating. Definitely a bad sign.

"Well, I'd better get myself off to bed," Aunt Phoebe said, startling us by thumping the floor with her makeshift walking stick—a flagpole we'd dragged in from the porch—as she struggled to her feet. "I want to look my best when I turn myself in tomorrow."

"Oh, Phoebe, no!" Mother cried.

"No help for it," Aunt Phoebe said. "I can't keep quiet any longer and run the risk that someone innocent will suffer for my crime."

"Ought to give you a medal, considering who you bumped off," Mrs. Fenniman remarked.

"It doesn't matter," Aunt Phoebe said, striking a noble pose. "I must pay the consequences of my actions."

"Ingrid Bergman," I said.

Everyone looked at me as if I were crazy. Except for Michael.

"In *Joan of Arc?*" he asked.

I nodded.

"I can see that," he said. "Although actually I thought more of a Katharine Hepburn."

"In what movie?" I asked.

"I hadn't quite figured out yet. It'll come to me."

"*Sylvia Scarlett,* maybe," I said. "Or, better yet, *Mary of Scotland.*"

"Oh, that's the ticket. Definitely *Mary of Scotland.*"

"You're both crazy," Mrs. Fenniman announced. "Rob, come help your aunt and your mother with the stairs; they both need their rest."

Michael leapt up to help as well, and after they'd hauled Aunt Phoebe and Mother upstairs, everyone drifted off to bed. Just as well. I was exhausted, too. I retrieved the folders I'd left by the umbrella stand, but then I stuffed them in my suitcase to look at in the morning and took myself to bed. I wasn't sure I could manage dawn, but I knew I'd have to get up pretty early to resume the hunt for Dad. And I wanted to tag along when Aunt Phoebe turned herself in. I didn't for a minute believe she'd murdered Resnick. I couldn't exactly say why, but her story sounded phony to me. Maybe I'd figure out why in the morning, after a good night's sleep.

Of course, a good night's sleep was exactly what I didn't get. The first couple of times I woke up, the storm had definitely gotten worse, as if the cottage were in a wind tunnel, with a herd of elephants pounding on the walls and tap-dancing on the roof. And Michael either had the world's worst case of insomnia or thought he could avert some danger by patrolling the cottage half the night, checking doors and peering out of windows. After about 2:00 or 3:00 A.M., either the hurricane started moving again or I got used to the noise, and I finally got a few hours of sleep.

Mother woke me up at dawn.

"Time to get up and start looking for your father again," she said, leaning over me.

Spike, sleeping on my chest again, growled at her. For once, I agreed with him.

"I don't dare get up till he does," I said, and closed my eyes again.

A few minutes later, I heard the refrigerator door opening and closing several times, followed by pots and pans rattling, and then the crinkling noise of a cellophane wrapper.

Spike lifted his head.

Mother appeared in the doorway, massaging a half-empty potato chip bag.

Spike jumped off my chest and ran over to her, wagging his tail. He followed her back into the kitchen and then out again.

She no longer held the potato chip bag, and from the look on Spike's face, I doubted he'd gotten any of the contents.

"You could at least feed him, if you're going to torture him like that."

"I'll feed him after you're gone," she said.

"Don't leave without me," came Aunt Phoebe's voice from above. She stumped down the stairs with her flagpole. Michael and Rob, both half-dressed, trailed after her, trying to help and being firmly shooed away.

"I'm going down to see the constable now," she announced when she reached the ground floor.

"It's only six A.M.; does the store open this early?" I asked.

"It doesn't matter; Jeb Barnes lives behind it," she said. "I don't want to put it off any longer."

"And what about the hurricane?" I asked.

"Moving out to sea," Mrs. Fenniman said. "We're just seeing the tail end of it now."

She could be right, I thought; I hadn't actually heard the wind slam anything into the side of the house for the whole ten or fifteen minutes I'd been awake. Probably a good sign.

"I can't let a little rain stop me," Aunt Phoebe said.

"I think you should have a good last meal first," Mrs. Fenniman announced, knocking over a clump of pink plastic flamingos on her way to the kitchen.

"No, I can't think of food right now," Aunt Phoebe said. "I just want to look around one last time. Who knows when I'll see my own hearth again?"

I wasn't sure she could see the hearth now, considering the amount of junk in the room, but I suppose she was speaking metaphorically.

"Hang on a minute while I throw some clothes on," I growled. "I won't let you go into the lion's den alone."

I suppose that struck the right melodramatic note; at any rate, she waited, tapping her foot, until I had dressed, gulped down a few ounces of coffee, and grabbed my knapsack. Then she, Michael, and I set off for the village.

Of course, we had to clear quite a bit of debris off the deck before we could escape the house. Leaves, twigs, branches, limbs, and even whole trees were strewn about everywhere, and the number of smashed lobster pots littering the landscape made me worry about how the fishermen would manage next season.

"What a morning," I grumbled as we preceded Aunt Phoebe down the path, moving the worst of the debris out of the way as we went.

"Oh, come on; think what an interesting adventure we're having," Michael said.

"Are you usually this cheerful in the morning?" I asked.

"Why? Is cheerful in the morning a good or a bad thing, in your opinion?"

"Cheerful's fine, as long as it's quietly cheerful until I'm completely awake."

"I'm not awake at all myself," Michael said. "Never am before ten. I'm only this cheerful because I'm sleepwalking."

"That's much better. Sleepwalking I can understand."

"Come on, you two!" Aunt Phoebe called out. "Look sharp up there! Can't keep the law waiting!"

"In a hurry to hang herself, isn't she?" Michael said.

"Do you mean that literally?" I asked. "I mean, does Maine actually have capital punishment?"

"Guess we'll find out," Michael said.

The worst of the storm appeared past, but Hurricane Gladys couldn't have gotten all that far away. It was still raining and blowing heavily, and we had trouble keeping upright. Aunt Phoebe let us help her over the rough spots until we got to the door of the general store. She insisted on walking up the steps and into the store on her own, with the help of the flagpole. Michael opened the door and Aunt Phoebe limped dramatically into the store.

Jeb Barnes already stood behind his counter, despite the early hour, and the usual collection of locals had already gathered around the stove, listening to a battery radio. Or perhaps they'd never gone home last night. Mayor Mamie sat among them, sipping a cup of coffee.

"I've come to turn myself in," Aunt Phoebe announced in ringing tones. "I killed Victor Resnick."

Chapter 17

The Return of the Prodigal Puffin

When the commotion died down, Aunt Phoebe described her confrontation with Victor Resnick with a great deal of gusto. Perhaps she had been too tired to go into much detail the night before, or perhaps she found the gang at the general store a more congenial audience. At any rate, she produced a great many more details than she had the first time around. The bit at the end, where she left Resnick lying senseless in the middle of his yard with the hurricane howling around him, was particularly effective. By the time she got to that part of her story, everyone in the general store was speechless with amazement. I was surprised no one applauded. Back home, my family would have.

"Well, I guess that about wraps it up," Jeb Barnes said, when he finally found his voice.

"So you might as well arrest me now," Aunt Phoebe said.

The constable frowned. I suspected he was wondering what to do. I doubted the island had a jail.

"Why don't you have her go back to the cottage and consider herself under house arrest?" I said. "It's not as if she can go anywhere before the ferry starts running."

"Just what I was thinking," Jeb Barnes said. "Consider yourself under house arrest, Miss Hollingworth. Don't leave the island."

"You'll know where to find me, Constable," Aunt Phoebe said. She turned and limped across the room, head held high. Her grand exit was a little spoiled by the blast of wind and rain that burst into the room when she opened the door, nearly knocking her over, but she recovered rapidly and slammed the door behind her.

"What a grand old lady," Jeb Barnes said.

Murmurs of agreement came from the crew around the stove.

"Yes, she is," I said. "She's not your murderer, of course; but she did make a grand confession. I almost believed it myself. But ever since she told us last night, something about her story's been bothering me, and I finally figured out what's wrong with it."

"So what's wrong with it?" Jeb said, giving me a wary look.

"You heard what she said: They were struggling over the gun, and she rapped him on the noggin."

Jeb looked blank.

"Oh, I see," Michael said. "Allow us to demonstrate."

He plucked two umbrellas from a stack dripping by the front door and handed one to me with a flourish.

"My umbrella represents Resnick's gun, and Meg's is her aunt's stick," he said.

Jeb nodded.

Then we pretended to grapple over the gun umbrella. Michael allowed me to wrest it away from him and then, when he tried to grab it back, I rapped him lightly on the head with the top of the walking-stick umbrella.

The crowd around the store was entranced. To my satisfaction, scattered applause greeted the conclusion of our reenactment.

"Notice anything?" I asked.

"Looked pretty authentic to me," Mamie said, sipping her coffee. "Pretty much as she described it."

"Exactly," I said. "So if they were struggling like that, how did she hit him on the back of the head? That's where the wound was; in fact, it was pretty far down the back of the head. I can manage the forehead—like this."

I tapped Michael on the forehead. Just at the hairline, where I remembered seeing the bruise on Resnick's face.

"I can even manage the top of the head," I continued, demonstrating.

"But there's no way I can manage the back of the head unless he turns his back to me. Her confession doesn't hold water."

"Then why'd she do it?" Mamie asked. "Confess, I mean."

"She probably feels guilty over having hit him on the head," I said. "She's had all night to stew about it; by this time, she probably really believes she killed him. You know my family; by tomorrow, she'll be convinced that she left him lying in a pool of blood with her stick stuck through his heart like a stake."

The nods and chuckles from the locals around the stove showed I'd hit home. I didn't mention the other possibility: that Aunt Phoebe might be covering for someone. Mamie and Jeb looked at each other.

"Go look at Resnick's wounds if you like," I offered. "I'm sure you'll see what I mean."

"No, no," Mamie said. "I think you're right. We'll pass that along to the police."

"And another thing. Jeb, remember we told you Aunt Phoebe was going up to Resnick's. And you went dashing up in Fred Dickerman's truck, right?"

He nodded warily.

"So why didn't you see this supposed murder? You couldn't have gotten there before she did, or you'd have seen her come storming up a few minutes later. And if she really left him lying dead in the middle of the yard, you'd have found him there. But you found him alive, remember? And madder than a wet hen; I believe that was the expression you used. And according to Aunt Phoebe, she left him lying dead in his yard. So how did he end up floating in the tidal pool?"

"That's right," Jeb said. "Guess it's not her after all."

"No problem," one of the locals said. "Not as if they have to look far for a suspect."

Murmurs of agreement followed this statement, and I could

see my worst fears coming true. By the time the police arrived, the locals would have Dad tried and convicted in the court of public opinion.

Of course, at the moment, they were doing it in absentia, which reminded me of my real mission, now that we'd defused Aunt Phoebe's confession.

"By the way," I began, but before I could get much further, the door burst open, letting in another blast of wind and water. We all turned to see who was coming in.

"Dad!" I cried, and ran over to hug the wet, bedraggled figure staggering into the store. I felt as if someone had just lifted an enormous weight from my shoulders, and I heard Michael sigh with relief.

Dad was covered with mud and had bits of leaves and twigs stuck in his eyebrows and clinging all over his clothes. The bandage was half off his head, and the gash had opened up again.

"Meg!" he said. "And Michael! I thought I saw you two in here. What are you doing out in the storm?"

"Never mind that; where have you been?" I asked.

"I got lost and had to spend the night under a bush on the far side of the island," he announced, as if he'd managed to pull off something clever. "Did you miss me?"

"You have no idea," I muttered.

"Meg, you should have seen what it was like, watching the hurricane hit!" he cried, waving his arms as if trying to imitate a gale-force wind. "It was awe-inspiring! Invigorating! Absolutely breathtaking! I feel reborn!"

"That's nice," I said. "Now come down to earth for a while; a lot of things have happened while you were out being reborn."

"Was anyone hurt?" Dad asked, no doubt sensing my serious mood.

"Victor Resnick's dead," I said.

"Oh dear," Dad said. "I suppose I should take that as a lesson.

I've been so busy enjoying the hurricane, I haven't stopped to think that it can be deadly as well as beautiful."

"Well, actually—" Jeb began.

"And now I shall always regret having parted on unfriendly terms with him," Dad went on.

"Parted on unfriendly terms?" I said while the rest goggled.

"Yes, I ran into him on my way to Green Point," Dad said. "I couldn't understand why he kept trying to invite me in for a drink. I'm afraid I treated him rather rudely. Never liked him much, actually; and I was in no mood to waste time on him when I could be watching the hurricane. Ironic, isn't it?"

"What is?" I asked.

"Well, at one point when I was stumbling around, trying to find my way back, I began to regret how uncivil I'd been to him. I promised myself that when I got safely back to the village, I'd go and have that drink with him and apologize for the way I'd acted. And now I'll never have the chance, with him taken by the very storm that spared me."

"Actually, he wasn't," I said. "Taken by the storm, that is. He was murdered."

"Murdered!" Dad exclaimed. "How dreadful!"

He didn't sound as if he thought it dreadful. In fact, he sounded suspiciously enthusiastic. I hoped Jeb and the rest wouldn't take his tone the wrong way. I made a mental note to explain to the police about Dad's obsession with murder mysteries.

Then again, maybe I should wait until the police caught the real murderer. They might not realize I was talking about fictional murder mysteries. No sense letting them jump to any more false conclusions.

"How was he killed?" Dad asked.

Several of the locals around the store guffawed.

"He was hit over the head," Jeb said. "But we don't know whether the blow actually killed him or just knocked him unconscious into a tidal pool, causing him to drown."

"Well, we'd better examine him to see if we can find out," Dad said.

"Examine him?" Jeb exclaimed.

"Yes," Dad said. "Of course, you'll need the coroner for the actual autopsy, but——"

He suddenly yawned prodigiously and blinked slightly.

"Sorry, where was I?" he went on. "Oh, yes: Examining the body early on could be very important. Have you done anything to preserve it?"

"You don't expect us to let a suspect just mess around with the body," Jeb said.

"A suspect?" Dad repeated. His face lit up. I should have known. For a mystery buff like Dad, being a suspect in a real, live mystery was probably the next best thing to playing detective.

"Everyone on the island's a suspect," I said.

"Why so they are!" Dad exclaimed. "It's like a classic locked-room mystery! How exciting! Still, it could be important for someone with medical knowledge to observe the body early on. There might be another doctor or two among the bird-watchers. Perhaps we could get together a panel and do a noninvasive examination, under close supervision, before the body deteriorates. Take pictures. And——"

He yawned again, even more broadly.

"Dad, the body's in a refrigerator, and it isn't going anywhere. You need some rest—why don't you take a nap while Jeb considers your suggestion?"

"Yes, but——"

"And Mrs. Langslow's worried sick about you," Michael put in. "Have you seen her yet? Does she know you're all right?"

"Oh, goodness!" Dad exclaimed. "I never realized. I'll go right up there. Meg, do explain to them how important the examination could be. I'll——" He yawned again, and made no protest as Michael and I hustled him out the door. Michael stood, watching him trot up the street while I turned back to Jeb.

"You know, he does have a point. You could do worse than have some doctors examine the body."

"Like I said, we can't have a suspect messing with the body," Jeb replied.

"Why not?" I said. "We did last night, when you and Mamie and Fred fetched it down to the Anchor Inn. Are you trying to tell me that none of you had any possible reason for disliking Resnick?"

Jeb looked taken aback, and chuckles from the locals confirmed that I'd hit the mark.

"Yeah, Jeb," one of them said. "Bet you killed him just to get him off your back."

"Off your back?" I repeated.

"Bastard wanted to buy my store," Jeb said. "I told him to take a hike, of course. Been in the family since my grandfather's day; not likely I'd want to sell it. And even if I did, I wouldn't have sold it to him. Wouldn't take no for an answer, always hanging around here, waving his damned checkbook."

"You see," I said. "You need to protect yourself from suspicion, as well. Of course, it's your jurisdiction, but if I were you, I'd think very carefully about seeing if you can't find another doctor or two among the bird-watchers, as Dad suggested, and letting them all examine the body to verify its condition."

"I'll think about it," Jeb said. I wasn't sure if this really meant he'd think about it or if, like beleaguered parents, he used "I'll think about it" as a gentle way of saying "Hell no!"

"And you may want to stop making such a big deal about any person in particular being a suspect," I said. "Of course, I'm not a lawyer, like my brother, but I imagine people do get sued for that type of thing. Especially since you have so many possible suspects."

"You ask me, Fu Manchu there did it," one elderly local piped up from his place by the stove. "They were having a big set-to just before he died."

"Fu Manchu?" Jeb repeated.

"Ayah," the old man said, and buried his nose back in his coffee.

"Ayah," Michael murmured to me. "They really do say that, then?"

"Only to amuse the tourists," I whispered back. "Fu Manchu?"

Michael shrugged. Jeb didn't seem very impressed with the revelation that Sax Rohmer's sinister pulp villain was alive and well and plotting on Monhegan. Could dacoits and Thugs be far behind? And then I saw someone passing outside the store windows, and enlightenment struck.

"Well, if I were you, I'd think about finding those doctors," I said. "Meanwhile, we'd better run along," I added, tugging at Michael's sleeve. After one plaintive glance at his coffee mug, he sighed and followed me outside.

"What's up?" he asked.

"We're going to interrogate Fu Manchu," I said.

Chapter 18

East of Puffins

"Interrogate Fu Manchu?" Michael said. "You're not serious."

"I think the old guy meant the Asian man we saw quarreling with Resnick yesterday," I said.

"The one too well dressed for a birder?"

"Exactly. And if I'm not mistaken, that's him right now."

I pointed across the street to the front porch of the Island Inn, where the Asian man was stamping his feet and shaking himself. He had a brightly colored bag with the name of the other, upscale grocery on it. With a bottle of wine inside, from the shape of it.

"You could be right," Michael said.

"I'm positive," I said. "If we had to find a middle-aged Caucasian woman with binoculars, we wouldn't have a chance in the world of figuring out which birder it was. But Monhegan in flyover season isn't exactly a hotbed of ethnic diversity."

The Asian man had disappeared by the time we entered the hotel lobby, but the desk clerk looked up.

"Good grief, he's fast," I said. "Sorry, but you know the man who just came back into the lobby?"

"Mr. Takahashi?" the owner said.

"Yes," I said. "He forgot to mention which room he's in, and we need to give him back something."

I pointed vaguely back at my knapsack.

"He's in room twenty-three," the clerk said. "You want me to call him?"

"We can just take it up, if that's all right," I said. "Won't be a minute."

Mr. Takahashi looked surprised when he opened his room door and saw Michael and me.

"Yes?" he said. I had to look up to see his face. He was young—thirty-five at most—and taller than I expected—he nearly matched Michael's six four.

"Mr. Takahashi, I hate to bother you, but it's very important," I said. "Yesterday, you were overheard in . . . well, in a rather heated discussion with—"

"Oh, good God," Takahashi said. "Just tell the bastard to lay off, will you? I won't harass him, I'll do my damnedest not to even see him, but I can't very well leave the island until this damned hurricane blows over."

I was surprised to notice that he had a faint southern accent. And obviously he had mistaken us for someone official. I decided not to enlighten him.

"I assume you're talking about Victor Resnick?" I asked.

"Well, who else?" Takahashi said. "You don't mean someone else has filed a complaint about me? If they have, I guarantee you Resnick's behind it."

"Just what is the nature of the relationship between you and Mr. Resnick?" I said.

"Relationship? We don't have a relationship; I came to see him on business."

"What's the nature of your *business* relationship, then?" I persisted.

Takahashi looked at me with exasperation. He glanced behind me at Michael, who tried to look stern and official while dripping audibly on the floor. Michael seemed to rattle him a little. Men Takahashi's size don't often run into people taller than they are.

Takahashi sighed and turned to pick up something from the bedside table. A card case. He handed each of us a business card.

Very nice cards, engraved on heavy off-white textured paper so thick, it was almost cardboard.

"Kenneth N. Takahashi," I read. "Vice President, Coastal Resorts, Ltd."

Takahashi nodded as if that explained everything. About the only thing it explained for me was his accent, since the firm was headquartered in Atlanta.

"What is Coastal Resorts, Ltd.?" I asked.

"What is it?" Takahashi's drawl got a little thicker when he got excited. "It's only the country's second-largest developer of luxury resort properties. Don't tell me you haven't heard about the hotel project?"

"Hotel project?"

"I came all the way up here from Atlanta in good faith to negotiate with Mr. Resnick about the purchase of some land that my company had planned to develop as a luxury resort," Takahashi said.

"A luxury resort? Here on Monhegan?" Michael asked, glancing at the window, which Gladys was pelting with sheets of cold, icy rain.

"I'm told it's very pleasant in the summer," Takahashi said, following Michael's gaze.

"Not much room here on the island for another hotel," I said. Takahashi shrugged.

"I didn't put the deal together," he said, frowning. "I'm just here to try to keep it from falling apart."

I got the feeling he would have a few interesting things to say to someone back in Atlanta.

"No offense," I said, "but the whole thing sounds a little far-fetched to me. I mean, does this look like the kind of place that could support a big hotel?"

"We weren't planning a big hotel," Takahashi said. "A very small one, in fact; very luxurious, very secluded. The sort of place where high-profile people could come with absolute assurance of their privacy."

"You mean over-the-hill movie queens recuperating from plastic surgery, reclusive, paranoid billionaires, people like that?" Michael asked.

"Exactly," Takahashi said. "People who appreciate the kind of tight security you can maintain in a place this isolated."

We must have still looked dubious. He walked over to the small rustic table under the room's one window and unrolled a large sheet of paper.

"Look, here are some of the project plans."

We gathered around and looked down at a three-foot-by-five-foot map of Monhegan. Only this wasn't the Monhegan we knew. A giant, sprawling building occupied the top of the hill where the lighthouse now stood. Labels indicated where the restaurant and the indoor pool would be located. A nine-hole golf course had been carved out of the undeveloped ocean side of the island. The meadow where the Central Monhegan Power Company's modest generator now chugged housed a sprawling complex of equipment and support buildings. I wondered if the owner of the Island Inn knew that one of his guests was plotting to raze his hotel and replace it with a heliport? Or if Aunt Phoebe had any intention of having her cottage torn down to make room for a set of indoor tennis courts?

"A lot of people would be pretty ticked with Resnick if they knew about this," Michael said, looking at me with one eyebrow raised significantly.

He was right. And one of them might have gotten mad enough to murder him. I couldn't decide whether to rejoice that we'd already discovered another plausible motive for Resnick's murder or feel depressed at the incredible number of possible suspects Takahashi had just revealed. I ran my hand through my hair in frustration, managing to shower Takahashi's map with drops of water in the process.

"I'm sorry," I said. "I forgot I was still wet."

"I don't think I'll ever be dry again," Takahashi muttered. "Don't worry, you can wave the damned thing out the window, for all I care; it's useless now."

Michael nodded, but my radar went on the alert. Useless? How could Takahashi know his maps were useless unless he already knew about Victor Resnick's death?

"What do you mean, 'useless'?" I asked.

"The bastard backed out of the deal," Takahashi said, rolling up the map. "Going with the competition. So the whole thing's completely useless. Would you like a souvenir of what Coastal Resorts could have done to bring this place into the twenty-first century?"

"I wouldn't give up yet," I said. "If he hasn't actually signed the deal, who knows, maybe you can win over Resnick's heirs, whoever they are. Of course, the whole thing could get caught up in probate for years."

"Heirs?" Takahashi said. "What do you mean, 'heirs'? The bastard was perfectly healthy yesterday."

"Yes, but someone bashed his skull in late yesterday," I said.

"Oh, damn," Takahashi said. He sat down heavily on the bed and buried his face in his hands. "Damnation. That's all I need."

"You sound awfully upset for someone who claims he hardly knew Victor Resnick," I said.

"Why shouldn't I be upset?" Takahashi said, looking up. "My boss will probably make me stay here to negotiate with the heirs. Do you know who they are?"

I winced, thinking about the damned biography. It didn't sound as if Resnick had much family left, apart from the long-lost illegitimate child. What if his death led to a massive, well-publicized search for the missing offspring? I fervently hoped he'd made a will leaving his estate to some second cousin. Or maybe his favorite charity. The Society for the Relief of Indigent Curmudgeons, perhaps.

"I don't imagine we'll find out until they probate his will," I said. "Guess you'll have to stick around for a while to find out."

"Not when the storm lets up," Takahashi said, glancing at the window. "As soon as that damned ferry starts running, I'm out of here. They can send someone else to clean up the deal."

"I know how you feel," Michael said.

We left the disgruntled Takahashi sitting in his room, staring out the window and muttering curses in the drawl that grew deeper when he got more upset. And struggling to open a bottle of pricey Chardonnay with one of those makeshift bottle openers they sell for people to take on picnics.

"Now what?" Michael asked.

"Now, if you're up for it, we're going to burgle Resnick's house," I said.

By the time we left the inn, the birders had started to emerge from shelter, although the absence of any birds to watch reduced them to wandering around marveling at the storm damage. Michael and I pretended to do the same as we strolled nonchalantly out of the village and up the path to Resnick's house.

"Would you look at that?" I said, pausing on a hilltop to look down at the glass monstrosity. "It's a good thing Resnick isn't here."

"You mean, apart from the fact that he'd have a clear shot at you standing there?" Michael said, joining me on the crest.

"No, I mean imagine how he'd feel if he saw what's happened to his house."

A large branch had crashed through one of the ten-foot square glass walls flanking the front door. I counted at least two more cracked panes, and we hadn't even seen the more exposed ocean side yet.

"People who live in glass houses . . ." Michael began.

"Should have some way of protecting them in nor'easters," I replied. "I wonder if he was killed before he had a chance to board it up, or if he was really fool enough to think all that glass would survive a hurricane."

"We'll never know. But he strikes me as the kind of guy who'd call his insurance company five minutes after it happened, demanding that they send someone out immediately to fix it."

"Only there wouldn't have been any phone service."

"True," Michael said. "That would really have set him off."

"Come on," I said very loudly as I started down the path. "We need to take care of this."

"Take care of what?" Michael called after me.

"Resnick's house."

"I thought that's what we were here for," Michael said. "To burgle—"

"Shh!" I hissed. "Not so loud; there could be birders lurking in the bushes."

"Oh, I get it," he hissed back, and then said more loudly, "The storm's passing; it's not likely to break any more windows."

"Yes, but there's enough wind and rain to do considerable damage to everything inside," I said. "Someone should make sure anything valuable is safely stowed away."

"Someone also wants to snoop around and see if there's any useful evidence," Michael added more softly as he caught up with me.

"Well, that's the whole idea of burgling his house, isn't it? You didn't think I'd suddenly decided to turn daring international art thief, did you?" I asked as I picked my way carefully through the leaves and glass shards to the gaping hole by the door where the glass panel used to be. "It's not as if anyone else is doing anything useful."

"Everyone else is wisely waiting until the mainland authorities arrive," Michael said, following me.

"By which time, anything could happen." I said, stepping into the house. "The wind and rain could reduce any important documents to papier-mâché. Or break any valuable antiques. And he's sure to have paintings—"

Yes, he had paintings. I stopped just inside the hallway and stared openmouthed at the one I saw there. Michael bumped into me.

"Sorry," he said, grabbing me to keep from knocking me over. "If you're going to snoop, better not get cold feet just inside the door, where your accomplices might trample you on their way in."

"Oh my God," I said. "Michael, look!"

Michael followed my finger with his eyes. He looked puzzled for a moment, and then I had the satisfaction of seeing his jaw drop in amazement.

"Is that who I think it is?" he asked.

"It can't possibly be," I said.

Resnick was mostly famous for his landscapes, but, if the picture before us was anything to go by, not from any lack of talent at painting interiors or the human figure. You could almost have warmed yourself at the roaring fire in the painted fireplace, and the way the half-filled champagne flute reflected the firelight was extraordinary. You could all but feel every hair of the white bearskin rug on your own skin, and I suspect had I been a man, I'd have felt an erotic response instead of envy at the flawless skin and perfect figure of the nude blond woman sprawled on the rug. Under other circumstances, I'd have admired the painting enormously. As it was . . .

"That can't possibly be Mother," I said finally.

Chapter 19

Nude Puffin Descending a Staircase

"It certainly looks like your mother," Michael said, tipping his head to scrutinize the painting. "Or at least looks like what I gather she would have looked like at that age, from the photo albums we looked at last night. The face anyway; I wouldn't know about the rest of it."

"Well, yes, that's what she looked like at that age," I said. "As far as one can tell from pictures of her in swimsuits. But surely you don't think Mother would actually have posed for something like that?"

"It's definitely got her attitude."

He was right. The woman in the picture lay full length on the rug, facing the viewer, her head and shoulders propped up by a couple of pillows covered with Oriental fabric. One hand was behind her head and the other held the champagne. One leg was bent slightly at the knee and the other outstretched fully, with a high-heeled fur mule dangling from the toes. Her face showed no sign of awkwardness or embarrassment, only an expression of pride and absolute confidence. I couldn't imagine Mother posing nude for a painting, but if she had decided to, I'm sure she would have stared out at the artist with just that air of arrogant self-assurance.

"She'd never wear a tacky fur slipper like that," I said defensively. "And the bearskin's pretty clichéd, too."

"He could have done it from photos," Michael said.

"Of course he did it from photos," I snapped. "*Clothed* photos. But why? And when?"

"Let's make sure it's out of the rain," Michael said. "We can worry about the rest later."

We took the nude down and carried it with us into the living room.

Michael gasped. "What a view!"

I frowned at him. My mind was still on the picture we carried, and it took me a second to realize he was talking about the room we'd entered.

A giant wall of glass gave a sweeping view of the shore and the sea—a very gray and turbulent view, at the moment. The inside was a mess, too. The panes of glass forming the wall were slightly smaller than the ones beside the door—perhaps because this was the ocean side of the house. Even so, something had bashed one of them in, and mud and leaves littered the room. Several paintings on the wall were getting a bit damp. Only landscapes, I noted with a sigh of relief.

We hauled the paintings to the driest corner of the living room and continued our explorations.

"Impressive kitchen," Michael said. "You could run a small restaurant out of this place."

"Pretentious," I said. "I bet he hasn't cooked a dozen meals here since he moved in. Look how spotless everything is."

"Maybe he's just a good housekeeper."

"No," I said. "There's a difference between spotless from regular cleaning and spotless from disuse. This is disuse. Trust me—I know what disuse looks like from the occasional flying visit to my own kitchen."

"Well, pretentiousness has its advantages," Michael said. "Take a look at this wine cellar."

"Pretentious is right," I said. His wine cellar was probably larger than all my closets combined. "But what use is it? Unless you're suggesting that we take advantage of Resnick's wine collection, since he's not around to complain?"

"It's a tempting thought," Michael said, examining the labels of a few bottles with obvious interest. "Actually, I thought we could stash the paintings in here. No windows, and the walls are designed to protect the contents."

"Good idea," I said. We stowed the nude safely along one wall, then put the slightly damp landscapes from the living room along the other.

The dining room would have seated a dozen people easily, although all the chairs except the one closest to the kitchen had a thin film of dust on them. The guest room was expensively furnished but rather cheerless. And long unused. Despite the shortage of rooms on the island, obviously Resnick hadn't offered his spare bed to anyone, and I doubted anyone had even asked. I suspected the birders we'd heard singing in the church the night before were happier there than they would have been here anyway.

The master suite rivaled the kitchen for pretentiousness. But the lush white carpet was already dingy from lack of cleaning. And strewn with wet leaves, which had probably blown in from one of the broken windows.

"Fancies himself quite the ladies' man," I said, frowning at the ornately canopied king-size bed. "I'm surprised he resisted the ceiling mirror."

"He ran out of mirrors after he finished in here," Michael's voice echoed from the bathroom.

I poked my head in.

"Ick," I said, stepping inside to gape at the interior. "It's like a fun house. Imagine having to look at yourself in all these mirrors first thing in the morning."

"The view doesn't look that bad to me," Michael said, coming up behind me and putting his arms around my waist.

"Thanks for the vote of confidence," I said, leaning back against him. "But now try imagining you're Victor Resnick."

"No thanks," he said, sighing. "I know it's stupid, but poking around in here actually makes me feel sorry for him."

"Me, too," I said.

Actually, until Michael said that, I'd been thinking what a pity the one place we'd managed to find five minutes alone together all weekend was the house of a murder victim. If Victor Resnick had been merely missing, I'd have suggested to Michael that we make ourselves at home and, if anyone ever caught us later, pretend that we'd taken refuge here during a bad part of the storm. But since an army of forensic experts would soon begin swarming all over the house, I knew we shouldn't do anything we couldn't explain away as part of our quest to minimize damage and secure the contents of the house.

Although I couldn't help noticing the extralarge sunken tub. More like a small wading pool, really, all lined with gold-flecked turquoise-colored tiles. There was even a small adjoining fireplace, though that showed little sign of use.

Like something out of *Lifestyles of the Rich and Famous*. Which Resnick was, of course. No sensible person would use a tub like that for ordinary daily bathing, especially on an island with a chronic water shortage. But fill it up, add lots of bath oil, set several dozen candles around the periphery, light the fire, and send Michael to the wine cellar to pick out a bottle or two of Resnick's undoubtedly expensive wine . . . I shook myself. This was not the time for erotic fantasies.

"Depressing," I said, reluctantly pulling away from Michael.

"Gee, thanks," he said.

"I mean this place," I said. I stepped over to the wide vanity counter and, using the corner of my shirt to avoid smearing— or leaving—fingerprints, popped open the medicine cabinet.

"Why the medicine cabinet?" Michael said. "He wasn't poisoned."

"You can learn a lot about someone from his medicine cabinet," I said as I poked through the bottles, jars, and tubes in the cabinet.

"Remind me to clean my medicine cabinet before you get another chance to rummage through it," Michael said, peering over my shoulder. "Anything suspicious?"

"No," I replied. "Apart from having an ulcer or some other serious stomach problems for a couple of decades, he was pretty healthy for someone his age."

"A couple of decades? How can you tell?"

"Fifteen-year-old leftover Tagamet pills; Zantac prescriptions from four and seven years ago—obviously he was one of those suicidal idiots who never threw out old medicine."

"On second thought, remind me to put a padlock on my medicine cabinet," Michael said. "Is this significant?"

"Probably not," I said. "The rest of the drugs are normal over-the-counter stuff. He wasn't on medication for anything like epilepsy or heart problems, anything that would account for his falling down into the tidal pool from natural causes."

"Well, we knew that from the gash on the back of his head."

"True," I said. "Well, one good thing: If he was this much of a pack rat about medicine, maybe there's a desk somewhere crammed with interesting papers."

"I think it's out in the living room," Michael said. "I noticed it while we were hauling the wet paintings down."

"Well, why didn't you say something?" I said, going back out into the bedroom. "Let's go and—"

"What now?" Michael asked, seeing that I'd stopped in the middle of the room.

I indicated the bearskin rug in front of the fireplace.

"Yes, the man liked bearskin rugs," Michael said. "They have their charms."

"He must have liked this one anyway," I said. "It must be older than God. Look how ratty it is."

"He probably had it for years."

"But he didn't have it lying here very long."

"The house hasn't existed very long," Michael said.

"Yes, but look at those paler areas of the carpet," I said. "Here, you can see it better if we move the bearskin."

I peeled back the bearskin rug and pointed to a rectangular area of white carpet still more or less the original snow white.

"I see," Michael said. "From the shape of the clean spot, he had another rug, a rectangular one, lying here up until very recently. And then he replaced it with the bearskin rug."

"After the storm began, most probably," I said. "See, a couple of wet leaves stuck to the underside of the bearskin."

"Which brings up the question of whether he did it or someone else?"

"Why on earth would someone sneak in here and unroll a ratty old bearskin in front of Resnick's bedroom fireplace?"

"Bloodstains on the other rug?" Michael suggested. "Maybe he wasn't killed outside; perhaps he was killed here and then the murderer replaced the bloodstained rug with the bearskin."

"It's possible," I said. "But I think it's more likely that Resnick did it himself. Shortly before he died, which would account for the wet leaves under it."

"And why would he do that?" Michael asked.

"To make Dad jealous," I said. "We know the bearskin rug hasn't been here all that long. How long has that picture been in the entryway?"

"Possibly as long as the house has been here. How many people brave the shotgun blasts to visit him?"

"Yes, but he had to have workmen, delivery people. I'm sure if it had been there any time at all, someone in the village would have seen it, and they would have said something about it by now. Mrs. Fenniman practically broadcast the news that Resnick was Mother's beau before Dad came along, and I'm sure other people know about it."

"But would they recognize who it was?" Michael said. "No offense; your mother's in wonderful shape for a woman her age, but would anyone really recognize her in the picture?"

"A stranger wouldn't, but at least a dozen people on the island right now knew her then. Maybe more. And that's not counting anyone who's leafed through Aunt Phoebe's photo albums; she's always dragging them out at parties."

"Well, that's true," Michael admitted. "They'd know it was a Hollingworth, at any rate."

"I bet he put it there deliberately, to make sure someone saw it and spread the word," I said. "Heck, maybe he planned to invite Mother and Dad for dinner and hope the sparks flew."

"There's another possibility," Michael said. "Maybe he wanted to stir up another kind of spark."

"What do you mean?"

"What if he planned to invite just your mother over? Show her the picture, claim he'd kept that ratty old bearskin all these years as a souvenir, and try to rekindle their romance?"

"I'm sure Mother has more sense," I said.

"Yes, but did Resnick?"

I pondered it for a while and sighed.

"I wish we wouldn't keep finding evidence that points at members of my family."

"Cheer up," Michael said. "Let's go through Resnick's desk. We're probably already on the hook for trespassing and interfering with a murder investigation; let's not stop before we find something useful."

"We're just making sure nothing's getting damaged," I repeated.

"Or we could always pretend we were taking advantage of the empty house to get a little privacy in which to . . . misbehave."

"You think they'd believe that?"

"They will if we show them that sunken tub," Michael said, quirking one eyebrow. "If the town decides to raze the house, do you suppose they'd give us the tub?"

"I'm not sure it would survive the move," I said.

"True. In fact, it may not have survived the hurricane," he said. "Perhaps we should check it out."

"Maybe later," I said, "when we've finished burgling."

"And when you're feeling less frantic about clearing your father," Michael said with a sigh. "Just a thought."

"Well, hold the thought, but let's worry about the desk for now."

Chapter 20

The Puffin Who Liked to Quote Kipling

Michael led the way back to the living room and pointed out Resnick's desk.

"Good work," I said. "I'd overlooked it somehow."

"Overlooked it?" Michael said, staring at the huge antique roll-top desk. "How could you overlook that thing? It's over five feet tall."

"I'm afraid my idea of a desk is a mound of papers with legs sticking out from under it," I said. "I never imagined that anything that tidy could be a working desk."

"You're describing your own desk, aren't you?" Michael said.

"Fraid so."

"And yet I'll bet you're going to say that, despite its messy appearance, you can find any piece of paper you need in five minutes."

"Are you kidding? Five days, working full-time, and that's if I'm lucky. Now that's more like it," I said as we rolled up the top, revealing a desktop computer and a reasonably promising quantity of paper. "A little too tidy for my taste, but at least there are signs of life here."

"Luckily, the desk is awfully close to that cracked window," Michael said. "See, it's getting wet already."

"I don't suppose we could possibly lift the desk," I said.

"I don't even want to try," Michael said. "We'll have to move the contents to safety. The wine cellar, I should think."

Most of the contents weren't all that interesting. We studied his bills and bankbooks as we transported them, but we didn't find any dirt. Victor Resnick was a rich man who spent a great deal of money on his own pleasures, but then, he had a great deal of it to spend.

Or did he? He didn't have a very large balance in any of his accounts. Maybe he had a broker somewhere managing the bulk of his money. Then again, we found an awful lot of dunning letters from creditors. Was he simply, like so many wealthy people, careless about paying on time, or was he going broke?

We found an entire drawerful of papers related to the publication of the book of his paintings I'd bought—contracts, proofs of the photographs, and about fifteen drafts of the text, each annotated lavishly in a bold, angular handwriting. Along with corrections, we saw a great many scathing remarks about the intelligence and ancestry of the writer. If by chance we found the writer on Monhegan, I'd add him to the top of the list of suspects.

"The handwriting on these matches the edits on the biography," I pointed out. "Resnick was definitely cooperating with James Jackson."

"Did Jackson write this, too?" Michael asked as he perused one of the drafts.

"No, someone named Edwards. Who can actually write. I don't know where Jamie boy came from, but he can't write for beans."

"Resnick didn't realize that," Michael said, flipping through a fat sheaf of papers from another drawer. "And Jackson's definitely a pseudonym. Here's another copy of the biography—dated a couple of weeks ago, with the author listed as James Jones; and Resnick crossed the name out, with these orders: 'Sounds too phony—pick another alias!' "

"And the biographer thought James Jackson sounded more plausible?"

"I suppose; tell that to the publishers of *From Here to Eternity*.

Resnick edited this version with just as heavy a hand; the whole manuscript looks as if it has the measles. But he's not as hard on Mr. Jones/Jackson as on poor Edwards."

"Another draft or two and I bet he'd have started ripping Jamie boy's liver out, too," I said.

"He didn't like the galleries that handled his work, either," Michael remarked.

We found several files of letters to and from various galleries. Resnick evidently considered the owners of several of the most prestigious New York and Boston galleries either fools who had no idea how to sell his work or scoundrels trying to take him for a ride. More suspects, if they were on the island, which I doubted, but I grabbed a piece of paper and jotted down their names anyway.

"You suspect the gallery owners?" Michael asked.

"I suspect everybody," I said. "Besides, haven't you heard that the value of an artist's work triples when he dies?"

"I don't suppose we could buy a few before word gets out on the mainland," Michael suggested.

"Probably not," I said. "And anyway, I don't know about you, but it's not as if I have fifty or a hundred thousand dollars to do it with."

Michael whistled.

"They sell for that much?"

"Well, that's nothing compared with what you'd have to pay for a painting by someone really famous. A major Wyeth, for example. I think they go for a million or two."

"But still, it's a motive. I wonder how we could find out who owns his paintings."

"Ask and ye shall receive," I said. "See, he keeps a list of everything he sells. Most artists do."

"That's great! Although I suppose they won't all still belong to the original buyers anymore."

"On the contrary, artists usually keep pretty close track of where all their paintings are. See, here's a painting he sold to someone in 1962, and a note that it was resold in 1970, with the selling price and the new owner's name. And here's one that was sold about the same time, then donated to the Cleveland Art Museum in 1981."

"Want me to help you copy the names down?" Michael asked.

"No," I said. "He printed out three copies; we can take one and still leave two for the cops."

Michael studied the list, looking over my shoulder.

"Notice anything odd?" he asked after awhile.

"Only that he wasn't selling very many paintings these days," I said, frowning. "And other people haven't been selling them much, either. Look at all these entries for the fifties and sixties. And in the eighties and nineties—practically zip."

"Maybe he stopped keeping track of sales and resales?"

"No," I said. "See, here's a sale from two years ago. And a resale from three months ago. He's keeping track, but there's not much to keep track of."

"Makes you wonder how he could afford to live like this," Michael said, looking around. "Imagine how much this house must have cost."

"We don't have to imagine," I said. "We've got the files right here."

From the house construction files, we deduced that Resnick had gotten along about as well with his architect and his general contractor as he had with the rest of humanity. He had withheld some of the money he owed them until they fixed various minute flaws. Strangely enough, though, considering the local uproar about the house, we found almost no paperwork on approval for the construction—just a standard building permit for "renovations" signed by Mrs. M. A. Benton, Mayor.

"Renovations?" Michael exclaimed. "Who did he think he was kidding? He definitely got special treatment. Wonder if he had some kind of hold over the mayor?"

"Pay dirt!" I shouted, holding up a stack of files. "Here's the stuff on the resort project."

I'd found a file marked "Coastal Properties, Ltd." and another marked "New England Development Associates." Both full of correspondence that would no doubt fascinate a corporate lawyer but which only reminded me how little sleep I'd gotten the night before. A third file was more interesting; it contained a map of the island, with all the property boundaries marked and a number assigned to each plot. Parts of the map were colored in solid blue, parts in blue and white stripes, and a few in pink. Behind that was a list of numbers from the map, with people's names written beside them.

"What's this supposed to be?" Michael said, studying the map.

"If I'm reading this list correctly, the blue is property he owned. See, here's where we are now, in blue. The gift shop by the dock, that's in blue, too. And the blue and white stripes are places where he'd negotiated some kind of option to buy."

"And the pink?"

"I'm guessing there are places he'd tried and been turned down flat. Yes, there's Jeb Barnes's store in pink. Remember what Jeb said? That Resnick had tried to buy the general store and Jeb told him to take a hike?"

"Yes, but isn't that your aunt Phoebe's cottage there?"

"You're right," I said, frowning.

"I think she'd have mentioned it if he'd tried to buy the place."

"Maybe it just means places he expected to have problems buying," I suggested.

"That sounds logical," Michael said. "He colored your aunt Phoebe's lot a particularly intense pink, compared with some of the others."

We went on through the rest of the files, which were all marked with the names of local citizens. Some of them—Mamie Benton's, for example—contained bills of sale. Apparently, Mamie had once owned the building in which her gift shop was located, but now she rented it from Resnick. Other files—including Frank Dickerman's file—contained long documents in legalese. Options to buy, as far as I could tell.

But he had a file on everyone on the island, not just the property owners. And along with the contracts or details of any negotiations he'd been conducting, all the files contained notes—sometimes pages and pages of notes—about the owners, including any dirt Resnick had dug up about their personal and financial peccadilloes.

"Michael, the man was a monster," I said after browsing in a few files. "He was blackmailing people into selling him their property."

"Well, he's a dead monster now, and these files could very well contain the motive for his murder," Michael said. "We have to turn these over to the proper authorities."

"You mean to Mayor Benton, who, according to her file, had to sell her building to him to pay off her gambling debts and then rubber-stamped the building permit for this house to keep him quiet? Or Constable Barnes, who hadn't yet agreed to sell the store, but might have changed his mind if Resnick had threatened to tell his wife about that fling he had with Candi, the hairdresser over in Port Clyde?"

"I see your point," Michael said. "The mainland authorities. Well, this is interesting."

"Whose file are you reading?"

"The Dickermans'. One of those blue-striped pieces is their house, and it was about to go solid blue."

"Why?" I asked. "The power company isn't making a profit?"

"The power company's doing fine, but they're probably going to lose that, too. Mr. Dickerman senior borrowed money from Resnick to bail two of his sons out of jail on charges of grand theft auto. And assault. Our charming friend Fred and a brother named Will, whom we probably won't be meeting, because he skipped out on his bail, bringing the whole family economy crashing down in ruins. Resnick threatened to foreclose on the loan in a few weeks."

"Now, there's a motive."

"And the assault consisted of Will hitting someone on the head with a lug wrench."

"Ooh, I like it!" I said. "I mean, it's terrible, of course; but I'm sure the mainland police will find it fascinating, having someone with a motive and a history of bludgeoning his victims."

"And consider Will Dickerman a far more likely suspect than any of your relatives."

"Him or Fred, either one," I said. "I've never met Will, at least not since we were kids, but if you asked me who of all the people I've met on Monhegan in the past few days was the most likely to have bashed someone's skull in, Fred Dickerman would be my number-two choice."

"Only number two?" Michael said, raising one eyebrow. "Who's number one?"

"The victim himself."

"And, unfortunately, he's out of the running."

"True," I said. "Suicide by blunt instrument's pretty hard to accomplish. Oh, good grief!"

"What's wrong?"

"Is there anyone on this island who doesn't have a guilty secret in their past?"

"I see you're holding your aunt Phoebe's file; don't tell me he dug up any dirt on her!"

I scanned her file quickly.

"No, thank goodness. The only charges he's logged against her are a complete lack of tact and caring more about birds than humans."

"Guilty on both counts, if you ask me," Michael said with a chuckle.

"Agreed. But I've never heard either of those is even a misdemeanor. Besides——"

"What's that?" Michael said, pointing to the glass wall behind me. I saw only the rain-soaked shrubbery outside.

"What did it look like?" I asked, going over to the window.

"I thought I saw someone behind that bush."

Just then, I saw a flicker of motion at the edge of the yard and caught a glimpse of someone disappearing into the woods.

"Rhapsody," I said. "Wonder what she's doing here?"

"Maybe she's researching her latest book," Michael said.

"*To Kill a Puffin,*" I suggested. "*The Happy Puffin Family Solves a Grisly Murder.*"

"Or *Silence of the Puffins?*" Michael countered.

"I know!" I said. "*The Puffin of the Baskervilles!*"

"You're right; that's it," Michael said as we dissolved into laughter.

"Ah, well," I said. "Maybe we should wrap things up here before someone else comes along snooping. I think we've found as much as we're going to. At least until the power comes on and we can get into his computer."

"By the time that happens, we'll have police all over the place," Michael said.

I didn't answer. He was right, of course.

"Let's check the studio," I said.

We locked the last of the papers up in the wine cellar and went back out the smashed window in the front hall. Unfortunately, the studio had weathered the storm far better than the house. The only broken glass was in the roof, way beyond our reach.

"I think if we had a rope, we could let ourselves down through that hole from one of those trees," I said.

"Aren't we supposed to have ropes in our knapsacks?" Michael asked, shrugging his off his shoulder.

"Yes, but we used them hauling Resnick's body up, remember? And we never got them back."

"That's right," Michael said, hefting the knapsack back onto his shoulders. "Not that I especially want those particular ropes back. We'd need the rope to get up into the tree, too. Not to mention a really good story in case we get caught."

"We have to," I said as my stubborn streak kicked in. I glanced over at Michael. He was looking down at the ground, and from the expression on his face, I suddenly feared that we were on the brink of an argument. That he would refuse to do any more unauthorized snooping, and try to stop me from doing it, too. And I couldn't exactly blame him; it wasn't his family.

Then he looked up, caught my eye, and sighed.

"Okay, let's go back to the house and get some ropes, then," he said.

Chapter 21

A Cat Among the Puffins

When we came to the intersection where Resnick's private path joined the main gravel road, I insisted that we lurk in the bushes for a few moments to make sure no one was around.

"I told you we wouldn't run into anyone else," Michael said as we finally stepped out into the road.

"We have to be careful," I said. "After all—"

"Hello!" called several voices from behind us. We whirled, to see half a dozen birders striding energetically down the path.

"Did you hear about the murder?" one of them asked eagerly.

"Yes, we found—" Michael began.

"Yes, but what's the latest word?" I asked, interrupting him before he could reveal our close connection to the case.

The birders swept us into their midst and, as we panted to keep up with them, talked nonstop and simultaneously all the way down to the village. Other birders joined us in progress, and by the time we reached the main square of the village, we formed part of a milling, chattering crowd that must have included half the birders on the island.

When the police arrived, they'd have a lot of fun interrogating all the birders. Not surprisingly, since they'd wandered all over the island since their arrival, their ranks contained possible witnesses to nearly everything that had happened over the past several days.

The police would find witnesses to Resnick shooting at Michael and me, and several witnesses who would testify, truthfully or not, that he'd shot at them. Witnesses to the fight with Ken Takahashi, several of whom had taken photographs. Witnesses to Aunt Phoebe's struggle with Resnick. I was relieved to hear confirmation that he had still been standing—actually jumping up and down, yelling his head off, according to the witnesses—when Aunt Phoebe stormed off. Of course, that didn't prove that he hadn't collapsed later on as a result of the rap on the head, but it was encouraging. Eyewitnesses to Aunt Phoebe pulling up at least one of Resnick's NO TRESPASSING signs and throwing it violently over the cliff, which could answer the question of how the sign ended up floating in the tidal pool. Though not, of course, the question of whether the murderer had used the missing signpost as a weapon. And from what we heard, the sign couldn't have landed on Resnick's head by accident when Aunt Phoebe had thrown it; too many witnesses had seen him alive and well afterward. Witnesses who saw Jeb Barnes's subsequent arrival and summary dismissal. Witnesses who saw Dad have some kind of altercation with Resnick a short time later, which terrified me, until I managed to extract the information that though they'd exchanged harsh words, Resnick had been very much alive when they parted. Witnesses who saw Resnick afterward, patrolling his borders in search of trespassers. Witnesses who saw him pottering about by the shore, throwing a few stones at the gulls. Even witnesses who'd seen Michael and me when we'd found the body. I'd have felt better if some of the witnesses were a little more reliable on the matter of time. They tended to think less in hours and minutes and more in terms of "before we saw the bay-breasted warbler, and just after I got that snapshot of the crested grebe feeding." But just by circulating through the crowd and listening, we could more or less put together a time line of exactly what Resnick had done up until shortly before Michael and I found him.

We also encountered potential witnesses who claimed they had actually seen Resnick shooting down puffins, which I took with a grain of salt under the circumstances, since we had it on good authority that the puffins had all long since departed for the Arctic Circle. And then there were the witnesses who claimed they'd seen a sinister stranger skulking about the island, pretending to be a birder, despite an almost complete lack of birding knowledge. I made a note to ask Rob what kind of pranks he'd been playing over the past day or so.

The one thing we didn't find was a witness who could explain Resnick's transformation from a live misanthrope strolling along the seashore with a small bump on his forehead to a dead body with a bloody gash on the back of his head. During the critical period, which, depending on the feeding schedule of the crested grebe, ranged anywhere from fifteen to forty-five minutes, no one had seen anything out of the ordinary.

"Well, our killer certainly picked his time well," I said to Michael in an undertone.

"Yes," Michael said. "Almost every birder on the island passed by his house sometime yesterday, and not a single one of them saw the murder."

"Where's your father?" someone asked. I turned, to see Jeb Barnes and Mamie Benton looking very stern.

"Up at Aunt Phoebe's cottage, recovering from his ordeal," I said.

"I got through to the police briefly," Jeb said. "They're going to want to talk to him."

"Talk to Dad?" I said, feigning innocence. "Why?"

"I'd say he's their prime suspect," Mamie said, sounding rather smug. "No alibi for the time of the murder, and everyone knows there was no love lost between him and the deceased."

"Oh, and everyone else on the island adored the old curmudgeon and has an ironclad alibi?" I said. "I can think of a few other possibilities. You might tell them to keep their eyes out for the missing Will, for example."

"What, Resnick's will?" Jeb asked.

"How do you know it's missing?" Mamie asked. "And what's the problem if it is? Far as I know, he used a mainland law firm; they'll have a copy on file."

"Not Resnick's will," I said. "Will Dickerman."

"Haven't seen him on the island in months," Mamie said.

"No, not since he skipped bail on those grand theft auto and assault charges, I expect," I said.

"What the devil—," Jeb began.

"How on earth did you find out about that?" Mamie asked.

Not wanting to admit that we'd rummaged through Victor Resnick's files, I settled for looking inscrutable.

"Well, he's not on the island anyway," Mamie said. "I'd have seen him get off the ferry."

"How do you know he didn't come over on a private boat before the hurricane hit?" I said.

Mamie blinked. Jeb chuckled.

"Yeah, normal weather, he could have come over most any-time," he said. "But even if he had, what does that have to do with the murder? I mean, you're not thinking that just because he's had a few brushes with the law, he's got to be the killer, are you?"

"No," I said. "But he's definitely someone we want to keep an eye on, considering that he's a fugitive from justice with a reason to hate Victor Resnick and a history of whacking people with blunt objects."

"Reason to hate Resnick?" Jeb echoed. "I'm sure he didn't like Resnick any more than the rest of us, but what reason does he have to hate him? With all those steam baths and cattle prods and such Resnick has up at that house, he's the Dickermans' best customer. *Was* their best customer. Why would Will want to spoil that?"

"Because Resnick had bought up Mr. Dickerman's loans and was about to foreclose on them," I said. "About to take away the power plant. So if you see Will Dickerman, he's a suspect all right. For that matter, I'm sure the police will take a very close look at everyone who has had adverse financial dealings with Victor Resnick."

I looked at Mamie Benton when I said it, and felt a guilty satisfaction at seeing her turn pale.

"Take a damn long time to do that," Jeb Barnes said. "Not a person on the island the bastard didn't try to rook sometime or other. Me included. Liked to run a tab with me, and then when I'd try to make him pay, he'd argue. Claimed he'd never gotten things. I finally cut him off, and now the bastard does—well, did—all his shopping over on the mainland."

"Then I suppose they'll cross-examine everyone on the island," I said.

"I suppose they will, which means you don't have to go poking your nose in it," Jeb retorted as he and Mamie turned to leave. "You just let us handle it until the police get here."

I stepped forward, about to tell them just what I thought of how they were handling things, but Michael grabbed my arm, pulled me back, and gave me a warning look. I fumed silently until Jeb and Mamie were out of earshot.

"I don't suppose there's any chance you're going to take that advice?" Michael asked.

"Not when they're trying to railroad my Dad, no," I said. "Let's get out of the rain a minute; I need to think."

We shook the standing water off two metal Adirondack chairs on the front porch of the Island Inn and sat down. The birders continued to mill about in the square in front of us, trading bird news and crime rumors.

"Okay," I said when I felt a little calmer. "Let's make a mental list of the things we need to do."

"A pity, you didn't bring along the notebook that tells you when to breathe," Michael said, referring to the organizer I normally took everywhere. For some reason, people interpret my attachment to my organizer as a sign that I am unnaturally organized. I'm not, really; just the opposite. I long ago accepted the fact that if I write something down, I'll probably get it done, and if I don't, all bets are off.

I'd left the organizer behind, though; which shows you just how complete a getaway from my day-to-day life I'd been planning. A pity, as I could have used it now. But before I could even begin my plan for the afternoon, Rob appeared out of the crowd, dragging Spike, who was making heroic efforts to bite unwary passing birders.

"Could you hang on to Spike while I run into the general store?" Rob asked, holding out the leash.

"They don't mind dogs in the general store," I said.

"They mind Spike, ever since he took a chunk out of that woman who runs the gift shop," Rob said. "And Mother sent me to fetch some cream for Dad's coffee when he wakes up."

"Oh, all right," I said.

I watched as Rob ambled across the muddy square and disappeared into the general store.

"Help me keep an eye out for Rob," I said.

"Why?" Michael asked. "Is he in danger?"

"He will be if he tries to sneak off and leave me with Spike," I said. "If the general store had a back door, I wouldn't have let him out of my sight."

But while we stared at the door, watching for Rob's reappearance, a commotion elsewhere in the square distracted us. Mrs. Peabody, the stout birder, had intercepted Jeb and Mamie and was haranguing them. She was thrusting something at them, and they were backing hastily away from her. After several attempts to give them whatever she was holding, Mrs. Peabody shook her finger at them.

"What's got them all fired up?" came a voice from behind us. I glanced up, to find Ken Takahashi looking over our shoulders. I deduced from the little bits of cork all over his clothes that he hadn't had much fun opening his Chardonnay.

"The murder, of course," Michael said. Takahashi shuddered.

"Do you have any idea if the ferry's running today?" he asked, zipping up his parka.

"No, but I bet they know over at the general store," I said. "Let's go and ask."

"Are we really that interested in the ferry's whereabouts?" Michael asked as the three of us strolled across the street.

"I'm more interested in Rob's whereabouts," I said. "He's been in there long enough to buy a case of cream. If he's gone off and left us with Spike, Jeb may have another homicide on his hands."

"She's only kidding," Michael said quickly. Takahashi looked as if he didn't quite believe him.

The locals all looked up when we entered, and several of them actually nodded. I stayed near the door, where they'd be less likely to object to my bringing in Spike. Evidently, Takahashi hadn't quite given up the idea of charming the locals out of their real estate. He pasted a bright smile on his face.

"My God, it's like the North Pole out there," he said, shoving back the hood of his parka and shaking himself.

A couple of the locals huddling around the fire frowned. I suspected that any second we'd start hearing mutters about "weak-livered city folk."

"What brings you here, Mr. Takahashi?" Jeb Barnes asked.

"Do you know if the ferry's running today?"

"Doubt it," Jeb said. "Why?"

"I'd like to know how much longer I have to stay in this hellhole," Takahashi said, his charm slipping for a moment.

The native Monheganites bristled visibly at this. Even Takahashi noticed, and he returned to full-blown salesman mode.

"I mean, it's all very well for you hardy New England types, but I'm from Atlanta," he said. The drawl was heavier than before; he made it sound as if the name Atlanta had at least twelve syllables. "I can deal just fine with ninety-eight in the shade and near one hundred percent humidity. But this kind of weather—

call me a wimp, but I just don't understand how y'all can bear it. I'd have double pneumonia half the time if I lived here. In fact," he said, sniffling audibly, "I think I am coming down with something now. I don't suppose I could buy a cup of hot tea?"

"I can put the teakettle on," Jeb said. "We don't have fancy herbal teas, though, like they do down the street. Just plain old supermarket tea."

"As long as it's hot," Takahashi said.

"I wouldn't mind some myself," Michael said. "What about you, Meg?"

"Actually, we're just looking for my brother, Rob," I said. "You haven't—"

Just then, the door flew open and a swarm of birders burst into the store.

"That's him! That's him!" they shouted, pointing to Ken Takahashi.

Chapter 22

Tell Me How Long the Puffin's Been Gone

I was afraid the birders planned to lynch Takahashi, for some unknown reason. And when I looked around for Jeb Barnes, I found that he'd slipped away into the store's back room. Ostensibly to put the teakettle on, I supposed, though surely he could hear the commotion out here in the store. Takahashi quailed behind Michael. I was relieved to see a few familiar faces entering at the tail end of the birder mob, including Winnie and Binkie.

"Now then, let's calm down," Binkie called out in a surprisingly penetrating voice. "Let's have a little order here!"

The shouting died down, and the birders stood back as Binkie pushed her way to the front of the crowd.

"One of you tell me what's going on here," Binkie ordered. "Just one!" she added as several birders began to speak.

Mrs. Peabody stepped forward and pointed a quivering hand at Ken Takahashi.

"He's the one!" she said.

"What one?" I asked. "Do you mean you think he's the murderer?"

"Well, that's for the police to find out, isn't it?" Mrs. Peabody said. "All I know is, he's the one pretending to be a birder."

"Pretending to be a birder?" I said. I glanced at Takahashi, somewhat disappointed. I'd hoped the phony birder would turn out to be our missing biographer. Ken Takahashi seemed too down-to-earth to have written that much purple prose. Still, a way of testing the possibility occurred to me.

"Walking around, pretending to be one of us, when he doesn't know a tern from a seagull," Mrs. Peabody said. "Probably in league with that lunatic who was trying to wipe out the bird population of the island."

Considering what Takahashi and Resnick had planned for the island, she wasn't that far off the mark.

"That's ridiculous," Takahashi said. He reached inside his coat, probably to pull out his business cards. "I'm—"

"Mr. Takahashi!" I snapped. He froze. In fact, everybody froze.

"Hold on a second," I told Mrs. Peabody, the ringleader.

"If you don't mind . . ." I said to Binkie. She looked puzzled, but nodded.

I handed Spike's leash to Michael, drew Takahashi aside, and spoke to him in an undertone.

"Are you sure you want to tell them what you do? These are rabid environmentalists. They're very militant about development."

Takahashi turned pale.

"What am I supposed to tell them?" he asked.

A thought struck me.

"What do you know about the *Unheralded Genius of the Down East Coast?*" I asked, recalling the subtitle of Resnick's biography.

"It's another of those birds, isn't it?" Takahashi said without enthusiasm.

" 'Who could have predicted this event, at once so joyous and so tragic?' " I quoted. " 'Who can calculate the import this occurrence would present upon his life and art?' "

Takahashi began edging away from me. Okay, so he wasn't the biographer. Just checking.

"Inside joke," I said. "Just leave it to me."

"What's going on anyway?" Mrs. Peabody asked, tapping her foot with impatience.

As Takahashi continued to sidle farther away, I beckoned Mrs.

Peabody to join me—which took her out of earshot of the other birders.

"You can't reveal this to a soul," I said in a low voice.

"No, of course not," she said eagerly.

"Are you familiar with the *Unheralded Genius of the Down East Coast?*" I said.

"No," Mrs. Peabody said, looking at Takahashi. "Is that him? What's he supposed to be a genius at?"

Okay, so neither of the Peabodys was masquerading as James Jackson, either. It was worth a shot.

"Well, I can't say too much—but would it surprise you to learn that a certain environmental organization had taken an interest in Victor Resnick's less savory activities?"

Takahashi looked as if it would surprise the hell out of him, but he managed a feeble smile when Mrs. Peabody put on her reading glasses and inspected him at length.

"Well, that's quite a different kettle of fish," she said finally. Takahashi must have passed muster; she grabbed his hand and shook it vigorously for several seconds. "Carry on, then!" she ordered before turning on her heel and beginning to shoo the other birders out of the room.

"No, it's not what we thought," I heard her telling several people. "I can't talk now, but I'll tell you all about it later."

So much for not telling a soul.

"What am I supposed to do now?" Takahashi asked.

"As little as possible, until the ferry comes," I suggested.

"Right," Takahashi said, looking around nervously. "You really think one of them would harm me?"

"I have no idea," I said. "But if I were you, I wouldn't take chances. For all we know, one of the birders could have knocked off Victor Resnick. If some kind of environmental vigilante is running around loose on the island, you don't want to make yourself the next target, do you?"

"But what am I supposed to do if they ask me why I'm here?" Takahashi said, looking perplexed.

"Tell them you're under orders not to reveal that information," Michael said.

"Whose orders?" Takahashi persisted.

"Mine," I said. "But don't tell them that, of course. Just say orders."

"Right," Takahashi said.

"And stop the masquerade; just carrying around a pair of binoculars isn't going to make anyone think you're a birder."

"Binoculars? I don't even own binoculars."

Well, that was odd. Had the birders imagined the binoculars, or was there another imposter masquerading as a birder?

But before I could interrogate him further, Mrs. Peabody burst back into the room.

"Is there something else wrong, Mrs. Peabody?" I asked.

"There certainly is," she boomed. "Look at this!"

She thrust something under my nose.

For a split second, I wasn't sure what it was. And then I realized that it was a puffin. Not one of the plush stuffed puffins from Mamie Benton's shop. Right general size, shape, and color. But even a stuffed puffin left out overnight in the hurricane wouldn't be quite such a limp, bedraggled mess. This was the real thing. Or had been, when it was alive.

"I thought the puffins were long gone by now," Michael said. "Out to sea for the winter or something."

"Well, this one obviously wasn't in any shape to make the trip," I said. "Where was it anyway?"

"Down by Victor Resnick's house," she said. "Near that tidal pool you found him in. The poor thing was probably his last victim."

"And when did you find it?"

"An hour ago," she said.

"An hour ago?" I echoed. Something about this didn't make sense. "Would you mind showing us where?"

"Not at all," said Mrs. Peabody. To my relief, she whisked the dead puffin out from under my nose and began striding toward the porch steps. "It's about time somebody did something about this! Clearly the local authorities aren't going to take any action!"

I looked around for Rob, but he had fled, and Mrs. Peabody was rapidly disappearing.

"Arg!" I exclaimed, taking the end of Spike's leash. "Come on, you little monster."

He followed me, barking with glee. As I expected, I had to pick him up and carry him after about fifteen feet—although, to his credit, he managed to pick up a remarkable amount of new mud during his short time on the ground.

To my dismay, other birders began following Mrs. Peabody as she strode through town. I suppose, given the weather, there wasn't all that much else for them to do, since most of the birds remained sensibly out of the rain. We had collected fourteen or fifteen stragglers by the time we reached Resnick's house. Mrs. Peabody led us past the house and down to the tidal pool, along the path the rising tide had prevented Michael and me from using yesterday.

"Right there," she said, pointing to a large flat rock. "It was lying right there."

"Lying how?" I asked.

"I'll show you," she said, reaching for her knapsack. For a second, I thought she was about to shed her knapsack and arrange herself on the rock in the place of the dead puffin. But instead, she pulled out a camera.

"I took pictures of the body," she said.

"The puffin's body, you mean?" I asked.

"Well, of course," she said. "What other body could I mean?"

"Victor Resnick's?" Michael suggested.

"Him," she said, shrugging. "Why would I bother? Here, I'll show you."

"Great," I said as she held out her camera. "We can have the film developed."

"You don't need to develop any film," Mrs. Peabody said with a scornful look. "This is a *digital* camera. Here."

She pressed a switch on the camera, looked at it for a few seconds, then turned it so we could see. The back of the camera had a little display screen, on which I could see a picture of a small evergreen tree.

"That's fantastic!" Michael said, looking over my shoulder. "You can see the pictures as soon as you take them! Does it use film?"

"No, it saves the pictures on a computer chip," Mrs. Peabody said.

"The things they do with computers these days," another birder said, shaking his head.

"And if you don't like what you've taken, you can erase them and try again," Mrs. Peabody said.

"Amazing!" Michael said.

"How much does a thing like that run anyway?" another birder asked.

"Later, guys," I said. "I thought you said you had a picture of a puffin. That's not a puffin; it's a cedar."

"No, it's a wren," she said. "See there, he's roosting inside the cedar.

"If you say so," I said. "What about the puffin?"

"Just press this button," she said.

I put down Spike so I would have my hands free. He galloped off to bark at the waves, which were creeping closer and closer; we'd have to adjourn to the top of the hill soon. I took the small camera, pressed the button Mrs. Peabody had indicated, and waited for several seconds as another picture of the cedar tree scrolled onto the screen.

"Keep going," she said. "It's been an hour; I may have taken quite a few pictures."

I kept pressing the button and waited while several more pictures of the cedar loaded. These were followed by pictures of other shrubbery, presumably containing other wrens. Interspersed with the nature photos were occasional off-center shots of the sky or of Mrs. Peabody's muddy hiking boots, which I assumed she'd taken by mistake. Michael and several male birders looked over my shoulder, exclaiming at the high quality of the pictures, and Mrs. Peabody explained how she took the electronic pictures and e-mailed them to her sister in California.

Finally, a puffin appeared on the tiny screen. It lay on its back on the flat rock, with its toes pointing straight to the sky, its wings neatly folded by its side, and its feathers carefully groomed and reasonably clean. It looked a lot better in the photo than it did now that Mrs. Peabody had hauled it around for an hour. It looked as if it'd been laid out for viewing at a wake, and I didn't for a minute believe it had landed in that position by accident.

"There's something odd about this," I muttered, glancing from the puffin on the camera screen to the flat rock. I took off my knapsack, fished around in it, and pulled out a small pamphlet called *The Pocket Guide to Monhegan.*

"Was the puffin there when you found the body?" Mrs. Peabody asked.

"No," I said, still leafing through the guide.

"How can you be sure?" she insisted.

"Well, in the first place," I said, "that was the rock where we put Resnick's body after we hauled him out of the water; if the puffin had been there, we'd have stepped on it."

Several birders who were leaning against the rock shuffled a few feet away from it.

"And, in the second place, I took a good look around for clues, and I'd have noticed something as unusual as a dead puffin. In the third place, that rock's underwater at high tide, so even if it had been there yesterday when we found the body, it'd have washed away by this morning. The tide came in after we found Resnick's body, you know. This whole place was underwater between ten P.M. and two A.M."

I waved the pocket guide, held open to the page with this year's tide tables on it.

"That's true," a birder said.

"Perhaps it washed out to sea after the murder and then washed back in again this morning," Mrs. Peabody said.

"Does it look as if it was washed in?" I said, pointing at the little screen. "It looks as if someone posed it there. Deliberately. But why?"

"Maybe the murderer did it," Michael said. "To confuse us."

"He's wasting his time, then," I said. "We're already as confused as we're ever going to get; he should save it for the mainland cops."

"Maybe someone's trying to give us a subtle clue to the murder?" Michael said.

"Well, they're going to have to try a lot harder, and be a lot less subtle," I said.

"This is all very odd," Mrs. Peabody announced, frowning at Michael and me as if the whole mess were our fault and we should do something about it.

"And speaking of odd," I said. "There's something else rather odd about that puffin. Let me take a look at it."

"Yes, of course," Mrs. Peabody said. She tried to hand me the small carcass. Spike growled and leapt up, trying to attack it. I backed away, happy to settle for a visual inspection. Yes, there was definitely something unusual about the puffin.

"Strange," I said. "I wonder why anyone would bother to keep a dead puffin around all this time."

"I beg your pardon! I'm not keeping it around, as you put it," she said. "I only brought it along to show what that horrible man was doing."

"I didn't mean you," I said. "I meant whoever had it before you."

"No one had if before me. I found it today, not even an hour ago, right here on this rock."

She pounded the rock with one plump fist by way of emphasis.

"Well, you may have found it there, but I doubt if it died there; and it didn't die today, or yesterday, for that matter," I said. "That is not a recently deceased puffin."

"Nonsense, it's still quite fresh," Mrs. Peabody said, thrusting it under my nose by way of proof.

"Possibly," I said, backing away. "I suppose whoever put it there could have had it in his freezer for the last couple of months."

"In the freezer?" she said. "Whatever makes you think someone had that poor puffin in a freezer?"

The other birders were muttering, "The freezer?" and looking at me as if I'd announced my intention of serving them southern-fried puffin with a side of pickled puffins' feet.

"This puffin is wearing mating plumage, or whatever you call it," I said. "I mean, that is what the white face and those bright orange-and-yellow plates on the beak mean, isn't it? That when this puffin died, he was still looking for his soul mate? Unless I've completely misunderstood all the puffin lore everyone's babbled at me, he would have shed the white feathers and the pretty little plates by the end of the spring, right? So he must have died before that."

The birders looked at each other and then at the puffin.

"She's right," one of them murmured. "She's absolutely right."

"Do you mind if we keep your camera for a while?" I asked Mrs. Peabody.

"Not at all," she said. "Or if you want to come by the Island Inn, I can have my husband transfer the pictures onto diskettes for you."

"Thanks," I said. "We'll probably do that."

"I've got some digital pictures, too," another binoculars-toting man said, bounding up holding his camera. "I've got pictures of that lunatic shooting at you!"

"That has nothing to do with the murder!" Mrs. Peabody said, elbowing him aside.

"Well, neither does your puffin," said the second birder. I almost expected him to say, "So there!"

Michael tried to defuse the confrontation by taking the man's camera and exclaiming over the pictures, but the two birders were squaring off for a verbal donnybrook, when a voice rang out from above us.

"What's going on here?"

I glanced up and saw Jeb Barnes, hands on hips, stumbling down the last few feet of the path.

Inspired by the interest we had shown in the puffin, Mrs. Peabody strode over and, with a flourish, tried to present it to Jeb, who began backing up the path to escape her.

I flipped through Mrs. Peabody's pictures of the puffin again. The remaining birders, sensing that I wasn't going to do anything else amusing, followed Jeb and Mrs. Peabody.

"This puffin is evidence!" Mrs. Peabody shouted.

"Nonsense!" Jeb shouted back.

"Mind if I take a look at the puffin?" I asked, looking up at the two.

"No," Jeb said. "I mean yes. I'm impounding it. As . . . as . . . as a danger to public health."

With that, he snatched the puffin from Mrs. Peabody's hands and, holding it at arm's length, fled up the path.

Mrs. Peabody frowned.

"I think he's going to lock it up for the police," I said.

"Well, that's all right, then," Mrs. Peabody said.

"And you people stay away from the crime scene," Jeb called from the top of the cliff.

"Yes, we'd better get off the beach before the tide gets any higher," Michael suggested.

We stowed our two borrowed digital cameras safely in my knapsack and headed for the path.

"So, what has the defrosted puffin told you?" Michael said as we picked our way up the side of the cliff.

"Not a thing; he's keeping his beak shut," I said in a passable imitation of a thirties movie gangster. "But give me a few minutes alone with our feathered friend and I'll make him sing like a canary."

Well, Michael thought it was funny. Mrs. Peabody said, "Humph!" and strode off ahead of us.

"Seriously, I don't know if the puffin tells us anything useful," I said in a more normal tone. "So far, it's just another puzzle: Why would someone keep a dead puffin around for months, then leave it at the scene of a murder the day after the body was discovered? It makes no sense."

"Maybe it's symbolic," Michael suggested. "That he was killed to revenge his crimes against puffinkind?"

"Possibly, but it doesn't narrow down our suspect list," I complained.

"Maybe it does," Michael said. "Whoever left the puffin here has to be a local with a freezer to keep it in, right?"

"Not necessarily," I said. "One of the birders could have brought it over on the ferry. Can you swear there wasn't a cooler containing a dead puffin somewhere in that mountain of luggage on the dock when we arrived?"

"True," he said.

"And even if a local put the puffin there, we don't know for sure that the puffin has anything directly to do with the murder."

"What other reason could anyone have for putting it there?" Michael asked. "To throw us off the scent?"

"When we find whoever put it there, we'll ask," I said.

"When *you* find whoever put it there?" Jeb echoed from above. "I thought I told you to keep your nose out of this."

"Well, I assume when the police find out who put the puffin there, they'll let all of us know," I said as I reached the top of the path. "Surely there's no harm in being curious."

Michael chuckled.

"Well, at least Jeb's taken custody of the puffin," Michael said in an undertone.

"Even if he's only doing it because he thinks we want it," I answered. "Whereas the only one who really wants the damned thing is Spike."

"Speaking of Spike, where is he?"

"Oh damn," I said, turning around. "Still down by the rock, chasing the waves, I suppose. I'd better get him before the tide carries him away."

"I don't see him down there," Michael said, frowning.

"Oh bloody hell," I said. "Your mother will kill us if anything happens to him."

"Well, with any luck, she'll only kill Rob," Michael said. "But it would break her heart. Let's go down and look for him."

We called back Jeb Barnes and Mrs. Peabody, and the four of us scrambled around the area by the tidal pool, frantically calling Spike's name and looking in every crevice. The waves started to wash over the rocky, flat area, drenching us and narrowing our search with every passing minute.

"We'll have to give it up," Jeb said finally. "The tide'll cover the path in a minute."

"No, we have to find him!" I said.

"Meg, he's right," Michael said.

He half-dragged me up the path behind Jeb and Mrs. Peabody. We had to wait for a moment between waves to cross one spot, but we made it up to the top of the hill and stood looking down at the churning mass of water occupying the spot where we'd been standing——well, wading anyway——only a few minutes before.

"I'm so sorry about the poor little dog," Mrs. Peabody said. She sounded genuinely sympathetic, probably because she hadn't known Spike very well. And probably never would now.

"Oh damn," I said. I was astonished and embarrassed to find tears welling up in my eyes.

Chapter 23

Puffin, Come Home

Of all the stupid things, I told myself as I scrubbed at my eyes with the back of a sleeve that was already sopping wet. I take everything in stride——a dead body, a murder, my own aunt confessing to the crime, both parents nearly managing to get themselves killed in a storm. And now I break down over Spike, of all things.

"Don't worry; he'll probably turn up," Michael said, putting his arms around me. "And if he doesn't, we'll figure out some cover story to tell Mom."

"No, we'll tell her the truth," I said, standing up straight and bracing my shoulders. "That I carelessly took him out in a hurricane and callously ignored him while the surf carried him away and it's all my fault."

"It's not your fault," Michael began.

"No, it's all my fault, and I'll never forgive myself," I said. "Please, let him turn up somewhere. If we could just find him safe and sound, I promise I'll——"

Just then, a familiar yapping broke out somewhere behind us. "Spike!"

We all whirled, and I was relieved to see Spike running toward us.

"What was it you were about to promise if Spike turned up safe and sound?" Michael asked.

"Not to feed him to the sharks on the trip home," I said.

Michael chuckled.

"Good dog!" I added, rather pointlessly, as Spike arrived at my feet, panting and still yapping.

His normally sleek black-and-white fur was now a uniform muddy grayish brown, and I didn't envy whoever had to wash him before Michael's mother saw him again. Not me, I vowed, no matter how glad I was to see him undrowned.

I quickly noticed that he wasn't just barking. He was running back and forth between my feet and a pile of rocks at the edge of the cliff, yapping all the way.

"Are you trying to tell us something?" Michael asked, leaning down toward Spike the next time he arrived at my feet. Spike growled at him and turned back to me.

"You're both watching far too many *Lassie* reruns," I said as Spike ran off again. "The bit where Lassie finds the lost child is an overdone cliché; and besides, we've already found all our lost relatives."

"Oh, you're no fun," Michael said, pretending to sulk. "Can't we just go see what he's found?"

"Dead fish washed up from the storm, I expect," Jeb put in.

"Never mind, then," Michael said.

"Let's head down and see how Dad's doing," I said. "And then—"

I heard a low rumble down by my ankles.

"Cool it, Spike," I said.

Spike growled again, then butted my ankle with his head. I glanced down and started.

"What the hell has that fool dog got there?" Jeb asked.

"Aunt Phoebe's walking stick," I said.

Noticing we were paying attention to him, Spike began wagging his tail and trying to bark, his efforts a little muffled by the walking stick in his mouth. He held it at one end—the lower, narrower end. The stick had been pretty battered and gnarled to begin with, but I could see several obviously new chips and scratches. And was I imagining the telltale dark stain on the top third?

"Is that blood on one end of it?" Jeb Barnes asked.

"Could just as easily be mud," Michael said.

"Careful!" I said as Jeb reached down toward the stick. "He bites!"

"Well, not with that stick in his mouth," Michael said. "But he could choke himself trying."

"We don't want him to run off with it," Jeb said.

"How fast can he run?" Michael said. "The thing's so heavy, he can barely drag it."

"Someone give me a handkerchief," I said. "I'll try to get it away from him."

Holding Michael's handkerchief behind my back with my right hand—fluttering cloth sometimes spooked Spike—I knelt in the mud and extended my left hand.

"Here, Spike," I called, fixing an insincere smile on my face. "Here, boy. Come here, boy."

Spike paused six feet away and looked at me, then at the others.

"Back away some more," I said, not taking my eyes off Spike.

"If we back any farther away, we'll fall off the cliff," Jeb said.

"Here boy," I called to Spike. "Come and give me the stick, you miserable little fur ball."

"You're not going to get him to come to you, calling him names like that," Jeb said.

"He doesn't care what names I call him," I said in my most coaxing voice, eyes still locked on Spike's. "It's the tone he's listening for. I could call him a mangy little cur, and as long as I smile when I say it, he won't care. Will you, Spike?"

Spike wagged his tail.

"Here, you ornery little mutt," I said, smiling harder and beckoning. "Come to Aunt Meg. Don't make me wring your wretched little neck."

Spike wagged harder, then staggered over to me, dragging the stick behind him.

"That's a good little monster," I said, patting him. Spike had to drop the stick to begin his usual pastime of licking me obsessively, which gave me the chance I needed to grab the walking stick with the handkerchief and hand it over to Jeb Barnes. I reattached Spike's leash while Jeb juggled the puffin and the stick.

"Yes, that's Phoebe's cane," Jeb said.

"Stick, not cane," I corrected. "Don't let Aunt Phoebe hear you calling it a cane; she'd kill you. Not literally," I added, seeing the startled expression on Jeb's face. "That was a figure of speech."

"Right," he said. I wasn't sure he believed me. "I thought she said she'd lost the . . . stick when she fell."

"No," I said, starting down the trail toward the village. "She told us she lost it before she fell."

"It could be evidence," Jeb said, falling into step beside me. "After all, she did confess to the murder this morning."

"She did?" Mrs. Peabody said with a gasp. "Well, I never!"

"Yes, but you'll remember I pointed out exactly why her confession didn't hold water."

"Good," Mrs. Peabody said. "I can hardly imagine a dedicated environmentalist like Phoebe committing murder."

"Not even of someone like Victor Resnick?" Michael asked.

Mrs. Peabody didn't answer. I glanced back. She had paused at a fork in the trail and seemed to be seriously thinking over the question. Much too seriously.

"That dark stuff on the stick really looks like mud to me," Michael said.

"We'll let the police decide that," Jeb said.

"Exactly," I said. "Let's just get the stick safely locked up until the police can do a forensic examination."

"Locked up where?" Jeb asked.

"In the locker with the body, I suppose," I said. "Bodies, if you include the puffin. After all, the damned stick's survived a hurricane; a little cold won't hurt it."

"Yes, that would work," Jeb said.

We watched as Jeb trudged off toward the Anchor Inn with the puffin and the walking stick in hand. Mrs. Peabody trailed after him, presumably to keep her eye on the puffin.

"Let's go get a rope and do our burgling," I said. Michael nodded and fell into step beside me as we headed back to Aunt Phoebe's cottage.

"Aunt Phoebe did say she lost her stick before she fell into the gully," I said. "She just didn't say how long before."

"Still, it doesn't look good, her walking stick turning up so near the scene of the crime. And with blood on it."

"You're the one who keeps saying it's mud."

"Could be mud," he said. "Could be blood, too."

"True," I agreed. "And that makes two possible murder weapons that have some association with Aunt Phoebe."

I brooded on that a while longer.

"Of course," Michael put in, "The sheer improbability of the story she told goes in her favor."

"Yes, except that if she were guilty and knew all the details of the crime, she could make up an improbable story better than anyone."

"Is she that devious?"

I had to think about that one.

"I don't think so," I said finally. "Normally, I tend to think of Aunt Phoebe as abrupt and straightforward. But if she'd brooded a lot about the crimes she thought Resnick had committed against the birds . . . who knows?"

"Or if she's particularly good at thinking on her feet."

"Exactly. And then again, there's the question of why she would tell such a howler in the first place."

"Because she's covering up for someone else?"

"Yes," I said. "And people would naturally assume that someone is Dad. Which isn't an idea we want to encourage."

Just then, I saw Jim Dickerman shambling along the path toward us.

"Afternoon," I said as he drew near.

"Yeah, I know," he snapped. "Give me a break."

"Pardon?"

"Look, I'll get it running as soon as I can, damn it. I stayed up all night trying to fix the damned thing. I'm going back up now, but I had to get a couple hours of sleep."

"Hey, calm down," I said. "Aunt Phoebe isn't even hooked up to your generator, remember? I wasn't asking when you'll have the thing fixed or giving you a hard time; I just said good afternoon."

"Sorry," he said, fighting a yawn. "Bad night."

His eyes were bloodshot, and he looked as if he hadn't shaved, combed his hair, or changed his clothes in several days.

"You look as if you could use a lot more sleep," I said. "Let the generator wait a few more hours."

"Too many people complaining," he said, stifling another yawn.

"One less than there used to be at least," I said.

"Yeah," he said with a startled laugh. "I guess so. And the bastard was the biggest complainer of all. Course, he was our biggest customer, too. Pity."

"I don't suppose you saw anything useful," I asked. "Any possible clues or anything?"

"I wasn't down by Resnick's yesterday," Jim said, shrugging. "Too busy with the generator."

"What about your windows?" I asked. "I should think you have a pretty good view from there."

"When they're not shuttered up," he said. "Got 'em nailed shut for the storm right now."

"That's true," I said. "When did you do that?"

He thought for a few seconds.

"Day before they stopped the ferry," he said. "That'd be Thursday afternoon."

"So I don't suppose you saw much of what went on around the island yesterday and today, then?"

He shrugged.

"Only when I went outside," he said. "Damn birders all over everywhere."

"You don't like the birders?"

"Can't see what the big deal is, but I've got nothing against them. Mess up the island less than most damn tourists."

What a relief to see that Resnick's death wouldn't completely deprive the island of curmudgeons. I wondered if Jim and Victor Resnick had actually gotten along in their own gruff way. And then a thought hit me. . . . Jim . . . James—what if Jim Dickerman was the phantom biographer?

"Tell me," I said. "Do you know anything about the *Unheralded Genius of the Down East Coast?*"

"The what?" Jim asked.

" 'Who could have predicted this event, at once so joyous and so tragic?' " I quoted.

" 'Who can calculate the import this occurrence would present upon his life and art?' " Michael added.

"If that's one of those word games, I don't get it," Jim said in a voice that suggested he didn't much care, either. If he wasn't the biographer, he was a phenomenal actor. Ah, well. I tried another angle.

"Before the storm. You could see what went on at Resnick's, right?"

"Yeah, I guess."

"Was he really electrocuting birds?"

"Yeah, but he wasn't killing them."

"Then what was he doing?"

"Running a low-voltage current through some of the metal

struts in his roof. Give 'em a hotfoot, scare 'em away so they'd stop crapping on his glass. Town made him stop, though."

"You mean he actually did what they asked?"

Jim snorted.

"Yeah. Well, he wouldn't have, except that it didn't really work anyway. Gulls just sat on the glass. Funniest thing you ever saw, watching him jump up and down in his yard, yelling at the gulls. Couldn't throw anything without breaking the glass."

"When did he stop?"

"May, maybe June. Before the tourist season anyway."

That made sense; the puffin could have still been in breeding plumage in May or June, as far as I could tell from the bird books. Maybe puffins were more sensitive to a hotfoot than gulls. Or maybe Resnick had experimented with higher voltages before the town pulled the plug on his bird-control program.

"Have you seen your brother recently?" I asked finally.

"Fred? Yeah, he's down in the village somewhere, I guess."

From the tone of voice, I got the feeling there was no love lost between the brothers.

"No, I actually meant Will."

Jim frowned but said nothing.

"Monhegan's own candidate for America's most wanted," I went on. "You haven't seen him around recently, have you?"

"No, not since—" Jim began, then stopped.

"Not since when?" I asked.

"Not since before they got arrested," he said slowly. "What does he have to do with anything? Will wasn't even on the island when . . ."

His voiced trailed off, as if something had just occurred to him.

"Well, if you find out he's on the island, tell him to see his lawyer," I said.

"Even if he didn't do it," Michael said.

"Especially if he didn't do it," I added. "Do you think the police will look far for another suspect if they find someone right under their noses with a prior history of whacking people over the head?"

At least I hoped that's what the police would do. I must have sounded pretty convincing. Jim frowned.

"I have to get back to the generator," he said, and strode off.

"Okay, I'll bite," Michael said. "What was last bit all about?"

"I'm not sure," I said. "I'm hoping if Will Dickerman is on the island, Jim will go and see him."

"To warn him, or to give him hell for jumping bail and jeopardizing the power plant?"

"Either one will do," I said.

"Shouldn't we do something? Like maybe follow him?"

"He knows every inch of the island; I think we'd be slightly conspicuous?"

"So we stir things up and then just sit around and wait to see if something happens?"

"No. Like I said, we get the rope and burgle Resnick's studio."

But before we got to the cottage, Winnie and Binkie came hiking briskly up behind us. Predictably, after we exchanged greetings, they asked if we'd heard any more news about the murder.

About ten seconds after we told them about Mrs. Peabody and the puffin, Michael and Winnie were deep in conversation about digital cameras. Binkie and I fell in step a little behind them.

"I have the awful feeling I'm going to hear a great deal about digital cameras over the next few months," I said with a sigh.

"Dear me, yes," Binkie murmured. "And, if your young man is anything like Winnie, spending a great deal of time saying, 'Yes, dear, that's a lovely picture.' "

I shuddered. I had no doubt she was right.

"Speaking of pictures," I said, "what do you think of Resnick's painting ability?"

Instead of answering, Binkie looked over her glasses at me and frowned. Was I just imagining things, or had I touched a nerve?

Chapter 24

The Puffin Who Knew Too Much

"Resnick's painting ability?" Binkie asked warily. "Why, what's that got to do with his death?"

"I don't know that it has anything to do with it," I said. "Unless you know of a reason."

"No, of course not," Binkie said. A little too quickly perhaps? "Well, anyone on Monhegan can tell you about Victor Resnick. He's probably the most distinguished local landscape artist—"

"The real scoop, not the Monhegan Chamber of Commerce spiel."

She looked over her glasses at me. I tried to look innocent, earnest, and discreet. Apparently, I pulled it off.

"Second rate, at best," she said. "A shame, really. He showed such early promise, but then he never developed."

"I'm no art critic," I said. "His paintings seem pretty good to me."

"Oh, they're good, of course," she said. "But they're no better today than they were fifty years ago. In fact, they're not the slightest bit different. Not the style, not the technical skill, not even the subject matter."

"Always landscapes, yes," I said.

"Always Monhegan landscapes," Binkie corrected.

"I thought he'd spent most of the last twenty years in the south of France," I said.

"Yes, and did nothing the whole time but paint pictures of

Monhegan. What kind of artist could live for twenty years on the Côte d'Azur and never once paint the Mediterranean?"

She frowned and shook her head. I followed suit, while privately thinking that it might take more strength of character than I possessed to pick up a brush at all if I were living on the Côte d'Azur.

"Maybe he was homesick," I suggested.

"If he was homesick, why didn't he come home a little more often, then?" Binkie said. "Lazy, more like. Did it from snapshots, of course. Only came home when he wanted more snapshots. If he were still alive, you'd see him running around with that Polaroid of his right now, taking pictures of the storm."

I had a sudden vision of Victor Resnick standing in his expensive greenhouselike studio, ignoring the glorious view as he peered at a curling Polaroid clipped to his easel.

"And honestly," Binkie went on, "if I have to look at one more painting of those eerie, foreboding, calm-before-the-storm skies . . . well, I suppose now I won't have to."

"You'll probably think I'm a total philistine for saying this," I said, "but I bought a book of his paintings down at Mamie's store largely because of those skies. I thought he did them rather well."

"Oh, he did do them well. Superlatively. It's just that he did them all the time. He figured out the technique early on, dazzled everybody, and couldn't let it go. Flip through that book of yours and see. Every other painting's got that same gray-green sky. That or the gnarled tree."

"Gnarled tree?"

"He used to have this charmingly gnarled tree on a rock near where his house is now," Binkie said. "I've lost count how many of his paintings I've seen it in, from one angle or another. The poor thing blew over in a nor'easter eighteen or twenty years ago, and I remember thinking, What a relief—no more gnarled tree; or at least he'll have to find another gnarled tree."

"Let me guess: He had photos of it."

"Hundreds, I imagine; from every conceivable angle. I don't think he even noticed it was gone for a year or two; and then only because he went out to take more snapshots. That's one reason why his sales are in such a slump. In his early days, when he was hot, every museum and major collector had to have a Resnick or two. But that's all you need, really. A seascape with the gnarled tree and the gray-green sky, and maybe a weathered saltbox with waves crashing on the beach behind it, and you've pretty much got Resnick covered."

"And that's not the case with most artists, right?"

"Oh, no," Binkie exclaimed. "Take someone like, oh, Picasso. There's no way you could mistake a painting from his twenties for one done in his fifties. With Resnick, you couldn't tell if he didn't date them. Of course, the critics took a while to realize he wasn't going any further, but he'd fallen pretty well out of the mainstream by the eighties, which means he missed out on all the real money, back when the Japanese started buying."

"So he wasn't all that wealthy, then?"

"Well, he hadn't made as much money as people like Wyeth, for example, but I shouldn't think he was broke, if that's what you mean," Binkie said. "I suspect he invested well enough to live quite nicely. No reason why he shouldn't have; apart from that eyesore of a house, he never spent much money on anything that I can see."

"And he never married or . . . um . . ." I said, bogging down with embarrassment in the middle of my attempt to pry into Resnick's love life.

"He never married, no; and as for uming—well, if he bedded any woman around here, she had the good sense to keep quiet about her bad taste. Of course, I have no idea what he might have gotten up to in France," she added with a slight frown.

"Mrs. Fenniman said he was an old beau of Mother's, before she met Dad," I said.

"Well, I don't know that you'd call him a beau," Binkie said, her frown deepening. "He was quite smitten with her, of course; all the young men were. But I don't think she took him seriously. Or any of them back then. She'd pretend to, of course, if she thought it would shock your grandparents. I think that's why she took up with Resnick, really. He was the most unsuitable young man she could find. Any of the older girls, I think your grandfather would have stuck them in a convent school after that, but your mother managed to wangle that trip to Paris she'd always wanted."

Binkie shook her head, as if in admiration of Mother's cleverness.

"Well, this is your turnoff," she said, stepping up to take Winnie's arm as we arrived at the foot of Aunt Phoebe's lane. "We'll see you later, dear. Don't worry. I'm sure it will all work out much better than you think."

With that cryptic encouragement, the Burnhams strode up the hill toward the Dickermans' house.

"So," Michael asked when they were out of earshot. "Did you learn anything useful?"

I sighed.

"Not really," I said. "Nothing we didn't already know. Damn, I'm getting tired of this. We come here for a little peace and quiet, to get away from it all, and we land right in the middle of another murder. This whole thing has been a disaster from start to finish."

"I'm crushed," Michael said, reeling back in mock dismay. "You don't think it's romantic, us trapped together on a remote island, like the Swiss Family Robinson?"

"More like a remake of *Ten Little Indians*," I said, and then instantly wondered if my answer had been a little too honest. Michael didn't seem insulted, though. "What a pity Mother and Dad didn't just stay in Europe for a few more weeks," I added, trying to change the subject.

"Yes, I think you might rather enjoy all this if you weren't worried that the police will suspect your family."

"Exactly," I said. "Besides, I always enjoy it anytime Mother's off traveling."

"That's rather a rotten thing to say about your own mother," Michael said.

"I don't see what's so rotten about it," I said a little defensively. He was kidding, wasn't he?

"Saying you don't want her around? That's not rotten?"

"I didn't say I don't want her around; I said I enjoy it when she's traveling," I corrected. He smiled, and I relaxed. Okay, he didn't think me an ungrateful daughter after all. "She sends home such interesting stuff," I added.

"What kind of stuff?"

"You never know with Mother," I said. "She thinks of traveling largely in terms of shopping, so of course she always sends home lots of loot. Though you never know when you open a package whether you're going to find a present for you, something she bought for herself, or some laundry she decided was easier to send home than get washed."

"Not much shopping on Monhegan," Michael said. "Unless you're into puffin-related tchotchkes."

"True. I wonder why on earth she agreed to come here."

"Your dad wanted to come," Michael said. "Isn't that reason enough?"

I glanced up. Michael was looking casually out to our right, apparently enjoying the view of the churning surf and dripping rain. But I had this sneaky feeling that was some kind of test question, as in "Wouldn't you do something like that for me?"

I hate that kind of test question. I always assume I've flunked them——even when it turns out later that I didn't, or that it wasn't a test question after all.

"Reason enough?" I said. "I guess it would be for most normal people. For Dad, certainly, or Rob, or just about anyone I can think of. But Mother?" I shrugged.

"You don't give your mother enough credit; I think she's very devoted to your dad."

She was certainly very intent on letting him get his rest. Before we even got in the door, she sent Mrs. Fenniman running out to shush us.

"Your dad's asleep," Mrs. Fenniman hissed. "And your aunt Phoebe's resting up for her ordeal."

"Ordeal?" I asked.

"When the mainland police come to haul her away," Mrs. Fenniman said.

I decided not to spoil Aunt Phoebe's grand drama just yet. Her idea of resting involved sitting in the kitchen with her injured knee propped up under an ice pack, helping empty the larder. Perhaps she thought they wouldn't feed her in jail. I inquired after the knee, dodged her questions about what we'd been up to, and settled down in the living room with two heaping plates of food—one for myself and one for Michael, who had gone upstairs to change.

As I sat there with my eyes closed, munching a ham sandwich, I felt a sudden, surprisingly intense surge of relief and pleasure. I hadn't felt this happy about things since arriving on the island— since shortly after setting foot on the ferry, for that matter. Illogical, I thought. The storm still rattled the windows. We might still see Dad or Mother or Aunt Phoebe arrested on suspicion of murder. And even if we escaped the forces of nature and the long arm of the law, we still had the ferry ride back to the mainland to dread.

"You look very cheerful," Michael said, plunking down beside me.

"Things are looking up," I said.

"You've solved the mystery?" he asked eagerly.

"No, but for the moment, we're all safe and sound under the same roof, the whole family. And we're warm and dry and fed."

"Some of us are fed," he said, frowning.

"Here, I brought you a plate, too."

"Thanks," he said. "So warm, dry, and fed is enough to make you happy?"

"For now," I said. "Later, we'll work on warm, dry, fed, and free of all suspicion in the death of Victor Resnick. Speaking of which . . ."

Chapter 25

Puffin or Tiger?

I rummaged through my suitcase until I found the files I'd dragged down from the attic.

"You're not going to slog away at that while we're eating?" Michael asked.

"There're only a few of them," I said. "I just want to get to them before something else interrupts us."

Michael rolled his eyes and returned to his sandwich.

Most of the files were pretty boring. My grandfather Hollingworth's correspondence with a contractor about renovations to the cottage. Bills from someone named Barnes—Jeb's father or grandfather, presumably—for groceries and supplies.

I came close to giving up on the files and sticking them back in the attic, when I ran across a file marked "Resnick."

I was relieved at first to see that it contained only a series of increasingly angry letters from Grandfather to Resnick. Apparently, Grandfather had bought a painting, which Resnick had procrastinated about delivering. How odd; as far as I knew, my grandfather had a reputation as a canny businessman, but he wasn't exactly a patron of the arts. Perhaps he'd been canny enough to recognize Victor Resnick as a young artist on the rise and had bought a painting as an investment. Then again, having seen the painting in Resnick's house I could think of another reason for the transaction. Especially when I found the last documents in the files: a canceled check for ten thousand dollars, made out to Victor Resnick, and two copies of a bill of sale.

"Michael," I said. "Where's that book of Resnick's paintings?"

"Good question," he said, looking around the living room.

"Help me find it, will you?"

After a prolonged search, we finally found the book behind a stack of flowerpots, sitting on a coiled garden hose. I flipped through the first chapter, searching for dates.

"What's up?" Michael said, leaning over my shoulder. I lost track, just for a moment, of why I was looking through the book. Oh, right, Resnick's paintings.

"Aha!" I said, when I found the right page. "Victor Resnick made his first major sale in 1956. For the princely sum of five thousand."

"Think what a bargain that would be today," he said. "Now that he's selling for a hundred times that much."

"More like twenty times, maybe, but yes, it's a bargain. But up till 1956, his sales were for peanuts. Where's that sales log of his anyway?" I asked, fishing through my knapsack. "Aha. See. Nothing over a thousand until 1956."

"True."

"So what would you say if I told you that in 1953, someone paid Resnick ten thousand for a painting?"

"I'd say the buyer was either very gullible, very farsighted, or buying something more than just a painting."

"And that it wasn't recorded in the sales log?"

"Scratch out gullible and farsighted."

"Right," I said, handing him the canceled check. "Take a look at this."

"R. S. Hollingworth—let me guess, your maternal grandfather," he said. "It doesn't say, but I'd bet anything we've seen the painting in question."

"The nude."

"So how does this relate to the murder?" Michael asked.

"I have no idea," I said. "Not at all, I hope. Though if the police start poking into the case, I'm sure it will all come out, whether it's related or not."

I began reading the letters in the file again. I looked up when I heard a snort of laughter from Michael. He was playing with the digital cameras again.

"What's so funny?" I asked.

"Nothing," he said, pressing a button on the camera.

"Let me see the camera," I said.

I had to wrestle with him for it, which would have distracted both of us from my original request if Mrs. Fenniman hadn't kept wandering in and out. He finally let me have the camera, and I turned it on to see what he was looking at.

This was the second camera, the one whose owner claimed to have photos of Resnick shooting at us. He had indeed caught some interesting shots of the confrontation. First, a none-too-flattering view of my rear end as Michael and I scrambled over the top of the hill. Then a shot or two of Resnick waving his gun around. And one of me looking very Neanderthal, standing on the top of the hill, threatening Resnick with my rock.

"I think I'll ask for a copy of some of these," Michael said.

"Very funny," I said, pressing the button to remove my picture from the little screen. "I really don't see why . . ."

I found myself staring at the next picture in the camera.

"What's wrong?" Michael said, looking over my shoulder.

"Look at this," I said.

"It's the tidal pool," he replied. "So?"

"You can see part of a figure there in the corner."

"Since we have no idea who it is, what's the use?"

"It's Rhapsody," I said.

"Rhapsody? How can you tell?" Michael asked, peering more closely at the camera.

"The lilac and black clothes, combined with that hunched-over, 'Please don't hurt me' posture."

Michael studied the photo.

"You could be right," he said. "But it looks pretty light in this picture. Must have been taken fairly early in the day."

"It was, obviously; before the pictures of us confronting him anyway."

"Then what's the point?"

"I don't know," I said. "I just think it's funny that she was there at all. And she was hanging around the house again today; I'm sure that it was Rhapsody we saw through the windows. We need to find a way to ask her about it."

"I'm sure you'll manage," Michael said.

"Oh, there you are, dears," Mother said, looking down from the balcony above. "Your father isn't up yet; I'll keep you company until he's awake. Let me just find my embroidery."

She disappeared again.

"Your mother does a great deal of embroidery, doesn't she?" Michael said.

Was that simple admiration in his voice, or was there some kind of subtext? As in "Why don't you do something decorative and feminine, instead of dragging me all over the island in the rain while you play sleuth?"

"She doesn't actually *do* a lot of embroidery," I said. "She carries it around all the time, but if you watch, she takes a stitch only occasionally. I don't really think she's that keen on it."

"Then why does she do it?"

Before I could answer, Mother limped into the room. She settled herself on the sofa opposite us. We watched as she laid out several dozen skeins of brightly colored embroidery thread on the sofa beside her and covered half the coffee table with the contents of her sewing basket. She fussed with the items for a while, like a decorator primping a floral arrangement. Then she picked up her hoop and her needle and looked at us with a smile, one eyebrow raised, as if asking whether the stage set looked just right. Or possibly hinting that we should entertain her while she worked.

Out of the corner of my eye, I could see Michael's mouth twitching.

"How's the new embroidery coming, Mother?" I asked.

She cocked her head to one side, like a wren, and studied the cloth on her lap.

"Slowly," she said with a sigh.

Michael made a strangled noise, and Mother took three or four leisurely stitches before stopping to examine her progress from several angles. Michael now sat with his elbow on his knee and his hand over his mouth, a very serious look on his face. In fact, he looked rather like the Thinker come to life, except that I somehow couldn't imagine the Thinker ever wheezing with suppressed chuckles.

I hated to put a damper on his fun, but something preyed on my mind. I glanced around to make sure no one else could over-hear before turning to Mother.

"Mother," I said. "We found an interesting painting up at Victor Resnick's house. A portrait."

I should have known better than to expect a dramatic reaction from Mother.

"Oh?" she said, pausing, her needle poised gracefully over the embroidery hoop.

"I didn't know he even did portraits," Dad put in, peering down from the balcony. So much for my carefully chosen moment. "Thought he only did landscapes."

"Well, apparently he did in his youth," I said.

"I've never heard of any," Dad said, rubbing his eyes as he ambled down the stairs. "And there weren't any in that book about him."

"Are you sure, Dad?" I asked.

"Well, yes, of course," he said. "I'll show you. Where's that book anyway?"

"Out in the kitchen, I think," I said, shoving the edge of the book in question out of sight under the couch. Dad trotted out to the kitchen.

"I doubt if he ever exhibited this painting," I said, my voice too low for Dad to hear in the kitchen. "I think it was done for his own private enjoyment."

Mother looked up again.

"Oh really?" she said. "What makes you think that?"

"The subject was . . . rather unconventional."

To my amazement, Mother smiled.

"Yes, he was rather unconventional as a young man," she said. "And terribly wild."

My jaw dropped.

"Gifted with an overactive imagination, of course," she said. "And not very honest, I'm afraid."

"Yes," I said. "Taking payment for something and then never delivering it isn't very honest, is it?"

"Well, he did deliver it eventually," Mother said. "I rather wish he hadn't; I was so provoked when your grandfather burned it."

"Burned it!" Michael and I echoed.

"Yes, can you imagine it?" Mother said. "Burning a genuine Victor Resnick! Of course, we didn't know then how famous he'd become, but still. I would so like to have that painting. It would bring back such fond memories."

Michael and I looked at each other in consternation. What kind of fond memories? I wondered. Memories of an affair with Resnick? Or just of the days when she looked the way she looked in the painting?

"Well, you may be in luck," I said. "Apparently, he painted at least one more portrait of you."

"Another portrait?" Mother asked, looking very interested. "What was it like?"

"Well," I said, and then froze. I looked at Michael for assistance.

"Not a painting I can imagine Meg's grandfather would approve of," Michael said.

"No, I imagine not," Mother murmured. "Well, that explains a lot."

"A lot of what?"

"I think he expected someone to come over and collect it this weekend," she said. "Perhaps you and Michael could take care of that?"

"No, at least not without some kind of proof that we're not pulling a million-dollar art heist," I said.

"Oh, well," Mother said. She dropped the embroidery into her lap, reached over to the end table for her purse—an impractical scrap of velvet, lace, and satin that would probably survive five minutes if I tried to carry it—and pulled out a small envelope.

"Here," she said, handing it to me.

There was no stamp. "Margaret Langslow" was written on the front in the same bold, angular hand I recognized from Resnick's files. I hesitated before opening it, and Mother gestured impatiently.

"My dear Maggie," it began.

"Maggie?" I said aloud.

"I never liked that nickname," she said, shrugging.

"I have something of yours that I'd like to give you—that painting your father admired so much. Come and see me; we can talk about old times. Vic."

It was dated Friday—the day after she'd arrived on the island. He hadn't lost much time.

"How did you get this?"

"Your aunt Phoebe found it slipped under the door sometime after we arrived."

"Did you go to see him?"

"Of course not," Mother said. "I had no interest in seeing him, and even if I had, why would I want to walk that far in this weather? And I thought he was lying about the painting."

"Maybe Grandfather lied about burning it."

"Oh, no," Mother said. "He made me watch while he burned it."

Somehow I could picture the scene: Grandfather sputtering like a firecracker while Mother coolly pretended indifference to the fate of the painting.

"Well, Resnick has this one hanging in his hallway," I said. "I don't think he'd had it there long, though, or everyone on the island would have heard about it."

"Is it still there?" Mother asked. She didn't look alarmed, just interested.

"No, we put it and some of the other paintings away where the rain couldn't damage them."

"That's nice," she said. "Well, go along and collect it. I'm sure it would cause all kinds of confusion if the police found it."

"It's not out there," Dad said, popping in from the kitchen.

"Oh, I'm sorry," I said. "I just found it here under the couch."

For the next half hour, I had to keep my composure while Dad thumbed through the book with one hand and ate with the other. And he commented all the while, with his mouth full, on what a genius Resnick was and what a shame such a great artist had been such a difficult person, and what a pity it was he had come to such an untimely end. Mother continued to fuss over her embroidery and practice her patented Mona Lisa smile, occasionally reminding Dad not to drop food on my new book.

Well, it wasn't as if Dad had ruined my chance to find out more about the painting. Mother had obviously said all she planned to say about it. Whether she had posed for it or whether Resnick had done it from memory or imagination, I'd probably never find out. In fact, I wasn't even sure I wanted to know.

I decided not to worry about the painting until tomorrow. In fact, I wasn't going to worry about anything until tomorrow. As soon as possible, I was going to go to bed. I might even take a nap right now, I thought, leaning back into Michael's arm and closing my eyes with a contented sigh. I felt Michael shift his weight and then felt his breath in my ear. Yes, I thought, a very nice time to whisper a few sweet nothings in my ear.

"Things would be a lot easier if we didn't have all these damned birders underfoot," he murmured.

"Yeah," I agreed. Not to mention my family. I opened one eyelid to check on what our unintentional chaperones were up to. Dad was studying a photo with a magnifying glass. Mother was contemplating her embroidery with a dreamy expression on her face.

"I mean, they're very useful for establishing the time line, but there are just too many of them, and any one of them could be the murderer. In fact . . . What's so funny?"

Mother and Dad both glanced up, wondering what the joke was, and Michael and I fled to the kitchen, where we could talk with more privacy.

"I thought you were talking about our situation, not the latest homicide," I said, giggling.

"Yeah, well, that, too," he said, sheepishly. "But you've got to admit, it's intriguing."

"It's completely baffling," I said. My sleepy mood had vanished. "Too many suspects, all with motive, means, and opportunity."

"I like Will Dickerman for it," Michael said. "Perfect casting for the murderer."

"Well, if you like Will, don't forget about Fred," I said. "To know him is to loathe him, and he'd have had much the same reasons Will had for doing Resnick in. And for all that southern-fried charm he puts on, I wouldn't put it past Ken Takahashi to do the old boy in. For ruining the deal, or just for dragging him out here in a hurricane."

"I don't know," Michael said. "I rather like Takahashi. I'd hate to see him turn out to be the one."

"Well, I'd hate for the police to suspect Dad or Aunt Phoebe."

"Perhaps it will turn out to be someone we don't know," Michael said. "One of the birders, or a local we haven't really met."

Just then, we heard the front door slam. We peeked out of the kitchen door to see what was up.

"This place is absolutely impossible," Rob said, striding in.

"What's wrong, dear?" Mother asked.

"They won't let me use the power in the Anchor Inn, even though they've got that generator going, doing nothing but running the freezer," Rob complained. "And then I tried to talk to the guy who does the generator, and all he wants is free legal advice."

"Let me guess," I said. "Was he asking what happens if someone who's jumped bail gets turned in? Or what happens to a foreclosure if the note holder dies while it's in progress?"

"Both, actually," Rob said. "What are you, psychic?"

"She's a very fine detective," Dad said, beaming.

"I'm just using the brain God gave me," I said. Well, that and the information from Resnick's files. "What did you tell him?"

"Basically, that I had no idea," Rob said. "I mean, that's the kind of stuff you don't know off the top of your head unless you work with it every day. And even if I did know, I'd know how it worked in Virginia. This is Maine. Things could be completely different here."

"He shouldn't ask for free legal advice," Dad said. "It's unfair; like asking me for free medical advice just because I'm a doctor."

"Not that I've ever heard you turn anyone down," I commented. "Or, for that matter, that you usually wait to be asked."

"Well, he should talk to a Maine lawyer," Dad said. "I don't know why he doesn't ask Binkie Burnham. She's an old friend of the Dickerman family; I'm sure she'd give him any legal advice he needs."

"That's right; Binkie's a lawyer," I said, remembering the private investigator's report. "Harvard Law School!"

"Oh, yes," Dad said. "Quite a famous litigator, too. She does environmental cases, mostly, plus the occasional criminal case. Of course, she's semiretired these days."

I pondered this fact for a moment.

"Let's get some fresh air," I said to Michael.

"Fresh——" he began, looking at the drizzle outside. "Oh, right, fresh air," he said. "Good idea."

What an actor, I thought as I grabbed my knapsack and stuffed some rope into it. I could almost believe him myself.

Chapter 26

Round Up the Usual Puffins

"Fresh air?" he repeated as we finished fastening our rain gear.

"The game is afoot," I said. "Let's go up to the Dickermans' for a minute."

"I can manage that far," Michael said as we turned down the road. "Barely. But why?"

"Every time I've seen Winnie and Binkie for the past few days, they've been going up or coming down the road from the Dickermans'," I said. "I just assumed it was for bird-watching purposes. Or because they've all been friends for decades. But now that we know Binkie's a crack criminal lawyer, it strikes me as odd that she would spend so much time near the house of the only two criminals on the island whose identity we already know. Let's go see what's up."

In the light of day, the Dickermans' house looked rather more run-down than usual, even for Monhegan. Signs that they could no longer afford the upkeep? Or just my overactive imagination?

I knocked on the door, and we waited awhile—I had a feeling someone was inspecting us from behind a curtain. Then the door opened and Mrs. Dickerman peered out.

"May we come in?" I asked.

She hesitated for a moment, then stepped aside. I walked into the living room, where Winnie and Binkie sat holding teacups. Mr. Dickerman stood before the fireplace, looking anxious.

"Meg, dear, how nice to see you," Binkie said, looking up with a smile. "And Michael. Mamie says you two are trying to play detective."

"We're trying to keep them from railroading my Dad, if that's what you mean," I said. "Just because Mother knew Victor Resnick half a century ago does not make Dad suspect number one."

"Quite right, I'm sure," Binkie said. "And how's your sleuthing going along, then?"

Chalk it up to tiredness, but I had no patience for drawn-out verbal fencing.

"Coming along about as well as you'd expect," I said. "I don't suppose I can persuade you to come clean about Will?"

The Dickermans started, and even Winnie looked mildly disconcerted. Binkie only smiled and sipped her tea.

"Come clean?" she said with a shake of her head. "My, that sounds so melodramatic. I can almost hear Cagney saying it, or Bogart. What on earth could Will Dickerman have to do with the events of the past few days?"

"Quite a lot, if he was on the island for the past few days," I said.

"I can assure you, Will Dickerman is not on the island today, and was not on the island at the time of Victor Resnick's death." Binkie said.

"How can you be so sure, if he's on the lam?"

Binkie sighed.

"Because just before Winnie and I came over to the island, I accompanied Will to the Port Clyde police station, where he surrendered himself to custody," Binkie said in a brisk, businesslike tone of voice. "Needless to say, there was no possibility of bail."

I thought for a moment.

"I notice you were very careful to say when Will wasn't on the island," I said. "Just for the sake of argument, suppose he had been on the island sometime after he skipped bail and before he went to the mainland to turn himself in."

Binkie raised an eyebrow but said nothing.

"Suppose he had hidden himself by camping out on the far side of the island, and Michael and I had found the remains of his campsite."

Mr. and Mrs. Dickerman started.

"I mean, if we were absolutely sure it had nothing to do with the murder, Michael and I wouldn't have to go out of our way to report the campsite to the police," I said. "In case they got the idea that someone on the island was aiding and abetting a fugitive by bringing Will food and beer."

Binkie thought for a moment.

"Hypothetically, if I were representing any parties involved in the situation you describe, I would work with the district attorney to arrange immunity from prosecution on the aiding and abetting charges in return for providing vital evidence in a homicide."

"But if what you say is true, the campsite isn't vital evidence, is it?"

"To the extent that a defense attorney might use the campsite to muddy the waters in a trial, the police might find the true explanation of its origin rather vital, now wouldn't they, dear?" Binkie smiled gently.

I gazed at her round weathered face and wondered how many sharp young district attorneys had, over the years, come to grief by mistaking Binkie for a harmless, well-bred New England matron.

"So in the unlikely event that we found this hypothetical campsite, we could safely assume it had nothing to do with the murder?"

"I imagine you could safely assume it was abandoned three or four days before the murder," Binkie said.

And from the look on her face, I doubted we'd pry any more information out of Binkie. I stood up to go.

"Sorry to barge in," I said, looking at the Dickermans. I felt sorry for them. Not their fault, really, how Fred and Will had turned out; or if it was, they were certainly paying for it now. "I hope you can work things out with the power plant and all. I know Aunt Phoebe's not sold on it, but I'm sure a lot of people around here would hate to see it shut down or change hands."

"Don't worry, dear," Binkie said. She smiled—not the gentle smile I'd seen previously, but the sort of smile that made me feel very, very sorry for anyone who might attempt to take the Central Monhegan Power Company away from the Dickermans.

Just then, we heard frantic knocking at the door. Both of the Dickermans leapt to answer it, then returned almost immediately with Mamie and Dad at their heels.

"Ah, Mamie thought we'd find you up here!" Dad exclaimed. I was about to ask what he wanted me for, but then I realized he was looking at Binkie.

"Dr. Langslow suggested that we might want a couple of doctors to examine Resnick's body," Mamie said. "Just in case there's anything significant that doesn't . . . uh, last. Seemed like a good idea."

"Yes," Binkie said. "Provided you have some responsible witnesses to supervise the proceedings, of course."

"We thought perhaps you could do that," Mamie said.

"Of course," Binkie said. "Shall we go now?"

"Well, first we have to find John Peabody," Dad said. "He's the only other doctor we know of on the island, and we haven't seen him all day."

"Off finding a bit of peace and quiet, I imagine," Winnie said. Having met Mrs. Peabody, I imagined he was right.

"Winnie and I can find John, then meet you at the Anchor Inn," Binkie said. "We'll see you later, then," she told the Dickermans, and shooed the rest of us out. She and Winnie hiked off in search of Dr. Peabody while Mamie, Dad, Michael, and I took what Mamie assured us was a shortcut to the Anchor Inn.

"Oh, Meg," Dad said as we strolled. "Mrs. Peabody said you had her digital camera and could take some pictures."

"What a great idea," Michael said.

I rolled my eyes, wondering whether I really wanted to be involved in this.

Just then, we rounded a turn in the path and I caught sight of a cottage I hadn't seen before.

"Mamie," I said. "That's Rhapsody's cottage, isn't it?"

"Why yes," she said, beaming. "How did you know?"

"Just a lucky guess," I murmured.

Chapter 27

Touch Not the Puffin

Unlike Aunt Phoebe's cottage, which was just a small weathered saltbox, this really looked like a fairy-tale cottage. Rhapsody had painted it various shades of lilac and lavender, with blue trim. The blue tile roof hadn't weathered the hurricane well, and several of the blue-and-lavender shutters had come loose, revealing, rather than protecting, the small diamond-shaped windowpanes. Dead vines covered the front. The vines probably bore purple flowers during Monhegan's brief summer, but they looked pretty stark now. Still, the effect was charming, in a cloying sort of way. I half-expected to see Hansel and Gretel walk around from the backyard, munching on chunks of marzipan windowpane and gingerbread woodwork. The door knocker was shaped like a unicorn's head, complete with a wickedly sharp horn, and I wondered how many people had impaled themselves on it.

"Isn't it cute?" Mamie said.

"Very cute," I said. Mamie smiled and Michael looked puzzled. Only Dad had known me long enough to realize that I'd just uttered my ultimate insult, but even Dad wasn't tactless enough to say so.

"Look, we'll catch up to you in a bit," I said. "I want to talk to Rhapsody."

"What about?" Mamie snapped.

Damn. I'd forgotten how protective Mamie was of her pet artist.

"Mother's interested in a painting," I said. Well, it wasn't a complete lie; if Mamie chose to think I meant one of Rhapsody's paintings, that was her problem.

"I'll come with you, then," Mamie said. "She's very shy, you know."

"I'd like to meet her," Dad said, falling into step beside Mamie.

We slipped and slid up the cobblestone path—nature never intended cobblestones for use in hurricanes—and Mamie knocked very gently on the front door.

After half a minute, I saw motion out of the corner of my eye. The curtain in the window to the left of the door fluttered slightly. I deliberately avoided looking at it, and pasted what I hoped was a friendly, harmless smile on my face.

Mamie had raised her hand to knock again when the door opened slightly, with the sort of creak they use in movies to suggest that maybe this is a door you'd be better off not entering. But there wasn't a monster or a wicked witch hiding behind the door. Just poor Rhapsody, who peeked through the narrow opening as if she were the one expecting monsters.

"Rhapsody, we're so sorry to intrude, but Meg's parents want to buy a painting," Mamie said.

Rhapsody didn't seem reassured by Mamie's words, but after staring at us blankly for a few seconds, she opened the door a little wider and scuttled back to let us pass.

"I'll make tea," she murmured, and fled down the tiny hallway while Mamie led us into the living room. I instantly wished I'd suggested inviting Rhapsody down to the general store or to Mamie's house. Her decor gave me galloping claustrophobia. Not so much the furniture, although she had too much of it—fussy little chairs that would collapse instantly under anyone over a hundred pounds; rickety-looking tables about to overturn under their loads of knickknacks; spindly cabinets whose glass fronts bulged outward from the further hoard of knickknacks within. You could have sewed all the frayed antimacassars and antique doilies together to make several bedsheets, and from the number of puffin-related items among the knickknacks, I gathered that Rhapsody was Mamie's best customer.

And apart from the black and white of the puffins and the various wood tones, everything in the room was colored some shade of lavender, purple, or lilac.

Everything also carried a visible coating of dust. I sneezed four times while poking around the room to find a chair I would feel safe sitting on.

Mamie beamed with pride at the decor. Dad gazed at me, clearly awaiting brilliant deductions. I could tell Michael wanted to make a break for the wide-open spaces. I tried to stifle my sneezes by concentrating on the pictures on the wall. She had about thirty of them, all book covers or illustrations from the Puffin Family series. At the lower left-hand corner of every painting was Rhapsody's signature—a fussy, overelaborate design, barely recognizable as the letter R, in luminous purple paint.

Rhapsody emerged from the kitchen, wearing a frilly lavender dress that served very well as camouflage, considering her decor. She carried a tray, from which she handed out tea in eggshell-thin antique china. The idea of actually grasping the delicate gold-and-lavender handle of the cup was more than I could manage; I was sure to break it. Besides, I could tell from the smell that she'd made some kind of odd-tasting herbal muck. So I cleared a space among the fragile-looking knickknacks on the doily-covered end table, set down my cup, and tried not to watch what Dad was doing with his.

"By the way, before we talk about the painting, I have a question about puffins," I said.

"I don't really know that much about them," Rhapsody said, her voice hardly more than a whisper. "I just paint them."

"Yes," I said. "That's what I wanted to ask you about."

She smiled nervously. I got the idea that four people were

almost more of an audience than she could handle. I felt a sudden surge of impatience and claustrophobia and decided not to waste time beating around the bush.

"You had a dead puffin you used as a model, right?" I asked. "You kept it in your freezer."

She stiffened but said nothing.

"Oh, come on, Rhapsody," I said. "We saw you down by Victor Resnick's house on the day of the murder and——"

Rhapsody shrieked, burst into tears, and threw herself on the sofa. Mamie Benton hurried over and began patting her back.

"There, there," she said, glaring at me. "That wasn't a very funny joke, but I'm sure Meg didn't mean anything by it."

Mamie acted as if she'd caught me torturing a small child, which I suppose wasn't far from the truth. Dad had that "I'm disappointed with you" look, and even Michael seemed rather uncomfortable.

"I didn't do it on purpose!" Rhapsody wailed. "It was an accident! Honestly!"

Rhapsody lapsed into hysterical sobs. The others gaped when they heard her words, and Mamie froze, her hand still outstretched toward the sobbing woman's shoulder.

"You don't mean——" She gasped.

"Aha!" Dad said. "I knew you'd solve this!"

"She can't possibly have done it!" Mamie wailed. "Oh, this is awful!"

"Oh, for heavens' sake," I said. "Stop carrying on; what she's done may be perfectly legal."

"Perfectly legal!" Mamie exclaimed. "I'm sure you could argue that killing Resnick was morally justified, but even if it was self-defense——"

"Oh, do be quiet for a few minutes and let Rhapsody talk," I said. I strode over to the sofa and nudged Mamie aside so I could take her place beside Rhapsody.

"Rhapsody," I said in a firm, matter-of-fact tone.

She continued to sob. Dealing with sobbing members of my own sex isn't my forte. I began to wonder if we should send for someone better equipped to deal with the situation—though I had no idea who that might be. Mrs. Fenniman or Aunt Phoebe would only scare Rhapsody to death, and Mother would enjoy the drama and encourage her to sob for a few more hours. We had no time for that.

"For heaven's sake, stop sniveling and sit up," I said, pulling her upright and giving her a firm shake. "No one cares about the stupid puffin; we just want to know the whole story so we can clear this thing up."

She collapsed back on the sofa with such violence that she knocked over the end table. I could hear the tinkle of breaking glass and china. So much for the knickknacks and antiques.

Michael suddenly appeared, kneeling at our feet.

"Let me try," he murmured. I scooted aside to let him sit closer to Rhapsody.

"Now Rhapsody," he said, in soothing tones, taking her hands in his. "It's all right. No one wants to hurt you. We just need to know what happened so we can take care of things."

He went on in much the same vein while gently chafing her hands. He was making progress; her sobs grew less violent. She finally sat up, took the tissues Michael had ready, and began swabbing at her face with them.

"They'll arrest me," Rhapsody moaned, looking at Michael with an expression of adoration. I resisted the impulse to knock her down and jump up and down on her, yelling, "Mine! Mine!" Michael was, I reminded myself, an actor. The expression of tender concern on his face wasn't real. Still, I was irrationally relieved to see that Rhapsody was not one of those women who can cry charmingly. Her entire face was beet red, and I upped my estimate of her age by a decade.

"Arrest you for what?" Michael asked.

"They'll think I killed the poor little p-puffin," Rhapsody said, sniffling slightly. "They'll arrest me for harming an endangered species."

"Puffins? Nonsense, they're not endangered," I said.

"But there are only twelve puffin nests on Egg Island," she said.

"And a couple million healthy puffins flying around northern Canada and Greenland," I said. "Isn't that right, Dad?"

"Oh, yes," he said. "It's threatened in this habitat, of course; they've all moved farther north, where humans don't impinge on their breeding grounds. But it's not endangered. Not in the least."

"But I can see your point," I said. "The birders around here wouldn't take kindly to anyone killing a puffin. But of course you didn't, did you?"

"N-no," she said. "That horrible man did, with his electric-shock things. I was trying to sneak past his house to go down to the point, where I could watch the live puffins, and I saw the poor thing die when it landed on the roof, and it fell off and was just lying there, and I couldn't resist. He was always calling my drawings lifeless and mechanical, but all I ever have to work with are photographs and bird books. I thought maybe if I used a real puffin, it would help."

"And did it?" I asked.

"No," she said. "I couldn't even look at it without wanting to cry. But by the time I found that out, they'd made him stop using his electric-shock things, and he was chasing people out, and I didn't have a chance to take it back."

"So you kept it."

"Why didn't you just leave it somewhere else on the island?" Michael asked.

"Because Puffin Point's the only place on the island where anyone ever sees puffins," she said.

"And certainly the only place on the island where you'd expect to find one electrocuted," I added.

"Yes," she said, sniffing. "And when the hurricane came along, I thought I could just leave it there, and people would think it had washed up in the storm, and even if they figured out it had been electrocuted, they'd think he was at it again. I didn't even know he was dead until after I did it."

"That must have been quite a shock," I said.

"I was so terrified someone had seen me and would think I'd done it," Rhapsody said.

"Well, you should never keep quiet about something like that," I said in my sternest tone. "These things always come out in a murder investigation, and you're always better off if you tell the truth from the start."

Michael quirked one eyebrow. I rolled my eyes to show I realized how stupid and pretentious that sounded. But Rhapsody, Dad, and Mamie all nodded with great enthusiasm.

"So," I said. "Tell us more about the puffin."

Chapter 28

Anatomy of a Puffin

And so for the next half hour, Rhapsody told us about the sad fate of the puffin. Now that she'd confessed her dread secret, she was pathetically eager to spill everything. I waited patiently and let Michael respond to her description of how she'd found the puffin and what had occurred while she'd had it in her custody. I cared more about her two most recent visits to Resnick's house.

"So anyway," she said finally. "I hid the puffin under a cloth in the bottom of my wicker basket and went up the path toward that horrible man's house."

"Weren't you afraid of meeting him?" I asked.

"Oh yes!" she said. "So I found a place to sketch where I could overlook the path and see when he went down to the village. I think I ruined my sketchbook, sitting out in the rain all that time."

She gestured toward the fireplace, where a book bound in lavender velvet stood on end, its pages fanned open toward the thin warmth of her fire.

"I was just looking around the house, trying to decide where to put the puffin, when I heard a noise down on the shore. I thought at first it was Mr. Resnick, coming back from another direction, but when I ran back down the path, I almost knocked him over. So he hadn't been down on the shore after all."

"Probably the murderer," Dad said with obvious relish.

Rhapsody looked stricken, and her hands flew to her mouth, stifling a shriek.

"Nonsense," I said. "Probably only a birder, taking advantage of Resnick's absence to look for that rare whatsit that's nesting by his house."

"Yes, I'm sure that's all it was," Michael said, patting Rhapsody's shoulder again. I braced myself for more hysterics, but our reassurances—well, Michael's anyway—did the trick.

"Do you really think so?" she said, gazing up at him with an expression of frail, helpless innocence that would have looked perfect on the face of a Victorian maiden. For that matter, it had probably served Rhapsody rather well in her twenties.

"After all that, I'm amazed that you managed to go back the next day," I said. "That took a lot of courage."

"Well, I had nightmares all night," she said. "I knew I just had to return the poor little puffin so he could rest in peace. I decided that even if that dreadful man tried to stop me, I was going to march right down there and put the poor little thing somewhere near Puffin Point, where he belonged. And I did. Not near the house, of course; but I thought he belonged by the shore."

A pity she hadn't chickened out again; if she had, we wouldn't have wasted so much time on a red herring.

Rhapsody had no other useful information to offer, at least none we could extract during another twenty minutes of questioning, so I decided to call it quits.

"Well, we'd better run along," I said, standing up. Surely Winnie and Binkie would have found Dr. Peabody by this time. My head felt far too near the ceiling—doubtless an optical illusion created by the busy lavender-and-white-patterned wallpaper overhead.

"Oh, can't you stay a little longer?" Rhapsody said. To her credit, she was looking at me, with barely a sidelong glance toward Michael. "I could make more tea."

"No," I said. "But if you like, come down to the cottage if the rain lets up a little. We can talk more, and Mother would enjoy the company. She gets out so little in this kind of weather."

As we all milled about in the tiny front hall, poking one another in the noses with our elbows as we struggled into our rain gear in the confined space, a thought hit me.

"Oh, by the way," I said. "May I borrow your sketchbook?"

"My sketchbook?"

"Yes, the one you had the day you staked out Resnick's house. Who knows, perhaps something you sketched may give us a clue."

"Staked out Resnick's house," Rhapsody repeated. "Oh, yes, of course! Let me find something to wrap it in!"

We set out finally, with her battered velvet-covered sketchbook wrapped in several layers of plastic in my knapsack. Rhapsody stood in her doorway, waving a fond good-bye to us.

"Now look what you've done," Michael said. "I'm sure she'll come down to the cottage in a few hours, panting to know what clues you've discovered in her sketchbook."

"The sooner the better," I said.

"Do you really want her hanging around?"

"I want to get her into Mother's clutches as soon as possible," I said. "Now that Dad's home safe, Mother will start getting restless and looking for something to do. I think Rhapsody's just the thing."

"And what's your mother supposed to do with Rhapsody?" Michael asked.

"Well, either Mother will decide to take Rhapsody in hand or Rhapsody will be overwhelmed with Mother and begin imitating her. Preferably both. Rhapsody's an attractive woman, but I get the feeling she's been stuck in that Haight Ashbury Pre-Raphaelite-style garb since the late sixties. She could do worse than pick up some of Mother's style. And Mother would love to have a docile, cooperative protégée; she's certainly had no luck working her magic on me."

"Thank goodness," Michael said. "Much as I adore your mother, I like you just fine the way you are."

Well, those were encouraging words, I thought. Not to mention the look that went with them, which went well past encouraging. As a teenager, I'd always resented how easily Mother charmed my boyfriends. With some of them, I'd never shaken the feeling that they only took up with me in the hopes that ugly duckling Meg would eventually blossom into a swan like Mother.

Just then, Mamie, who had stayed behind to talk to Rhapsody, came out of the lavender cottage. She saw us standing there and strode up.

"I heard Jeb tell you to keep your nose out of this," she began.

"Yes, but when Mrs. Peabody insisted on dragging that miserable puffin up, I knew we had to do something," I said. "I mean, if we hadn't cleared this up, Rhapsody might have had to talk to the police!"

I tried to give my voice an authentic quaver, calculated to create the impression that Rhapsody was in genuine danger of being beset by the minions of the law, bearing handcuffs, rubber hoses, and truncheons. Whatever truncheons were. Mamie frowned, then nodded and walked off.

"Bring the damned camera," she said over her shoulder.

We followed Mamie to the Anchor Inn, where Jeb, Binkie, and Dr. Peabody already waited.

Considering how cold, wet, and miserable conditions still were outside, I found myself surprisingly reluctant to step inside the Anchor Inn. Get a grip, I told myself. It's dry, warmer than outdoors, and solidly built. Compared with some of the island buildings, the Anchor Inn, I felt sure, could withstand whatever huffing and puffing the departing Gladys could manage outside.

Yes, quite solidly built, and rather well insulated. Once we all stumbled inside and slammed the door shut behind us, the noise of the storm was a lot less overpowering. Almost muted. For some reason, that wasn't comforting. In fact, it was downright spooky.

"Quiet as a tomb in here," Jeb remarked. He sounded nervous.

"Let's not waste time, then," Dad said.

"This really isn't my specialty," Dr. Peabody said apologetically. "I'm a dermatologist."

Smart man, I thought. In grade school, when Dad had managed to give us the impression that as Langslows we were doomed to medical careers, Rob and I had debated at length what kind of specialist to become, our main criteria being the ease of avoiding dead bodies and large quantities of blood. I'd opted for psychiatry, but I had to admit dermatology seemed a reasonable choice for someone like Rob, who fainted at the sight of rare roast beef. Fortunately for the skins and minds of our countrymen, neither of us had actually allowed Dad to bully us into medical school. Evidently, Dr. Peabody's parents had found him more malleable. He looked greener than any of us, and we hadn't even gotten near the deceased yet.

Jeb led the way through the silent front room of the restaurant and back into the kitchen. We stood around looking at the door to the meat cooler as he fumbled through his pockets and finally located the key to the padlock holding the door closed.

"In here," he said after he'd unlocked and opened the cooler door.

Dad and Dr. Peabody peered in. I looked over their shoulders at the blanket-covered bundle on the floor of the cooler.

"Well, let's get him out here where we can take a look at him," Dad said.

Jeb and Michael looked at each other. Having taken my turn carrying Resnick's body when Michael and I first found it, I decided I could honorably wimp out this time and let the men do the heavy lifting.

"You'll need more light," I said. "I'll see if I can find some lanterns."

I uncovered a stash of oil lamps in a cabinet, and enough lamp oil to fill half a dozen of them. While I bustled about trimming wicks and lighting lamps, the four men, after a bit of nervous hemming and hawing, picked up Resnick and laid him on the long wooden table I had cleared. Binkie stood watching them with her arms crossed, looking stern and vigilant.

Dad whisked back the blanket to reveal the late Victor Resnick. He didn't look much like the distinguished figure on the back of the book I'd bought. From our brief acquaintance, I suspected the angry expression on his face was a lot more characteristic than the lofty, noble, far-seeing expression the photographer had captured. His face was pale and had a sort of weird bluish color to it. His eyes were open, and his hair and beard wildly disheveled. The impulse to run screaming out of the room fought in my mind with an irrational urge to close his eyes, smooth his hair, and remove a little bit of seaweed tangled in his beard.

"Hmm," Dad said. That knocked some of the fright out of me, and replaced it with irritation. I hate it when doctors do that. "Hmm" can mean just about anything. "How soon can I get this disgustingly healthy person out of my office and go on to someone with an interesting ailment?" or "Yikes! How can I possibly break it to her that she's got maybe six weeks to live?" or "Chinese or tacos for lunch?" Give me a doctor who babbles out exactly what he's thinking.

Dr. Peabody looked faint. He examined the body visually, but from rather a distance, with his hands clasped tightly behind his back. Dad was doing his Sherlock Holmes act, inspecting every inch of Victor Resnick with great attention. Jeb scrutinized the Anchor Inn's kitchen fixtures as if he planned on buying the joint. Michael was snapping pictures frantically. Only Binkie and I paid attention to Dad's examination. I wondered what he found so interesting about Victor Resnick's fingernails.

"Let's turn him over," Dad said after a while.

Binkie and I supervised again while the men did the turning.

Dad repeated his detailed inspection on this side of Resnick, with particular attention, naturally, to the head wound, which didn't look all that bad now. I thought I had seen quite a lot of blood on Resnick's head when we first found him floating face-down in the pool, but there wasn't much when you looked at it close-up. Had a lot of it washed off while we were hauling him up here to the Anchor Inn? Or had I overreacted when I first saw him—when I thought, for a heartbeat, that it might be Dad. Close-up, the wound looked so small that I wondered how it could have been fatal.

"Very interesting," Dad said at last. "Let's turn him over again."

"So, did he die of drowning or from getting hit on the head?" Jeb asked when the body was right side up again.

"Neither," Dad said.

"Neither? Then how the blazes did he die?"

"Electrocution."

Chapter 29

I Am the Only Running Puffin

"Electrocution?" we all chorused.

"How can you tell?" I asked.

"See this small burned spot?" Dad said, indicating the corner of Resnick's mouth. "And this discoloration?" He pointed to the fingernails.

"Don't tell me those tiny burns killed him."

"No, undoubtedly the ventricular fibrillation killed him."

"The what?" Jeb asked.

"Ventricular fibrillation?" I echoed, stumbling over the half-familiar term. "Isn't that what they do in emergency rooms to revive people?"

"That's defibrillation," Dad said. "If a person's heart has stopped or is irregular, you can use a controlled electrical current to get it started, or steadied. But if you take someone with a normally functioning heart and subject them to an electrical shock, it can slow or stop the heart, or mess up the rhythm. Can be fatal."

"So that's why in emergency rooms they always yell, 'Clear!' and make sure no one's touching the patient before they try to defibrillate," I said.

"Oh, right," Jeb said, nodding. "I've seen that on TV."

"Essentially, yes," Dad went on. "Most people who die in low-voltage electrical accidents don't die from burns; it's the v-fib that kills them."

"Dr. Peabody, what do you think?" Jeb asked.

"Oh, Langslow's diagnosis sounds fine to me," Dr. Peabody said. "Electrocution, definitely."

"You can really tell that, without an autopsy?" I asked.

"Well, not for certain," Dad said. "We won't really know for sure until the local ME does a formal autopsy. But I'd put my money on electrocution."

Dr. Peabody nodded vigorously and glanced at his watch.

"What about the wound to the head?" Jeb asked.

"Superficial," Dad said. "If he walked into my office with that, I'd have given him a few stitches and had his family watch for signs of concussion."

"Can you tell what did it?"

"A rock, most probably," Dad said.

"Not a stick?" I said, thinking of Aunt Phoebe's walking stick and the NO TRESPASSING sign reposing back in the cooler. "Or a board?"

"Oh, no," Dad said. "Much too jagged for either of those."

"Could the blow have knocked him out?" Jeb asked.

"It's not impossible," Dad said. "But unlikely, I'd say. And even if it did knock him out, it wouldn't have caused his death. Unless he fell on a live wire when he lost consciousness."

"And he didn't fall on a live wire; he fell into the tidal pool," Jeb said.

"Unless someone put him there," Michael suggested. "To make it look as if he'd drowned."

"Or unless there was an electrical charge in the tidal pool," I said. "Remember how the birders accused Resnick of shocking the puffins to scare them away from his land? According to Jim Dickerman, he did run a charge through some of the metal parts of his roof to keep the birds from sitting on it and messing it up. But I only saw seagulls on his roof. Puffins are waterbirds—so maybe he ran a wire along the shoreline."

"And the gash could have happened if he was thrown back by

the shock," Dad said. "In fact, considering the angle, I'd say it was probable."

"Good heavens," Jeb said. "Maybe it wasn't murder after all. Maybe the whole thing was a horrible accident. Probably reached in to retrieve his precious NO TRESPASSING sign, not realizing that the power was on."

He suddenly looked very cheerful. Obviously an accident, however horrible, would cause the town a lot less trouble than a murder.

"I don't suppose you could rule it a death by misadventure," he said.

"The coroner may, when he or she gets here," Dad said. "I have no jurisdiction. Still, I shouldn't be surprised."

He looked so downcast that I was almost tempted to pat him on the back and say, "Never mind, Dad; I'm sure we'll find you another murder soon."

"It's possible," I said instead. "But until they're positive, I'm sure the police will take every precaution. Treat it as a possible homicide until they're sure it's not."

"She's quite right," Dad said, brightening again at the thought that the investigation would continue, even if it was only pro forma.

"And while you're at it, why not take a look at the dead puffin?" I asked.

"The puffin?" Dad echoed. "Why?"

"Evidence," I said. "I'm sure the police will want to know how and when it died. Just to confirm Rhapsody's story."

Jeb pulled out the puffin and Dad bent over to examine it.

After blinking once in surprise, he shrugged and began giving the puffin the same careful scrutiny he'd previously given Resnick.

"Good thing Meg already figured out that Rhapsody had it in her freezer, or I'd worry about him," he said, jerking his thumb over his shoulder at Resnick.

"I think he's past worrying about," I said.

"I mean, from the point of view of an accurate autopsy," Dad said. "Could complicate things if you'd been running the meat locker cold enough to freeze the body. But, of course, you already figured out that the puffin was frozen elsewhere."

"Because of plumage," Michael put in.

"The plumage?" Dad said, looking blank.

I explained about the breeding plumage.

"Oh, very good!" Dad exclaimed. "Actually, I wasn't thinking of the plumage at all; it was the texture."

"Your medical expertise confirms Meg's deduction, then?" Michael asked.

"Actually, it's my culinary expertise," Dad said. "From my bachelor days. You can tell by the limpness that it's been thawed," he said, waggling one of the puffin's legs in a disgusting fashion. "And from the smell that it wasn't thawed recently enough to be safe," he added, bending over to smell the puffin and wrinkling his nose.

"It's not an entrée, Dad; it's evidence," I said with exasperation.

"Although I do hope we're not having poultry tonight," Michael murmured.

"Can you tell how the puffin died?" I asked. "Was it electrocuted, for example?"

"Can't really tell without an autopsy, which I don't suppose you want me to do," Dad said, looking around with an eager expression. Jeb shook his head, and Dad sighed.

"Could be electrocution," Dad said. "Could be a lot of things."

"Well, it's probably irrelevant to Resnick's accident anyway," Jeb said.

"Look, about this accident idea," I said. "How do we know it was an accident? I mean, even if you assume he had the bad luck to touch something electrified during one of the rare moments yesterday when we had power, what was the something? And if you think he had some kind of electrical bird trap hooked up among the shoreline, where is it?"

"Probably washed away with the storm," Jeb said.

"Possibly, but why didn't Michael and I see it when we found the body?"

"You saw the wound, and you were looking for something that could have hit him," Dad said. "You probably didn't see the bird trap."

"I'd have noticed," I said. I glanced at Michael for support.

"She did look around," he said. "She said that the tide was about to cover up the crime scene, and she looked around very carefully so she could describe it later."

"A really strong electrical shock could have thrown him back some distance," Dad said. "Maybe whatever shocked him wasn't all that nearby. If he touched something, got a shock, and fell back into the pool, landing on a rock that caused the gash, and then floated to the other side of the pool . . ."

"Hell, maybe it was a lightening bolt from the storm," Jeb put in.

"It was a hurricane, not a thunderstorm," I said.

Jeb shrugged.

"Well, whatever it was, it's gone now," Dad said, patting my shoulder.

"Maybe the waves got it and washed it away just before we got there," Michael said. "They were awfully close to washing Resnick away by the time we found him."

"We'll let the mainland authorities worry about it," Jeb said.

Everybody took that as a signal that the examination was over. I followed them out of the cooler, still irritated.

"You don't look very pleased," Michael murmured to me.

"Oh, I'm thrilled," I said softly. "Dad's just removed any need for us to run around the island investigating the murder."

"What's wrong with that?"

"We still haven't found James Jackson, the biographer, remember? Even if they rule the death accidental, he'll probably try to capitalize on it. If it really was accidental."

I tried not to take my irritation out on him, but I suspect it still showed. Was it just hurt pride, because I'd failed to notice Resnick's electrical contraption lying around? Or was there something to my feeling that this was suddenly turning out much too easy?

Jeb secured the meat locker again and we left the Anchor Inn. Dad and Dr. Peabody strode ahead, eagerly sharing the news with everyone they met.

"I'm sorry," Michael said as we followed along more slowly.

I shrugged.

"Well, maybe after this, Dad will stop bragging about my detective abilities," I said.

"Not necessarily," he said, with a chuckle. "You did figure out about the puffin."

To my relief, Michael had the good sense not to keep trying to cheer me up, and we hiked back to Aunt Phoebe's cottage in companionable silence.

Word of Dad's and Dr. Peabody's findings spread throughout the island, and within half an hour people began turning up at the cottage for a spontaneous celebration. People swarmed up and down the stairs, carrying all the lawn furniture and yard ornaments up to the bedrooms, which would make bedtime a whole lot of fun. Jeb Barnes was one of the first to arrive, and he brought along a case of cheap champagne.

"I got through to the Coast Guard!" he announced over the popping corks.

A ragged cheer went up from the twenty or so people gathered around the crate, and Rob asked, "When's the ferry going to start running?"

"Maybe tomorrow, maybe Tuesday," Jeb said. "They're going to wait and see. But the Coast Guard will bring the police over from the mainland tomorrow so we can tie up all the loose ends about Resnick's death."

Another cheer, this time accompanied by clinking glasses.

Death. No one was calling it a murder any longer. Even Dad seemed to have gotten over his disappointment that our homicide had turned into death by misadventure. Jim had the generator running again, and Dad put a collection of big band music on the portable player. I was the only one not in high spirits. After all, even if the police declared the death an accident and eliminated the danger of assorted members of my family being arrested for murder, Resnick was still news. James Jackson, the biographer, was still here on the island, sitting on the latest draft of his manuscript. And I suspected that whether he'd uncovered the truth about Mother's past or jumped to a totally wrong conclusion wouldn't matter to a pack of reporters hungry for sensational headlines. We had to find Jackson and deal with him, somehow, before he made his story public.

Dad was telling a group of birders some kind of story. From his gestures, I deduced he was describing Resnick's wounds.

"Absolutely understandable," I heard him say during one of those chance lulls in the general noise level. I saw several of the birders glance my way. "Electrocution is remarkably hard to—"

Drat. I'd hoped no one had noticed my ineffectual attempts to play detective, but from the looks on the birders' faces, I suspected they had all noticed. Irrational of me to resent that. Equally irrational to resent Dad's not being around earlier to give his verdict on the cause of death.

I glanced around the party, trying to convince myself that everyone present wasn't pointing at me and snickering at my failure. I saw that Rhapsody had arrived and, as I expected, had immediately become enthralled with Mother. She followed Mother around, literally sitting at her feet, absorbing her every word and gesture as if the fate of the world depended on it. She had already picked up some of Mother's mannerisms. Mother, of course, was eating it up and acting even more charming and elegant than usual.

Damn. On top of everything else, I didn't need to feel like one of Cinderella's ugly stepsisters.

"Don't be so gloomy," Michael said, handing me a glass of the champagne. "Aren't you glad it turned out to be an accident?"

"It isn't an accident until the police say it is," I said. "Sorry, I don't mean to take it out on you."

"I understand," he said. "It's not as if you can take it out on your dad; he didn't mean to get lost just at the one moment when we really could have used his expertise. Look, don't worry so much about Jackson; I'm sure we'll figure out some way to——"

"Great news," said Kenneth Takahashi, appearing beside us. "I mean, I'm sorry the old goat's dead, but thank God it was an accident."

I noticed that Takahashi had learned one thing from the birders at least. He had grasped the concept of protective coloration, and now he wore clothes as faded and mud-stained as the best of them.

"Well, don't let your guard down yet," I said. "Some of the birders would still give you quite a hard time if they knew why you came here."

"Oh, that's all right," he said, waving his glass genially. "If they ask me what I do, I'll tell them I'm in land use. Sounds vaguely conservationish. They seem to like that. They keep trying to feed me."

I had a sudden mental image of birders trying to coax him out of a tree with handfuls of sunflower seeds and cracked corn.

"Pity there isn't a decent restaurant on the island," he added.

"Is that your latest development project?" I asked, fearing the worst.

He shuddered.

"Good heavens, no!" he exclaimed.

"That's good," I said. "I think the people who come here like roughing it a little."

"Obviously," he said. "Each to his own; me, I plan to do everything I can to make sure I never have to come back here in my entire life. Up till now, my idea of roughing it was staying at a hotel without a four-star restaurant nearby."

Somehow, I had a feeling that Ken Takahashi's rather jaundiced view of Monhegan would soon make the rounds to every real estate development firm on the East Coast. Which should do much, I thought with satisfaction, to discourage any other developers who might have their eyes on the island.

"That reminds me of something," Michael said. "Could I have a word with you?"

He dragged Takahashi off into the corner and the two of them began an animated discussion about something. I leaned back and tried to concentrate on a yoga breathing technique that was supposed to improve one's mood.

"Meg?"

Of course, you had to do the breathing for a little more than ten seconds before it started to have any effect. I bit back an oath and opened one eye. Rob stood in front of me.

"Dr. Peabody and that other birder want their digital cameras back," he said.

"We have to give the photos to the police," I said.

"But if it's not a murder . . ."

"We don't know that until the police say so," I said.

"But can't we just—"

"No."

"I could download the photos if you like," Rob offered. "Then we could just give the data files to the police."

"Good idea," I said. "Want to do it now, since the power's on?"

Rob looked plaintively at his champagne glass.

"Then I'll hold on to them until you're ready," I said. I picked up the knapsack containing cameras in question then stormed into a corner, where it was quieter.

Get over it, I told myself. What harm would it really do to let them have their silly cameras? I took the other birder's camera out of my knapsack and began flipping through the photos. I was brooding over one that showed the fateful tidal pool when Mother came up behind me and looked over my shoulder.

"Oh, what a lovely view of the shore," she said. "You should print that out and have it framed, dear."

I wondered if I should tell her that this picture showed where we'd found the body of her late beau. Better not, I decided. I flipped to the next photo, one of the tidal pool from a slightly different angle.

"I liked the first one better," Mother said. "More unspoiled."

I peered at the photo. It looked much the same as the first, except that in one corner you could see a tiny flash of orange.

"I know the electricity makes it so much easier, especially for the islanders who live here year-round," Mother said. "But I do wish they'd find a way to bury the wires, instead of having all those blue pipes and orange extension cords all over the place. So . . . untidy, really."

I opened my mouth to explain the impossibility of burying pipes and wires in the island's rocky terrain, then closed it again.

Mother was right. An orange extension cord.

I flipped through the rest of the photos. The extension cord appeared in several, snaking down toward the tidal pool. No wonder all the birders thought Resnick had been killing puffins. They *had* seen some kind of electrical gadget near the tidal pool.

I closed my eyes and thought back to how the pool had looked when Michael and I had found the body. No, I thought. I'd have seen an orange extension cord. It hadn't been there.

Who had moved it? And when? And for that matter, exactly where had the extension cord come from? Hard to tell from this angle. For all I knew, it came from out in the ocean.

I had to go back to Resnick's house and see.

Chapter 30

The Scene of the Puffin

I grabbed two flashlights, snagged one of Dad's hiking knapsacks, stuffed the digital cameras inside, and went in search of Michael.

I found him backed into a corner, enduring a lecture from two birders.

"—vital for every educated citizen to take action!" one of them was exclaiming as I walked up. He shook his finger in Michael's face. "We cannot afford to sit idly by and watch these large corporations—"

"Sorry," I said, coming up and taking Michael's arm. "Hate to interrupt you, but we have to be somewhere, remember?"

Michael started and looked at his watch.

"Oh, sorry . . . yes . . . have to run," he said as we backed away. From their expressions, I could tell the birders wanted to ask what kind of urgent appointment we could possibly have elsewhere on the island at this time of night.

"Hurry!" I stage-whispered to Michael.

We made it to the front door, grabbed two ponchos from the pile of several dozen identical drab, damp ones, and slipped out onto the front deck. Michael looked surprised when I turned on my flashlight, pulled up my hood, and headed for the driveway.

"We're not really going anywhere, are we?" he asked.

"Oh, would you rather stay here and talk to the bird-watchers? I got the distinct impression you didn't mind being rescued."

"I would rather be with you any day, even if it means circum-navigating the island again," he said with an exaggerated bow.

"Only it's night, not day; and it's still rather cold and wet out here. Couldn't you have found some way to rescue me that didn't involve going outdoors?"

"We need to go back to Resnick's house," I said. "Something's bothering me."

"What?"

"I'll show you when we get there."

We hiked along in silence. I concentrated on not tripping and falling down, or at least not landing in any large puddles when I did so.

Maybe I shouldn't have dragged Michael out on this wild-goose chase, I thought. For all I knew, he might be getting tired of my amateur attempts to solve the murder and protect my family. But I felt better with his tall form striding along beside me. Not safer, really—I wasn't expecting any danger—just more natural. The idea of going back to Resnick's house, or anywhere else on the island, for that matter, and not having Michael along seemed unthinkable. Quite a remarkable change in attitude for me; stubborn independence and the need for a certain amount of solitude had always been my hallmarks. How odd, I thought, then put the subject away for further consideration after the present crisis. We'd arrived at Resnick's house.

It definitely hadn't fared well. Rain had ruined the finish on the polished wood floor of the entry, and the wood itself had buckled in several places. When we entered the living room, we startled several birds roosting on the exposed high beams of the cathedral ceiling.

"We should chase the damn things out," I said.

"They'd only get back in again," Michael said. "Besides, I thought you hated this place. Wanted it torn down."

"Yes, but I feel bad just seeing it fall apart like this. Even if it is a pretentious eyesore."

"Is that what we came back for? To make sure Resnick's place isn't falling apart? Or something about the biography?"

"No, it's about the murder."

"I thought we found out it was an accident, not murder."

"We found out it was electrocution instead of a blow to the head," I said. "The accident or murder question is still open. Very open."

"Okay," he said. "So what are we looking for?"

I pulled out the digital camera and showed him the best shot of the tidal pool.

"See that?" I asked, pointing to the orange cord.

"So what?" he said. "They're underfoot all over the island, as the state of my poor mistreated shins can testify. Along with those pestilential pipes."

"Yes, but there wasn't one there when we found the body," I said. "And I don't remember seeing one when we searched the house before. I want to make sure."

"We came up here in the middle of the night to search the house for orange extension cords?"

"Humor me," I said. "Please."

Was my idea so off-the-wall that even Michael wouldn't take it seriously? To my relief, he smiled, shrugged, and began rummaging through the hall closet.

Searching the house didn't take that long. I took the kitchen, while Michael did the rest of the house. Sooner than I expected, we met again in the living room, empty-handed.

"Nothing here," I said.

"The shed!" Michael said, snapping his fingers. "We forgot the shed."

"I hadn't forgotten it," I said. "I'm working up my nerve."

"Strikes you as a little creepy, does it?" Michael said.

I nodded as I pulled my hood over my head and turned for the entrance.

"No reason to feel that way," he said, following me. "Just because Resnick's body was there for—what, half an hour? No reason to get squeamish about the place."

"You're right," I said. "Then I assume you'll have no problem dining at the Anchor Inn if we come back to Monhegan next summer? It's probably the best restaurant on the island."

"On the other hand," Michael said, "who am I to criticize a perfectly normal human reaction?"

"I thought so," I said, throwing open the shed door.

It took us only five minutes to make sure the shed concealed no orange extension cords. Stumbling around the yard with our flashlights took more like half an hour, but still no extension cords.

"Tide's still fairly low," I said. "Let's go down to the shore."

It was still a little wet, but we reached the tidal pool, and after a great deal of peering back and forth between the photo and the landscape, I identified the place where I'd seen the orange electric cord in the picture. I wasn't surprised to see that instead of running along the shore toward Resnick's house, it would have climbed up the cliff toward the center of the island.

"That's odd," Michael said.

"Very odd," I said. "For one thing, it was on the inner side of the pool, so how could it have washed away before his body?"

"And for another, what was it connected to?" Michael said. "Do you suppose the old skinflint ran the extension cord up there and tapped into the power line before it hit his meter?"

"I don't think he ran that extension cord anywhere," I said, craning to look up. We were out of sight of the village, and Resnick's house was dark. The only light I could see was a thin ray shining down from high above us. Probably from the ridge at the top of the island. It reminded me of the glint of light I'd seen when we'd found the body; the glint I'd thought was the reflection from a birder's binoculars.

"Of course," I said. "It's obvious who did it; I'm an idiot not to have seen it sooner."

"I still don't see it, whatever it is," Michael said. "Care to give me a clue?"

"Jim Dickerman," I said. "He's the only one who could have done it. When we thought someone had whacked Resnick on the head, we had too many suspects. Anyone on the island could have done that. In fact, Aunt Phoebe did. But now that we know he was electrocuted, there's only one possibility. Jim. No one else could possibly have arranged for the power to come on just when Resnick reached into the tidal pool. He could wait until Resnick touched the water and then flip the switch to turn the generator on. He may have boarded his windows up, but I bet he left enough chinks to see through."

"And his motive?" Michael asked quietly.

"He was afraid of losing the power plant, of course. He didn't know about Binkie negotiating restoration of bail. All he knew was that Resnick was going to take away his precious power plant, and all his mechanical toys. He could easily have rigged the extension cords going down; no one would pay any attention to Jim doing something electrical. Maybe he was the imposter the birders kept talking about, if he slung his binoculars around his neck when he came down here to do it. He probably planned to wait until Resnick picked up the cord. Aunt Phoebe throwing in the sign was just another fantastic bit of luck. Remember how at least one time that day the power came on for only a few seconds? I bet that was him, throwing the switch that killed Resnick."

We stood there for a few moments, watching as the receding waves uncovered more and more of the rocky ledge.

"You're right," Michael said. "It's the only logical solution. Brilliant."

"Thanks," I said. "Come on, we've got work to do."

"Are we going up to the power plant to confront Jim?"

"Are you crazy? You're definitely watching *way* too much TV," I said. "That's the sort of stupid thing that gets people killed, or at least gets them into the kind of trouble that they can't get out of until just before the last commercial. We'll tell the police tomorrow and then let them confront Jim."

"Then what are we doing?"

"Burgling Resnick's studio," I said, opening my knapsack and pulling out the ropes I'd brought.

"But why?" Michael asked. "If we're sure Jim is the murderer—"

"We still haven't found James Jackson," I said. "I want at least a chance to talk him out of mentioning Mother in his wretched biography. And the studio's the only place we haven't looked where Resnick might have left some clue to Jackson's identity, and tonight's probably the last chance we'll have to search before the police arrive tomorrow. With the press hot on their heels, no doubt."

"Let's get it over with, then," Michael said.

Chapter 31

Abandon Puffins, All Ye Who Enter Here

I'd spotted a useful tree next to Resnick's studio. One branch spread over the yard, where we could throw a rope over it and shinny up, while another was perfectly positioned for using the same rope to climb through the broken pane of glass in the studio roof.

Actually doing all this proved a lot harder than we expected.

"I hadn't realized how long it's been since I've climbed a tree," I said as I examined the knees, elbows, and palms I'd skinned during our travels.

"Obviously, there are significant gaps in my fitness program," Michael said from where he sat on the floor, puffing. "Please tell me we're going to figure out a way to leave at ground level."

"We can probably unlock the door," I said, limping over to it. "Damn, I think it needs a key on both sides."

"Try that," Michael said, pointing to a key on a hook a few feet from the door.

"Perfect," I said. "Voilà! Our exit."

"Unlock it, and leave the key in the lock," Michael said. "In case we need to make a quick getaway."

"Good idea," I said. "And let's take the rope down, too, so no one passing by will spot us."

"The place has glass walls," Michael said. "Anyone passing by will spot us even without the rope. Even if we only use our flashlights."

"Well, if we take down the rope, at least we can pretend we found the door open and we didn't actually break into the place."

"That's what I like about you," Michael remarked. "Your finely honed sense of deviousness."

We teased the rope out of the tree, and I buried it in the very bottom of my knapsack, where you could hardly see it beneath the Gatorade, first-aid kit, flare gun, water, and candy bars. Michael was groping around the walls of the studio.

"What are you looking for?" I asked.

"The light switch," he said. "If we're going to pretend we found the door open, we may as well search in comfort, instead of creeping around with our flashlights like burglars. Ah, here it is."

The lights came on, and we both turned to survey the studio.

And saw Mother. Two Mothers, in fact; both nude and staring straight out of their canvases at us. One stood, her weight resting on one hip, her head cocked to one side, and a petulant look on her face, as if she were about to open her mouth and complain about how long she'd been standing there, and ask how much longer was this going to take. The other sat on the side of a bed, her arms raised, her hands either putting up or, more likely, taking down her hair, and judging by the look on her face, any words she was about to say would be edited out for broadcast on network television.

"Oh my God," I moaned. "More of them!"

We continued to search the studio, under Mother's watchful eyes, and turned up several more nude Mothers, stacked against various walls. Mother lying on a red velvet couch with a black velvet ribbon around her throat, rather reminiscent of Manet's *Olympia*. Mother, seen from above, sprawled in a giant claw-footed bathtub. Mother holding an old-fashioned large porcelain doll that somehow just barely managed to avoid covering any erogenous zones.

After a while, I began turning the paintings to the wall. The cumulative effect of so many naked Mothers unnerved me.

"Somehow I don't think we're going to have much luck hushing this up," I said, sitting down in the middle of the studio and burying my head in my hands. "Between the damned biographer and these ghastly paintings—Oh!"

"What?" Michael asked, looking up from another painting.

"Well, we've solved the mystery of the disappearing bedroom rug anyway," I said, pointing to the Oriental rug beneath me. "Of course, we still have the mystery of why he dragged it out here."

"Are you sure it's the same rug?"

"Well, I see little bits of white carpet fuzz sticking to the underside," I said, examining the back of the rug.

"Redecorating, I suppose," Michael said, shrugging.

"All my best clues turn out to be useless," I complained.

"This is weird, too," Michael said. He had pulled out another painting and was staring at it with a puzzled frown.

"What?" I asked. I glanced over. Michael stood between me and the painting, but I could see that this nude Mother was waving a gauze scarf, which I somehow suspected would emphasize, rather than conceal, anything of potential prurient interest.

"Would you look at this!" he said.

"Do I have to?" I replied. "I'd really rather not. I've seen enough. Much more than enough, actually."

"You haven't seen anything like this," he said, stepping aside so I could see the latest painting.

I glanced up, expecting to see another smiling, unblushingly nude Mother. I was right about the scarves; they left absolutely nothing to the imagination. But instead of Mother's face, I saw a patch of blank canvas.

"Has he painted out her head in that one?" I asked.

"More like he never painted it in at all," Michael said. "Or could he have taken the face off with turpentine or something?"

I went over and looked at the head. Or rather, the lack thereof.

"No, if he'd wiped off the head, he'd have taken the background, too," I said. "But that's still perfectly fine."

"All ready to paint the head in," he said. "This is really weird."

"And she's standing on the migrating rug," I pointed out.

Michael nodded. He moved the nude with scarves aside, revealing yet another headless nude, this one posing brazenly in a clearing in the woods. Resnick had finished the background in elaborate detail, right down to a bee hovering above a clover blossom in the grass and the delicate fluff of a dandelion in the nude woman's hand. But again, no head. The coloring of the skin and body hair made it obvious that the woman was blond, and she definitely had Mother's tall, slender build. But the head was completely missing.

"What the devil's going on here?" I muttered.

Michael began to move the latest painting aside. A piece of paper fell from behind it, and he stooped to pick it up.

"You know," he said, glancing at what he'd picked up. "This may sound crazy, but—"

"Put your hands on your heads!" barked a voice from behind us. "And don't move!"

Since the two halves of that order were obviously contradictory anyway, I decided to risk turning around as I raised my hands.

Jim Dickerman stood in the studio doorway, holding a gun.

Assuming we survived the night, I was going to have a long talk with Dad. He was always so excited at the idea of my investigating a real murder case. But here, I would explain to him, we had a perfect example of why this was such a stupid hobby. If you go around trying to hunt down criminals, some of them resent it, and sooner or later they take matters into their own hands.

"Should have known your snooping would cause trouble," Jim said.

"Don't be a fool, Jim," Michael said in his most earnest, persuasive tones. "You'd never get away with it. Just put it down."

It sounded sensible to me; I'd have dropped my gun in a heartbeat. Jim wasn't buying it.

"If I have to shoot you, I'll just put the gun back in my brother's truck and they'll think he did it," Jim said.

"You'd set up your own brother for a murder rap," I exclaimed. I still felt guilty enough over setting my brother up for a disastrous blind date, and that was years ago. Jim, however, shrugged casually.

"If I have to. Back up a bit," he added, gesturing slightly with the gun. "And lie down. Facedown. And stick your hands up behind your backs."

We followed orders. Then he walked over to Michael's side. I braced myself. Was he going to shoot Michael? Should I throw myself at Jim? Then he dropped something by Michael's head. A roll of duct tape.

"You," he said, obviously meaning me. "Tape his wrists."

He backed up and pointed the gun at me while I did as he ordered. And then he made me lie back down again, and he taped my wrists.

I should have been terrified that I was probably about to die, but instead, I found myself fuming over the fact that he'd taped my arms behind my back. Don't male thugs ever stop to think that although lying on your stomach on a hard wooden floor may not be relaxing for men, it's downright torture for any woman with larger than an A cup? Obviously not. I growled to myself and shifted slightly so I could see what Jim was doing. I had a hard time looking over my knapsack, which lay open just in front of my face. The knapsack—was there anything in it I could use to get us out of this?

Jim puttered about the studio, looking for things. I noticed he was wearing work gloves, which meant he wouldn't leave any telltale fingerprints.

Not worth worrying about, I told myself. If things got to the point where the police were looking for fingerprints, I'd be past caring.

He dragged something out in the middle of the floor—a rather ancient-looking kerosene space heater. He rummaged about some more until he found a large tin can. He unscrewed the can, filled the heater most of the way, then dropped the can. Some kerosene spilled out, but apparently not enough for his purposes. He picked up the can, poured the remaining kerosene on the floor, then dropped the can again.

While Jim did this, I scanned the contents of the knapsack for possible weapons. Gatorade, rope, compass, first-aid kit—alas, Dad's emergency survival plans had never included exchanging gunfire with armed desperadoes. I could try the flare gun, of course, but I had no idea if it would do any damage, even assuming I got a chance to snatch it up. And I wasn't even sure I could fire it, since my hands were taped behind my back. Still, I had to try. First, though, I'd need to distract him.

"You're not really going to burn down the studio, are you?" I asked.

"Why not?" Jim said. He was rummaging through the trash can, pulling out paint- and turpentine-stained rags and scattering them about the studio. But not at random—he was making a path. Toward the back of the studio, where I could see what looked like a gas generator.

"You'd destroy the work of a great artist," I said. Yes, definitely a path; now he took a can of turpentine and shook splashes of it along the path.

"Yeah, right," Jim said. "They've got museums full of his art; they won't miss what's here. All looks alike anyway; the old bastard hasn't painted anything new in forty years."

Michael began laughing.

"Oh no?" he said. "Take a look at one of those canvases before you light the torch."

The sight of his bound, helpless captive convulsed with laughter must have roused Jim's curiosity. He glanced around at the canvases—all of which I'd turned to face the wall. He went over to one of the easels and turned the canvas around. It was the picture of Mother taking down her hair. His eyes widened, his jaw dropped, and I seized my chance.

I rolled over so my bound hands could reach the knapsack, scrabbled until I had the flare gun, and then rolled the other way and fired when I thought I had the gun pointed in his general direction. I missed—big surprise—but the flare passed close enough to his head to startle him.

Unfortunately, firing a flare gun in a room filled with spilled kerosene and paint-covered rags wasn't exactly a move that would endear me to fire-safety experts. The flare hit one of the easels, then skittered into some of the spilled kerosene, setting it on fire and splashing Jim's jeans, which also caught fire.

He yelped with pain and began beating at his pants with both hands. Not the best idea when you're holding a loaded gun; the gun went off, though, to my disappointment, he didn't actually shoot himself in the foot.

He turned and ran to the door. Michael and I were awkwardly struggling to our feet. Jim fired several wild shots in our direction—causing us to fling ourselves back on the floor—then yanked the key out of the lock, opened the door, and ran out while Michael and I were still struggling to our feet again.

"We've got to stop him, damn it!" Michael cried, and ran for the door like a charging bull.

Too late. I heard the key turn. Michael twisted at the last minute and threw himself at the door, trying to break it down with his shoulder.

"Oww!" he yelled as he fell over.

"Are you all right?" I called.

"I think I've broken my shoulder," he said. "Please tell me that the door cracked or something."

"It looks the same as before," I said, jumping as something—an aerosol can, I think—exploded across the room.

"That always works in the movies," he said, lurching to his feet again.

"They use wooden doors in the movies," I said. "Not metal ones. Maybe we should tackle the glass."

"And impale ourselves on glass shards?" Michael said. "Maybe we can kick the door in."

He began trying, but I could tell from his expression that the effort hurt him a lot more than it did the door.

"Maybe we need a battering ram," he muttered, looking around, without success, for something large enough to serve.

The fire was spreading rapidly. I had to dodge a few stray patches of flame to make my way to the largest canvas—the standing portrait of Mother. I backed up to it, got a grip on it, and began dragging it toward the nearest glass wall.

"Don't worry about saving the damned art," Michael said.

"We're not saving it; we're sacrificing it to save ourselves," I said. "Here, help me wedge it up against this glass wall."

"What good will that do?" he asked.

"It may keep me from being impaled on shards when I try to break the glass," I said.

"Brilliant," he said. "But let me do it; I'm heavier."

He backed up and ran again, this time at the painting. I noticed he led with his other shoulder. I heard a cracking noise.

"Let me take a turn," I said.

Instead of running, I gave the painting a few swift karate kicks. I could hear glass shattering; after half a dozen kicks, we pulled the painting away and found a space large enough to climb through.

"After you," Michael said.

"Keep your eye open," I said. "Remember, Jim's out here somewhere with the gun."

We both managed to climb out, then crouched down and ran for some nearby bushes. Starting nervously at every stray noise, we sat back-to-back and I pulled the duct tape off Michael's hands. He was just untaping mine when something exploded. The flames, which had grown steadily, suddenly shot ten feet into the sky at the back of the studio. We both leapt to our feet and backed up some more.

"Reached the kerosene stove, I guess," Michael said.

"That or the generator," I agreed.

"Are you okay?"

"I'm fine," I said. "I'm a mass of cuts, bruises, scrapes, and burns, and I think I singed off a few inches of hair on one side, but I'm alive."

"We're both alive, thanks to you," Michael said.

I had hoped for a more enthusiastic demonstration of gratitude, but Michael stood there for a moment, looking at the fire, frowning. Then he reached in his back pocket and took out his wallet.

What on earth?

"With any luck, the fire will destroy all of those very interesting paintings," he said. "But we still have a few loose ends to tie up."

He took a piece of paper out of the wallet. I recognized it: the map, the one with Dad's printing on it that I'd found at the murder scene.

"We don't need this anymore," he said, and he wadded it up and threw it at the fire.

"Michael!" I said, launching myself at him.

"Watch the shoulder," he said.

Making allowances for his injuries, I found the demonstration of gratitude that followed quite satisfactory. At least the beginning of it; after a few minutes, the Monhegan volunteer fire department arrived and we postponed any further celebrations until their departure.

Chapter 32

Much Ado About Puffins

"I think the coast is clear," Michael said as he shook me awake.

"Or as clear as it's going to get," I said, peering out the door of Resnick's garden shed, where we'd taken refuge until the crowds died down. Jeb Barnes had drafted most of the spectators into the search parties that were, even now, combing the island for the missing Jim. Only two people stood guard by the studio, and both of them were swathed in wraps, huddled against a tree, and, most important, facing in the other direction. We slunk across the lawn and paused in the shadows outside the entry to make sure no one had seen us. The guards hadn't moved.

"Some guards," Michael muttered. "Probably asleep. And why did they have to leave guards at all; do they really think Jim's likely to come back here?"

"No, but given the way everyone feels about Resnick's house, I think they want to make sure it doesn't go up in smoke, too."

"And this would be a bad thing?"

"No, as long as we get one more chance to snoop around before it happens. After all, Jim proving himself the murderer only solves one of our problems. There's still the biographer to deal with. Before he or she tries to capitalize on the notoriety of Resnick's death. Maybe if we can get into Resnick's computer, we can find a clue to the biographer's identity."

"Actually, I think I know his identity," Michael said, giving me a hand through the broken glass into Resnick's front hallway.

"You do!" I exclaimed. "Who?"

"I'll tell you in a second. Stay here while I check out something."

"But——"

"Humor me, just this once," he said.

So I stood in the hallway while Michael padded softly into the living room.

"Aha!" he called back. "I thought so."

"Thought so what?"

"Resnick's biographer is no longer in any condition to reveal anything," Michael called back.

"You don't mean——"

"Yes," Michael said. "Come and see who is——or rather, was—— writing the biography."

I took a deep breath and walked into the living room, expecting to see a bloody corpse lying on the floor. Instead, I saw Michael. He held up an eight-by-ten print of a photo——the photo of Resnick that had appeared on the back of the book of paintings.

"You mean Resnick?" I said. "He's the biographer?"

"Bingo," Michael said, setting down the photo.

"How do you know?"

"Well, right at the moment, it's sort of a hunch, but now that the power's on, I bet we can find the drafts of the thing in his computer."

"Okay," I said, reaching for the switch to turn on the computer. "So you think it was an autobiography?"

"No, I think he wanted it published under a pseudonym, so it would look like a genuine critical biography."

"Fat chance," I said. "Only one person in the world has that high an opinion of Victor Resnick. That should have given us a clue right there."

"Too true."

"Yeah, and I guess if he planned to reveal the scandals of his youth, it was a lot easier to pretend that someone else had dug it up, instead of having to face the criticism if anyone like Mother objected. It makes sense, but I still don't understand what gave you the idea that Resnick was the biographer."

"The paintings," Michael said

"The paintings? What about them?"

He held up his hand to show me a smear of blue paint on the palm.

"He did those paintings recently," Michael said. "Recently enough that the one we used to help escape from the studio was still wet——I got this on my hand helping you carry it."

"You're sure it wasn't just melting from the fire?"

"No, the painting wasn't hot when we picked it up, and it wasn't wet on the surface——I put my finger on a blob and paint squished out. That's what happens when you put on a thick layer of oil paint; it dries from the outside in."

"But how does that explain the headless paintings?" I asked. "He was getting them ready, but he couldn't do the heads until Mother showed up? It's not as if he could use the present-day Mother as a model, you know."

"I also found this," Michael said, plucking something out of his shirt pocket.

A faded photograph of Mother as a teenager. Clothed. In fact, she wore the same bathing suit we'd seen in Aunt Phoebe's photo album.

"I suspect we've just solved the mystery of the missing photos," he said. "And maybe he only recently managed to get into your aunt Phoebe's cottage to filch these."

"Everyone kept telling us he painted from photos," I said, shaking my head.

"Yes, and that his style hadn't changed appreciably during his whole career," Michael said. "So if he just waited until they dried, who would have any doubt that they were older paintings?"

"I think they have ways of figuring out the age of a painting," I said. "For example, do you really think they're still manufacturing the same oil paint, canvas, and varnish he used forty or fifty years ago, with no modern improvements that would show up in an analysis?"

"But why would they even bother if they got it from the artist and it was clearly in his style?"

"Yes, and why would anyone bother to forge a Resnick when for the same amount of effort they could forge the work of someone a lot more famous? And for that matter, does it really count as forgery if the only thing false is the date he painted it?"

"I don't understand why he painted them in the first place," Michael said. "Was writing about his youth making him nostalgic? Or did he think he had to have some paintings of the people involved to prove the truth of his biography?"

"More likely, he just wanted to stir up trouble," I said. "That's perfectly in character. In fact—my God, that's it!"

"What's it?" Michael said.

"Consider the detective's report."

"You're right," Michael said, his shoulders slumping. "That doesn't add up. I can see why he would have the detective's report on your mother, maybe to try to find out what she'd done with her life after they'd parted. But why those other women— unless maybe it was camouflage," he added, looking up with a hopeful expression.

"No, I think the detective's reports were just what they looked like—he wanted to find out more about those women to see who could be his long-lost sweetheart."

"But surely he knew who she was."

"Not if he invented the whole love affair," I said. "And wanted to find out which woman had a gap in her life that would match the story he'd made up."

"Made up? But why? That's an absolutely crazy idea!"

"Crazy like a fox," I said. "I know exactly why he did it. Just look at that stack of books on his desk."

"Books?" Michael said, glancing over. "They're art books; wouldn't you expect a painter to have them?"

"Yes, but these aren't books with pictures of paintings. They're biographies. The one on top's a dead giveaway: a biography of Andrew Wyeth."

"So?"

"So remember the whole Helga thing? When Andrew Wyeth revealed that for fifteen years he'd been painting this beautiful redheaded model without his wife knowing it? And suddenly, he's on the cover of *Time* and *Newsweek*. Of course, I don't know if it did Wyeth's career good or harm in the long run, and I don't suppose it would ever have occurred to Resnick that Wyeth might be a better painter. All Resnick saw was that after the Helga paintings came out, Wyeth got more media attention than he could handle. And Resnick wanted some."

"And what better way to get it than to rake up an old scandal and suddenly reveal that he's got a collection of highly erotic paintings featuring a beautiful underage model," Michael said, shaking his head. "It's tailor-made for the tabloids."

"And I bet there's not a word of truth in it anywhere. Look, there're also books about van Gogh, Picasso, Franz Liszt, and even Byron, for heaven's sake. He was going for notoriety."

"So let's search his computer and see what we find," Michael said, hitching a chair up to the desk.

What we found was six earlier drafts of the book, stretching back over a period of two years.

"Obviously practice doesn't always make perfect," I said. "I don't think his drafts were getting any better."

"Oh, I don't know," Michael said. "I don't recall seeing this bit about her turquoise eyes rolling on the floor in the draft we found. Sounds more like a game of marbles than a love scene."

"Sounds painful, if you ask me. Yes, and some instinct for self-preservation made him take out all the bits about him nurturing other artists' careers. I somehow doubt that he even met Keith Haring and Basquiat, much less nurtured them."

"I think we've pretty well established who the biographer is," Michael said. "Now we have to decide what to do about it."

I sighed. For my part, I wanted to reformat the hard drive and burn every scrap of evidence that the biography had ever existed. But I had a dreadful feeling Michael wouldn't consider this ethical.

"What do you think we should do?" I asked, and braced myself for an answer I wasn't going to like.

"Reformat the computer and burn every scrap of paper," Michael said readily. "Don't you agree?" he asked, seeing my jaw drop. "I mean, we have to reformat it; you can recover deleted files with a good utility program. We can back up the nonbiography stuff to diskettes before we do it."

"Sounds great to me," I said. "But I wasn't sure you'd see it that way."

"We know Jim Dickerman killed Resnick," Michael said. "At best, all this stuff will only embarrass your family. At worst, Jim's lawyer could use it to cast doubt on his guilt."

"What about the painting?" I asked.

"We'll take it with us."

"Take it with us?"

"The old coot owes us something," Michael said. "After all, we solved his murder, at considerable personal risk."

"And if someone catches us with it?"

"We've got the bill of sale from your grandfather's files, remember?"

"I like the way you think," I said, grabbing an armload of papers and heading for the fireplace. "Let's do it."

"No, no!" Michael said. "Not that fireplace; do you want everyone on the island to see? We'll use the one in the bathroom—there's no window in there. You work on the computer; I'll take care of the fire."

I sat and watched the computer grinding away, first backing

up Resnick's other files—there weren't many—then reformatting. Michael ferried armload after armload of papers back to the bathroom fireplace.

"How's it going?" he asked, coming up behind my chair and putting his hands on my shoulders.

"Nearly there," I said. "How's the fire?"

"It'll take a while," he said. "But I figure we'll have to hang out here until all the firemen go home or fall asleep, so that's no problem." He straightened up and went out into the kitchen.

Checking for papers there, I assumed. Probably not a bad idea. I heard a sudden loud *pop* from the kitchen.

"Michael?" I called. "Is something wrong?"

"Everything's fine," he said, reappearing with two filled champagne flutes. "Absolutely fine."

"Isn't that Resnick's champagne?" I asked.

"Yes, and a very fine one at that," he said, handing me one flute. "Like I said, the old coot owes us one. To our host!"

"To our host!" I echoed, and sipped the champagne.

"Why don't you take these in and keep an eye on the fire?" Michael said, handing me his flute. "I'll see what we have in the pantry. Oh, and I found a jar of bath salts; goodness knows what Resnick wanted with that."

The bathroom was warm and wonderfully scented. Steam rose from the tub, and the fire blazed away merrily. From the size of the paper mound, I knew we'd need quite a few hours to burn them all. And who knows how many glasses of champagne.

"To our host," I said again, raising my glass. And then I fed a few more pages of the biography into the fire and kicked off my sneakers.

Chapter 33

Hair of the Puffin

"You'd think after all we went through to steal the damned painting, we'd get a little gratitude," I muttered.

Gaahhh! replied the seagull to whom I was speaking. I sighed and fed another handful of trash into the rusty barrel that served Aunt Phoebe as an incinerator. Given Monhegan's astronomical trash-removal fees, most residents only paid for hauling away things they couldn't possibly burn or feed to the gulls. As a kid, I'd always adored the giant trash fire that marked our last day on the island.

Of course, as a child I'd never had to burn the trash with a raging champagne hangover. Or all by myself. The police had dropped in to question us far earlier than I'd planned on getting up. Then Dad hauled off both Michael and Rob to help him with a project, leaving me stuck with all the chores and errands that Mother, Aunt Phoebe, and Mrs. Fenniman together could think up. At least as long as I stayed down here at the water's edge burning trash, they couldn't dump any more work on me. And it was relatively quiet. And I was getting very, very good at feeding trash into the fire without moving my throbbing head or, for that matter, opening my eyes.

Pyromania was a lot more fun last night, I thought, examining my fingers, whose tips still looked faintly prunelike, although the garbage and kerosene had long since overpowered the faint lingering scent of the bath salts.

I closed my eyes. Yes, the aspirin had begun to work. I'd given up trying to recall last night's rapture; all I asked was a slight lessening in the severity of my headache.

"Good Lord, there's more trash now than when I left," came Michael's voice, startling me out of my concentration.

"Last day's like that," I said, stirring up the fire in the barrel and managing a feeble smile. "Heard anything more from the police?" He shook his head, and I breathed a sigh of relief. Luckily for us, the police had found searching for Jim much more inter-esting than poking though Resnick's house; they'd taken at face value our story of rescuing papers and paintings by hauling them into the wine cellar. And I suspected he'd had a word with the younger of the two detectives to explain the still-damp sunken tub.

"Your Dad's been running us ragged, going all over the island taking pictures with the digital cameras and downloading them into your brother's laptop," Michael said, massaging his shoulder. He'd been at the aspirin bottle, too.

"Pictures of what?"

"Resnick's house, the Anchor Inn, the place where we found the body—everything. Documenting your latest detective tri-umph, as he calls it."

"Good Lord," I muttered. "He does remember that those aren't his cameras, doesn't he?"

"Yes, eventually we filled up Rob's hard drive and had to give the cameras back to their owners," he said. "And by the way, it's still looking good for the ferry tomorrow, or possibly even this afternoon," he added. "In fact, your Dad went up to the cottage to get everyone started packing. We should probably head up there, too."

"Give it a few minutes," I said. "I want to stay out of Mother's way right now."

"Why?"

"She's presenting Dad with a late wedding present, and I'm wondering how he's going to like it."

"A late wedding present?" Michael echoed. "What?"

"The painting."

"The painting—my God, you've got to be joking!"

"No. Hang on, here they come."

They strolled out onto the deck, Mother limping gracefully, with the support of Dad's arm. Dad was beaming from ear to ear.

"Oh, good," I said. "I think he likes it."

"She must not have presented it yet."

"Yes, she has; see, I can see the back of the easel through the window; the cloth's thrown back."

"Your father's a strange bird," Michael said, shaking his head. "This is not how I would react under these circumstances, a fact I hope you'll keep in mind if any lecherous painters express an interest in immortalizing your charms quite that completely, with or without your cooperation."

"I'll definitely keep that in mind," I said. "Shove another wad of trash in the barrel, will you?"

"In fact," Michael said, warming to his subject, "I'm not even sure—What the devil's this?"

He held up a piece of paper and stared at the half-dozen giant purple letter *R*'s writhing and curling across its surface.

"Well, what does it look like?" I asked, suppressing a smile.

"It looks like Rhapsody's signature."

"Yes, it does, doesn't it?"

"Dozens of signatures," he said, picking up another stray piece of paper.

"Yes, it took quite a few tries before we got it right," I said.

"Got what right?"

"Rhapsody's signature, of course. Mother and I worked at it for several hours before we finally decided I could do it well enough to try it on the canvas."

"By canvas, I presume you mean the portrait of Mother?"

"Naturally. How could Dad possibly object to Mother commissioning a female painter to do a glamour portrait of her as a young woman as a present for him?"

"Oh Lord," Michael said, closing his eyes.

"Of course, that does leave us with one small problem," I said.

"Dare I ask?"

"We haven't quite figured out what to do with the painting we bought from Rhapsody," I said. "I mean, we needed it to copy the signature from, and we bought the biggest one she had so we can pack the two paintings together and sneak the portrait off the island that way. But we haven't quite figured out what to do with it when we get it home. I don't suppose you'd like a larger-than-life portrait of a puffin, would you?"

"What's he doing—sledding, trimming Christmas trees, mowing the lawn?"

"Nothing silly like that. It's a nature study, not an illustration from one of her books. He's just sort of loitering about on the rocks, with a dead fish dangling from his beak. Very picturesque."

"No thanks," he said. "Unless, of course, you have developed an inexplicable fondness for the thing and want to see it on a regular basis."

"No," I said. "I'd be just as happy never to see it again."

"I'll pass, then," he said. "Although if you need a place to hide it, I'd gladly offer my attic. Or my basement. When I have an attic or a basement again."

"I'll keep it in mind," I said. "Oh my God!"

"What?" he asked, whirling about. With Jim still loose somewhere on the island, everyone startled easily.

"Rhapsody's coming," I said. "Help me stuff the rest of the forgeries in the trash barrel!"

We were backing away slightly from the roaring blaze that resulted when Rhapsody reached us. And unfortunately, Dad spotted her and came dashing down the path. Mother fixed me with a gimlet eye and raised an eyebrow in a signal for me to deal with the situation.

"What a wonderful painting!" Dad exclaimed as he reached us. "I can't tell you how much it means to me!"

"Why . . . thank you," Rhapsody replied. She was pleased, although obviously a bit taken aback by the force of Dad's enthusiasm.

"It's a masterpiece," Dad said, taking both of her hands in his and shaking them vigorously. "It really transcends everything else you've ever done."

"Do you really think so?" Rhapsody said. "I wasn't sure it worked, really. It's the first time I've done anything like it, and the first time I've worked from life, so to speak."

"Well, you should do more like it," Dad said. "Truly astounding. The skin tones are absolute perfection!"

"Skin tones?" Rhapsody echoed in a puzzled voice.

"Of the feet and the beak, I suppose," I murmured in an undertone. "He tends to anthropomorphize."

"And the way you've captured the fur!" Dad went on.

Rhapsody's confusion deepened.

"Fur, feathers—he gets them mixed up when he's this excited," I stage-whispered.

"I know we'll always treasure it as a reminder of a special time in our lives," Dad said.

"Yes, it has been quite a weekend—" Rhapsody began.

"Dad," I broke in. "When are you going to show us the painting?"

"Show us?" Michael repeated, his voice so strangled, it was almost a squeak.

"Why—" Dad's jaw suddenly dropped, and he blushed bright red. "No," he said, finally. "It's . . . well, it's rather personal. I'm sure your mother would rather not. You understand," he said, looking at Rhapsody and then retreating back to the cottage. Mother smiled her thanks at me as she followed him inside, and for the next few minutes we could hear the fuss and bother Dad kicked up as he ransacked the cottage in search of a quiet, discreet place to hide the painting.

"Personal," Rhapsody repeated.

"He's very sentimental about presents Mother gives him," I improvised. "Hides them away where he thinks no one but the two of them can find them. And keeps them forever; she's learned the hard way never to give him anything edible. Bottles of vintage wine turned to vinegar in their closet; ten-year-old chocolate truffles petrifying in the bureau drawers. A nuisance, I suppose, but we've always thought it rather sweet."

"Yes, I see," Rhapsody said. "I'm sure that's very nice for your mother. So many men aren't sentimental at all. Well, I must be going. Oh, I almost forgot. Mamie sent me up here to tell you that the ferry's definitely going this afternoon, and she has your tickets, but you'd better come down soon and claim them before someone else does."

"Right, thank you," I said. Rhapsody headed back to town, looking back now and then as if she wasn't quite sure what to make of us.

"Will you consider me an oaf if I confess that I ate the chocolate dinosaur you sent me last week?" Michael asked.

"I'd consider you an idiot if you hadn't," I said. "You didn't really buy that nonsense about the ten-year-old chocolate, did you?"

"Just checking," Michael said. "And if I ever bring you a bottle of vintage wine, I'll bring a corkscrew, as well."

"Now you've got the idea," I said. "Let's go down and claim our tickets before the birders filch them."

Chapter 34

A Farewell to Puffins

We hustled everyone down to the docks, only to find that the ferry wasn't taking off quite as soon as originally planned. Another Coast Guard cutter had arrived, carrying more police to join the search for Jim. A dozen or so police and Coast Guarders swarmed all over the docks, inspecting every piece of luggage larger than a hatbox and affixing stickers over the latches and fastenings of the containers when they finished. Loading the ferry would definitely take longer than usual.

Michael, Dad, and I arranged the family's luggage in a giant mound along one side of the dock and ordered Rob to guard it.

"I wish we could persuade him to relax a little," I said, glancing over to where Rob sat.

"Rob or Spike?" Michael asked, following my gaze.

Rob had perched on top of a trunk, with the strap of his laptop over one shoulder and Spike's leash wrapped around the other wrist. He clutched the wooden crate containing Mother's portrait and Rhapsody's puffin painting—clutching it so tightly with both hands that his knuckles had turned white. Spike strained at the leash, barking at a seagull that seemed to enjoy sitting just out of his reach, on top of another larger crate that someone was shipping some paintings in. And someone with more courage than sense had managed to paste one of the police inspection stickers to the back of Spike's head.

"Spike's a lost cause," I said. "But you'd think Rob could control his nerves better."

"Yes," Michael said. "Someone should explain to him that the key to pulling off a daring daylight art heist is to look nonchalant and unconcerned."

"I did," I said. "Several times. We'll just hope they chalk up that anxious, furtive look to worry about his computer."

"I wouldn't count on it," Michael said. "Luckily, with Spike around, even the police won't want to get close enough to question him."

"I just wish Rob would move away from that other crate," I fretted. "It's so obviously a painting-shaped crate; what if someone notices the similarity in shape and makes the connection?"

"Don't worry; we do have bills of sale that will serve for both paintings, remember?" Michael said.

"I'm not worried that they'll think we're stealing it; what if they insist on unwrapping it out here on the dock?"

"We'll insist they take it inside, out of the rain," Michael said, jerking a thumb at the ramshackle baggage shed near the end of the dock. "Oh, hang on a minute; there's Ken Takahashi. I need to ask him something."

He strolled over to the other side of the dock and greeted Takahashi. I wondered what they kept finding to chat about. Suddenly, they both glanced over at me. Takahashi pulled something out of his inside jacket pocked, scribbled on it, and handed it to Michael. Then they laughed and shook hands.

No one talked to me, of course. I'd blown the whistle on Jim, and apparently some of the birders had dubbed him a hero. An environmental warrior, doing battle against a bloodthirsty bird-killer. I more than half-suspected they might help him hide. I hoped the police realized this; they'd have to keep a sharp eye out when the ferry began loading, in case someone tried to sneak Jim aboard in their party.

The birders were also taking up a collection, although the reason for donating varied from birder to birder. Some thought they were contributing to Jim's defense fund, others to a fund to rescue the Central Monhegan Power Company, and a few to the expense of tearing down Resnick's house and restoring Puffin Point to its natural, unspoiled condition.

I found myself resenting the great outpouring of sympathy for Jim and the Dickermans. After all, no matter how nasty Victor Resnick had been, that didn't give anyone the right to kill him. Not to mention trying to kill Michael and me, which they were all conveniently overlooking. And had it dawned on anyone that if I hadn't already fingered Jim as the murderer, they'd probably all still be stuck on the island being questioned and investigated? Or maybe they didn't resent me for fingering Jim, just for losing him. Yes, that was it; they thought it was my fault we were looking over our shoulders nervously every five minutes while the police ransacked our luggage.

And then there was Michael. He was astonishingly cheerful about leaving. Granted, this hadn't exactly been an ideal vacation. And looking back, I realized that I had rather neglected him, taken him for granted while we chased up and down the island looking for miscreants and lost relatives. But still, did he have to look so damned happy about escaping? Had last night made up for the several miserable days before it, or would this weekend manage to kill our grand romance before it really got off the ground?

"Hello!" came a soft voice from my elbow.

Rhapsody. With luggage.

"I didn't know you were leaving the island," I said. "I thought you stayed here year-round."

"Well, usually I do," she said. "But the puffins are gone for the winter, and who knows when they'll manage to arrest that horrible murderer? So when your mother invited me to visit all of you in Yorktown, I thought, Why not?"

"How nice," I said with as much sincerity as I could muster. Had Mother gone mad? For that matter, had she completely forgotten how many stray relatives we already had staying with us? And with Rhapsody underfoot, how could she continue to pull the wool over Dad's eyes about who had painted the nude?

"I'm so excited," she said. "I'm so looking forward to studying you."

"Studying us? Why?"

"Well, you mostly."

"Me?"

"Yes," she said, beaming. "You've inspired me!"

"Inspired you how?"

"I'm planning a whole new series of books based on you!"

"On me?" I squeaked.

"Yes!" she said, clasping her hands. "You'll be a friend of the Puffin Family, a brave and clever girl detective! Can't you just see it?"

Unfortunately, I could. Did she really mean a girl detective, or did she plan to puffinize me? Either way, I could see it all too clearly: a tiny, round Meg conversing stiffly, in profile, with little Petey and Patty and all the beady-eyed members of the Happy Puffin Family. Probably carrying a magnifying glass and wearing a deerstalker hat. I supposed I should have been happy that someone wasn't mad at me, but the idea of becoming a badly drawn cartoon character filled me with despair. *The Puffin of the Baskervilles* didn't sound so funny now that I thought it might become a reality.

Rhapsody must have noticed my lack of enthusiasm.

"Don't you like the idea?" she asked.

She looked so fragile that I couldn't bring myself to confess how much I hated it, so I settled for saying, "Well, I'm having a hard time seeing myself as a puffin."

"So was I," Rhapsody confessed. "So I've decided to branch out. I'm going to make you an owl! A wise, clever owl!"

Well, marginally better than a puffin, I thought.

"And Michael will be a falcon!" she added, eyes shining.

I managed to keep a straight face, but I suddenly felt very sorry for Rhapsody's editor—she had an editor somewhere, didn't she, seeing that she never went beyond a certain level of inanity? I had a feeling the editor would have quite an eye-opening experience when Rhapsody's first owl and falcon adventure landed on his desktop, no doubt seething with barely repressed eroticism.

"Don't you think murder's a little much for a kid's audience?" I asked.

"Oh, yes," she said. "So I'm going to start with having them find Patty Puffin's little lost kitten."

Did she have any idea what a real owl or falcon would probably do to a little lost kitten if they found it? Oh, well. Editor's problem, not mine.

I glanced down. Rhapsody was making a few tentative sketches of her owl detective. They were, alas, enough like me to be identifiable. In fact, if I crossed my eyes and pasted feathers all over my face, the likeness would be uncanny.

I made a solemn vow to evict the sculptor squatting in my studio within the next two weeks, even if I had to break the doors down and hire a forklift to move his fifteen-foot work in progress.

"Well, I guess we'll see you back for the trial," Jeb said, coming up to shake my hand.

"Assuming they ever find Jim," I said.

"He'll turn up sooner or later," Michael said, rejoining me.

"That's so," Jeb said. "Hard to hide that long on an island this small. Course, they'll probably have the trial over on the mainland. Don't want to inconvenience all the summer folk."

"I'm sure we summer folk will all be properly grateful," I said.

"Well," he said, clearing his throat. "Some of you aren't so bad. Time comes that you want to get away from the craziness over there, you call one of us up. Someone'll have a room free."

With that, he nodded and stumped away up the hill.

"I'm not entirely sure, but I think that counts as an extravagant compliment," I said.

"Sounded that way to me," Michael said.

"A pity we couldn't just convince Mother to leave the painting here until the trial," I said. "When there won't be quite so many police swarming around."

I glanced back at Rob, who still crouched by the painting, looking so guilty that I wasn't surprised several Coast Guarders had already come up to check his ID. Spike was still barking obsessively at the seagull.

No, actually the seagull had flown. Several other seagulls perched nearby, but Spike ignored them. He was barking obsessively at the crate.

The crate. I strolled over, trying to look casual, and inspected it. About six feet tall, four wide, and maybe a foot deep. I glanced from it to several of the Coast Guard officers and then back again. Tight quarters for a grown man, but if he was desperate enough . . . I glanced at the label. One of the New York galleries whose name I'd seen in Resnick's files. No return address. No official stickers or labels to indicate what shipping company would claim it on the mainland, though it did have one of the ubiquitous inspection stickers plastered rather haphazardly on one side.

I flagged down the officer in charge of the Coast Guard squad.

"Did your people really open this to inspect it?" I asked.

"Didn't need to," she said, frowning at me in irritation. "It was in the baggage shed over there. Been locked up there all night. Can't you keep that thing quiet?" she added, gesturing at Spike.

"I'd check that one again," I said. "Guy you're looking for has a brother who does a lot of the local baggage hauling. I wouldn't be surprised if he had a key to that shed."

Her head snapped around. I could see her measuring the crate with her eyes. And then she barked orders at several of the enlisted men around her. They lowered the crate gently on its flat side and then, with a couple of police standing by, weapons drawn, two of the Coast Guarders began prying at the top with their chisels.

With a snap, the lid popped open and the Coast Guarders shoved it aside. Jim Dickerman lay sprawled in an X shape, like a giant squashed bug, blinking in the sudden light.

"Jim Dickerman?" asked one of the police.

"That's him," Jeb said.

"Miserable mutt," Jim growled. I almost opened my mouth to point out that I, not Spike, had finally convinced the Coast Guard to open the crate, then thought better of it. I'd made it my new policy never to annoy suspected murderers—at least not ones with whom I still shared a planet.

Jim had obviously hidden in the box for hours; he was so stiff that several of the police had to help him up.

"You have the right to remain silent," the policeman began as mingled cheers and catcalls from the crowd drowned out the rest of the Miranda warning. Several overexuberant birders came to blows and fell into the water in the excitement, which gave the Coast Guard something to do while the police handcuffed Jim.

"A flighty bunch, these birders," Michael remarked. "A few minutes ago, they were all calling Jim an environmental martyr, and now some of them are happy to see him arrested."

"Well, they're not stupid," I said. "They may sympathize with what they think he's done, but they're not eager to have an armed fugitive running around the island."

"Look what I've got!" Dad said, trotting up, beaming.

"Puffins," I said, closing my eyes. He carried an assortment of plush stuffed puffins in all sizes.

"A souvenir of your latest adventure!" he said.

"Where do you want me to put the rest of them?" Mamie Benton said. I could see two local men behind her, both carrying boxes of stuffed puffins.

"What a splendid idea!" Mrs. Peabody trumpeted. "Do you have any left?"

"A few," Mamie said. "And of course I can always take your orders and have them shipped directly to your homes."

The birders, led by Mrs. Peabody, began swarming into the gift shop and trickling out with large parcels for the Coast Guard to inspect.

Adding half the contents of Mamie Benton's store to the already-substantial load destined for the ferry made it doubly difficult for the captain and his crew to embark. We took off a full hour later than planned, close behind the Coast Guard cutter carrying Jim, and even then, one woman came running up the gangplank at the last minute, clutching an armload of puffin coasters and tea towels.

I spent the intervening hour, and most of the crossing, being congratulated by the birders, having my picture taken with them, and autographing their stuffed puffins. I think I had liked it better when they avoided me. Spike took a violent dislike to the entire puffin tribe, and he barked whenever he saw one. I could see his point of view. The birders finally gave me some peace and quiet when I managed to drop a rather large stuffed puffin down where Spike could get hold of it. He immediately pounced on it, buried his teeth in its neck, and spent the rest of the trip noisily trying to dismember it. The birders all found this either so shocking or so entertaining that they finally left me alone.

"Good Lord," I said as we approached the Port Clyde docks, where the Coast Guard cutter had just landed. "It's a media circus over there."

We could see three or four television sound trucks and a police line holding back several dozen people laden with cameras and notebooks.

"Well, the man wasn't completely unknown," Michael said.

"Unheralded Genius of the Down East Coast," I muttered, shaking my head.

Luckily for the rest of us, the press latched onto the police, their prisoner, and Binkie Burnham. The older cop said about two sentences, and then Binkie took the floor, making a folksy but no-nonsense statement. The reporters scribbled and filmed madly. Most of the birders stood around watching, some of them hoping, no doubt, to use their proximity to a notorious murder to capture their allotted fifteen minutes of fame.

Michael and I collected our baggage and crept round the edge of the crowd, hoping to make it to his convertible before anyone spotted us.

"Oh, there you are," Dad said, appearing at our side with a double armload of stuffed puffins. "Can you find some space for a few of these?"

We piled our luggage in the trunk, then filled the remaining space, as well as the space behind the seats, with puffins.

"I might have a few smaller ones that could fit in the crevices," Dad said, and headed back for the docks.

"There you are," Rob said, appearing on the driver's side of the car just as Michael opened the door. "Why don't you take him back with you?"

"Well," Michael began.

Spike, spotting the pile of puffins behind the seat, began barking and straining at the leash.

"With all these stuffed puffins?" I said. "You've got to be kidding. Besides, we're not going directly back to Yorktown. Michael has to get back for his classes, and I have to evict that damned sculptor."

Rob tried on his patented pitiful look. Impressionable coeds eat it up, but Michael and I were immune.

"See you," Michael said, getting into the driver's seat.

"Later," I added, taking the passenger's side.

Rob slouched off, dragging Spike behind him.

"Good thinking," Michael said. "By the way, what do you say to a small detour on the way home?"

"What kind of a detour?"

"Well, did you know that Coastal Resorts owns a small but very exclusive hotel outside Rockport? About an hour south of here."

"Oh, is that what you and Kenneth Takahashi were talking about?"

"Yes, and Ken feels very grateful to us," Michael added as he started the engine. "So he gave me a voucher for three nights' stay. I think we should drop by on the way home and check the place out. See if we want to come back and stay there sometime."

"Not tonight, of course," I said. "Because you have to get back to teach your classes."

"Oh, no; we'll just cruise by and check it out, and then head straight on home. Assuming we don't have car trouble again, of course. I really don't like the sound of that knocking in the engine."

"What knocking?" I said, cocking an ear. I heard only the usual smooth purr of a well-maintained engine.

"You're not getting into the spirit of the thing," Michael complained as he guided the car through the rut-infested gravel parking lot, heading toward the exit. "I'm sure if you try, you can hear it."

"Now that you mention it, I do hear a funny noise," I said with a chuckle. "Although I would have called it more of a ping than a knock."

"You're right," Michael said. "It's pinging and knocking. Do you think it's safe to drive?"

"Well, let's try it on the road for a while," I said.

"Maybe an hour," Michael said. "I think if it's going to break down, it won't do it before we get to Rockport at least. Why don't we—Oh my God!" he said suddenly, jamming on the brakes.

"What?"

"Look at that!"

He pointed out toward the harbor, beyond the crowded, noisy dock. I followed his finger and saw . . . a puffin. Even a bird-watching amateur like me could recognize it. It flew so clumsily, I was sure it would fall at any second. In fact, I thought it had when the stocky black-and-white figure plummeted toward the choppy water just beyond the end of the dock. But instead of falling in, it skimmed along the top of the waves and then rose again with a wriggling fish in its beak.

"Shall we go tell the bird-watchers?" Michael asked. We both glanced at the docks. The cluster of reporters had broken up and spread out in search of new camera fodder. Birders happily offered themselves up to the cause. Mother and Aunt Phoebe, sitting on a pile of luggage with their injured legs elevated, had already collected a quorum. Aunt Phoebe gestured wildly with her makeshift walking stick while Mother smiled and looked elegantly enigmatic.

"They're bird-watchers," I said. "If they did their jobs, they'd spot it."

The puffin headed toward the open ocean, wings flapping madly, looking as if at any moment it might lose the battle with gravity and plunge into the water. None of the birders noticed.

Except for Dad, who stood a little apart from the pandemonium. He glanced around, saw us, smiled, pointed at the puffin, and turned back to the harbor. The three of us watched until the puffin disappeared.

And as Michael eased out of the parking lot, I could see Dad in the rearview mirror, still standing at the edge of the crowd, waving cheerfully at us with a toy puffin in each hand.

"Andrews's talent for the lovably loony makes this series a winner; to miss it would be a cardinal sin."

—*RICHMOND TIMES-DISPATCH*

Fill your nest with these high-flying mysteries

Murder with Peacocks

Murder with Puffins

Revenge of the Wrought-Iron Flamingos

Crouching Buzzard, Leaping Loon

We'll Always Have Parrots

Owls Well That Ends Well

No Nest for the Wicket

The Penguin Who Knew Too Much

Cockatiels at Seven

Six Geese A-Slaying

Available wherever books are sold

Visit www.MinotaurBooks.com for a chance to win free books and connect with your favorite authors!

St. Martin's Griffin

www.DonnaAndrews.com
www.MinotaurBooks.com

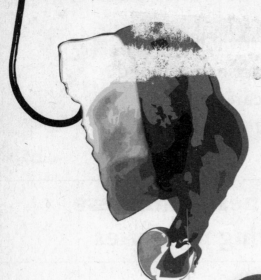
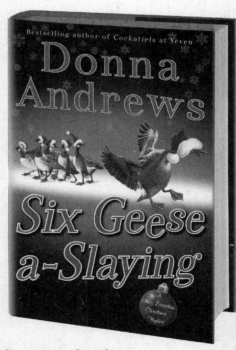